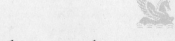

SelectEditions

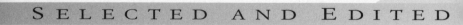
SELECTED AND EDITED

SelectEditions

BY READER'S DIGEST

VOLUME 3 1999
THE READER'S DIGEST ASSOCIATION, INC.
PLEASANTVILLE, NEW YORK

READER'S DIGEST SELECT EDITIONS

Editor-in-Chief: Tanis H. Erdmann
Executive Editor: Marjorie Palmer
Volume Editor: Paula Marchese
Book Editor: Laura Kelly
Volume Copy Editor: Marilyn J. Knowlton
Copy Editors: Maxine Bartow, Tatiana Ivanow
Art Editor: Clair Moritz
Art Associate: Janine L. Megna

CONTENTS

THE HAMMER OF EDEN

KEN FOLLETT

A man-made earthquake?
Death and destruction on a massive scale?
Who would believe such a thing is possible?

But one FBI agent is taking the threat seriously.
The question now is, Can she stop the
Hammer of Eden before it's too late?

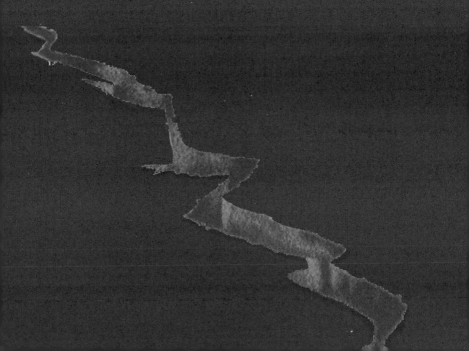

WHEN *he lies down to sleep, this landscape is always on his mind: A pine forest covers the hills, as thick as the fur on a bear's back. The sky is so blue in the clear mountain air that it hurts his eyes to look up. Miles from the road there is a secret valley with steep sides and a cold river in its cleft. Here, hidden from strangers' eyes, a sunny south-facing slope has been cleared, and grapevines grow in neat rows. When he remembers how beautiful it is, he feels his heart will break.*

Men, women, and children move slowly through the vineyard, tending the plants. These are his friends, his lovers, his family. One of the women laughs. She is a big woman with long dark hair, and he feels a special warmth for her. As they work, some of the men quietly pray to the gods of the valley and of the grapevines for a good crop. At their feet a few massive tree stumps remain, to remind them of the backbreaking work that created this place twenty-five years ago. Beyond the vineyard is a cluster of wooden buildings, plain but well built. Smoke rises from a cookhouse.

This is a holy place.

But now the vision changes.

Something has happened to the quick, cold stream that used to zigzag through the valley. Instead of a rush of white water, there is a dark pool, silent and still. The pool widens. Soon he is forced to retreat up the slope. He cannot understand why the others do not notice the rising tide. As the black pool laps at the first row of vines, they carry on working. The buildings are surrounded, then flooded. Why don't they run? he asks himself.

Now the sky is dark with iron-colored clouds, and a cold wind whips at the clothing of the people, but still they move along the vines. He is the only one who can see the danger.

In the vineyard the water rises to the workers' knees, then their waists, then their necks. He tries to tell the people he loves they must do something now, quickly, in the next few seconds, or they will die, but though he opens his mouth, no sound comes out. The water laps into his open mouth and begins to choke him.

This is when he wakes up.

PART ONE
FOUR WEEKS

1

A MAN called Priest pulled his cowboy hat down at the front and peered across the flat, dusty desert of south Texas.

The low, dull green bushes of thorny mesquite and sagebrush stretched in every direction as far as he could see. In front of him a ridged and rutted track ten feet wide had been driven through the vegetation. On one side of the track, at fifty-yard intervals, bright pink plastic marker flags fluttered on short wire poles. A truck moved slowly along the track.

Priest had to steal the truck.

He had stolen his first vehicle at the age of eleven—a new 1961 Lincoln Continental, parked, with the keys in the dash, outside the

Roxy Theatre in Los Angeles. Priest, who was called Ricky in those days, could hardly see over the steering wheel, but he drove it ten blocks and handed the keys proudly to Jimmy "Pigface" Riley. That's how Ricky became a member of the Pigface Gang.

But this truck was not just a vehicle.

As he watched, the powerful machinery behind the driver's cab lowered a massive steel plate, six feet square, to the ground. There was a pause; then he heard a low-pitched rumble. A cloud of dust rose around the truck as the plate began to pound the earth rhythmically. Priest felt the ground shake beneath his feet. This was a seismic vibrator, a machine for sending shock waves through the earth's crust. The shock waves were reflected off rock or liquid in the earth, and they bounced back to the surface, where they were picked up by listening devices called geophones, or jugs.

Priest worked on the jug team. They had planted more than a thousand geophones at precise intervals in a grid a mile square. Every time the vibrator shook, reflections were picked up by the jugs and recorded by a supervisor working in a trailer known as the doghouse. This data would later be fed into a supercomputer in Houston to produce a three-dimensional map of what was under the earth's surface. The map would be sold to an oil company.

The vibrations rose in pitch; then the sound stopped abruptly. Priest ran to the truck, opened the door, and clambered up into the cab. A stocky black-haired man of about thirty was at the wheel. "Hey, Mario," Priest said as he slid into the passenger seat.

"Hey, Ricky."

Richard Granger was the name on Priest's commercial driving license (class B). The license was forged, but the name was real.

He was carrying a carton of Marlboros, the brand Mario smoked. He tossed it onto the dash. "I brought you something."

"Hey, man, you don't need to buy me no cigarettes."

"I'm always bummin' your smokes." Priest picked up the open pack on the dash, shook one out, and put it in his mouth.

Mario smiled. "Why don't you just buy your own cigarettes?"

"Hell, no. I can't afford to smoke."

"You're crazy, man." Mario laughed.

Priest lit his cigarette. He had always had an easy ability to make people like him. On the streets where he grew up, people beat you up if they didn't like you, so he had developed an intuitive feel for what they wanted from him—deference, affection, humor, whatever. In the oil field, what held the men together was humor.

Although he had been here only two weeks, Priest had won the trust of his co-workers, but he had not figured out how to steal the seismic vibrator. He had to do it in the next few hours, for tomorrow the truck was scheduled to be driven to a new site seven hundred miles away, near Clovis, New Mexico. His vague plan was to hitch a ride with Mario. At some point he would get Mario drunk or something, then make off with the truck.

"My car's dying," Priest said. "You want to give me a ride as far as San Antonio tomorrow?"

Mario was surprised. "You ain't coming all the way to Clovis?"

"Nope. Texas is so beautiful, man, I never want to leave."

Mario shrugged. "Sure, I'll give you a ride." It was against company rules to take passengers, but the drivers did it all the time. "Meet me at the dump at six."

Priest nodded. The garbage dump was a desolate hollow on the outskirts of Shiloh, the nearest town.

He needed this truck. His palms itched to grab Mario right now and throw him out and just drive away, but that was no good. The theft had to go undiscovered for a few days. Priest needed to drive the truck to California and hide it before the nation's cops were alerted to watch out for a stolen seismic vibrator.

There was a beep from the radio, indicating that the supervisor in the doghouse had checked the data from the last vibration and found no problems. Mario raised the plate, put the truck in gear, and pulled up alongside the next pink marker flag. Then he lowered the plate again and sent a ready signal. Priest watched closely, making sure he remembered the order in which Mario moved the levers and threw the switches. If he forgot something later, there would be no one he could ask.

They waited for the signal from the doghouse that would start the next vibration. This could be done by the driver in the truck, but generally supervisors preferred to start the process themselves by remote control. Mario nodded toward Priest's car, parked a quarter of a mile away on the blacktop. "That your woman?"

Priest looked. Star had got out of the dirty, light blue Honda Civic and was leaning on the hood. "Yeah," he said.

"Lemme show you a picture." Mario extracted a photograph from his billfold and handed it to Priest. "This is Isabella."

Priest saw a pretty Mexican girl in her twenties, with a baby on her hip and a dark-haired boy by her side. "Your children?"

Mario nodded.

"Good-looking kids. Where do they live?"

"El Paso."

An idea sprouted in Priest's mind. "You get to see them much?"

Mario shook his head. "I'm workin' and workin', man. Savin' my money to buy them a nice house."

The radio beeped again, and the truck began to shake. The noise was like rolling thunder. It began on a profound bass note and slowly rose in pitch. After exactly fourteen seconds it stopped. In the quiet that followed, Priest said, "Say, I got an idea."

"What?"

"I just thought, you know, your wife is so pretty and your kids are so cute, it's wrong that you don't see them more often. I could drive the truck to New Mexico while you go visit them."

"No, man, it ain't possible."

"Let's see, if we set out early tomorrow and drove to San Antonio together, I could drop you off at the airport there. You could be in El Paso by noon. You'd play with the kids, have dinner with your wife, spend the night, get a plane the next day. I could pick you up at the Lubbock airport. How far is Lubbock from Clovis?"

"Ninety, maybe a hundred miles."

"We could be in Clovis that night or next morning at the latest, and no way for anyone to know you didn't drive the whole way."

"But you want to go to San Antonio."

"I've never been to Lubbock. Buddy Holly was born there."

"You'd drive all that way just for me?"

"Sure I would. As long as you let me smoke your Marlboros."

Mario shook his head in amazement. "You're a heck of a guy, Ricky, but I don't know. I don't want to lose my job."

"Think about it," Priest said. "You going to the bar tonight?"

"Sure."

"Well, why don't you let me know then?"

"Okay, that's a deal."

"I got to get back to the jug team," Priest said. He returned the family photo and opened the door. "I'm telling you, man, if I had a girl that pretty, I wouldn't leave the house." Priest grinned, then jumped to the ground and slammed the door. He walked away toward where Star was parked.

She had been famous once, briefly. During the hippie era she had lived in the Haight-Ashbury neighborhood of San Francisco. Priest had not known her then, but he had heard the stories. She had been a striking beauty, tall and black-haired, with a generous hourglass figure. She had made a record, reciting poetry against a background of psychedelic music with a band called Raining Fresh Daisies. The album had been a minor hit, and Star was a celebrity for a few days.

That was long ago. Now Star was a few weeks from her fiftieth birthday, and there were streaks of gray in her hair. Her figure was no longer like an hourglass—she weighed a hundred and eighty pounds—but she still exercised extraordinary sexual magnetism. Even now, when she was worried and hot, there was a sexy flounce to the way she paced and turned beside the old car.

"What happened?" she said as soon as he was within earshot.

"Looking good," Priest said, and told her the offer he had made to Mario. "The beauty of it is, Mario will be blamed."

"How so?"

"Think about it. He gets to Lubbock; he looks for me; I ain't there, nor his truck either. Is he going to make his way to Clovis and tell the company he lost their truck? At best he'd be fired. At worst he could be accused of stealing it. I'm betting he won't even go to Clovis. He'll fly back to El Paso and disappear. Then the police will be sure he stole the truck, and Ricky Granger won't even be a suspect."

Star frowned. "It's a great plan, but will he take the bait?"

"I think he will."

She leaned back against the car. "I wish I felt sure."

He stroked her cheek. "You need a ride, lady?"

"Yes, please. Take me to my air-conditioned hotel room."

"There'll be a price to pay."

She opened her eyes wide in pretended innocence. "Will I have to do something nasty, mister?"

He slid his hand into her cleavage. "Yeah."

"Oh, darn," she said, and started kissing him.

THE crisis had entered its final, decisive phase exactly three weeks earlier. They were sitting at the table in the cookhouse, eating their midday meal, when Paul Beale walked in with an envelope in his hand. Paul bottled the wine that Priest's commune made, and he was their link with the outside. He had been Priest's friend since the two of them were fourteen-year-old hoodlums in the early '60s.

Priest guessed what was in the letter but waited for Paul to explain.

"It's from the Bureau of Land Management," Paul said. "Addressed to Stella Higgins." He handed it to Star. Stella Higgins was her real name, the name under which she had first rented this piece of land from the Department of the Interior in 1969.

Around the table everyone went quiet. Even the kids shut up.

Star ripped open the envelope and took out a single sheet. She read it with one glance. "June the seventh," she said.

Priest said reflexively, "Five weeks and two days from now."

Several people groaned in despair. A woman called Song began to cry quietly. Priest's ten-year-old son Ringo said, "Why, Star?"

Priest caught the eye of Melanie, the newest arrival. She was a tall woman, twenty-eight years old, with pale skin, long hair the color of paprika, and the body of a model. Her five-year-old son, Dusty, sat beside her. "What?" she said in a shocked voice. "What is this?" Everyone else had known this was coming but not Melanie.

Priest said, "We have to leave the valley. I'm sorry, Melanie."

Star read from the letter. " 'The above-named parcel of land will become dangerous for human habitation after June seventh; therefore your tenancy is hereby terminated on that date.' "

Melanie stood up. Her pretty face twisted in sudden rage. "No!" she yelled. "No! They can't do this to me. I've only just found you! I don't believe it. It's a lie." Her child began to cry.

Everyone started shouting at the same time.

Priest was beside Melanie in a couple of strides. He put his arm around her. "You're frightening Dusty," he said quietly.

"Tell me it isn't true," she said.

Priest gently pushed her into her chair. "It's true, Melanie."

When they had quieted down, Priest said, "Come on, everyone, let's wash the dishes and get back to work."

"Why?" said Dale, the winemaker. After Priest and Star, he was the most important person in the group. "We won't be here for the harvest. We have to leave in five weeks. Why work?"

Priest fixed him with the Look, the hypnotic stare that intimidated all but the most strong-willed people. He let the room fall silent. At last he said, "Because miracles happen."

PRIEST went on his own to a bar called the Doodlebug in Shiloh, Texas, with cheap draft beer, a country-western band, and waitresses in tight blue jeans and cowboy boots. He did not want Star to show her face and risk being remembered later. He wished she had not had to come to Texas, but he needed someone to help him take the seismic vibrator home. Priest had changed his appearance before arriving in Shiloh. He had grown a bushy beard and tied his long hair in a tight plait that he kept tucked up inside his hat.

When he arrived at the Doodlebug, Mario was already there, sitting at a table with five or six of the jug team and the party boss, Lenny Petersen, who controlled the entire seismic exploration crew. Priest got a Lone Star longneck and joined Mario's table.

Lenny was a balding man with a red nose. He had given Priest the job two weekends ago. Now, as Priest sat down, Lenny said in his slow Texas accent, "So, Ricky, you're not coming with us to Clovis."

"That's right," Priest said. "I like the weather here too much."

"Well, I'd just like to say very sincerely that it's been a real privilege and pleasure knowing you, even for such a short time."

The others grinned. This kind of joshing was commonplace.

Priest put on a solemn face and said, "Lenny, you're so sweet that I'm going to ask you one more time. Will you marry me?"

They all laughed. Mario clapped Priest on the back.

The conversation turned to baseball. Priest had no interest in sports, so he waited impatiently, joining in now and again with a neutral comment.

After an hour Mario went to the men's room. Priest followed.

He stood beside Mario and said, "Listen, I got to leave. My woman's waiting back at the motel."

Mario grinned. "I saw you and her this afternoon, man."

Priest shook his head in mock regret. "She's my weakness. I just can't say no to a pretty face."

"Now, about tomorrow . . ." Mario said as Priest held his breath. "If you're willing, let's go for it. You still want to?"

"Sure I do." Priest put an arm around Mario's shoulders as they left the men's room. "Hey, what are buddies for?"

"Thanks, man. You're some guy, Ricky."

IT WAS still dark when Priest and Star got up on Saturday morning in Shiloh. Priest got coffee from the diner next door and brought it to their motel. When he came back, Star was poring over a road atlas. "You should be dropping Mario off at the San Antonio airport around nine thirty this morning. Then you'll want Interstate 10."

Priest did not look at the atlas. Maps baffled him. He could follow signs for I-10. "Where shall we meet?"

Star calculated. "I should be about an hour ahead of you. There's a place called Leon Springs on I-10 about fifteen miles from the airport. I'll park where you're sure to see the car."

"Sounds good."

Star asked, "What will we do with the Honda?"

Priest had bought the car three weeks ago for a thousand dollars cash. "We'll find a wooded spot off the interstate and dump it."

"Can we afford to?"

"Money makes you poor." Priest was quoting one of the Five Paradoxes of Baghram, the guru they lived by.

Priest knew how much money they had, to the last cent, but he kept everyone else in ignorance. Most of the communards did not even know there was a bank account. And no one knew about Priest's emergency cash—ten thousand dollars in twenties taped to the inside of an old acoustic guitar in his cabin.

Star shrugged. "I haven't worried about it for twenty-five years, so I guess I won't start now." She took off her reading glasses and gave him a sideways glance. "Are you looking forward to seeing Melanie?"

Priest and Melanie were lovers.

He took Star's hand. "Sure," he said. "You're not unhappy about Melanie, are you?"

"Marriage is the greatest infidelity," she said, quoting another of the paradoxes.

He nodded. They had never asked each other to be faithful, but for the last few years, though they still believed in the principle of free love, neither of them had actually taken advantage of it. So Melanie had come as kind of a shock to Star, but that was okay. Their relationship was too settled anyway. Priest did not like anyone to feel he or she could predict what he was going to do. He loved Star, but the anxiety in her eyes gave him a pleasant feeling of control.

She toyed with her Styrofoam coffee container. "I just wonder how Flower feels about it all." Flower was their thirteen-year-old daughter, the oldest child in the commune.

"She hasn't grown up in a nuclear family," Priest said. "That's the point of a commune."

"Yeah," Star agreed. "I just don't want her to lose you."

He stroked Star's hand. "It won't happen."

She squeezed his fingers. "Thanks."

"We got to go," he said.

Their few possessions were packed into three plastic grocery bags. Priest took them outside to the Honda. Star followed. They had paid their bill the previous night. The office was closed, and no one watched as Star took the wheel and they drove away.

They reached the dump a few minutes before six o'clock. There was no sign of Mario or the seismic vibrator.

Priest kissed her. "Mario will be here any second," he said. "Get movin' now. Put some miles behind you." He got out of the car.

She turned around in a wide circle and drove away fast.

Priest looked around. He found it amazing that such a small town could generate so much trash. The place was a wasteland of twisted bicycles, baby carriages, refrigerators, cardboard boxes, tinfoil, and plastic bags. In Silver River Valley there was never much garbage. They did not use baby carriages or refrigerators, and they rarely bought anything that came in a package. A shiny metal object glinted at his feet. He picked up the object. It was a heavy Stillson wrench.

Priest heard a vehicle and dropped the wrench. A tan pickup came bouncing along the rough track. Mario's car. What did this mean? Mario was supposed to show up in the seismic vibrator.

Mario pulled up and got out of the pickup. He shook his head sadly. "I can't do it, man. I gotta say no."

Priest gritted his teeth and made his voice sound casual. "What happened to change your mind, buddy?"

"After you left the bar last night, Lenny gave me this long speech, man, about how much the truck cost and how I don't gotta give no rides, pick up no hitchhikers, and how he's trustin' me and stuff. This is an okay job. I don't want to lose it."

"Hey, no problem," Priest said with forced lightness. "So long as you can still take me to San Antonio."

"I better not after what Lenny said. That's why I brought my own car here, so I can give you a ride back into town. So, uh, what do you say? You wanna get going?"

Priest had spent two weeks in this hot, dusty desert, working at a stupid, worthless job, and had wasted hundreds of dollars on airfares and motel bills. He did not have time to do it again. The deadline was now only two weeks and one day away.

Mario frowned. "Are you listening to me? Come on, man, let's go. You want a ride into town or not?"

"Sure," Priest said. *Sure, you yellow-dog coward. I want a ride.*

Mario turned around, and Priest's eye fell on the wrench he had dropped a few minutes earlier. A new plan unfolded in his brain.

As Mario walked the three paces to his car, Priest stooped and picked up the wrench. He glanced past Mario, along the track that led to the road. There was no one in sight. No witnesses.

Priest took a step forward just as Mario reached to open the door of his pickup. He had a sudden disconcerting flash—a photograph of a pretty young Mexican woman with a child in her arms and another by her side—and for a split second his resolve wavered. Then he saw a worse vision—a pool of black water slowly rising to engulf a vineyard and drown the men, women, and children tending the vines.

He ran at Mario, raising the wrench high over his head.

Mario must have seen something out of the corner of his eye, for he suddenly let out a roar of fear and flung the car door wide. Priest crashed into it, and it flew back at Mario, knocking him sideways. Both men stumbled. Mario lost his footing and went down on his knees. His Houston Astros baseball cap landed on the ground. Priest fell backward, dropping the wrench. It landed on a plastic half-gallon Coke bottle and bounced a yard away.

Mario gasped, "You crazy—" He got to one knee and reached for a handhold to pull himself up. His hand closed around the doorframe. Priest, still on his butt, drew back his leg and kicked the door. It slammed on Mario's fingers and bounced open. Mario cried out with pain and fell, slumping against the side of the pickup.

Priest leaped to his feet. He snatched up the wrench. He stepped close to Mario and raised the tool.

Mario half turned toward him. The expression on his young face showed infinite puzzlement. As Priest brought the wrench down, he said in a questioning voice, "Ricky?"

The heavy end of the wrench made a sickening thud as it smashed into Mario's head again and again. His scalp tore; his skull cracked. Mario's corpse fell slowly sideways until his head hit the ground.

Priest fell to his knees and closed his eyes. "Dear God Almighty, forgive me," he said, and knelt there shaking.

To quiet his brain, he chanted to himself, reciting his mantra: "Ley, tor, pur-doy-kor . . ." The syllables soothed him, and soon he stood up, his heart cold, his face set in a determined expression. He had purged himself of emotion. He felt no regret or pity. Priest picked up his cowboy hat, brushed off the dirt, and put it on his head.

He took a screwdriver from the pickup's tool kit and used it to detach the license plates. He walked across the dump and buried them in a mass of garbage. Then he bent over the body. With his right hand he grasped Mario's belt. With his left he took a fistful of the checked shirt. He grunted as he lifted the heavy body off the ground.

The door of the pickup stood open. With one big heave Priest threw Mario's body into the truck's cab; then he threw in the wrench. He siphoned gas out of the gas tank using the flexible plastic pipe that led from the windshield washer reservoir. Priest filled the half-gallon Coke bottle with the gas, then emptied it over the corpse. He filled the Coke bottle again and doused the entire interior of the cab.

He noticed Mario's Houston Astros cap on the ground. He picked it up and threw it into the cab with the body. Then he took a book of matches from his jeans, struck one, and used it to light all the others. He threw the blazing matchbook into the cab of the pickup and swiftly backed away. There was a whoosh of flame, and in a second the inside of the cab was a furnace. Then there was an explosion as the gas tank blew up.

Priest knew that if the cops examined the pickup, they would probably find Mario's belt buckle, the fillings from his teeth, and maybe his charred bones, but Priest had done all he could to conceal the evidence of his crime. Now he had to steal the seismic vibrator.

He turned away from the burning body and started walking.

AT THE commune in Silver River Valley there was an inner group called the Rice Eaters. There were seven of them, the remnants of those who had survived the winter of 1972–73, when they had been isolated by a blizzard and had eaten nothing but brown rice boiled in melted snow for three weeks. The day the letter came, the Rice Eaters stayed up late in the evening, sitting in the cookhouse.

Song, who had been a fifteen-year-old runaway in 1972, was playing a guitar. Star was singing along in a smoky, intimate contralto, making up words. She had the sexiest voice in the world.

Melanie sat with them, although she was not a Rice Eater, because Priest did not care to throw her out, and the others did not challenge Priest. She was crying silently and saying, "I only just found you."

"We haven't given up," Priest told her. "There has to be a way to make the governor of California change his mind."

Oaktree, the carpenter, a muscular black man the same age as Priest, said in a musing tone, "You know, it ain't that hard to make a nuclear bomb." He had been in the marines but had deserted after killing an officer during a training exercise, and he had been here ever since. "We could blackmail the governor. If they don't do what we want, we threaten to blow Sacramento all to hell."

"No!" said Aneth. She was a motherly type in her forties. "You can't save the world with bombs."

Star stopped singing. "I gave up trying to save the world in 1969. All I want now is to save this—what we have here, our life—so our children can grow up in peace and love."

Aneth said, "We could kidnap someone."

Priest nodded. This could work, but something bothered him. "Say some big shot gets kidnapped," he said. "So what? If you're going to scare people, you can't pussyfoot around."

At this point Melanie spoke. "You know, there are ten or fifteen places in California where the faults in the earth's crust are under such tremendous pressure that it might take only a teeny little nudge to make the tectonic plates slip and then *boom!*"

Oaktree said, "Melanie, baby, what you talking about?"

"I'm talking about an earthquake," she said. "Forget kidnapping. Forget nuclear bombs. Why don't we threaten the governor with an earthquake?"

"No one can cause an earthquake," Priest said. "It would take such an enormous amount of energy to make the earth move."

"That's where you're wrong. It might take only a small amount of energy if the force was applied in just the right place."

Oaktree said, "How do you know all this stuff?"

"I studied it. I have a master's in seismology. I should be teaching in a university now, but I married my professor and that was the end of my career. I was turned down for a doctorate."

Her tone was bitter. Priest had talked to her about this, and he knew she bore a deep grudge. Her husband had been on the committee that turned her down. He had to withdraw while her case was discussed, but Melanie felt he should somehow have made sure of her success. Priest guessed that she had not been good enough to study at the doctoral level, but he told her that the men on the committee were so terrified of her beauty and brains that they conspired to bring her down. She loved him for letting her believe that.

She went on. "My soon-to-be ex-husband developed the stress-trigger theory of earthquakes. At certain points along the fault line, shear pressure builds up over the decades to a high level. Then it takes only a relatively weak vibration in the earth's crust to dislodge the plates, release that energy, and cause an earthquake."

Priest studied Melanie's face. She had an otherworldly air. Her pale skin, startling green eyes, and red hair made her look like a beautiful alien. Did she know what she was talking about? "If it's so easy," he said, "how come it hasn't already been done?"

"I didn't say it would be easy. You'd have to be a seismologist to know exactly where the fault was under critical pressure."

Priest's mind was racing now. "How would you cause a vibration in the earth's crust?"

"That would be the hard part," she said.

WALKING back to the town of Shiloh, Priest found himself thinking that killing Mario had been the easy part. Next he had to pull the wool over Lenny's eyes. But how?

He was jerked back to the immediate present by the sound of a car. It was coming from behind him, heading into town.

In these parts no one walked. Most people would assume his car had broken down. Priest tried to think of a reason why he would be walking into town at six thirty on Saturday morning. Although the morning air was cool, Priest began to perspire.

The car passed him slowly. He could see the driver checking him out in the mirror. Priest had the impulse to turn and run.

The car stopped and reversed. The driver lowered the nearside window. He was a young Asian man in a business suit. He said, "Hey, buddy, want a ride?"

"I'm a little dusty," Priest said, looking down at his jeans.

"Who isn't, in these parts?"

Priest got into the car. His hands were shaking. He fastened his seat belt just to have something to do to disguise his anxiety.

As the car pulled away, the driver said, "What the heck you doing walking out here?"

At the last second Priest thought of a story. "I had a fight with my wife," he said. "I stopped the car and got out and walked away. I didn't expect her to just drive on."

"Would that be a good-looking dark-haired woman in a blue Honda that I passed twenty miles back?" The guy smiled, then said, "When you're crossing this desert, every car is interesting."

"No, that ain't her," Priest said. "My wife's driving my pickup. What about you? How come you're up early on Saturday morning?"

"I didn't fight with my wife. I'm going home to her. I live in Laredo. I travel in novelty ceramics."

"Is that a fact?"

"I might stop in Shiloh for breakfast. Got a recommendation?"

Priest would have preferred the salesman to drive through town without stopping, so that he would have no chance to mention the bearded guy he had picked up near the dump. But the man was sure to see Lazy Susan's along Main Street. "There's a diner."

"How's the food?"

"Grits are good. It's right after the stoplight."

When the car pulled into a slot by Susan's, Priest thanked the man and got out. "Enjoy your breakfast," he called as he walked away.

A block from the diner was the local office of the small seismic exploration firm Priest had been working for. The office was a large trailer in a vacant lot. Mario's seismic vibrator was parked in the lot alongside Lenny's red Pontiac Grand Am.

Priest stopped and stared at the truck for a moment. It was a ten-wheeler, with big off-road tires like dinosaur armor. Underneath a layer of Texas dirt it was bright blue. He itched to jump in and drive it away, but if he stole it now, every highway patrolman in Texas would be looking for him within a few minutes.

He went into the trailer. The office was busy. A surveyor was arguing on the phone, and Lenny's secretary, Diana, was checking a list.

Priest stepped through an open door into the inner office. Lenny was drinking coffee with a phone to his ear. After a minute he hung up the phone and said, "Hey, Ricky, you seen Mario this mornin'? He should've left here a half hour ago."

"Yeah, I seen him," Priest said. "He's let you down. He was missing his wife and kids so bad, he got into his pickup and left town."

"That's great. How did you find out?"

"He passed me on the street this morning headed for El Paso."

"Well, I just hope he keeps going across the border and doesn't stop until he drives into the ocean."

"He's got a young family, Lenny. Don't be too hard on him."

"Hard? Are you serious? He's history."

"He really needs this job."

"And I need someone to drive his rig to New Mexico."

Priest tried to sound casual. "I'll drive the truck to Clovis if you promise to give Mario his job back." He held his breath.

"You have a commercial driver's license, class B?"

"Since I was twenty-one years old." Priest took out his billfold, extracted the license, and tossed it onto the desk. It was a forgery.

Lenny checked it, then looked up and said, "I thought you didn't want to go to New Mexico."

"Suddenly I could use another five hundred bucks."

"Would you do it for two hundred?"

Priest hesitated. "Two hundred is low for three days' work."

"It's two days, maybe two and a half. I'll give you two fifty."

Anything! Just give me the keys! "Listen, Mario's a nice kid. I want to help him. Pay me whatever you think the job's worth."

"All right, three hundred."

"You got a deal." *And I've got a seismic vibrator.*

Lenny opened a drawer and took out a sheet of paper. "Just fill out this form for insurance."

Priest could not read or write. He stared at the form in fear.

Lenny said, "Come on, take it. It ain't a rattlesnake."

Priest reached out slowly and took the form. "I'll fill it in outside."

He walked out into the main office and looked at the form. There was no big X to show you where to put your name. Priest could write his name, sort of. However, he could not write anything else.

As a kid, he was so smart he didn't need to read and write. He could add in his head faster than anyone, and his memory was infallible. In school he found ways to avoid reading aloud. If there was a writing assignment, he'd get another kid to do it for him.

Later on he had managed to run a thriving liquor wholesaling business. He never wrote a letter but did everything on the phone and in person. He kept dozens of phone numbers in his head. He knew exactly how much money was in the bank. He had made a million dollars at the age of twenty-one. He had lost it all by the time he met Star—not because he was illiterate, but because he defrauded his customers, failed to pay his taxes, and borrowed from the Mob.

He sat down in front of Lenny's secretary's desk and smiled at Diana. "You look tired this morning, honey," he said.

She sighed. She was a plump blonde in her thirties, married to a roustabout. "Ricky, I got so much to do. I wish I had two brains."

He put on a crestfallen look. "That's bad news. I was going to ask you to help me with something."

She hesitated, then smiled ruefully. "What is it?"

"My handwriting's so poor, I wanted you to fill out this form for me. I sure hate to trouble you when you're so busy."

"Well, I'll make a deal with you." She pointed to a stack of cardboard boxes up against the wall. "I'll help you with the form if you'll put all those files in the green Chevy Astro van outside."

"You got it," Priest said gratefully. He gave her the form.

She picked up her pen. "Now, first we need your full name and date and place of birth."

Priest gave her the information, and she filled out the blanks on the form. Then she drew a big X next to a dotted line, handed the paper to him, and said, "You sign here."

He took her pen and wrote laboriously. The R for Richard, then the G for Granger. After RG he just did a wavy line like a snake. It was not pretty, but people accepted it.

This was why his forged license had to be in his own name. It was the only one he could write.

He gave Diana back the form. "Thanks for your help."

"You're welcome. I'll get you the keys to the truck from Lenny's office as soon as he gets off the phone."

After Priest had loaded all the boxes, Diana took the form into the inner office.

She emerged from Lenny's office with a key ring in her hand and gave Priest the keys to the seismic vibrator.

"Thank you," he said. He could hardly wait to get out of there. "Bye, everyone. See you in New Mexico."

"You drive safely, now, you hear?" Diana said.

"Oh, I'll do that," Priest replied. "You can count on it."

Outside, he climbed into the truck and turned over the engine. He checked the gauges. Mario must have filled the tank last night.

He headed north, following the route Star had taken in the Honda. As he approached the dump, he began to feel strange. Then he pulled himself together. Mario was not the first man he had killed.

Jack Kassner had been a cop, and he had robbed Priest's mother. When Ricky was fifteen, his mother had been a prostitute, working with three other women out of an apartment in Los Angeles. Jack Kassner was a vice-squad detective who came once a month for his shakedown money. One day he saw Priest's mother getting the bribe money from the back room. That night the vice squad raided the apartment, and Kassner stole fifteen hundred dollars. He thought he was in no danger from three B-girls and a fifteen-year-old, but the next evening, in the men's room of a bar on Broadway, little Ricky Granger stuck a six-inch knife into Kassner's back. Looking back, Priest marveled at his cool assurance. He had felt no fear, no guilt.

He passed the dump and drove on, heading north.

"WE'LL do it tonight," Priest had said when the letter came. "We'll tell the governor there'll be an earthquake four weeks from today."

Star was dubious. "We're not even sure this is possible. Maybe we should do everything else first, then issue the ultimatum."

"No!" Priest said. The suggestion angered him. He knew that the group had to take a risk and feel there was no turning back.

"But an earthquake might kill people," Aneth said.

Priest said, "We'll cause a small harmless tremor out in the desert, just to prove we can do what we say. Then when we threaten a second earthquake, the governor will negotiate."

Oaktree said, "How should we make the threat?"

"An anonymous phone call or letter, I guess," Priest said.

Melanie said, "We could post it on an Internet bulletin board. If we used my laptop and mobile phone, no one could trace it."

Priest had never seen a computer until Melanie arrived. "All right," he said.

"How will we sign the message?" Star said. "We need a name."

Song said, "Something that symbolizes a peace-loving group who have been driven to take extreme measures."

"I know," Priest said. "We'll call ourselves the Hammer of Eden."

It was just before midnight on the first of May.

PRIEST became tense as he reached the outskirts of San Antonio. In the original plan Mario would have driven the truck as far as the airport, but now Priest was alone as he entered the maze of freeways that encircled the city. He began to sweat. There was no way he could read a map, and even road signs were difficult for him.

Eventually, by asking directions, he got out of San Antonio on the right road. A few minutes later, passing through a small town, he was relieved to see the blue Honda parked at a McDonald's.

He hugged Star gratefully. "What happened?" she said worriedly. "I expected you a couple of hours ago."

He decided not to tell her he had killed Mario. "I got lost in San Antonio," he said.

"I was afraid of that, but you're here now. Let's go."

When they drove on, Star took the wheel of the truck. They planned to drive nonstop to California. It would take at least two days and nights. One would sleep while the other drove.

They left the Honda in the McDonald's lot. As they pulled away, Star handed Priest a paper bag with scissors and a battery-powered electric shaver inside. "Now you can get rid of that beard," she said.

He turned the rearview mirror toward himself and started to cut. His own face reemerged as he used the shaver to finish the job. Finally he took off his cowboy hat and undid his plait.

He looked at his reflection. His hair fell in waves around a gaunt face. He had a nose like a blade and hollow cheeks, but he had a sensual mouth. Many women had told him that. However, it was his eyes they usually talked about. They were dark brown, almost black, and people said they had a forceful, staring quality that could be mesmerizing. He practiced the Look now, in the mirror.

"Handsome devil," Star said, laughing at him affectionately.

"Smart, too," Priest said.

"I guess you are. You got us this machine anyway."

Priest nodded. "And you ain't seen nothing yet."

2

N THE Federal Building at 450 Golden Gate Avenue in San Francisco early on Monday morning, FBI agent Judy Maddox sat in a courtroom on the fifteenth floor, waiting. She spent a lot of time waiting in courtrooms. Most law-enforcement personnel did.

She was worried. Months of work, sometimes years, went into preparing a case, but there was no telling how it would go once it got to court. Four men were on trial today: the Foong brothers and two of their executives. In cooperation with a Hong Kong triad, they had set up a network for laundering money from the northern California dope industry. It had taken Judy a year to figure out how they were doing it and another year to prove it.

She had one big advantage when going after Asian crooks: She looked Oriental. Her father was a green-eyed Irishman, but she took more after her late mother, who was Vietnamese. Judy was slender and dark-haired, and her eyes slanted upward. The middle-aged Chinese gangsters she had been investigating had never suspected that this pretty little half-Asian girl was a Stanford Law School graduate and a hotshot FBI agent.

She was working with an assistant U.S. attorney whom she knew well. His name was Don Riley, and until a year ago they had been living together. He was her age, thirty-six, and he was experienced, energetic, and as smart as a whip. She had thought they had a watertight case, but the accused men had hired the top criminal law firm in the city and put together a clever, vigorous defense.

Judy had a special reason to be worried about this case. Her immediate boss, the supervisor of the Asian organized crime squad, was about to retire, and she had applied for the job. The overall head of the San Francisco office, the special agent in charge, or S.A.C., would support her application, but she had a rival: Marvin Hayes, another high-flying agent in her age-group. Marvin's best friend was the assistant special agent in charge. Right now the contest between Judy and Marvin Hayes was close.

She wanted that job. She was a good agent, she would be an outstanding supervisor, and someday she would be the best S.A.C. the Bureau had ever had. The S.A.C. had hinted to Judy that she rather than Marvin would get the job if she won her case today.

In court with Judy were most of the team on the Foong case, but to her surprise neither the A.S.A.C. nor the S.A.C. was there. This was a big case. She felt a twinge of unease. She wondered if something going on at the office that she did not know about. She started to step outside to call, but the clerk of the court entered and announced that the jury was about to return. She sat down. Don gave her shoulder an encouraging squeeze.

The jury entered. The judge emerged from his chambers and took his seat. Judy crossed her fingers under the table.

"Members of the jury, have you reached a verdict?" asked the clerk.

The foreman stood up. In a quiet voice he said, "We have."

"And how do you find the accused—guilty or not guilty?"

"Guilty as charged."

There was a second of silence as the news sank in. Judy looked at Don, who was smiling broadly at her.

The judge thanked the jury, adjourned the case, and went out.

I did it, Judy thought. I won the case. I put the bad guys in jail, and my promotion is in the bag. Supervising Special Agent Judy Maddox, only thirty-six, a rising star.

"You did a great job," she told Don. "Thanks."

"You gave me a great case," he said, hugging her.

She turned to her colleagues and went around thanking them for their work. Then the defense lawyers came over. The senior of the two was David Fielding, a partner in the firm of Brooks Fielding. "Congratulations, Ms. Maddox, on a well-deserved win," he said.

"Thank you," she said. "It was closer than I expected. I thought I had it buttoned up until you got started."

He acknowledged the compliment with a tilt of his head. "Well, if you ever get tired of the FBI, please come and see me. Your preparation was immaculate. With my firm you could earn three times your present salary."

"That's a nice offer, but I want to put bad guys in jail, not keep them out."

"I admire your idealism," he said, and turned to speak to Don.

Judy picked up her briefcase and left. The FBI office was in the same building as the court, on two lower floors.

As she entered the FBI office lobby, she wondered again why the S.A.C. and the A.S.A.C. had not come to court for the verdict. She headed for the S.A.C.'s office. Milton Lestrange had always had a soft spot for her and had been an early supporter of women agents. As soon as she entered his outer office, she knew something was wrong. His secretary had obviously been crying. Judy went to comfort her, but she waved Judy away and pointed to the door of the inner office.

Judy went in.

Sitting behind Lestrange's desk, with his jacket off and his tie loosened, was A.S.A.C. Brian Kincaid, a big barrel-chested man with thick white hair. He looked up and said, "Come in, Judy."

"What is going on?" she said. "Where's Milt?"

"Milt is in the hospital," he said. "He's been diagnosed with pancreatic cancer. He'll be having an operation, some kind of intestinal bypass, and he won't be back here for a while, at best."

"Oh, no! Poor Milt!" Judy sat down.

"I've been made acting S.A.C. in Milt's absence."

Judy's heart sank. "Congratulations," she said.

"I'm moving you to the Domestic Terrorism desk." Brian picked up the phone and spoke to his secretary. "Ask Matt Peters to come in and see me right away." Peters was supervisor of the DT squad.

"But I just won my case," Judy said indignantly.

"Well done. That doesn't change my decision."

"Wait a minute. You know I've applied for the job of supervisor in the Asian organized crime squad."

"I think you need to broaden your experience."

"And I think you want Marvin to get the Asian desk."

"You're right. I believe Marvin is the best person for that job."

What a jerk, Judy thought furiously. He gets made boss and uses his new power to promote a buddy. "You can't do this," she said. "We have Equal Employment Opportunity rules."

"Marvin is better qualified than you," Kincaid said.

"I've put a lot more bad guys in jail."

Kincaid gave her a complacent smile and played his trump card. "But he's spent two years at headquarters in Washington."

He was right, Judy thought despairingly. She had never worked at FBI headquarters, and headquarters experience was thought desirable in a supervisor. Judy fought back tears.

Matt Peters came in. He was a stocky bald guy. Like Marvin Hayes, he was close to Kincaid. Judy began to feel surrounded.

"Congratulations on winning your case," Peters said to Judy. "I'll be glad to have you on my squad."

"Thank you." Judy could not think what else to say.

Kincaid said, "Matt has a new assignment for you."

Peters had a file under his arm, and now he handed it to Judy. "The governor has received a terrorist threat from a group calling itself the Hammer of Eden."

Judy opened the file. "What are they demanding?"

"A freeze on the building of new power plants in California. They gave us four weeks to comply. They say they're the radical offshoot of the Green California Campaign."

Green California was a legitimate environmental pressure group. It was hard to believe they would do something like this.

"And what's the threat?"

"An earthquake."

Judy looked up from the file. "You're putting me on. No one can cause an earthquake. How was this threat communicated?"

"It appeared on an Internet bulletin board on the first of May."

She looked at Matt. "There's something you're not telling me. Today is the twenty-fifth. We've ignored the message for three and a half weeks. Now, with four days left to the deadline, we're worried?"

"John Truth saw the bulletin board. He talked about the threat on his show Friday night, and he got a lot of calls."

"I get it." John Truth was a controversial talk-radio host whose show was syndicated live on stations all over California. "John Truth pressured the governor to do something about the terrorist message, so the FBI has to go through the motions of an investigation that no one really believes in."

"That's about it," Matt said.

Judy took a deep breath. She addressed Kincaid because she knew this was his doing. "This office has been trying to nail the Foong brothers for twenty years. Today I put them in jail." She raised her voice. "And now you give me a stupid case like this?"

Kincaid looked pleased with himself. "If you want to be in the Bureau, you'll have to learn to take the rough with the smooth."

"I learned, Brian! Ten years ago, when I was new, I was given assignments like this. I took them cheerfully, did them conscientiously, and proved that I deserve to be trusted with real work."

"Ten years is nothing," he said. "I've been here twenty-five."

She tried reasoning with him. "Look, you've just been put in charge of this office. Your first act is to give one of your best agents a job that should have gone to a rookie."

"You're right, I just got this job. And you're already telling me how to do it. Get back to work, Maddox. This meeting is over."

Judy could not take it. Her rage boiled over. "It's not just this meeting that's over," she said. She stood up. "Damn you, Kincaid. I quit."

And then she walked out.

"You said that?" Judy's father said.

"Yeah. I knew you'd disapprove."

"You were right about that."

They were sitting in the kitchen drinking green tea. Judy's father was a detective with the San Francisco police. He did a lot of undercover work. He was a powerfully built man, very fit for his age, with bright green eyes and gray hair in a ponytail.

He was close to retirement and dreading it. Law enforcement was his life. He was horrified by the idea of his daughter quitting when she did not have to.

Judy's parents had met in Saigon during the days when American troops there were still called advisers. Her mother came from a middle-class Vietnamese family. Judy's father brought his bride home, and Judy was born in San Francisco. As a baby, she called her parents Bo and Me, the Vietnamese equivalent of Daddy and Mommy. The cops caught on to this, and her father became known as Bo Maddox.

Judy adored him. Her mother had died in a car wreck when Judy was thirteen. Since then she had been close to Bo. After she had broken up with Don Riley a year ago, she had moved into her father's house.

She sighed. "I don't often lose it, you have to admit."

"Only when it's really important."

"But now that I've told Kincaid I'm quitting, I guess I will." Judy was still boiling with fury inside. "He's such a fool."

"He must be, because he just lost a good agent." Bo sipped his tea. "But you're dumber. You lost a great job."

"I was offered a better one today. Brooks Fielding, the law firm. I could earn three times my FBI salary."

"Keeping mobsters out of jail!" Bo said indignantly. "Why don't you marry Don Riley and have babies? Grandchildren would give me something to do in retirement."

Judy winced. She had never told Bo the real story of her breakup with Don. The simple truth was that he had had an affair. Feeling guilty, he had confessed to Judy. She had tried to forgive him, but her feelings for Don were not the same afterward. Bo did not know any of this. He saw Don Riley as the perfect husband: handsome, intelligent, successful, and working in law enforcement.

Bo stood up. "I've got to go. We have a raid going down tonight." He pulled on a jacket and kissed her cheek. "I love you."

"Bye."

Judy turned on the TV and looked in the fridge, thinking about dinner, but she did not feel hungry. She decided to write her résumé. She would go into the office and do it on her computer.

She picked up her gun, then hesitated. Agents were on duty twenty-four hours a day and were obliged to be armed except in court, inside a jail, or at the office. *But if I'm no longer an agent, I don't have to go armed.* Then she changed her mind. *If I see a robbery in progress and I have to drive on by because I left my weapon at home, I'm going to feel pretty stupid.*

It was a standard-issue FBI weapon, a SIG-Sauer P228 pistol. Judy also had a Remington model 870 five-chamber shotgun. Like all agents, she did firearms training once a month. Her marksmanship was tested four times a year. Like most agents, she had never fired her gun except in training. FBI agents were investigators. It was perfectly normal to go through an entire career with the Bureau and never get involved in a shoot-out, but they had to be ready for it.

Judy put her weapon into a shoulder bag. She was wearing the ao dai, a traditional Vietnamese garment like a long blouse, with a little upright collar and side slits, always worn over baggy pants. It was her favorite casual wear because it was so comfortable, but she also knew it looked good on her. The white material showed off her shoulder-length black hair and honey-colored skin, and the close-fitting blouse flattered her petite figure. She would not normally wear it to the office, but it was late in the evening.

She went outside. Her Chevrolet Monte Carlo was parked at the curb. It was an FBI car. When she was a defense lawyer, she could get something more exciting—maybe a little European sports car.

Judy took the expressway downtown. Rush hour was over and traffic was light, so she was at the Federal Building in a few minutes. She entered the office of the Asian organized crime squad. The room was empty. She turned on the lights, sat at her desk, and booted up her computer, to write her résumé.

She needed to give a clear account of her ten years in the Bureau, but instead her memory produced a disjointed series of flashbacks: the serial rapist who had thanked her for putting him in jail; the man who had kidnapped two small children, and how she had persuaded him to give her his gun. She could hardly tell Brooks Fielding about those moments. They wanted Perry Mason, not Wyatt Earp.

She decided to write her letter of resignation first. She put the date, then typed, "To the Acting Special Agent in Charge."

She wrote, "Dear Brian: This is to confirm my resignation."

It hurt. She had given ten years of her life to the FBI. Other women got married and had children or started their own businesses. She had dedicated herself to being a terrific agent. Now she was throwing it all away. The thought brought tears to her eyes.

Then Simon Sparrow came in. Like Judy, he was dressed casually. He had a doctorate in linguistics and had spent five years with the Behavioral Science Unit at the FBI Academy at Quantico, Virginia. His specialty was threat analysis. He had a file in his hand. "Your earthquake threat is fascinating," he said. "I was going to leave this on your desk, but I'm glad I've caught you. Congratulations on winning your case today. You must be pleased."

"I should be, but I had a fight with Brian Kincaid afterward."

"Oh, him." Simon dismissed their boss with a flap of his hand. "If you apologize nicely, he'll have to forgive you. He can't afford to lose you. You're too good."

It was almost as if Simon had known beforehand, but if he knew she had resigned, why had he brought her the report?

Intrigued, she said, "Take a seat and tell me about your analysis of the threat."

"It had me mystified for a while." He handed her a printout of the message as it had appeared on the Internet bulletin board.

Judy had seen the message before. It was in the file Matt Peters had handed her earlier today. She studied it again.

> May 1st
> To the state governor
> Hi!
> You say you care about pollution and the environment, but you never do nothing about it; so we're going to make you.
> The consumer society is poisoning the planet because you are too greedy, and you got to stop now!
> We are the Hammer of Eden, the radical offshoot of the Green California Campaign.
> We are telling you to announce an immediate freeze on building power plants. No new plants. Period. Or else!
> Or else what you say? Or else we will cause an earthquake exactly four weeks from today. Be warned! We really mean it!
> —The Hammer of Eden

"What do you make of it?" Simon asked.

Judy thought for a minute. "I see a nerdy young student sitting at his computer fantasizing about making the world obey him."

"Well, that's about as wrong as could be," Simon said with a smile. "He's an uneducated low-income man in his forties."

"How do you know?"

"Vocabulary and sentence structure. Affluent people start a letter with 'Dear Sir,' not 'Hi.' And college graduates generally avoid double negatives such as 'you never do nothing.' "

Judy nodded. "So you're looking for Joe Bluecollar, age forty-five. That sounds pretty straightforward. What puzzled you?"

"Contradictory indications. Other elements in the message suggest a young middle-class woman. The spelling is perfect. There's a semicolon in the first sentence, which indicates some education. And the number of exclamation points suggests a female."

"How do you know she's young?"

"Older writers are more likely to use initial capital letters for a phrase such as 'state governor' and hyphenate words such as 'off-shoot' that young writers run together. Also, the use of a computer and the Internet suggests someone both young and educated."

Judy studied Simon. Was he deliberately getting her interested to stop her from resigning? "Are you about to tell me this message was written by someone with a split personality?"

"No. Simpler than that. It was written by two people: the man dictating, the woman typing." Simon went on, "I ask myself why he dictates. It might come naturally to an executive who was used to having a secretary, but this is just a regular guy. I wonder if he's illiterate."

"He could simply be lazy," Judy said. "All right, you've got a nice college girl in thrall of a street guy. She's probably in danger, but is anyone else? The threat of an earthquake just doesn't seem real."

Simon shook his head. "I think we have to take it seriously."

Judy could not contain her curiosity. "Why?"

"As you know, we analyze threats according to motivation, intent, and target selection. Motivation is either emotional or practical. In other words, is the perpetrator doing this just to make himself feel good or because he wants something?"

"On the face of it, these people have a specific goal: They want the state to stop building power plants," she said.

"Right. And they hope to achieve their aims by making a threat."

"Whereas the emotional types would rather kill people."

"Exactly," Simon said. "Next, intent is either political, criminal, or mentally disturbed."

"Political, in this case, at least on the surface."

"Right. Political ideas can be a pretext for an act that is basically insane, but I don't get that feeling here, do you?"

Judy saw where he was heading. "You're trying to tell me these people are rational. But it's insane to threaten an earthquake!"

"I'll come back to that. Finally, target selection is either specific or random. Trying to kill the President is specific; going berserk with a machine gun in Disneyland is random. An earthquake would kill a lot of people indiscriminately, so it's random."

"All right, you've got practical intent, political motivation, and random targeting. What does that tell you?" she asked.

"The textbook says these people are either bargaining or seeking publicity. I say they're bargaining. If they wanted publicity, they would have put their message on TV or in the newspapers, not on an obscure bulletin board on the Internet. I think they simply wanted to communicate with the governor."

"They're naïve if they think the governor reads his messages."

"I agree. These people display an odd combination of sophistication and ignorance, but they're serious."

"So who are these people?" Judy asked.

"We don't know. The typical terrorist shows an escalating pattern. He begins with threatening phone calls and anonymous letters; then he writes to the newspapers and TV stations; then he starts hanging around government buildings. By the time he shows up for the White House tour with a Saturday night special, we've got quite of lot of his work on the FBI computer. But not this one. I've had the linguistic fingerprint checked against all past terrorist threats on record at Quantico, but there's no match. These people are new."

"So we know nothing about them?"

"We know plenty. They live in California, obviously."

"How do you know that?"

"The message is addressed 'To the state governor.' If they were in another state, they'd send it to the governor of California."

"What else?"

"They're Americans, and there's no indication of any particular ethnic group in their language."

"You left out one thing," Judy told Simon. "They're crazy."

He shook his head. "They're sane, serious, and focused. And that means they're dangerous." He stood up. "I'm beat. Want to go for a beer?"

"Not tonight, but thanks for the report. You're the best."

"You bet. So long."

Judy was sure now that Simon had been trying to persuade her not to resign. Kincaid might think this was a nothing case, but Simon's message was that the Hammer of Eden might be a genuine threat, a group that needed to be put out of action. In which case her FBI career was not necessarily over. She could make a triumph of a case that had been given to her as an insult. The prospect was enticing.

She looked at her computer screen. She had written, "Dear Brian: This is to confirm my resignation." After erasing the sentence, Judy wrote, "I would like to apologize for my rudeness. . . ."

THE Tuesday morning sun was coming up over I-80. Priest's 1971 Plymouth 'Cuda headed for Berkeley.

He had bought the car new, at the height of his business career, when the only cool car to own was a Volkswagen Beetle. Driving the bright yellow 'Cuda, Priest looked like a pimp, Star used to tell him. So they gave it a trippy paint job: planets on the roof, flowers on the trunk, and an Indian goddess on the hood, in purple, pink, and turquoise. In twenty-five years the colors had faded to a mottled brown, but you could still make out the design.

He had set out at three a.m. Melanie had slept all the way. She lay with her head in his lap, her fabulously long legs folded on the worn black upholstery. As he drove, he toyed with her hair. She had '60s hair, long and straight, although she had been born around the time the Beatles split up. The kid was asleep, too, lying on the back seat. Priest's German shepherd, Spirit, lay beside him.

Priest was worried. He had promised an earthquake. If he failed, he would lose everything that was dear to him. And if he was caught, he would be in jail until he was an old man.

But he was extraordinary. He had always known he was not like other people. The rules did not apply to him. He did things no one else thought of.

And he was already halfway to his goal. He had stolen a seismic vibrator. The truck was now hidden in a lonely valley in the foothills of the Sierra Nevada. Today Priest was going to find out exactly where to place it so as to cause an earthquake. And Melanie's husband was going to give him that information.

According to Melanie, Michael Quercus knew more than anyone about the San Andreas Fault. His accumulated data was stored on his computer. Priest wanted to steal his backup disk and make sure that Michael would never know what had happened.

For that he needed Melanie. Which was why he was worried. He had known her only a few weeks. In that time he had become the dominant person in her life, but she had been married to Michael for six years. She might suddenly regret leaving her husband; she might be struck by the danger and the illegality of what they were doing.

In the rear seat her five-year-old son woke up. Dustin, known as Dusty, suffered from allergies. He sneezed uncontrollably, his eyes bulged, and he broke out in skin rashes. Melanie carried powerful suppressing drugs, but they mitigated the symptoms only partially.

Now Dusty started to fret. "Mommy, I'm thirsty," he said.

Melanie came awake. She sat upright, turned around, and said, "Drink some water, Dusty. You have a bottle right there."

"I don't want water," he whined. "I want orange juice."

"We don't have any damn juice," she snapped.

Dusty started to cry.

Melanie was obsessive about her son's health, so she was over-protective, but her tension also made her cranky with him.

Priest took charge. He said, "Hey, whoa, what the heck is that coming up behind us?" He made himself sound really scared.

Melanie looked around. "It's just a truck."

"That's what you think. It's disguised as a truck, but really it's a

Centaurian fighter spacecraft with photon torpedoes. We'll know he's firing his torpedoes if we see an orange light flashing on his port fender. Dusty, you better watch for that."

The truck was closing in on them fast, and a minute later its left-side indicator flashed, and it pulled out to pass them.

Dusty said, "It's firing. It's firing!"

"Okay, I'll raise our magnetic armor while you fire back."

Dusty made zapping noises. Spirit joined in, barking furiously at the truck as it passed. Melanie started to laugh.

When the truck pulled back into the slow lane ahead of them, Priest said, "Whew. We were lucky. I think they've given up."

"Will there be any more Centaurians?" Dusty asked eagerly.

"You keep watch out the back and let me know what you see."

"Okay."

Melanie said quietly, "Thanks. You're so good with him."

I'm good with everyone: men, women, children, and pets. I got charisma. It's a way of making people do what you want. Anything from persuading a faithful wife to commit adultery, all the way down to getting a scratchy kid to stop whining. All you need is charm.

A few minutes later they left the freeway and entered the leafy university town. Melanie directed Priest to Euclid Avenue, a street of modest houses and apartment buildings.

"I still think I should go in alone," she said.

It was out of the question. "No," he said.

"Okay, okay," she said hastily.

Dusty said excitedly, "Hey, this is where Daddy lives!"

"That's right, honey," Melanie said. She pointed to a low-rise stucco apartment building, and Priest parked outside it.

"He stays in the car," Priest said.

"He might get scared," she said.

Priest twisted around to speak to Dusty. "Hey, Lieutenant, I need you and Ensign Spirit to stand guard over our spacecraft. Think you can handle the guard duty assignment?"

"You bet!"

"Very good. Carry on." Priest got out of the car.

Melanie took her purse and got out, too.

They walked up the path to the building door. Melanie pressed the entry phone buzzer and held it down. Her husband was a night owl, she had told Priest. He liked to work in the evening and sleep late. That was why they had chosen to get here before seven o'clock in the morning. Priest hoped Michael would be too bleary-eyed to wonder whether their visit had a hidden purpose.

Melanie said he was a workaholic. He spent his days driving all over California—checking the instruments that measured small geological movements in the San Andreas Fault—and his nights inputting the data into his computer. But what had finally driven her to leave him was an incident with Dusty. She and the child had been vegetarian for two years. She believed the strict diet reduced Dusty's allergy attacks. Then one day she discovered that Michael had bought Dusty a hamburger. To her that was like poisoning the child. She left that night, taking Dusty with her.

Priest thought she might be right about the allergy attacks. The commune had been vegetarian ever since the early '70s, and the communards were a remarkably healthy bunch. But unlike Melanie, he was not obsessive about diet. He still liked fish, and now and again he would unintentionally eat meat in a soup or a sandwich.

A grouchy voice came through the intercom. "Who is it?"

"Melanie."

There was a buzz, and the door opened. Priest followed Melanie inside and up to the second floor. Michael Quercus stood in a doorway. Priest was surprised by his appearance. He had been expecting a weedy professorial type. Quercus was about thirty-five. Tall and athletic, he had a head of short black curls and wore a dark blue robe.

As Melanie reached the top of the stairs, Michael said, "I've been very worried. Where the hell have you been?" Priest could see he was barely controlling his stored-up rage.

"I'm here to explain," Melanie said. "This is my friend Priest. May we come in?"

Michael stared at her angrily. "This had better be pretty good, Melanie." He turned his back and walked inside.

Melanie and Priest followed him into the living room.

This was clearly his office. As well as a couch and a TV set, there was a computer on a table and a row of electronic machines with blinking lights on a deep shelf. One wall was taken up with a huge map. "What is that?" Priest said.

Michael gave him a who-the-heck-are-you look and said nothing. "It's the San Andreas Fault," Melanie answered. "Beginning a hundred miles north of here in Mendocino County, all the way south and east, past Los Angeles and inland to San Bernardino. A crack in the earth's crust seven hundred miles long."

Melanie had explained that Michael's specialty was the calculation of pressure at different places along seismic faults. It was partly a matter of precise measurement of small movements in the earth's crust, partly a question of estimating the accumulated energy based on the lapse of time since the last earthquake. His work had won him academic prizes. But a year ago he had quit the university to start his own business, a consultancy offering advice on earthquake hazards to construction firms and insurance companies.

Melanie was a computer wizard and had programmed Michael's machine to back up every day between four a.m. and six a.m., when he was asleep. Everything on his computer, she had explained to Priest, was copied onto a disk. When he switched on his screen in the morning, he would take the disk out of the disk drive and put it into a fireproof box. That way, if his computer crashed or the house burned down, his precious data would not be lost. Now they just had to get Michael out of the room long enough for Melanie to snatch the disk from the drive.

Michael said to Melanie, "Now, are you going to tell me why you disappeared?"

"It's very simple," she said. "A friend offered me and Dusty the use of her cabin in the mountains. We can't afford vacations, so I grabbed at the chance."

That was when Priest had met her. She and Dusty had been wandering in the forest and got lost. Priest was out on his own, fishing that spring day. He had been sitting on the bank of a stream when he heard a child crying. Following the sound, he found Dusty and Melanie. She was close to tears. When she saw Priest, she said, "Thank heavens. I thought we were going to die out here!"

He had stared at her for a long moment. She was a little weird, with her long red hair and green eyes, but in the cutoff jeans and a halter top she looked good enough to eat. He asked her if she was from Mars. "No," she said. "Oakland."

Priest knew where the vacation cabins were. He picked up his fishing rod and led her through the forest. It was a long walk. On the way he asked her sympathetic questions and found out all about her. She was a woman in deep trouble.

She had left her husband and moved in with a bass guitarist in a rock band, but the bassist had thrown her out after a few weeks. She had no one to turn to. She was working in a supermarket, leaving Dusty with a neighbor all day. She lived in a slum that was so dirty it gave the kid constant allergy attacks. She needed to move to a place with clean air, but she could not find a job outside the city. She was desperate when a girlfriend had offered her this vacation.

Priest liked people in trouble. He knew how to relate to them. All you had to do was offer them what they needed, and they became your slaves.

By the time they reached the cabin, it was suppertime. Melanie made pasta and salad, then put Dusty to bed. When the child was asleep, Priest seduced her on the rug. She was frantic with desire.

Now her supercilious handsome-professor husband was complaining: "That was *five* weeks ago. You can't just take my son and disappear without even a phone call!"

"You could have called me. I have a mobile."

"I tried. I couldn't get an answer."

"The service was cut off because you didn't pay the bill. You're supposed to pay it. We agreed."

"I was a couple of days late, that's all! It doesn't matter *why* I couldn't reach you. I couldn't. That's why you have to call me before taking Dusty away on vacation."

Melanie said, "There's something I haven't told you yet."

Michael sighed and said, "Sit down." He sat behind his desk.

Melanie sank into a corner of the couch while Priest perched on the arm. "I'm going to move to the mountains permanently," Melanie said. "I'm living with Priest and a bunch of people."

"Where?"

Priest answered. He did not want Michael to know where they lived. "It's in Del Norte County." That was at the northern end of California. In fact, the commune was in Sierra County, near the eastern border of the state. Both were far from Berkeley.

Michael was outraged. "You can't take Dusty to live hundreds of miles away from his father!"

Melanie persisted. "There's a reason. In the last five weeks Dusty hasn't had a single allergy attack. He's healthy in the mountains."

Michael was skeptical. "It's the desert, not the mountains, that normally suits people with allergies."

"Don't talk to me about normally!" Melanie flared. "I can't go to the desert. I don't have any money. This is the only place I can afford where Dusty can be healthy. It's a commune."

"Melanie, what kind of people have you fallen in with now? First a junkie guitar player, now a godforsaken hippie commune—"

Priest interrupted. "Why don't you ask Dusty how he feels about this, Michael? He's right outside, in my car."

Michael flushed with anger. "You left my son in the car?"

"He's okay. My dog's with him."

Michael glared furiously at Melanie. "What is wrong with you?" he shouted, and stormed out.

"Why did you tell him Dusty was outside?" Melanie wailed.

"To get him out of the room. Now grab that disk."

Melanie went over to the row of machines on the shelf. She pressed a button, and a flat plastic square popped out of a slot. She opened her purse and took out another disk. "Damn!" she said.

"What?" Priest said worriedly. "What's wrong?"

"He's changed brands. Mine is a Sony; Michael's is a Philips."

"Will he notice?"

"He might. He'll probably start work as soon as we've gone.

He'll eject the disk and swap it with the one in the fireproof box, and if he looks at them, he'll see they're different."

"He's sure to connect that with us." Priest felt a surge of panic. "Does he keep spare disks?"

"He should." She looked around. "I wonder where they are."

"Melanie," he said, "put both disks in your purse."

She obeyed him automatically.

Priest heard the building door slam. Michael was on his way back. Priest felt perspiration break out in the small of his back. "Think: Does Michael have a stationery cupboard?"

"Yes. Well, a drawer." She pointed to a white chest.

Priest yanked open the top drawer. He saw a package of yellow pads, a box of cheap ballpoints—and an open box of disks.

He heard Dusty's voice coming from the vestibule of the apartment. With shaking fingers he fumbled a disk out of the packet and handed it to Melanie. "Will this do?"

"Yes. It's a Philips."

Priest closed the drawer.

Michael walked in with Dusty in his arms, and Melanie froze with the disk in her hand. Dusty was saying, "And you know what, Daddy? I didn't sneeze in the mountains."

Michael's attention was fixed on Dusty.

Melanie regained her composure. As Michael bent to put Dusty down on the couch, she slid the disk into the disk drive.

"You didn't sneeze?" Michael said to Dusty. "Not once?"

"Uh-uh."

Melanie straightened up. Michael had not seen what she did. Priest closed his eyes. The relief was overwhelming. They had Michael's data, and he would never know.

Michael said, "That dog doesn't make you sneeze?"

"No. Spirit is a clean dog. Priest makes him wash in the stream, and then he comes out and shakes himself, and it's like a rainstorm." Dusty laughed.

"Is that right?" his father said.

Melanie said, "I told you, Michael."

"Okay, okay," Michael said in a conciliatory tone. "If it makes such a difference to Dusty's health, we'll just have to work it out."

She looked relieved. "Thanks."

Priest smiled. Now they just had to hope that Michael's computer did not crash. If that happened and he tried to retrieve data from the disk, he would discover that it was blank. But Melanie said that crashes were rare. And tonight the computer would back up again, overwriting the blank disk with Michael's data.

Michael said, "Well, at least you came here to talk about it. I appreciate that."

Melanie said, "I'll bring Dusty to see you as often as you like."

Priest could see into her heart. She was being nice to Michael, but she did not love him, not anymore. Michael was different. He was angry with her for leaving him; that was clear. But he still cared for her. A part of him still wanted her back.

Priest felt jealous. *I hate you, Michael.*

JUDY woke up early on Tuesday wondering if she had a job. Last night she had left a note on Brian Kincaid's desk. Would he accept her apology, or would he insist on her resignation?

She was stiff with tension as she drove to work. She went straight to the S.A.C.'s office.

Brian Kincaid was behind the big desk. He looked up at her. "Good morning," he said coldly.

"Morn—" Judy's mouth was dry. She swallowed and started again. "Good morning, Brian. Did you get my note?"

"Yes, I did. Your apology is accepted."

She felt weak with relief. "Thank you."

"Move your stuff into the Domestic Terrorism squad room and get to work on the Hammer of Eden case right away. We need something to tell the governor."

Judy was surprised. "You're seeing the governor?"

"His cabinet secretary. A Mr. Albert Honeymoon."

"I've heard of him." Honeymoon was the governor's right-hand man. The case had taken on a higher profile, Judy realized.

"Let me have a report by tomorrow night."

That hardly gave her time to make progress. Tomorrow was Wednesday. "But the deadline is Friday."

"The meeting with Honeymoon is on Thursday."

"I'll get you something concrete to give him."

"You can give it to him yourself. Mr. Honeymoon insists on seeing what he calls the person at the sharp end. We need to be at the governor's office in Sacramento at twelve noon."

"Wow. Okay. I'll get right on it."

She carried her stuff down the corridor to Domestic Terrorism. Her new supervisor, Matt Peters, allocated her a desk. He had assigned a young agent to work with her on the Hammer of Eden case. Raja Khan was a fast-talking Hindu with an M.B.A. Although inexperienced, he was intelligent and keen.

Judy sent him to check out the Green California Campaign. "Be nice," she told him. "Tell them we don't believe they're involved, but we have to eliminate them."

"What am I looking for?"

"A couple: a blue-collar man of about forty-five who may be illiterate, and an educated woman of about thirty who is probably dominated by the man. Get the names of all the officers of the organization and run them through the computer to see if any of them have any record of criminal or subversive activity."

"You got it," Raja said. "What will you do?"

"I'm going to learn about earthquakes."

WHEN Judy got home that night, Bo was watching television. "I solved a murder today," he said, turning off the TV.

Judy knew he had several unsolved cases. "Which one?"

"The Telegraph Hill rape-murder."

"Who did it?"

"A guy who's already in jail. He was arrested a while back for harassing young girls in the park. I had a hunch about him and searched his apartment. He had a pair of police handcuffs like the ones found on the body, but he denied the murder. Today I got his

DNA test back from the lab. It matches the semen from the victim's body. I told him that, and he confessed. Jackpot."

"Well done!" She kissed the top of his head.

"How about you?"

"Well, I still have a job, but it remains to be seen whether I have a career. I didn't make much progress with my case."

"Last night you thought it was a dumb assignment anyway."

"Today I'm not so sure. The linguistic analysis showed that these people are dangerous, whoever they are."

"But they can't trigger an earthquake."

"I don't know."

Bo raised his eyebrows. "You think it's possible?"

"I spoke to three seismologists today. One said it was unlikely, one said the possibility was vanishingly small, and the third said it could be done with a nuclear bomb."

"Could these people have a nuclear device?"

"Possibly. But why not just threaten us with their bomb?"

"Yeah," Bo said thoughtfully. "That would be just as terrifying and a lot more credible. What's your next step?"

"I have one more seismologist to see, a Michael Quercus. He's the leading authority on what causes earthquakes."

She had already tried to interview Quercus. Late that afternoon she had rung his doorbell. He had told her, through the entry phone, to call for an appointment.

She drove back to the office, fuming. She did not make appointments. Agents rarely did. She preferred to catch people off guard. But she called him and made an appointment for the next day.

"What I really need," Judy told Bo, "is someone to explain the science to me in such a way that I can make my own judgment about whether a terrorist could cause an earthquake."

"And you need to find these Hammer of Eden people and bust them for making threats. Any progress there?"

She shook her head. "I had someone interview everyone at the Green California Campaign. No one there matches the profile. None have any kind of criminal or subversive record."

"Don't be discouraged. You've only been on the case a day."

"True, but that leaves only two clear days to their deadline."

"You'd better start early tomorrow." He got up off the couch.

They both went upstairs. Judy paused at her bedroom door. "Night, Bo."

"Good night, kid."

3

A S SHE drove across the Bay Bridge on Wednesday morning heading for Berkeley, Judy wondered what Michael Quercus looked like. His manner on the phone suggested a peevish professor. Or he could be an academic fat cat in a pin-striped suit.

Judy parked on Euclid Avenue. She rang his bell, and when she gave her name, there was a buzz and the entry door opened. She climbed two flights to his apartment. Michael's door was open. She walked in and found herself in his office-cum-living room.

He was sitting at his desk in khakis and a navy-blue polo shirt. Michael Quercus was neither a peevish professor nor an academic fat cat. He was a hunk: tall, good-looking, with dark curly hair.

He, too, was surprised. His eyes widened, and he said, "Are you the FBI agent?"

Judy gave him a firm handshake. "I've been one for ten years."

He grinned. "Okay," he said.

She got right to the point. "I need to know if a terrorist group could trigger an earthquake."

"Have you had a threat?"

"You haven't heard? It's been talked about on the radio. Don't you listen to John Truth?"

He shook his head. "Is it serious?"

"That's what I need to establish."

"Okay. Well, the short answer is yes."

Judy felt a frisson of fear. "How could they do it?"

"Take a nuclear bomb, put it at the bottom of a deep mine shaft, and detonate it. But you probably want a more realistic scenario."

"Yeah. Imagine you wanted to trigger an earthquake."

"Oh, I could do it."

Judy wondered if he was just bragging. "Explain how."

"Okay." He reached down behind his desk and picked up a plank of wood and a house brick. He obviously kept them there for this purpose. He put the plank on his desk and the brick on the plank. Then he lifted one end of the plank slowly until the brick slid down the slope onto the desk. "The brick slips when the gravity pulling it overcomes the friction holding it still," he said. "Okay so far?"

"Sure."

"A fault such as the San Andreas is a place where two adjacent slabs of the earth's crust are moving in different directions. They don't move smoothly: They get jammed. Then when they're stuck, pressure builds up slowly but surely over the decades."

"So how does that lead to earthquakes?"

"Something happens to release all that stored-up energy." He lifted one end of the plank again. This time he stopped just before the brick began to slide. "Several sections of the San Andreas Fault are like this—just about ready to slip any decade now. Take this."

He handed Judy a ruler. "Tap the plank in front of the brick."

She did so, and the brick began to slide.

Quercus grabbed it. "When the plank is tilted, it takes only a little tap to make the brick move. And where the San Andreas is under tremendous pressure, a little nudge may be enough to unjam the slabs. Then they slip, and all that pent-up energy shakes the earth."

Quercus was a clear thinker, and he explained himself easily. Judy enjoyed talking to him, and not just because he was good-looking. "Is that what happens in most earthquakes?"

"I believe so. There are natural vibrations that resound through the earth's crust from time to time. Most earthquakes are probably triggered by the right vibration in the right place at the right time."

"So how does that help our terrorists?"

"They need a ruler, and they need to know where to tap."

"What's the real-life equivalent of the ruler? A nuclear bomb?"

"They don't need anything so powerful. If they know exactly where the fault is vulnerable, they might do it with dynamite."

"Anyone can get hold of dynamite if they really want to."

"The explosion would have to be underground," Quercus said. "A terrorist group would obviously need drilling equipment, expertise, and some kind of pretext to get permission."

Those problems were not insurmountable. "Is it really so simple?" Judy said.

"Listen, I'm not telling you this would work. I'm saying it might. You'll have to make your own assessment of the risk."

Judy nodded. "So knowing where to place the charge is everything. Who has that information?"

"Universities, the state geologist . . . me. We all share information. It's not secret, though you would have to have some scientific knowledge to interpret the data."

"So someone in the terrorist group needs to be a seismologist."

"Yes. Could be a student."

Judy thought of the educated thirty-year-old woman who was doing the typing. She could be a graduate student.

Quercus went on. "And then there's the earth tides. The oceans move this way and that under the gravitational influence of the moon, and the solid earth is subject to the same forces. Twice a day there's a seismic window when the fault line is under extra stress because of the tides, and that's when an earthquake is most likely—or most easy—to trigger. Which is my specialty. I'm the only person who has done extensive calculations of seismic windows for California faults."

"Could someone have gotten this data from you?"

"Well, I'm in the business of selling it." He gave a rueful smile. "But I have only one contract, with a big insurance company."

"Someone might have taken the information without your knowledge. Have you been burgled lately?"

"Never."

"Could your data have been copied by a friend or relative?"

"No one spends time in this room without my being here."

Judy picked up a photo of a pretty redhead with a child from his desk. "Your wife or girlfriend?"

Quercus looked annoyed and took the picture out of her hand. "I'm separated from my wife, and I don't have a girlfriend."

"Is that so?" said Judy. She had got everything she needed from him. "I appreciate your time, Professor."

"Please call me Michael. I've enjoyed talking to you. You pick up fast. That makes it more fun."

He walked her to the door of the apartment and shook her hand. "Anything else you want to know, I'll be glad to help."

She risked a gibe. "So long as I call for an appointment, right?"

He did not smile. "Right."

Driving back across the bay, Judy reflected that the danger was now clear. A terrorist group might conceivably be able to cause an earthquake. They would need accurate data on critically stressed points on the fault line. They had to have someone to interpret the data, and they needed some way to send shock waves through the earth—a difficult task, but not out of the question.

She had the unwelcome task of telling Mr. Honeymoon, the governor's aide, that the whole thing was horrifyingly possible.

PRIEST woke at first light on Thursday.

One more day.

From the governor's office there had been nothing but a maddening silence. They acted as if no threat had been made. So did the rest of the world. The Hammer of Eden was rarely mentioned in the news broadcasts Priest listened to on his car radio.

Only John Truth took them seriously. He kept taunting Governor Mike Robson on his daily radio show. Until yesterday all the governor would say was that the FBI was investigating, but last night Truth had reported that the governor had promised a statement today.

If that statement was conciliatory and gave a hint the governor would consider the demand, Priest would rejoice. But if the statement was unyielding, he would have to cause an earthquake.

Priest wondered if he really could. Melanie sounded convincing when she talked about the fault line and what it would take to make it slip, but no one had ever tried this.

He rolled over. Melanie's head lay on the pillow beside him. He studied her face in repose. A strand of long ginger-colored hair fell across her cheek. He sat up. He was in the one-room house that had been his home for the last twenty-five years. As well as the bed, it had an old couch in front of the fireplace and a table in the corner with a fat yellow candle in a holder. There was no electric light.

In the early days most people lived in cabins like this, and the kids all slept in a bunkhouse. But over the years some permanent couples had formed. They had built bigger places with separate bedrooms for their children, although Priest and Star had kept their own individual houses. Now there were six family homes, as well as the original fifteen cabins. The commune consisted of twenty-five adults and ten children, plus Melanie and Dusty. One cabin was empty.

Priest picked up a towel and went outside. His dog, Spirit, greeted him with a quiet snuffle. The sun had not yet appeared over the mountains. No one else was about.

He walked downhill through the village, and Spirit followed. Priest knew the place might not be beautiful to other eyes. The paths were muddy, the buildings rickety, yet everything about the place warmed his heart. And when he looked farther away and saw the forested hillsides soaring steeply from the gleaming river to the blue peaks of the Sierra Nevada, he had a view that was so beautiful it hurt.

Beside the river, a wooden box on a boulder held soap, cheap razors, and a hand mirror. Priest shaved, then bathed in the cold stream. He dried himself briskly with a coarse towel.

He went back up the hill and dressed quickly in blue jeans and a work shirt. He walked to the cookhouse. Inside, he built up the fire with logs and lit it, put on a pan of water for coffee, and went out.

Priest liked to walk around when the others were all abed. He whispered their names as he passed their homes. "Moon. Dale. Poem. Giggle." He imagined each one lying there sleeping. Apple, a fat girl, lying on her back with her mouth open, snoring; the kids in the bunkhouse—his own Flower and Ringo; Melanie's Dusty;

the twins, Bubble and Chip, all pink cheeks and tousled hair . . . *My people. May they live here forever.*

He passed the barn where the wine from last year's harvest stood in huge wooden casks, almost ready to be blended and bottled.

He paused outside the temple, which was built five years ago. The temple meant a lot to Priest. It showed that his community was mature. They could feed themselves and still have the time and resources to spare for building a place of worship. They were no longer a bunch of hippies trying out an idealistic dream. The dream worked; they had proved it. The temple was the emblem of their triumph.

Priest stepped inside. It was a simple wooden structure with a single skylight and no furniture. Everyone sat cross-legged in a circle on the plank floor to worship. It was also the schoolhouse and meeting room. The only decoration was a banner Star had made. Priest could not read it, but he knew what it said.

> MEDITATION IS LIFE: ALL ELSE IS DISTRACTION.
> MONEY MAKES YOU POOR.
> MARRIAGE IS THE GREATEST INFIDELITY.
> WHEN NO ONE OWNS ANYTHING, WE ALL OWN EVERYTHING.
> DO WHAT YOU LIKE IS THE ONLY LAW.

These were the Five Paradoxes of Baghram. Priest said he had learned them from an Indian guru he had studied under in Los Angeles, but in fact, he had made them up.

He stood in the middle of the room, eyes closed, arms hanging loosely at his sides, focusing his energy. He prayed that Governor Mike Robson would announce a freeze on the building of new power plants in California. He imagined the governor saying, "I have decided to give these people what they want—not just to avoid an earthquake, but because it makes sense." After a few minutes Priest's spiritual strength was renewed. He felt alert, confident, centered.

When he went outside again, he decided to check on the vines. There had been no grapes originally. When Star arrived, there was nothing in the valley but a ruined hunting lodge. For three years the commune had lurched from crisis to crisis. Then Priest came.

It took him less than a year to become Star's acknowledged equal as joint leader. Under Priest's direction they had terraced the hillside, diverted a brook for irrigation, and planted a vineyard. Now their chardonnay wine was sought after by connoisseurs.

Priest walked along the neat rows. The vines were sprouting. It was late May, so the annual peril of frost killing the new shoots was past. At this point in the cycle most of the work consisted of tying the shoots to trellises to train their growth and prevent wind damage. Priest had learned about wine during his years as a liquor wholesaler, and Star had studied the subject in books, but they could not have succeeded without old Raymond Dellavalle, a good-natured winegrower who helped them because, Priest guessed, he wished his own youth had been more daring.

Priest's vineyard had saved the commune, but the commune had saved Priest's life. He had arrived here a fugitive—on the run from the Mob, the Los Angeles police, and the IRS. He was a drunk and a cocaine abuser—lonely, broke, and suicidal. He had driven down the dirt road to the commune, following vague directions from a hitchhiker, and had found peace, a new religion, work, friends, and lovers. There would never be any other existence for him. This place was all he had, and he would die defending it.

He would listen to John Truth's radio show tonight. If the governor was going to open the door to negotiation, it would surely be announced before the end of the broadcast.

When Priest came to the far side of the vineyard, he decided to check on the seismic vibrator. He walked up the hill. There was no road, just a well-trodden path. A quarter of a mile from the houses, he arrived at a muddy clearing. Parked under the trees were his old 'Cuda, a rusty Volkswagen minibus, Melanie's orange Subaru, and the communal pickup, a dark green Ford Ranger. From here a dirt track wound two miles through the forest, disappearing into a mud slide and passing through a stream, until at last it reached the county road.

Once a year, eight months after the harvest, the entire commune would roll barrels of wine through the trees to this clearing, to be loaded onto Paul Beale's truck for transport to his bottling plant in

Napa. In return for the wine, Paul Beale brought food for the communal kitchen and kept the free shop stocked with supplies: clothing, candy, cigarettes, books, toothpaste, everything anyone needed. The system operated without money. However, Paul kept accounts, and at the end of each year he deposited surplus cash into a bank account that only Priest and Star knew about.

From the clearing Priest headed along the track for a mile, then turned off and followed an invisible way through the trees. He came to a hollow and stopped at a pile of branches heaped twelve feet high like a bonfire. He pushed aside some of the brush to confirm that the truck was still there under its camouflage.

Spirit gave a low bark, as if he had heard something. Priest nervously replaced the branches he had moved, then headed back through the trees to the track and turned toward the village.

When they came within sight of the parking circle, Priest saw why Spirit had become agitated. There in the muddy clearing, parked beside his 'Cuda, was a police car. Priest's heart stopped as a cop stepped around the trunk of a tree.

Spirit barked fiercely. "Quiet," Priest said, and the dog fell silent. The cop saw Priest and waved.

Priest waved back, then reluctantly walked up to the car. He breathed evenly, smiled, and said, "Howdy."

"Are there any residences near here?" the cop asked.

Priest was tempted to lie, but it was risky. The cop had only to walk a quarter of a mile to stumble upon the houses. So Priest told the truth. "You're not far from the Silver River Winery."

"I never heard of it before."

That was no accident. In the phone book its address and number were Paul Beale's. None of the communards registered to vote. None of them paid taxes, because none had any income.

"It's pretty small," Priest said.

"You the owner?"

"No, just a worker."

"So what do you do here, make wine?"

"Yeah, that about sums it up. What brings you to these parts so early in the morning? We haven't had a crime here since Charlie got drunk and voted for Jimmy Carter." Priest grinned. There was no Charlie: He was trying to make the kind of joke a cop might like.

"I'm looking for the parents of a girl named Flower."

Priest felt cold as the grave. "What's happened?"

"She's under arrest."

"Is she okay?"

"She's not injured in any way, if that's what you mean."

"Thank heavens. I thought you were going to say she'd been in an accident." Priest's brain began to recover from the shock. "How can she be in jail? I thought she was here, asleep in her bed!"

"Obviously not. How are you connected with her?"

"I'm her father."

"Then you'll need to come to Silver City."

"Silver City? How long has she been there?"

"Just overnight. We didn't want to keep her that long, but she refused to tell us her address. She broke down an hour ago."

Priest's heart lurched to think of his little girl in custody.

The cop went on. "Even so, you were awful hard to find. In the end, I got directions from a bunch of gun-toting freaks about five miles down the valley from here."

Priest nodded. "Los Alamos."

"Yeah. Had a big sign up saying 'We do not recognize the jurisdiction of the United States government.' "

"I know them," Priest said. They were right-wing vigilantes who had taken over a big old farmhouse and guarded it with high-powered firearms. "Why is Flower in custody? What did she do?"

"She was caught stealing from a store."

"From a *store?*" Why would a kid who had access to a free shop want to do that? "What did she steal?"

"A large-sized color photograph of Leonardo DiCaprio."

PRIEST thanked the man for coming and promised that he and Flower's mother would appear at the sheriff's office in Silver City within an hour. Satisfied, the cop drove away.

Priest went to Star's cabin. It doubled as the commune's clinic. Star had no medical training, but she had picked up knowledge from her physician father and nurse mother. Her room was full of bandages, jars of ointment, aspirin, and cough medicines.

He woke her and told her the bad news. She jumped out of bed, yelling, "We have to go get her out *now!*" Star hated the police.

"Right," he said. "Just get dressed first, okay? It won't help Flower if you go in there mad and get yourself arrested, too."

She got control of herself. "You're right." She pulled on her jeans.

Priest had always believed it was best to be conventionally dressed when dealing with the police. He put an old dark blue suit on over his work shirt. Then he and Star got in the 'Cuda.

When they reached the county road, Priest said, "How come neither of us noticed she wasn't at home last night?"

"I went to say good night to her, but Pearl told me she had gone to the privy." Pearl, the daughter of Dale and Poem, was twelve years old and Flower's best friend. "I never imagined—"

"Why would you? The darn kid has spent every night of her life here. No reason to think she was anywhere else."

They drove into Silver City. The sheriff's office was next door to the courthouse. They entered a gloomy lobby. A deputy in a khaki shirt and green tie said, "Help you?"

Star said, "My name is Stella Higgins; you have my daughter here."

"Just one moment, please," the deputy said, and disappeared.

Priest spoke to Star in a low voice. "I think we should be respectable, law-abiding citizens who are appalled that a child of ours is in trouble with the police."

"Gotcha," Star said tightly.

A door opened, and the deputy let them in. "Mr. and Mrs. Higgins, follow me, please." He led them to a conference room.

Flower was waiting. She was going to be formidable and voluptuous like her mother one day, but at thirteen she was still a lanky, awkward girl. Now she was sullen and tearful at the same time. Star hugged her silently; then Priest did the same.

Star said, "Honey, have you spent the night in jail?"

Flower shook her head. "At some house," she said.

The deputy explained. "California law is very strict. Juveniles can't be jailed under the same roof as adult criminals, so Flower stayed at the home of the sheriff's sister."

Priest began to feel better.

The deputy said, "Sit down, please. I'm the probation officer."

They sat down.

"Flower is charged with stealing a poster worth ten dollars."

Star turned to her daughter. "I can't understand this. Why would you steal a poster of a movie star?"

Flower was suddenly vocal. She yelled, "I just wanted it, okay?"

Priest addressed the deputy. "We'd like to take our daughter home as soon as possible. What do we need to do?"

"Mr. Higgins, I should point out to you that the maximum penalty for what Flower has done is imprisonment until the age of twenty-one. However, I wouldn't expect such a harsh punishment for a first offense. Tell me, has Flower been in trouble before?"

"Never."

The deputy probed their homelife to establish whether Flower was well cared for. Priest answered most of the questions, giving the impression that they were simple agricultural workers.

The deputy seemed satisfied with the answers. Flower had to sign a promise to appear in court in four weeks' time. The deputy asked for one of the parents to countersign, and Star obliged.

Outside the sheriff's office, Priest said, "Flower, you did a dumb thing, but we love you as much as we always did. Just remember that. And we'll all talk about it when we get home."

As they drove back to the winery, Priest reflected on the wider implications of Flower's arrest. The commune had never before attracted the attention of the police. But now the place was on the map, and it was the worst possible moment for this to happen.

He switched on the car radio. At the top of the hour there was a news bulletin: "Governor Mike Robson meets with FBI agents this morning to discuss the terrorist group the Hammer of Eden, who have threatened to cause an earthquake."

When they got home, Melanie's car was gone from the parking circle. She had taken Dusty to his father's for the weekend.

Most of the group were weeding in the vineyard. When they saw Priest and Star returning with Flower, they all headed for the temple. When there was a crisis, they always met to discuss it.

On their way to the temple Priest and his family were intercepted by Dale and Poem with their daughter, Pearl. "There's something you should see," Dale said.

Flower shot an accusing glare at Pearl, who looked frightened.

Dale, a small man with neat, short hair, was the most conventional one in the group. He was a key person because he was an expert winemaker who controlled the blend of each year's vintage, but Priest sometimes felt he treated the commune as if it were any other village.

Dale led them all to the one empty cabin. The ceiling had a trap-door leading to a crawl space with a stepladder beneath it. Dale lit a candle and went up the ladder. Priest and Star followed. In the roof space they saw the girls' secret cache: a box full of cheap jewelry, makeup, fashionable clothes, and teen magazines.

Priest said quietly, "All the things we brought them up to consider worthless."

Dale said, "They've been hitchhiking to Silver City. They've done it three times in the past four weeks. They take clothes and change out of their jeans and work shirts when they get there."

Star said, "What do they do there?"

"Hang out on the street, talk to boys, and steal from stores."

Priest put his hand into the box and pulled out a narrow-bodied T-shirt, blue with a single orange stripe. It felt thin and trashy. With the shirt in his hand he retreated down the stepladder. Star and Dale followed. The two girls looked mortified.

Priest said, "Let's go to the temple and discuss this."

By the time they got there, everyone else in the group was sitting cross-legged on the floor, waiting. Priest sat in the middle, as always.

"Who wants to begin?" he said.

Aneth spoke up. "Maybe Flower and Pearl should begin by telling us why they wanted to go to Silver City."

"To meet people," Flower said defiantly.

Aneth smiled. "Boys, you mean?"

Flower shrugged.

Aneth said, "Well, I guess that's understandable, but why did you have to steal?"

"To look nice!"

Star asked, "What's wrong with your regular clothes?"

"Mom, be serious," Flower said scornfully.

Star leaned forward and slapped her face. "Don't you dare speak to me that way," she said. "I've had to get you out of jail for stealing, so don't talk as if I'm the stupid one."

Pearl started to cry.

Priest sighed. He should have seen this coming. There was nothing wrong with the clothes in the free shop. They had jeans, denim work shirts, T-shirts, heavy wool sweaters for the winter, waterproof coats for working in the rain. But the same clothes were worn by everyone. Of course the children wanted something different. Thirty-five years ago Priest had stolen a Beatle jacket from a boutique called Rave.

Poem said to her daughter, "Pearl, you don't like your clothes?"

Between sobs Pearl said, "We wanted to look like Melanie."

"Ah," Priest said, and he saw it all. Melanie was still wearing the clothes she had brought here: skimpy tops, miniskirts and short shorts, funky shoes, and cute caps. She looked chic and sexy. It was not surprising the girls had adopted her as a role model.

Dale said, "We need to talk about Melanie."

Priest felt defensive. He had brought Melanie here, he was her lover, and she was crucial to the plan. She was the only one who could interpret the data from Michael's disk. Priest could not let them turn on her. "We never make people change their clothes when they join us," he said. "They wear out their old stuff first."

Alaska, a former schoolteacher, spoke up. "It's not just her clothes. She doesn't do much work."

Priest argued, "I've seen her washing dishes and baking cookies."

Alaska persisted. "Some light domestic chores. She doesn't work in the vineyard. She's a passenger, Priest."

Now Garden spoke. A former junkie, she was twenty-five but looked forty. "Melanie's a bad influence. She talks to the kids about pop records and TV shows and trash like that."

Priest said, "Obviously we need to have a discussion with Melanie about this when she gets back from San Francisco."

Dale was not satisfied. "What bugs a lot of us—"

Priest frowned. This sounded as if the group had been talking behind his back. "Well? What bugs a lot of you?"

Dale swallowed. "Her mobile phone and computer."

There was no power line into the valley, and there had grown up a kind of puritanism about things like TV and videotapes. Melanie's equipment, which she recharged at the public library in Silver City, had drawn some disapproving stares.

There was a special reason why Melanie had to keep her mobile phone and her computer, but Priest could not explain it to Dale. He was not a Rice Eater. Priest could not be sure he would go along with the earthquake plan. He might freak.

Priest realized he had to end this. It was getting out of control. "I feel we're discussing these things in a bad atmosphere," he said. Most of them nodded. "What do we do about it?" Priest looked at his ten-year-old son, a dark-eyed, serious child. "What do you say, Ringo?"

"We meditate together," the boy said. It was the answer any of them would give.

"Then let's make ourselves ready," Priest said.

Each of them assumed the position they liked. Priest and some others sat cross-legged, hands loose on their knees, eyes closed.

A contemplative peace descended on the room, and Priest said a slow, deep syllable: "Om."

With one voice the congregation replied, "Omm . . ."

My people. May they live here forever.

THE meeting at the governor's office was scheduled for noon. Sacramento, the state capital, was a couple of hours' drive from San Francisco. Judy Maddox left home at nine thirty to allow for traffic.

Officially, the aide she was to meet, Al Honeymoon, was a cabinet secretary. In fact, he was hatchet man. Anytime Governor Robson needed to run a new highway through a beauty spot, build a nuclear power station, or fire a thousand government employees, he got Honeymoon to do the dirty work. Honeymoon had been selected for his bad-guy role because he was black, and the governor had shrewdly calculated that the press would hesitate to vilify a black man. Honeymoon was a political operator of great skill and utter ruthlessness. No one liked him, but plenty of people were scared of him.

For the sake of the Bureau, Judy wanted to make a good impression. The FBI liked to appear all-powerful, but Judy had made so little progress with the case that it would be kind of difficult to play that part. Her plan was simply to appear efficient and inspire confidence.

She decided to call ahead and check the parking. She dialed the governor's office on her cell phone and got Honeymoon's secretary. "I have a twelve noon meeting with Mr. Honeymoon, and I'm wondering if I can park at the Capitol Building."

The secretary was a young man. "We have no visitor parking, but there's a parking garage on the next block, on Tenth Street. However, your meeting isn't at noon. It's at eleven thirty."

"What? Has it been changed?"

"No, ma'am. It always was eleven thirty."

Judy was furious. To arrive late would create a bad impression. "I guess someone made a mistake." She checked her watch. If she drove like hell, she could be there in ninety minutes. "It's no problem. I'm running ahead of schedule," she lied. "I'll be there."

"Very good."

She put her foot down and watched the Monte Carlo's speedometer climb to a hundred. Fortunately, the road was not busy.

Brian Kincaid had told her the time of the meeting, so he would be late too. Judy dialed the San Francisco office and spoke to his secretary. "Linda, would you call Brian and tell him the governor's aide is expecting us at eleven thirty, not noon, please?"

"I think he knows that," Linda said.

"No, he doesn't. He told me twelve. See if you can reach him."

"Sure will."

"Thanks." Judy hung up and concentrated on her driving.

A few minutes later she heard a police siren. She looked in her mirror and saw a California highway patrol car.

"I do not believe this," she said. She pulled over and braked hard. The patrol car pulled in behind her. She opened her door.

An amplified voice said, "*Stay in the car.*"

Judy took out her FBI shield, held it at arm's length so the cop could see it, leaving the door open. The patrolman approached her. "You were doing ninety-nine miles per hour—"

"Just look at this," she said, shaking her shield. "It's an FBI shield! I'm an agent on urgent business, and you've delayed me."

"Well, you sure don't look like—"

"Don't tell me I don't look like an agent. You don't recognize an FBI shield, so how do you know what an agent looks like?"

"Can I see your license, please?"

"No. I'm leaving now, and I'm going to drive to Sacramento at ninety-nine miles per hour. Do you understand?"

"You can't do that," he said.

"Write your Congressman," she said, and she slammed the door and drove off.

She had lost her temper with the patrolman. He would tell his superior, who would complain to the FBI. Judy would get a reprimand, but if she had been polite, she would still be there.

She reached the turnoff for downtown Sacramento at eleven twenty. By eleven twenty-five she was entering the parking garage on Tenth Street. She found a slot and ran across the street.

The Capitol Building was a white stone palace that looked like a wedding cake. Judy hurried along a marble hall to a large doorway with GOVERNOR carved over it. She stopped and checked her watch. It was exactly eleven thirty. She had got there on time.

Inside was a large lobby presided over by a secretary behind an enormous desk. On one side was a row of chairs where, to Judy's surprise, she saw Brian Kincaid waiting, looking cool and relaxed and not at all like someone who had rushed to get here. When Kincaid caught her eye, she saw a flash of surprise in his expression.

She said, "Uh . . . hi, Brian."

"Morning." He looked away.

She asked, "What time did you get here?"

"A few minutes ago."

That meant he had known the correct time for the meeting. But surely he had not deliberately misled her?

A young black man emerged from a side door and spoke to them. "Mr. Honeymoon will see you now."

They followed him along the corridor and around a corner. Then they were shown into Honeymoon's room.

He was a big man with close-cropped hair turning gray. He had taken off the coat of his gray pin-striped suit to reveal black suspenders. He had a dark, sculptured face that wore a don't-mess-with-me expression. Despite his intimidating appearance, his manner was courteous. He stood up, shook their hands, and said, "I appreciate your coming here all the way from San Francisco."

"No problem," said Kincaid.

They sat down.

Without preamble Honeymoon said, "What's your assessment of the situation?"

Kincaid said, "Well, sir, I'll let Judy here fill you in."

Judy said, "We haven't caught these people yet, but we're fairly sure they're not connected with the Green California Campaign. That was an attempt to lay a false trail. We don't know who they are, but we've found out some things about them."

Honeymoon said, "Go ahead, please."

"First of all, linguistic analysis of the threat message tells us we're dealing not with a lone individual, but with a group."

Kincaid said, "Well, two people, at least."

Judy glared at Kincaid, but he did not meet her eye. "The message was composed by a man and typed by a woman, so there are at least two. Point two: These people are not insane."

Kincaid said, "Well, not clinically. But they sure aren't normal." He laughed as if he had said something witty.

Judy silently cursed him for undermining her. "People who commit violent crimes can be divided into two kinds—organized and disorganized. The disorganized act on the spur of the moment, use whatever weapons are handy, and choose their victims randomly. The organized plan their crimes, carry their weapons with them, and attack victims they've selected beforehand."

"All right," Honeymoon said. "The Hammer of Eden people are organized."

"Judging by their threat message, yes."

"You rely a great deal on this linguistic analysis," Honeymoon said skeptically.

Kincaid answered, "It's no substitute for careful investigative work, but in this case it's all we've got."

The implication was that they had to fall back on linguistic analysis because Judy had failed to do the legwork. Desperately she struggled on. "We're dealing with serious people. If they can't cause an earthquake, they may attempt something else."

"Such as?"

"One of the more usual terrorist acts. Explode a bomb, take a hostage, murder a prominent figure. However, I'm not prepared to rule out the possibility that they really could cause an earthquake. It's not likely, but it's conceivable. That's what I was told by California's leading expert, Professor Quercus."

Kincaid leaned back in his chair. "Judy has told you the textbook answers, Al," he said in a we're-all-boys-together tone of voice. "Now maybe I should tell you how it looks from the perspective of a certain amount of age and experience. These people can't cause an earthquake, and they don't care about power plants. My instinct tells me this is a guy trying to impress his girl. He's got the governor freaked out, the FBI running around, and it's all on the John Truth radio show every night. Suddenly he's a big shot, and she's, like, wow!"

Judy felt humiliated. Kincaid had let her lay out her findings and then poured scorn on all she had said. He had obviously planned this, and he had deliberately misled her about the time of the meeting.

Honeymoon stood up. "I'm going to advise the governor to take no action on this threat." He added, "Thank you both."

Kincaid said, "Anytime we can be of assistance, let us know."

A moment later they were outside.

Judy remained silent as they walked through the lobby into the hallway and left the building. There Kincaid stopped and said, "You did just fine in there, Judy. Don't you worry about a thing."

She wanted to scream at him, but she forced herself to say calmly, "I think we did our job."

Judy watched him walk away. Then crossing the street, she went into a See's candy store and bought some chocolates.

Driving back to San Francisco, she ate the whole box.

AFTER the meeting in the temple, Priest and Star sat in Priest's car and turned on the radio. The news bulletin was identical to the one they had heard earlier. Priest ground his teeth in frustration. "The governor has to say something soon!"

Star said, "Well, we figured all along we'd need to give a demonstration before he'd listen."

"Yeah." Priest hesitated. "I'm just scared the seismic vibrator won't work. There'll be no earthquake, and then we'll be lost."

They got out of the car and started walking to the vineyard to do some weeding. Along the way Star said, "Spend time with Flower tonight. Do something with her. You're always playing with Dusty."

Dusty was five. It was easy to have fun with him. Flower was thirteen, the age when everything grown-ups did seemed stupid.

"What'll I do with her?" Priest asked.

"She wants to learn the guitar."

Priest was not much of a guitarist himself, but he could play enough to get her started. "Okay, we'll start tonight."

They went to work, but a few minutes later they stopped. Priest saw a man coming down the hill, followed by a woman carrying a child. As the figures got closer, he said, "Is that Bones?"

"Yes!" Star said delightedly. She hurried toward the newcomers.

Priest followed more slowly. Bones, whose real name was Billy Owens, was a Rice Eater, but he liked to be drunk or stoned or both, and he had not joined the commune to find work and self-discipline. So after a couple of years Bones took off. He had not been seen since. Now, after more than twenty years, he was back.

Star hugged him hard. They had been a serious item for a while. When they let each other go, Priest could see that Bones did not look well. He had always been thin, but now he looked as if he was dying of starvation. His clothes were dirty. *He's here because he's in trouble.*

Bones introduced the woman as Debbie. She was no more than twenty-five. Her child was a boy about eighteen months old. She and the kid were almost as thin and dirty as Bones.

It was time for their midday meal. They took Bones to the cookhouse for pearl barley casserole. Debbie ate ravenously and fed the child too, but Bones took just a couple of spoonfuls.

Later, as they cleared the table, Bones took Priest aside and said, "Got something I want to show you. Come on."

Priest shrugged and went with him. As they walked, Priest took out a little bag of marijuana and rolled a joint.

Bones licked his lips. "You don't have anything with, like, more of a kick, do you?"

"What are you using these days, Bones?"

"A little brown sugar to keep my head straight."

Heroin. So that was it. Bones had become a junkie.

"We don't have any smack here," Priest told him. "No one uses it." *And I'd get rid of anyone who did.*

When they reached the clearing where the cars were parked, Bones said, "This is it."

At first Priest could not work out what he was looking at. It was a truck, but what kind? It was painted with a bright red-and-yellow design. Along the side was a picture of a monster breathing fire and some lettering in the same gaudy colors. Bones, who knew that Priest could not read, said, "The Dragon's Mouth. It's a carnival ride."

Priest saw it then. A lot of small carnival rides were mounted on trucks. The truck engine powered the ride in use. Then the parts of the ride could be folded down and the truck driven to the next site. Priest passed him the joint and said, "Is it yours?"

Bones said, "I been making my living from this for ten years, but it needs work." He drew on the joint. "I have to sell it. It's worth fifty thousand dollars. I'm asking ten. Maybe you guys should buy it."

"What would I do with a carnival ride, Bones?"

"It's a good investment. If you have a bad year with the wine, you could go out with the ride and make some money."

Priest shook his head. "No way. But I wish you luck."

"Hey, Priest, you want to know the truth of it? I'm in bad shape. Could you loan me a thousand bucks? That'd get me straight."

It would get you stoned out of your head, you mean. "We don't have any money," Priest said. "We don't use it here, remember?"

Bones nodded. "That's a bummer, man. I'm in serious trouble."

"Don't try to go behind my back and ask Star, because you'll get the same answer." Priest put a harsh note into his voice. "Are you listening to me?"

"Sure, sure," Bones said, looking scared. "Be cool, man, be cool."

"I'm cool," Priest said.

WHEN Melanie showed up at the end of the afternoon, Priest told her about Flower's being arrested and warned her that people wanted to put the blame on Melanie and her cute clothes. She said she would get some work clothes from the free shop.

After supper Priest sat outside his cabin with Flower and tuned his guitar. "Most songs have three chords," he began. "If you know three chords, you can play nine out of ten songs."

He showed her the chord of C. As she struggled to press the strings with her soft fingertips, he studied her face in the evening light: her perfect skin, the dark hair, green eyes like Star's.

"I'll teach you a song your mommy used to sing to you when you were a baby," he said.

As Flower struggled to play the chord of A minor, Priest toyed with the idea of returning to normal society. He fantasized going every day to a job, owning a TV. The thought made him queasy.

He recalled the one regular job he had ever had. At eighteen he had worked for the Jenkinsons, a couple who ran a liquor store. His intention had been to work just long enough to figure out where they kept their money, then steal it. But he discovered he had a queer talent for arithmetic. As customers bought liquor and got change, Priest either served them himself or heard one of the Jenkinsons sing out the total, "Dollar twenty-nine, Mrs. Roberto," or "Three bucks even, sir." And the figures seemed to add themselves up in his head. He soon knew the wholesale and retail prices of every item in the store and was awestruck by how much they were making without stealing from anyone.

He arranged for them to be robbed four times in a month, then made them an offer for the store. When they turned him down, he arranged a fifth robbery and made sure Mrs. Jenkinson got roughed up this time. After that Mr. Jenkinson accepted his offer.

Priest borrowed the deposit from the neighborhood loan shark and paid Mr. Jenkinson the installments out of the store's takings. Within a year he had four stores. Two years later he had a wholesale liquor warehouse. After three years he was a millionaire, and at the end of his fourth year he was on the run.

He sometimes wondered what might have happened if he had paid off the loan shark in full, given his accountant honest figures to report to the IRS, and made a plea-bargain deal with the LAPD on the fraud charges. Maybe today he would have a company as big as Coca-Cola and be living in a mansion in Beverly Hills.

But he knew it could never have happened. Priest could never live in the square world and obey other people's rules. That was why he had to live here. *In Silver River Valley I am the rules.*

Flower told him her fingers hurt.

"Then it's time to stop," Priest said.

"Does it hurt you?"

"No, but that's only because I'm used to it. When you've practiced the guitar a little, your fingertips get hard pads on them. Do you think you might like to be a musician someday?"

"No. I want to be a writer."

"That's good! What kind?"

"For a magazine. Like *Teen,* maybe."

"Why?"

"You get to interview stars and write about fashions."

Priest tried not to let his revulsion show. He knew she was not planning to spend her life in the valley. But when she was old enough to decide for herself, he hoped she would have a different view.

Star came over. "Time for John Truth," she said.

Priest took the guitar from Flower. "Go and get ready for bed."

He and Star headed for the 'Cuda. They found Melanie already there, sitting in the back seat, listening to the radio.

John Truth was saying, "I'm going to read that statement made by the governor's cabinet secretary, Mr. Honeymoon."

Priest's hackles rose. Honeymoon was the man behind the scheme to flood Silver River Valley, and they hated him.

John Truth went on. " 'The FBI has investigated the threat which appeared on an Internet bulletin board on the first of May. They have determined that there is no substance to the threat.' "

Priest's heart sank. He had hoped for at least some slight hint of appeasement, but Honeymoon sounded completely intractable.

Truth carried on reading. " 'Governor Robson, following the FBI's recommendation, has decided to take no further action.' "

Priest said, "That means we have to do it."

Melanie said, "Well, I never expected the governor to cave in without a demonstration."

"We can do this without hurting anyone," Priest said. "Melanie has picked the perfect location." He turned to her. "Tell Star."

Melanie unfolded a map so that Star and Priest could see it. "Here's the Owens Valley fault," she said. "There were major earthquakes in 1790 and 1872, so another one is overdue."

Star said, "Surely earthquakes don't happen according to a regular timetable?"

"No. But enough pressure builds up over about a century, so we can cause one now if we give a nudge in the right place."

"Which is where?" Star said.

Melanie pointed to a spot on the map. "Round about here. I can't be exact until I get there. When I look at the landscape, I should be able to pinpoint the spot by evidence of earlier earthquakes."

"Okay," Star said.

"Now, the best time, according to Michael's seismic window, will be between one thirty and two twenty."

"How can you be sure no one will get hurt?"

"Look at the map. Owens Valley is thinly populated. The point I've chosen is miles from any human habitation."

Priest added, "We can be sure the earthquake will be minor. The effects will hardly be felt." He knew this was not certain, and so did Melanie, but she did not contradict him.

Star said, "If the effects are hardly felt, no one's going to care."

She was being contrary, but that was just a sign of how tense she was. Priest said, "We said we would cause an earthquake tomorrow. When we've done it, we'll call John Truth and tell him we kept our promise. Then we threaten to do it again. But this time we give them a week. And it'll be someplace where real damage will be done." He caught an apprehensive look from Star. "We don't have to mean it. Once we've shown our power, the threat ought to be enough."

IT WAS pitch-dark when they left the next morning.

The seismic vibrator had not been seen in daylight within a hundred miles of the valley, and Priest wanted to keep it that way. He planned to leave home and return in darkness. The round-trip would be about five hundred miles, eleven hours of driving. They would take the 'Cuda as a backup car, Priest had decided. Oaktree would come with them to share the driving.

Priest sat behind the wheel of the truck, slid the key into the ignition, and turned on the engine. Melanie climbed in beside him. He steered the heavy vehicle through the trees to the dirt track, then headed for the road. Star and Oaktree were behind in the 'Cuda.

By sunup they were on U.S. 395, across the border in Nevada. They took a break at a truck stop and ate breakfast.

When the road swung back into California, it climbed into the mountains and the scenery was majestic. They dropped down again beside what Melanie said was Mono Lake. Soon they were on a two-lane road that cut a straight line down a long, dusty valley.

The ground on either side of the road was tan-colored and stony.

Melanie said, "This is Owens Valley."

They passed through a sleepy small town every twenty miles or so. There was little traffic, and the seismic vibrator was stared at every time they waited at a stoplight. It was a big vehicle, and the machinery in the back looked kind of intriguing. Plenty of men would remember it. "Yeah, I seen that rig. Looked like she might be for layin' blacktop or somethin'. What was she anyway?"

Melanie switched on her laptop and unfolded her map. "Somewhere in the next five or ten miles," she said.

"What's the time?" Priest asked.

"Just after one."

They had cut it fine. The seismic window would open in half an hour and close fifty minutes later.

Melanie directed Priest down a side turning that crossed the flat valley floor. It was not really a road, just a track.

"Pull up here," Melanie said at last.

Priest stopped the truck, and they both got out. The 'Cuda pulled up behind the truck, and Star and Oaktree joined them.

"See the dry gulch?" Melanie said. "Now look to the right."

Where she was pointing, the gulch came to an abrupt end, then began again just as abruptly and continued toward the middle of the valley. "That's the fault line," Priest said. "Last time there was an earthquake, one whole side of this valley shifted five yards."

Oaktree said, "And we're about to make it happen again?"

"We're going to try." Priest turned to Melanie. "Is the truck in exactly the right place?"

"I guess," she said. "A few yards one way or another up here on the surface shouldn't make any difference five miles down."

"Okay." He hesitated. "Well, I'll get started."

Priest got into the truck and threw the switch that lowered the steel plate to the ground. He set the vibrator to shake for thirty seconds in the middle of its frequency range. Then he picked up the remote control and got out of the truck. "All set," he said.

The four of them got into the 'Cuda. Oaktree drove it back to the road, crossed it, and headed into the scrub on the far side. They went partway up a hill; then Melanie said, "This is fine."

Oaktree stopped the car. They got out and stood looking across the valley at the truck.

Priest pressed the button on the remote control. He heard the roar of the vibrator, though it was muted by distance. He felt the vibration in the soles of his feet, a faint but definite trembling sensation. A cloud of dust billowed around the truck.

All four of them were taut as guitar strings, their bodies tensed for the first hint of movement in the earth. Seconds passed. Priest's eyes raked the landscape, looking for signs of a tremor.

Come on, come on!

The seismic exploration crews normally set the vibrator for a seven-second sweep. Priest had set this one for thirty seconds. It seemed like an hour. At last the noise stopped.

Melanie said, "Damn it. Try it again."

Priest pressed the button one more time.

The distant roar started up, but nothing happened.

Despair engulfed Priest. Perhaps the Silver River Valley commune was a dream that had come to an end. But Melanie was not ready to give up. "Let's move the truck a ways and try again."

They got into the 'Cuda and drove fast across the baked earth to the seismic vibrator. Then Priest and Melanie climbed into the truck, and he drove while Oaktree and Star followed in the car.

Melanie scanned the landscape. After half a mile she pointed at what looked like a miniature cliff about four feet high. "Fault scarp," she said. "About a hundred years old. Let's try here."

Priest stopped and lowered the plate. He set the vibrator, programmed a sixty-second sweep, and jumped out of the truck.

Again they drove the 'Cuda across U.S. 395 and up the hill on the far side. They all got out of the car and looked across the valley. Priest pressed the button.

The truck roared, the earth trembled faintly, and the dust rose for a full minute, but there was no earthquake.

Star said, "This isn't going to work."

Melanie threw her a furious look. Turning to Priest, she said, "Can you alter the frequency of the vibrations?"

"Yes," Priest said. "I can go up or down. Why?"

"There's a theory that pitch may be a crucial factor. Maybe a vibration has to be just the right pitch to dislodge the fault. You know how a musical note can shatter a glass?"

"I know what you mean. When they use the vibrator in seismic exploration, they vary the pitch over a seven-second sweep. I didn't select that feature, but I can."

"Let's try it."

"Okay, but we need to hurry. It's already five after two."

They jumped into the car. Oaktree drove fast, skidding across the dusty desert. Priest reset the controls of the vibrator for a sweep of gradually increasing pitch over a period of sixty seconds. As they raced back to their observation point, he checked his watch again. "Two fifteen," he said. "This is our last chance."

Priest pressed the button.

This time the roar did not stay at the same moderate pitch but started at a profound bass rumble and began slowly to climb.

It happened. The earth beneath Priest's feet seemed to ripple like a choppy sea. He felt as if someone had taken him by the leg and thrown him down. He landed on his back, hitting the ground hard. He saw Star and Melanie fall, Melanie next to him and Star a few steps away. Oaktree staggered, stayed on his feet, and fell last. There was a noise like an express train thundering past. The ground continued to move as if someone had hold of the end of a rug and would not stop shaking it. It was terrifying.

Priest struggled to his knees. Then Melanie grabbed his arm and pulled him down again. He screamed at her, "Let me go!" But he could not hear his own words.

The ground heaved up and threw him downhill. Melanie rolled on top of him. He curled up in a ball and waited for death.

The shaking stopped as suddenly as it had started. Priest rubbed the dust out of his eyes and stood up. He extended a hand to Melanie and pulled her up. "Are you okay?" he said.

"I think so," she replied shakily.

The dust in the air thinned, and he saw Oaktree getting to his feet unsteadily. Where was Star? Then he saw her. She lay on her back with her eyes closed. *Not dead, please God, not dead.* He knelt by her side. "Star!" he said urgently. "Are you okay?"

She opened her eyes and said, "That was a blast!"

Priest grinned with relief. He helped her to her feet.

He looked across the valley and saw the truck. It was upright and seemed undamaged. A few yards from it there was a great gash in the ground that ran north and south as far as he could see.

"Well, I'll be darned," he said quietly. "Look at that."

"We did it," Oaktree said. "We caused an earthquake!"

Priest grinned at them all. "That's the truth," he said.

He kissed Star, then Melanie; then Oaktree kissed them both. They all laughed. Then Priest started to dance, his boots kicking up the newly settled dust. Star joined in, then Melanie and Oaktree, and the four of them went round and round in a circle, shouting and whooping and laughing until tears came to their eyes.

PART TWO
SEVEN DAYS

4

JUDY Maddox was driving home on Friday at the end of the worst week in her FBI career. Nothing good had happened since her meeting yesterday with Al Honeymoon. She had been interviewing seismology professors, asking who had access to their data and did any of those people have connections with terrorist groups. The seismologists had not been helpful. Most of today's academics had been students in the '60s and '70s. To them the FBI was the enemy.

The Hammer of Eden's deadline ran out today, and there had been no earthquake. Judy was deeply relieved. Maybe this would be the end of the whole thing.

Her car phone rang. "This is Judy Maddox," she said.

"This is your father. Turn on your radio, quick, to John Truth."

She got the station that broadcast *John Truth Live*, and his nasal twang filled the car. "The California state seismologist has confirmed that there was an earthquake today—the very day the Hammer of Eden promised it—at twenty minutes after two in Owens Valley, just as the Hammer of Eden said when they called a few minutes ago."

Judy was electrified. *They did it.*

John Truth was saying, "In a moment we will play you a recording of the message left by the Hammer of Eden."

They're on tape! That could be a crucial mistake. A voice on tape would provide a mass of information to Simon Sparrow.

A commercial for a furniture warehouse came on, and Judy muted the volume. "Are you still there, Bo?"

"Sure."

"They did it, didn't they?"

"Sure looks like it."

Judy tried to calm her racing heart. "I'd better go back to work." She made a right turn. "Thanks, Bo. You're a great daddy."

He laughed. "You're a great kid, too. Bye."

She turned up the radio and heard a low, sexy voice saying, "This is the Hammer of Eden with a message for Governor Mike Robson."

The picture that came into her mind was of a mature woman with a wide smile, likable but kind of off the wall.

The tone changed, and the woman muttered, "Damn, I didn't expect to be talking to a tape recorder." She resumed her formal voice and continued. "Like we promised, we caused an earthquake today, four weeks after our last message. It happened in Owens Valley, a little after two o'clock. You can check it out."

A faint background noise caused her to hesitate.

What was that? Simon will find out.

A second later she carried on. "We do not recognize the jurisdiction of the United States government. Now that you know we can do what we say, you'd better think again about our demand. Announce a freeze on construction of new power plants in California. You have seven days to make up your mind. After that we will trigger another earthquake. But the next one won't be out in the middle of nowhere."

John Truth came on. "There it is, the voice of the Hammer of Eden, the group that claims to have triggered the earthquake that shook Owens Valley today."

Judy turned down the volume and dialed Raja's home number.

When he answered, she said, "Hi, this is Judy. There was an earthquake in the eastern part of the state this afternoon, and the Hammer of Eden claims they triggered it."

"Wow! Maybe these people are for real after all."

"John Truth just played a recorded message from the perpetrators. I need you to go to the radio station and get the tape. Take the tape to Simon and tell him I need something in the morning."

"You got it."

She broke the connection and turned John Truth up again. He was saying: "A minor earthquake, magnitude five to six. No one injured, no property damage, but a tremor that was definitely felt by the residents of Bishop, Independence, and Lone Pine."

Judy realized that some of those people must have seen the perpetrators within the last few hours. She had to get over there and start interviewing them as soon as possible. Where exactly was the earthquake? She needed an expert. She dialed Michael Quercus's number.

He picked up after six rings. "Quercus."

"This is Judy Maddox from the FBI. I need to talk to you. It's urgent, and I'd like to come to your place right away."

"It's out of the question. I'm with someone."

He had a woman there, Judy guessed. But he had told her that he was not seeing anyone. Perhaps he had lied.

"Have you been listening to the radio?" she asked him. "There's been an earthquake, and the terrorist group we talked about claims to have triggered it."

"Are they telling the truth?"

"That's what I need to discuss with you."

"I'd like to help you, but . . . No, wait." His voice became muffled as he covered the mouthpiece with his hand, but Judy could still distinguish his words. "Hey, have you ever met a real-live FBI agent?" She could not hear the reply, but after a moment he said, "Okay. My guest would like to meet you. Come on over."

"Thanks. I'll be there in twenty minutes."

Judy drove over the bridge, found Euclid Street, and parked. She rang Michael's bell, and he buzzed her into the building. He came to the apartment door barefoot, looking pleasantly weekendish. She followed him into his office-cum-living room.

There, to her astonishment, she saw a little boy of about five, with freckles and fair hair, dressed in pajamas with dinosaurs on them. After a moment she recognized him as the child in the photograph on the desk: Michael's son. This was his guest.

Michael said, "Dusty, meet Special Agent Judy Maddox."

The boy shook hands politely. "Are you really in the FBI?"

"Yes, I am. Want to see my badge?" She took her shield from her shoulder bag and gave it to him. He held it reverently.

Michael said, "Dusty likes to watch *The X-Files*."

Judy smiled. "I don't work in the alien spacecraft department. I just catch regular earth criminals."

Dusty said with elaborate politeness, "We were just going to have some Cap'n Crunch. Would you care to join us?"

"I'm real hungry. I'd love some Cap'n Crunch."

"Come into the kitchen."

The three of them sat at a table in the little kitchen and ate breakfast cereal and milk out of blue pottery bowls. "My goodness," Judy said, "I'd forgotten how good Cap'n Crunch is."

Michael laughed. Judy was amazed at the difference in him. He was relaxed and amiable. She was beginning to like him.

When supper was eaten and they had left the kitchen, Judy heard Dusty whisper, "She's nice, isn't she?"

"Yes," Michael replied.

Judy went back into the living room while Michael got Dusty ready for bed. Michael joined her a few minutes later. He said, "You were great with him."

"It wasn't difficult. He's a charmer."

Michael nodded. "Gets it from his mother."

They were both silent for a moment. Then Michael said, "Tell me about the earthquake."

"It took place in Owens Valley this afternoon at twenty minutes past two."

"Let's get the seismograph." Michael sat at his desk and tapped the keys of his computer. "When your terrorists made their threat four weeks ago, did they specify the location?"

"No."

"There's an earthquake in California more or less every day. Maybe they just claimed responsibility for something that happened naturally."

"Can you tell me exactly where today's tremor took place?"

"Yes. I can calculate the epicenter by triangulation. I'll just print out the coordinates." After a moment his printer whirred.

Judy said, "Is there any way of knowing how the earthquake was triggered?"

"Yes, I should be able to tell." He turned from the screen to face her. "A normal earthquake is preceded by a gradual buildup of fore-shocks, or lesser tremors, which we can see on the seismograph. By contrast, when an earthquake is triggered by an explosion, there is no buildup—the graph begins with a characteristic spike." He turned back to his computer. "That's odd," he said. "I don't see a spike."

"So the earthquake happened naturally?"

Michael shook his head. "I'm not sure. There are foreshocks, yes. But I've never seen foreshocks like this."

"What's peculiar about them?" she asked.

"They're too regular. They look artificial. I don't know what caused these vibrations, but they don't look natural. I believe your terrorists did something. I just don't know what it is."

"Can you find out?"

"I hope so. I'll call a few other seismologists."

Judy guessed she had got all she could out of Michael tonight. Now she needed to get to the scene of the crime. "Thanks for seeing me," she said. "I appreciate it."

"I enjoyed it." He smiled at her, a big hundred-watt smile.

She left the apartment and got into her car. She would go to the office and look up airline schedules on the Internet, see if there was a flight to somewhere near Owens Valley early tomorrow morning.

Judy returned to FBI headquarters. As she walked past Brian Kincaid's office, she heard voices. She tapped on the open door.

"Come in," he called.

She stepped inside. Her heart sank when she saw that Kincaid was with Marvin Hayes. She and Marvin disliked each other intensely, but Brian liked him, and Brian was now the boss.

"Am I interrupting something?" she said.

"Did you hear about the earthquake?" Brian asked.

"Of course. I just interviewed a seismologist who says the foreshocks are like nothing he's ever seen before. He's sure they're artificial. I want to go to Owens Valley to look for witnesses."

A significant glance passed between the two men. Brian said, "Judy, no one can cause an earthquake."

Marvin said, "I've talked to two seismologists myself tonight, and they both told me it was impossible."

Brian said, "We think this group never went near Owens Valley. They found out about the earthquake and claimed credit."

Judy frowned. "This is my assignment," she said. "How come Marvin is calling seismologists?"

"This case is becoming very high-profile," Brian said. "I'm not confident you can deal with that."

"You can't reassign me without a reason."

"Oh, I have a reason," he said. He picked up a fax from his desk. "Yesterday a California highway patrolman stopped you for speeding. According to this, you were uncooperative and abusive, and you refused to show him your license."

Judy struggled to control her rage. "I showed him my badge!"

Brian ignored that. "I'm setting up a special squad to deal with the Hammer of Eden," he went on. "I've asked Marvin to take charge. He won't be needing your help. You're off the case."

PRIEST could hardly believe he had done it.

I caused an earthquake. I really did. Me.

As he drove the truck north on U.S. 395, heading for home, he found it surprising that the world was carrying on as if nothing had happened. Cars and trucks passed up and down the freeway; people parked at Burger King. They should all have been in shock. He began to wonder if the earthquake had really happened.

In the late afternoon Priest pulled into a filling station. The 'Cuda followed. Priest and Oaktree filled the tanks while Melanie and Star looked for the ladies' room.

Priest went inside to pay. The clerk had a radio on. It occurred to Priest that he might hear the news; it was five to six. Priest paid, and Melanie and Star came out of the rest room. At last the news began.

To give them a reason for hanging around, Priest slowly selected some candy bars and took them to the counter while he listened. The first item was a report on the President's visit to India. The clerk added up the cost of the candy bars, and Priest paid again. The next story was about a shooting in a school in Chicago.

Priest walked slowly toward the door, followed by Melanie and Star. Finally the newscaster said, "The environmental terrorist group the Hammer of Eden has claimed responsibility for a minor earthquake that took place today in Owens Valley, California."

Priest whispered, "Yes!" and smacked his left palm with his right fist in a triumphant gesture.

"The claim was made in a phone call to *John Truth Live*."

Then Priest was shocked to hear Star's voice. He stopped dead. She was saying, "Now that you know we can do what we say, you'd better think again about our demand. Announce a freeze on construction of new power plants in California. You have seven days to make up your mind."

Star exploded, "That's me!"

"Hush!" Priest said as the newscaster continued. "The governor has not responded to this latest threat, but the head of the FBI's field office in San Francisco has promised a press conference tomorrow morning. In sports today—"

They stepped outside.

Star said, "They broadcast my voice! What am I going to do?"

"Stay calm," Priest told her. "Nobody outside our commune knows your voice. You haven't said more than a few words to an outsider for twenty-five years."

"I guess you're right," Star said doubtfully.

Oaktree was waiting at the wheel of the 'Cuda. "Come on, you guys, what's the holdup?" he said.

Star explained what they had heard. "Luckily nobody outside the commune knows my voice. Oh, no!" She turned to Priest. "The probation officer—in the Silver City sheriff's office."

Priest cursed. Of course. Star had spoken to him only yesterday. If he heard the radio broadcast and remembered Star's voice, the sheriff and half a dozen deputies might be at the commune right now, waiting for Star to return. But maybe he had not heard the news. Priest had to check. "I'm going to call the sheriff's office. Wait here."

He went to the pay phone, got the sheriff's number from information, and dialed. "I need to speak to Mr. Wicks," he said.

A friendly voice said, "Billy ain't here. He flew to Nassau last night. Back in a couple a weeks. Anyone else help you?"

Priest hung up and went outside. "The guy went on vacation," he told the others. "He's in Nassau for two weeks. We're safe."

Star slumped with relief. "Thank the Lord for that."

Priest opened the truck door. "Let's get back on the road."

IT WAS approaching midnight when Priest steered the seismic vibrator along the rough winding track that led through the forest to the commune. He returned the truck to its hiding place.

After parking the 'Cuda, they walked down the hill to the village. Most of the cabins were dark and silent. They said good night quietly and trudged off to their individual homes.

It was a warm night. Priest lay on his bed, thinking. No comment from the governor, but an FBI press conference in the morning. That bothered him. What was the FBI up to? He had to find out more. Then it occurred to him that he could go to the press conference. It would be dangerous, but the idea appealed to him.

He rolled off the bed, stepped into his sandals, and went outside. In the moonlight he found his way to Melanie's cabin. She was sitting on the edge of her bed, brushing her long red hair. As he walked in, she looked up and smiled. "Hello," she said.

"I need to use your cell phone," he said.

She pouted. That was not the reaction she wanted.

Priest gave her his bad-boy grin. "But I may have to throw you to the ground and ravish you, then use your phone."

She smiled. "It's okay. You can phone first."

He picked up the phone, called information, got the number of the FBI in San Francisco, and dialed it.

A man's voice answered, "FBI."

"This is radio station KCAR in Carson City. Dave Horlock speaking," Priest said. "We want to send a reporter to your press conference tomorrow. Could you give me the address and time?"

"It's at twelve noon, here in the Federal Building."

"Do we need an invitation, or can our guy just show up?"

"All he needs is his regular press accreditation."

"Thanks for your help." Priest hung up. He would show up at the press conference tomorrow and see what the enemy was up to.

Melanie lay back on the bed and said, "It's been a long day."

Priest gazed at her body. He needed to calm his mind. The second-best way of doing that was meditation. The best was in front of him.

MELANIE went to sleep afterward. Lying beside her, Priest worried over the problem of press accreditation until he thought of the solution. At dawn he got up.

He went to the kids' bunkhouse and woke Flower. "I want you to go with me to San Francisco," he said. "Get dressed."

Priest made breakfast for her in the deserted cookhouse. As she ate, he said, "You remember we talked about you being a writer? And you told me you'd like to work for a magazine?"

"Yes, *Teen* magazine," she said.

"Well, today you're going to find out what it's like to be a reporter. I'm taking you to an FBI press conference."

"I never read about the FBI in *Teen*."

"Well, Leonardo DiCaprio isn't giving a press conference today. "

She grinned sheepishly. "Too bad. What's the press conference about?"

"A group who claim they caused an earthquake. Now, I don't want you to tell anyone about this. It has to be a secret, okay?"

"Gotcha."

Priest thought about putting on the dark blue suit. However, it was so old-fashioned, it would be conspicuous in San Francisco, so he wore blue jeans and a checked flannel shirt with a long tail, which he wore untucked. He stuck a knife in the waistband of his jeans, at the back, where it was concealed by the tail of his shirt.

He was high on adrenaline throughout the four-hour drive to San Francisco. They reached the city at eleven a.m. and put the car in a parking lot. At a drugstore Priest bought Flower a spiral-bound notebook. Then he took her to a coffee shop. While she was drinking a soda, he said, "I'll be right back," and left.

He walked toward Union Square, searching for a man who looked like him. The streets were busy with Saturday shoppers. There were plenty of dark men in their forties, but most of them were twenty or thirty pounds heavier than Priest.

Then he struck it lucky: a thin-faced guy of about fifty, wearing glasses. He was dressed in navy slacks and a green polo shirt but carried a worn tan attaché case. Priest guessed he was going to the office to do some Saturday catching up. Priest followed him around a corner, waiting for an opportunity.

The man turned into a street of office buildings. There was no one in sight. Priest drew the knife, ran up to him, shoved the knife in his face, and screamed, "Gimme your wallet, or I'll slit your throat!"

"It's in my case."

Priest grabbed the briefcase, took the guy's glasses, and ran away. He dropped his knife into a garbage bin and walked on. At the next corner he stopped by a building site and opened the case. Inside was a file folder, a notebook, some pens, and a leather billfold. Priest took the billfold and threw the case into a Dumpster.

He returned to the coffee shop and sat down with Flower. He opened the billfold. It contained money, credit cards, business cards, and some kind of an identity card with a photo. Priest pulled out a business card and handed it to Flower. "My card, ma'am."

"You're Peter Shoebury, of Watkins, Colefax and Brown."

"I'm a lawyer?"

"I guess."

He looked at the photo on the identity card. It did not look exactly like Priest, but neither did it look much like Peter Shoebury. Still, Priest could improve the resemblance. Shoebury had short hair. Priest said, "Can I borrow your hair band?"

"Sure." Flower took a rubber band out of her hair and shook out her locks. Priest pulled his hair into a ponytail, tied it with the band, and put on the glasses. He showed Flower the photo.

"How do you like my secret identity?"

"H'm. Daddy, did you pick someone's pocket?"

"Sort of." Priest could see she thought that was roguish rather than wicked. He looked at the clock on the wall. It was eleven forty-five. "Are you ready to go?"

"Sure."

They walked along the street and entered the Federal Building. They took the elevator up to the FBI floor. Priest led Flower into the FBI office and followed a sign to a conference room off the lobby. There was a table with microphones at the far end of the room. Near the door stood four men, all tall, wearing business suits, white shirts, and sober ties. They had to be agents.

Priest sensed that the leader was the older man with thick white hair. He was talking to a man with a black mustache.

A young woman carrying a clipboard approached Priest. "Hi. Can I help you?"

"Well, I sure hope so," Priest said. "My name is Peter Shoebury. I'm an attorney with Watkins, Colefax and Brown. My daughter, Florence, is editor of the school newspaper. She heard on the radio about your press conference, and she wanted to cover it for the paper. I hope it's okay."

Everyone looked at the white-haired guy. He held out his hand and said, "I'm Associate Special Agent in Charge Brian Kincaid, head of the San Francisco field office of the FBI."

Priest shook hands. "Good to meet you, Brian."

"Would you have any kind of ID?"

"Oh, sure." Priest opened the stolen wallet and took out the card with the photo of Peter Shoebury. He held his breath.

Kincaid looked at it, then checked the resemblance to Priest. He handed it back. Priest breathed again.

Kincaid turned to Flower. "What school are you at, Florence?"

"Um . . ." Flower hesitated. Priest was about to answer for her. Then she said, "Eisenhower Junior High."

Priest felt a surge of pride. She had inherited his nerve. Just in case Kincaid should happen to know the schools in San Francisco, he added, "That's in Oakland."

Kincaid seemed satisfied. "Well, we'd be delighted to have you join us, Florence," he said.

"Thank you, sir," she said.

The conference room was filling up with photographers, reporters, and a couple of TV crews.

Kincaid said, "We need to start the press conference now, Florence. I hope you'll stay to hear what we have to announce."

"Yes, thank you," she said.

The agents moved to the table at the far end. Priest and Flower sat at the back and waited. He had not gained much hard information yet, but he did have a sense of the people he was dealing with. He was reassured by what he had learned. Neither Kincaid nor the others struck him as brilliant. They seemed like ordinary plodding cops, the kind who got by with a mixture of dogged routine and occasional corruption. He had little to fear from them.

Kincaid stood up and introduced himself. "I would like to begin by making one thing very clear. The FBI does not believe that yesterday's earthquake was triggered by a terrorist group. Nevertheless, a terrorist threat has been made, and the Bureau intends to catch the people who made it. Our investigation is headed by Special Agent Marvin Hayes. Over to you, Marvin."

Hayes stood up. "FBI agents have this morning questioned all five paid employees of the Green California Campaign and visited the headquarters of the campaign here in San Francisco."

Priest had laid a false trail, and the feds were following it. There was more, but it did not change the basic story. Priest was pleased that the FBI investigation was so far off course.

At last Kincaid drew the session to a close. Priest and Flower made for the door but were stopped by the woman with the clipboard. "You two didn't sign in." She handed Priest a book and a pen. "Just put your name and the organization you represent."

Priest froze with fear. *I can't. I can't!*

"Sure." He took the book and pen and handed them to Flower. "I think Florence should sign for us. She's the journalist."

Flower wrote in the book and handed it back to the woman.

"You, too, sir, please." The woman gave Priest the book.

He took it reluctantly. Now what? If he just scrawled a squiggle, she might ask him to print his name clearly. As Priest hesitated, he heard Kincaid say, "I hope that was interesting for you, Florence."

"Yes, sir, it was," Flower said politely.

Priest drew a scrawl where he was supposed to write his name. Then he closed the book before handing it back to the woman.

Kincaid said to Flower, "Will you remember to send me a copy of your class newspaper when it's printed?"

"Yes, of course."

The woman opened the book and said, "Oh, sir, would you print your name? I'm afraid your signature isn't really clear."

"You'll need an address," Kincaid said to Flower. He took a business card from the breast pocket of his jacket. "There you go."

"Thank you."

Priest remembered that Peter Shoebury carried business cards. He opened the wallet and gave one to the woman. "My handwriting is terrible. Use this," he said. He shook Kincaid's hand. "I'll make sure Florence sends you the clipping." They left the room.

Outside, Flower said, "Why did we have false names?"

"Well, I never like the pigs to get my real name," Priest said. She would accept that. She knew how her parents felt about cops.

But she said, "Well, I'm mad at you about it."

He frowned. "Why?"

"I'll never forgive you for calling me Florence," she said.

Priest stared at her for a moment; then they both burst out laughing. "Come on, kid," he said fondly. "Let's go home."

ON SATURDAY morning Judy drove to Gala Foods and shopped. Back at home, Bo helped her unload the groceries and said, "I hear Marvin Hayes raided the Green California Campaign."

"It can't have done him much good. They're all clean. Raja interviewed them on Tuesday. If they're terrorists, I'm Kojak."

The doorbell rang. Judy opened the door to Simon Sparrow. She was surprised but pleased. "Hey, Simon, come on in."

Bo shook hands with Simon. Judy said, "Simon is one of the FBI's top linguistic analysts."

Simon was carrying a cassette tape and a manila envelope. "I brought you my report on the Hammer of Eden tape," he said.

"I'm off the case," Judy said. "It's Marvin Hayes's case now."

"I know, but I thought you'd still be interested." Simon saw Bo's radio-cassette on the kitchen counter. He slipped his cassette into the player. "Let me talk you through the tape."

Judy shook her head. "You should talk to Marvin first."

"Yeah, but Marvin is an idiot. Just hear me out, okay? I'd like your opinion." Simon turned up the volume and started the tape.

The voice of the woman said, "This is the Hammer of Eden with a message for Governor Mike Robson."

Simon said to Bo, "Who do you visualize when you hear that?"

Bo grinned. "I picture a large, sexy woman, about fifty."

Simon nodded. "Your instincts are reliable. Untrained people can tell a lot about a speaker just by hearing them. You can tell how old they are and generally estimate their height and build. Sometimes you can even guess at their state of health. It's because the sound of the voice comes from the body. Pitch, loudness, resonance, huskiness—all have physical causes. Tall people have a longer vocal tract; old people have creaky cartilage. My computer picks up the same cues as people do and is more accurate." Simon took a typed report out of the envelope he had been carrying. "This woman is between forty-seven and fifty-two. She's tall, within an inch of six feet. She's overweight but not obese, probably just generously built."

"I like this woman," Bo said. "Does the computer say if she's good in bed?"

Simon smiled. "The reason you think she's sexy is that her voice has a whispery quality." He wound the tape to the beginning. "Listen to her accent." He played the first two sentences. "This is the Hammer of Eden with a message for Governor Mike Robson. Damn, I didn't expect to be talking to a tape recorder."

He stopped the tape. "It's a northern California accent, of course, but did you notice anything else?"

Bo said, "She's middle-class."

Judy frowned. "She sounded upper-class to me."

"You're both right," Simon said. "Her accent changes between the first sentence and the second."

"Is that unusual?" said Judy.

"No. Most of us get our basic accent from the social group we grew up with, then modify it later in life. Usually people try to upgrade. Occasionally it goes the other way: a politician from a patrician family might make his accent more down-home to seem like a man of the people, but we revert to our childhood speech patterns when we're under stress. Okay so far?"

Bo said, "Sure."

"This woman has downgraded her speech. She makes herself sound more blue-collar than she really is. First she says 'Guvnuh Mike.' This is street talk. But listen to the next bit. The voice mail announcement has put her off guard, and she speaks naturally."

"Damn, I didn't expect to be talking to a tape recorder."

"She pronounces the word recorder very correctly. A blue-collar type would say recawduh, pronouncing only the first *r*. The average college graduate says recorduh, pronouncing the second *r*. Only very superior people say recorder the way she does, carefully pronouncing all three *r*'s."

Bo said, "Who'd have thought you could find out so much from two sentences?"

Simon smiled, looking pleased. "Just listen to this."

"It happened in Owens Valley a little after two o'clock. You can check it out." There was a faint background noise.

Simon paused the tape. "I've enhanced that odd little murmur." He released the PAUSE switch. Judy heard a man's voice, distorted with a lot of background hiss but clear enough to understand, say, "We do not recognize the jurisdiction of the United States government." The background noise returned to normal, and the woman's voice repeated, "We do not recognize the jurisdiction of the United States government." Simon stopped the tape.

Judy said, "She was speaking words he had given her, and she forgot something, so he reminded her."

Bo said, "Didn't you figure the original Internet message had been dictated by a blue-collar guy, maybe illiterate, and typed by an educated woman?"

"Yes," Simon said. "But this is a different woman—older."

"So," Bo said to Judy, "now you're beginning to build up profiles of three unknown subjects."

"No, I'm not," she said. "I'm off the case. Come on, Simon, you know this could get me into more trouble. I think you should take your report to Marvin now."

"Okay." He took the tape out of the machine. "I've told you all the important stuff anyway." Judy saw him to the door.

When she came back, Judy said, "It must be a cult, and the man behind all this must be a charismatic figure with power over women. But something's not right. That demand for a freeze on new power plants—it's just not wacky enough. They must have some down-to-earth selfish reason to want this freeze."

"Maybe they have an interest in one particular power plant," Bo said. "Like, it's going to pollute their salmon river or something."

She felt he was onto something. "The freeze on all plant construction is a cover, then. They're afraid to name the one they're really interested in for fear that would lead us to them."

"But how many possibilities can there be? Power plants aren't built every day, and any proposal has to have been reported."

"Let's check."

They went into the den. Judy switched on her laptop and accessed the files of the San Francisco *Chronicle,* searching for references to power plants in the last three years. "Okay, here's a scheme for a nuclear plant in the Mojave Desert, a hydroelectric dam in Sierra County—"

Bo said, "Sierra County? That rings some kind of bell."

Judy clicked on the article. "Yeah. The proposal is to dam the Silver River. Isn't there a vigilante group around there?"

"That's right!" said Bo. "They're called Los Alamos."

"They're armed to the teeth, and they refused to recognize the U.S. government. They even used that sentence on the tape. Bo, I think we've got 'em."

"What are you going to do?"

Judy's heart sank as she remembered she was off the case. "If Kincaid finds out I've been working this case, he'll bust a gut. But Los Alamos has to be checked out. I think I have to see him."

Bo just shrugged. "You don't have any choice, do you?"

Judy could not risk people getting killed just because she was afraid to confess what she had been doing. "No, I don't," she said. Then she got into her car and drove downtown.

Marvin would have to organize a raid on Los Alamos. There might be trouble: Vigilantes were crazy. It needed to be meticulously handled. The Bureau was terrified of another Waco.

She went straight to Kincaid's office. His greeting was chilly. "What can I do for you, Judy?"

"Simon Sparrow brought his report to me because he hadn't heard I was off the case. I told him to give it to Marvin, but he told me what he had found. I speculated that the Hammer of Eden is a cult that feels threatened by a planned building project for a power plant."

Brian looked annoyed. "I'll pass this on to Marvin," he said.

"There are several power plant projects in California right now. I checked. And one of them is in Silver River Valley, where there is a right-wing vigilante group called Los Alamos. I think Los Alamos must be the Hammer of Eden and we should raid them."

"Is that what you think?"

"Is there a flaw in my logic?" she said icily.

"You bet there is. The flaw is, you're not on the damn case. Do you understand me? Go home and leave this case to Marvin and me."

"Brian—"

"Good-bye, Judy. Have a nice weekend."

She stared at him and fought back the angry retorts that sprang to her lips. After a long moment she walked out of the room.

5

RIEST parked the old Plymouth 'Cuda at the side of the road in the faint light of early dawn. He took Melanie's hand and led her into the forest. After a few minutes they emerged on a bluff that looked over the width of the Silver River Valley.

"This is where they want to build the dam," Priest said.

It was still too dark to see the river, but as the light strengthened, they could distinguish the dark crane and giant earthmoving machines below them, silent and still, like sleeping dinosaurs.

Priest had given up hope that the governor would now negotiate. It was the second day since the Owens Valley earthquake, and still there was no word. There would have to be another earthquake.

"It'll create a lake ten miles long," he told Melanie. "Upstream from here, everything you see will be underwater."

She said, "Surely someone tried to stop the dam."

Priest nodded. "There was a big legal battle. Some of the wealthier residents hired lawyers, and the environmental groups sided with the local people. It did no good."

"How come?"

"Governor Robson backed the dam and put this guy Al Honeymoon on the case. He got the whole thing turned around so that the media made folks here look selfish, like they wanted to deny electric power to every hospital and school in California. So Coastal Electric got permission to build the dam. Everyone gets compensation except us, because we don't own our land. We get nothing for the best vineyard between Napa and Bordeaux."

"And the only place I ever felt at peace."

"We'll make certain it stays the way God made it." Priest took Melanie's hand and led her through the trees back to the car.

Driving along the narrow road up the valley, he said, "Are you going to pick up Dusty from San Francisco today?"

"Yeah. I'll leave after breakfast."

Priest heard a strange noise. He glanced up out of the side window and saw a helicopter. He stopped the car and jumped out.

Melanie got out, too. "You think it's looking for us?"

"I think it's the feds," Priest said. He cursed.

Melanie said, "Why are they here?"

"I think they've come for Los Alamos. Those nutcases must be on file with every law-enforcement agency in the United States. And when Star called the John Truth show, I had her say their slogan: 'We do not recognize the jurisdiction of the United States government.' "

"Are we safe, then?"

"No. After they draw a blank at Los Alamos, the feds may look at the other people in the valley. They'll see the vineyard from the chopper and pay us a visit, so we'd better warn the others."

Priest got back into the car. As soon as Melanie was in, he floored the pedal. He wondered who at the FBI had ordered this raid. Yesterday Kincaid and Hayes had seemed a long way from tracking him down. There had to be someone else on the case.

As he approached the Los Alamos spread, Priest rolled down his window, listening for gunfire. He heard none. He rounded a bend and saw that the wooden five-bar gate that had blocked the entrance was smashed to splinters. He guessed the FBI had driven their armored trucks right through it without stopping.

Priest drove slowly, like a curious passerby, until he was out of sight. Then he stepped on the gas.

When he got back to the commune, he told Star about the FBI raid on Los Alamos. "They may decide to check out the other residences in the valley. We just have to maintain our usual pretense. If we're itinerant workers with no long-term interest in the valley, there's no reason we should care about the dam."

It was midmorning when two agents stumbled down the hill. The younger man was tall and blond, the older an Asian man. Priest was sure neither had been at the press conference.

Most of the adults were spraying the vines with diluted hot sauce to keep the deer from eating the new shoots. The children were in the temple, having a Sunday school lesson from Star.

Priest took a deep breath, then walked across the hillside to the vineyard. Dale greeted the two agents, as arranged. Priest filled a watering can with the pepper mixture and began to spray, moving toward Dale so that he could hear the conversation.

The Asian man spoke in a friendly tone. "We're FBI agents making some routine inquiries in the neighborhood. I'm Bill Ho, and this is John Aldritch. Are you in charge here?"

"I'm the foreman," Dale said. "How can I help you?"

Aldritch said, "Do you folks live here?"

"Most of us are seasonal workers," Dale said, following Priest's script. "The Napa Bottling Company provides accommodation because this place is so far from anywhere."

Ho glanced toward the cluster of buildings on the far side of the vineyard. "Mind if we take a look around?"

Dale shrugged. "Sure, go ahead." He resumed his work.

The agents wandered around the cabins, peeking in. They checked out the grape press, the barns where the wine was fermented, the barrels of last year's vintage. They walked down to the stream and seemed to contemplate crossing. But apparently they did not want to get their feet wet, for they turned around and came back.

At last they returned to the vineyard, and Aldritch said to Dale, "Y'all have some of these cabins tricked out kind of nice for 'temporary accommodation,' don't you?"

"Yeah," Dale said. "Some of us come back year after year. And a few of us live here all year-round."

Aldritch said, "I want a list of who lives or works here."

Ho added, "We also need ages and permanent addresses."

Dale looked nonplussed. "Gee, I guess you'll have to go round asking them all. I sure as heck don't know everyone's birthday."

Priest could not allow the agents to question everyone. They would give themselves away a dozen times. He stepped forward. "Maybe I could assist the gentlemen. I've been coming here a few years. I guess I know everybody and how old they are."

"Okay, go ahead," Dale said, looking relieved.

"Why don't you come to the cookhouse?" Priest said to the agents. "I bet you'd like a cup of coffee."

Ho smiled and said, "That'd be real good."

Priest led them back through the rows of vines and took them to the cookhouse. He put a pot of water on the fire, and the agents sat at the long pine table. Ho opened his notebook.

"The foreman is Dale Arnold; he's forty-two."

"Permanent address?"

"He lives here. Everyone does."

"I thought you were seasonal workers."

"That's right. Most of us will leave come November, when the harvest is in, but we ain't the kind of folks who keep two homes."

"So the permanent address for everyone here would be—"

"Silver River Valley Winery, Silver City, California."

Priest poured them coffee as he made up a list of names. To help him remember who was who, he used variations of their commune names: Dale Arnold, Peggy Star, Richard Priestley.

Priest went slowly, dragging out the session as long as possible. Ho was closing his notebook when Priest said, "More coffee?"

"No, thanks." Aldritch looked at Ho. "I think we're done here."

Ho said, "Is this land owned by the Napa Bottling Company?"

"No," Priest said. "The company operates the winery, but I believe the land is owned by the government."

"So the name on the lease would be Napa Bottling."

Priest hesitated, then said, "Matter of fact, I think the name on the lease may be Stella Higgins." He hated to give Star's real name to the FBI. "She was the one who started the vineyard years ago." He hoped it would not be of any use to them. He could not see how it gave them any clues.

Ho wrote down the name. "That's all, I think," he said.

Priest hid his relief. "Well, good luck with the rest of your inquiries," he said as he led them out through the vineyard.

SUNDAY afternoon Judy and Bo went for a beer at one of Bo's joints, a cops pub with a TV over the bar. The news came on. When Judy saw footage of the raid on Los Alamos, she smiled sourly. Brian Kincaid had screamed at her for interfering; then he had adopted her plan. The newscaster was saying that no arrests had been made. Bo said, "They don't even say they seized evidence. I wonder what the story is."

"We can go find out," Judy said.

They left the bar and got into her car. Judy picked up her car phone and called Simon Sparrow. "What do you hear about the raid?" she asked him.

"We got zip. They have no computers, so it's hard to imagine they could have left a message on the Internet. Nobody there has a college degree, and I doubt if any of them could spell seismologist. And they're happy with the compensation they're getting from Coastal Electric for their land."

"Well, whose dumb idea was it to raid them anyway?"

It had been hers, of course. "At this morning's briefing Marvin claimed it was his," Simon said. "Brian has another meeting with Mr. Honeymoon in Sacramento tomorrow afternoon. Looks like he'll go empty-handed."

Judy smiled grimly. She had no sympathy for Kincaid, but she could not take pleasure in the failure of the raid. It meant the Hammer of Eden were still out there somewhere, planning another earthquake. "Thanks, Simon."

As soon as she hung up, the phone rang. It was the switchboard operator at the office. "A Professor Quercus called with a message he said was urgent. He has some important news for you."

Judy dialed Michael's home. When he answered, she said, "This is Judy Maddox. What have you got?"

"Can you come over? I really need to show you."

"Do you have any Cap'n Crunch?"

"I think there's a little left."

"Okay. I'll be there in fifteen or twenty minutes." She hung up. "I have to go see my seismologist," she said to Bo. "Shall I drop you at the bus stop, or do you want to ride to Berkeley with me?"

"Why not? I'm curious to meet your handsome seismologist."

She made a U-turn and headed for the Bay Bridge. "What makes you think he's handsome?"

"From the way you talked to him," Bo said. "He's married?"

"Separated."

They reached Berkeley and parked on Euclid Street. There was an orange Subaru parked in Judy's usual space.

When Michael opened the door of his apartment, Judy said, "Hi, Michael. This is my father, Bo Maddox."

"Come in," Michael said abruptly.

His mood seemed to have changed in the short time it had taken to drive here. When they entered the living room, Judy saw why. Dusty was on the couch, looking terrible. His eyes were watering, his nose was running, and he was breathing noisily.

Judy knelt beside him. "Poor Dusty! What happened?"

"He's having an allergy attack," Michael explained. "I've given him the drug he needs to suppress the reaction."

"How fast does it work?"

"It's already working, but he may stay like this for days."

"I wish I could do something for you," Judy said to Dusty.

A female voice said, "I'll take care of him, thank you."

Judy stood up and turned around. The woman who had just come in had a pale oval face and red hair that fell past her shoulders.

"This is Melanie, Dusty's mom," Michael said. "Melanie, meet my friend Judy Maddox."

Melanie nodded curtly. So that's his wife, Judy thought.

"This is my father, Bo Maddox," Judy said.

Melanie did not trouble to make small talk. "I was just leaving," she said. She was carrying a duffel bag with a picture of Donald Duck on the side. She looked at the child on the couch. "This never happens in the mountains," Melanie said coldly.

Michael looked anguished. "What am I going to do, not have him stay with me?"

"If he doesn't sleep over, he won't get like this."

"I know. I'll carry him to your car." Michael picked up Dusty from the couch. "Come on, Tiger, let's go."

When Michael returned, he was grim-faced and preoccupied. He sat at his computer. "Look at this," he said without preamble.

Judy and Bo stood behind him and looked over his shoulder.

"Here's the seismograph of the Owens Valley tremor, with the mysterious preliminary vibrations. Now here's a typical earthquake of the same magnitude. This has normal foreshocks. See the difference?"

"Yes." The normal foreshocks were uneven and sporadic, whereas the Owens Valley vibrations followed a regular pattern.

Michael then brought a third chart up on the screen, showing a neat pattern of even vibrations, just like the Owens Valley chart.

"What made those vibrations?" Judy said.

"A seismic vibrator," Michael announced triumphantly.

Bo said, "What's that?"

Michael said, "It's a machine used by the oil industry to explore underground. Basically, it's a huge jackhammer mounted on a truck. It sends vibrations through the earth's crust."

"And those vibrations triggered the earthquake?"

"I don't think it can be a coincidence."

Judy nodded solemnly. "That's it, then. They really can cause earthquakes. But the Owens Valley tremor was really quite minor."

Michael said, "We can't take comfort from that. The size of the earthquake bears no relation to the strength of the triggering vibration. It depends on the pressure in the fault."

"What are we going to do?" Judy said.

Bo said, "You're off the case."

Michael frowned, puzzled. "Why?" he asked Judy.

"Office politics," Judy said. "We have a new boss who doesn't like me. He assigned the case to someone he prefers and has ordered me not to interfere."

"But you can't just ignore what I've told you," Michael said.

"Don't worry. I won't do that," she said. "If we can find out where the seismic vibrator came from, we may have a lead on the Hammer of Eden. How many of these machines are there in the continental United States? A hundred? A thousand?"

"In there somewhere," Michael said.

"Anyhow, not many. So the people who manufacture them probably have records of every sale. I'll track them down tonight."

Bo said, "I could have the San Francisco PD put out a multistate query on the CLETS Computer." CLETS was the California Law Enforcement Telecommunications System. "And I could get the newspapers to print a picture of one of these trucks, get people looking out for it. I won't say this is connected with the Hammer of Eden, just that we're looking for a stolen seismic vibrator."

"Great," Judy said. "Michael, can you print out the graphs?"

"Sure." He touched a key, and the printer whirred.

Judy put a hand on his shoulder. "I sure hope Dusty feels better."

He covered her hand with his own. "Thanks." His touch was light. She felt a frisson of pleasure.

Michael said, "After you two have made these phone calls, would you like to meet for dinner?"

"Not me," Bo said. "I have a bowling match."

"Judy, how about you?"

Judy realized that there was not a thing she would rather do this evening than have dinner with Michael. "Okay, sure."

MICHAEL TOOK JUDY TO A small downtown restaurant that served vegetarian Indian dishes. She put her mobile phone on the table. "I know it's bad manners, but Bo promised to call me if he got any information about stolen seismic vibrators."

"Okay by me," Michael said. "Did you call the manufacturers?"

"Yeah. I got a sales director at home. He promised me a list of purchasers tomorrow, and he faxed me a picture." Judy took a sheet of paper from her purse and showed it to him.

"It's just a big truck with a piece of machinery on the back."

"But after Bo puts this picture out on CLETS, every cop in California will be watching for one. And if the newspapers carry the picture, half the population will be on the lookout, too."

The food came. It was delicious, and Judy ate with gusto. After a few minutes she caught Michael looking at her with a faint smile. She raised an eyebrow. "Did I say something witty?"

"I'm pleased you're enjoying the cuisine."

She grinned. "I'll try to be more dainty."

"Please don't. It's one of the things that attracts me to you. You seem to have a big appetite for life. You like Dusty, and you have a good time hanging out with your dad, and you're proud of the FBI. You even enjoy Cap'n Crunch."

Judy flushed, but she was pleased. She changed the subject. "We're assuming that the Hammer of Eden has data similar to yours about pressure points along the San Andreas Fault."

"They must have, to pick the locations where the seismic vibrator could trigger an earthquake."

"Could you go through the same exercise? Study the data and figure out the best place?"

"I guess I could. Probably there would be a cluster of five or six possible sites. Then, I suppose, the FBI could stake out the sites and watch for a seismic vibrator."

"Yes—if I were in charge."

"Maybe I'll fax the list to Governor Robson."

"Don't let too many people see it. You might cause a panic. If everyone tries to leave San Francisco at the same time, there'll be riots. And if I'm associated with an outbreak of mass hysteria, I don't think I could survive at the Bureau."

"Is that important to you?"

"Yes and no. Sooner or later I plan to get out and have children."

"Do you have anyone in mind to have children with?"

"No." She gave him a candid look. "A good man is hard to find."

Michael waved at a waiter to bring them coffee. "Being a parent can be painful, but you never regret it."

They drank their coffee, talked about Dusty, and then Michael paid. He walked her to her car. "This evening has gone so fast," he said. "Do you want to go to a movie sometime?"

The dating game. It never changes. "Yes, I'd like that."

"May I kiss you good night?"

"Yes." Judy grinned. "Yes, please."

It was a soft, tentative kiss. Without thinking, she pressed her body against his. He squeezed her briefly, then broke away.

ON MONDAY morning Judy was assigned to investigating a militant Muslim group at Stanford University. She found it hard to concentrate on a harmless bunch of religious fanatics when she knew the Hammer of Eden were planning their next earthquake.

Michael called at five past nine. "How are you, Agent Judy?"

The sound of his voice made her feel happy. "I'm fine."

"Are you free tomorrow night?"

"I gucss." That sounded too cool. "I mean, yes."

"Let's meet in the bar of Morton's at six. Then we can pick a movie together."

"I'll be there."

At lunchtime Judy went to Simon Sparrow's office.

He was talking on the phone and watching the screen of a wave analyzer at the same time. "Mrs. Gorky, tell me what you can see from your front window." As he listened to the reply, he watched the spectrum of Mrs. Gorky's voice, comparing it with a printout he had. After a few moments he drew a line through a name on a list. "Thank you for your cooperation, Mrs. Gorky. Good-bye."

Judy said, "Why do you need to know what Mrs. Gorky sees when she looks out the window?"

"I don't," Simon said. "That question generally elicits a response of about the length I need to analyze the voice. By the time she's finished, I know whether she's the woman I'm looking for."

"And who's that?"

"The one who called the John Truth show, of course." Simon tapped the ring binder on his desk. "The Bureau, the police, and the radio station have so far received a total of one thousand two hundred and twenty-nine calls telling us who she is."

Judy leafed through the file. In most cases there was a name, address, and phone number for the tipster and the same for the suspect. One tip gave no name but said, "I know I've heard her voice on the radio or something. It was so sexy, I remembered it. But it was a long time ago. Maybe I heard it on a record album."

Simon said, "I've eliminated one hundred of them today."

Judy continued leafing through the file. She came across another call that mentioned a record. The caller said, "I'm sure I've heard the voice on an album. Something from way back, like the '60s."

Judy asked Simon, "Did you notice that two of the tip-offs mention a record album?"

"They do? I missed that!"

Raja Khan passed the door and caught her eye. "Oh, Judy, your father called. I thought you were at lunch."

Judy rushed back to her desk and dialed Bo's number.

He picked up right away. "Lieutenant Maddox here."

"What have you got?"

"A suspect. Get this. A seismic vibrator went missing two weeks ago between Shiloh, Texas, and Clovis, New Mexico. The regular driver disappeared at the same time, and his burned-out car was found at the local dump, containing what appear to be his ashes. The prime suspect is one Richard Granger, age forty-eight. They called him Ricky, and he has a record."

"You're a genius, Bo!"

"A copy should be coming out of your fax machine now. He was a big-time hoodlum in L.A. around the late '60s, early '70s, but he disappeared in 1972. The LAPD thought he must have been whacked by the Mob—he owed them money—but they never found a body, so they didn't close the file."

"Do we have a picture of Ricky?"

"There's one in the file, but it's a photo of a nineteen-year-old. He's pushing fifty now. Luckily, the sheriff in Shiloh prepared an E-fit likeness." E-fit was the computer program that had replaced the old-style police artist. "He promised he would fax it to me."

"Re-fax it to me as soon as you get it. I'm going to Sacramento."

IT WAS four fifteen when Judy stepped through the door that had GOVERNOR carved on it. The secretary recognized Judy and registered surprise. "You're one of the FBI people, aren't you? The meeting with Mr. Honeymoon started ten minutes ago."

"That's okay," Judy said. "I've brought some important information that just came in. Did a fax arrive here for me?"

"I'll check." She spoke into the phone. "Yes, your fax is here." A moment later Judy was given a sheet of paper, and she stared at the face on it. This was the man who might kill thousands.

She saw a handsome man who had gone to some trouble to hide the true shape of his face. His head was covered by a cowboy hat. The bottom half of his face was concealed by a bushy beard and mustache. By now, she guessed, he was clean-shaven. He had deep-set eyes that stared hypnotically out of the picture.

Since his beard was dark, Ricky Granger probably had dark hair. From the attached description Judy learned that he was about six feet tall, and slim. It was not much, but it was better than nothing. And nothing was what Brian and Marvin had.

Honeymoon's assistant appeared and ushered Judy into Honeymoon's office. Judy allowed herself to enjoy the shock and dismay on the faces of Brian Kincaid and Marvin Hayes.

Honeymoon looked at Judy with raised eyebrows and said, "Agent Maddox, Mr. Kincaid just got through telling me he took you off the case because you're a ditz."

Judy was floored, but she recovered fast. "Brian's full of it," she said. "I'm the best agent he has, and I just proved it. I know who's sending terrorist threats to Governor Robson. Marvin and Brian don't. You can make your own decision about who's the ditz."

Hayes was bright red. "What are you talking about?"

Honeymoon asked, "Agent Maddox, did I hear you say you know who's making the threats?"

"Correct." She put a fax picture on Honeymoon's desk. "This is Richard Granger, a hoodlum from Los Angeles who was believed, wrongly, to have been killed by the Mob in 1972."

"And what makes you think he's the culprit?"

Judy handed him another piece of paper. "Here's the seismograph of a typical earthquake. Look at the vibrations that precede the tremor. There's a haphazard series of different magnitudes." She showed him a second sheet. "This is the Owens Valley earthquake. Nothing haphazard here. Just a neat series of regular vibrations." She put another sheet on his desk. "Look at this chart."

Honeymoon studied it. "Regular, just like the Owens Valley graph. What makes vibrations like these?"

"A machine called a seismic vibrator, used in oil exploration."

Honeymoon looked skeptical. "Are you saying the earthquake was man-made?"

"I'm not theorizing. I'm giving you the facts. A seismic vibrator was used in that location immediately before the earthquake. You can make your own judgment about cause and effect."

He gave her a hard, appraising look. Finally he said, "Okay. How does that lead you to the guy with the beard?"

"A seismic vibrator was stolen a week ago in Shiloh, Texas. Richard Granger is the prime suspect in the theft—and in the murder of the truck's regular driver. Granger was working for the oil exploration team that was using the vibrator."

Honeymoon turned to Kincaid. "What have you got to say about all this?"

Kincaid said, "I don't think we should bother you with internal disciplinary matters—"

"Oh, I want to be bothered," Honeymoon said. "Look at it from my angle. You come here and tell me the earthquake was definitely not man-made. Now it appears that it very likely was. You tell me you can't find the perpetrators, then in walks Agent Maddox with a name, a police record, and a picture."

"I think I should say—"

"I feel like you've been jerking me around, Special Agent Kincaid," said Honeymoon. He stood up. His face was dark with anger. "And when people jerk me around, I get kind of tetchy."

Kincaid tried to gather the shreds of his dignity. "What do you want me to say?"

"That you're putting Agent Maddox in charge of this case. If you have a problem with that, I'll have Governor Robson call the director of the FBI in Washington."

"That won't be necessary," Kincaid said.

"So put Maddox in charge."

"Okay."

"Now get out of here," Honeymoon said, and they all got up.

Honeymoon said, "Maddox, call me once a day."

That meant Honeymoon would continue to support her, and Kincaid knew it. "You got it," Judy said.

They went out.

6

DUSTY was sick all day Monday.

Melanie drove into Silver City to pick up more of the allergy drug he needed. She came back in a panic.

Priest was in his cabin when Melanie burst in with a newspaper in her hand. "Look at this!" she said, waving the paper in front of his eyes.

He was shocked to see a photograph of a seismic vibrator.

He took the newspaper from her and looked at the picture. It was of a truck just like the one he had stolen.

"Damn," he said. "Tell me what it says."

"The police are looking for a stolen seismic vibrator. It doesn't say anything about earthquakes. It's just, like, a funny story. Who'd want to steal one of these things?"

"I don't buy that," Priest said. "This can't be a coincidence. They know how we made the earthquake happen, but they haven't told the press yet. They're scared of creating a panic."

"So why have they released this picture?"

"To make it hard for us to drive the truck on the open road. Every highway patrol officer in California is on the lookout."

"What if we drive at night?"

He shook his head. "Still too risky."

"I have to go check on Dusty," Melanie said. "Oh, Priest, he's so sick. We won't have to leave the valley, will we?"

Priest hugged her. "I'm not beaten yet."

While Melanie went to see Dusty, he headed for Star's cabin, worrying over the problem of the truck. Maybe there was a way they could disguise the seismic vibrator so that it looked like some other kind of vehicle, a Coke truck or something.

Priest stepped into the cabin and noticed Bones. He was lying on the bed, fully clothed but fast asleep—or more likely passed out. There was an empty bottle of Silver River Valley chardonnay on the rough wooden table.

The sight of Bones gave Priest inspiration, and his mind was working feverishly. He told Star about the problem of the seismic vibrator. Then he told her the solution.

PRIEST, Star, Melanie, Oaktree, and Bones stood looking at the carnival ride, the Dragon's Mouth. Then Priest spoke to Oaktree. "We drive it up the track and park it next to the seismic vibrator. Then we take off the painted panels and temporarily fix them to our truck. The cops are looking for a seismic vibrator, not a carnival ride."

Oaktree looked at how the panels were fixed. "No problem."

Priest looked at Bones. The great snag with this scheme was that Bones had to be in on it. In the old days Priest would have trusted Bones with his life. He was a Rice Eater, after all. However, since Bones had become a junkie, all bets were off.

But Priest had to take the risk. He was desperate. He had promised an earthquake four days from now, and he had to carry out his threat.

Bones agreed readily to the plan.

Oaktree and Star climbed into the cab of the carnival ride with Bones, who handled the rig confidently. Melanie and Priest took the 'Cuda for the milelong ride to where the seismic vibrator was hidden.

Priest wondered what else the FBI knew. He turned on the car radio, hoping for a bulletin. The news came on just as they drew near the hiding place of the vibrator. Priest turned up the volume.

"Federal agents investigating the Hammer of Eden terrorist group have issued a photographic likeness of a suspect, Richard or Ricky Granger, age forty-eight, formerly of Los Angeles."

Priest slammed on the brakes.

"Granger is also wanted for a murder in Texas nine days ago."

"That's not true," Priest said to Melanie. "I didn't kill anyone."

"Is that your real name?" Melanie said. "Ricky Granger?"

He had forgotten that she did not know. "Yeah."

Melanie said, "How did they get a photo of you?"

"Not a photo," he said. "A photographic likeness. That must mean one of those Identi-kit pictures that they make up."

"Only they use a computer program now."

Priest was now glad he had changed his appearance before taking the job in Shiloh. With luck the likeness would not resemble the way he looked today. But he needed to be sure.

"I need to get to a TV," he said.

The carnival ride pulled over near the hiding place of the seismic vibrator, and Oaktree and Star got out. In a few words Priest explained the situation to them. "You make a start here while Melanie and I drive into Silver City," he said.

He and Melanie headed for town. On the outskirts of Silver City there was an electronics store. Priest parked, and they got out.

The store's window displayed several TV sets all showing the same program, some kind of game show. Priest looked at his watch: almost seven. The news would be on in a few seconds.

Suddenly the multiple screens showed a black-and-white picture of a heavily bearded man in a cowboy hat. Priest stared at it. The picture did not look like him at all.

He relaxed. "What do you think?" he said.

"I wouldn't know it was supposed to be you," Melanie said.

The screens all flickered, and Priest was shocked to see a police photo of himself at nineteen. He was so thin, his face looked like a skull. "Would you recognize me there?" he said.

"Yes," Melanie said. "By the nose."

She was right; the picture showed his distinctive narrow nose.

Melanie asked, "Where did they get that picture?"

"From my police record, I'm assuming."

She looked up at him. "I didn't know you had a police record."

"I gave up crime when I came to the valley. I didn't do anything wrong for the next twenty-five years—until I met you."

The scene shifted to the Federal Building, where the FBI had its San Francisco office. A demonstration in support of the Hammer of Eden was going on. The camera focused on a young woman with an Asian cast to her features. She caught Priest's eye because she was beautiful in the exotic way that strongly appealed to him.

Melanie said, "Oh, it's her!"

Priest was startled. "You know that woman?"

"I met her on Sunday at Michael's apartment. Michael just introduced her as Judy Maddox. He didn't say anything about her."

"What's she doing at the Federal Building?"

"It says on the screen, 'FBI agent Judy Maddox, in charge of Hammer of Eden case.' She's the detective who's after us!"

Priest was fascinated. Was this his enemy? She was gorgeous and one heck of a detective. She caught on about the seismic vibrator, found out where it came from, and got his name and picture. And she had met Melanie. She was too close.

Melanie went on. "Michael didn't say she was with the FBI. I thought she was a new girlfriend."

"Girlfriend or not, I don't like her getting this close to us." He turned away from the store and walked slowly back to the 'Cuda.

They sat in the car, but Priest did not start the engine. "This is bad for us," he said. "Agent Maddox is asking, 'Where will the Hammer of Eden strike next?' Michael can help her with that by figuring out the most likely places for an earthquake. Then the FBI can stake out those locations and watch for a seismic vibrator."

"I never thought of that." Melanie stared at him. "My husband and his FBI floozy are going to mess this up for us."

"Wait a minute." Priest was getting an idea. "We have to know whether the FBI has staked out possible earthquake locations—and if so, which ones. Michael might tell you."

"Why would he do that?"

"I believe he's still carrying a torch for you. He'd tell you anything if you slept with him."

"I won't do it. I won't!"

"I hate to ask you, but I have no choice."

"Forget it," Melanie said.

"Okay," Priest said. "I'm sorry I asked." He started the car.

They were silent driving through the mountains. They turned off the road and drove down the long, rough track toward the commune. The carnival ride was no longer visible. Priest guessed that Oaktree and Star had concealed it for the night.

He parked in the cleared circle at the end of the track. They walked through the woods to the village and went to Melanie's hut to check on Dusty.

He was sleeping peacefully. Priest watched as she tucked the sheet around the boy and kissed his forehead. She looked at Priest and whispered, "This is the only place he's ever been okay."

"It's the only place I've ever been okay. It's the only place the world has ever been okay. That's why we have to save it."

"I know," she said. "I know."

THE Domestic Terrorism squad of the San Francisco FBI worked in a narrow room on one side of the Federal Building. It looked like a million other offices except that the men and women wore guns in holsters on their hips or under their arms.

At seven o'clock on Tuesday morning they were standing, sitting on desk corners, or leaning against the wall, ready to take notes. The whole squad had been put under Judy's orders.

The noise of conversation died away when Judy stood up and said, "Pay attention, everyone. We're going to divide into two teams. Peter, Jack, Sally, and Lee will check out tips based on the pictures we have of Ricky Granger. Dave, Louise, Steve, and Ashok will work with Simon Sparrow, checking tip-offs based on the recorded voice of the woman who phoned John Truth. And Raja, I want you to prepare a short briefing to go out to all police departments telling them how to recognize a seismic vibrator." She held up a hand. "No vibrator jokes, please." They all laughed.

"Now I'm going to get us some extra manpower and more workspace. Meanwhile, I know you'll do your best. One more thing. These people are trying to blackmail the governor of California. They say they can make earthquakes happen." She shrugged. "I'm not telling you they can, and I'm not telling you they can't. Either way, you need to understand that this assignment is very very serious." She paused, then finished: "Let's get to it."

Judy left the room and walked briskly along the corridor to Brian Kincaid's office. She knocked on the door and went in.

"I have a thousand leads to follow up on the voice of the woman on tape. I'm guessing we'll get even more calls about the picture of Ricky Granger. I can't begin to evaluate them all by Friday with nine people. I need twenty more agents."

Kincaid was sitting in the big chair behind his desk. He laughed. "I'm not putting twenty people on this assignment."

She ignored that. "I want to convene the Joint Terrorist Task Force so we'll have delegates from police departments, customs, and the U.S. Federal Protective Service. And starting at sundown on Thursday, I plan to stake out likely locations for the next earthquake."

"There isn't going to be one."

"There isn't enough room here at the office. We have to set up our emergency operations center elsewhere. I checked out the Presidio last night." The Presidio was a disused military base near the Golden Gate Bridge. "I'm going to use the ballroom of the officers club."

Kincaid stood up. "You are like hell!" he shouted.

"I never wanted to fight with you, Brian," Judy said. She went to the door. "I'm going to talk to Honeymoon at nine thirty. By then I'd like to have a logistics person assigned to my team with the authority to organize the manpower I need and set up a command post at the officers club. If I don't, I'll tell Honeymoon to call Washington. Your move." She went out, slamming the door.

She returned to the Domestic Terrorism office. The phone on her desk was ringing. She picked up. "Judy Maddox."

"John Truth here. I'm at home, but my producer just called me. My voice mail at the radio station was maxed with overnight calls about the Hammer of Eden woman. I got two people who remembered the name of the record of this woman reading poetry over a background of psychedelic music."

"That's great!" Judy was thrilled.

"The album was called *Raining Fresh Daisies*. That's also the name of the band, or 'group,' as they used to call them then."

Judy said, "I never heard of them."

"Me either, but Haight-Ashbury is full of secondhand record stores with clerks who live in a time warp. I'd check them out."

"Good idea. Thanks."

She hung up and called Raja Khan into her office. "I have another job for you," she said. "We're looking for an album called *Raining Fresh Daisies*. It's from the '60s."

"No kidding."

She grinned. "Yeah, it does have kind of a hippie feel to it. The voice on the record is the Hammer of Eden woman, and I'm hoping we'll get a name for her. I want you to contact all the major recording companies, then call stores that sell rare records."

"I'll get started."

Raja went to his desk, and Judy called her father. She said, "Bo, it's me. Cast your mind back to the '60s. I think the Hammer of Eden woman made a record with a band called Raining Fresh Daisies."

"Sorry, Jude, I never heard of it. But I'm glad you called. I've been thinking about your guy, Ricky Granger. He's such a planner, he must be dying to know what you're up to. I think the FBI has probably talked to him already."

"You do?" There was a type of perpetrator who insinuated himself into the investigation, approaching the police as a witness or kindly neighbor, trying to befriend officers and chat with them about the progress of the case. "But Granger also seems ultracareful."

"There's probably a war going on inside him between caution and curiosity. My guess is, curiosity will win out."

Judy nodded into the phone. Bo's intuitions were worth listening to. They came from thirty years of police experience. "I'm going to review every interview in the case. Bye."

She hung up, frowning. She would have to go over every interview Marvin's team had done with the Green California Campaign people, plus all the notes from the raid on Los Alamos. When she got her extra personnel, she would put a team on it. She also had to arrange stakeouts on likely earthquake sites. Michael had said he could make a list. Judy dialed his number.

He sounded pleased to hear from her. "I'm looking forward to our date tonight."

"I've been put back on the Hammer of Eden case."

"Does that mean you can't make it tonight?"

She could not contemplate dinner and a movie. "I'd like to see you, but I won't have much time. Could we meet for a drink?"

"Sure."

"I'm sorry, but the case is developing fast. I called about that list of likely earthquake sites. Could you bring it tonight?"

"Sure. Morton's at six?"

"See you there."

"Listen . . . I'm really glad you're back on the case. I feel safer knowing you're after the bad guys. I mean it."

"Thanks." She hung up hoping she merited his confidence.

Three days left.

BY MIDAFTERNOON THE emergency operations center was up and running. The officers club looked like a Spanish villa. Inside, it was a gloomy imitation of a country club, with cheap paneling and ugly light fixtures.

The cavernous ballroom had been fitted out as a command post. In one corner was the head shed, a table with seats for the heads of the agencies involved in managing the crisis—the police, firefighters, the mayor's office of emergency services, a representative of the governor, and experts from FBI headquarters in Washington.

Around the room, tables were set up for the different teams. Laptop computers were on each table. Notice boards covered the walls: lead status boards, event boards, subject boards, demand boards, and hostage boards. Key data and clues would be written up here. Right now the subject board had one name—RICHARD GRANGER—and two pictures. The lead status board had a picture of a seismic vibrator.

The room was big enough for a couple of hundred people, but so far there were only about forty. Judy had divided them into teams, each with a leader. There was an air of subdued urgency.

She was called to the head shed for a call from Michael.

"Hi. I've got a problem tonight. I can't make it."

He sounded curt and unfriendly. "What is it?" she said.

"Something came up. I'm sorry to cancel on you."

"Michael, what is wrong?"

"I'm in kind of a rush. I'll call you." And he hung up.

Now what was all that about? Just as I was getting fond of the guy.

Carl Theobald, the leader of the team reviewing Marvin Hayes's files, interrupted Judy's thoughts. He looked troubled. "Hayes has some paper records in his office," he said. "But when I said I needed to see them, he pretty much told me to shove it."

"Don't worry, Carl," she said. "Come with me."

They went outside and jumped into her car. It took fifteen minutes to reach the Federal Building. They went up in the elevator.

Judy opened the door to the organized crime squad room and went in. Carl followed.

Marvin was on the phone, grinning broadly, telling a joke.

Judy leaned on his desk and said loudly, "What's this crap you're giving Carl?"

"Someone's interrupting me, Joe," he said. "I'll call you right back." He hung up. "What is it with you? What do you mean by going over my records as if I must have made some mistake?"

"I think you may have talked to the perpetrator," she said. "Where are these paper records?"

He smoothed his yellow tie. "All we have are some notes from the press conference that never got keyed into the computer."

"Show me."

He pointed to a box file against the wall. "Help yourself. You won't find a thing."

She riffled through the papers. There were some faxes from newspapers, a guest list, a form on which the journalists attending had been asked to put their names and the publications they represented. Judy ran her eye down the list. "What is this?" she said suddenly. "Florence Shoebury, Eisenhower Junior High?"

"She's a kid who wanted to cover the press conference for the school newspaper," Marvin said. "Her father brought her."

There was a business card stapled to the form. "Peter Shoebury, from Watkins, Colefax and Brown. Did you check him out?"

Marvin hesitated, realizing he'd made a mistake. "No," he said.

Judy handed the form with the business card to Carl. "Call this guy right away," she said.

Carl sat at the nearest desk and picked up the phone.

A few minutes later Carl hung up and said, "Peter Shoebury has never been inside this building, and he has no daughter. But he was mugged on Saturday morning, and his wallet was stolen."

Judy was excited by the news. "I guess he didn't look like the E-fit picture we got from Texas," she said to Marvin.

"Not a bit," Marvin said. "No beard, no hat. He had big glasses and long hair in a ponytail."

"What about his build? Dark hair, dark eyes, about fifty?"

"Yes, yes, and yes."

Judy almost felt bad for Marvin. "It was Ricky Granger, wasn't it?"

Marvin looked at the floor. "I guess you're right."

"I would like you to produce a new E-fit, please."

He nodded, still not looking at her. "What kind of terrorist brings a little girl along with him?"

"One who is completely ruthless. What did the kid look like?"

"About twelve, thirteen. Dark hair and eyes. Slim. Pretty."

"Better do an E-fit of her, too. Is she really his daughter?"

"That's how they seemed. She showed no signs of being under coercion, if that's what you're thinking."

"Yes. Okay, I'm going to assume they're father and daughter, for now." Judy turned to Carl. "We're out of here."

LATE that evening Judy got the first edition of the San Francisco *Chronicle* with the two new pictures: the E-fit of Florence Shoebury and the new E-fit of Ricky Granger disguised as Peter Shoebury. Studying them, Judy was struck by the resemblance between Granger and Florence. *They're father and daughter; they have to be. I wonder what will happen to her if I put her daddy in jail.* She yawned. It was time to go. The night shift was already here.

Driving home, Judy reviewed the day and what she had achieved. While sitting at a stoplight, she realized that Michael had not faxed her the list of likely earthquake sites. Judy dialed his number on the car phone, but there was no answer. She tried again, and the line was busy. She called the office switchboard and asked them to check with Pacific Bell. The operator called her back and said the phone was off the hook. So he was home but not picking up. Judy felt uneasy.

She checked the dashboard clock. It was just before eleven. She turned the car around and headed for Berkeley.

Judy reached Euclid Street at eleven fifteen. There were lights on in Michael's apartment. She parked behind an old orange Subaru and rang Michael's doorbell. There was no answer.

She was troubled. Michael had crucial information. Today he abruptly canceled their date; then he became incommunicado. She wondered what to do. Maybe she should call for police backup and break in. He could be tied up or dead in there.

A young woman approached the building. She stopped at the door and fumbled in her briefcase for keys.

"Good evening," Judy said. She showed her badge. "FBI special agent Judy Maddox. I need access to this building."

"Something wrong?" the woman said anxiously.

"I hope not. Just go to your apartment and close the door."

The woman entered a ground-floor apartment, and Judy went up the stairs. With her knuckles she rapped on Michael's door. There was no reply, so she knocked again, three times, hard. She put her ear to the door and listened. She heard a scream.

That did it. Judy took a step back and kicked the door as hard as she could. It burst open. She drew her gun. "FBI," she shouted. "Drop your weapons and put up your hands!"

Michael's bedroom door was open. She entered with her arms extended and aimed into the room. What she saw stunned her.

Michael was on the bed making love to his wife.

They both stared at Judy in fear and disbelief.

Judy felt like a fool. "Oh, I'm sorry," she said. "I'm sorry."

AT DAWN on Wednesday, Priest stood beside the Silver River looking at the way the morning sky was reflected in the water. It was a tranquil moment, but Priest's soul was not at peace.

His deadline was only two days away, and still Governor Robson had said nothing. It was maddening.

As he stood musing, Star appeared. She slipped out of her purple robe and stepped into the cold river to wash. When she had toweled herself dry, Priest said, "Let's go get a newspaper. I want to know if Governor Robson said anything last night."

After Star got dressed, they drove to a gas station. Priest filled the tank of the 'Cuda while Star got the San Francisco *Chronicle*.

She came back white-faced. "Look," she said, showing him a picture of a young girl on the front page. It was Flower.

Stunned, he picked up the newspaper. Beside the computer-generated image of Flower was one of himself based on his appearance at the FBI press conference.

Flower had not been in disguise. Her computer picture was like a poorly drawn portrait—not her, but like her. A month ago it would not have mattered: No one outside the commune knew Flower. But she had been going secretly to Silver City to meet boys. She had been arrested and spent a night in custody. Would people recognize her?

He stared at the paper while Star read the text. "Is there a statement from the governor in the paper?" Priest asked.

"No. According to this, a lot of people are saying he should give in and negotiate, but he refuses to comment."

WHEN Judy woke up, she could not remember why she felt so bad. Then the whole ghastly scene came back in a dreadful rush. Last night had been a mistake. Michael had been a mistake. She had to put it all behind her. What was really important was that she had two days to prevent an earthquake.

Judy called Michael on her way to work. "I'm sorry about your door," she said. "I couldn't understand why you didn't answer, and I thought you must be in some kind of trouble."

"What brought you here so late?" He sounded more curious than angry.

"You didn't send me that list of earthquake sites."

"Oh, that's right! It's on my desk. I just forgot. I'll fax it now."

"Thanks," she said, and hung up.

When Judy reached the officers club, Michael's fax was waiting for her. She showed it to Carl Theobald. "We need surveillance teams at each of these locations."

"Okay." Carl frowned. "You know, these locations are awful big. One team can't watch an area a mile square. Should we put on multiple teams? Or could your seismologist narrow it down?"

"I'll ask him." Judy picked up the phone and dialed Michael again. "Thanks for the fax," she said, and explained the problem.

"I'd have to visit the sites myself," he said. "Signs of earlier earthquake activity would give me a more precise fix."

"Could you do that today?" she said immediately. "I can take you to all the locations in an FBI helicopter."

"Uh . . . I guess," he said. "I mean, of course I will."

"Can you find your way to the officers club in the Presidio?"

"Sure."

"By the time you get here, the chopper will be waiting."

"Okay."

IT WAS a long day. Judy, Michael, and Carl covered a thousand miles in the helicopter. By nightfall they had set up round-the-clock surveillance at the five locations on Michael's list.

They returned to the Presidio. The helicopter landed on the deserted parade ground. Judy had to go inside to report to a big shot from FBI headquarters in Washington. But first she walked Michael to his car. "Is there some way I can get notified real fast if there's a tremor anywhere in California?" she asked him.

"Sure. I could set up on-line seismography at your command post tomorrow."

"Good," Judy said. She looked up at his shadowed face. "Michael, you gave me the impression you were growing fond of me. Why did you sleep with your wife?"

"I guess I owe you an explanation."

"I think so."

"Until yesterday I was sure it was over. Then last night she reminded me of the things that had been good about our marriage. She was affectionate. She made me forget all the things that were bad."

"Such as?"

He sighed. "I think Melanie is drawn to authority figures. I was her professor. She wants the security of being told what to do. I expected an equal partner. She resented that."

"I get the picture. And last night?"

"I forgot all that. She seemed to want to try again, and I thought maybe we should for Dusty's sake."

She wished she could read his expression, but it was too dark.

"I'm glad you told me. Good night." Judy walked away.

"Good night," he said, then called after her, "Are you angry?"

"No," she said over her shoulder. "Not anymore."

PRIEST EXPECTED MELANIE TO return to the commune around midafternoon. When nightfall came and she still had not arrived, he was frantic. What had happened to her? Had she decided to go back to her husband? Had she confessed everything to him?

He took a candle lamp and waited at the parking circle. Finally he saw her Subaru lights approach through the trees.

Melanie parked erratically, got out, and slammed the car door.

"I hate you," she said to Priest. "I hate you for making me do that. I feel like a prostitute."

Priest was silent for a minute. Then he said, "A prostitute does it for money. You did it to save your child. I know you feel bad, but you're not bad."

He put his arms around her and hugged her. Slowly she relaxed. He could feel the tension leave her bit by bit.

"You were right about the list," Melanie said. "That FBI woman had asked Michael to work out the best locations for an earthquake. He was just finishing it when I got there."

"So what happened?"

"I made him dinner. Later, when the phone rang, I told him not to answer; then I took it off the hook. But she came over anyway, and when Michael didn't answer the door, she broke it down. Boy, did she have a shock. She almost died of embarrassment."

"Did he give her the list?"

"Not then, but she called this morning, and he faxed it to her."

"And did you get it?"

"While he was in the shower, I got to his computer and printed out another copy." She reached into her back pocket, pulled out a single sheet of folded paper, and gave it to Priest. "They're going to stake out each of these locations, looking for a seismic vibrator."

"Now listen carefully. Could you look over the data and pick the five *next* best locations?"

"Yes."

"And could we cause an earthquake at one of them?"

"It's maybe not as sure, but the chances are good."

"Then that's what we'll do. Tomorrow we'll look at new sites."

7

AT FIVE a.m. the guard at the entrance to Los Alamos was yawning. He became alert when Melanie and Priest pulled up in the 'Cuda. "How are you?" Priest said as he walked up to the gate.

"Who are you, and what do you want?"

Priest hit him in the face very hard, then kicked the guard's legs from under him. The man fell onto his back, and his rifle went flying through the air. Priest kicked him in the ribs three or four times. Then the man curled up in a ball, sobbing in pain.

Priest knelt and took the handgun from the man's belt. This was what he had come for. Now he was armed.

PRIEST rejected the first location Melanie took him to.

It was a small seaside town fifty miles north of San Francisco. The location was a long distance from the freeway, so there could be no quick getaway.

"Let's look at another place," he said.

Melanie directed him south on Interstate 280. "Right where the San Andreas Fault crosses Route 101, there's a town called Felicitas."

They drove for twenty minutes. The exit ramp for Felicitas led to a vantage point overlooking the town. Priest stopped the car and got out. Felicitas was laid out in front of him like a picture. Main Street ran from left to right and was lined with clapboard stores and offices. There was a small wooden church with a bell tower. At either end of the town the street became a country road and disappeared among fields. In the distance was a railway track. Behind Priest the freeway ran along a viaduct on high concrete arches.

Stepping down the hill was a cluster of six huge bright blue pipes. "What's that?" Priest said.

Melanie thought for a moment. "It must be a gas pipeline."

Priest breathed a sigh of satisfaction. "This place is perfect."

They made one more stop that day.

After the earthquake Priest would need to hide the seismic vibrator. It was going to become more and more difficult to drive it on public roads, so he needed to hide it someplace where he could, if necessary, trigger a third earthquake without moving far.

They drove into San Francisco, and Melanie directed him to Third Street, a run-down industrial neighborhood of derelict factories and empty warehouses.

"This is good," Priest said. "It's half an hour from Felicitas, and it's the kind of district where nobody takes much interest."

Realtors' signs were optimistically fixed to some of the buildings. Melanie, posing as Priest's secretary, called the number on one of the signs and asked if they had a warehouse to rent.

An eager young salesman drove out to meet them an hour later. He showed them a crumbling cinder-block ruin. There was a broken sign over the door, which Melanie read aloud: "Perpetua Diaries." There was plenty of room to park the seismic vibrator. The place also had a working bathroom and a small office with a hot plate and a big old Zenith TV left by the previous tenant.

Priest paid the man four weeks' rent in advance, cash. The salesman gave Melanie the keys, shook hands, and hurried away.

Priest and Melanie drove back to Silver River Valley.

THURSDAY evening Judy Maddox packed an overnight bag and returned to the officers club at ten p.m. The command post was quiet, but the atmosphere was tense.

There were now more than a hundred people in the old ballroom. The on-scene commander was Stuart Cleever, a big shot from Washington. Despite Honeymoon's orders, there was no way the FBI was going to let a lowly agent take charge of something this big. Judy's title was investigative operations coordinator. That gave her all the control she needed. Alongside her was Charlie Marsh, commander of the SWAT team. Between the head shed and the investigation team table were Michael Quercus and his young assistant seismologists, sitting at their screens, watching for signs of earthquake activity.

The phone on Judy's desk rang. She picked it up. "Maddox."

The operator said, "A call for you from Ricky Granger."

"Trace it!" She waved at Cleever and Marsh, indicating that they should listen.

"Judy Maddox here."

A male voice said, "You're smart, Agent Maddox. But are you smart enough to make the governor see sense?"

He sounded irate, frustrated. Judy imagined a man of about fifty losing his grip on life and feeling resentful. She said, "Am I speaking to Ricky Granger?"

A male voice said, "You know who you're speaking to. Why are they forcing me to cause another earthquake?"

"*Forcing you?* Are you kidding yourself that all this is someone else's fault?"

This seemed to make him angrier. "It's not me who's using more and more electric power every year. I don't use electricity."

"You don't? So what's powering your phone—steam?"

"Don't mess with me, Judy. You're the one that's in trouble."

Next to her, Charlie wrote in large letters on his notepad: "Pay phone—Oakland—I-980 & I-580 Texaco."

"We're all in trouble, Ricky," she said more reasonably.

"Your voice changed," Granger said. "What happened?"

Judy felt out of her depth. She had no special training in negotiating skills. All she knew was that she had to keep him on the phone. "I suddenly thought what a catastrophe there will be if you and I don't manage to come to some agreement."

"Have you traced this call already?" Granger said. "Are you trying to keep me on the line while your SWAT team comes after me? Forget it! I got a hundred and fifty ways out of here."

"But only one way out of the jam you're in."

"It's past midnight," he said. "Your time is up. I'm going to cause another earthquake, and there's not one damn thing you can do to stop me." He hung up.

Judy slammed down the phone. "Let's go, Charlie!" She ripped the E-fit picture of Granger off the subject board and ran outside.

The helicopter was waiting on the parade ground, its rotors turning. She jumped in, with Charlie close behind.

As they took off, he said, "I've ordered the major freeways closed in a twenty-five-mile radius."

"What about other roads?"

"If he gets off the freeway, we lose him. This is one of the busiest road networks in California. You couldn't seal it off watertight if you had the whole U.S. Army."

ON I-80 PRIEST heard the throb of a helicopter and looked up to see it passing overhead. "They can't be after us, can they?"

"They can trace phone calls instantly," Melanie said. "Can't we get off the freeway?"

"There are side roads, but they don't cross the water. There's no other way to get home to get the seismic vibrator."

Priest approached the Carquinez Bridge toll plaza, slowly fishing in his jeans pocket for change. A highway patrol officer was in the booth, behind the attendant, staring at Priest. The attendant took Priest's money but did not turn on the green light. The officer stepped out.

"Good evening, sir," the officer said. He was wearing a bullet-proof vest. "Please pull over to the right side of the road."

Priest did as he said. His old car could not outrun the cops.

There was another officer waiting in a highway patrol car. He got out when Priest pulled up. He, too, was wearing a bulletproof vest. The first officer came over from the tollbooth.

Priest opened the glove compartment and took out the revolver he had stolen that morning. Then he got out of the car.

IT TOOK Judy only a few minutes to reach the gas station from which the phone call had been made. The police had moved fast. In the parking lot four cruisers were parked at the corners of a square, facing inward, their blue lights flashing, their headlights illuminating a cleared landing space. The chopper came down.

Judy jumped out. A police sergeant greeted her. "Take me to

the phone," she said. He led her inside. The pay phone was in a corner next to the rest rooms. Behind the counter were two clerks.

"Any other witnesses?" she said to the sergeant.

"Nope. There may have been other customers in here at the same time, but they're long gone."

Charlie Marsh came hurrying up with a mobile phone to his ear. "Granger's been spotted," he said to Judy. "Two CHPs stopped him at the toll plaza at Carquinez Bridge."

"We have him in custody?" Judy asked.

"No," Charlie said. "He shot them in the head and got away."

"Did we get a make on his car?"

"No. Tollbooth attendant didn't notice."

"And the two highway patrol officers?"

"Both dead."

The police sergeant paled. "God rest their souls," he whispered.

Judy turned away, sick with disgust. "And God help us catch Ricky Granger," she said, "before he kills anyone else."

OAKTREE had done a great job of making the seismic vibrator look like a carnival ride. The gaily painted red-and-yellow panels of the Dragon's Mouth completely concealed the massive steel plate, the large vibrating engine, and the complex of tanks and valves that controlled the machine. As Priest drove across the state to the coast on Friday afternoon, other drivers smiled and children waved from the rear windows of station wagons.

Priest drove the truck, with Melanie beside him. Star and Oaktree followed in the 'Cuda. They reached Felicitas in the early evening. The seismic window would open just after seven p.m.

Priest pulled off the freeway and stopped the truck. At the end of the exit ramp there was a gas station and a Big Ribs restaurant, where several families were eating dinner. He could see a school and a small wood-frame chapel on the road leading into town.

Melanie said, "The fault line runs right across Main Street."

"In twenty minutes there's going to be the biggest panic California has ever seen," Priest said.

"All right!" Melanie said. She was tense but excited.

Secretly Priest was full of doubt. *Will it work this time? Only one way to find out.* He drove down the hill.

Priest swung onto Main Street. There was a coffee shop right on the fault line. Priest pulled onto the parking apron in front. "Go buy some doughnuts," he told Melanie. "Look natural."

She jumped out and sauntered across to the coffee shop.

Priest engaged the parking brake and flicked the switch that lowered the hammer of the seismic vibrator to the ground. He checked the dials of the vibrating mechanism. Everything was green.

Melanie reappeared. "Go get in the 'Cuda with the others," Priest told her. "I'll be right there."

He set the machine to vibrate on a signal from the remote control, then jumped out, leaving the engine running.

Priest got into the passenger seat of the 'Cuda. "Drive back up the hill where we stopped before," he told Oaktree.

Priest turned on the radio and tuned to John Truth.

"Seven twenty-five on Friday evening, and the threat of an earthquake by the Hammer of Eden has failed to materialize."

Priest turned to Melanie. "Call him on your cell phone."

Melanie tapped out the number. "It's busy."

"Keep trying."

Oaktree stopped the car at the top of the hill, and they looked down on the town.

"I got through," Melanie said. "Hello? . . . Yes, I'll hold for John Truth. I want to talk about the earthquake," she went on. "It's . . . Melinda. . . . Oh! He's gone. I nearly told him my name!"

Priest said, "Give me the phone."

She handed it over, and Priest put it to his ear. Suddenly he heard, "Hello, Melinda. You're on *John Truth Live.*"

Priest said, "This isn't Melinda. It's the Hammer of Eden."

"Buddy, you better not be kidding," Truth said, "because if you are, you could go to jail, you know?"

"I guess I could go to jail if I'm not kidding," Priest said.

Truth did not laugh. "Why are you calling me?"

"We just want to be sure, this time, that everyone knows the earthquake was caused by us."

"When will it happen?"

"Within the next few minutes."

"Where?"

"I will only tell you that it will take place on Route 101."

RAJA Khan jumped on a table in the command post. "Everyone, shut up and listen!" They all heard the shrill note of fear in his voice, and the room went dead. "A guy claiming to be from the Hammer of Eden is on *John Truth Live.*"

There was a burst of noise as everyone asked questions. Judy stood up. "Quiet, everyone! Raja, what did he say?"

Carl Theobald, who was sitting with his ear to the speaker of a portable radio, answered, "He just said the next earthquake will take place on Route 101 within a few minutes."

"Turn up the volume, Carl." Judy swung around. "Michael, does that fit any of the locations we have under surveillance?"

"Nope," he said. "I guessed wrong."

"Then try to figure out where these people might be."

An alarm sounded on Michael's computer. "It's just coming on screen," he said. "It's not a tremor. It's a seismic vibrator."

"Where is it?" Judy said. "Give me a location."

"Okay. Here are the coordinates."

Judy and Charlie Marsh went to the wall map. "Here," Judy said triumphantly. "Right on Route 101, south of San Francisco. A town called Felicitas. Charlie, I'm coming with you in the chopper."

Michael warned, "The vibrator could be anywhere within a mile or so of the coordinates."

"How can we narrow it down?"

"If I look at the landscape, I can spot the fault line."

"You better come in the helicopter. Grab a bulletproof vest."

"IT'S not working!" Priest said, trying to control his alarm.

"We have to move the truck and try again," Melanie said. "I

think the earth here is too soft. The town is close to the river. Soft, wet ground soaks up vibrations."

Priest turned to her accusingly. "Yesterday you told me earthquakes cause more damage on wet ground."

"I said buildings on wet soil are more likely to be damaged, but for transmitting shock waves to the fault, rock is better."

"Where do we try next?" Priest asked.

She pointed up the hill. "Where we came off the freeway. It's not directly on the fault line, but the ground should be rock."

Priest shouted, "Drive, Oaktree! Back to the truck!"

Oaktree tore down the hill and stopped in front of the coffee shop. Priest leaped out, jumped into the truck, raised the plate, and pulled away, flooring the gas pedal.

When the truck was halfway up the hill, a police car came off the freeway ramp and sped past them heading into Felicitas.

At last the truck arrived at the spot from which Priest had first looked over the town. He stopped across the road from the Big Ribs restaurant and lowered the vibrator's plate.

Priest saw the police cruiser coming back up the hill from the town. Glancing up, he spotted a helicopter in the distant sky. He had no time to get clear of the truck and use the remote. He would have to activate the vibrator sitting in the driver's seat.

He put his hand on the control, hesitated, and pulled the lever.

FROM the helicopter Felicitas looked like a town asleep. Judy could see Main Street. A woman in a straw hat stood still on the sidewalk; two boys stopped their bicycles in the middle of the road. There was movement on the freeway that flew past the town on the elegant arches of a viaduct. She spotted two police cruisers approaching the town at high speed, coming, she assumed, in response to her emergency call. But in the town no one moved.

After a moment she figured out what was going on. They were listening to the seismic vibrator. But where was it?

The chopper flew low enough, but she could not see a vehicle big enough to be a seismic vibrator.

Judy spoke to Michael over a headset. "Where's the fault line?"

"It crosses the railroad, the river, the freeway, and the gas pipeline. Dear Lord, there's going to be some damage."

"But where's the vibrator?"

"What's that on the hillside?"

Judy followed his pointing finger. Above the town, close to the freeway, she saw a fast-food restaurant. On the road near the restaurant were a mud-colored coupe, a police cruiser pulling up behind it, and a large truck painted all over with dragons in red and yellow. "It's a carnival ride," she said.

"Or a disguise. That's the right size for a seismic vibrator."

"I bet you're right!" she said. "Charlie, are you listening?"

Charlie Marsh was sitting beside the pilot. Six members of his SWAT team were seated behind Judy and Michael, armed with stubby MP-5 submachine guns. "I'm listening," Charlie said. "Pilot, can you put us down near that carnival truck on the hill?"

"It's awkward," the pilot replied. "I'd rather come down in the parking lot of that restaurant."

"Do it," Charlie said.

The chopper came down, and a figure jumped out of the truck. Judy saw a tall, thin man with long dark hair, and she felt sure he was Granger.

As the helicopter touched the ground, there was a noise like the crack of doom.

THE bang was a thunderclap so loud it drowned the roar of the seismic vibrator and the thrash of the helicopter rotors.

The ground seemed to rise up and hit Priest like a fist. He was watching the chopper land in the Big Ribs parking lot, thinking that his scheme had failed. The next moment he was flat on his face. He rolled over, gasping for breath, and saw the trees all around him bending and twisting as if a hurricane were blowing.

A moment later he realized it had worked! He had caused an earthquake. And he was in the middle of it.

The air rang with a terrifying rumble. He scrambled to his knees, but the ground would not stay still, and in trying to stand up, he fell over again. He rolled over and managed to sit upright.

The chapel down the road seemed to fall over sideways. Its walls went down in a cloud of dust, leaving a massive carved-oak lectern standing in the middle of the wreckage.

The windows of Big Ribs smashed, and the screams of terrified children pierced the air. One corner of the roof sagged, then dropped on a group of five or six teenagers, crushing them. The other patrons rose in a wave and surged toward the now glassless windows as the rest of the roof started to come down on them.

The air was full of the pungent smell of gasoline. The tremor had ruptured the tanks at the filling station. Priest saw a sea of fuel spilling out. An out-of-control motorcycle came weaving off the road. The rider fell off, and the machine slid across the concrete, striking sparks. The spilling gas caught alight with a whoosh, and a second later the entire plaza was ablaze.

THE helicopter lifted off a second after it had touched down. Judy saw the ground beneath her shimmer like a block of Jell-O. She saw a motorcyclist crash into a filling station, and she cried out in grief as the gasoline caught on fire and the flames engulfed the fallen rider.

The helicopter swung around, rising, and her view changed. Now she saw a freight train crossing the flat fields. It came off the rails, and the loaded cars piled into the back of the engine.

Judy could see the town. Desperate people were running into the street, mouths open in screams of terror, trying to escape as their houses collapsed. Main Street seemed to be on fire and flooded with water at the same time. There was a flash like lightning, then another, and Judy guessed power lines were snapping.

As the helicopter gained height, the freeway came into view, and Judy's hands flew to her mouth in horror as she saw that one of the giant arches supporting the viaduct had twisted and snapped. A tongue of road now stuck out into midair. At least ten cars had piled up on either side of the break. A big old Chevrolet hurtled toward the precipice, tumbled in the air, and finally crashed onto the roof of a house below, bursting into flames.

A sudden wind blew away the cloud of black smoke over the filling station, and Judy saw the man she thought was Ricky Granger. He struggled to his feet and ran to the brown coupe, shouting and gesticulating to the people inside.

The police cruiser was right behind the coupe, but the cops seemed slow to act. Judy realized the terrorists were about to flee.

"Go down, pilot!" she screamed through the headset. "Those people did this, and now they're getting away!"

The helicopter swooped toward the ground.

PRIEST yelled at Oaktree through the open window of the 'Cuda. "Let's go!" He pointed. "That old road leads back to San Francisco."

Priest saw the two local cops getting out of their cruiser. He leaped into the truck, raised the plate, and pulled away. Oaktree scorched a U-turn in the 'Cuda and headed down the hill. Priest turned the truck around more slowly.

One of the cops was standing in the middle of the road, pointing his gun at the truck. He was shouting, "Police! Stop!"

Priest drove right at him. The cop dived out of the way.

Then the FBI helicopter landed in the middle of the road a quarter of a mile ahead. Priest saw the 'Cuda screech to a halt.

Okay, you asked for it. Priest floored the gas pedal.

Agents in SWAT gear leaped out of the chopper and took cover at the roadside. Priest's truck careered down the hill and roared past the stopped 'Cuda. "Follow me," he muttered, hoping Oaktree would guess what was expected of him.

He saw Judy Maddox jump out of the chopper holding a shotgun. A man tumbled out after her. It was Melanie's husband.

Priest glanced in his mirror. Oaktree had the 'Cuda tucked in right behind him. Behind the 'Cuda was the police cruiser.

Priest's truck was heading for the chopper. An FBI agent stood up at the roadside and aimed a machine gun at the truck.

The chopper lifted off the ground.

JUDY CURSED. THE HELICOPTER pilot had landed too close to the approaching vehicles. There was hardly time for the SWAT team to spill out and take positions before the carnival truck was on them.

Michael staggered to the side of the road. "Lie flat!" Judy screamed. She saw the driver of the truck duck as one of the SWAT team opened fire. The windshield frosted, but the truck did not stop. Judy fired her gun at the tires, but her shot went wide.

The chopper was lifting out of the way, but then Judy saw, to her horror, that the pilot had been a split second too slow. The roof of the truck's cab clipped the undercarriage of the helicopter. The aircraft tilted suddenly. The truck charged on, unaffected. The brown 'Cuda raced by, close behind the truck.

Judy fired wildly at the retreating vehicles.

The helicopter wobbled in midair as the pilot tried to correct its lurch. But a rotor blade touched the ground, and then suddenly the helicopter nose-dived into the road. The pursuing police cruiser braked desperately and skidded into the crashed helicopter. There was a deafening bang, and both vehicles burst into flame.

PRIEST saw the crash in his side mirrors and let out a victory whoop. Now the FBI looked stuck: no helicopter, no cars.

Behind him the 'Cuda was swaying in a peculiar way. After a minute he figured it must have a flat in a rear tire.

They reached a crossroads. Three cars had piled up at the junction: a Toyota minivan, a battered Dodge pickup, and an old white Cadillac. None was badly damaged, and the minivan's engine was still running. Priest could not see the drivers anywhere.

He steered around the pileup and turned right, away from the town. They were now more than a mile from the FBI team and well out of sight. He jumped out of the truck.

The 'Cuda pulled up behind, and Oaktree got out, grinning broadly. "Mission successfully completed, General," he said.

Priest gave him a high five. "But we need to get away fast."

Star and Melanie got out of the car. Melanie's cheeks were pink with exhilaration. "We did it. We did it!" she said.

Star bent over and threw up at the roadside.

"It's not over yet," Priest said. "Every cop in California will be looking for a carnival ride called the Dragon's Mouth." He turned to Oaktree. "How fast could we get these panels off?"

"In a few minutes."

Working fast, the two of them took the carnival panels off the truck and tossed them over a wire fence into a field.

When they had finished with the truck, Oaktree said, "Now the damn thing looks like a seismic vibrator again."

"I know," Priest said, "but I don't have far to drive. Let's go."

"First I need to change a wheel. I have a flat."

"Don't bother," Priest said. "We gotta ditch the 'Cuda anyway. The FBI will be looking for it." He pointed back toward the cross-roads. "I saw three vehicles back there. Grab yourself a new ride."

Oaktree hurried off.

Star looked at Priest with accusing eyes. "I can't believe we did this," she said. "How many people have we killed?"

"We had no choice," he said angrily. "We'll talk later, okay?"

"You're so calm about it." Star shook her head as if amazed. "I spent twenty-five years with you and never really knew you."

Oaktree came back driving the Toyota minivan.

Priest said to Star, "Go with him."

She hesitated for a long moment; then she got into the car.

Oaktree pulled away and disappeared fast.

"Get in the truck," Priest said to Melanie. He got behind the wheel and reversed the vehicle to the crossroads. They both jumped out and looked at the remaining two cars. The keys were in the ignition of the white Cadillac. "Follow me in the Caddy," Priest said.

She got into the car and said, "Where are we headed?"

"Perpetua Diaries warehouse."

As they were leaving, there was a huge explosion. Priest looked toward Felicitas and saw a jet of flame shoot high in the evening sky.

Melanie said, "Wow, what's that?"

"I guess the gas pipeline just caught on fire," he said. "Now that's what I call fireworks."

CHARLIE WAS TALKING INTO A mobile phone. "The pilot is dead and so are two local cops. There's a pileup on Route 101, which needs to be closed. You'll need to call the governor's office of emergency management."

Michael Quercus was sitting on a patch of grass at the side of the road, looking shocked and helpless. Judy went over to him.

"Pull yourself together," she said. "People die every day."

"I know," he said. "It's not the killings—although they're enough. It's something else. Did you see who was in the car?"

"I saw there was a black guy driving it."

"But in the back? A woman."

"Did you recognize her?"

"I sure did," he said. "It was my wife."

THEY were on the outskirts of San Francisco when Priest got through to the John Truth show. Priest said he was from the Hammer of Eden and got connected right away.

"You have done a terrible thing," Truth said.

"You're wrong," Priest told him. "The people who are turning California into a poison wasteland have done a terrible thing. I'm just trying to stop them."

"By killing innocent people?"

"Pollution kills innocent people."

Truth said, "I appeal to you to turn yourself in, right now."

"I have one thing to say to you and the people of California," Priest said. "Governor Robson must announce a freeze on power plant building. Otherwise there will be another earthquake."

"You would do this again?" Truth sounded genuinely shocked.

"You bet. And the next earthquake will be worse than this one."

"Where will it strike?"

"I can't tell you that."

"Can you say when?"

"Oh, sure. Unless the governor changes his mind, it will take place in two days' time." Priest hung up. "Now, Mister Governor," he said aloud, "tell the people not to panic."

PART THREE

FORTY-EIGHT HOURS

8

JUDY and Michael got back to the emergency operations center a few minutes before midnight. The horror of the earthquake was still with her, but Michael's revelation had given her new hope. If Judy could find Melanie, she could find the Hammer of Eden. And if she could do it in two days, she could prevent another earthquake.

She went into the old ballroom that had become the command post. Stuart Cleever, the big shot from Washington, stood at the head shed. Beside him stood Brian Kincaid.

"What went wrong?" Brian said when he saw her.

"We were too late, by a few seconds," she said wearily. "But I have a new lead. I know who their seismologist is. Her name is Melanie Quercus. She's the estranged wife of Michael, who's been helping us. She got the information about where the fault is under tension from her husband, stole it off his computer. And I suspect she stole the list of sites we had under surveillance."

Kincaid said, "Quercus could be in cahoots with her!"

Judy had anticipated this. "I'm sure he's not," she said, "but he's taking a lie detector test right now, just to make sure."

"Good enough," Cleever said. "Can you find the wife?"

"She told Michael she was living in a commune in Del Norte County. We're searching our databases for communes there."

ON SATURDAY morning at breakfast Dale and Poem stood up in the cookhouse in front of everyone. "We have an announcement," Dale said solemnly. "We're leaving the commune today."

Priest was dumbstruck. People did not leave unless he wanted them to. These folk were under his spell. Dale was the oenologist, the key man in winemaking. They couldn't afford to lose him.

If Dale had only heard the news—as Priest had an hour ago—he would know that California was in a panic. Airports were mobbed, and freeways were jammed with people fleeing the cities close to the San Andreas Fault. The governor had called out the National Guard. More and more people were urging him to give in to the demand made by the Hammer of Eden. But Dale knew nothing of all this.

Melanie was the first to speak. She said, "But Dale, why?"

"You know why," he said. "This valley is going to be flooded. We have three children. We can't stay here hoping for a miracle."

Priest said, "This valley is not going to be flooded."

Dale said, "We know that something's been going on, Priest. But whatever you're up to, you haven't shared it with us. And we can't risk the future of our children on your faith. We're not staying."

Torn between rage and the need for restraint, Priest walked silently out of the cookhouse and went to his cabin.

Star came in. She had not spoken to him since she and Oaktree had driven away from Felicitas last night in the minivan.

She said, "I'm going to the police."

Priest was astonished. "You're out of your mind," he said.

"We killed people yesterday," she said. "At least twelve people died, and more than a hundred were hospitalized."

He reached for her hand. "I didn't intend to hurt anyone. I knew there was a risk, and I decided to take it because what was at stake was so important. I thought you made the same decision."

"I did, and it was a wicked decision." Tears came to her eyes. "Can't you see what's happened to us? We were the kids who believed in love and peace. Now we're killing people!"

"So you feel you made a mistake, and you want to redeem yourself by punishing the whole commune. You want to betray us."

Star was taken aback. "I hadn't looked at it that way," she said.

"What you really want, I think, is to be sure it's over."

"I guess so, yeah."

He reached out to her. "It's over," he said softly. "There will be no more earthquakes. The governor will give in. You'll see."

THE next day Judy went to Sacramento for a meeting at the governor's office. Unfortunately, a search of the communes in Del Norte County had failed to turn up anyone who'd ever seen Melanie or Dusty. Consequently, Judy's spirits were low.

Judy, Stuart Cleever, and Charlie Marsh met at noon on Saturday at the Capitol Building in the conference room of the governor's suite. Al Honeymoon was in the chair.

"There's a twelve-mile traffic jam on I-80 with people trying to get away from the San Andreas Fault," Honeymoon said.

Cleever said, "The President called the director of the FBI."

"He called Governor Robson, too," Honeymoon said.

"We do not yet have a serious public order problem," Cleever said. "However, if there should be another earthquake . . ."

"There can't be another earthquake," Judy said.

Honeymoon made a sardonic face. "You have a suggestion?"

"There's only one thing I can think of," she said. "Set a trap. Tell Ricky Granger that Governor Robson wants to negotiate a freeze on power plant building with him personally."

Cleever said, "I don't believe he'd fall for it."

"He's smart, but he's a psychopath, and they love controlling others. The idea of personally negotiating with the governor of California is going to tempt him mightily. Is it a possibility?"

"I wouldn't recommend it, but maybe it could be made to work. However, I know the governor won't do it," Honeymoon said.

"But he could pretend," Judy said. "We tell Granger the governor will announce the freeze but only under the right conditions. He wants to talk personally with Granger to agree to those conditions."

"I don't know if Granger will buy it," Honeymoon said, "but I guess we have to try. Let's do it."

PRIEST and Melanie drove into Sacramento in the white Cadillac on Saturday afternoon. The town was thronged with people.

Listening to the car radio soon after midday, Priest heard the voice of John Truth, although it was not time for his show. "Here is a special message for Peter Shoebury of Eisenhower Junior High." Shoebury was the man whose identity Priest had borrowed for the FBI press conference, and Eisenhower was the imaginary school attended by Flower. Priest realized the message was for him. "Would Peter Shoebury please call me at the following number?"

"They want to make a deal," he said to Melanie. "We've won!"

While Melanie drove around downtown, Priest made the call from her mobile phone. It was answered by a woman.

"This is Peter Shoebury from Eisenhower Junior High."

The response was instant. "I'm going to connect you with Al Honeymoon. I need to verify your identity first. Could you give me the name of the student reporter who was with you a week ago?"

"It was Florence."

"Connecting you now."

A moment later the deep voice of Honeymoon said, "Mr. Granger, the governor wants to meet with you today, with the object of negotiating a resolution to this crisis."

"Is the governor willing to announce the freeze we want?"

Honeymoon hesitated. "Yes, but there must be conditions. The announcement of this freeze will have to be handled delicately."

"Where do we meet?"

"In the governor's office, here at the Capitol Building. No police, no FBI. You would be guaranteed freedom to leave the meeting without hindrance, regardless of the outcome."

"I'm not falling into your trap. I'll tell you where we'll meet. Set up a little round table and two chairs on the front lawn of the Capitol. Have the governor there at three o'clock. In his pocket he must have a signed letter guaranteeing me immunity from prosecution."

"I can't agree to all this—"

"Have a photographer there. I want a picture of him handing me the letter of immunity, for proof. Got that?"

"Got it."

"No tricks. My seismic vibrator is already in place, ready to trigger another earthquake. This one will strike a major city. If the governor doesn't appear today at three o'clock . . . *bang.*"

Priest broke the connection.

THERE were at least thirty agents within sight of the table that sat on the lawn, but Judy could not see them. She was playing the part of the photographer. Her gun was in a camera bag slung from her shoulder. She wore a blond wig so Granger wouldn't recognize her.

Tour parties were wandering across the lawn and following their prescribed routes around the Capitol. Judy scrutinized every tall, thin man of middle age through her camera lens.

At one minute to three she still had not seen Ricky Granger.

Michael, who had met Granger face to face, was also watching from a surveillance van parked around the corner.

Judy spoke into a little microphone clipped to her bra. "I think Granger won't show until after the governor appears."

A tiny speaker behind her ear crackled, and she heard Charlie Marsh reply, "We were just saying the same thing."

A moment later the governor emerged from the front entrance. He looked bulkier than usual on account of the bulletproof vest under his jacket. He walked across the lawn and sat at the table.

Then, out of the corner of her eye, Judy saw movement. An old Chevrolet Impala approached slowly on Tenth Street. It stopped at the curb right opposite Governor Robson. Her heart beat faster.

The door of the car opened. The figure that stepped out wore blue jeans, a checked work shirt, and sandals. He was about six feet tall, and thin, with long dark hair, and he wore large-framed sunglasses.

Judy's earpiece crackled. "Judy, is it him?" Charlie asked.

"I can't tell," she said. "It could be."

The man looked around and started toward the governor.

Judy placed herself between him and the governor. "I don't think it's him," she said. All the pictures had shown a nose like the blade of a knife. This man had a broad, flat nose.

He stepped around Judy and approached the governor. The man put his hand inside his shirt.

In her earpiece Charlie said, "He's reaching for something!"

Judy dropped to one knee and fumbled for the pistol in her camera bag. The man began to pull something out of his shirt. Judy saw a dark-colored cylinder. She yelled, "Freeze! FBI!"

Agents burst out of cars and vans and came running from the Capitol Building. The man froze.

Judy pointed her gun at his head and said, "Pull it out real slow and pass it to me."

"Okay, okay!" The man drew out a rolled-up magazine.

Judy took it from him. It was this week's *Time*. There was nothing inside the cylinder.

The man said in a frightened voice, "Some guy gave me a hundred dollars to hand it to the governor."

Agents bundled the governor back into the Capitol.

Judy looked around. *Granger is watching this. He has to be. Where is he?* A tour group was coming down the steps of the grand entrance. As Judy watched, a man in a Hawaiian shirt peeled off from the group and walked away, and something about him caught Judy's eye. She went after him, walking fast.

He turned the corner of the building. Judy broke into a run.

She heard Charlie's voice in her earpiece. "Judy, what's up?"

"Just checking someone out," she said. "Probably a tourist."

She saw the Hawaiian shirt disappear into the Capitol Building.

Judy ran inside, too. She went left off the grand lobby, raced past an elevator bank and into the rotunda, which extended up two floors to a richly decorated dome. She glanced up to the circular gallery at the second-floor level and caught a glimpse of a brightly colored shirt.

She bounded up one of the paired grand staircases. At the top she looked across the gallery. On the far side was an open doorway leading to a modern corridor with strip lighting. The Hawaiian shirt was in the corridor. He was running now.

Judy went after him. There was no one in the corridor: It was Saturday. She followed the shirt around a corner, then another and a third. Coming full circle, he returned to the gallery. She lost sight of him momentarily and guessed he had gone up again.

Breathing hard, she went up another ornate staircase to the third floor. In a corner she noticed a sign that read NORTH STAIR—NO ROOF ACCESS. Judy opened it and found herself in a narrow functional stairwell. She could hear her quarry clattering down the stairs, but she could not see him. She hurtled down.

She emerged at ground level in the rotunda. To her left a corridor led to an exit door. She saw the shirt going out.

She followed. Granger was darting across L Street, dodging traffic. Drivers swerved to avoid him and honked indignantly. Judy sprinted across, taking the same mad risks with the traffic.

Granger sped along Eleventh Street, then darted into a parking garage. Judy flew after him, going as fast as she could. Then something hit her, a mighty blow in the face.

Pain exploded in her nose and forehead. She fell onto her back, hitting the concrete. She lay still, paralyzed by shock and pain. A few seconds later she heard Michael saying, "Judy, are you alive?"

Judy opened her mouth. "It hurts," she mumbled.

He pulled a handkerchief from the pocket of his khakis and wiped her mouth with surprising gentleness. "Your nose is bleeding."

She sat upright. "What happened?"

"I saw you turning inside, going like greased lightning; then the next minute you were flat on the ground. I think he was waiting for you and hit you as you came around the corner." He helped her up.

Judy's face hurt, but she could see clearly and her legs felt steady. She tried to think straight. *Maybe I haven't lost him yet.* He must have gone up the ramp. She knew this garage—she had parked here when she came to see Honeymoon.

"I'm going after him," she said.

She ran up the ramp. Michael followed. They reached the first parking level and started across the floor. Suddenly a black car shot out of its parking slot straight at them. Judy leaped sideways, fell to the ground, and rolled underneath a parked car.

She saw the wheels of the black car as it turned with a squeal of tires and accelerated down the ramp like a shot from a gun.

Judy stood up, searching frantically for Michael.

She saw him a few yards from her, on his hands and knees, white with shock. "Are you all right?" she said.

He got to his feet. "I'm fine, just shook up."

Judy looked to see the make of the car, but it had disappeared.

As JUDY was entering the officers club at seven p.m., Raja Khan came running out. He stopped when he saw her. "What happened?"

"I let Ricky Granger punch me in the nose," she said. She had a bandage across her face. The pills they had given her at the hospital in Sacramento had eased the pain, but she felt battered and dispirited. "Where are you going in such a hurry?"

"We were looking for a record called *Raining Fresh Daisies,* remember? I've located a copy at a store called Vinyl Vic's."

This could be the lead Judy needed. "I'm coming with you."

They jumped into Raja's car and headed for Haight-Ashbury.

He explained as he drove. "The record was released in 1969 on a San Francisco label, Transcendental Tracks. It sold a few copies, but the label went out of business after a few months."

Vinyl Vic's was a small store stuffed with old records. At the back, a thin man in a tie-dyed T-shirt stood beside a cash register.

Raja introduced himself. "You must be Vic. I spoke to you on the phone a few minutes ago."

Vic stared at them. "Oh, right."

"What about this record?" Judy said impatiently.

"Here it is." She saw that Vic had a turntable behind the cash register. He lowered the stylus. A burst of manic guitar introduced a surprisingly laid-back jazz-funk track. Then the woman's voice came in. It was the voice on the John Truth tape without question. Younger, clearer, gentler, but with that same unmistakable low, sexy tone.

"Do you have the cover?" Judy said urgently.

Vic handed it to her. The front had a swirling design and the words "Raining Fresh Daisies." Judy turned it over and skipped the liner notes. At the bottom of the album cover was a row of five photographs, just head and shoulders—four men and a woman. The caption under the woman read "Stella Higgins, poetry."

"Stella Higgins," she said. "I believe I've heard that name before." But she could not remember where. The small black-and-white head shot showed a girl of about twenty, with a smiling, sensual face framed by wavy dark hair. "She was beautiful," Judy murmured. "Can we borrow this?"

"I'm here to sell records, not lend them," Vic said. "It's fifty bucks."

She was not going to argue. "Okay." And she paid him.

Driving back in Raja's car, Judy said, "Stella Higgins. Where have I seen that name?"

Raja shook his head. "It doesn't ring any bells with me."

As they got out of the car, she gave him the album. "Make blowups of her photo and circulate them to police departments."

They entered the command post, and Judy went to her computer. She initiated a search of criminal records. There was a Stella Higgins in the files. The woman had been fined for possession of marijuana and been given a suspended sentence for assaulting a police officer at a demonstration. Both convictions were dated 1968, and there was nothing since. Stella's record was like that of Ricky Granger, who had dropped off the radar in the early '70s.

Judy felt a hand on her shoulder. It was Bo. "My baby, what happened to your face?" He touched the bandage on her nose.

"I guess I was careless," she said.

He kissed the top of her head. "I'm on duty tonight, but I had to stop by and see how you are. When are you going home?"

"I don't know. I just made a breakthrough." She told him about *Raining Fresh Daisies*. "The way I see it, she's a beautiful girl living in San Francisco in the '60s. In the '70s she hooks up with a charismatic guy who is on the run from the Mob. They start a cult. It survives for three decades; then somehow their existence is threatened by a plan to build a power plant. As they face the ruin of all they've worked for, they look for a way to block this power plant. Then a seismologist joins the group and comes up with a crazy idea."

Bo nodded. "They probably don't own their house or farm or whatever. If they owned it, they'd get compensation and they could start again somewhere else. I'm guessing they have a lease."

Carl Theobald came up and said, "Three hits in the phone book. Stella Higgins in Los Angeles is a woman of about seventy. Mrs. Higgins in Stockton has a strong African accent. And S. J. Higgins in Diamond Heights is a man called Sidney."

"Damn," Judy said. She explained to Bo, "Stella Higgins is the voice on the John Truth tape. I'm sure I've seen the name before."

Bo said, "Try your files. If the name seems familiar, that could be because it has already come up during the investigation."

"Good idea."

"I gotta go," he said. "Good luck—and get some rest."

"Thanks, Bo." Judy activated the search function on the computer and had it go through the entire Hammer of Eden directory for Stella Higgins. Carl watched over her shoulder. The search took a while. Finally the screen flickered and said, "1 file(s) found."

Two more agents looked over Judy's shoulder as she opened the file. It was a large document containing all the notes made by agents during the raid on Los Alamos six days ago.

Stuart Cleever appeared. "What's all the fuss about?"

"We've found the woman who called John Truth!" Judy said. She used the search function to locate the name in the notes.

Stella Higgins had not been at Los Alamos. Two agents had visited a winery a few miles up the valley. The site was rented from the federal government by a Stella Higgins.

Judy read on. The agents had conscientiously noted the name and age of every adult at the winery. Most gave their address as that of the winery. So they were living there. Maybe it was a cult, and the agents simply had not realized that.

"We've got them," Judy said.

Stuart Cleever said, "I think you're right." He turned to the SWAT team table. "Charlie, call the Sacramento office and organize a joint raid. We'll hit them at first light."

Judy said, "We should raid them now. If we wait until morning, they may be gone."

Cleever said, "Nighttime is too risky. We raid at dawn."

"So be it," she said. "What time do we head out, Charlie?"

Marsh looked at his watch. "Leaving here at two a.m."

"I may grab a couple of hours' rest."

On the way out she met Michael. "You look exhausted," he said. "Let me drive you home."

"Then how will I get back here?"

"I'll nap on your couch and drive you back."

Judy stopped and looked at him. "I have to tell you, my face is so sore I don't think I could kiss, let alone anything else."

"I'll settle for holding your hand," he said with a smile. "Will you let me watch you sleep?"

He read her expression. "I think I'm hearing yes," he said.

She smiled. "Yes."

PRIEST was mad when he got back from Sacramento. Governor Robson had had no thought of making a deal. The whole thing had been a setup. The FBI had thought he was some dope. They would learn the truth, and the lesson would be dear.

It would cost them another earthquake.

Everyone at the commune was still stunned by the departure of Dale and Poem. It reminded them that tomorrow they were all supposed to leave the valley. Although it was Saturday night, nobody wanted to party. Melanie went to the bunkhouse to read to the children. Priest sat outside his cabin watching the moon go down.

Star came into view, backlighted by moonlight. She bent over Priest and kissed him. "It's almost midnight. Your deadline is about to run out. The governor isn't going to give in."

"He has to." Priest stood up. "I have to listen to the news."

She walked with him as he crossed the vineyard and climbed the track to the cars. "Let's go away," she said suddenly. "Just you and me and Flower. Let's get in a car right now and leave. We won't say good-bye. We'll just take off."

Without answering, Priest got into the Cadillac and turned on the radio. Star sat beside him. "Come on, Priest, what do you say?"

The news came on, and he turned up the volume: "Suspected

Hammer of Eden terrorist leader Richard Granger slipped through the fingers of the FBI in Sacramento today. Meanwhile, residents fleeing neighborhoods near the San Andreas Fault have brought traffic to a standstill on many freeways within the San Francisco Bay Area. And a Haight-Ashbury rare-record dealer claims FBI agents bought from him an album with a photograph of another terrorist suspect."

"Album?" Star said. "What the—"

"Store owner Vic Plumstead told reporters the FBI called him in to help track down a '60s album, which they believed featured the voice of a Hammer of Eden suspect. The album is by an obscure rock band, Raining Fresh Daisies. The FBI would not confirm or deny they are seeking the vocalist, Stella Higgins."

"They know my name!" Star burst out.

Priest's mind was racing. Star had not used the name for almost thirty years. No one knew where Stella Higgins lived.

Yes, they did. The name Stella Higgins was on the lease for this land. And he had said that to the two FBI agents who came here on the day they raided Los Alamos. Sooner or later someone at the FBI would make the connection.

Silver River Valley was a secret no more.

Priest's original plan had been that the authorities would never know who the Hammer of Eden were or why they had demanded a ban on new power plants. Now the FBI was about to find out, but maybe they could be forced to keep it secret. That could become part of Priest's demand.

It was outrageous, but to do it, he would have to stay out of the clutches of the FBI. He got out of the car. "Let's go. I've got a lot to do."

Star got out slowly. "You won't run away with me?" she said.

"No way." He slammed the door and walked away.

She followed him across the vineyard and back to the settlement. Star went to her cabin without saying good night.

Priest went to Melanie's cabin. She was asleep. He shook her roughly to wake her. "Get up," he said. "We have to go. Quickly."

JUDY WATCHED AND WAITED while Stella Higgins cried her heart out. She was a big woman, and though she might have been attractive in different circumstances, now her face was contorted with grief. They sat in the tiny cabin that was her home.

Judy went to the door and looked out, giving Star a minute to recover her composure. Michael appeared, leading Dusty by the hand. "How is he?" Judy asked.

"He's just fine," Michael said.

"Have you found Melanie?"

"She's not here." He nodded toward Star. "What does she say?"

"Nothing, yet." Judy went back and sat on the edge of the bed. "Tell me about Ricky Granger," she said.

Star said, "He was a hoodlum before, I know, but in the more than twenty-five years we were together, he didn't hurt anyone—until now, until someone thought up the idea of this stupid dam."

"All I want to do is find him before he hurts more people."

Star nodded. "I know."

Judy made Star look at her. "Where did he go?"

"I'd tell you if I knew," Star said, "but I don't."

9

RIEST and Melanie drove to San Francisco in the commune's pickup. They reached the city a little after five on Sunday morning. The waterfront district was deserted. They found the Perpetua Diaries warehouse, and Priest unlocked the door. The real estate agent had had the power turned on.

Priest checked the seismic vibrator. He started the engine, then lowered and raised the plate. Everything worked.

They lay down to sleep on the couch in the small office, close together. When they woke, it was ten o'clock in the morning.

Priest put a pan of water on the hot plate for coffee. He had brought from the commune a can of organic coffee and some cups.

Melanie turned on the TV to watch the news.

Priest watched with her to see if there was anything about him. It was *all* about him.

"Authorities in California are taking seriously the threat of an earthquake today as the terrorist deadline looms closer," said the anchor, and there was footage of city employees erecting a tent hospital in Golden Gate Park.

The sight made Priest angry. "Why don't you just give us what we want?" he said to the TV.

The next clip showed FBI agents raiding log cabins in the mountains. After a moment Melanie said, "It's our commune!"

They saw Star, her face a picture of grief, being walked out of her cabin by two men in bulletproof vests.

Priest cursed. He was not surprised—it was the possibility of a raid that had led him to leave so hastily last night—but all the same, he found himself plunged into rage and despair by the sight. He saw Judy Maddox, looking grim. She was not so pretty today. She had two black eyes and a large Band-Aid across her nose.

Melanie gasped. There was a shot of her husband carrying Dusty. "Oh, no!" she said. "Where will Michael take him?"

"Does it matter?"

"It does if there's going to be an earthquake!"

"Michael knows better than anyone where the fault lines are. He won't be anywhere dangerous." Priest had watched enough. "Let's go out. Bring your phone."

Melanie drove the pickup out, and Priest locked the warehouse behind them. "Head for the airport," he told her as he got in.

They were close to the airport before they hit traffic. Priest called the John Truth show on Melanie's phone.

John Truth himself answered. "I have a new demand," Priest said. "I want a presidential pardon for everyone in the Hammer of Eden, as well as the freeze on new power plants."

"Wait a minute," Truth said. "Now that everyone knows where your commune is, you don't need a statewide freeze. You just want to stop your valley from being flooded, don't you?"

Truth was right. Still, Priest decided not to agree. "Heck, no," he said. "I've got principles. California needs less electric power, not more. Our original demand stands. There will be another earthquake if the governor doesn't agree."

"How can you bring such suffering to so many people?"

"I'm trying to save California."

"By killing people."

Priest lost patience. "Shut up and listen," he said. "The next earthquake will hit at seven tonight." Priest broke the connection.

They came to a junction. Melanie turned and headed back. She was thoughtful. "Will we ever return to the valley?" she said.

"Yes," he said. "I know it looks bad, and we may have to stay away for a while, but the media will forget about us eventually. Then we can slip quietly back."

Melanie smiled. "Yeah," she said.

She believes it. I'm not sure I do. "Now let's head for the city and find a restaurant that's serving brunch. I'm starving."

JUDY and Michael took Dusty to Stockton, where Michael's parents lived. They went in a helicopter. Dusty was thrilled.

Michael's father was a retired accountant, and they had a neat suburban house that backed onto a golf course. Judy drank coffee in the kitchen with Mrs. Quercus while Michael settled Dusty in.

Judy's mind was on the seismic vibrator. It had not been sighted since Friday evening, though the panels that made it look like a carnival ride had been discovered at the roadside near Felicitas.

She had found out what Granger was driving by asking the commune members what car was missing. He was using a pickup truck, and she had put out an all-points bulletin on it.

A small TV set on the kitchen counter was on with the sound muted. The news began, and Judy asked Mrs. Quercus to turn up the volume. There was an interview with John Truth. He played a tape of his conversation with Granger, who said, "The next earthquake will hit at seven tonight."

Judy shivered. She went to the kitchen door and called, "Michael, we have to go!"

She would have liked to leave Michael here with Dusty where they would both be safe, but she needed him at the command post.

He came in with Dusty. "I'm about ready," he said. The phone rang, and Mrs. Quercus picked it up. After a moment she held out the receiver to Dusty. "Someone for you," she said.

Dusty took the phone and said tentatively, "Hello?" Then his face brightened. "Hi, Mom."

Judy froze. It was Melanie.

Dusty said, "I woke up this morning, and you were gone. Then Daddy came to get me."

Melanie was with Priest and the seismic vibrator, almost certainly. Judy grabbed her mobile phone and dialed the command post. She got Raja and said quietly, "Trace a call. Melanie Quercus is calling a number in Stockton." She read the number off the instrument. "Call started a minute ago, still in progress."

"I'm on it," Raja said, and Judy broke the connection.

Dusty was listening, nodding and shaking his head occasionally. Then he offered the phone to his father. "She wants you."

Judy whispered to Michael, "Find out where she is."

He took the phone from Dusty and held it against his chest, muffling it. "Pick up the bedroom extension."

Judy darted into the bedroom across the hall, threw herself across the bed, and grabbed the phone from the bedside table.

She heard Michael say, "Melanie, where are you?"

"Never mind. I saw you and Dusty on TV. Is he okay?"

"Dusty's fine. We just got here. Can you speak up?"

"No, I can't, so just listen harder, okay?"

She doesn't want Granger to hear her. That's good. It may be a sign that they're beginning to disagree.

"Okay, okay," Michael said.

"You're going to stay there with Dusty, right?"

"No," Michael said. "I'm going into the city."

"What? For heaven's sake, Michael, it's dangerous!"

"Is that where the earthquake will be—in San Francisco?"

"I can't tell you."

"Will it be on the peninsula?"

"Yes, on the peninsula, so keep Dusty away!"

Judy's cell phone beeped. Keeping the mouthpiece of the bedroom phone covered, she put the cell phone to her other ear. It was Raja. "She's calling on her mobile in downtown San Francisco. They can't do better than that for a digital phone."

"Get some people out in the streets looking for that pickup."

"You got it." And Judy broke the connection.

Michael was saying, "If you're so worried, why don't you just tell me where the seismic vibrator is?"

"I can't do that!" Melanie hissed. "You're out of your mind."

"*I'm* out of my mind? You're the one causing earthquakes!"

"I can't talk anymore." There was a click.

Judy replaced the handset and rolled over onto her back, her mind racing. Melanie had given away a great deal of information. She was somewhere in downtown San Francisco. The earthquake would be triggered on the peninsula, the broad neck of land between the Pacific Ocean and the San Francisco Bay. The seismic vibrator had to be somewhere in that area. And Melanie was worried about Dusty. How could that be used against her?

Judy heard footsteps and opened her eyes. Michael came into the room. He gave her a strange look. "This may seem inappropriate," he said, "but you look great lying on a bed."

She remembered she was in his parents' house. She stood up.

He wrapped his arms around her. "How's your face?" he said.

Judy looked up at him. "If you're very gentle . . ."

He kissed her lips softly.

"Mm," she said. "When this is all over . . ." She closed her eyes for a moment. Then she started thinking about Melanie again. She detached herself from Michael's embrace. "Melanie is worried that Dusty might be in the earthquake zone."

"He's going to be here."

"But you didn't confirm that. You said if she was worried, she should tell you where the seismic vibrator is."

"Still, the implication— Why would I take him into danger?"

"I'm just saying, she may have a nagging doubt. And wherever she is, there's a TV. What if we had a reporter interview you at the emergency operations center in San Francisco, and Dusty was, like, just in the background somewhere?"

"Then she'd know he was in San Francisco. She'd be scared."

"But would she stop Granger from operating the vibrator?"

"Maybe. If she could."

DOWNTOWN San Francisco was a ghost town. The restaurant was half empty. Priest ordered eggs and drank three Bloody Marys. Melanie was subdued, worrying about Dusty.

When they left the restaurant, Priest did not want to return to the warehouse, so he and Melanie walked around Fisherman's Wharf, making like tourists, enjoying the salty breeze off the bay.

As a precaution, they had altered their appearance. She had put up her long red hair and concealed it under a hat. Priest had greased his dark hair and plastered it to his head, giving him a Latin air.

They got back to the truck a few minutes after four. Priest did not see the cop until it was almost too late. He was only ten feet from the pickup when he noticed a uniformed cop staring at the license plate and speaking into a walkie-talkie.

Priest stopped dead, but by then it was too late. The cop glanced up from the license plate and caught Priest's eye.

Priest looked at Melanie. She had not seen the cop. He said, "Look at my hand." He turned his palm up.

She stared at it, then said, "What am I supposed to see?"

"Keep looking at my hand. We're going to walk right past the truck. There's a cop taking the number. He's noticed us."

She looked up from his hand to his face. Then, to his astonishment, she slapped him and cried, "And now you can just go back to your dumb blonde!"

"What?" he said angrily.

She strode past the pickup truck.

The cop looked at Priest with a faint grin.

Priest walked after Melanie, saying, "Now just wait a minute!"

The cop returned his attention to the license plate.

Priest caught up with Melanie, and they turned a corner.

"Very cute," he said, "but you didn't have to hit me so hard."

A POWERFUL portable spotlight shone on Michael, and a miniature microphone was clipped to the front of his dark green polo shirt. A small television camera on a tripod was aimed at him. In front of him sat Alex Day, a twentysomething television reporter.

Dusty stood beside Judy, holding her hand trustingly, watching his daddy being interviewed. Michael was saying, "Yes, we can identify locations where an earthquake could most easily be triggered, but unfortunately, we can't tell which one the terrorists have chosen until they start up their seismic vibrator."

"And what's your advice to citizens?" Alex Day asked. "How can they protect themselves if there is an earthquake?"

"The motto is 'Duck, cover, and hold,' " he replied. "Duck under a table or desk, cover your face to protect yourself from flying glass, and hold your position until the shaking stops."

Judy whispered to Dusty, "Okay, go to Daddy."

Dusty walked into the shot. Michael lifted the boy onto his knee. Alex Day said, "Anything special we can do to protect youngsters?"

"Practice the 'Duck, cover, and hold' drill with them right now so they'll know what to do if they feel a tremor. And keep them close so you don't have to go searching for them afterward."

"Anything people should avoid?"

"Don't run out of the house. Most injuries in earthquakes are caused by falling debris from damaged buildings."

"Professor Quercus, thank you for being with us today."

Alex Day smiled at Michael and Dusty for a long frozen moment; then the cameraman said, "Great." Everyone relaxed.

Dusty said, "When can I go to Grandma's in the helicopter?"

"Right now," Michael told him.

Judy said, "How soon will that be on the air, Alex?"

"It will go right out. Within half an hour, I'd say."

Judy looked at the clock. It was five fifteen.

PRIEST AND MELANIE GOT BACK to the warehouse at six twenty, forty minutes before the promised earthquake. He went to the bathroom, and while he was washing his hands, he heard Melanie scream. He ran out and found her staring at the TV. "What is it?" he said.

"Dusty," she said, pointing at the screen.

Priest saw Michael being interviewed. He had Dusty on his knee. A female anchor was saying, "That was Alex Day, interviewing one of the world's leading seismologists, Professor Michael Quercus, at the FBI's emergency operations center in the Presidio."

"Dusty's in San Francisco," Melanie said hysterically.

"Maybe he was, but by now he's miles away," Priest said.

"You don't know that!"

"Of course I do. Michael's going to take care of his kid."

"I wish I could be sure," Melanie said in a shaky voice.

"Go make coffee," Priest said, just to give her something to do.

"Okay." She took the pan from the hot plate and went to fill it with water in the rest room.

JUDY looked at the clock. It was six thirty. Her phone rang.

She snatched up the handset and held it to her ear. "Yes?"

The operator said, "Melanie Quercus asking for her husband."

Judy pointed at Raja. "Trace the call." Then she said to the operator, "Put her on."

The suits from the head shed gathered around Judy's chair. They stood silent, straining to hear. Judy said, "Agent Maddox here."

"Where's Michael?" Melanie sounded frightened and lost.

"Where are you, Melanie?" Judy asked.

"Please, just tell me where he's taken Dusty."

"Let's make a deal," Judy said. "I'll make sure Dusty's okay if you tell me where the seismic vibrator is."

"Can I speak to my husband?"

"Are you with Ricky Granger?"

"Yes."

"And you have the seismic vibrator, wherever you are?"

"Yes."

"Melanie, do you really want to kill all those people?"

"No, but we have to."

"You won't be able to take care of Dusty while you're in jail." Judy heard a sob on the line. "By the time they let you out, he'll be a grown man. Tell me where you are, Melanie."

She whispered something, but Judy could not hear it. In the background a man shouted, "Who the hell are you calling?"

Judy said, "Quickly, quickly! Tell me where you are."

Melanie said, "Perpetua—" Then the connection was broken.

Raja said, "She's somewhere on the bay, south of the city."

"That's not good enough!" Judy cried. "She said something like 'Perpetual.' Carl, check for a street called Perpetual."

Raja said, "We should check for a company, too."

Cleever said, "What do you want to do now?"

"I'd like to get in the air," Judy said. "We can fly down the shoreline. Michael can come with me and point out where fault lines run. Maybe we'll spot the seismic vibrator."

"Do it," Cleever said.

PRIEST stared at Melanie in fury. She had tried to betray him. He would have shot her right there and then if he had had a gun. But the revolver he had taken from the guard at Los Alamos was in the seismic vibrator. He switched off Melanie's phone, dropped it into his pocket, and tried to make himself calm.

Had the FBI been able to trace Melanie's phone? If so, they would soon be cruising the neighborhood, looking for a seismic vibrator. He had run out of time. The seismic window opened at six forty. It was now six thirty-five. To hell with his seven-o'clock deadline. He had to trigger the earthquake right now.

The seismic vibrator stood in the middle of the empty warehouse. Priest jumped into the cab and started the engine. It took a minute for pressure to build up in the vibrating mechanism. He watched the gauges impatiently. At last the readings went green.

The passenger door of the truck opened, and Melanie climbed in. "Don't do it!" she yelled. "I don't know where Dusty is!"

Priest reached out to the lever that lowered the plate of the vibrator to the ground.

Melanie knocked his hand aside. "Please, don't!"

Priest hit her across the face. "Stay out of the way!" he yelled. He pulled the lever to the down position, and the plate descended.

"Please," she said. "Don't!"

What am I going to do with this stupid woman? He remembered the gun under his seat. He reached down and snatched it up. He pointed it at Melanie. "Get out of the truck."

To his surprise she reached across him, pressing her body against the barrel of the gun, and threw the lever back up.

He pulled the trigger.

The bang was deafening in the little cab of the truck. She was thrown back across the seat. The door was still open, and she fell out, hitting the floor of the warehouse with a sickening thud.

Priest did not stop to see if she was dead.

He pulled the lever again. Slowly the plate descended to the ground. When it made contact, Priest started the machine.

JUDY sat next to the helicopter pilot, Michael behind. As they flew south along the shore of the San Francisco Bay, Judy heard in her headphones the voice of one of Michael's student assistants. "This is Paula. It's started up—a seismic vibrator!"

Judy shouted into her microphone, "Give us the location," and then she grabbed a map. As Paula read the numbers on her screen, Judy found the location and said to the pilot, "Due south two miles, then about five hundred yards inland."

They were flying over the old waterfront neighborhood. Judy looked for a truck that could be the seismic vibrator. To the south she saw two patrol cars speeding toward the same location. Soon half the law-enforcement vehicles in northern California would be heading for the map coordinates Paula had given out.

The pilot said, "This is it. We've arrived at the coordinates."

Judy and Michael stared out, searching frantically for the seismic vibrator. On the ground nothing moved.

PRIEST CURSED. THE VIBRATING machinery was operating, but there was no earthquake.

This had happened before. Both times the vibrator hadn't triggered an earthquake until the second or third try. Boiling with frustration, Priest turned off the mechanism and raised the plate. He had to move the truck.

He jumped out. Stepping over Melanie, who was crumpled up against the wall, bleeding onto the concrete floor, he ran to the entrance of the warehouse. There was a pair of old-fashioned high doors that folded back to admit big vehicles. Inset into one panel was a people-size door. Priest threw it open.

OVER the entrance to a small warehouse Judy saw a sign that read PERPETUA DIARIES.

She had thought Melanie was saying "Perpetual."

"That's the place!" she yelled. "Go down!"

The helicopter descended rapidly, avoiding a power line that ran from pole to pole along the side of the road, and touched down in the middle of the deserted street. As soon as she felt the bump of contact with the ground, Judy opened the door.

PRIEST looked out.

A helicopter had landed in the road. As he watched, someone jumped out. He recognized Judy Maddox.

There was no time to open the big doors. He dashed back to the truck, got in, and backed up as far as he could into the warehouse. Then he revved the engine high. He pressed the pedal to the floor. With the engine screaming, the big truck gathered speed the length of the warehouse and crashed into the old wooden doors.

Judy Maddox was standing right in front of one of the doors, gun in hand. Shock showed on her face as the truck burst through. She dived sideways, and the truck missed her by an inch.

The helicopter was in the middle of the road. A man was getting out. Priest recognized Michael Quercus, then steered toward the helicopter and accelerated.

JUDY ROLLED OVER, AIMED AT the driver's door, and squeezed off two shots. She thought she might have hit something, but she failed to stop the truck.

The chopper lifted quickly, but the rotor blade caught in the roadside power lines. The helicopter's engine faltered. One of the power-line poles tilted under the strain and fell. The rotor blade began to spin freely again, but the chopper had lost lift, and it fell to the ground with a mighty crash.

PRIEST had one hope left.

If he could drive a quarter of a mile, then get the plate down and the vibrator operating, he might yet trigger an earthquake before the FBI could get to him. And in the chaos of an earthquake he might escape, as he had before.

He wrenched the wheel around and headed down the road.

JUDY fired again as the truck swung away from the downed helicopter and lumbered down the potholed road.

Michael ran up to her. "Are you okay?"

"Yes. See if you can help the pilot. I'll go after Granger."

Judy holstered her pistol and ran after the truck. It was a sluggish vehicle, taking long moments to accelerate. At first she closed the distance rapidly. Then Granger changed gear, and the truck picked up speed. Just when she thought she would never catch it, Granger shifted gears again, and in the momentary slowdown Judy leaped for the tailgate. She got one foot on the bumper and grabbed the spare wheel. She thought she would slip and fall, but she managed to clamber onto the flatbed among the tanks and valves of the machinery.

Granger could not operate the vibrator while the truck was in motion, so she remained where she was, waiting for him to stop.

But he had seen her. Judy heard glass shatter and saw the barrel of a gun poke through the rear window of the driver's cab. She ducked instinctively. The next moment she heard a slug ricochet off a tank beside her. She heard another shot, but it missed her.

The truck swerved violently to the right. Judy saw that Granger was heading suicidally straight for the brick front of a factory. At the last moment he braked hard and swerved, but the truck's fender plowed into the brickwork. Judy felt an agonizing pain in her ribs as she was crushed against the tank she was holding. Then she was thrown into the air.

She hit the ground, landing on her left side. Her head banged against the road. She hurt, but she could move.

Judy had fallen near the rear corner of the truck, close to its enormous wheels. If Granger reversed a yard, he would kill her.

She looked up and down the street and could see Michael struggling to get the pilot out of the crashed helicopter. She got to her feet and drew her weapon, expecting Granger to jump out of the cab and shoot at her, but he did not.

If she approached on the driver's side of the truck, he would surely see her in his side-view mirror. She dropped to her knees, lay flat on her belly, and crawled under the truck. She wriggled forward until she was almost beneath the driver's cab.

Judy heard a new noise above her. Glancing up, she saw a huge steel plate. It was being lowered onto her.

Frantically Judy rolled sideways. Her foot caught on one of the rear wheels. For a few horrendous seconds she struggled to free herself as the massive plate moved inexorably down. At the last moment she pulled her foot out of her shoe and rolled clear.

She was out in the open. If Granger leaned out of the passenger door now, gun in hand, he could shoot her easily.

There was a blast like a bomb in her ears, and the ground beneath her shook violently. He had started the vibrator.

She had to stop it. Now. Judy jumped onto the step, grabbed the door handle, flung it open, and came face to face with Richard Granger. She pointed her gun at him. "Turn it off!" she screamed.

"Okay," he said, and he grinned and reached beneath his seat.

The grin alerted her. Judy knew he was not going to turn off the vibrator. His hand came up holding a revolver.

As the long barrel swung toward her, she aimed her pistol at his head and squeezed the trigger. The bullet hit him in the face.

Granger shot her a split second later. She felt a burning pain across her right temple.

She had been taught always to fire twice. Automatically Judy pulled the trigger again. This time she hit his shoulder. He spun sideways and fell back against the door, dropping the gun.

Judy fought a wave of faintness and nausea. She held the gun pointed at Granger.

The machine was still vibrating. She stared at the mass of switches and dials. There must be a key. There was. She reached over the inert body of Ricky Granger and turned it.

Suddenly there was quiet.

Outside the warehouse, the helicopter was on fire. *Michael!*

Judy climbed out of the truck, fighting to stay conscious, and saw a patrol car approaching. She waved it down. "FBI," she said weakly. "Take me to that chopper." She opened the door and fell into the car.

The cop drove the four hundred yards to the warehouse and pulled up a safe distance from the burning aircraft. Judy got out. "Michael!" she yelled. "Where are you?"

"Over here!" He was behind the busted doors of the warehouse, bending over the pilot. Judy ran to him. "This guy needs help," Michael said. He looked at her face. "So do you!"

"I'm all right," she said. "Help is on the way." She pulled out her cell phone and called the command post. She got Raja.

He said, "Judy, what's happening? The vibrator stopped."

"I know. I stopped it. Any tremors?"

"No. Nothing at all."

Judy slumped with relief. She had stopped the machine in time. There would be no earthquake.

Another patrol car pulled up. "What in the world went on here?" the officer said. "Where's the perpetrator?"

Judy pointed. "He's in the front of that truck," she said. "Dead."

"We'll take a look." The lieutenant got back into his car and tore off down the street.

Michael had disappeared. Looking for him, Judy stepped inside the warehouse. She saw him sitting on the concrete floor in a pool of blood, but he was unhurt. In his arms he held Melanie. Michael's face was contorted with grief.

Judy went and knelt beside him. She felt for a pulse in Melanie's neck. There was none. "I'm sorry, Michael," she said.

He swallowed. "Poor Dusty," he said.

Judy touched his face. "It will be all right," she said.

MOMENTS later the officer reappeared. "Pardon me, ma'am," he said. "Did you say there was a dead man in that truck?"

"Yes," she said. "I shot him."

"Well," the cop said, "he ain't there now."

10

STAR was jailed for ten years. Flower was placed with foster parents, a Methodist minister and his wife. Oaktree disappeared, but his fingerprints showed up a couple of years later on a stolen car that had been used in an armed robbery in Seattle.

Brian Kincaid retired. Marvin Hayes resigned and became security director for a supermarket chain.

Michael Quercus became moderately famous. Because he was nice-looking and good at explaining seismology, television shows always called him first when they wanted a quote about earthquakes. His business prospered.

Judy was promoted to supervisor. She moved in with Michael and Dusty. When Michael's business started to make money, they bought a house together and got married. Bo cried at the wedding.

Judy figured out how Granger had got away.

The wound to his face was nasty but not serious. The bullet to his shoulder had nicked a vein, and the sudden loss of blood caused him to lose consciousness. Judy should have checked his pulse before going to help Michael, but confused and weakened by her injuries, she had failed to follow routine.

Granger came around a few seconds after she left. He crawled around the corner to Third Street, where he was lucky enough to find a car waiting at a stoplight. He got in, pointed his gun at the driver, and demanded to be taken to the city. En route he used Melanie's mobile phone to call Paul Beale, the wine bottler who was a criminal associate of Granger's from the old days. Beale gave him the address of a disbarred surgeon who patched Granger up. Granger stayed at the doctor's apartment overnight, then left.

Judy never found out where he went after that.

THE *water is rising fast. It has flooded all the houses. The cookhouse and the temple are also awash.*

He has waited weeks for the water to reach the vineyard. Now it has, and the precious plants are drowning.

He has drunk a bottle of his favorite wine. He throws the bottle away and takes from his pocket a big joint of marijuana laced with enough heroin to knock him out. He lights it, takes a puff, and walks down the hill.

When the water is up to his thighs, he sits down.

He takes a last look around his valley. It is almost unrecognizable. Only the roofs of the buildings are visible, and they look like upturned shipwrecks floating on the surface of a lagoon. The vines he planted twenty-five years ago are now submerged.

He draws the deadly smoke deep into his lungs. He feels the rush of pleasure as the chemicals flood his brain.

He rolls over and falls into the water. He lies facedown, helpless, stoned out of his mind. Slowly his consciousness fades, like a distant lamp becoming dimmer, until at last the light goes out.

KEN FOLLETT

Could a man-made earthquake like the one in *The Hammer of Eden* actually occur? According to Ken Follett, at least one scientific theory suggests it might be possible. And that possibility was enough to kick his story into gear. To make his novel both authentic and exciting, Follett— who began his career as a journalist— drew on thousands of eyewitness accounts of famous earthquakes. He also sat in on a massive FBI training exercise that involved hundreds of agents in a simulated terrorist incident.

Follett and his wife, Barbara, who is a member of the British Parliament, live far from the world's earthquake zones. They divide their time between houses in London and Stevenage, England.

WELCOME TO THE WORLD, BABY GIRL!

FANNIE FLAGG

In a more innocent time the glowing light of the small-town radio tower was a beacon of neighborliness and comfort.

That light seems like a quaint relic in these days of tabloid news and hype. Yet it exerts a mysterious pull on one ambitious woman who finds herself torn between the bright lights of success and the warm beacon of home.

"Utterly irresistible."
—*Time*

Preface

✤

IN THE late '40s Elmwood Springs, in southern Missouri, seems more or less like a thousand other small towns scattered across America.

Downtown is only a block long, with a Rexall drugstore on one end and the Elmwood Springs Masonic Hall on the other. If you walk from the Masonic Hall to the Rexall, you will go by the Blue Ribbon cleaners, a Cat's Paw shoe repair shop with a pink neon shoe in the window, the Morgan Brothers department store, the bank, and a little alley with stairs leading up to the second floor, where the Dixie Cahill School of Tap and Twirl is located. If it is a Saturday morning, you'll hear a lot of heavy tapping and dropping of batons upstairs by the Tappettes, a troop of blue-spangled Elmwood Springs beauties—or at least their parents think so. Past the alley is the Trolley Car diner; just beyond is the New Empress movie theater; next is the barbershop, and then there's the Rexall on the corner. Walk down on the other side of the street and you'll come to the First Methodist Church and then Nordstrom's Swedish Bakery and Luncheonette, with the gold star still in the window in honor of their son, Gene. Farther on is Dr. Orr's "painless" dentist's office. Warren and Son hardware is next. The son is eighteen-year-old Macky Warren, who is getting ready to marry his girlfriend, Norma, and is nervous about it. Then comes the A&P and the V.F.W. Hall on the corner.

Elmwood Springs is mostly a neighborhood town, and almost everyone is on speaking terms with Bottle Top, the white cat with a black spot who sleeps in the window of the shoe repair shop. There is plenty of fresh air, and everybody does his own yard work. There are three churches—Lutheran, Methodist, and Unity—and church suppers and bake sales are well attended. Nobody is rich, but despite that fact, this is a town that likes itself. You can see it in the fresh paint on the houses and in the clean white curtains in the windows. Elmwood Springs, Missouri, is not perfect by any means, but as far as little towns go, it is about as near perfect as you can get without having to get downright sentimental about it or make up a bunch of lies.

EVERYONE in Elmwood Springs remembers the day they put the radio tower in Neighbor Dorothy's backyard and how excited they were that night when they first saw the bright red bulb on top of the tower glowing like a cherry-red Christmas light way up in the black Missouri sky. Because the land was flat, that light could be seen for miles, and over the years it came to be a familiar and comforting sight. It made people feel connected somehow.

Every day between nine thirty and ten a.m. most likely you'd listen to the *Neighbor Dorothy* radio show just like everybody else—except for old man Henderson, who still thought that radio was a silly invention for silly people. Farm wives for miles around stopped whatever they were doing and sat down with a pad and pencil at the kitchen table to listen. By now Dorothy Smith was one of the most-listened-to radio homemakers in the Midwest, and if she gave out a recipe for maple swirl pound cake that day, most men would be eating it for dessert that night.

The show was broadcast live from her living room Monday through Friday and could be heard over station WDOT, 66 on your dial. All sorts of people would drop by to talk on the radio or sing or tap-dance. A Mrs. Mary Hurt even played the spoons once. Mother Smith played organ interludes, and Neighbor Dorothy also had a visit from the Hawaiian Fruit Gum Orchestra, all the way from Yankton, South Dakota. This is not to mention two local gals, Ada and Bess Goodnight, who would sing at the drop of a hat, and the news, which was mostly good.

In 1948 Neighbor Dorothy was a plump, sweet-faced woman in her fifties with the big, wide-open face of a young girl. Her husband, Doc Smith, was the pharmacist down at the Rexall. After high school Dorothy graduated from the Fannie Merit School of Home Economics in Boston and came home and married Doc and taught school for a while until she had her first child, Anna Lee. While she was home all day, Neighbor Dorothy began baking cakes—and more cakes. Tea cakes, lemon, banana, caramel, cherry, chocolate, maple, and jelly roll cakes. You name it, she baked it. But her specialty was theme cakes. There was not a child in Elmwood Springs or thereabouts who had not had a pink-and-white circus cake with a miniature toy carousel on top for her birthday party.

Which is how Dorothy came to be at the Mayfair Auditorium over in Poplar Bluff on Home Demonstration Day giving out the recipe for her circus cake on the radio. She just happened to mention that she used Golden Flake flour for all her cakes, and the next day, when Golden Flake flour sales doubled in four states, she was offered a show of her own. Which is how the radio tower came to be put up in her backyard in the first place and how her younger child, Bobby, happened to grow up on the radio. Bobby does not remember a time when there wasn't a radio show in the living room.

Although WDOT is only a two-hundred-watt radio station, because the land is flat, the signal from WDOT can tear a hole straight through the Midwest all the way up into Canada, and on one particularly cold day it was picked up by several ships at sea. You can't say her show is clever or sophisticated or anything like that, but one thing you can say for sure is that over the years Neighbor Dorothy has sold a heck of a lot of Golden Flake flour and pancake mix.

Her house is located on the left side of First Avenue North. It is the last house on the corner, with a wraparound porch—a two-swing front porch, one swing on one end and one on the other. It has a green-and-white canvas awning all the way around to the side of the house.

If you were to walk up the porch stairs and look to your right, you would see WDOT RADIO STATION, NUMBER 66 ON YOUR DIAL written in small gold-and-black letters on the window. As you walk in, to the right is a large room with a desk, and a microphone on it that says WDOT. The desk sits in front of the window so Neighbor Dorothy can report what the weather is doing firsthand. Mother Smith's organ is to the left, and about ten chairs are set up so people can come in and sit down if they want to. The floors are dark wood, and Neighbor Dorothy has some nice scatter rugs here and there. The curtains are green, with a yellow and deep pink floral print of what looks like might be palm trees. She has recently put up brand-new venetian blinds, a Christmas present from Doc.

The dining room has a nice brass chandelier, some lovely lace swag curtains on the bay window, and a pretty white tablecloth. The kitchen is still where everybody usually eats. Off the kitchen to the back is a large screened porch; Bobby sleeps there in the summer. On the other side is a group of miniature tables and chairs, where all the children in town have their birthday parties and where Anna Lee and her friend run a nursery school in the summer to make extra money for clothes. The other two rooms on the left side of the house are Anna Lee's bedroom—a seventeen-year-old girl's room with a white canopy bed and a dresser with a mirror—and a sunroom. Three bedrooms are off the hall: Doc and Neighbor Dorothy's, Mother Smith's, and Bobby has the room at the end.

Neighbor Dorothy's backyard is like everybody else's, except for the radio tower, with lots of open space all the way back to the railroad tracks, and behind that are the cornfields. Apart from the fact that Neighbor Dorothy's house has WDOT painted on the front window in gold-and-black letters, an organ in the living room, a radio tower in the backyard, and a nursery school on the back porch, it is just an ordinary house.

AND TODAY IS JUST ANOTHER ordinary day. At exactly nine thirty an announcer from the main station comes on and says, "And now, Golden Flake flour and pancake mix takes you to that little white house just around the corner from wherever you are, as we join your neighbor and mine, the lady with a smile in her voice, Neighbor Dorothy, with Mother Smith on the organ."

The minute they get the on-air signal, Mother Smith starts the show off with a rousing rendition of "On the Sunny Side of the Street." In a moment Neighbor Dorothy greets her radio listeners with a pleasant, "Good morning, everybody. How are you today? Fine, I hope. It is a beautiful day over here in Elmwood Springs, and I hope it's just as pretty where you are. We've got so many exciting things lined up for you today . . . so just sit down, put your feet up, and have a cup of coffee with me, won't you?

"Ooh . . . I want to start with some good news for all the gals that went to Norma's bridal shower yesterday. They were mighty worried when all the lucky-dime cake had been eaten and nobody had gotten the piece with the dime in it, but Norma's mother, Ida, called this morning and said they found the dime in the kitchen— she had forgotten to put it in—so you gals can rest easy. None of you will have to be x-rayed after all. As you all know, Norma is our little June bride-to-be. She is marrying Macky Warren at twelve noon on June the twenty-eighth down at the Unity Church, so if you are in town, drop in at the reception at the V.F.W. Hall afterwards. They say everybody is welcome.

"Speaking of brides . . . June is such a busy month, so many events—weddings, graduations—and if you're wondering what to get the special lady, Bob Morgan of Morgan Brothers department store says wonder no more because it's pearls, pearls, and more pearls. Pearls for the graduate, pearls for the June bride, pearls for the mother of the bride, pearls for everyone.

"And let's see, what else do I have this morning . . ."

Twenty-five minutes later Neighbor Dorothy ends the show with, "Well, I see by the old clock on the wall that it's time to go. It's always so pleasant to sit with you and share a cup of coffee. You make our days so happy. Until we see you again, you'll be missed, so come back again tomorrow, won't you? This is Neighbor Dorothy and Mother Smith from our house to yours, saying, have a good day. . . ."

THAT evening Neighbor Dorothy and her family were sitting on the porch, all of them eating bowls of homemade peach ice cream that Doc had made on the back porch earlier. Macky Warren and his fiancée, Norma, passed in front of the house. Norma had her little four-year-old cousin by the hand.

Dorothy called out and waved. "Hey, how're you tonight?"

They waved back. "Fine. We've just been up to the picture show. We saw *The Egg and I,* with Claudette Colbert and Fred MacMurray. It was a good one. Be sure to see it."

"We will," Neighbor Dorothy said.

Macky called up to the porch, "How are you doing, Doc?"

"Just fine," Doc said. He nodded at the little blond girl and said to Macky, "I see she's got you baby-sitting tonight. Well, might as well get used to it. You'll be having your own soon."

Macky smiled and nodded. "Yes, sir. Good night."

"Good night."

After they had gone on, Dorothy looked over at Anna Lee and sighed. "It seems like only yesterday when both my children were babies. Time . . . how fast it passes. Next thing I know, Anna Lee will be married and Bobby will be a grown man."

They sat for a while and waved and spoke to a few more people walking by, and then Dorothy said, "Don't you wish you could just stop time in its tracks? Keep it from moving forward?"

"Mother," Anna Lee asked, "when would you stop it?"

"Oh, honey, I guess if I could, I'd stop time right now, while I have all my family around me, on this very night." She looked over at her husband. "What about you, Doc?"

He took a puff of his pipe. "Now would be a good time to stop it. No wars. Everybody's healthy." He looked at Dorothy and smiled. "And before Momma loses her pretty figure."

She laughed. "Too late for that. What about you, Anna Lee?"

Anna Lee sighed. A recent high school graduate, she had suddenly become very wise. "Oh, if I had only known then what I know now, I would have stopped it last year, when I was still young."

Dorothy smiled at her daughter, then asked, "When would you stop time, Mother Smith?"

Mother Smith mused. "Well, I don't think I would. I think I'd just let it go on like it has been."

"You would?"

Mother Smith had been taken to the great world's fair in St. Louis in 1904 and had looked forward to the future ever since. "Oh, yes. I'd hate to take a chance on missing something good that might be coming up just around the corner, wouldn't you?"

"I guess you're right, Mother Smith," Dorothy said. "We just have no idea of what the future holds, do we?"

"No, we don't. Why, just imagine what life will be like twenty-five years from now."

Anna Lee made a face. "I'll be an old woman with gray hair."

Mother Smith laughed. "Maybe so, but I'll be long gone by then. At least you'll be around to see what's going on!"

The News

ELMWOOD SPRINGS, MISSOURI   APRIL 1, 1973

NORMA Warren was a nervous wreck waiting for Macky to come home and have his breakfast. She was about to burst with the news. He had only gone two blocks to take Aunt Elner a bag of birdseed. Aunt Elner had called at the crack of dawn and said her blue jays were practically knocking the house down because she had run out of seed. Norma loved poor old Aunt Elner; after all, she was deaf as a post. But why, of all mornings, did she have to pick this one to run out of seed? Norma knew that Macky would get waylaid, stopping to yaya with everybody and his brother up and down the street. Usually she didn't mind, but she did today. She sat there for a few more minutes, then put Macky's breakfast in the stove to keep warm, got the broom out, and went onto the front porch and started sweeping, all the time looking for him.

After a few minutes she could not stand it any longer. She went into the kitchen and called. The phone rang and rang until finally Aunt Elner picked up.

"Hello."

"Aunt Elner, are you all right?"

"I'm fine, honey," she said in a cheerful voice. "How are you?"

"I'm fine. I was just worried. You took so long to answer the phone."

"Oh, well, I was way out in the backyard. Macky is helping me plant some sweet williams."

Norma rolled her eyes but said sweetly, "Oh, I see. Well, no rush, but would you tell Macky when he gets through there to come straight on home? His breakfast is getting cold."

"All right, honey, I'll tell him. Oh, and Norma, my blue jays say thank you kindly. Well, bye-bye now."

"Bye, Aunt Elner."

Norma, a pretty brunette of forty-three, glanced at herself in the mirror over the sink. Her face was flushed with excitement.

About twenty minutes later, after she had almost swept the paint off the front porch and swept halfway up the block, she spotted Macky on the horizon, nonchalantly strolling toward home, waving and how-are-youing to everybody he passed by, including two dogs and a cat. She called out frantically, "Macky, come on, hurry up!"

Macky, a stocky, sandy-haired, friendly-looking man, smiled happily and waved back. Norma ran back inside, took his plate out of the oven, put it down on the table, and got the coffeepot as the screen door slammed behind him.

"Macky, get in here and sit down before I have a stroke."

He sat down. "Hey, what's up, kiddo?"

She poured his coffee, was back in her chair staring at him before he could take the first bite of his scrambled eggs.

"You will never guess who called here in a million years."

"Who?"

"Not three minutes after you left, maybe not even that long—"

"Who?"

"Are you ready?"

"Yes, honey, I've been ready. Who called?"

Norma paused as a trumpet played a fanfare in her head, then blurted out, "Baby Girl, that's who!"

Macky was sufficiently surprised and put his fork down.

"You're kidding. Where was she?"

"New York City, and guess what? She's coming home."

"She's coming here? Well, I'll be . . . Did she say why?"

"Well, she said she had been under a lot of pressure at work and would it be all right for her to come visit."

"What did you say?"

"I said of course. I said, 'We've done nothing for years but tell you we want you to come home, would *love* to have you come.' Haven't we said that I don't know how many times?"

"Absolutely. What else did she say?"

"Well, she said hello, how are you; then she said she needed to get away from something and would we be home. I said yes, of course, and she said for us not to go to any trouble."

Macky frowned. "You don't think she's sick or anything?"

"No, I don't think so. She sounded tired, maybe a little down— eat your eggs while they're hot—but she didn't sound sick."

Macky picked up his fork. "I told her she was working herself to a frazzle. I told her to slow down. I said that, didn't I?"

Norma nodded. "You did. When we were in New York, you told her she was working too hard and needed a vacation."

Norma saw that Macky was having a difficult time cutting into his scrambled eggs.

"Do you want me to fix you some more eggs?"

Macky, who would eat anything, said, "No, these are fine. I *like* well-done eggs. Is Baby Girl still seeing that guy with the initials? What's his name?"

"J.C.? I don't know, and I didn't ask," Norma said.

"He didn't show me much."

"Well, she likes him, and that's all that matters. All I know is that she's coming home, and I intend to do everything in my power to make sure she feels like she has some family in this world that loves her. She doesn't have any other relatives besides me and Aunt Elner. It just breaks my heart. All these years she's been living from pillar to post, jerked here and there, with nobody who really cares. What if she really did get sick, Macky? Who would she have?"

"She'd have us, honey. We told her that, and she must have believed it or she wouldn't have called."

Norma reached for a paper napkin from the red plastic holder and blew her nose. "Do you think so?"

"Of course I do. There's no use crying over it."

"Oh, I know. I'm just so happy it was us she called."

"She give you any idea about when she was coming?"

"No. I guess it could be as soon as tomorrow or the next day. Want some more coffee?"

"Just a little."

Norma gasped. "Oh, my Lord."

"What's the matter?" Macky looked concerned.

"I just realized I don't know whether she drinks coffee or tea. Or what she likes for breakfast. I need to have everything here she likes, so I can have it just in case. Do you think we should go up to the bakery and buy a cake, or should I make one?"

"Honey, a cake is a cake. They all taste the same to me."

"To you, maybe, but don't forget her grandparents owned the bakery before Edna Buntz; she could tell. No, I'll make a cake. What room should we give her? Should we give her ours?"

"No, honey. She wouldn't take it. Let's put her upstairs."

"I'll go up there later and make sure everything's okay, check out the bedding and all. We need to get those curtains washed and the rug cleaned for her. Thank heavens I'm getting my hair fixed this afternoon." She squinted at Macky. "You need to go up to Ed's and get a haircut yourself."

"Now, Norma, she's not gonna care if I get a haircut or not."

"Well, I will. We don't want to embarrass her, showing up at the airport looking like a couple of Elmer Fudds."

Macky laughed. "Well, I guess I do need to get the car washed."

Norma looked at Macky with a pained expression. "Why didn't you let me get the house painted like I wanted to?"

"Now, Norma, just calm down. She said not to make a fuss."

"Yes, but I just can't help myself. I still can't believe it. Just think. After all these years Baby Girl is coming home!"

NEW YORK CITY   APRIL 1, 1973

WHEN Dena Nordstrom opened her eyes, she had that three-to-four-second grace period before she remembered who she was and where she was. Before her body announced its condition. And, as always after a night like last night, it started with a blinding, pounding headache, followed by a wave of nausea and soon the agonizing cold sweats.

Slowly, one by one, the events of the previous night came back to her. The evening had started out the way it usually did when she agreed to have a drink with J.C. After cocktails they had gone on to the Copenhagen on Fifty-eighth for dinner, slugging down who knows how many glasses of ice-cold aquavit with the smorgasbord. She vaguely remembered insulting some Frenchman and then walking over to the Brasserie for Irish coffee. She did recall that the sun was up by the time she got home, but at least she was in her own bed alone—J.C. had gone home, thank heavens. Then it hit her. J.C. What had she said to him? For all she knew, they might very well be engaged again. And she'd have to think up a way to get out of it again. Always the same thing.

Dena tried to get up, but the pain throbbing in her temples was so intense she saw stars. She slowly eased out of bed sideways, holding her head. The room was as dark as a tomb, and as she opened the door, the light she had left on in the hallway almost blinded her.

She made it to the bathroom and held on to the sink to keep from spinning around. Her hands were shaking as she took two Alka-Seltzers, three Bayer aspirin, and a Valium. All she needed now was an ice-cold Coca-Cola, and she might live.

She walked down the hall to the kitchen, and when she got to the living room, she stopped. J.C. was sound asleep on the couch.

Dena tiptoed back down the hall to the bathroom and drank water from the tap. She took a cold washcloth for her head, went in and locked her bedroom door, praying to a God she didn't believe in. Please make him go home . . . please. She got back into bed, turned her electric blanket up, and went back to sleep.

It was around eleven a.m. when Dena woke again and needed more aspirin. Now her stomach was screaming for carbohydrates. She quietly tiptoed down the hall and looked in the living room. She was delighted. J.C. had left. Hooray. She called the Carnegie Deli across the street and ordered two grilled cheese sandwiches, french fries, a chocolate shake, and two packs of Viceroys. She went into the kitchen to wait. A note J.C. had left was taped to her refrigerator: "See you at eight for dinner."

She spoke to the note. "Oh, no, you won't."

The food arrived, and she devoured it all in less than five minutes. Then she went back to her bedroom and fell into bed with relief. She smiled to herself and thanked her lucky stars that this was only Saturday and she would be able to sleep until Monday morning. She closed her eyes for seconds—and then they flew open.

She had just remembered: The affiliates were in town for the National Association of Broadcasters convention. Today was the day she was supposed to be guest of honor at their luncheon.

She moaned. "No, please don't tell me I have to go to that luncheon. I'd rather be beaten to death with a baseball bat."

She lay there for ten more minutes, debating whether she should try calling with a sudden attack of appendicitis. As hard as she tried to convince herself that she had a right not to go, that the luncheon was just public relations for the network and not real work, she finally came to the conclusion that she had to go. If she didn't, she would feel so guilty she wouldn't be able to sleep anyway. She always liked to be dependable. *Especially* when it could do her some good, too. The affiliates had come from all over the country, and most of the men brought their wives along just for this occasion, to meet Dena Nordstrom in person. She was popular with almost all the wives, who watched her morning show every day. So she crawled out of bed and went back into the bathroom to see if there was any hope of getting herself together. She looked in the mirror expecting the worst but was pleasantly surprised at what she saw. Her blue eyes seemed to shine, and there was a wholesome flush on her cheeks.

At twelve thirty in the Tavern on the Green, a roomful of excited wives and their affiliate husbands kept glancing at the door to see if she had arrived yet. At twelve fifty-seven all attempts at conversation stopped. Every eye was on the tall, stunning blond woman standing at the door. There she was, in person, Dena Nordstrom, looking just like herself, with that fresh, open midwestern face of hers flashing that million-dollar smile.

At the podium microphone, she apologized to everyone. "I'm so sorry I'm so late. Wouldn't you know it, just as I was walking out the door, the phone rang, and it was my sister calling long-distance from Copenhagen to tell me she was in the emergency room with a broken ankle. I had to run and dig out all the insurance information and give it to her. So please forgive me. . . ."

She stopped. Why did all of her excuses somehow involve family? She didn't have any family. But had she announced that she had just slaughtered six nuns with an axe, this crowd would have forgiven her. Afterward they rushed toward her, wondering if they might have just one picture with her. Flash cameras began snapping until she saw nothing but little white dots. But she kept on smiling.

MACKY had flushed the toilet and turned on all the faucets to make sure they were working. Norma was wondering if they needed a new bedspread and called him out of the bathroom. Macky looked at the old one. "I don't think so, and I'll tell you why. I think it's best if we just leave things the way they are. After the places she's been, what we need to do is try and make her feel at home."

As they were walking downstairs, Norma said, "Macky, what about Aunt Elner? Baby Girl said for us not to tell anybody she was coming. Do you think she meant Aunt Elner, too?"

"Did she mention Aunt Elner?"

"No. She didn't say a word about her."

"There's your answer, then. If she had wanted us to tell Aunt Elner, she would have mentioned it."

"But she hasn't seen Aunt Elner since she was four. Why *wouldn't* she want to see her?"

"Honey, why not let her decide when she wants to?"

Norma put a load of washing in, closed the lid, and sat down with him at the kitchen table. "Okay, this is what we will do. After she's been here awhile and gotten settled in and all, I'll just casually say in conversation, 'Baby Girl, I'm sure you will want to see your aunt Elner. She's so proud of you and brags to everyone in town when she sees you on TV.' "

"In other words, you're gonna blackmail the girl into going."

"Don't be silly. Then, when she decides, I'll call and say, 'Aunt Elner, guess what? Baby Girl has just flown into town as a surprise.' That way Aunt Elner can be surprised."

Macky offered another suggestion. "Why don't you just take Baby Girl over there, knock on the door, and *really* surprise her?"

Norma looked at Macky in utter disbelief. "Macky, you can't just go up and knock on a ninety-three-year-old woman's door and yell *surprise*. She could have a heart attack and drop dead right there, and wouldn't that be wonderful for Baby Girl to come home and kill her aunt, just like that, right off the bat."

"Well, at least she'd be in town for the funeral."

Norma looked at Macky and shook her head. "You know, Macky, sometimes I worry about you. I really do."

As DENA entered her apartment, she headed down the hall for the medicine chest and took three huge swallows from the bottle of Maalox Liquid to help put out the fire in her stomach. The luncheon had gone well, but it had not ended one minute too soon. She noticed her hands shaking. That was something that had never happened to her before, and it frightened her. But she soon dismissed the thought. It's just because you're tired. You're not an alcoholic, for heaven's sake. You've just been pushing yourself lately. Well, lately for about fifteen years. The hangovers were getting worse and worse, and she wondered why she kept drinking like that. Her career was going great. She was on the highest-rated morning show on TV. You couldn't get any better than that, except for prime time, and that might be in her future if things kept going well. She had finally gotten over the guy from D.C. It had taken her almost five years, but she hardly thought about him anymore. Well, hardly. It must be I'm not getting enough rest, she thought. That's all. I'm not unhappy.

She ran a tub of hot water, hoping it would help soothe her aching body. Going to the kitchen for a beer, she remembered— Before she went back to sleep, she had to call J.C. and think of some reason she could not go to dinner.

As she got into the tub and began to relax, she thought about poor old J.C. He was such a good egg, really. He was fun, made the perfect escort, and he was so much in love with her that she could do pretty much what she wanted to on a date. But most of all, he kept other guys away. There was one other reason she wanted him around. She did not love him, and that was just fine with her. She had no interest in love. Love had taken her into the back room and beaten her up pretty badly. Falling head over heels for a slick, handsome, fast-talking Washington lobbyist had done nothing but break her heart and keep her upset. She had been completely obsessed with him and spent years waiting for him to call, waiting for him to come back to town, catching him in lies. It had been too painful.

Now she was perfectly happy being the one who was loved, and she was going to keep it that way. Sex maybe, friendship yes, but love *no*. If she ever felt love coming toward her, she would cross the street to the other side.

After the bath she got into bed and called J.C. and was pleased he was not home. She left a message with his answering service. It wasn't until she put the phone back on the table and took the receiver off the hook that she noticed her address book lying wide open—to the letter W. And a wave of hangover anxiety came over her when she saw the names Norma and Macky Warren, Elmwood Springs, Missouri. She began to have a recollection of calling someone at six o'clock that morning when she had been out of her mind. Oh, please don't tell me I called them. Surely I couldn't have done something that stupid. But deep down she knew very well that she might have. She didn't want to think about it, so she pulled the covers over her head and went to sleep.

DENA awakened at four a.m. on Monday, rested but still a little guilty. She had slept all Sunday. She showered, dressed, and was ready when the car picked her up at five and took her to the studio. She liked the city at that time of morning. The streets were quiet and almost empty. Sixth Avenue looked as long and as wide as a football field.

She went into the building at the studio entrance. After four years she still had a hard time believing she actually worked at Rockefeller Plaza. Her high heels cracked like gunshots on the marble as she walked down the empty halls to those smooth brass elevators that shot her up twenty-six floors in five seconds. The only side effect of her lost weekend was that her eyes were puffy from so much sleep, but the makeup woman would fix that by putting tea bags on her eyes.

Her interview with Helen Gurley Brown went very well. It was supposed to have been a fluff piece on the *Cosmopolitan* editor, but it turned out to be sharp, funny, and just spicy enough, so Dena was in a good mood when she got to her office and found a beautiful bouquet of flowers from Julian Amsley, the network president, with a card that said, "Heard you wowed them at the luncheon. Thanks from your network family." Then she saw a message that had come in while she was on the air: "Baby Girl, we are thrilled you are coming home! Please call and let us know what flight you will be on so we can pick you up at the airport. Your Elmwood Springs family, Norma, Macky, and Aunt Elner."

The people standing outside her door at the water fountain heard a loud, "Oh, no." Dena leaned over her desk with her head in her hands, wondering what in the world had possessed her to call and tell them she was coming to Missouri, of all places! Elmwood Springs was nothing more than the name of a town she had lived in for a short time as a child. Her father and grandparents were buried there, but she didn't even know where it was. And why Norma and Macky? She couldn't even remember how they were related. Sure, no matter where she moved, they always sent her birthday cards and some kind of weird brown preserves at Christmas, but she hadn't even seen them but once, and that was years before, when they had come to New York for a few days. As nice as they were, it had been a strain.

Dena was baffled. Why, of *all* the people in her address book, had she picked them to call? Maybe it was because she had been having that old dream about her mother and that house again; maybe it had been the aquavit. Whatever the reason, she wondered how she was going to get out of this one.

FOR the past two days Norma had been testing several recipes out of *The Neighbor Dorothy Cookbook*. She told Macky that she just felt like trying something new for a change, no big deal, but he knew she was trying out dishes to fix when Baby Girl came home. He had been served Minnie Dell Crower's meatloaf delight, Leota Kling's lima bean and cheese casserole, Virginia Mae's scalloped turnips, and Gertrude's bing cherry salad. Everything passed muster with the exception of the turnips. Whoever Virginia Mae was, she was destined not to go to good-recipe heaven. After that, Macky could hardly move and was stretched out in the living room watching television. Norma was in the kitchen listening to the last of the turnips being ripped to shreds in her garbage disposal, when the phone rang.

Five minutes later she came into the living room with a dejected look on her face, sat down, and looked at Macky. "She's not coming."

"Why?"

"Well, she said she had made all the arrangements to come and was going to call us from the New York airport. She was packed, was actually headed out the door, when her telephone rang. And wouldn't you know it, it was her boss, and he was frantic because there was this very important interview already set up out of the country and the reporter that was supposed to go had a sudden attack of malaria and couldn't go."

"Malaria?"

"Yes. So she didn't have a choice, because the plane was waiting at the airport at that very moment. Bless her heart, it's a wonder she had time to call us at all. It's a good thing she did call, though. I reminded her to take a coat. She could have gotten over to Siberia and frozen to death in a snowstorm."

"Siberia? Who is she going to interview in Siberia, I wonder."

"She doesn't know. She said that it was so important and evidently so secret that they didn't even tell her."

"Norma, are you sure she didn't say Sicily or Sardinia?"

"No. She said Siberia. Why would I tell her to take a heavy winter coat? I can tell the difference between Sardinia and Siberia."

"Did she say she might be able to come after she gets back?"

"No, she can't. This was the only time she could take off."

"Well, it's a shame the way they work her. She hasn't had a vacation since she started there. That girl works too hard."

Norma said, sighing, "Well, I guess I better call Aunt Elner and let her know she's not coming."

"She never knew she was coming in the first place, Norma."

But she had already dialed. "Aunt Elner, it's Norma." She said, louder, "Go get your hearing aid, dear." She waited. "Well, now the tale can be told because it's not going to happen. You will never guess who was coming home for a visit. *And* was going to come over to your house and surprise you. Guess. . . . Well, I know you don't know, but guess. . . . No, even better than Wayne Newton . . ."

How She Got There

❦

FAME is a funny thing. It knows who it wants and starts stalking people at an early age. Dena was only fifteen when it went after her. A photographer from *Seventeen* magazine came to the Sacred Heart Academy, and Dena was one of ten girls chosen to be photographed that day. Albert Boutwell, the makeup man, had been putting makeup on giggling teenage girls all over the country, and when the slim, lanky kid walked in, she was just another face. He noted that she was particularly pale, so he used a slightly darker base and a little more eyeliner to bring out her eyes. When he had finished, looking back at him was what had become, at a touch, one of the most beautiful faces he had ever seen. Dena, who had never worn makeup before, was as shocked as he was. Albert asked her what her name was. "Well, Miss Dena Nordstrom," he said, "look at yourself. You are a knockout!"

A month later, back in New York looking at proofs, the photographer came to the Nordstrom girl's picture, viewing it through a magnifier. "Look at this kid," he said. "You can't get a bad shot of her! She has a golden, million-dollar face."

"I told you," Albert said. "When she walked in, she was nothing. I slapped a little makeup on and whammo."

The photographer was still studying the picture. "Look—just *look* at that bone structure. What is she, Swedish?"

"Name's Dena Nordstrom."

"I knew it," the photographer said. "We got us a baby Garbo here or another Ingrid Bergman. How old is this girl?"

"Fifteen."

The photographer was disappointed. "Oh, well, I can dream, can't I?" He sighed. "Call Hattie over at the agency and tell her we are sending over some pictures—but tell her we get to use her first."

Two days later, after a phone call was made to Dena's school and Dena's mother was finally located at work, Hattie Smith explained that she handled only the top teenage models and that she wanted to sign Dena to a five-year contract and start her to work right away. "You have quite an exceptional daughter. We think with the right representation she is capable of making money—a *lot* of money—posing for magazines or doing commercials."

There was a silence. Dena's mother was alarmed. She had not known that Dena had been photographed. "I appreciate your interest, Mrs. Smith, but I intend to have my daughter receive an education before we consider anything else for her future."

"We have no intention of interfering with her education. We can schedule her shoots around school hours."

"Mrs. Smith, I do not want my daughter photographed. I am trying to be tactful, but thank you, no." And she hung up.

THREE years later, when Dena was on her own, they called back, and her first professional photo shoot put her on the cover of *Seventeen*. After which she was offered a scholarship to study drama at Southern Methodist University in Dallas. Dena was pleased, but after her sophomore year she quit to take a job as a weather girl at a television station in Fort Worth. As much as she loved the theater, she found out that television was where the money was, and she was good at it from the start.

After eleven months she began to move from station to station, almost every time to a little larger market and, in her mind at least, working closer and closer to New York. Dena didn't mind going from place to place; she was used to it. Her mother had moved all over the country from the time she was four.

Dena worked in Arkansas; Billings, Montana; then Oklahoma, Kentucky, back to Billings, and on to Richmond, Virginia, where she worked as cohost of the local morning program, doing features about art shows, horse shows, dog shows, and occasionally interviewing celebrities. When the actress Arlene Francis came to Richmond, she liked the way Dena handled the interview and mentioned it to her agents. Sandy Cooper was a young talent agent on the lookout for bright new female talent. The women's movement was gaining momentum. Sandy knew the networks had quietly started searching for more women to groom in the news departments, and he wanted to get in on it from the start.

One weekend he and his wife, Bea, drove to Richmond and stayed over to watch this Dena Nordstrom on the show Monday morning. He liked what he saw. Nordstrom's beauty was certainly distinctive, but she was also smart, quick, and she had that nice-girl-next-door quality coupled with a smile that lit up the screen. All Sandy had to find out now was if this girl was ambitious. That question was answered in less than five minutes after they met, and an hour later she was signed as a client of the William Morris Agency. Three months later Sandy set up an interview for Dena with Ira Wallace, head of the news department of a local New York station.

Dena flew in from Richmond the next week. Sandy picked her up at the hotel. Sandy wanted to walk so he would have a little time to prepare her for Ira Wallace and warn her not to be put off by his personality. Even from as far away as Richmond, Dena had already heard stories, but she was ready for this job, and she knew it.

When they reached the right floor, Sandy gave the receptionist their names. She told them to have a seat. After thirty-five minutes they heard a loud, impatient voice bark on the intercom, "Those two yahoos still there?"

"Yes, Mr. Wallace."

"Oh, all right. Send them in."

Sandy motioned for Dena to go first. The room reeked of cigar smoke. Wallace, a fat, bald man who looked exactly like a big sea bass wearing a white shirt, black plastic glasses, and smoking a cigar, was sitting behind a ten-foot-long desk. He was on the phone and did not get up. He glanced at Dena for a second and cursed into the receiver, leaving them standing. They waited while the little man with the shiny, sweaty head continued to berate whomever he was talking to. The longer Dena remained standing and ignored, the madder she got. If there was anything she had inherited from her mother, it was pride, and she was not going to let this little toad humiliate her, no matter how much she wanted the job.

The second he hung up the phone, she walked right up to Ira Wallace's desk and forced him to shake hands. "How do you do, Mr. Wallace? I'm Dena Nordstrom. What a pleasure to meet you. No, don't bother to get up. We will have a seat, thank you."

Wallace looked at her as if she had just dropped in from Mars.

She sat down and smiled at him. "Now, Mr. Wallace, tell me a little about yourself. I like to really get to know people before I make any decision about accepting a job."

He looked at Sandy Cooper, who was clearly confused, too. Wallace took the cigar out of his mouth. "Is she kidding?"

Sandy tried to recover. "Uh, Mr. Wallace, did you by any chance get to take a look at the tapes?"

Before Wallace could answer, Dena looked at her watch and said, "Oh, darn it all. I wish I could stay. I am *so* sorry, Mr. Wallace, but unfortunately, I'm already late for another appointment."

She stood up and shook his hand again. "It's always so nice to meet such a charming gentleman with such lovely manners."

Both men, their mouths open, watched as she left.

As Dena waited for the elevator, she said, "That man is a pig."

The receptionist, without looking up, said, "Tell me something I don't know."

Back in the office, Wallace shouted at Sandy, "Is she nuts?"

"I'm sorry, Mr. Wallace. I know she wanted the job. She's very responsible. I don't know what to tell you . . . except she's from the Midwest. She might be a little sensitive."

"Sensitive? Well, I liked her tapes, but I'm not putting up with any prima donna stuff."

Sandy said, "You liked her tapes?"

Wallace shrugged. "She might have potential. She's got the kinda look we want. That sappy, fresh-off-the-farm face and, well, some sort of class. So we might be willing to try her out."

Sandy changed gears in a hurry. "You're right about that, Ira.

That's why I brought her to you before somebody snapped her up. Not only is she beautiful but she has a lot of experience—six local stations, Richmond's most popular on-air personality."

"I don't care if she was Miss America. She starts at the bottom here. We'll give her seventy-five thousand a year with a thirteen-week out clause. Ours, not hers."

Sandy said, "Great, great. And I can tell you she's not afraid of work. She does a great interview."

"All right. Don't oversell."

Sandy started to back out of the office before Wallace had a chance to change his mind.

After the agent left, Wallace had to laugh. The decision to hire Dena Nordstrom had been made a week before, based on her tapes. They had been head and shoulders above the rest. But he liked to see people cower. Of course, she hadn't. She had thrown it right back in his face. Quite a change from the usual sweaty-palmed types that crawled in and out of his office all day. She just might have what he was looking for. *If* she was smart enough to do what she was told.

SANDY ran to his office and called Dena at the hotel. "It's Sandy. Dena, are you sitting down?"

Dena started to apologize. "Sandy, I'm so sorry. I know that was a stupid thing to do. I didn't mean to embarrass you."

"Dena."

"I know you are disappointed. I am, too, believe me. But my mother did not raise me to be insulted by some puffed-up little mutant. I wouldn't work with that man for a million dollars. How did he even get into television?"

"Dena, are you finished?"

"Yes."

"You got the job."

"Oh, yes, I'm sure I did—"

"Dena, *listen* to me. He liked your tapes. He's starting you at a pretty low salary . . . but it means you're in."

There was a pause. "Are you serious?"

"Yes. He thinks you have something."

"Really?"

"Yes."

"Oh. Well." There was another pause. "How much are they going to pay me?"

"Like I said, it's a little low to start, but—"

"How much?"

"Seventy-five thousand. And Dena, remember, you do well, and one day you've got a shot at network, okay?"

"Okay," said Dena. "Fine. I'll take it."

DENA worked for three long years on the morning show at the local station in New York, smiling and nodding at the male cohost with the bad wig and interviewing authors of books about child rearing, interior decorating, and cooking, three subjects in which she had absolutely no interest.

Finally, in the early '70s, she landed what she wanted and became cohostess of the network's morning show. It had been an easy transition. Still, although it was network, she found herself smiling and nodding at another male cohost with another bad hairpiece and doing the same sort of interviews.

It was the best job most women could expect at the time, and most would have been satisfied. But she had her eye on the new hour-long prime-time evening news show that her old boss, Ira Wallace, had created and was now producing. Soon Sandy talked the network into letting her do several interviews on the evening show. Although they were fluff pieces, she was good at it.

And yet after a year she continued to be thought of as nothing more than a pretty girl who could fill in and handle a few lightweight interviews. Wallace or any other producer was not ready to assign serious hard-hitting news-making interviews to any woman. She knew that if she was going to ever get one, she would have to go out and get it herself.

One day she found her man. Everybody suspected that when Senator Orville Bosley switched political parties and became a

Democrat, he was positioning himself for something big, maybe the vice presidency. The press were curious. Reporters had tried in vain to get to him, but he was, uncharacteristically, very discreet and not granting interviews. Luckily for Dena, the pompous Bosley thought he was God's gift to women.

She found out he would be at a reception for Democratic Senators and Congressmen at the Shoreham Hotel in Washington. That afternoon Dena took the train to Washington and that night timed her entrance for about an hour after the reception had started. She arrived alone, wearing a long black dress with a slit up the side. The only jewelry she wore was a gold choker around her neck. She did not want to look like a Senator's wife, and she didn't.

Bosley was over in the corner of the room, surrounded, as usual, by a group of men who all had on identical suits and ties. He looked to be puffed up with his usual macho self-importance and was holding forth on trade policy when he glanced up.

She stood in the doorway long enough to stop conversation, then walked straight through the crowd toward Bosley. People stepped aside like the parting of the Red Sea, and she did not stop until she was standing in front of him. Her hair was parted on one side, and when she turned her head slightly as she spoke, her hair fell forward, enough to intrigue him. She looked him directly in the eyes, smiled, and said, "So, Senator, I hear you and I smoke the same brand of cigar."

Three weeks later he was sitting across from her in the studio, preparing to give his first major interview since switching parties. Ira Wallace was impressed. The regular male anchors were furious and hoped Dena would fall flat on her Scandinavian face. But all the audience at home saw was this nice-looking young woman in a simple, neat red-and-black wool suit—with huge, clear blue eyes and a peaches-and-cream complexion—who seemed as calm and composed as if she were in her own living room chatting with an old friend. She smiled at her guest and looked sympathetic when he told her about growing up in the Depression. They laughed over a photograph of little Orville in tattered overalls. After he was completely relaxed, she said with a smile, "Senator, people have said that even though you are a Democrat, your voting record is actually more like a conservative Republican's. Don't you feel it would be fair to inform your Democratic constituency that while your party has changed, your position has remained the same?"

Bosley was caught off guard. He began to stutter. "Well, uh . . . I think that charge is completely unfounded. Everybody who knows me and knows my voting record . . ."

Having been carefully prepped by Ira's team of researchers, Dena knew his record cold, and she sat back and drew out his position issue by issue. The male interviewers' hopes for her demise slowly faded. Bosley's voting record contradicted everything he had just said. She had busted him big time, and she had done it in prime time in less than ten minutes.

After the director called, "Off the air," Dena had the feeling she had just scored a touchdown at the last minute.

As she was being escorted off the studio floor, being congratulated by a pleased Ira Wallace and by Sandy, she glanced back at Bosley. He sat there, completely devastated.

A week later, when she read that after the interview Bosley probably would not get enough votes to be reelected, let alone make a vice presidential candidate, a wave of guilt flooded over her. But she could not look back, not now. Ira had hinted that if she played her cards right, in a year or so she might be the first female to be offered a permanent spot on the show.

She was definitely on the way up. Yet there had been a price to pay for Bosley—and for her. His career was wrecked, and she started to wake up during the night with terrible stomachaches.

EVERY year the Reverend Charles Hamilton was named as one of the ten most admired men in America. His church in New York was not the largest, but he had become well known nationally because of his books. Although he and his wife, Peggy, had both come from humble beginnings, a small town in rural Kentucky, over the years he had become known as the man who inspired millions and counseled Presidents. Still, apart from his popular public appearances, he kept a low profile in his personal life. Dena had met the Hamiltons at several charity fund-raisers and found them to be exactly what they seemed to be—two extremely nice and genuinely kind people.

For years everyone had sought a personal interview with the Hamiltons, and they had declined, but now, for a reason dear to their hearts, they agreed to give Dena an interview in their home. Years ago Peggy had quietly founded Children, Inc., an organization that had escalated into a worldwide operation that fed and clothed children. But contributions had slowed, and Dena promised to devote half the interview to promoting Children, Inc., and the other half to talking about their family life and successful marriage. Dena was excited. It couldn't have come at a better time. She knew Ira Wallace was getting closer to a decision about adding her to the major news show.

Four days before the taping Wallace called Dena into his office. When she walked in, she saw three men, two of whom she recognized as staff researchers. The third person, a ferret-faced man, was a stranger. For once, Wallace, who never bothered with introductions, said, "Dena Nordstrom, say hello to Sidney Capello, freelance reporter. He just made you a star, kid."

Dena glanced at the man and nodded. "How do you do." She sat down.

Ira looked like a wolf licking his chops. "I didn't tell you this," he said, "but I've had my best people on this for weeks, and they kept coming up with zero, zilch, nothing. That s.o.b. was as clean as a baby's bottom."

Dena was confused. "Who . . . are you talking about?"

"Who? Your reverend friend, Mr. White Bread. I knew this was probably the only chance we'd get to nail him, and we got him, thanks to Sidney here. Not Hamilton, but the next best thing. The little wife, and we've got it on paper, sworn witness."

Dena felt a knot in her stomach.

"Sidney went to Kentucky to nose around, and he scored big.

Before Little Miss Holier Than Thou married Hamilton, she went and got herself knocked up. Not only that—she gave the kid away."

"Oh, no, Ira, I can't believe that," Dena said, stunned. "Where did this come from?"

Wallace picked up a paper. "Straight from the hayseed who knocked her up. I can't wait. You'll get them going on that happy marriage routine, and then you slip it in. 'So, Mrs. Hamilton, how long has it been since you've seen your first child?' She'll be confused, she'll say whatever the name of her first kid is with Hamilton, and you'll give her that innocent look of yours and say, 'No, I was speaking of the daughter you gave up for adoption.' Then all we do is sit back and watch them sweat. Oh, I love it."

Dena felt ill. "Does Charles Hamilton know about this?"

"Who knows? Who cares? Biggest scoop of the year, and you got it, thrown right in your lap. Do I take care of you or what?" Wallace waited for Dena to thank him.

"Ira, they'll think I set them up just to trap them."

Wallace looked at the others. "And what bait, right?"

They laughed. Wallace looked at Capello. "Don't let that innocent, corn-fed mug of hers fool you, Sid. She has the instincts of a killer. They'll never know what hit them."

Dena said, "Ira, could I talk to you alone, please?"

Wallace was getting concerned now. "Sure. Boys, take a hike."

The three men got up and left the room.

Wallace looked at her. "What's the matter with you? Do you know how lucky we were? Capello could have taken this thing and sold it for a fortune. I had to promise to make him an associate producer, but I got the story for you. You should be grateful."

"I am. It's not that. It's just that . . ." Dena leaned forward and looked him in the eye. "Why do it?"

"What? Are you kidding me? It's news."

"Is it? I'm not sure. It seems so, I don't know, unnecessary. Yes, crooks and frauds deserve to be exposed, but Peggy Hamilton is a sweet lady who never hurt anybody. What's the point?"

"What's the *point?* The point is, people have a right to know what phonies they are. You're gonna be a hero. Your fans are gonna love you for exposing the truth about these two."

"Ira, don't make me do this. They have children. Think how this will affect them. And what if Peggy Hamilton did make a mistake? She's human. Haven't you ever made a mistake?"

"Sure, but I'm not passing myself off on the public as some kind of saint. You want to be a do-gooder? This is your chance. People need to know the truth about these bums. That's your job."

Wallace waved a hand to dismiss her. Dena sat for a moment, went to the door, and turned back. "Why do you hate Charles Hamilton so much?"

Wallace looked up at her, genuinely surprised. "Hate him? I don't hate him. Hell, I don't even know him."

DENA went to lunch, but she couldn't eat. Ira had taught her well, and she knew it was not the answer Peggy Hamilton would give that could hurt her. It was the question. Once asked, it would open a floodgate of inquiries. And if Dena refused to ask it, she could destroy her chances of getting the network job. Nobody crossed Ira Wallace. If you did, you were out. She knew that Ira had started doing some pretty low stuff to get ratings, but this was a new low, even for him.

Dena had been back from lunch a few minutes when Sidney Capello, without knocking, walked into her office and went over and flopped down on her red leather couch as if he belonged there. Dena looked at him with the same revulsion as if a snake had suddenly crawled into her office.

Capello did not bother to look at her. "Ira wants you to run your questions by me, make sure you get it right. You know, the knocked-up preacher's wife. He wants us to work together."

Dena stood up. "Oh, no. You and I are not working together on anything, you creep."

Capello's eyes darted in her direction. "Hey, I don't have to take any lip off any bimbo. You don't want to work with me, that's your problem, sister."

Dena did not hear the last sentence; she was storming down the hall. She barged into Wallace's office. "Did you tell that slimebag Sidney Capello he could work with me?"

Wallace seemed puzzled. "Yeah, so?"

"Ira, it's bad enough I have to work with those other two cretins you call researchers, but this guy is disgusting. How can you trust him? He may be lying about the Hamilton piece."

"He ain't lying. We double-checked. He may be a slimebag, but he's an expert slimebag. Trust him? Please, he'd sell his grandmother for fish bait if he thought he could make a dime, but that don't mean he ain't good."

"How can you work with somebody you don't trust?"

"Hey! What's trust got to do with work?"

DENA sat in her living room at four thirty Saturday morning eating a plate of Stouffer's frozen macaroni and cheese. She had been up all night struggling with herself about the Hamilton piece. In the past she had always been crystal-clear about her career goal and had kept her eye on it even if it meant leaving people in the dust. But there was something about this interview that made her deeply uneasy. Was she afraid that if she crossed the Hamiltons, she would never be accepted by the right people again? Or was it simply because Peggy Hamilton was a woman and seemed so vulnerable, so defenseless? Was it because she had loathed Sidney Capello on sight? Why did she feel so threatened? She went into the bathroom and glanced up at herself in the mirror and was startled at what she saw. For a split second it could have been her mother's face looking back at her.

Dena set up a meeting with Peggy Hamilton for that afternoon at Laurent on Fifty-sixth. It was a lovely old-world place, and she was positive that Ira—or anyone Ira knew—would not be there. She showed up at the restaurant ten minutes early wearing a scarf and sunglasses and feeling as if she were in a bad Joan Crawford movie. At ten minutes after four she was a nervous wreck and had already put away two screwdrivers when Peggy Hamilton came in.

The older woman smiled. "Oh, I almost didn't recognize you in those sunglasses. Sorry I'm late. Will you forgive me?"

"Of course. I just got here myself. Would you like a drink . . . or tea or coffee? I'm having a drink."

"I guess I'll just have a cup of tea."

Dena ordered the tea and another drink for herself. Her hands were shaking as she tried to light a cigarette.

"Are you all right?" Peggy asked. "Is something bothering you?"

Dena had just lit the filter end of her cigarette. "Well, yes, there is. I think I really don't know how to ask you this. It's sort of personal. Well, actually, it's very personal. . . ."

Peggy Hamilton waited, then asked, "What is it?"

"Oh, this is hard. . . . My boss wants me to ask you about the fact that you might have . . . had a baby before you married."

The color drained out of Peggy Hamilton's face.

"Oh, Peggy, I was hoping they were wrong. I am so sorry. I wasn't even supposed to ask you about this until we got on the air."

"How did you find out?"

"It wasn't me, Peggy, I promise you. Some lowlife who does this kind of thing went to Kentucky and found this guy who claims to be the father and was willing to swear to it."

Peggy Hamilton was devastated. "Why? Why would he tell anybody that now? Why after all these years?"

"Maybe he thought he could get something out of it. Maybe it's his one chance at fame. People do this kind of thing."

"I see."

"Does Charles *know* about this?"

"Yes. It's my daughter who doesn't know." She looked at Dena. "I don't understand. Why would they want to ask me about this?"

"Oh, Peggy, I don't know." Dena shook her head. "It's part of the business. They want ratings. It's as simple as that. I feel just like a low-down dirty dog, but all I can do is warn you."

"You know, it's funny. I was always terrified that one day it would come out, and now that it has, I just feel numb. I think I will have that drink, if you don't mind."

Dena said, "Oh, please, me too. I need another." She motioned for the waiter to bring two more. "Peggy, I am so sorry. Believe me, I tried my best to talk them out of it, but I couldn't. I'm just supposed to ask the questions."

"I see. Well, I wonder where we go from here."

"Tell me, what happened? What were the circumstances?"

"I was barely fifteen, and he was twenty-three. I was so stupid. I didn't know anything about sex. He told me he loved me and that I was special, and the next thing I knew . . . It only happened once, but about a month later I found out I was pregnant. I went to live with my mother's sister. I had the baby, and the next day she was gone, and there hasn't been a day since that I haven't wondered about her. You don't know how hard it has been not to try to find her, but I couldn't do that to her—expose her. And now this."

Dena was suddenly upset again. "Well, I'll tell them that if they pursue this, I'll quit. I'll probably get fired anyway if they find out I told you. So I'll just walk in there Monday morning and quit."

"No, you can't do that, Dena."

"Think about it. This is going to ruin your lives. People put you two up on a pedestal. They are not going to care who you are trying to protect. All they are going to care about is that you had a baby when you weren't married and hid it." Dena touched her arm. "Listen to me, Peggy. Cancel the damn interview. Say you're sick. Say your mother is dying. Say you're dying. Say anything. Just don't do it. It's nobody's business anyway. They're not playing fair. Why should you?"

"I have to talk to Charles. I don't know what to do."

"I'm telling you what to do. Lie."

"But it's the truth. I couldn't do that."

Dena glanced around and realized that the restaurant was beginning to seat early dinner customers. "Look, I think we better get out of here. Go home and talk to Charles."

"Dena, I don't know how to thank you for warning me. In the meantime, no matter what happens, promise me you won't quit over this. I couldn't live with that on my conscience, too."

Dena nodded. "All right, I promise."

Peggy squeezed Dena's hand. "Thank you."

When Dena got up and walked through the restaurant, she found that her knees were weak and realized she was not as brave as she thought she was.

FOR the next few days at work Dena waited like an inmate sitting on death row. Would Ira call? As the time for the interview grew closer, she began to get terrified and had trouble breathing. This morning she was just about to take a Valium when the intercom buzzer almost made her jump out of her skin.

Wallace barked, "Come in here!"

As she walked down the hall, her heart was pounding. This last mile could be the end of her career. She knocked lightly.

"Come in." Wallace got up and closed the door. "Sit down." He scowled at her across the desk. "I know this ain't gonna break your heart, but we are going to have to pull the question about the Hamilton kid."

"Why?"

"Julian Amsley's afraid of a lawsuit."

"Why?"

Wallace slammed his fist down and yelled, "Because the damn corncob that Capello dug up is now claiming he lied about it and it never happened. So we have to scrap it. Can you believe he's denying it? He reneged on a deal. But that's what you're dealing with now—liars, cheats, bums, no-good bums. People don't have any ethics anymore."

Dena had no idea how the Hamiltons had managed to talk the father into denying it, but she pulled herself together and put on an act that would have made her college drama teacher proud.

"Are you telling me, Ira, after all you put me through on this piece, that now I can't use it? I just cannot believe it!" She stood up and started to pace the office. "Well, I don't care if Julian Amsley is the president of the network, I'm going to ask the question anyhow. He can't interfere with the news!"

Wallace panicked. "Do you want to get us all fired?"

"It's the principle of the thing. I had planned the whole interview around it. Now I'm left with some softball piece."

Wallace tried to calm her. "I know, I know, but what can I do?"

"So Capello is the best! He didn't even check out his source."

"Okay, okay, it was stupid. How can I make it up to you? What do you want? Tell me."

The next thing Dena said surprised her, but once said, she knew she meant it. "I want you to fire Capello."

"I can't do that. He has a contract. We're talking money here."

She leaned on his desk. "Let me put it this way, Ira. If he's not out of here in the next hour, I'm going to be too upset to do the interview, and the Hamiltons won't do it without me. And you'll be left with twenty minutes of dead air."

Dena had a determined look Wallace had not seen before. They stared at each other. After a while he said, "All right, all right, but this is blackmail."

"One more thing. I want to be here when you do it."

Now Wallace could not believe what he was hearing. "What's happened to you? You used to be such a nice, sweet kid."

FORTY-FIVE minutes later Dena was sitting across from Sidney Capello when Wallace fired him.

Capello immediately turned on Dena. "I'll get you for this. You just wait, you—"

Wallace came around the desk and more or less pushed him toward the door. "Yeah, yeah, yeah. We all know how tough you are, Sidney. Now get out of here." He shoved him out the door and slammed it behind him.

Wallace went back to his desk. "Satisfied?"

Dena smiled. "Wouldn't have missed it for the world."

As she walked down the hall, she felt a surge of something that made her feel strong. For the first time in her life she felt that heady rush of power, and she suddenly understood why men fought for it. It felt good.

SIDNEY CAPELLO WAS bitterly disappointed. This had been maybe his one chance to get into big-time television. Wallace was the only one who would ever have hired him, and now, thanks to that blond bimbo, he was right back where he started. Still nothing more than a paid informant working out of a seedy hotel room.

As he packed up the office he had had for only a few days, he pacified himself somewhat by reading the plaque he kept on his desk: REVENGE IS A DISH BEST SERVED COLD. He smiled.

Life is a long time.

Let's Have Lunch

❧

NEW YORK CITY   1973

TWO weeks after the Hamilton piece ran, Dena and J.C. attended the Heart Fund dinner at the Waldorf-Astoria. The Heart Fund man of the year was Howard Kingsley, the grand old man of news broadcasting. He was introduced as the man whose face and voice had become the one the country depended on for the past thirty years. Dena was thrilled to be in the same room with him.

Kingsley was now sixty-four years old and still a handsome man, distinguished for his thoughtfulness and balance, and beautifully spoken. His acceptance speech was gracious. He thanked his wife of forty years, Lee, for sticking with him through thick and thin ("mostly thick"), and he said that she and his daughter, Anne, had always been "his safe harbor on the rocky and stormy sea of broadcasting." After his short speech he received a five-minute standing ovation. Dena looked over at his wife and daughter and felt that old feeling whenever she saw a father and a daughter—a sadness tinged with envy. All she had ever seen of her father was a photograph.

After the dinner, as they were walking out, J.C. said, "By the way, we have an invitation to the private reception for Kingsley." J.C. was a fund-raiser and knew a great many people.

Dena did not want to go. "I won't know anyone. I'm not a friend of his. He might think I'm too pushy. You go, and I'll wait for you."

But J.C. would not take no for an answer, and five minutes later she found herself upstairs in a suite, at a party with the heads of all three networks, including Julian Amsley, the man who ran hers. After about thirty minutes of trying to hide in a corner, Dena got in line with J.C. to meet the guest of honor. She watched as Howard Kingsley came closer, shaking each person's hand. When Dena was introduced, she managed to look calm and say, "Congratulations, sir. I enjoyed your speech."

Howard looked at her with a little smile and said, "Thank you very much, young lady." As she started to move away, he said, "Oh, by the way, Miss Nordstrom, I caught the Hamilton piece. Good work. Let's have lunch sometime."

Dena managed, "Oh, thank you," just as another guest came up.

Had she heard right? Had he actually said, "Good work, let's have lunch," or was she hallucinating? Maybe she misunderstood. He had really said, "Bad work, hated it a bunch." Dena grabbed J.C. "Did you hear him say, 'Let's have lunch'?"

"Yes."

"Oh, my God. What do you think he wants?"

J.C. laughed. "What do you think he wants? He wants to tell you you are the most talented and brilliant woman in New York."

"Don't be silly. Did he really say, 'Good work'?"

"Yes, Dena. Am I going to have to carry a tape recorder around to gather all these little kudos from now on?"

"No. It's just that you never figure that someone like him would be watching me. I mean, I'm a silly little fill-in interviewer. You know, J.C., I never told you, but he's been sort of a hero of mine. It really would have been enough just to go to the dinner—but to actually meet him . . ."

When she got home, she was still on cloud nine. She took a bath and crawled into bed and tried to go to sleep but couldn't. She wished she had someone to call. It was at times like these, when she was the happiest, that she missed her mother the most.

DENA HAD MANAGED TO resist telling everyone at work what happened when she met Howard Kingsley, and now she was glad. It had been two weeks, and she had not heard from him.

Maybe he had forgotten, or maybe he said "Let's have lunch" to everybody, and why not? she thought. I must tell ten people a day let's have lunch. What an egotistical fool she had been to think he would actually waste time with her. The phone rang.

"Miss Nordstrom?"

"Yes?"

"This is Howard Kingsley. I was calling to see if you might be free this Thursday for lunch."

"Oh, ah, um, Thursday. Let me check. . . ." She pretended to look at her datebook and to flip through imaginary pages. Suddenly she stopped. "Oh, who am I kidding? Of course I'm free, Mr. Kingsley, and I would love to meet you for lunch."

Kingsley laughed. "Good. I like the Carlyle dining room. It's quiet, and the food's good. Thursday at, say, twelve thirty?"

"Oh, yes, fine. I'll be there."

"Good. Looking forward to it."

Thursday finally rolled around eight years later, or so it seemed, and Dena was talking to herself all the way to the Carlyle. "You have been in this business almost seven years. You're not an amateur. You're a grown woman. He is not going to bite you. If you seem nervous, you will make him nervous. You have no blemishes; your nails are clean. You won't have a drink unless, of course, he does. . . ." The cab jerked to a stop. She overtipped the driver, took a deep breath, and walked in.

The maître d' saw her at once. "Ah, yes, Miss Nordstrom. Mr. Kingsley is expecting you. Right this way." He led her all the way to the back corner. The roomful of ladies who lunch and businessmen all glanced up and tried not to stare at the great-looking blonde with the great legs. As she approached, Kingsley stood up.

"So glad you could make it. I know you must be a busy lady."

"Well, thank you," Dena said. "I'm flattered, but believe me, I'm not as busy as you may think."

He smiled. "Enjoy it while you can. You will be soon enough. May I order you a drink?"

She looked to see if he had a drink. He did. She tried to sound casual. "Sure. I'll take a martini as well."

"Fine." He motioned the waiter, then turned back to her. "I can tell all these men are jealous and all the women whispering because I have such a lovely young lady at my table. It happens every time I take my daughter out, and I must say I enjoy it."

Dena realized she did not have to worry that he was on the make. He was a gentleman to let her know in such a nice way.

"Mr. Kingsley, I saw your daughter the other night at the dinner, and she is a beautiful girl."

"Thank you. We're lucky she got all her mother's good looks."

The waiter brought her martini, and she took a big sip before she realized it was gin and not vodka. But she kept smiling so he wouldn't notice that her eyes were tearing. He asked her how she had gotten started. She gave him a short account of the long history of the jobs she had had before New York.

They ordered lunch, and when they had finished, he ordered coffee for each of them. "I think I mentioned the Hamilton piece to you the other night," he said.

"Yes, you did."

He cleared his throat. "I understand you went your own way on that . . . broke ranks with the network, so to speak."

Dena panicked. How did he know? "Well, I, uh . . ."

"Charles and Peggy Hamilton are friends of mine."

"Oh, I see."

"You could have lost your job pulling a stunt like that. It was foolhardy to do at the beginning of your career."

Dena's heart sank. She felt ten years old. "Yes, I guess it was."

"But personally, I thought it was a damn decent thing to do."

"You did? I mean, you do?"

He smiled. "Yes, I do. You went out of your way to save somebody else's skin. It was not an easy decision. I've been there myself. You took the high road, and it worked."

"Just barely," Dena said. "My boss was pretty mad at me."

"Ira Wallace?"

"Yes. Do you know him?"

He said with a weary look on his face, "Oh, yes, I know him." Kingsley sat back and seemed to be deciding something. "You know, Miss Nordstrom, I like you. You've got style, presence, and you've got class. You're just what they want, but by God, I just hate to see them get ahold of you." He grimaced. "Be that as it may, you gave my friends fair warning, so I'm giving you fair warning." He looked directly at her. "People like Wallace don't want news, they want audience, and to get it, they want ratings, and they don't care how they get them. But I'm sure you are aware of that."

"Yes," said Dena, "I am."

"I've covered three wars and have seen a lot of killing in my time, but this new bunch taking over scares me. Mark my words, as soon as they can get rid of all of us old guys, they're going to replace us with pretty young men and women, like yourself, to do their dirty work. To push their garbage down everyone's throats while they hide behind their office doors making millions, laughing at us, and the whole country falls apart."

People in the restaurant were looking over as Kingsley's voice got louder. When he realized what was happening, he said softly, "I'm sorry. I don't know why I subjected you to all my rantings. I'm probably just a senile old fool thinking the worst."

"Mr. Kingsley, you mustn't say that. You're not old or a fool, and you have a right to be upset."

He caught the waiter's eye and motioned for the check. "Call me Howard, please. You know, my wife says I should retire. Maybe I should, but until then somebody has got to keep reminding people we aren't all the scum they are trying to turn us into."

"All the more reason why you can never retire. We need you."

He smiled while signing the check. "Miss Nordstrom, I guess what I was trying to say to you is, try not to let them use you too much. Fight back when you can."

"Oh, I will. And it's Dena, please."

As they walked out, she said, "You know, I really appreciate your talking to me. Truth is, I don't think I'm going to be offered a new contract. I think I might not have what it takes."

Howard opened the glass door leading to the street. "Oh, you are going to get offered a contract, all right. Julian Amsley's smart enough to know what he's got, and he's not about to lose you."

Dena looked at him, dumbfounded.

He laughed. "No, I'm not a psychic. I play poker with Amsley every Friday, and he likes to talk."

He hailed a cab for her and helped her in. "Oh, listen. On that contract thing. They've got two hundred thousand a year budgeted. Don't let your agent settle for less. They won't tell you, but your popularity rating is through the roof. They'll offer one. Hold out for four and settle for three. When Amsley hears we had lunch together, that ought to scare him at least a hundred thousand."

He closed the door and handed the driver a ten-dollar bill. "Take this young lady where she wants to go for me, will you? And be careful. She's valuable property."

The driver beamed. "Yes, sir, Mr. Kingsley."

AT THE end of the week, Sandy Cooper called. "Dena, you got the contract!"

"Wow, great, Sandy."

"I knew we could do it. And wait until you hear this. I had to work like the devil, but I finally got them up to two hundred thousand a year. Isn't that great news?"

"Sandy, tell them I won't do it for less than four."

There was a long pause. "Are you trying to kill me?"

Two weeks later a battle-weary Sandy called. "All I could get them up to was three."

"Fine," Dena said. "I'll take it."

A FEW weeks later Dena was in the editing room working on an interview with Bella Abzug when her secretary buzzed and told her she had an urgent long-distance call from a Mrs. Sarah Jane Poole.

"Who's that?"

"I don't know, but she says she's a close personal friend."

"Oh, Lord. I have no idea who that is. . . . Put her through."

An excited woman's voice was on the other end. "Dena?"

"Yes, this is Dena Nordstrom."

"It's me!"

"Who?"

"Don't tell me you've forgotten your old college roommate, Sarah Jane Simmons Krackenberry from Selma, Alabama?"

"Sookie? For gosh sakes, why didn't you say it was you? How could I forget you, crazy thing? How are you?"

"Fine!"

"Are you still busy fighting the Civil War?"

Sookie screamed with laughter. "Of course, honey. You know me. Never say die!"

"How is Earle?"

"He's fine. But I am mad at you. My mother-in-law read where you were coming to Atlanta to get some big award, and you didn't even call and tell me you were coming."

Dena was confused. "I thought you still lived in Alabama."

"I do, silly, but I'm not going to let you get this close without getting a chance to see you. I'm only a few hours from Atlanta. I could run over there and pick you up and bring you here for a couple of days, and we could catch up on old times."

"Oh, Sookie, that would be great. But unfortunately, I'm only going to be there for one night, just for the dinner."

"Can't I see you at all? Maybe before the dinner or after?"

"I'm coming in and going straight to the dinner, and those things go on for hours. The next day I get right back on a plane."

"Well, I'm coming anyway. I don't care if I see you just for five minutes. I know you, Dena Nordstrom. If I don't hog-tie you while you're down here, who knows when I'll ever see you?"

Dena had to laugh. "Sookie, you are still the silliest girl I've ever met."

Sookie said, "Well, at least that's something."

"I'm not in my office, so I'll have to call you and let you know where and what time."

"Now you better call me back, because you're not getting off the hook, Dena Gene Nordstrom!"

When Dena hung up, she had to smile. Of all the girls she had been in school with, Sookie had been her closest friend, so maybe it might not be so bad. It could even be fun.

A WEEK later, after Dena had given her speech in Atlanta, she did not get to sleep until three a.m. When her wake-up call came the next morning, she had to drag herself out of bed. What had possessed her to set up a breakfast date with Sookie? As she showered and dressed, she thought the only consolation was that at least she would not have to do much but listen, because Sookie would do all the talking.

Walking into the hotel coffee shop, she immediately saw Sookie over in the corner, waving madly. Dena would have known her anywhere. She had on a neat cotton shirtwaist dress and still wore her short red hair in bangs, exactly as in college. Sookie stood up and ran over and hugged her. She still had the personality of a game show contestant. "Oh, Dena, I am *so* excited! I'm so glad to see you. Oh, sit down and let me look at you. I'm so nervous, I'm about to have an epileptic fit. Here you are in person, and I hate to say it, but you still look the same—same gorgeous pale skin, absolutely glamorous!" They sat down.

"Sookie, you look great, too."

"I do? Well, I'm just an old married woman, with children now. My youth is a thing of the past, gone with the wind."

Dena laughed. "Oh, stop it. You don't look a day older than the last time I saw you. Now tell me what's going on with you."

"Nothing. Same old stuff—raising my kids, you know, nothing. But forget about me. You're the one with the exciting life. I want to hear about everything. Tell me about the dinner last night."

Dena dismissed it. "It was all right as those things go."

"Didn't they give you some big award?"

"No. It was just a plaque."

"Oh," Sookie said, taken aback. "Well, I'd take any award they handed me and run like a thief."

"I tell you what," Dena said, smiling, "next one I get, I'm going to put a blond wig on you and send you. Come on, you know what I've been up to. Tell me about yourself."

"Me? Like I said, everything's the same. Earle's still a dentist. We moved out of his mother's old house downtown and moved to this cute little house in the suburbs, and we love it, and I do some work in the community, you know, all that stuff."

The waitress came up to the table. Dena ordered coffee, but Sookie said, "I don't want anything with caffeine. I'm so nervous now I'm about to faint. Bring me some Sanka, iced."

"How many children do you have?" Dena asked.

"Honey, I have three now. Can you believe it? Three little girls— Ce Ce, Dee Dee, and Le Le." Sookie whipped out a photograph of herself and three little miniature Sookies, bangs and all.

"They are very pretty."

Sookie beamed. "I think so, but I'm their mother. Earle is beside himself; he thinks all three are going to grow up and become Miss Alabama."

"What about *you*, Sookie? Are you still trying to be Miss Popularity? You ran for every office on campus, I remember."

"Honey, what did I know? When I hit S.M.U., I was straight out of Selma. Besides, that's not my fault. My mother told me if you can't be smart, be bubbly . . . and Lord knows, I bubbled."

The waitress served them their coffee, and a woman came up to the table just after that and spoke to Dena. "Excuse me, could I have your autograph, please? I'm one of your biggest fans."

Sookie was pleased and chatted happily with her while Dena had to dig through her purse looking for a pen and a piece of paper because the woman had neither.

Dena signed her name and handed the woman the paper. After she left, Sookie turned to Dena, excited. "I'll bet you get people coming up to you all the time. Doesn't that make you feel important?

I feel important just sitting here with you. Don't you just love it?"

"No, not really."

"You do too love it—all that attention. Who wouldn't?"

Dena smiled. "It's all right. It's just . . . Sometimes I don't feel like being nice."

Sookie sat back. "I always had to force you to be social. If it hadn't been for me pushing you, you wouldn't have ever been a Kappa. You wouldn't have known anybody except those weirdo theater majors. I pushed you out into the world. As a matter of fact, I am completely responsible for your success today. And don't you dare tell anybody any different."

"Okay."

"We had fun, didn't we? Remember that crazy song you wrote for the Kappa skit?"

Dena looked puzzled.

"Oh, you know! You made us all put balloons in our sweaters, and we all sang 'Thanks for the Mammaries.' We were silly and happy as clams. We'd laugh from morning till night."

"Really? I remember being sort of unhappy at school."

"Oh, pooh! You were just a little moody, that's all. And I just chalked that up to dramatic temperament. You had all the leads in those awful plays. You used to spend so much time over at that theater—everybody thought you had a secret boyfriend. What were you doing?"

"Lord knows. Acting, I guess, fooling with the lights."

"Well, it paid off. Here you are a big star." Sookie was beaming. "Oh, Dena, I always knew you were going to be famous. I used to tell you that all the time, didn't I?"

"You did?"

"Yes. Don't you remember anything?" Sookie looked at her wistfully. "Dena, don't you miss the good old days? I hate having to be a grown woman. Of course, I wouldn't take anything for Earle and my girls, but don't you wish we could go back and not have to worry about anything?"

Dena glanced at her watch. "Oh, Sookie, I've got to go."

Sookie wailed, "We just got started good."

Dena said, "I know, but we'll do it again soon. I promise."

Sookie walked with her out to the limo and hugged her good-bye. "Promise me . . . Promise that if you ever get back south of the Mason-Dixon line, you'll call me and let me know. Because if you don't, I'll find out and show up and embarrass you."

Dena, laughing, got into the car. "I promise."

As she drove off, Sookie waved and called, "Love you!"

ON THE plane Dena ordered a Bloody Mary and sat there and thought about the girl Sookie had described. Could it possibly have been her? The girl she remembered being had always been a sort of sad, dreamy kid who used to cry a lot, longing for something so hard that it hurt. But what she had been longing for or where those feelings had gone, Dena did not know. The truth was, she could barely remember that girl at all.

WHEN Dena was seven, her mother got a job at Bergdorf's in New York City and sent her to boarding school in Connecticut. Dena hated it—long, empty, dark halls and waiting to see her mother again. After about two months the mother superior wrote a letter to her mother: "We expect a certain amount of homesickness from our boarders, especially when the child is an only child, but it is clear that the child simply adores you and is terribly unhappy here. I wonder if she might have more weekends at home?"

Dena loved her mother's new apartment. It was off Gramercy Park on a pretty street lined with trees. She would sleep on the living-room couch. The apartment was on the ground floor, with the windows almost at street level. Lying there late at night, she could hear couples walking past the windows. Sometimes she would hear the music on a radio as a car swished by, its headlights shining through the ornate black bars on the windows and turning the small living room into a magical light-and-sound show.

Dena was full of dreams and curiosity. She longed to someday live in a white house like the one she often dreamed about. White against a green lawn, and her mother was always smiling. That Christmas her mother had let her come for a whole week. It had been a wonderful visit. They walked all the way up Fifth Avenue, looking at hundreds of people, Santa Clauses on each corner, and windows full of miniature things swirling and moving to music, then on to Radio City to see the Christmas show. The Rockettes were dressed in red-and-gold uniforms and looked like live toy soldiers. She could hardly breathe watching all the lights, fascinated by the way they changed from one color to another, again almost like magic. And if that wasn't enough, her mother astonished her when she told Dena that she knew one of the Rockettes and that they were going backstage to meet her.

When they got backstage, her mother's friend, a pretty blond lady named Christine, gave them a complete tour, from the huge mirrored rehearsal hall to the dressing rooms. Backstage was teeming with Rockettes, musicians, stagehands, and other costumed ladies, but Dena wanted to know only one thing: Who made the lights way up in the curved ceiling of the auditorium change from one color to another, and how did they do it? Christine had laughed at the question coming from such a small girl and introduced her to a man named Artie. He showed her the main control console, with its four thousand three hundred and five colored handles that controlled the amber, green, red, and blue lights. That night Dena's head was still whirling. She had never been so excited in her entire life. She slept with her mother and held her hand all night and dreamed about the lights.

Then, two months later, without warning, her mother suddenly quit her job and moved to the Altamont Towers apartments in an older section of Cleveland, Ohio, and Dena didn't see her at all until the summer. But she never forgot that night at Radio City and had been fascinated with lights ever since, any kind of light—sunlight, moonlight, lamplight—so much so that it was the lighting that first attracted her to the theater. She became totally obsessed with light, and eventually the light became obsessed with her, pulling her all the way back to New York.

Who Are You?

❧

DENA woke dreading her doctor's appointment, but she had to go. Dr. Halling would not prescribe any more medicine unless he saw her. After her examination she sat in his office, dying for a cigarette, while the doctor read the results of the G.I. series tests he had forced her to go through. He did not look happy.

"Dena, your ulcer is not healing as it should. In fact, it looks worse." He looked at her. "And you're not smoking?"

"No."

"No coffee, no alcohol?"

"No."

"And you are watching your diet?"

"Oh, absolutely." She had eaten a bowl of oatmeal last week.

He sighed. "Well, the only thing I can figure that is causing this is just plain old stress. I should put you on complete bed rest."

Dena's alarm system went off. "Bed rest! What does that mean?"

"Dena, it means just what you think it means. I'm going to put you to bed for at least three weeks. You don't want to wind up with a bleeding ulcer and have to have emergency surgery. Or worse, bleed to death."

"But I have to work. Really. I'll lose my job if I stop now."

"Dena, this is your health. You could kill yourself."

"Look, now and then I might not have eaten like I should have. And I smoked a little. I have been running around, maybe too much, but I promise I'll do better. Please?"

Dr. Halling sat back. "This is against my better judgment, but I'll make a deal with you. I want you back here in two months, and if it's not better, I'm going to order you into the hospital, do you understand?"

"Oh, yes. I understand."

"But in the meantime, I want you to talk to a friend of mine. See if he can't do something to help you try to figure out what's causing all this stress. You're too young to be in this condition."

Dena was relieved. "Fine. I'll see anybody you say."

He wrote down a name and address. Before he let her take the paper, he said, "*Promise* me you'll see this man at least twice a week."

"I swear I will. I'll call as soon as I get home."

She called this O'Malley that afternoon, and three days later she walked into his building and looked on the wall directory in the lobby: DR. GERALD O'MALLEY, PSYCHIATRIST. 17TH FLOOR.

Dena was appalled. A psychiatrist! What in the world was Dr. Halling thinking about?

She got out on 17, knocked on his door, and heard a voice say, "Come in." Dena walked into the office, and a young man, not much older than she, stood up and shook her hand.

"Hello, Miss Nordstrom. I'm Dr. O'Malley."

He was a neat, preppy-looking man in horn-rimmed glasses. He had blue eyes and fair, almost baby skin. He looked as if his mother had dressed him and combed his hair this morning.

"You're the doctor?"

"Yes. Won't you have a seat?"

"I don't know why," she said, sitting down, "but I was expecting an older man with a beard."

He laughed. "Sorry. I haven't had much luck with beards."

He sat down, took out a pad and pen, and waited for her to speak. Something she would soon find out he did a great deal.

Finally she said, "Umm, I'm not here because I think I need a psychiatrist, believe me."

He nodded. Something else he would do a lot.

"I have an ulcer. I just have a little stress, job related."

"Uh-huh." He nodded. "And what is your job?"

Dena was taken aback. "Television! You might have seen me. I do interviews on an evening news show."

"Sorry. I'm afraid I don't get the chance to watch much TV."

Dena was thrown. "Oh, well. It's an important job, and . . ." Suddenly she felt irritated at having to explain who she was and what she did. She began to bounce her right foot up and down, legs crossed. "Look, I don't know what I'm supposed to say. Don't you want to ask me some questions or something?"

"Is there anything you'd like to tell me?" Dr. O'Malley said. He looked at her and waited.

She looked around the room. "Listen, I'm sure you are a nice person, and I don't want to hurt your feelings, but I don't believe in all this stuff. All this whining and bellyaching about what your mother and daddy did when you were three. Really, I'm the least screwed-up person I know."

Dr. O'Malley continued to listen.

"I'm not depressed. My job is going great. I don't think I'm Napoleon. My parents didn't beat me—"

Dr. O'Malley said, "Tell me a little about your parents."

"What?"

"Your parents."

"They're fine. They're dead."

"Any brothers or sisters?"

"No. Just me."

"I see. How old were you when your parents died?"

"My father was killed in the war before I was born."

He waited. She looked around the room. "How long does it take to become a psychiatrist?"

Dr. O'Malley said, "A long time. And your mother? How old were you when she died?"

"I forget. Does it take less time to be a psychiatrist than it does to be a real doctor?"

"No, it doesn't. What was the cause of death?"

"Oh, hit by a car." Dena began to rummage around in her purse.

"I see. How did you feel about that?"

"Just like anyone would feel if their mother was run over. But you get over it. Do you have any gum or anything?"

"No, I'm sorry."

He waited for her to continue, but she did not. After a minute she became more agitated. "Look, I'm sorry to disappoint you, Doctor, but I basically am a very happy person. Things couldn't be better. All I have is a bad stomach."

He nodded and made notes. What *was* he doing, playing tic-tac-toe? When the session ended, Dena couldn't wait to leave. She wondered what the hell she was going to say to this cold fish for the next two months. How could she possibly talk to this guy? He didn't even watch television, for heaven's sake!

FOR weeks Dena dragged herself to Dr. O'Malley's office two times a week, and two times a week she sat there bored to tears. He too just sat and waited for her to say something interesting or something he could analyze. Today, fatigued with her own conversation, she decided to use her skills.

"So why don't you tell me a little bit about yourself. You seem a little young to be a doctor. Are you married? Children?"

He looked up from his notebook. "Miss Nordstrom, I'm the doctor, and you're the patient. I'm here to talk about you."

"What do you want me to say? Tell me."

"Anything you want, Miss Nordstrom. This is your time."

"I find this very uncomfortable. I mean . . . I'm paying you. Shouldn't you be the one who's talking to me, asking questions?"

He smiled but continued writing. After a moment she decided to try another tack. "Dr. O'Malley, you are a very handsome man, did you know that? Are you married?"

Dena thought she saw a faint blush, but he put his pen down and said, "Miss Nordstrom, you have tried everything that patients usually try, but we will eventually talk about you. I am interested in how you feel about you—outside your work."

"What do you mean?"

"How you relate to people, how you feel people relate to you."

"But they relate to me . . . about my work."

"You're mistaking a profession for a personal identity. Who are you *other* than what you do? That's what I'm trying to get at."

"I think you are trying to fit me into some box. What I do is not that simple. It's who I am. I am not a plumber or a construction worker who quits at five o'clock. What I do is a twenty-four-hour career. I'm on television. That's how people 'relate' to me."

"I'm not saying that other people may not be able to separate you from what you do. I'm wondering if you can."

Dena looked out the window. Snow was falling, luminous against the yellow streetlights. It reminded her of another late snowy afternoon when she and her mother had walked in the streets of New York, from midtown to her mother's apartment building, but she quickly pushed it out of her mind. She did not like to think about her mother. And it was not something she wanted to discuss with O'Malley. It was none of his business.

At the end of the session he closed his notebook. "Miss Nordstrom, I am afraid I have a scheduling problem. A former patient of mine is in a serious crisis, and I am going to be forced to give up your time."

Hooray, thought Dena.

"I am going to have to transfer you to another doctor—one I think can help you a lot more with your sleeplessness and nervousness. She specializes in hypnotherapy and—"

"Hypnotherapy? I don't want to be hypnotized."

Dr. O'Malley said, "Before you balk, I think you should consider giving it a try. We are finding that hypnotherapy can be very helpful with deep-seated . . . ah . . . relaxation problems."

Dena made a face. "I'm not crazy about the idea of going to a woman either. Don't you have a man you can recommend?"

"No. This therapist is the one person I can recommend with complete confidence. She will see you on Friday at our time. Her name is Elizabeth Diggers, and I think you're going to be quite pleased with her." He handed her Dr. Diggers's card.

"Oh, well. . . . All right. Whatever."

He stood up and shook her hand. "Well, good-bye, Miss Nordstrom—and good luck."

Walking home in the snow, Dena felt as if she had been let out of school, yet at the same time strangely sad and a bit rejected. Maybe it was just that Christmas was coming up. She hated Christmas. It was always the same, so many people pulling at her. Being single at Christmastime was a pain. She had to make up so many excuses, so many lies. J.C. was already badgering her to go home to Minnesota with him, but she had no intention of spending Christmas in the bosom of somebody else's family. She usually slept through Christmas and then had to lie about what a great time she'd had. It was getting harder and harder.

AFTER Dena had left his office for good, Gerry O'Malley sat back down, feeling ill. Sending her to someone else was the last thing in the world he wanted. But ethically and professionally, he had to do it. He had fallen hopelessly head over heels in love with Dena Nordstrom and could not be objective if he tried. That first day when she had come into his office, her beauty had almost taken his breath away. But it was not beauty alone that made him constantly want to get up and hold her. It was the vulnerable, terrified girl inside the woman he wanted to put his arms around.

He looked at his watch and dialed the phone.

"Liz, it's Gerry."

"Oh, hi, doll. What's up?"

"I just wanted to let you know she'll be there on Friday. So I'll send my notes on over, all right?"

"Good. How are you doing?"

"Other than feeling like a complete idiot, I'm doing just great. I finally found someone as sexy and beautiful as you, and she turns out to be a patient."

Elizabeth Diggers's laugh was low and hearty.

"Seriously, I appreciate your seeing her on such short notice. Liz, you are the only person I would trust with her."

"Happy to do it. And Gerry—want some highly technical professional advice? Go out and have a few drinks."

"You tell an Irishman that?"

"On second thought, don't. I'll have the drink. And Gerry?"

"Yes?"

"You're one of the good guys."

"Thanks, Elizabeth."

DENA had made an appointment with Dr. Diggers. She sounded nice, as if she might have a little more personality than O'Malley. Her office was on Eighty-ninth and Madison Avenue. The doorman who sent her up recognized Dena. Oh, great, she thought. Now everyone in New York is going to know I'm seeing a shrink.

Dena rang the bell of the apartment, and after a few minutes the door opened. A small Hispanic woman said, "Come right this way," and led her down the hall to Dr. Diggers's office. The woman knocked lightly. "Dr. Diggers, your five o'clock is here."

"Come in."

Dena was surprised. Dr. Elizabeth Diggers was a large black woman in a wheelchair.

"Hello, Miss Nordstrom. I'm Dr. Diggers." She smiled. "Didn't Gerry tell you I was a big black woman in a wheelchair?"

"No."

"I see. He tends to be short on small talk."

"Yes, I know," Dena said.

"Is that going to be a problem for you?"

"Excuse me?"

"How do you feel about my being black?"

Dena, who could lie like a dog, was caught off guard. "How do I feel about it? I couldn't care less. I'm the one who should be worried. I'm the patient. Does it bother you that I'm white?"

Dr. Diggers was opening a notepad and did not answer.

"Look," Dena said, "if this is some sort of test, I don't care what color you are, but you might as well know I don't want to be here. I promised my doctor I would—so here I am."

"I see."

"I just want to start off being honest."

"It's a good start," Diggers said. "It wasn't a test, but you passed." She laughed. "Have a seat."

Dena finally sat down.

"I have a few notes from Gerry, but if you don't mind, I'd like to find out some basic information. And by the way, I've seen you on television, and I think you do a wonderful job."

Dena liked that. "Oh, thank you."

"Now, Gerry mentioned you seem to be having some biological effects from stress. Stomach problems."

"What? Oh, yes. I tried to tell him it's from my job, but I don't think he gets it. He doesn't know what television is."

"I see. And how long have you had stomach problems?"

"Oh, a long time. Since I was maybe fifteen or sixteen."

"Tell me a little bit about your history, Miss Nordstrom."

"Well, I started in local television in Dallas when—"

Dr. Diggers stopped her. "No, I mean your family history."

"Oh." She sighed. "My father was killed in the war . . . and my mother's dead."

"How old were you when your mother died?"

"Ah, fourteen or fifteen, I think. It's hard to remember. She was sick for a long time, and I was in boarding school."

"I see. . . . And what was her illness?"

"Tuberculosis."

"I see." Suddenly Dr. Diggers remembered something from Gerry's notes. "Wasn't somebody in your family hit by a car?"

"Yes, she was, on her way to the hospital for treatment. She got hit by a car. Actually, a car hit her bus. Anyhow, the reason I'm here is I am having terrible trouble sleeping. I wondered—"

"Do you have living relatives?"

"One or two distant relatives. On my father's side. A distant cousin and an aunt, I think, but I don't see them much."

"On your mother's side?"

Dena leaned over to look at Dr. Diggers's pad. "Are you writing this down so if I go completely insane, you can call them?"

Dr. Diggers laughed. "No. Just making a few notes for myself. And on your mother's side?"

"No."

She looked up. "No?"

"No. All dead."

"I see." The doctor made a note: "Patient agitated, kicking foot."

LATER that evening, when Elizabeth Diggers had finished her dinner, the phone rang. She wheeled over to the wall phone. "I wondered how long it would be before you called."

"Well, did you see my girl today?"

"Oh, yes." There was a pause. "Mercy, son, you are either the bravest man I ever knew or the dumbest. Are you sure you want to take all that on?"

He chuckled. "No, but I don't have much of a choice. I am absolutely so crazy about that woman that I can't see straight."

"I'll do my best to help her, Gerry, you know that, but at this point I'm not even sure if she will come back."

"Isn't she the most beautiful thing you have ever seen?"

"Yes, she is a good-looking woman, but—"

"And smart."

"Oh, yes, and smart."

"Really, isn't she just a classic natural beauty?"

"Yes, Gerry, she puts the moon and the stars to shame. Does this girl have any idea how you feel?"

"No. I mean, I don't think so. And now is certainly not the time to tell her. So I'll only ask one more thing, and then I'm out of the picture, okay? What do you think—was I off on my evaluation?"

"Not much. I think you pretty much pegged it. Shut down. Definitely symptoms of some sort of severe rejection trauma."

"Yeah. It could be around her mother's death. She wouldn't let me get near that. But it's in your hands now, Elizabeth."

"Well, okay, buddy. I'll do my best. But in the meantime—it could be a long meantime—I suggest you see other people."

"Oh, really? So what are you doing this Saturday night?"

"What I always do—boogie till I drop."

He laughed.

"Good night, Romeo."

DR. DIGGERS WAS SOMEWHAT surprised when Dena showed up for her second appointment. She strolled in five minutes late and flopped down in a chair.

Dr. Diggers smiled. "Back to let me have another crack?"

"Yes," Dena said. "What are we supposed to talk about today?"

"Well, I would like to try to get to know you a little better, find out about your background. Where are you from?"

"I was born in San Francisco, but we moved around a lot."

"What is your heritage?"

"My what?"

"Your heritage. Where do you come from? Your roots."

"My roots? Like the book? Oh, my father was Swedish . . . or Norwegian or something like that."

"And your mother?"

"Just plain old American, I guess. She never said. Her maiden name was Chapman, so she's—what—English? I don't know."

Dr. Diggers was always astonished at how so few people cared about their heritage. "Aren't you curious to find out more?"

"Not really. I'm an American. That's all that matters, isn't it?"

"Let's play a little game. I want you to give me three answers to this question: Who are you?"

"I'm Dena Nordstrom, I'm blond, and . . ." She was having a hard time. "And I'm five foot seven. Did I pass or fail?"

Dr. Diggers put down her pen. "It's not a question of that. Think how you answered. All three describe your image."

"What was I supposed to say? What else is there?"

"Some people say, 'I'm a wife. I'm a mother. I'm a daughter.' In all three answers you did not connect yourself with a personal relationship—and that usually indicates you may have an identity problem. And some of our work here will be to find out why."

Dena felt alarmed. Identity problem?

"It is just something to think about. Right now let's talk about your immediate problems. You say you're not sleeping well."

"No, I'm not. But let's go back to the other thing. That test, or whatever it was, is dead wrong. I know exactly who I am. I always knew exactly what I wanted and what I wanted to be. I already told Dr. O'Malley that once."

"As I said, it's not a test," Diggers said. "It's just a question."

As THE weeks passed, Dena continued working at a breakneck pace, and almost every night J.C. had her going from one party to another. Lately she was having a hard time trying to keep up, and her stomach was beginning to hurt again. She needed a short rest. She had to get away, go somewhere far off the beaten path.

But where? Where could she go without running into any of J.C.'s crowd? Then it came to her. Sookie.

As DENA stepped off the plane in Selma, a gush of hot, almost tropical heat engulfed her. The sun was blinding, but she soon saw an excited Sookie waiting for her. As they walked to the car, Sookie said, "Now, Dena, as you asked, not a soul knows you are coming for the weekend, except Earle, and Toncie—she works for us—and the children have been instructed not to say a word. So I promise you, you are going to be left alone. Tomorrow I'm making Earle go down to the club, and you and I will just laze around by the pool, or you can sleep."

"Is it always this hot?"

"Honey, this is nothing. Wait until July and August." They got into an enormous blue Lincoln Town Car.

About twenty minutes after leaving the airport, Sookie turned down a road that seemed to run right through the middle of a pecan grove.

Dena said, "Are those cows out there?"

"I told you I lived out in the suburbs, honey. We're just old Alabama hillbillies."

After about five minutes of pecan groves Dena saw a huge house and suddenly realized that the road they had been driving on was Sookie's driveway. Sookie pulled up and said, "Here we are." Dena looked up at the rambling two-story white-columned building.

"Good Lord, Sookie, it looks like a governor's mansion."

Sookie dismissed it with a wave. "Oh, honey, it's not that big."

They got out of the car, and a woman in a white uniform came out. "Dena, this is Toncie."

Toncie beamed from ear to ear. "I know who you are, and I haven't said a word. No, ma'am."

"Thank you."

They stepped into a vast entry hall with a grand staircase leading up to the second floor. Sookie said, "Where's my brood? They are so excited you are coming, I almost had to sedate them."

At this point three little redheaded girls—all starched and pressed, with big bows in their hair—appeared at the top of the landing, peering through the railing at Dena.

"Well, you might as well get it over with, Dena." Sookie called up, "All right, girls, come on down, but don't run."

The three girls were down the stairs like a shot and stood staring up at Dena in awe. Sookie said, "This is Dee Dee, this is Ce Ce, and this is the baby, Lenore, but we call her Le Le. Girls, this is your aunt Dena."

Dena looked down at them. "Well, hello, girls. May I shake your hands?"

The two oldest were delighted, and they giggled as if shaking hands were the funniest thing they had ever done. The smallest walked over and hugged Dena's leg. Then all three began babbling and tugging at her. "Come on and see our room," they said, and tried to pull her up the stairs. Le Le had attached both hands to Dena's belt.

"All right, girls," Sookie said, "that's enough. She'll go upstairs later. Let go of her."

They disappeared with Toncie.

Off the kitchen in the back of the house was a long, screened-in brick patio filled with white wicker furniture and floral pillows. Sookie said, "During the summer we just practically live out here. It's so nice and cool at night." They walked across a courtyard with what seemed like an Olympic pool to where Dena would be staying—a charming, smaller version of the main house, decorated in gentle pastels and filled with fresh flowers. The minute Dena walked in, Sookie started to apologize. "It's not much, but I thought it would be quieter out here."

"Sookie, all I ever see is hotel rooms. This is great."

Sookie brightened. "Well, good. Now I'm going to drag myself away, like I promised, so you can take a nap or watch TV . . . or whatever. I thought we'd eat dinner around seven. Is that too early?"

"No. That's fine."

Sookie left, saying, "Rest now."

Dena unpacked and went out on her screened-in patio. She turned on the overhead fan and lay down. She closed her eyes, and before she knew it, she was in a deep sleep.

Dena did not wake up until eleven o'clock the next morning. She stumbled into the living room and smelled fresh coffee. A note was on her coffeemaker: "Come over when you wake up . . . or when you feel like it. Love, Sookie."

After an hour Dena got dressed and headed over to the big house. Sookie was in the kitchen. "Sookie, I'm sorry I missed dinner."

"Well, thank heavens you are alive. I could see the headlines: 'Dead Celebrity Found in the Pooles' Pool House'!"

"No, I'm not dead, but I swear I feel drugged."

Sookie went over to the refrigerator and pulled out a frosty glass of iced tea and handed it to Dena. Then, picking up her own glass, she opened the door to the back patio and walked out. They sat by the pool under the canopy. Dena said, "Everything is so green."

Sookie seemed surprised. "It is?"

"Yes. And it's so quiet here. You're lucky to have lived in one place all your life, Sookie. I'll bet you know everybody here."

"I guess between the Simmonses, the Krackenberrys, and the Pooles, we're probably related to everybody in town."

"Did you go to the same grammar school and high school?"

"I had no choice." Sookie took a sip of her tea.

"How great. And in high school were you a cheerleader or majorette or something?"

Sookie looked at Dena in horror. "Dena, surely you don't think I was ever a majorette. A cheerleader, yes, but a majorette? There was never a Kappa that was a majorette, Dena."

"Well, I don't know. What's the difference?"

"If you don't know, I'm certainly not going to tell you. Honestly, Dena, sometimes I wonder where you've been all your life."

Toncie came out with more iced tea. "Those girls are having a jumping-up-and-down fit to get out here, Mrs. Poole."

They looked up at the second story of the house. In the window were little faces staring at them longingly.

"Oh, Sookie, let them come down. Don't make them stay inside."

"All right, if you say so." Sookie raised her arm and announced to Toncie, "Release the prisoners. Free all the infidels at once."

A minute later the three girls, dressed in matching bright pink-and-white polka-dot bathing suits, came running and screaming out the back door, headed straight for Dena.

She spent the day at the pool with Sookie and her girls, and it was not until Dena had been upstairs in the girls' room and had been introduced to seven hamsters by name, looked at every doll, every dress, and every pair of shoes that Dee Dee, Ce Ce, and Le Le finally calmed down and went to sleep. All three passed out in one bed, exhausted.

It was dark out when Sookie and Dena went back downstairs so they could relax. Dena was unwinding, and the feeling was pleasant. "Sookie, tell me about your life down here."

"My life? It's just a plain old normal life. You're the one who hobnobs with the stars. We are just plain old people. Dull, dull, dull."

"No, really, tell me, what do you do?"

"We do the same old thing just about every day, year in and year out. Dinner at the club once a week, church every Sunday, and brunch with Mother every Sunday. That's what my life has been, just the same old thing from the day I was born."

A wave of sadness swept over Dena. Sookie had no idea how lucky she was.

Looking Through Windows

❀

DENA woke with tears running down her face. She wondered what that was all about. Then she remembered her dream, that same old dream that had popped up again. She would be on a merry-go-round and see a white house but lose sight of it as she went around. Then it would come to her that her mother was dying and needed her. She would rush to the phone and try to call her, but she would dial the wrong number over and over. Then she would start to panic and wake up crying, lost and helpless. That was not a feeling she could understand. Ask any man who had ever loved her. She had always taken care of herself, didn't want to need anybody, didn't want anybody to need her.

She was no good at love, and she knew it. Last week she had to tell J.C. that she couldn't see him anymore. Her job was getting harder and harder, and J.C. had become more and more demanding. So she told him it was best that he find someone else.

J.C. got the picture and gave up. When he hugged her good-bye and held her for a long time, it made Dena feel even worse. She did not like displays of emotion or affection. They always made her feel embarrassed and uncomfortable. Her mother had never really been affectionate with her, not like Dena had wanted. Her mother had been so beautiful, but there was something about her that was far away, removed, and even when Dena was a small child, it frightened her. As a little girl, she used to crawl into her mother's lap and take her face and look into it, trying to see what was the matter. She would ask over and over. Her mother would look at her and smile and say, "Nothing, darling," but Dena knew something was wrong.

In her personal life Dena did not like to get too close to people or have them get too close to her. She was much more comfortable speaking to a group of five thousand behind a lectern than talking with one person alone. When someone tried to hang on to her, it made her feel claustrophobic.

Dena made a promise to herself: Never get involved again.

AT HER next session with Dr. Diggers, Dena figured she might as well get something for her money.

"Let me ask you something, Dr. Diggers. Is it normal for people to keep having the same dream all the time?"

Dr. Diggers thought, This is the first real question Dena has asked. "Yes. Why?"

"I was just wondering. I keep having the same stupid dream."

"How long have you been having this dream?"

"Oh, I don't know. Since I was a child. It's always pretty much the same. I see this house, and it has a merry-go-round in the front yard, or sometimes in the backyard, but sometimes it's *in* the house, and I want to go in, but I can't find the door."

"Can you see yourself in the dream?"

"No. I just know that it's me, but I don't see myself. Anyhow, I just wonder what the stupid thing means."

"I wonder if you wonder," Dr. Diggers said.

Dena said, "What is that supposed to mean?"

"I think on some level you know you just don't want to look at it. Now, for the hundredth time, what was your mother like?"

Dena rolled her eyes. "Oh . . . I don't know."

"Try. Was she a loving mother? Mean? What was your impression of her?"

Dena started to tap her foot irritably. "I've told you. She was just a mother—two eyes, two ears. What was yours like?"

"My interview. Do you think maybe you left something unsaid before she died?"

Dena moaned. "I am not some weak, damaged little person unable to function. I am just under a lot of pressure at work right now, and it has nothing to do with any deep-seated secrets locked away in my psyche, and you didn't answer my question."

"What question?"

"What was *your* mother like?"

"She had fourteen ears and twelve legs and was polka-dotted. You know, Dena, you are harder than a hickory nut to crack, but I will. You can bat those big blue eyes at me all you want; I'm *not* giving up. You have finally met your match."

Dena laughed. She liked Dr. Diggers in spite of herself. "Do any of you psychiatrists ever get shot?"

"Oh, yes. I have to frisk my patients all the time."

Later, when she was leaving, Dr. Diggers went with her to the door. As Dena was putting on her coat, she said, "By the way, I broke up with J.C."

Dr. Diggers said, "Oh."

"Yes. He was a nice guy, but he got too serious."

DENA'S lunch with Howard Kingsley had become a weekly event. They discussed theater and books and rarely talked about the news business anymore. But as the weeks went by, she began to see a weariness that she had not seen before. One day, as they were having their coffee, he said, "Dena, you know what's wrong with the new bunch taking over? There's not an ounce of compassion in the whole lot. They don't like people." He looked into his cup. "And they don't have any loyalty except to themselves. You can't have compassion unless you have a certain loyalty to the human race."

Dena nodded in agreement but felt like a fraud. Howard had just described her to a tee. She didn't know if she particularly liked people, and as far as loyalty was concerned, she had no idea what she could be loyal to other than herself.

She went home that night and thought about what Howard had said. She did not feel connected to anything. Or anybody. She felt as if everybody else had come into the world with a set of instructions about how to live and someone had forgotten to give them to her. She had no clue what she was supposed to feel, so she had spent her life faking at being a human being, with no idea how other people felt. What was it like to really love someone? To really fit in or belong somewhere? She was quick and a good mimic, so she learned at an early age to give the impression of a normal, happy girl, but inside she had always been lonely.

As a child, she had spent hours looking in windows at families— from trains, buses—seeing the people inside who looked so happy and content, longing to get inside but not knowing how to do it. Was she the only one to feel alone out there in the world? She had been flying blind all her life, and suddenly she had started to hit the wall. She sat drinking red wine and thinking. What was the matter with her? What had gone wrong?

DENA was now making more money than she knew what to do with, and one of the first things she did was to move to a new apartment in Gramercy Park, where she had always wanted to live. She had been out of town covering the bicentennial in Washington and in Philadelphia and had not had a chance to finish decorating. After living in her new apartment for six weeks, she still had not hung her pictures on the living-room wall, and so she asked a studio set designer, Michael Zanella, to come over on Friday night to help her. He was now trying to place a large mirror in the middle of the wall. Dena was eating a sandwich, guiding him, when the phone rang. Before answering, she told Michael, "A little more to the left. . . . Hello," she said, not taking her eyes off the wall.

"Dena? Uh . . . . Miss Nordstrom?"

"Yes."

"It's Gerry O'Malley. Dr. O'Malley."

After all these months? "Oh, yes, Doctor. How are you?"

"Fine," he said. "How are you doing?"

"Just fine, Doctor." She made an okay gesture to Michael. "What can I do for you?"

"Well, there is something I need to ask you. But before I do, I think I owe it to you to be completely up-front. I think it's only fair that you know exactly how I feel before you make a decision."

"Uh-huh," Dena said, only half listening. She walked over and touched the next picture and pointed to where she wanted it.

"You know, all my life I have heard that I would meet someone somewhere, and no matter how well I knew them or how much or little time we had spent together, that person would just be *it* for me. And I have known for a long time that you are that person for me. And the truth is, I am, well, totally and completely mad about you. And have been from the first time you came into my office."

"Oh?" Dena said.

"I know this call must seem out of the blue, but I have waited to give you some time. I wanted to call sooner. . . . Would you have dinner with me sometime?"

Dena did not answer.

"You must think this is really bizarre of me to put you on the spot like this . . . or if you are involved with someone else—"

"Dr. O'Malley," Dena said, "can I call you back in a few minutes? I have someone here, and—"

"Oh. Oh, I'm sorry. Sure."

Dena hung up, not really believing what she had heard. It *was* so out of the blue, it was bizarre. Maybe he was crazy or drunk or kidding or something. She did not know what to think, so she forgot about it for the moment and kept on with the picture hanging.

Gerry, on the other hand, was shaken. He had just made the most important phone call of his life, and he had forgotten to give her his home phone number. He was too embarrassed to call back and hoped she would look it up. But she did not call back.

A week after his call Gerry came in late one night and called his exchange for his messages. There was one from Dena: "So—you call and tell me you're crazy about me, and then I don't hear from you?" He stood still in shock. At least she was still speaking to him; that was something. But what in the world did that message mean? He was a psychiatrist, and even he didn't know.

As for Dena, she had called the way she usually did when it came to something personal. She had come in from having drinks with a boring PR man and had called on a whim. It didn't mean anyth~~

On another impulse Dena decided to have a few pe~~
her new apartment for cocktails on Sunday. Although s~~

say so, it was her birthday, a day she would have forgotten if Norma and Macky and Aunt Elner hadn't sent her birthday cards, as always.

She had invited Ira Wallace and his wife. She liked Mrs. Wallace; she was a lovely lady. She also invited her agent, Sandy, and his wife, and a few others, including Gerry O'Malley.

When Sunday came around, Gerry was a nervous wreck. He had changed ties five times and wished he had not gotten his hair cut. But Dena made him feel welcome and acted as if he had never called and made a fool out of himself. He managed to get through the party without doing anything worse than crossing his legs and kicking a glass of Chardonnay off the coffee table.

Dena, on the other hand, looked at him several times when he didn't know it and decided he was not bad-looking. She needed somebody she could take places when a date was required. Someone nice, not in the business. Maybe she would give him a try.

DR. DIGGERS knew that Dena had been out with Gerry. However, Dena had said nothing about it. But one day as Dr. Diggers went down the hall with her to the door, Dena said offhandedly, "Oh, by the way, did I tell you that Dr. O'Malley called me?"

"No," Dr. Diggers said. "I don't believe you mentioned it."

Dena got her coat from the closet. "Anyhow, I went out with him a couple of times, but he doesn't say much of anything. All he does is sit there and stare at me and drop things."

Oh, dear.

Dena put on her coat. "Do you know anything about him?"

"All I can tell you is he is extremely well thought of, personally and professionally."

"Oh, I'm sure he's a great guy and all. He's cute, but I guess just not my type. You know, he's . . . Well, he's sort of dull."

"Dull? Gerry O'Malley?"

"At least he is to me. He doesn't even watch television."

"I see."

After Dena left, Dr. Diggers wondered how long it would be before she would be hearing from Gerry.

It was three weeks and one day. Dena had turned down date after date with Gerry, and he was baffled. "I know you can't get in the middle of this, but she seemed to like me. We had dinner, went to a couple of shows, but all of a sudden she stopped seeing me, and I don't understand what happened. I was a gentleman. I didn't push myself on her. I let her do most of the talking. I just don't get it."

Diggers listened to him go on and on for another twenty minutes. Finally she had to put him out of his misery. There was no other way. "Gerry, she thinks you're dull."

Gerry was taken aback. "Dull?"

"Dull. The only reason I'm telling you this is because she mentioned it out of session, so I'm not betraying patient-doctor privilege. But there it is."

"That's all she said?"

"Gerry, she doesn't know you. You are the last person I would call dull. Does she know anything about you at all?"

"No, not much. But what am I going to do? Give her a résumé?"

"You're one of the funniest, most interesting people I know. Tell her about yourself. Now get with it, boy."

Gerry hung up the phone and racked his brain. He put his jacket on and his lucky red baseball cap. The first thing he was going to do was buy a television set.

HE DID not give up asking Dena out. A few times she said yes and then canceled at the last minute. One night Gerry invited her to a concert at Carnegie Hall and said rather insistently, uncharacteristically, "Dena, promise me you won't back out. These tickets were almost impossible to come by. *Please,* give me your word."

Dena looked through her appointment book. She hated to be pinned down. "When is it again?"

"Next Friday."

"I have a cocktail party at five. I'll have to meet you there."

"All right. Carnegie Hall. At eight."

"Okay. Okay, I'm writing it down."

On Friday at about seven forty Dena looked at her watch and

groaned. Late already. She knew she shouldn't have made this date. He was there waiting for her, and she was all the way downtown.

By the time her cab made it through the theater district and up to Carnegie Hall, it was ten after eight. Everybody had already gone in except for a young man standing with a bouquet. She pulled the big brass handle of the glass door and walked into the lobby. The man with the roses ran after her. "Miss Nordstrom? I am supposed to take you to your seat."

Dena said, "Oh," and followed him to the left, down the stairs into a small auditorium. He held the door open. "Right this way." The auditorium was empty, but he did not give her a chance to say anything. He walked her down the aisle, seated her in the fourth row center, handed her the roses and a program, and was gone.

The stage was empty except for a piano, a bass, and a set of drums. She looked around. She must be in the wrong place. She glanced at the program and then read more intently: "A SPECIAL CONCERT FOR MISS DENA NORDSTROM, PERFORMED BY G. O'MALLEY & CO., WITH HIGH HOPES OF FAVORABLY IMPRESSING THE LADY WITH DR. O'MALLEY'S UNDYING DEVOTION."

At that moment the lights on the stage came up, and Gerry O'Malley walked out, dressed in black tie, with two other tuxedoed men. He bowed and sat down at the piano.

After a moment he nodded, and the trio started to play an old Lerner and Lane tune that said exactly what he had been unable to say. And he sang it right to her in an astonishingly good voice:

> *"You're like Paris in April and May*
> *You're New York on a silvery day*
> *A Swiss alp as the sun grows fainter*
> *You're Loch Lomond when Autumn is the painter*
> *You're moonlight on a night in Capri*
> *And Cape Cod looking out at the sea*
> *You're all places that leave me breathless*
> *And no wonder*
> *You're all the world to me."*

Dena, horrified, wanted to drop through the floor. Among the thousands of things she did not know about Gerry O'Malley was that he had worked his way through college with his own jazz combo, playing at parties. As he continued to play every love song he knew and a few really funny ones with lyrics she suspected were his, Dena had no choice but to smile. She also wanted to run. He was either completely off his rocker or else he thought she could get him on TV. Whichever it was, it was very embarrassing, but after a while she began to relax and enjoy herself.

When it was over, she stood and applauded, then walked to the stage and handed him the roses. He came down and said, "Well?"

He stood there smiling and waiting, and she said, "Well, wow! You really can play. Great! What can I say?" He introduced the other musicians to her, and she told them how much she had enjoyed the concert. Then they said good-bye.

Gerry took Dena to dinner next door at the Russian Tea Room. He had heard that it was a place show-business people liked. "I just thought this might be a way for you to get to know me a little better—and give you a better idea of how I feel about you."

"Gerry, that was very sweet of you. And don't think I didn't enjoy it and appreciate it. But don't you think this is all a little sudden? I'm really not ready for any kind of serious relationship. My job takes up most of my time."

"Dena, you can have all the time in the world, all the time you need. I'm here. If it's one year or five years, whenever you are ready. All I want you to know is that I'm in love with you."

"Are you serious?"

"Absolutely," Gerry said. "But listen: Just because I know that you are the one for me, I may not be the one for you. All I'm asking for is a chance."

At home later on, Dena thought about the evening. She had certainly heard many lines from many men, but this one was unique. She had to give him that. But he'd get over it. They always did. She'd heard that J.C. was already engaged to a stewardess. Anyway, she didn't have time to get involved with anyone, much less a piano-playing shrink who thought he was in love with her. If she was going to stay on top of her career, she had to make sure she was irreplaceable, strike while the iron was hot—and right now she was hot. She had just been on the cover of *TV Guide,* and there was talk of an Emmy.

Tour

❦

HOUSTON, TEXAS   FEBRUARY 1976

DENA had been in seventeen cities in seventeen days on a twenty-eight-day promotion tour for the network. Because of her increasing popularity, they had decided that she was the perfect person to send across the country to their local affiliates. The publicity department filled almost every minute of her time in each town with television, radio, and newspaper interviews, along with luncheon speeches and other personal appearances. Before she flew on to the next city, she'd try to get three or four hours' sleep, and then she would start all over again the next day.

Thank goodness they had sent their top publicist, Jonni Hartman, with her. Jonni was a master at getting Dena from one place to another. Dena had been doing a terrific job charming everyone, until Pittsburgh, when her stomach began to hurt again. She tried to drive herself through it by living on Maalox and Tums.

Right after she finished speaking at a big benefit dinner in Houston honoring the great heart surgeon Dr. Michael E. DeBakey, she and Jonni had to rush upstairs in the hotel, quickly change clothes, and leave immediately for the airport to catch a ten forty-five plane to Dallas. They had dragged their luggage halfway through the hotel lobby when the pain hit Dena so hard that she had to stop. Jonni caught her just before she passed out cold.

When she came to, she was in a hospital emergency room, with doctors examining her. After a few minutes, like a parting of the waters, the doctors and nurses stepped aside as Dr. Michael DeBakey, still in his tux from dinner, walked in and took over.

He smiled and talked to Dena as he examined her. "Well, young lady, it looks like you have decided to stay with us for a while. You know, you were a hit at the banquet. You had quite a few doctors who volunteered to take your case, but I said, 'No luck, fellows. She came here in my honor, so I'm the one who gets her.' How long have you had trouble with your stomach?"

"Not long," Dena lied.

He continued to check her out thoroughly, then took her hand. "You're going to live. We're going to take a little blood; then we're going to take you upstairs and put you to bed. Okay? I'll stop in and see you in the morning."

The next day Dena was still asleep when Dr. DeBakey looked in. Jonni, tired and frazzled after a night in the waiting room, said, "Doctor, is she all right? It wasn't a heart attack, was it?"

"No, Miss Hartman. Her heart is fine. She had a severe attack of gastroenteritis—inflammation of the stomach lining—probably brought on by stress."

"Thank goodness it happened here, Doctor. And I hate to bother you, but I need to know how long it will be before she might be back on her feet. I don't care, but the head of network publicity has already called to see when she'll be able to continue her tour."

Dr. DeBakey pointed to the paper Jonni was holding. "Is that Dena's schedule?"

"Yes."

DeBakey put on his glasses and studied it.

Jonni said, "You can see she has quite a few cities coming up."

"Oh, yes, I can see that. Now, just who wants this information?"

"It's my boss. Mr. Andy Brill."

"Do you have his number? I'll get back to the gentleman."

"Oh, thank you. That would be great."

DeBakey, a tall, thin man, walked down the hall, went into his private office, and handed his secretary, Sylvia, the phone number. "Get this guy on the phone for me, will you?" When she buzzed, he picked up. "Mr. Brill, this is Dr. DeBakey in Houston. I understand you are anxious to have a report on Miss Nordstrom's condition."

"That's right. We need to have some idea when she might be able to pick up her schedule. People are screaming all over the country. Do you think she can get back by, say, Tuesday?"

"Let me ask you a question, Mr. Brill. Are you people trying to kill her? Miss Hartman showed me her schedule. How could you expect anyone to keep going at that pace?"

"Yeah, well, I don't think you understand. This thing has been booked for over six months. We've got commitments here."

"Mr. Brill, I don't think *you* understand. She's suffering from serious stomach distress brought on by exhaustion and stress."

"What are you saying?"

"I'm saying that as long as this girl is my patient, she is not leaving the hospital for at least two weeks. You can expect her back at work in maybe a month. If she does go back any sooner, and if anything happens to her health as a result, I'm perfectly prepared to go on record that your network was forewarned."

"Forewarned? We can't just cancel. This is going to cost us—"

DeBakey interrupted. "If you have any other questions, please feel free to call my office—collect—at any time."

AFTER Dena had been in the hospital for a few days, she began to feel better and was eager to get back on tour. Dr. DeBakey had come to see her every afternoon, and when he came in today, she explained to him why he had to let her out.

He took her hand. "Honey, I know you are disappointed you can't go back to work. You feel a little better, so you think you're ready to get up and start running again. I've heard it from my patients more times than I can tell you, but let me tell you something: *Nothing* is worth ruining your health. Nothing in the world is really important except life and death, and that's it."

Dena did not give up. "I understand that, and I will take it easy from now on, but I made a *commitment* to the network."

He smiled. "Those people in New York may try to make you

think they can't do without you, but they can. Take some advice from an old man. No amount of success is worth pushing yourself like you are doing. I'm not trying to scare you, but if you keep on going like you have been, you won't live another five years. This flare-up is a warning that your body just cannot go on at this pace. Now, I called your family, and Mr. and Mrs. Macky Warren have already made arrangements to come here on Thursday the twelfth and take you home."

Dena was alarmed. "What?"

"Mrs. Warren has instructions as to what you can eat."

"Dr. DeBakey, you don't understand. I don't even know these people. I mean, not well. We are related . . . but I can't go home with them. I can take care of myself."

"No, you can't. You are going to need someone to prepare all your meals, keep people away from you, not let you use the phone. You have to rest."

"Why can't I rest in New York?"

"I don't want you anywhere near New York for at least three weeks. It's not you— It's those people you work for I don't trust."

And so on Thursday afternoon Dena found herself wrapped in a blanket, lying in the back seat of a brown-and-tan Oldsmobile, on her way to Elmwood Springs, Missouri, while Norma Warren happily chatted nonstop through the entire state of Texas and on into Missouri about people Dena did not know, or care to know, for that matter. She was too busy plotting her escape.

THAT first morning in Elmwood Springs, Dena woke up in a strange room, with a roly-poly gray-haired woman sitting in a chair across the room staring at her. The old lady said, "I know you were glad to get out of that old hospital, weren't you, honey?"

Dena managed a weak, "Yes," wondering who this was.

"Well, we are sure glad you are home where you belong. I kept saying to Norma, 'When is Baby Girl getting out of that hospital and coming home?' I don't envy anybody in the hospital. Did I tell you about the time Norma carried me up there for a checkup?"

"No," Dena said.

"That bed they had me in could do anything you wanted it to—go up and down, flat or tilted. Everything but dance the polka and kiss you good night. When they had me there, they looked at me up and down, every which way, and after they finished, I said to the doctor, 'You're just like that TV show *Star Trek.*' 'How so?' he asked. I said, 'Honey, you've been places where no man has dared to go.' "

Norma came into the room with a tray. "Good morning."

"I was telling Baby Girl about my hospital stay, how they checked me out, and how all my numbers looked good. Whatever that meant. But it finally calmed Norma down, didn't it, Norma?"

Norma said begrudgingly, "Yes, but everybody needs a checkup once in their life." She placed Dena's tray in front of her. "Here, honey. I want you to try and eat this."

Dena sat up and looked at a bowl of milk with a piece of toast floating in it. Norma went over and opened the windows, saying, "Seriously, Aunt Elner, you could be watering your sweet peas one minute and the next topple over with a stroke. You can make fun of me, but you never know from one minute to the next."

"All the more reason to enjoy every one of them. It tells us that in the Bible. *Can any of you by worrying add a single hour to your span of life?* Luke twelve: twenty-five."

"Well, that's fine for Luke," Norma said. "He didn't have you and Macky driving him crazy. Do you want some iced tea?"

Dena shook her head. Aunt Elner held her glass up. "I'll take some more while you're up." She had the sweet smile of a child.

After Norma left the room, Aunt Elner said, "That girl worries herself into a frazzle over everything. If I don't call her by seven a.m., she has me dead and buried. I said to her, 'Norma, when I finally do go, it's gonna be anticlimactic. You won't even be surprised, you've been practicing for so many years.' "

Norma came back, and Aunt Elner said, "Are you going to take Baby Girl out to eat while she's here?"

"Of course. She can go anywhere she wants, but I have to watch her diet. I have specific instructions."

"You know that catfish place closed."

"That didn't last long, did it?"

"No," said Aunt Elner. "But I told Verbena, 'They can stick a neon catfish up outside the door, but everybody knows that's where the mortuary used to be. Nobody's gonna want to eat fish in a place where they came to see their relatives laid out.'"

Dena could not believe what she was hearing.

But Aunt Elner went on. "Baby Girl, since you were last here, Hatcher's mortuary moved, and now they put in a new, drive-through funeral home."

"Sorry?" asked Dena, who was trying, in self-defense, to eat.

"They have a drive-by window to view the remains," Norma put in. "It's some lamebrained idea James Hatcher came up with."

Aunt Elner said, "Instead of ordering a burger and fries, you look at a dead relative. No, I'll just get myself cremated, thank you. I don't care a thing about wasting money on a coffin that you're only gonna use once. I'd rather spend my money over at the mall."

"Uncle Will already bought a burial policy for you, Aunt Elner."

"I know he did, but I'd rather have the money now. Do you think they'd give it to me, or do I have to die first?"

"Aunt Elner, the subject of death gives me the willies, and I am sure Baby Girl does not want to sit here and listen to you talking about getting yourself burned up."

"Oh, Norma, you don't burn up. It says so in the brochure. It's like looking into the sun. You feel the bright light, and then you just disappear." She snapped her fingers. "Just like that. And you still get a headstone over at the cemetery, so you can come and decorate me every Easter. Don't worry about that." Aunt Elner put down her iced tea. "Well, guess I better get on home. I just wanted to come over and cheer you up." She patted Dena on the hand. "I'll come back tomorrow. Maybe I'll even bring you my cremation brochures."

"Come on, Aunt Elner," Norma said. "Let's let her rest now."

"Bye, honey."

When the door closed, Dena thought, I have to get out of here.

THE SECOND MORNING, DENA had another visitor. At eight o'clock Dr. Gerry O'Malley arrived at the front door dressed as a fifteenth-century troubadour, complete with pink tights and a plumed hat, and carrying a dozen red roses and a mandolin.

Macky came to the door. "Hi. Can I help you?"

Gerry felt like a complete fool, but he was determined to go through with it. "Mr. Warren, I am a friend of Dena's, and I wonder if I could see her for just a few minutes."

"She's upstairs. Can I tell her who—or what—is here?"

"Uh, well . . . It's sort of a Valentine's thing. A surprise."

"Okay. Wait just a second. I'll see if I can get her down here."

As Macky passed Norma, he said under his breath, "You're *not* going to believe what's out on the porch."

Dena was still sound asleep when Macky knocked. "Baby Girl, there is somebody downstairs to see you."

Dena sat up in bed, startled. "Who?"

"He said it's a surprise. He has something for you."

"Oh. Can you just get it for me?"

"No, I don't think so. I think you need to get it yourself."

Dena put on her robe, came downstairs, and went to the door. She did not see anybody at first, but she looked down and saw roses spread out on the porch floor in a big heart-shaped design, with a card in the middle. As soon as she walked out the door, she heard music. She saw Gerry O'Malley standing in the yard dressed in some idiotic costume, playing a mandolin and singing something about love. She could not believe her eyes.

After his song he took off his hat and bowed and drove off, leaving her standing, still in a sleepy daze, trying to figure out what Gerry O'Malley was doing in Elmwood Springs, Missouri, at eight o'clock in the morning. Or was she having some sort of hallucination? She reached down and picked up the card and read it: "No pressure. Just know I adore you! Happy Valentine's Day. Love, Gerry."

She picked up the roses and went back inside. Norma poked her head around the kitchen corner. "Oh, aren't those flowers beautiful! I'll put them in a vase, and you can have them in your room. Well, wasn't your friend nice to bring you these. He seemed like a very nice person." Norma was just dying to know who he was but did not ask.

Dena started back upstairs. "He's nice, but I'm beginning to think he's a little crazy or something."

GERRY was on the road headed back to the Kansas City airport and still a little shaky, when, going ten miles over the speed limit, he passed a Missouri highway trooper.

The trooper slugged down the last of his coffee, turned on his siren, and started after the offending driver.

Twenty minutes later the trooper stood and watched as the man drove away. He thought, I sure would have loved to have taken him in; the boys would never have believed it. He got back in his patrol car and jotted down his report: "February 14, 8:36 a.m. Detained white male. Lovesick fifteenth-century troubadour in pink tights, pantaloons, and doublet." He wondered how to spell doublet, crossed it out, and added, "Hat with plume, and shoes that curled up on the end with tiny bells. First offense. Let off with warning."

BY THURSDAY morning Dena had been in Elmwood Springs almost a week. For the first time, Norma let her come downstairs to eat breakfast. When Norma saw Dena, she said, "Good morning. Come on in and sit down. I am so glad to finally see some color back in those cheeks. What would you like—pancakes, waffles, or French toast? I'm making Macky pancakes, but you can have whatever your little heart desires."

"I'll take pancakes, too. Where is Macky?"

"He's out in the yard fly-fishing."

"Do you have a lake or pond or something?"

"No. He's just out there practicing, and I warn you, as soon as you even look like you might be feeling better, he's gonna start pestering you to go fishing with him. But you don't have to go. Just remember that. Uh-oh. Here he is."

Macky was coming in the back door, happy to see Dena. "Well, hey, look who's up."

"I've never slept so much in my entire life."

"Well, you needed it, Baby Girl," Macky said. "Maybe, if you're up to it, Saturday we can take a run out to the river."

"Macky, she does not want to go. Do you?"

Dena was caught. "Oh, I wouldn't mind. It's just that I don't know anything about fishing."

Macky's face lit up. "I can give you a few pointers. When you feel like it, come to the store, and we can pick out a few things."

"Macky, she does *not* want to spend five hours looking at fishing lures. Do you, Baby Girl?"

They both looked at Dena.

"Well . . . I don't mind. That sounds interesting."

"Come on down this afternoon if you feel like it."

"She can't come this afternoon."

"Why not?"

"Because I promised Aunt Elner to bring her over for a visit." Norma looked at Dena. "You don't mind, do you, Baby Girl?"

THAT afternoon Dena found herself on Aunt Elner's sunporch. When Aunt Elner handed Dena and Norma glasses of iced tea, Norma looked at the tea, an unusual shade of brown, dark at the top and lighter at the bottom. "What kind of tea is this?"

"It's instant, but it's all I had. I used my last tea bag this morning. I've had that jar for a couple of years, or maybe five, but I don't guess it will poison us." She laughed. "How are you doing, Baby Girl? Are you getting a chance to rest up?"

"Oh, yes."

Norma took a sip of tea and tried not to make a face. She caught Dena's eye and gestured to her not to drink hers.

"Nobody's been bothering you, have they?" asked Aunt Elner.

Dena put her glass down. "No, they really haven't."

"And they better not," said Norma. "That's all I can say, or they will have Mr. Macky Warren to answer to. But I tell you, Aunt

Elner, you have never seen people act so silly in your entire life. If I've had one phone call, I had a hundred, wanting Dena to do this or to do that. Even Mary Grace called all the way from St. Louis, wanting her to come up to the phone company and give a talk."

"You remember my niece Mary Grace, don't you, Baby Girl?" Aunt Elner said.

"No, I don't think I ever met her." Dena took the opportunity to ask a question. "Ah . . . are you my aunt, too? How are we related? I'm a little confused."

Norma answered, "Your grandmother, Gerta Nordstrom, was Aunt Elner's sister, so that makes her your great-aunt. Her other sister, Zela, was my mother, so that makes her my aunt . . . so you and I are second cousins on your father's side."

"What is Macky, then?" Aunt Elner wondered. "My nephew?"

"No, honey, he is not related to you by blood. He is your— I guess he's your nephew by marriage. Here, this will make it easier for you, Baby Girl: Your daddy, Gene, was my first cousin, so you must be my second cousin, and Macky is your second cousin by marriage. That's right, isn't it? Or maybe you're my third cousin. Isn't that right, Aunt Elner?"

"Oh, Lord, honey, I don't know anymore."

"Well, Gene's mother was my aunt Gerta so . . . Wait a minute. Aunt Elner, you must be my great-aunt."

At this point Dena was wondering how fast she could get out of there and back to New York.

After they got back to Norma's, Dena said casually, "You know, I think I really would like to see those fishing things. Is the hardware store hard to find?"

Norma laughed. "No. Downtown is only a block. You can't miss it. It's right past the flower shop. Do you want me to drive you?"

"No. I'll walk, thanks."

The real reason Dena wanted to go downtown was not to look at fishing lures. She wanted to get to a phone. As soon as she turned the corner, she went into the Rexall drugstore and called her agent.

"Get me out of here," she said to Sandy Cooper.

"What? You don't have to go back to work for two weeks."

"I don't care. Just get me out of here now."

When she hung up and came out of the booth, several people were waiting to say hello to her and to say how glad they were to see her home. In a moment she walked by a place that seemed vaguely familiar. It was the bakery they said her grandparents used to own, still called Nordstrom's Swedish Bakery. She peered inside, but nothing looked familiar. It was odd to walk down the street; people she had never seen before in her life stopped and told her stories about her grandparents and father. Finally, what seemed like hours later, she reached the hardware store.

Soon Macky had shown her all his fishing flies and explained each one by name. She said, "Macky, did you know my father?"

He nodded. "Very well. And your grandparents. Fine people."

She realized that even though everybody in town had wanted to tell her about her father or grandparents or talk about seeing her when she was little, no one mentioned her mother. She suddenly began to wonder what it was that had caused her mother to move away. What had happened?

The next morning at breakfast Dena said, "Norma, what did you know about my mother?"

Norma was caught off guard for a moment. "Well, Baby Girl, not much. What would you like to know?"

"Oh, what she was like when she was here, things like that."

Norma put a plate in the dishwasher and closed it and sat down across from Dena. "Well, she wasn't here all that long, and she stayed mostly to herself. I do remember we would go up to Aunt Gerta's house to see you, and she was always so proud of you."

"Did you like her?"

"Oh, yes, very much. But don't forget I was still in high school and didn't get to know her all that well. Aunt Elner could probably tell you more than I could."

Right after breakfast they were on Aunt Elner's sunporch again.

"Aunt Elner, I wonder what you remember about my mother."

Norma said, "I've told Baby Girl everything I remember."

"Well, honey, let me sit here and tax my memory. Lord, that was a piece ago, wasn't it? But I remember the first day she came here. You were just a tiny baby. We went down to the train station to meet Gene's wife. He had written of how pretty she was, but here this glamorous creature steps down from the train. We had never seen anything like her in Elmwood Springs. Beautiful red hair and that creamy white skin and those green eyes—you got Gene's eyes, but you got your mother's figure. She was tall, and she held herself just like a queen. When we saw you, we were all tickled to death. You were Gene's baby, all right, with that towhead of white hair and those big blue eyes."

Dena said, "How did my mother seem?"

"If anything, she was shy. She wouldn't let anyone take her picture. I said as pretty as you were, you needed to have your picture made—but she wouldn't."

"Did she seem unfriendly?"

"Oh, no. She was perfectly friendly and pleasant, but you could tell right away that she was not one of those flighty young girls that some of the boys brought home. Not only was your mother pretty, she was refined, well educated, and from a good family, but she never talked about them, and we never asked. After losing her entire family in a fire, then to lose Gene . . . I don't know how she lived through it. Do you, Norma?"

"No. I kept thinking that she would talk about it, but she never did the whole time she was here."

"It must have been terrible for her, a young girl like that all alone in the world. I don't know how she stood it, but you could tell it had affected her. She always seemed a little sad."

"I read in the *Reader's Digest* that a person who survives a tragedy goes through guilt for being the one left alive," Norma said. "She should have gone for some help, but back then they didn't have any. She did seem nervous, though, didn't she, Aunt Elner?"

"Well, I wouldn't go so far as to say nervous, but she always seemed a little uneasy. You were her only joy, Baby Girl, the only thing I ever saw her eyes light up over. She got a job and just went to work every day and came home and played with you at night. Otherwise she never went out, never saw anybody. And then one day when you were about four, she just packed your things, took you out of nursery school, and left. And she never came back. It broke your poor grandparents' hearts."

"Did anybody at all ever come to see her?" Dena asked.

Aunt Elner thought. "No. She never had anybody come and see her—nobody except that Italian man that time."

Norma said, "Italian? You never told me about any Italian man."

"Well, I forgot. I think he was an Italian or Greek or something, some kind of foreigner. I only saw him through a screen door, but he had kind of slicky hair. He walked up on the porch and knocked on the door. The minute your mother saw him, she took him way out on the sidewalk and away from the house. Whoever he was, your mother was not happy he showed up, I can tell you that. And after about ten minutes he was gone. When she came back in the house, you could tell that she was still upset."

Norma was amazed. "And she never said who he was?"

"No."

"And you didn't ask?"

"No, Norma, I don't poke in other people's affairs."

"Did he ever come back?" Dena asked.

"No, not to my knowledge."

Norma said, "Couldn't you hear *anything*?"

"Oh, I could hear them, all right, but I couldn't understand what they were saying. They were talking in German."

Norma was puzzled. "Aunt Elner, now, are you *sure* it was German? Could it have been Italian or maybe Spanish?"

Aunt Elner said, "No. Don't forget your uncle Will's father was a Shimfessle. All he spoke was German, so I know German when I hear it. It was German, all right—that much I'm sure of."

"Baby Girl knew her mother spoke German, didn't you?"

Dena said, "Oh, yes, I knew that." Suddenly she began to feel anxious. Why had she lied? She had no idea her mother spoke German. She quickly changed the subject.

The next morning a telegram arrived for her: AM SORRY TO INFORM YOU THAT YOUR BELOVED AGENT AND SHOW BUSINESS ICON, SANDY COOPER, PASSED AWAY SUDDENLY LAST EVENING. PLEASE RETURN TO NEW YORK AT ONCE. JULIAN AMSLEY, NETWORK PRESIDENT.

Later that night, when she got off the plane at La Guardia, Sandy said, "Well, how do I look for a dead man?"

Dena said, "Beautiful!" and kissed him, thrilled to be back.

ONE of the first things she did when she got back to her apartment was to sit down and type a letter:

> Dear Gerry,
>
> Thank you so much for your flowers. I know you went to a lot of trouble to bring them to me, and I really do appreciate it. However, I think it would be unfair of me to keep you from pursuing a relationship with the kind of woman you deserve to be with. You are too nice a guy to lead on.
>
> I hope we can be friends in the future, and I wish you all the best in everything you do.
>
> Sincerely,
> Dena Nordstrom

Rumors

NEW YORK CITY   1976

AS THE months went by, Dena was getting better and better interviews. Sandy even heard serious rumblings. They were considering moving her to a coanchor spot on the six-o'clock news, but in the meantime, Ira Wallace was happy with her work. The ratings were still climbing, and upstairs was pleased, too. News shows were suddenly big business.

Competition was heating up, and Dena's interviews were getting rougher and rougher. It made her uneasy, particularly when she remembered that Howard Kingsley might be watching.

Pete Koski had been elected governor of his state mostly because he had been a football star, but after twelve years in politics he had turned out to be a respected member of his party, and now there was a lot of talk about him being asked to run for President. Ira asked her to his office to brief her for the interview. As soon as she sat down and saw that look on Ira's face, she knew something was coming, and she prepared herself for the worst.

"Your Mr. Macho, Super Governor, has a son that's as queer as a three-dollar bill. Got kicked out of the army for playing house with some other fairy, but Koski had it fixed so it wouldn't show up on his record. How's that for a nice little cherry bomb?"

"Oh, Lord, Ira, why won't you let me just have one interview without trying to turn it into an ambush?"

"It's the truth!" Wallace yelled defensively. "Capello got the report out of the damn military files."

Dena stared at him. "Ira, I told you before, I wouldn't work with Capello. You lied. You didn't fire him, did you?"

"You think I would quit working with the best s.o.b. in the business just because you don't like him? Ya think I'm stupid? I got him outta your face. What else do you want from me? Now I'm not asking you, I'm telling you. You work for me, not Howard Kingsley. Me! You ask the questions that I tell you to."

"What does Howard Kingsley have to do with this?"

"Don't play innocent with me. Everybody knows what's been going on with you two. Who do you think you're kidding?"

"Ira, I hope you're not serious. You know that's not true."

"Hey, what you do is your own business."

"Ira, you are disgusting, do you know that? A disgusting pig."

"Oh, yeah, I'm terrible. Meanwhile, your sainted governor just got caught abusing his power. He bribed the United States Army. That's a crime, kid, so don't get all high and mighty with me. Here, read this." He pushed a copy of a medical discharge toward her and an army psychiatrist's private notes.

Dena looked at him in disbelief. "Ira, we can't use this. This is illegal. How did Capello get this?"

"I don't ask. I don't care. He got it. Just ask the question."

"Ira, this guy should be in jail, and that's where you'll wind up if you're not careful. I'm not doing it."

"That's final?"

"Yes," said Dena, and she meant it.

Wallace sat back. "You know, kid, you are beginning to worry me. And when I worry, I start looking around."

"What does that mean?"

"You figure it out."

As Dena was leaving, Wallace said, "By the way, I hear your boyfriend Kingsley is retiring."

"What?"

"He's retiring, all right. I got it on good authority. They are giving him an ultimatum. Either he retires or gets canned officially."

"I don't believe it."

"Believe it. Do you know what he was doing? He was redlining stories, leaving segments out. That senile old alligator was trying to control the news." He laughed mirthlessly. "About time somebody knocked him on his holier-than-thou, sanctimonious butt."

Dena went back to her office, sick at what Wallace had said about Howard and particularly about their relationship. Was he just trying to shake her up and knock her off-balance, or did everybody else think that, too?

Two months later Howard Kingsley finished his broadcast as he usually did, "And so ends another day." But this night after the sign-off he took his glasses off, looked into the camera, and said, "As some of you may know, tonight ends for me what has been as exciting and as rewarding a career as a man can have. I have been proud and humbled by the support and trust you have so graciously allowed me throughout the years, and I only hope I have been worthy of the task. I wish you well, and may God bless you all. Good night and good-bye."

After the news went off the air, Howard stood up and removed his mike and quietly shook hands with a few cameramen. Then he walked over to the edge of the set, where his wife and daughter were waiting to take him home.

THANKSGIVING, then Christmas came and went. Dena's schedule, especially for travel, was more hectic than ever. Then one day her secretary handed her a news report that had just come in over the wire: "SAG HARBOR—Howard Kingsley, the 'conscience of broadcasting,' died of heart failure last night. He was 68 years of age."

DENA arrived home from Howard Kingsley's memorial service in Sag Harbor at about twelve thirty that night, and the minute she came in the door, she opened a bottle of vodka and put her nightgown on. At about four a.m., drunk as a loon, she got the idea that she would finally tell Ira Wallace what she thought of him. She sat down at her typewriter and started typing:

Dear Dirtbag,

How dare you even say all those terrible things about Howard Kingsley? You aren't fit to wipe his shoes. You laugh at anybody who has integrity. You belittle everybody, strip everybody of any dignity. You are not loyal to anyone but yourself. People are going to learn to hate and suspect each other just like you do, and when it's not safe to go out your front door, what do you care? I don't think you are a good American either, you fat buttermilk-pancake face. I quit. So long, good-bye, and good riddance.

Sincerely,
Dena Nordstrom

P.S. Howard was the top. You're the bottom!

Dena felt a great weight off her. She felt free, went to bed, and slept like a baby for the first time in weeks. At around one o'clock that afternoon she woke with a new hangover and a terrible stomachache. She made herself coffee, had Maalox and three aspirin, and read the letter she had typed. What a pile of sanctimonious rubbish. Who was she to point the finger at anyone? Who did she think she was to imagine herself in the same category with Howard Kingsley? Last night she had been so sure she believed all this stuff, but today she had no earthly idea of what she really thought or felt about anything anymore. Did she really care about anybody but herself? She ripped the letter to shreds.

ACROSS town Gerry O'Malley was leaning over the center-island counter in his kitchen, wearing his red baseball cap, scribbling out another one of the many letters he had started:

Dear Dena,

There are so many things I want to say to you, but I don't want words that skim lightly over the top of what I feel for you. I want words that will produce a long, deep boom of explosion, that will jar you to your very bones and stay ringing in your ears forever. I want you to drink my words in like rich red wine, to reach down in every part of you until there is not a place left untouched. I want you to know I love you in every cell of your brain, in every sleeping and waking thought. I want it to be in the air you breathe . . . so with every breath you will know there is someone on this earth who is yours, knows who you are, loves you forever and, if there is anything after forever, even after that.

Gerry stopped writing, reread what he had just written, and thought, That's the most sickening, most embarrassing pile of hooey I've ever read in my life. And he threw it into the trash can.

He said out loud, "Just call her, you idiot!" He went to the phone and dialed her number. But she had unplugged the phone.

The object of all these earth-shattering emotions was unaware of them. Dena Nordstrom did not believe in love, true or not. It almost killed Gerry when he later read in the paper that Dena had started dating Julian Amsley, the president of her network. Every time he saw a picture of them together in the paper, which was often, it almost broke his heart. But there was nothing he could do.

SIX MONTHS AFTER HOWARD'S death Dena spoke at the Mississippi College for Women, and Sookie offered to drive her to Atlanta to catch her plane back to New York. Sookie was extremely quiet on the drive. Dena said, "All right, Sookie, what's going on?"

Sookie looked somber as she began a speech. "Dena, on May the twenty-second I invited the Lord to come into my life, and I have completely accepted Him as my Lord and Savior. As my best friend, I wanted to share with you that I now have a personal relationship with Jesus Christ."

"What? Sookie, surely you're not serious."

"Of course I'm serious. I would not joke about this."

Dena was at a complete loss for words. "Oh . . . well, uh . . . I hope you two will be very happy. I mean, what can I say?"

"Dena, the other thing I wanted to share is that two weeks ago Jesus spoke to my heart and told me that you needed to be saved, and I would like the opportunity to personally witness for Christ and introduce Him to you."

Dena was horrified at the prospect. "Sookie, I love you, but let's don't talk about this. Let's talk about something else."

Sookie was clearly disappointed. "All right. I promise I won't talk about it anymore now. But I'm not going to give up on you, Dena. I am not going to heaven without you."

Dena stared at her friend in disbelief as they rode along in silence for a while. Then she asked, "Sookie, have you ever spent any time alone? I mean really alone."

Sookie thought about it. "Why would I want to?"

"Don't people get on your nerves?"

"No. And if you ask me, *you* are alone too much. You need to have somebody to talk to, to share your innermost thoughts with."

"Don't worry. I have a psychiatrist I pay a lot of money to share my innermost thoughts."

Sookie, alarmed, almost ran the car off the road. "A psychiatrist? Don't tell me you're going to a— Oh, my Lord, see, I knew something was wrong."

"There is nothing wrong. A lot of people go to psychiatrists."

"You don't need to go to some psychiatrist, Dena Nordstrom. I can tell you what's wrong with you absolutely free. You think you don't like people, but you do, and you're just scared of them, so you stay alone."

Dena sighed. "Sookie, I have so many people around me all day, believe me, I am not alone."

"I mean when you go home at night. And on holidays, for instance. Who are you with on Christmas? You sure won't come to Selma to spend it with us. I think you sit up there in that apartment of yours all by yourself—that's what I think."

"Sookie, I'm not like you. I like to be alone. I really do. Anyhow, let's get off me. Why can't we just have a nice visit without you constantly badgering me?"

Sookie kept driving. For a long time she did not answer. "Dena, I have something I have to tell you."

Dena could tell by her tone that it was going to be something she did not want to hear, and she moaned, "This isn't going to be more about your new religious experience, is it?"

"No." Sookie stared straight ahead, then took a deep breath. "Dena, I know about your mother."

Dena, startled, said, "What?"

"There, I've said it. I didn't mean to find out. It was an accident."

"What are you talking about?"

"We . . . Well, all the girls in the sorority used to think you had a secret boyfriend. And . . . they put me up to looking to see if you had any love letters stashed away, and I accidentally read a letter from your grandfather. It mentioned that your mother had been listed with the Bureau of Missing Persons."

Dena felt her face getting hot, and her heart was racing.

"I know I shouldn't have done it, and I'm sorry," said Sookie. "Are you just ready to kill me?"

Dena lit a cigarette and remained silent.

Sookie was miserable. "Dena, if you don't say something, I am going to have a heart attack. You're going to have to say something eventually. I don't know what gate your plane leaves from. . . ."

Dena spoke. "Who else did you tell?"

"Nobody!" Sookie was emphatic. "Do you think I would tell anybody else? I didn't even tell *you* until now. I wanted you to like me, and you kept telling me you were spending all your holidays with your mother and what a wonderful time you had. I couldn't very well just come out and say I knew you were lying, could I?" Sookie's chin began to quiver, and she was on the verge of tears. "I'm sorry I read that letter, Dena . . . but that's why I worry about you and badger you. I think you still lie to me about what you do on holidays. You spend too much time alone, and that's not good for a person. I don't care what you say."

"Sookie, you knew about my mother. Then why do you insist on babbling on and on about how happy and how great everything was back then, when you knew better?"

Sookie threw her hands up in the air. "Oh, I know, I know . . . Don't ask me why. I always felt so guilty about it. I guess I couldn't face the fact that I let you down, because I couldn't deal with it myself. Or maybe I could have helped you." Sookie glanced at Dena. "Why did you lie to me? I was your best friend."

Dena put her cigarette out in the ashtray and said, "Because I was embarrassed."

"Embarrassed? But why? It's nothing to be ashamed of."

"I'm not ashamed."

"It must have been terrible for you, Dena. Did you ever find out what happened?"

"No. Listen, Sookie, there are only a few people who know anything about it. And I'd like to keep it that way. It's not something I want out in public. Can you understand?"

"Of course," Sookie said. "I understand perfectly, and as far as I'm concerned, it's forgotten. And you know you can trust me with your life."

An hour later, when they arrived at the airport, Sookie hugged her good-bye. Dena paused a moment before she left, and said, "Sookie, you really are a good friend."

"That's what I've been telling you for years, goofy!"

A Dish Best Served Cold

❧

DENA Nordstrom had ruined Sidney Capello's one chance to be big in network television, but like a rat in a maze, he had quickly scurried in another direction. In the tabloid business, where speed does count, Capello had shot to the top like a silver bullet. He had tired of being a freelance, so he started his own paper. Stripped of the dead weight of ethics, a conscience, or fear of the law, Capello and his paper were soon way ahead of the pack. Not fussing over facts was an economy. In less than a year his cheaply produced paper outsold everything on the supermarket rack.

The main reason for Sidney's success was his ability to look to the future, to put away something for a rainy day. He had what he called a hot file, his get-them-before-they're-famous time bombs. He sent his staff out gathering information on anybody he even suspected might become newsworthy one day—kid actors, musicians, public servants, do-gooders.

This is how the Dena Nordstrom file had come into being and now sat ticking away, waiting for the right moment. Capello was usually strictly business, but he took a personal interest in her story. If it had not been for Nordstrom, he might be producing television today. He put his most expensive, tough-digging researcher, Barbara Zofko, to work on this one.

If Sidney Capello was the queen bee, Barbara Zofko was the perfect drone. She served him well. A lumpy, misshapen sort of woman, not ugly, not pretty, she had the kind of face that could walk past a thousand people a day and not one would remember her. She was perfect for her job. She had no human relations to interfere with her work.

As Capello's top bird dog, she had tracked Dena's career from one local television station to another, but . . . nothing. They all said the same thing. Nice girl. We knew she would do well. A blind alley.

As for the immediate family, they had been dull—typical small-town churchgoing well-liked people. Nothing Zofko could use. The father, Gene, had once gotten in trouble for swimming inside the town's water tower with a bunch of other boys. Certainly nothing that even Capello could work up a good smear over. The only item where there might be something was the mother.

Zofko had her resources. She got the mother's Social Security number and tracked down every state employment record on her. The job data records were always the same: Name: Marion Chapman Nordstrom. Born: December 9, 1920, Washington, D.C. Parents: Deceased.

Her record of employment was odd. She had gone to work in a dress shop in New York City in 1942 and remained at that job until 1943, when she went to Gumps in San Francisco. From then on she seemed to go from one job to the next, from one town to another. Zofko sat in her apartment eating a bag of Fritos, studying the chart she had made. She read and reread the copies of all the employee records and job applications she had managed to get hold of, and this time she noticed something she had not caught before. A Lili's dress shop had been listed in all her references, then suddenly, after 1946, did not appear on any more applications. Why had she left that job out? Could something have happened there that might be the reason she was running?

Zofko was hopeful. She went to the New York City library newspaper reference room, searching through the advertisements in the New York area at the time, and she found it. Lili's Exclusive dress shop, "clothes for the discriminating woman," 116 Park Avenue. She went to the city records and looked up the list of owners for that address. The building at 116 Park had been purchased from a Rickter, William J., and sold to Steiner, Lili Carlotta, in 1935. From there it was easy. Zofko called a woman who worked for the New York Census Department and was on Sidney Capello's payroll as well and told her to send everything she had on Lili Carlotta Steiner.

Then Zofko went back to her office and waited. The information came by messenger. She ripped open the envelope with relish:

Steiner, Lili Carlotta
Born: Vienna, Austria, 1893
    Moved to New York, resided in Yorkville section at 463 East 85th Street. Owned and operated fashionable dress shop until the time of her arrest. Closely associated with American Nazi Party members and accused of spying and on December 13, 1946, was convicted and served ten years in prison. Died in 1962 at the age of sixty-nine in Milwaukee, Wisconsin.

When Capello read all the information Barbara Zofko handed him, he looked at her. "What can I say? It doesn't get better than this. You're the best."

Zofko was happy. She liked to please her boss.

"How long did the mother work for Steiner?"

"About eight months."

Capello nodded. "It's enough—more than enough. Write it. Hitler, holocaust, death camps, the whole deal."

Zofko went back to her office and knocked out a few sample headlines and phrases: "Dena Nordstrom's Shameful Nazi Past . . . Daughter of Nazi spy now in American broadcasting. Mother close friend of Hitler . . . aided the Nazi cause . . . Nazi war criminal confesses, names top American broadcaster as the daughter of Nazi spy . . ." She would finish a full rough draft later. It wasn't airtight. It wasn't complete. It might not be true, but it would do the job. When Zofko finished, she put it in the file with the rest. This little hand grenade would wait for a time when Sidney Capello decided to pull the pin and throw it at Nordstrom, the all-American girl.

DENA had turned down Julian Amsley's invitations week after week, but finally he had said something that changed her mind. "Going out with me will give you more stature, more clout. Think of it as business, if nothing else." That appealed to Dena.

But it wasn't easy. Amsley was an older man, but he was not harmless. He was trying to prove that he was still a virile man, and it came to be exhausting having to fight him off.

Because she was dating him, there was a feeling in the air that Dena was moving up. The pressures mounted. Amsley's friends had the mistaken idea that she was one of their crowd. She wasn't. She was a working girl. Her social life was work to her. When the wealthy wives were busy the mornings after all the parties—shopping, getting their faces lifted—Dena was at the studio, and she was getting worn out. Again.

One night she went with Julian to see the musical *Mame,* a benefit performance for the Actors Fund, and it seemed as if all of New York was there. It was a glittering evening, and Dena admitted to herself that she enjoyed hearing people whispering, "There's Dena Nordstrom," as she walked down the aisle. Seated, Dena was thoroughly enjoying the show, when halfway through the first act she started to break out in a sweat. Her heart began to pound, and she heard a ringing in her ears; everything became distorted. The entire audience seemed to be moving in on her, and she was gasping for breath. She felt as if she was either going to die or pass out.

She stood up and was stepping over people, trying to get to the aisle. Julian turned and half rose, but she was gone before he had a chance to ask her what was wrong. Somehow Dena made her way out the door to a taxi and home, leaving Julian in his third-row center-aisle seat wondering what had happened to her.

THE next morning she woke up scared to death, and for the first time she was glad she had an appointment with Dr. Diggers. She really needed to talk to someone. She told the doctor exactly what had happened the night before.

Elizabeth Diggers said, "Dena, you had an anxiety attack."

"What? Are you sure?"

"Yes, I'm sure."

"I'm perfectly fine. Everything is going great. Why would anxiety attack me all of a sudden?"

"Sometimes it's environmental. Sometimes it's subconscious."

"Great. It's not enough that I have to fight off Julian Amsley every night. Now my subconscious is after me."

"Let's talk a little bit about last night," Diggers said. "Tell me exactly what you were doing."

"I told you, I was just sitting there watching *Mame*."

"Try to remember exactly what was going on at the moment you started to feel anxious."

Dena thought for a moment. "It was something about Christmas. They were singing they wanted a little Christmas early, and there was a tree. That's all I remember."

"Ah, yes, that was the 'We Need a Little Christmas' song. Does anything about Christmas trigger anything for you?"

Dena looked at her blankly. "No. I don't even like Christmas. Why are you asking me all these questions?"

"What did you and your mother do at Christmas?"

"I don't remember what we did. Nothing. We just did nothing." Dena started to break out in a cold sweat.

"Dena? Are you feeling anxious right now?"

Dena had dug her nails into the chair and was breathing heavily. "A little. . . . I don't know why."

Diggers wheeled over to her. "Okay, you're all right. I'm here. Let's go in the kitchen, put some cold water on your face."

They made it to the kitchen, and Dena put water on her face and held on to the sink. The woman who worked for Diggers stood in the kitchen over in the corner, saying nothing. Diggers said, "Louisa, go in the medicine chest and bring me a ten-milligram Valium." She gave it to Dena and made her lie down on the couch, then sat talking to her. "You're okay. Just keep breathing."

Dena felt herself calming. "I hate this."

"I know you do."

"Is my time up yet?"

"No. You stay right where you are."

They sat in silence. Five minutes later Dena said, "Something did happen on Christmas. But I thought I was over it."

WHEN DENA WAS FIFTEEN, HER mother was living in Chicago in a large red brick apartment building called the Berkeley. Dena's boarding school was outside Baltimore, and she couldn't wait to see her mother for the holidays. She had called and called from school, but each time, she missed reaching her at home. She called the department store, and they told her that her mother was no longer working there. Her mother changed jobs quite a bit and sometimes forgot to tell her, so Dena wrote a letter saying what time her train would be arriving. All the way across the country she was humming with excitement.

When her train finally pulled into the station, Dena was the first person off. Her mother was not there. She waited almost two hours. She didn't know what to do. Maybe her mother had not received her letter or had to work late. So she went outside and took a cab to her mother's apartment building. Her heart jumped with joy when she saw her mother's name written on the small strip of paper next to the buzzer. She pushed the button, but there was no answer. The air was freezing, and the wind was so cold it hurt.

It was getting dark when a man came, took a key, and opened the big glass front door leading into the lobby. Dena said, "Excuse me, is there a superintendent? I need to get into my mother's apartment. I don't have a key, and she's not home yet."

The man let her in and pointed her to the brown door, saying, "Ring that bell." Dena saw that it said MRS. CLEVERDON, MANAGER. A middle-aged lady in an apron opened the door.

"Hello. I'm Mrs. Nordstrom's daughter, and I just got here, and I was wondering if she left me a key."

The woman smiled. "Well, no, dear, she didn't leave a key. But I'll take you up and let you in. Your mother's on the sixth floor."

"Thank you. Guess she's working late because of Christmas."

"I imagine so," Mrs. Cleverdon said.

They took the elevator up, and Dena followed her down the hall to apartment 6D. Mrs. Cleverdon opened the door. "I know your mother will be glad to see you. Have a nice visit, now."

"Thank you."

Dena walked into the apartment and noticed unopened mail lying on the floor. Her letter was right on top. Then it dawned on her. Her mother must have gone on a buying trip for the store. She often did that; she was probably on her way home right now.

The minute Dena walked into the bedroom, it smelled familiar—her mother's Shalimar—and she felt at home. She liked this apartment. It had a little kitchen and a nice-sized living room. She noticed that her mother had put a small white ceramic tree on the dining table by the front window. It had tiny colored lights. She plugged it in, and it lit up in red and green and blue.

After unpacking, Dena opened the front closet to hang up her coat. Four beautifully wrapped Christmas packages were on the floor. Each one said "To Dena. From Mother." She put her gifts for her mother by the little tree and sat down to wait, wondering what was in the packages, especially the big one. That night, every time she heard the elevator door open and heard someone come down the hall, she held her breath; she just knew it was her mother. But it never was. At about ten o'clock she was starving, and there was nothing in the refrigerator, so she wrote a note: "Mother, I am here! I have gone to get something to eat and will be right back."

She put her coat on and had to leave the door unlocked because she didn't have a key. She went down the street to a coffee shop and got a grilled cheese sandwich and a Coke and a piece of chocolate pie, but when she got back to the building, it was locked, and she couldn't get back in. She buzzed her mother's apartment. There was no answer, so she had to buzz the manager again.

The next day she fooled around the apartment, killing time. Each time she went out, she left the same note. Two days later she called her school, asking if her mother had called and left her a message. They said she hadn't.

Christmas morning she got up early, put on her good dress, and sat by the window. Every time she heard the elevator door open, her heart jumped. And then sank again as whoever it was walked on down the hall. She sat there all day. At about six o'clock she went into the kitchen and heated up a frozen turkey dinner and ate it.

She watched the Perry Como Christmas special on the television set in the living room. She waited until eleven o'clock, and then she opened her presents. She saved the big one for last. She cleaned up all the paper and went to bed.

All through the rest of the holiday she waited for her mother. By the end of the week she was numb. On her last day she packed, called a cab, put on the new blue wool pea coat that her mother had given her for Christmas, went over and turned off the lights on the Christmas tree, then went downstairs to wait for her taxi.

Upstairs in apartment 6D, a note was on the table: "Mother, I was here. Love, Dena." Three weeks later the note she had left on the table in the living room was still there. Mrs. Cleverdon told her so on the phone. Her mother had not come back. Her mother had disappeared off the face of the earth. But Dena did not cry. Not once. Back at school, if anyone asked how her Christmas had been, she lied. She pretended it had never happened. It took years for Dena to really believe that her mother was not coming back.

"AND you never heard from her after that?" asked Dr. Diggers.

"No. Nobody did. Anyhow, that was a long time ago."

"Wait a minute. So you don't know if she's living or dead."

Dena dismissed it. "I don't know, and I don't care. Really, it doesn't matter to me one way or another."

"Why didn't you tell me this before?"

"Because it's not anything I'm particularly proud of."

"What do you mean?"

"I don't know. It's just embarrassing."

"Let's talk about it."

"Let's don't. I'm not interested in the past. I'm a little old to sit around hugging a teddy bear, whining about my mother. I don't have time for that, and I don't need anybody to feel sorry for me. I didn't have a great childhood, but I'm not going to dine out on it."

Diggers rolled over closer to Dena. "Sweetie pie, I do feel sorry for you. That was a *terrible* thing that happened. You are going to have to talk to someone. It might as well be me. Okay?"

It was the first time Dr. Diggers had called her anything but Dena, and it caught her off guard. She heard herself say, "All right."

"Good girl. We have to look at this thing head-on and not sweep it under the rug, because until you deal with it, you are not going to know what you are feeling about anything. I won't lie to you. It is going to be a long, hard process, but we have to start somewhere."

Dena was really listening to her for the first time.

"Are you willing to start to work with me now?"

"Yes."

WHEN Elizabeth Diggers looked at Dena, she saw the fifteen-year-old who never got out of that room. She was still sitting there looking out the window, still waiting for her mother to come home. Diggers's job was to go inside that room, take that girl by the hand, and bring her out. Get her out into the sun and fresh air so she could continue to grow. Dena's heart had been broken, and she had never gotten over it.

Session after session Dena would close her eyes and try to remember what her mother was like. She was unable to come up with anything but the shadow of a person. What had her mother thought about? What had she felt? Had Dena loved her? Had she really loved Dena?

Dr. Diggers persisted, asking Dena the same question over and over. "Let's start again, Miss Hickory Nut. How did you feel when your mother did not come home?"

Weeks went by without much progress, and then one day, out of the blue, Dena burst into tears and started to cry uncontrollably.

"What is it?" Diggers asked. "What are you thinking about?"

"I always thought she'd come back, but she never did," Dena blurted out between sobs. "And I don't know what I did wrong."

Finally Dena stopped fighting. Dr. Diggers's hypnotherapy began to help her relax, and she was remembering more and more each session. One day Dr. Diggers put her under a little deeper. Dena had her eyes closed and could almost see her mother, but she was still an indistinct figure. Then Dena said, "She had taken me shopping in . . . New York, maybe. I remember we walked by this big store, and it had all these pianos in the window. She stopped, and we went in. Way in the back she saw a piano she must have liked. She sat down and opened it up, and she had this odd look on her face."

"Like what? Describe it."

"Oh, I don't know. Like I wasn't there or something. And all of a sudden she started to play some sort of waltz. I was so surprised. I didn't even know she could play. I remember she looked so happy. I had never seen her look so . . . well . . . transported. After we left, I said, 'Mother, why didn't you tell me you could play the piano?' And she acted like it was nothing."

"Did she ever talk about her parents?"

"No. Just that they were killed in a fire."

"Weren't you curious?"

"Talking about them upset her, so I just didn't."

"You spent a lot of time not upsetting your mother. Why?"

"Why? Because I was enough trouble as it was."

"Why do you think that?"

"Well, because she had to look after me."

"Let's talk about your feeling of being afraid. What were you afraid of?"

"I don't know."

"Did something make you think your mother was frightened?"

Dena said, "I think she was afraid of that man, one time."

"What man?"

"Some man she saw when we were still living in New York. We were coming home, and it was snowing. We turned the corner, and when we got to the apartment building, she stopped. I looked up at her and saw that she was staring at the man talking to the clerk at the desk. He had his back to us, a big man in a black-checked overcoat. I said, 'What's the matter?' Before I had finished, she grabbed me by the arm and almost dragged me down the street. She was walking so fast that I had to run to keep up with her. I said, 'Did I do something, Momma?'

" 'No,' she said. 'Come on.' She practically ran to the subway, and we caught the first one, and she sat down and just looked straight ahead. I was convinced I had done something wrong, and I started to cry. She said, 'Why are you crying?'

" 'I'm scared,' I said. 'I don't know what's the matter.'

" 'Oh, Dena, don't be so sensitive. I just saw someone I didn't want to see, that's all.'

"I asked, 'Who is he?' She said, 'Stop asking so many questions.' Then she looked up for the first time and noticed where we were headed. At the next stop we changed subways and went all the way to the Village. It was really snowing, and it was hard to walk, but we got to West Twelfth or maybe Eleventh Street. We stopped at a coffee shop, and she made a phone call. After she came back, she seemed a little more herself. She said, 'We're going over to see Christine.' "

"Who was Christine?" asked Diggers.

"A friend of my mother's who was a dancer at Radio City. She said, 'She's invited us to spend the night. Won't that be fun?'

"She lived in a basement apartment on St. Luke's Place and was very glad to see us. She let me play with her cat, Milton. I slept on a pad that Christine made up for me, and Momma slept on the couch. At about daybreak I woke up. I looked over and saw that my mother was sitting by the window. I remember having that cold, scared feeling in the pit of my stomach again. I knew she was unhappy, and I didn't know why. I was scared to ask her, because I thought maybe it was me. Maybe she wished she did not have a little girl."

"Dena, I'm going to count to three, and when you wake up, you will feel rested and peaceful. One . . . just like you have slept for hours. Two . . . feeling calm and serene. . . . Three."

Dena slowly opened her eyes.

"How do you feel?"

"Fine." Dena yawned. "Hate to disappoint you, but I don't think I was hypnotized. I remember everything you said."

Diggers smiled. That's what everyone she hypnotized said.

Secrets Can Kill

❀

IRA Wallace was listening to an idea Sidney Capello had for a television news show. Although Wallace did not trust Capello, the more he heard about the idea, the more he liked it. Capello elaborated. "We cover all the Hollywood stuff. I can feed you enough material from my files to keep you supplied for years. We set it up as a news thing—legit gossip, headline stuff, cutting-edge, hard-hitting red-hot items. We get some hair-spray head or some good-looking broad to sit up there, tell them to smile, and I guarantee you got a hit."

"You talking network?"

"No, I'm talking syndication. That's where the money is—millions, maybe billions, Ira. We own it, we sell it, no regulations. We can cover stuff the networks won't touch."

Wallace leaned back and looked at Capello. The dirt digger had not seen the light of day for years and had unhealthy blue-white skin, and lips the color of raw liver. Wallace, who was no beauty, wanted to throw up at the sight of him. But he was smart enough to know a good idea. "What's the deal?"

"Sixty-forty."

"Whew," Wallace said.

"Hey, without me you got no show."

Two months and what seemed like forty-eight lawyers later Sidney Capello and Ira Wallace were, as they say in the business, in bed together, and Wall-Cap Productions was formed. As the thing took shape, they again discussed talent. Capello dropped his bombshell. "I want Dena Nordstrom."

"And I want the Queen of England, but she ain't available."

"Why not? We'd have a built-in audience. Mass plus class."

"Sidney, she's now the most popular female newscaster in the business. Nordstrom would be anybody's first choice. But she hates your guts, so forget it. We'll get some other blonde."

"It doesn't hurt to ask, Ira. You never know—people change."

"Yeah, but they don't change that much."

But Capello would not give up. After a week Wallace gave in. "All right, we'll ask. I guess it can't hurt to ask."

SANDY Cooper asked Dena to meet him after work to discuss an offer. She said, "Can't you just tell me over the phone?"

"No. This is too big. This could change your life."

That night she met him across the street at a restaurant on Sixth Avenue. They ordered drinks—Dena chocolate milk because her ulcer had been giving her trouble. Cooper ordered a gin and tonic because he was nervous. He took a gulp. "So, Dena, how would you like to be a millionaire by the time you are thirty-five?"

Since she was now thirty-four, he had her attention.

"Just hear me out before you say anything, okay?" And he went on to tell her all about the new show she had been offered.

"Who's producing this? Do they have the money?" she asked.

"It's a new company, just formed." Cooper looked around the room and confided, "I'm not really supposed to tell you until it is announced, but it's Ira Wallace . . . and a partner."

"Ira?"

"Yes. He's handing in his resignation to the network and forming his own company. And you know he knows what he is doing and has the money behind him, but the best part is, he's offered to make me executive vice president."

Dena sat back in her chair. Something was off. Why would Ira need to bring Sandy in? "What's the name of this company?"

Cooper couldn't hedge. "Uh . . . Wall-Cap Productions."

"Wall-Cap Productions? Who is Cap?"

"Well, that's the one thing Ira thought you might have a little problem with. He said you didn't like this guy, but Dena, where this much money is concerned, you don't have to like them."

"What guy? Who are you talking about?"

"A guy named Capello."

Dena reacted with horror. "Capello? Sidney Capello? Forget it. Absolutely not."

"We are talking a *lot* of money here. Couldn't you just try?"

"Sandy, there is nothing—and I repeat *nothing*—in the world that could make me work for that sleazebag."

Sandy could see by the look on her face that the odds of his becoming a vice president had just gone from slim to none.

BARBARA Zofko wandered down the hall in a lump and went back to her office. She sat down and pulled the sleeves of her gray cable-knit sweater up on her plump forearms, kicked off her shoes, and rolled a sheet of paper into her typewriter:

> Dear Ms. Nordstrom,
>
>   I could lose my job for doing this, but I can no longer stand by without warning you. Sidney Capello is a dangerous man. Please do not cross him. He is an evil man, and he will print this information! I beg you to reconsider your decision.
>
>   A Friend

She picked up a plain manila envelope and put a copy of the Dena Nordstrom file into it. She searched for her shoes under her desk, found them, and went back to Capello's office. He nodded his approval.

That Friday night Dena's doorman handed her the envelope. "Miss Nordstrom, a lady dropped this by for you earlier."

Dena took it, with thanks. As she rode up the sixteen floors, she opened the envelope.

All her life she had lived with some low-grade dread, a fear of something unknown, and now here it was. When the elevator doors opened on her floor, she was almost unable to move. She somehow reached her door, but she could hardly get the key into the lock. The door open, she walked in and slid down to the floor, leaning back against the wall. Surely this could not be true. But there it was in black and white, with Capello's name attached to it:

NORDSTROM, MARION CHAPMAN.
MOTHER OF AMERICAN BROADCASTER DENA (GENE) NORDSTROM.
EMPLOYEE AND CLOSE ASSOCIATE OF STEINER, LILI CARLOTTA,
    HIGH-RANKING OFFICIAL AMERICAN NAZI PARTY, CONVICTED
    OF SPYING DEC. 13, 1946, SERVED TEN YEARS, DIED IN 1962.
CHAPMAN HAD CLOSE CONTACT WITH KNOWN MEMBERS OF THE
    AMERICAN NAZI PARTY, SUSPECTED OF SPYING.
CHAPMAN/NORDSTROM REPORTED AS MISSING PERSON, JAN. 1960.
WHEREABOUTS UNKNOWN.

After a moment Dena got up off the floor and sat down on the sofa, still in shock. Maybe it was true. Dena remembered what Aunt Elner had told her about her mother speaking German. She realized that even if this weren't true, it didn't matter. If the implications of this ever got printed, her career would be over. Just like that. Gone.

Dena knew what Capello could do to her and the awful power he had. With this information, saying no to him would be playing Russian roulette with her life. All night she struggled, wondering how to save herself. Maybe she should take the job.

But she knew that however hard she tried, and as much as she wanted a career or did not want her name or her mother's dragged through the mud, she could not work for him. She could not let herself become a part of the garbage she knew that Sidney and Ira would be pushing on television to get ratings. Howard Kingsley had warned her, and he had been right. Even if she were to take the job, Capello would never stop threatening her. He would own her for life. And she would rather be dead than have that happen.

When Sandy called again, on Capello's orders, Dena was particularly brave. She was as terrified as ever, but she still said no.

As always, there was a price to pay.

ON MONDAY morning when the cleaning woman let herself into Dena's apartment, she was not prepared for what she saw. Blood was everywhere. Smeared on the walls, on the floor, in the hall.

When she saw her employer lying on the floor in the doorway to the kitchen in a pool of dried blood, she ran out of the apartment screaming, "Missus Nordstrom's been murdered!" When the police arrived, they entered with guns drawn, but nobody was there except Dena's dead body, or at least what looked like her dead body. When the doctor came and started to examine her, he looked up and said, "Call an ambulance. This girl is still alive."

The paramedics felt a weak pulse. She had lost so much blood the emergency-room doctor did not hold out much hope, but he started a transfusion anyway. They checked her for bullet or stab wounds but could not find any. Later they discovered that she had bleeding ulcers. One had hemorrhaged, and she had almost bled to death. They got her into emergency surgery.

As sick as Dena was, being unconscious was at least some relief from what she had been going through. Since receiving the letter, she had tried not to think about it, but it haunted her. Suddenly it seemed like everything about her mother that she had worked so hard to remember had become suspicious. Dena had canceled all her appointments, including Dr. Diggers. The only way she could get any sleep was to drink until she passed out. At four o'clock in the morning on Monday she sat up in bed and started to throw up blood and could not stop. She tried to crawl down her hall to buzz the doorman, but she became unconscious.

For days it was touch and go. Her doctors felt that after all the blood she had lost, it was a miracle she was alive at all. When it was announced on the news that she had been rushed to the hospital and was on the critical list, Dena, who did not believe in God, had the most unlikely people praying for her in the most unlikely of places. Elizabeth Diggers and the entire congregation of the A.M.E. Baptist Church on 105th Street said a prayer for her. When Norma Warren heard about Dena, she was so frightened that she completely bypassed hysteria. She immediately picked up the phone and called her minister. That night in Elmwood Springs, people in all three of the churches came to pray for her. In Selma, Sookie, who was now on a first-name basis with Jesus Christ, had a lot to say and, just to be on the safe side, alerted all the Kappa Bible-study groups in the country to say a special prayer for their sister.

Most likely the prayer that might have done the trick was Aunt Elner's, who talked to God every day. She went out into her yard and looked up and said, "Please don't take her now, Lord. She's just getting started, and that poor little thing has had so many hard knocks. And if You need a family member, just go ahead and take me. I'd be tickled to death to see You, and I don't have a thing planned except for putting up some preserves."

After three days Dena was taken off the critical list. Whether or not it had been all those prayers or the skill of the doctors, nobody could say for sure, but to put it in Elner's words, "It sure didn't hurt her any."

A lot of things went on during those long days that she was totally unaware of. Visitors came and went. Reporters and fans tried to get in but were turned away. Julian Amsley had called several times and sent flowers, and he had come to the hospital once, but Gerry O'Malley came every day, often sitting outside Dena's room. And Dena never knew Gerry had been there.

WHEN Dena woke, she wondered where she was. She could not quite figure it out. Then she heard a familiar voice.

"Hello there, Miss Hickory Nut." Dr. Diggers was sitting in the wheelchair by her bed. "Do you remember what happened?"

"No. . . . Kind of. . . . No."

"You hemorrhaged and passed out. Do you remember that?"

Dena was still confused.

"Go on back to sleep and rest. You are going to be fine."

Macky and Norma had been packed, waiting for the doctor to tell them they could come, but he asked them to wait a little while until Dena was stronger. Sookie paid no attention to the doctor. She flew to New York, and when she walked into the room, she burst into tears. Dena looked like a ghost. She had lost fifteen pounds in the past few days. When Sookie had composed herself, she sat by the bed. "Dena, you have just got to get better. If you die on me after I have crossed the Mason-Dixon line to see you, I'll just be furious."

Sookie had cheered her up, but at night when Dena was all alone in her room, she was filled with that old black dread. She knew she could not stay in New York. She had to get out, get as far away from Capello as she could. She needed time and distance to try to figure out what she was going to do, or the fear would eventually kill her. Sookie begged her to come back to Selma for a while, but Dena found herself saying the oddest thing. "Sookie, that is so sweet, but I really want to go home for a while."

Like a good omen, the next morning a telegram arrived: YOUR ROOM IS READY. WHEN ARE YOU COMING? LOVE, NORMA AND MACKY.

The day before she was to leave, Gerry O'Malley came into the room with an enormous bouquet of roses.

"Hi. How are you doing?" he said.

"Hi. Come on in. I'm fine. Or nearly fine."

"I heard you were pretty sick."

"Yes, I was, but I'm leaving tomorrow for Elmwood Springs."

"Yes, that's what I heard." He put the flowers down on a chair.

"They're beautiful. I'll get a nurse to put them in some water."

Gerry was happy to see that she looked a hundred percent better than the last time, when she was still unconscious. The sight of her sitting there in bed looking like her old self took his breath away. He was suddenly nervous. "So, you look good. When do you think you're coming back?"

"I don't know. I'm really not sure."

"Ah . . . well. If there's anything I can do for you while you are gone, just let me know. You have my number. Just call, uh, if you think about it. Or call Dr. Diggers. Keep us posted, okay?"

"I will."

Gerry left the hospital, aching. He knew by looking into her eyes that she was a hundred miles away. He had no idea if he would ever see her again, but he was so much in love he still hoped that maybe someday, some year, she might give him another chance.

That night Dena could not sleep. She thought about what Elizabeth Diggers had asked her that first time. Who are you? She thought she had known then, but who was she now? She had no idea. She had lost herself somewhere along the way.

She was like the front of a bombed-out building, still standing but empty. She knew the truth of what Dr. DeBakey had told her. If she didn't slow down, she'd be dead. She had come close.

The next morning she flew home.

IT WAS good to be in Elmwood Springs. It was quiet in her room. The weather was warm. She went to sleep with her windows open and slept soundly. On the fourth day she awakened at seven and felt strong enough to get up. She went downstairs to the kitchen. Norma said, "Baby Girl, what are you doing up so early?"

"I couldn't go back to sleep, but I feel better."

"Well, the kitchen's a mess, but come on in if you can stand it."

Dena noticed one cup and a saucer in the sink. Other than that, it was, as usual, spotless, but Norma, horrified, quickly rinsed them off.

"Sorry the place is such a wreck, but I got a little behind this morning. Aunt Elner has already been on the phone three times wanting you to come over and see her. She's all excited because she found a four-leaf clover in her yard, and she wants to show it to you, as if you have never seen a four-leaf clover before."

Dena sat down. "Actually, I don't think I ever have."

"Really? Well, she's all worked up about it." Norma opened the icebox and pulled out the eggs and milk. "I don't know how she can see well enough to find one. Imagine, at her age. I couldn't find one even with my glasses on, but she has eyes like a hawk."

After a big breakfast Dena decided to walk over to Aunt Elner's house. People waved to her and said, "Good morning." As she paused on Aunt Elner's porch, she could hear her inside, singing away. She knocked, and Aunt Elner came to the door.

"Well, hey there, Baby Girl. Come on in."

Elner was wearing a faded floral blue-and-white housedress and white mesh tie-up shoes. The house smelled like bacon.

"Have a seat if you can find one. Let me go turn my bacon off."

Dena went into the living room and sat down. Aunt Elner came back with a little white bowl full of water, with a four-leaf clover floating on top.

"I found it this morning, and I said, I'm giving it to Baby Girl for good luck."

"Thank you, Aunt Elner, that's very sweet."

"Well, that's all right, honey, bless your heart. You need a little good luck to come your way. How are you doing? You look good, but I worry about you. Are you getting enough to eat?"

"I'm getting plenty to eat, and more."

"Well, good. Norma doesn't eat enough to keep a twig alive, and on top of it she runs around all day cleaning and scrubbing."

"She's a good housekeeper, all right."

"Too good, if you ask me. She's a neat-aholic. Little things drive her crazy, but I'll tell you, in a natural disaster she calms down right when everybody else is falling apart. That's when Norma is at her best."

"What kind of natural disaster?"

"Any kind, you name it. A while back, when we had all those terrible floods and so many people lost their homes, Norma went down to the high school and had it up and running, organized into a shelter and a hospital in no time. Saved all kinds of lives."

"Really?"

"Oh, yes. She has an earthquake kit you wouldn't believe."

"Are there earthquakes here?"

"There was one a hundred years ago, but if there is ever another one, Norma's ready. She's prepared for a tornado, a drought, floods, the atomic bomb, germ warfare. You name it, she's ready."

"Well, that's good to know."

"You're not gonna run off back to New York, are you?"

"I'm not sure."

"I wish you'd stay here with us. Nobody's gonna bother you. Macky Warren has seen to that. In fact, the whole town is gonna see to that. This is your home. You don't need to be pestered to death in your own hometown."

AS DENA WALKED HOME WITH her four-leaf clover, she wondered just what she was going to do. She had thought it might be good to be alone, but now she was finding that it was sort of nice to have relatives around. She began to toy with the idea of staying in Elmwood Springs for a while. Maybe she would even find a place she could rent for a few months.

When she got back, she looked in the phone book and saw an ad in the business section. It had a picture of a woman in a hat talking on the phone, and it said FOR ALL YOUR REAL ESTATE NEEDS, CALL BEVERLY. Two weeks later, when Macky and Norma went out of town for a hardware convention, she called Beverly.

BEVERLY showed up wearing a huge hat and driving a big blue Lincoln. She was elated to have a potential customer, especially Dena. "Well, am I happy to meet you. When my husband and I first moved here, we heard this was where you were from, and I always hoped you'd come back."

Beverly was a dynamo, and within an hour they had seen everything. They looked at a duplex, even a condo, and several new apartments way out by the mall, but Dena did not warm to any of them. They were too cold and sterile. Beverly was stumped. "We just don't have that many apartment rentals here."

Dena said, "Do you have any houses for rent?"

"A whole house? Let's see. I do have a little one, but it's way out in the country. And you don't want that. I have one in town I can show you. Now, I don't know what shape it's in, but we can look."

They drove to the older section of town. Large elm trees lined the street, and Beverly stopped and parked in front of a white frame house with a green-and-white awning around the front porch. They got out of the car, and Beverly rattled on. "It might be a little big for you, but you don't see many houses these days with two swings, do you? The house stayed in the family. The daughter and her family lived here up until a couple of months ago, but her husband got emphysema so bad they had to move to Arizona." As Beverly tried the front door, Dena noticed something written on the front window. She walked over to look closely and could just make out WDOT RADIO STATION, NUMBER 66 ON YOUR DIAL. Beverly, who was furiously pushing on the door, noticed what she was looking at. "They say the woman who used to live here had a radio show." Finally, with one more push, the door opened.

"Here we go. I didn't think it was locked. Come on in." It was dark inside, all the curtains drawn, and as Beverly quickly went around the front room opening them, Dena noticed a certain smell, a sweet smell, as if someone had been baking. The house still had the original venetian blinds. The curtains in the living room were thick and floral, green and yellow and maroon, with what looked like palm leaves. There was some furniture left. A small desk was in the living room over by the window, and there were several old Aladdin lamps, yellow with white flowers, and a stand-up lamp that still had the original shade, with a maroon silk ruffle. Beverly switched it on, and the old lamp gave off a soft yellow light, almost golden in color. As Beverly turned on more lamps, all the light seemed to glow in a soft, muted way that Dena found soothing.

She asked, "When was this house built, do you think?"

"Oh, I'd say probably around 1925. No later than the '30s, I would guess by the transoms over the doors and the wallpaper. I think this is the original wallpaper." The ceilings were about twelve feet high. Dena had lived in apartments and hotel rooms so long she had forgotten about high ceilings. It seemed so strange to have all that space up there. The floors were in excellent condition, a beautiful oak. The bathrooms all had huge claw-foot bathtubs and large pedestal sinks.

They walked to the back of the house. As soon as they entered the kitchen, Dena said, "Smell that? Someone has been baking a cake or something in here." The kitchen was huge; a lone lightbulb hung over the white wooden table. There was a big white enamel sink and drainboard with a floral-print skirt around it, a huge icebox, and a 1920s white O'Keefe & Merritt stove in perfect condition. "Look at this pretty stove," Beverly said, and she turned on a burner. The flames popped right up. "And it works, too!" They walked out of the kitchen onto a large screened-in back porch and saw that beyond the backyard there was a field. Beverly said, "Oh, look, there's an old sweetheart swing. I just love those, don't you?"

"Oh, yes," said Dena, not having any idea what a sweetheart swing was.

"They say there used to be a big radio tower out in the backyard and that people could see it for miles around."

"Really?" Dena went back to the front porch and sat on the swing by the window with the writing on it and waited for Beverly. When Beverly emerged, Dena said, "I'll take it."

"Oh. When would you want it?"

"Today, if possible."

THE next afternoon Aunt Elner's friend Merle brought over a couple of old mattresses and a hideous brown sofa that Dena had bought at the Goodwill store out on the highway to use just until she figured out what all she wanted to put in the house. She borrowed some sheets and a few pillows from Norma's linen closet. After Merle left, Dena walked down to the grocery store and bought coffee, cream, milk, eggs, and a few frozen dinners, and came home and wandered around the house.

She found a bucket and Octagon soap under the sink and started cleaning the venetian blinds. They were in perfect shape. While she was cleaning, she looked up and saw a black-and-white cat sitting in the window, glaring at her. Dena walked to the front door and opened it, and the cat shot by her into the house, like a person trying to get the best seat in a crowded bus. There was a green tin wastebasket that had tipped over, and the cat ran to it and curled up in it and went to sleep. Dena was a little afraid of it and left it alone.

She went back to the blinds and opened them, and she could see the outline of the round rug that used to be on the floor. At about six thirty she was tired. She went out in the yard and sat in the swing and watched the sun go down over the field. When she came back in, she remembered dinner, turned on the oven, and heated up a frozen dinner and ate the entire thing.

As she sat at the table, she noticed how quiet it was in the kitchen. Dena got up and walked around the house, turning on all the lights, thinking about furniture she might put in all the rooms. After a while she went out on the front porch. A few minutes later the cat came and sat there with her. It was a warm and balmy evening, but a small breeze kept the air moving, and she could smell the flowers that were just starting to bloom on the side of the house. A few cars drove by; other than that, there was no activity.

At about eleven o'clock she and the cat went inside. She went into the bathroom and ran the water for a bath. The deep white tub took a long time to fill up, and when she got in and sat down, the water was almost up to her neck, and she had to laugh. It was like getting into a small swimming pool. After her bath she went into the bedroom, put her nightgown on, and bent down to pull her bed covers back. The cat jumped up on the bed and crawled under the sheet. A minute later she felt something pushing at her arm and heard the cat purring away, happy and contented to have her for a bed partner. She reached over and petted it. She had not slept with a cat since that night so many years ago at her mother's friend Christine's apartment, when Christine's cat, Milton, had slept beside her in the living room. It felt good.

IN THE morning she went over to pick up a little ivy plant for her window that Aunt Elner wanted her to have. Aunt Elner was overjoyed that she was going to be so close by. "I'm just tickled to death you are going to be living in Neighbor Dorothy's old house. Oh, honey, many is the broadcast I heard from there." Aunt Elner sat down at her kitchen table.

Dena reached over and took a fresh biscuit. "Was it a kind of news show?"

"A news show? You could call it that, but she had all kinds of things on there. People used to sing or play or do whatever they had a mind to. She gave out household hints, recipes, and had talks."

"What kind of talks?"

"Oh, all kinds. Anybody that wanted to come on and talk on the radio could. People used to stick their heads in the window and chat about things. One time Bess Truman came."

"What was Neighbor Dorothy like?"

"Oh, she was just a nice lady, had two children . . ."

"What did she sound like?"

"Real sweet, like she was glad you were listening. I sure do miss hearing her. Neighbor Dorothy was a lot of company, I can tell you that. Not that I didn't love living on the farm while Will was alive, but one of the bad parts about living way out in the country is I'd get so lonesome for people. My closest neighbor was twelve miles up the road. Will wasn't much of a talker, and I used to be starved for the sound of another person's voice. Neighbor Dorothy's show was like having a next-door neighbor to visit with every day. I don't know what kind of a show you'd call it, but it always made me feel better. Eat all the biscuits you want, honey. I was just going to give them to the birds."

Dena took another one and put butter and jam on it.

"Did you ever meet her, Aunt Elner? Neighbor Dorothy?"

"Oh, lands, yes. She was a good friend of your grandmother's. Come to think of it, you met her, too. Don't you remember?"

"No. When?"

"Oh, lots of times. Anna Lee, her daughter, and her friend Patsy ran a little nursery school out there on the back porch. That's where you used to go to nursery school. I remember one time, you must have been four, and you had your birthday party there with all your little nursery school friends. Your mother dressed you up like a china doll. Your grandparents came. Norma came. We all came."

Dena was surprised. "Really?"

"You were so happy, a happy little child, such a sweet thing."

"I was happy?"

"Oh, yes. I think that was the happiest time of all our lives, when we had our Baby Girl with us. We hated to lose you."

"I don't remember ever having a birthday party."

"You sure did. You know, I think we took a picture that day, if I'm not mistaken. Hold on and let me go find the box."

Dena could hear her opening and closing drawers.

Then she said, "Here it is!" and came back into the kitchen and handed a photograph to Dena. "Looka there. Now if that isn't you, a happy child, I'm a monkey's uncle."

Dena looked. It was a picture of a little blond girl sitting at the end of a small table full of other children. And there was her mother, leaning against the wall with her arms behind her. Her head was turned toward Dena, and she was smiling with love in her eyes. Dena had never seen her mother look at her like that; she had never felt that love she saw now.

Something else in the picture caught her eye. It was a cake with what looked to be a miniature merry-go-round on top.

"What's this?"

"Neighbor Dorothy made that. She made you one of her famous carousel cakes. It was pink and white. Don't you remember?"

On the way home, Dena thought there was something familiar about that cake, and yet she couldn't quite place it. It was something she had seen before. Then all of a sudden it hit her.

When Dena got to the house, she walked out on the back porch and stood there staring at the picture in her hand and crying. This was the same merry-go-round she had been dreaming about for years. This was the place she had been trying to get back to, where she had once been happy.

Welcome to the World, Baby Girl!

❧

ELMWOOD SPRINGS, MISSOURI   1944

"GOOD morning, everybody. It's another beautiful day here in Elmwood Springs, and we have hardly been able to contain ourselves waiting for this morning. First of all, I want to start by saying a great big welcome to the world to little Miss Dena Gene Nordstrom, who entered into the human race yesterday afternoon at four twenty. The baby girl is the brand-new granddaughter of Lodor and Gerta Nordstrom and the daughter of their son, Gene. We all remember what we went through when we lost Gene in the war, but by some miracle we have a little piece of him back, and we couldn't be happier. Gerta says that as soon as baby Dena is able to travel, her mother will be bringing her to Elmwood Springs, and we can't wait to see you, so hurry up and get here so we can all give you a proper welcome. . . . We have lots more good news today. We have a big winner in the Who's the Most Interesting Guest You Ever Had in Your Home? contest. And wait until you hear this one. I know it's not nice to toot one's own horn, but Mother Smith and I are so proud of Doc. For the second year in a row he has won the Rexall award for proficiency in dispensing drugs. So if you are listening down there at the drugstore, Doc, we are mighty proud of you.

"And now here are the Goodnight Twins to sing for you that old favorite, 'I'll Keep a Light Burning in the Window, Dear, 'Cause I'm Still in Love with You.' "

1978

AS THE days went by, Dena sat with the cat, wondering what she was going to do with the rest of her life. She had not thought much about life other than her work and pushing for success. What was left? Who was left? She had even forgotten why she had wanted to succeed in the first place. And why was she so devastated to think of life without success? What difference did it make anyhow?

After Dena's first week in the house Norma had brought over an old copy of *The Neighbor Dorothy Cookbook*. Lately Dena had spent hours staring at the picture of the smiling lady on the cover. Her eyes seemed to be looking right at Dena. She looked so alive, but she was gone. Dena began to wonder about the past. Was it gone forever? Or late at night, when all was dark and still, did it come back? Was Neighbor Dorothy still there somewhere, her voice still up in the air? All Dena knew was that she felt the presence of something in that house. Whatever it was, it did not scare her, and that was some relief, not to be afraid.

In the meantime, as the weeks went by, New York and the Ira Wallaces and Sidney Capellos of the world seemed farther and farther away. When Dena had arrived in Elmwood Springs, her nerves were in such bad shape that any loud noise caused her to jump, but now she felt safe here, a million miles away from the real world with its harsh lights and loud noises. As her ears adjusted to the quiet, she began to hear birds, crickets, and at times the sound of children playing. She could hear the church bells, and lately she could even tell which bells were ringing—the Unity, the Methodist, or the Lutheran. Each had a distinctive sound.

Sometimes she would go outside and look in at the house with the lights on, and a wave of homesickness would sweep over her, a feeling so powerful it brought tears to her eyes. She would stand alone and cry, not knowing what she was crying about. She began to feel like she did after she had been to the dentist and the Novocain started to wear off; it was painful, but a bittersweet pain. Slowly she was beginning to feel like the girl she used to be, the one that had gotten lost along the way.

Fall approached, and the network kept calling Sandy, wanting to know when Dena was coming back. She sent him a telegram: DEAR SANDY, TELL THEM I'M SORRY BUT THEY WILL HAVE TO START THE FALL SEASON WITHOUT ME. I FIND THAT I CANNOT COME BACK AT THIS TIME. NOT YET. LOVE, DENA.

DR. DIGGERS had told Dena to take her time making any decisions about her future, but as the weeks went by and she began to feel stronger, it became clear to her what she had to do first. She had to find out the truth about her mother, as painful as it might be.

But she needed help. She needed someone she could trust. Someone who was not in the business, someone who wouldn't turn around and sell information or talk to the press.

On September 21 she was sitting out in the yard in the sweetheart swing when a name popped into her head: Gerry O'Malley. She didn't know him all that well, but she trusted him. He certainly was not connected to the television business. That night Dr. Diggers called, and Dena asked, "You know Gerry O'Malley very well. Do you trust him?"

"With my life. Why?"

Dena told her that she had decided to find out about her mother. Dr. Diggers was pleased; this was what she had hoped for. "Good for you. Is there anything I can do?"

"Thank you, but the problem is, I can't look for her myself, for obvious reasons. What I need is to find a middleman who would be willing to say that it was *his* relative he was looking for, so my name would not be involved. Do you think Gerry would help?"

Diggers thought that Gerry would probably jump off the Chrysler Building if Dena asked. She said, "Call him. Now."

"GERRY, it's Dena."

"Well, hello," he said. "Are you back?"

"I'm still in Missouri."

"Are you coming back soon?"

"Gerry, that's just it. I don't know. I need some help."

"Oh," he said. "What's going on?"

She told him everything about her mother and read the letter she had gotten from Capello. Gerry said, "Who is this idiot?"

"He's a man I know, and he's dangerous."

"But that's just a bunch of stuff he's trying to scare you with. You know it's not true. Why can't you call his bluff?"

"Because I don't know if it's true or not. Gerry, you didn't know my mother. I always felt that there was something . . . wrong. Why else would somebody just run off like that?"

"There could be a thousand different reasons. Maybe she met a guy. Who knows? But Dena, you can't let this jerk drive you out of your job. This is blackmail!"

Dena said, "I don't have a choice. I don't want my mother's name dragged through the papers. And my name would make it news. Don't you understand? I don't have the strength to fight anymore."

Gerry realized she was right. "No, of course you don't. What am I thinking about? Let's concentrate on what we can do so you won't have to think about this anymore. The first thing we need to do is to find out what happened to your mother. Dena, do you trust me?"

"Yes."

"Okay. I have a friend in Washington I can call. You can trust him, too. The sooner we find out, the better. Are you up for that?"

"Yes. I think I am."

"You have been living with this all these years, all by yourself, but you're not alone anymore. I'm with you. Do you hear me?"

Dena felt as if a hundred-pound weight had been lifted off her chest. "Yes."

MACKY, Norma, and Aunt Elner were in the Warrens' living room when Dena told them that she had decided to try to find out more about her mother.

Norma looked at Macky with a horrified expression.

Macky slowly leaned forward in the chair and said thoughtfully, "Baby Girl, if that's what you want to do, then that's what you need to do. But is there any particular reason other than I'm sure you'd like to know what happened to her?"

She had not told them about Capello's threat. "I just think it's time I found out. I'd like to know if there's a chance she's still alive. I know my grandfather hired some people and they didn't find her, but that was—what—twenty years ago? They have all kinds of new ways to track people now."

Norma wailed, "Oh, I just knew we would make the wrong decision, no matter what we did. I told Macky that at the time. Now look what's happened."

"Norma, calm down. Just go get the box."

Dena appealed to Macky. "What's she talking about?"

Norma stood up and started for the bedroom, muttering, "I am going to have a complete nervous breakdown before I die."

Aunt Elner, not really clear about what was going on, smiled. "I'll tell you one thing about your mother— She was a pretty thing."

Norma came back in and handed Macky a tin box. "Here, you give it to her. I can't."

"What is it?" asked Dena.

"It's a letter, Baby Girl," Macky said, "from the detective agency your grandfather hired. I didn't think it would do you any good to see it at the time, but now, if you're gonna go ahead with this thing, you need to know about it."

Dena took the letter and skimmed it.

> Dear Mr. Nordstrom,
>
> Using all the information at hand from your daughter-in-law's marriage certificate, her Social Security number, and the birth date and place given, we have not found a Marion Chapman born on that date in Washington, D.C., listed in any official records. We have repeatedly checked all our national research sources and have found only eleven Marion Chapmans born around that date, all of whom have been accounted for. According to our files, no such person exists. If you have any further information, we will be happy to assist you in the future.
>
> Yours truly,
> A. A. Dunbar, Dunbar & Straton

One sentence jumped out at her: *According to our files, no such person exists.*

"Macky, what does that mean?" Dena asked.

"It means that for some reason she was using a different name than her own."

Aunt Elner said, "Maybe she didn't like her real name. I know if I hadn't married a Shimfessle, I would never have called myself that. I would have changed it to Jones . . . but I didn't tell them that!"

THE next afternoon Dena's phone rang.

"This is Richard Look with the State Department."

Dena's heart pounded. "Yes?"

"I understand from Gerry O'Malley that you might need a little help locating someone?"

Dena sat down. "Yes. What has Gerry told you?"

"Miss Nordstrom, just so you know, Gerry informed me of the

entire situation, and I understand completely the need for confidentiality. Your name will be kept out of the investigation."

The word investigation made her uneasy, but she said, "Thank you. I really appreciate that. Did he tell you about the letter?"

"The German spy stuff? Yes, but don't worry. We've handled these kinds of things before. All I need you to do for me is to send whatever you have—papers, letters, photographs, the names of anyone who might have known her. Can you do that?"

"Yes, I can do that."

"Fine. Then we'll go from there."

All there was to send him was the one photograph, plus the letter Macky had given her the night before, the letter about Capello's file, and the first name of a Rockette. Other than that woman, her mother had no friends that she knew of.

The minute Dena mailed the letter, she regretted it. Walking home, she began to wonder again why her mother had changed her name. Had she been a spy? What if they found her and arrested her? By the time Dena reached the house, she was so rattled she could hardly dial the phone.

Gerry was with a patient, and she left a message. By the time he called back twenty minutes later, she was almost hysterical.

Gerry said, "Dena, calm down. Listen to me. It's not too late. Nothing's happened. I can call Dick right now and stop it."

"Will you call right now? Tell him to forget it, please."

"All right, I'll call him now."

Five minutes later Gerry called back. "Okay. Everything is fine. He's not going to proceed. But he said when and if you ever need his help, he's there. Okay?"

"Gerry, I'm sorry. I guess I'm not as ready as I thought. Are you disappointed?"

"Of course not, Dena. You called me, didn't you?"

A FEW days later Dena, to her own surprise, called New York. A woman answered, "Radio City Music Hall. Personnel office."

"I wonder if you can help me. I am trying to locate a woman

named Christine. I think her last name was Whitten, or something like that. She was a Rockette, and she worked there around 1950 or '51. I know she lived in Greenwich Village at the time, and I was wondering if you had a present address for her."

"I'll have to look in my files."

"That's all right. I'll hold."

After some minutes the woman came back on. "I found a Christine Whitenow, but we don't have a current address, just the one she gave us at the time, Twenty-four St. Luke's Place."

"I see. Would you have any idea how I might find her?"

"No, but there were a few of the gals that used to keep up with one another. Try calling Dolly Berger in Fort Lauderdale, Florida." She gave her the number. "She might be able to help you."

A CHEERY woman picked up, and after Dena explained, Dolly Berger repeated the name. "Christine Whitenow? Oh, we used to send each other Christmas cards, but we stopped. If you can hold on, I might find it on one of my old lists. Hold on."

After a moment Dolly picked up in another room. "Hello, are you still there?"

"Yes, I'm here."

"Bear with me while I go through this. I'll tell you, sweetie, you know you are getting old when half of your Christmas card list is crossed off. It seems like people are dropping like flies."

Dena had a sinking feeling. It had never occurred to her that Christine could be dead. Then Dolly announced, "Here it is! Now, I'm not sure if she's still living there, but this is the last address I have on her. It's Mrs. Gregory Bruce, 4023 Massachusetts Avenue, Washington, D.C. The zip is 20019. And when you talk to her, tell her that Dolly is still alive. And, as we all say, kicking."

"I will, Mrs. Berger. And thank you so much."

A WEEK later Dena was in a car in Washington, D.C., listening to Gerry talk but not really hearing him. He was telling her to knock on the door and see if the woman was at home. They were parked across the street, where—according to Richard Look, who had checked it out—a Mrs. Gregory Bruce was still living. Massachusetts Avenue was a wide residential street in what looked to have been a nice upper-middle-class neighborhood at one time but was now beginning to decline. They had driven up and down the block but had not seen a living soul. Richard Look had advised Dena to show up unannounced. He said that on the off chance Mrs. Bruce might know about her mother's employer having been convicted of spying, she might not be so eager to discuss old times. Dena had agreed, but now that the moment was actually here, she was anxious. She turned to Gerry. "What's the signal again? I forgot."

"If it is her, and you feel like you need me to come in with you, wave, and I'll come. Otherwise I'll be here waiting for you."

She opened the car door and said, "Wish me luck." As she started up the cement steps, she thought, A coward dies a thousand deaths; a hero dies but one. This is just another interview, that's all.

She reached the front door, took a deep breath, and pushed the bell. She stood there and waited, then heard the sound of footsteps coming toward the door. A figure opened the door halfway, leaving the barred outer door closed. In the dim light Dena could see it was a dignified-looking woman who wore her silver-gray hair pulled straight back from her face.

"Yes?"

"Sorry to bother you. I'm looking for Mrs. Gregory Bruce."

The woman said, somewhat leery, "Yes, I'm Mrs. Bruce."

Dena was caught off guard for a moment. "Ah . . . I believe you used to know my mother, Marion Chapman?"

The woman frowned slightly. "Who?"

"Marion Chapman. You knew her around 1950 or 1951?"

The woman did not respond. Dena continued, "She had a daughter, and they came to see you at Radio City Music Hall. And one time we spent the night at your apartment in the Village on St. Luke's Place. You had a cat named Milton?"

Dena heard the sound of a loud iron lock clicking. The woman opened the door and stood staring at her in amazement.

"Dena? Are you Dena?"

"Yes."

Her entire demeanor changed. "Oh, for heaven's sake. Well, come in, come in."

Dena stepped inside. "Do you remember me?"

"Of course I do. I just can't believe it. How did you get here?"

"A friend brought me. He's going to wait in the car for me."

"Here, let me have your coat. Go on into the living room."

Dena went in and sat down. It was a dimly lit, rather formal room, furnished with furniture that looked as if it had been there for a long time. Christine came in, smoothing her hair. "I wish I had known you were coming. I just got in from a church meeting, and I don't have a thing to offer you as far as food goes. Here, let me put some lights on. What a surprise. I thought you looked familiar, but couldn't place where I'd seen you before."

As Christine went around switching on the lamps, Dena was able to get a good look at her. She was conservatively dressed in a gray dress and pearls. Somehow Dena had expected her to be blond and somewhat jazzier. This woman was reserved in speech and manner. Her features could have been Greek or Italian, and she was still quite attractive. Christine sat down across from her and asked, "Now tell me, where is Marion? How is she doing?"

A good interviewer, Dena wanted to let her talk a little longer and answered her question with another question. "How long has it been since you two have seen each other?"

"Oh, too long. We just lost touch with—" She did not finish. "Wait a minute. I know you. You're Dena Nordstrom!"

Dena smiled. "Yes."

Christine put her hand over her heart. "That's you? You grew up to be Dena Nordstrom? Oh, I can't believe it." She laughed. "No wonder you looked familiar." Christine kept shaking her head. "How in the world did you find me after all these years?"

"Believe it or not," Dena said, "I called Radio City Music Hall, and they told me to call a woman named Dolly Berger, who had your married name and address."

Christine smiled. "Dolly Berger, that crazy thing. But you still haven't told me about your mother. Is she all right?"

This was tricky. Dena needed to see what Christine knew.

"Actually, she's the reason I'm here. I was wondering if you could tell me when was the last time you saw or heard from her."

Christine thought. "Oh, I think it must have been— Well, I know it was before I got married, in 1953. I remember I wrote her at the last address she gave me—I think you and she had moved to Boston or Philadelphia by then—and I never heard back. Why? Is she all right? Did something happen to her?"

Dena could see by the genuine concern in her face that she was not hiding anything.

"That's just it. I don't know where she is or if she is still alive."

After Dena told her the whole story about that Christmas in Chicago, Christine looked stricken. "Oh, no. And she didn't leave a note or anything?"

"No, nothing. Just my gifts—and she just vanished."

Christine's eyes filled with tears. "Oh, no. That poor girl." She sat sadly shaking her head. Dena handed her a Kleenex. "I'm sorry. It's just so terrible. It breaks my heart to hear it. But I'm not surprised."

Dena spoke as calmly as possible. "You're not surprised?"

"No. From the beginning she was scared to death somebody might find out who she was. That you might be disgraced or thrown out of school."

Dena's heart began to pound.

"A lot of them disappeared like that, just dropped out of sight, couldn't stand the pressure. But to leave your child . . ." Christine started to cry again. "Oh, that poor girl, what she must have been going through."

Dena's face became chalk white, and she felt as if she might faint. Her worst nightmare was coming true. She was surprised to hear herself saying, "But she trusted you."

Christine blew her nose. "Oh, yes. She knew I would never have told anybody. Listen, how she wanted to live her life was her business, but there were a lot of people who didn't feel that way. And after all that mess about Theo hit the papers, she almost went crazy, she was so scared. She was convinced she was next."

Dena was pulled back into reality. "Theo? Who is Theo?"

"Her brother, Theo," Christine said, as if Dena should know.

Dena stopped her. "Wait a minute. My mother had a brother who was also a Nazi?"

Christine frowned at Dena. "A Nazi? Theo wasn't a Nazi. He was a violinist. Where did you hear that?"

"Well, isn't that what you said? Didn't you just say my mother was a Nazi spy?"

Christine was completely taken aback. "A spy? Your mother was not a Nazi spy. Who told you such a thing?"

"Didn't my mother work for a woman named Lili Steiner, who had a dress shop in New York?"

"She worked for some woman named Lili something. But what does that have to do with anybody spying?"

"Lili Steiner was convicted for spying and spent ten years in jail."

Christine said emphatically, "Well, I don't *care* what that woman was convicted of. Your mother was not a Nazi. My Lord, she hated the Nazis. Your poor grandfather had to get out of Vienna, leave everything he owned just to get away from them."

Dena's mind was reeling. So that was it—her mother was Jewish! That's why she changed her name, why no such person as Marion Chapman existed. This was the last thing in the world she had expected to hear . . . but what was the big deal about that? Why was her mother so afraid? Something was still not right. Her mind raced in a hundred different directions. If she was not a German spy, who was she running from?

Dena, distracted, said, "I don't understand. Why did she change her name?"

"A lot of people did. I did. You have to remember, things were very different back then. You couldn't get a job; you couldn't even get in most places. Whitenow was not my real name. If anybody looked at me funny, I used to say my mother was Spanish."

"Do you think my father knew?"

"No," she said. "I know for a fact he didn't."

"Would it have made a difference to him?"

"You never knew if it would or not. No, I think your mother just wanted to get married, have a baby, and forget it. It just broke poor Dr. Le Guarde's heart. First Theo and then your mother—"

"Who's Dr. Le Guarde?"

"Your grandfather."

Dena tried to recover. "Oh, I knew about my grandfather, but I didn't know he had been a doctor."

"Oh, yes," Christine said almost reverently. "Your grandfather was one of the most respected doctors in Washington. He was chief of staff at Freeman Hospital right over here and head of the medical school at Howard University for years. He was very well known."

"Really," was all that Dena could manage. This was the first time she had ever heard her mother's real last name. She looked at Christine. "Le Guarde. That doesn't sound like a Jewish name to me. Why would they have to change it?"

"Jewish?" Christine said with a puzzled expression. "Dr. Le Guarde was not Jewish."

"He wasn't? Was it my grandmother?"

"No, neither one. Where did you get that idea?"

Dena felt herself getting ready to be pulled through a knothole. Either she had completely lost her mind or Christine was purposely trying to confuse her. "Didn't you just get through telling me that my grandfather had to leave Vienna to escape the Nazis?"

"I said they had to leave, but not because they were Jewish."

"What are you talking about, then?"

Now it was Christine's turn to be confused. "Didn't you tell me you knew about your grandfather?"

"I said I knew I *had* a grandfather. But all my mother ever told me about her family was that they all burned to death in a fire."

"A fire? What fire?"

"Was that not true?"

All of a sudden Christine realized what had happened. She gasped, "Oh, my God in heaven, I thought you knew."

"Knew what? I thought you told me that you and my mother were Jewish. Isn't that what you just told me?"

Christine shook her head. "No."

"Then you're not Jewish either."

"No."

"You're not." Dena scanned her face once more, looking for an answer. "Are you Italian? Is that it? Does it have something to do with the Mafia?"

Christine was clearly torn. "Dena, please don't ask me anything else. I promised your mother."

Dena's eyes got big. "Then she *was* in the Mafia!"

"No, your mother was not in the Mafia."

Dena's head began to throb. "Then what is it? I can't imagine what it was that was so terrible . . . that she would just leave like that. What didn't she want me to know—"

Dena suddenly stopped talking. Slowly it began to dawn on her—what Christine had assumed she knew all along. What had been right before her eyes and had been so obvious from the start. Something she had missed completely until this very second. All at once everything began to clear, and things started to fall into place, like pool balls dropping into pockets. Christine was not Italian or Greek or anything else. Christine was a light-skinned black woman.

Dena and Christine sat there for a moment staring at each other, both in shock but for different reasons. After a time Dena went outside and motioned to Gerry to roll his window down. "Gerry, I think you'd better come in."

Gerry got out of the car quickly. "Did she tell you anything?"

"Oh, yes. You're not going to believe this—"

"What?"

"Wait."

WHEN Dena and Gerry got back to the hotel, Dena was worn out. She felt as if she had been riding a giant Tilt-A-Whirl at the carnival, whipped first one way and then the other. Gerry registered them under his name but had gotten a suite with two bedrooms. At eight thirty he called her from his room. "How are you? Sure you don't want me to order you some dinner?"

"No. I just want to sleep." Then she asked, for the twentieth time, "Do you *believe* this?"

"Well . . . it's different from what we expected."

Later Gerry was rereading *What's Doing in Washington* magazine when the phone rang. It was Macky Warren, wanting to know how things were going. Dena had said Macky might be calling and to let him know what was going on.

Gerry said, "Well, we found the woman we were looking for."

"Great. What did she say?"

"She told Dena that her mother was a black woman."

"A what?" Macky was quite sure he had not heard right.

"A black—you know, like Lena Horne. Light but black. The woman didn't know what happened to her, but at least now we know the mother's real name. That's a start. Dena's asleep in the other room, but I'm sure she'll call you when we know more."

MACKY walked slowly back into the living room, where he had left Norma and Aunt Elner cracking pecans.

Norma sat waiting for news like a bird waiting for a worm. "Well?" she asked, her eyes wide. "What did she say?"

"I didn't talk to her. I talked to her friend. She was asleep."

"Yes . . . And?"

"And he said they found the woman."

"What did she say about Dena's mother?"

Macky tried to sound casual. "She said that Dena's mother was a black woman." He sat down and picked up the paper.

Norma looked at him incredulously. "What?"

"Black."

She squinted at him. "What? You mean Amos and Andy black?"

"No. He said more like Lena Horne black."

Norma waved him off. "Oh, you are making this up."

He looked over the top of his paper at her. "I'm telling you, he said she was black. That's what the woman said. I'm just repeating."

"Oh, don't be ridiculous. She was no more black than I am!" Norma cracked a pecan to make her point.

"Norma, you asked, and I told you."

"Well, he's wrong. Don't you think somebody would have noticed if Gene had married a colored girl? Not one person did. Did they, Aunt Elner?"

"Not that I recall."

"Of course they didn't. She was a white person, for goodness' sake. How can you be black if you are a white person? It makes no sense at all. Lena Horne, my foot."

Aunt Elner looked up, confused. "How did Lena Horne get in this? Was she there?"

"Oh, she's not in it, Aunt Elner," said Norma. "He's making it up just to get my goat. He is determined to drive me insane."

Macky heaved a sigh. "Have it your own way, Norma."

Minutes passed. Norma cracked more pecans. "The very idea of saying a white person is black. I knew her; you didn't."

"Norma, I'm not saying it. The woman said it. I don't know!"

Aunt Elner said, "Well, whatever she was, she was a pretty thing. Isn't that what they say? That black is beautiful?" She emptied her bowl of shells into the paper bag at her feet. "And I'll tell you another thing. They ought to put Amos and Andy back on the radio. Where did Amos and Andy go, is what I want to know."

Who Was My Mother?

❧

Washington, D.C.   1978

THE next day Dena went back to see Christine. They sat in the kitchen drinking coffee. "Last night after you left," Christine said, "I racked my brain trying to think of someone who might know where Theo is. I called my brother and a few other people who knew him, and they all said the same thing. They have no idea. And your mother? Well, God only knows. I know I'm the only one besides Theo who knew that she was passing." She sipped slowly. "I'm as baffled as you are. All I know is that your mother adored you. After your father was killed, you were the only thing she cared about."

"If she cared about me so much, how could she just leave?"

"I don't know." Christine sighed. "Your mother was a complicated girl, even when she was young."

"What was she like?"

Christine weighed her words. "Well, she and Theo were both different. They had been raised in Vienna. Your grandfather went there to study medicine, and that's where he met your grandmother."

"Was my grandmother black?"

"No. She was German, a doctor's daughter, came from plenty of money. I don't think your grandfather would ever have left Vienna if it had not been for the war. He may have had blond hair and green eyes, but his visa still said Negro, and don't forget Hitler didn't like blacks any more than he did Jews.

"You can imagine what a shock it was for your mother and Theo when they came back. One day they were white Viennese people, and the next thing they knew, they were colored people living in a colored neighborhood. But your mother was such a little lady. She spoke perfect French and German, played the piano. Both she and Theo were so well behaved. And oh, how they loved their father."

"Do you remember him?"

"Oh, yes. Dr. Le Guarde and my daddy were good friends. We used to love to go over there all the time. It was a beautiful home, so tastefully decorated. Your grandfather and grandmother both loved music, and they always had music playing—Brahms, Schumann, Strauss—and the parties they had. . . . A library second to none, as my daddy used to say, and the art. They brought a lot of wonderful paintings from Europe. Their home was their haven."

"What did my grandfather look like?"

"Oh, he was a good-looking man. Tall, very distinguished."

"I see." Dena wanted to ask the next question but was concerned it might sound like an insult. "How dark was he?"

Christine was not offended. "About as dark as you with a tan. He was a real blue vein."

"A blue vein?"

Christine laughed and turned her arm over. "So light you can see the veins. His mother had been one of those light-skinned quadroons from New Orleans and had married a Frenchman."

"What did Theo look like?"

"Theo? Oh, well, if it's possible for a man to be beautiful, then he was. I was in love with Theo. He looked more like his mother, with those big brown eyes and long lashes. I used to sit and watch him practice his violin for hours, but he never looked at me or any girl. All he cared about was playing that violin."

Dena sat there trying her best to keep up. "If my mother's mother was full-blooded German and her grandfather was French, how much black blood did my mother have?"

"About a drop, if there is such a thing as black blood, which there isn't. Back then, one sixteenth of a drop of Negro blood was one drop too much. You were still Negro under the law."

"Do you think my father would have cared?"

Christine shrugged. "I don't know. But that was just it—you never knew how people were going to feel. And don't forget that was in the '40s, and it was illegal in some states for a person to marry outside their race. People were still being put in jail for it."

"Why didn't my mother tell me? It wouldn't have made any difference to me."

Christine's smile was sad and weary. "Oh, yes, it would have. Maybe not as much as your mother thought, but she figured you were better off not knowing. Think about it. Could you have gone to the same schools, dated the same boys, walked through the same doors? Oh, you might have made it eventually because of your looks and talent, but everywhere you went, they would have been looking at you with that in mind."

"It wouldn't have changed the way I felt about my mother."

"No, maybe not, but it would have changed the way you looked at the world. And how the world looked back. It changes you.

Believe me. Your mother was just trying to spare you heartache."

"Did she ever tell you why she decided to pass for good?"

"No, but I figured she felt the same way Theo did. He was pulled one way and then the other till he didn't know what or who he was. Finally he was just pulled apart, all because of a newspaper article. He had to choose between his daddy and his music. He didn't want to be the great new Negro musician; he just wanted to be a musician. And believe me, they weren't going to let a Negro in any symphony orchestra, not then. You still don't see all that many today."

"No, you don't."

"I could have passed for good if I had liked it, but I just felt more comfortable with my own people. Still, I don't judge those who did. When you get as old as I am, you realize that life is hard, and if you can get a break in this world, why not take it? But I don't envy those who passed. It's like going to another country and never being able to go home again." Christine sighed. "I tell you the truth, I'm so tired of this race thing, the things it does to people. I don't know what caused your mother to run off like that, but whatever it was, she must have had a good reason. Because I know she loved you."

AFTER Dena's morning with Christine she got into the car, where Gerry was waiting. He looked at her. "How are you?"

"Fine." But she wasn't. She had been strangely touched by Christine. There was something about her, a look in her eyes. She had seen the same look at times in her mother's. She started to cry. "I'm sorry. I don't know what's the matter with me."

"That's all right, Dena. You're going through a lot right now."

She had learned much in two days, but she still had not found out what happened to her mother that Christmas. But at least they had a little more information to pass on to Richard Look.

That night as Gerry was walking her to the plane back to Missouri, he reassured her. "Richard said this is plenty to work with. I promise, the minute he finds anything, I'll call you."

When they reached the gate, Dena shook his hand. "Gerry, I don't know how to thank you. You've really been a good friend."

He shrugged it off. "Hey, that's what I'm here for." He smiled and waved back as she went through the gateway. He wanted to get on that plane with her so badly it almost made him dizzy, but he knew he had to let her go. Gerry thought of nothing but Dena as he drove back to New York.

On the plane home, Dena could think of nothing except a family she never knew she had until yesterday.

THE minute Dena walked in the door, she called Dr. Diggers and told her about her mother.

Diggers sounded as surprised as Dena had been. "Well, I must say, of all the things I suspected, this was not one of them, and I should have guessed. Me of all people! When I first started in practice, half of my patients were passing. Oh, yes. Unfortunately, I know all about it. But the point is, how do you feel about it?"

"Betrayed. Confused. Lost, like I never really knew my mother."

"Sweetie pie, there was a big part of her you didn't know, but at least now we have a pretty good explanation of why she seemed so remote. Passing is a complicated issue, with a lot of serious problems that go along with it. Guilt, confused identity, feelings of isolation, deception, abandonment. It's very stressful."

"I understand all that, but I just can't understand why she didn't tell me. I could have helped her. I was her daughter."

"Yes, but don't forget you were the closest thing to her. She might have been afraid of losing you, afraid if you knew, you wouldn't love her. I've seen it happen before. People push away the very ones they don't want to lose trying to hold them."

"I know, but why did she just disappear like that? And why at Christmas? Why couldn't she have waited?"

"Oh, sweetie, it could have been one of a hundred different reasons. She may have met someone, or she may have just reached a breaking point living with that much stress every day. A good possibility is that it built up over the years, and she couldn't take the pressure any longer, and one day she had some sort of psychic break, lost touch with reality. Just snapped and took off."

"Is that what you think happened?"

"Well, that would be my guess, based on what we know. But the important thing is she gave you all the love she was capable of giving under the circumstances. It wasn't as much as you needed, but there it is. It's unfair and it's lousy, but that's life, and at least now we know the basic cause of your problems. The next thing for us to do is to try to get beyond them and get on with your life. All right. Now, when are you coming back to New York?"

"I'm not sure. I haven't thought about it yet."

"No. You are probably still in a state of shock. Do me a favor and take some time before you make any decisions. Okay?"

THAT night Norma and Macky brought over a hot supper.

When Dena told them what Dr. Diggers thought had happened, a look of relief came over Norma's face. "I am so glad to finally find out what was the matter. I was always afraid it was something that we had done, or maybe it was just us she didn't like."

For the next three days Dena still felt dazed. But a week later, as her mind began to clear, she woke in the middle of the night and sat straight up in bed. Something did not add up. She was too good a reporter not to know when a piece was missing from a story.

Her mother had loved her. She knew that now. She would not have left unless something was terribly wrong. But what? Why had her mother left Elmwood Springs so abruptly in 1948? Who was the man who spoke German?

As soon as the sun came up, Dena made her first call.

"Christine, it's Dena."

"Oh, hello. How are you?"

"I have a question for you. You mentioned that there had been something in the papers about my mother's brother, Theo, and I was wondering what year that was."

"Oh, dear, it must have been in the early '40s. This stupid woman Ida Baily Chambless, who set herself up as a black society columnist of sorts, wrote the story. I never read it. Daddy said she was nothing but a Georgia nobody who thought she should be invited everywhere. She had a run-in with your grandfather years before, and she went after poor Theo with a vengeance. Pretended she was on some crusade, but she was just jealous. If she couldn't pass, nobody was going to pass. Honey, I was lucky she didn't come after me."

"Is she still alive?"

"No, thank heavens. She finally got herself murdered."

Dena's heart skipped a beat. "Murdered? When?"

"Oh, a long time ago. I was still living in New York. It must have been 1948, somewhere around then."

Dena's heart skipped two beats. That was the same year she and her mother had left Elmwood Springs in such a hurry.

SAN FRANCISCO, CALIFORNIA   1942

FROM the moment Carlos Maurice Montenegro began to play, Joseph Hoffman knew that the young man before him was one of the most extraordinarily gifted violinists he had ever heard. Hoffman took him under his wing, and in less than six months Carlos Montenegro was named first violinist of the San Francisco Symphony. He had one flaw—he was almost too pretty.

When he played, most women could not take their eyes off him. Carlos had never talked about himself or where he was from, but there had been rumors that he was probably the son of a Spanish count. Many dreamed of those beautiful hands and long, delicate fingers and the way the shadow of his eyelashes fell across his cheek. But there was something else that concerned his teacher. Without his violin Carlos seemed unusually shy and unsure of himself. He seemed content to just play in the orchestra and to compose. Hoffman was eager to have such a talent exposed to the world, and he took it upon himself to enter one of Carlos's concertos in an international music competition held in Quebec.

The winner was assured of a year's worth of concerts around the world. All the boy needed was this chance to tour. Then he would have the world at his feet. A month later, to Hoffman's great joy and to Carlos's great surprise, he won. But there was, shortly, another surprise waiting for Carlos.

SOCIETY SLANTS
by Ida Baily Chambless

There is exciting news today. It came to my attention that last week's happy headline "American Wins International Music Competition" should have read "American Negro Wins International Music Competition." The celebrated recipient is none other than Theodore Karl Le Guarde, who has of late adopted the nom de plume Carlos Maurice Montenegro, for "artistic" reasons, no doubt. His father is Dr. James A. Le Guarde, a prominent Negro doctor here in Washington.

Despite Mr. Le Guarde's stage name, nothing could keep us from shouting from the highest rooftops that one of us is on his way to the big time. It is with great glee and salutations to the world that I announce that Carlos Maurice Montenegro, *né* Theodore Le Guarde, has just been named Negro of the Year by this newspaper. We are proud of so many high achievers who share our Negro heritage, and I for one shall be awaiting his return to our fair city with a great big welcome home. Move over Cab Calloway, Duke, Jelly Roll, and Louis, and make room for a new genius on the block!

When Theo's photograph, along with Ida Baily Chambless's press release announcing that he had been named Negro of the Year, appeared in newspapers around the country, all hopes of a classical career went down the drain. His colleagues were stunned by the news. Suddenly they saw him as an impostor who had lied to them. Hoffman was devastated for Theo and went immediately to his apartment but found that Theo would not let him in. He would speak to no one. The day after the article appeared, he was flooded with invitations from the leading Negro organizations. They were proud of him. As the Negro newspaper the Washington *Bee* put it, "We add a new star in the crown of Negro accomplishments."

White newspapers took a different tack. The caption under his photograph read NEGRO CAUGHT MISREPRESENTING ANCESTRY.

The International Music Committee reconvened for an emergency meeting and voted to a man to stand by its decision, but there was a war in Europe, most of Carlos's concerts had been planned for America, and one by one they began to be canceled. After several weeks and much pressure all around, a press release was sent:

> The International Music Committee has reconvened for the second time and announced today that it has withdrawn its cash prize and canceled all concert dates of recent first-prize winner Carlos Montenegro. A spokesman said this decision was made with deepest regrets and was based not on the fact that he is a Negro, but that he withheld that fact from the committee.

His sister, Marguerite, was working in New York. When she read about what had happened to Theo, she immediately went to San Francisco. But by the time she arrived, he had disappeared.

AFTER he left San Francisco, Theo wandered aimlessly about the country. He tried to work at a factory job, but in a few days he collapsed with what the doctors termed a nervous breakdown, and he spent a year in a charity ward in a hospital outside of Lansing, Michigan. After he was released, he slowly made his way back to Washington, D.C., washing dishes, sweeping floors, anything to get by. Once back, he managed to make a fair living giving private violin lessons to the children of wealthy diplomats. He often thought about his sister. He hoped she was safe and happy.

For the next four years he lived less than a mile from his father, but it might as well have been a thousand miles. He wanted to see his father, but he had caused him enough pain, and as much as he missed him, he couldn't face him. Theo sometimes bought a copy of the Washington *Bee* just to see if it had any mention of his father. It was there he learned of his death. The day of the funeral he stood in the back of St. Augustine Church and listened to the priest eulogize his father as a great man and a great doctor. No mention was made of his two children. It was as if they had never existed.

Theo left before the service was over, shaking with regret, sorrow, anger. He hated himself. How could he have turned his back on his daddy? If only he could go back. But it was too late. He was completely alone now. All he had was his sister.

Word had reached Mrs. Chambless that someone who looked like Theo had been spotted leaving the church, but the sister had not been spotted, and it confirmed what Chambless had already begun to suspect. Two days after the funeral she wrote:

SOCIETY SLANTS

I have dipped my spoon into the thick, rich soup of Negro history of our fair city and have pulled out a tasty morsel. Our reluctant Negro musical genius, Theodore Le Guarde, has a sister, Marguerite, who has all but vanished into thin air. Could it be that she too has chosen to take the same traitorous route leading into white society? As the children at play call, Come out, come out, wherever you are. It is a sad fact that there are those of our race who do not have the decency to come out in the open of their own accord, and if I am the chosen to spur you to acknowledge you to your duty, so be it.

You will not be allowed to sit at the table of acceptance until all Negroes are seated. And a word to the wise to all you *others* out there resting your pretty heads upon the soft white pillows of deception: Rest not, for your days are numbered.

THAT night Theo Le Guarde walked with Chambless's column in his pocket to her house in Le Droit park. The house was dark except for a light in a room on the second floor. He went to the front door and knocked. No one answered. He tried the door, and it was unlocked; in fact, it swung wide open. Mrs. Chambless had no fear. What man would dare to rob her? Theo stepped in and closed the door behind him. He could hear the sound of typing, and he followed the stairs to the room where she sat, enormous in a pink housecoat, completely absorbed in her work.

She did not see him until he was standing right in front of her. She let out a, "Whooo! Good God Almighty. You nearly scared me to death. What do you mean coming in here and sneaking up on me like that?" She peered at the gaunt figure before her. "Who are you? Do I know you?"

Theo began to shake and struggled to get the words out. "Why—Why are you doing this? Why did you ruin my life?"

Suddenly Mrs. Chambless sensed who he was and sat back in her chair with a smug, mocking smile. "Well, well, well. If it's not the great Theodore Le Guarde himself." Then her expression changed as she lunged forward and hissed at him with a voice filled with contempt. "Listen. . . . If your life got ruined, it was you that ruined it, not me. You and that high-and-mighty family of yours." She dismissed him with a wave of her hand. As an afterthought she added, "And tell that sister of yours she's next."

At that moment something deep inside Theo broke loose, and he heard a roaring in his ears so loud that he could not hear Ida Baily Chambless's screams as he grabbed her by the throat. He was choking the very life out of her, and he could not stop.

The next thing he remembered, he was outside in the cold, wringing wet with sweat. He walked for a mile, not knowing where he was going until he was at the Lincoln Memorial. He looked up at the statue of the man and suddenly heard a woman's screams in his ears and saw the grotesque face of Mrs. Ida Chambless. He looked down at his hands, and he began to sob. He had to find his sister. He would be safe with her.

Living a Lie

✤

NEW YORK CITY   1942

DENA'S mother, Marguerite Le Guarde, had not intended to lie about who she was. It just happened. She had taken a trip to New York to help a friend shop for her trousseau. When she spoke to the owner of the shop in German, Lili Carlotta Steiner recognized at once that the young girl had been raised in Vienna, as she had.

Delighted with the pretty young woman who obviously knew about fine clothes, Steiner offered her a job. Excited, Marguerite wrote her father and asked him if she might stay for the summer. Her father wrote back and said yes. Her mother had died recently, and he thought the change might be helpful.

When she went for her work permit, she gave the made-up name of Marion Chapman. Why take the chance of someone recognizing her real name? By now her father was well known in medical circles, and his name had appeared in the paper numerous times connected with various Negro organizations. Why go through the humiliation of trying to convince people that she was the daughter of a famous Negro doctor? No one ever believed her, and besides, the job was only for a few months.

But as the weeks went by, she found she liked being Marion Chapman, an ordinary working girl. Lili had found her a small apartment in a predominantly German neighborhood. She ate German food, heard familiar music, and as she wrote to her father, it was "somewhat like being back home in Vienna."

She was completely unaware of Lili's political activities. To Marguerite, Lili was just a nice woman who had given her a job. All she knew or cared about was that as much as she missed her father, she was happier in New York. She liked being around her own people again. But it was only to last a short time. When she read in the newspaper about Theo's losing the award, she was devastated for him. Music was his life. He had always been delicate and highstrung, and she was frightened of what he might do to himself. She tried to call but could not reach him, so she immediately took a train to San Francisco. By the time she arrived, he had disappeared again. She stayed in San Francisco and took a job at a department store, hoping Theo might come back. But he didn't.

She finally gave up waiting and was about to go home to her father in Washington. Then she met Private Gene Nordstrom. He looked as if he had just stepped off a marine recruiting poster. He was at least six feet three, with blue eyes and white-blond hair. She had not meant to fall in love, but his joy and enthusiasm for life had been so infectious that there was nothing she could do about it. She had every intention of telling Gene about her father and her brother, but after what happened to Theo when people found out about him, she was afraid to tell him. The more deeply in love she fell, the more and more frightened she became of losing him. He was so open, he might not care, but in matters of race you could never be sure.

Then he proposed. There was a war going on, and everything was happening so fast. That year it seemed that everybody in San Francisco was in a mad rush to get married, desperate to have a few days together before the men went off to war. After they got word that Gene's unit was shipping out immediately, there was no time to tell him, or so she told herself.

When they arrived at the courthouse the next morning, she told the clerk she did not have a birth certificate, that it had been lost in a fire. The clerk was annoyed, but he issued them a license anyway. She should not have lied, but she was hopelessly in love, and Gene was leaving. They just wanted to get married.

It was not until Gene was gone for a week that she realized the seriousness of what she had done. Then she became filled with remorse. Had she been in such a daze that she actually believed she was Marion Chapman, that there was no such person as Marguerite Le Guarde? She made a vow that she would tell Gene the truth the minute he came home. But he never came back.

Gene had been dead only a month when she discovered she was pregnant. After many nights of crying and wondering what to do, she finally decided. She wanted her baby to be raised free of those problems, free of her. After the baby was born, she would take the child home to Gene's parents in Elmwood Springs. After a few days she would just leave, disappear, and it would be as if Marion Chapman had never existed at all.

Her plan was to go back to Washington, to her father, and resume her life as it had been. She took her daughter to Elmwood Springs, but the one thing she had not planned on was just how much she would love the little blond baby girl who had Gene's eyes.

As hard as she tried, she could not leave. The Nordstroms had taken her in with open arms and without any questions about her past. She found small-town life out in the middle of the country to be as wonderful as Gene had described and was enjoying seeing her child grow up such a happy little girl. Dena had just had her fourth birthday party when suddenly her mother's world fell apart again.

Five days after Dena's party Theo came to Elmwood Springs looking for her. At first she was upset at him for just showing up like that. Then Theo told her of her father's death. And he showed her the column Ida Baily Chambless had written about her, wanting to know her whereabouts. He broke down and confessed that he had murdered the woman and that the police might be after him. When she heard that, Marion was terrified. He begged her to hide him, to let him stay, but she refused and sent him away. As much as she loved her brother, her first thought was of Dena. She could not let the Nordstroms be dragged into a murder investigation, find out who she really was. She had implored Theo to please stay away from her, but in the state he was in, she could not be sure he would not come back.

The next day she took Dena and left Elmwood Springs. She and Dena began moving from place to place so Theo would not find them, but it wasn't easy. Time and time again he found her. Each time he became more desperate, needed greater sums of money. And each time she told him it was the last time. As frightened as she was, it broke her heart to send him away, but it was too late to undo the past. She had to think about Dena now. She had gone back to using the name Chapman instead of Nordstrom at work, so if there was to be trouble, she and Dena would have different names.

Over the years, without anyone she could trust or talk to, her fears grew worse and worse that one day her brother would be arrested and all the details of the murder and his family would come out. Simple gestures of friendship from co-workers, or anyone attempting to get close to her, frightened her. She did not want anyone to have too much information in case the police might be looking for her brother.

Theo fared no better. Over the next decade he had fled from imaginary police all over the world. Everywhere he looked, he saw them lurking in the shadows, waiting to grab him. In 1953, with money from his sister, he somehow managed to sneak onto a steamer headed for South America, and after two more years he worked his way back to Vienna, where he hid out in a damp basement in a seedy part of the city.

Although the brother and sister had no way of knowing, the Washington police had closed the investigation of the murder of Mrs. Ida Baily Chambless two months after it took place. As far as the police were concerned, those people were always killing each other, and as long as they didn't bother any white people, the police couldn't have cared less.

CHICAGO, ILLINOIS   DECEMBER 1959

MARION had been jumpy and on edge more than usual. The phone call she had gotten a few days before from a stranger wanting to use Dena's picture on the cover of *Seventeen* magazine had rattled her so that she was having a hard time trying to get things together for Dena's Christmas. It was only a week away, but the same nagging questions were gnawing at her: Why did that woman really want to put Dena's picture in a magazine? Was someone trying to connect her and her daughter? She was so distracted that she had to wrap and unwrap the last of Dena's presents, something she was usually expert at. Lately, even at work, the simplest of tasks seemed so difficult that she could hardly get through them.

She had just put the last present in the closet when the phone rang and startled her. Who could be calling at this time of night?

It was long-distance from Vienna. Theo was in the hospital, dying. The man said Theo had given her name as next of kin, and if she wanted to see him, she had better come right away.

When she put the phone down, her heart was pounding so hard she could scarcely think. All she knew was that she had to get to Theo. He needed her, and there was no time to waste. She quickly packed a bag, ran out in the freezing rain, and hailed a cab for the airport. Thank heavens she had kept her Austrian passport. Eighteen sleepless hours later she arrived at the hospital.

When she was led into the ward where they had him, she was shocked to see the person the nurse pointed out. At first she could not be sure if it was her brother. The man lying there was so small; his face was so old and drawn; it couldn't be Theo.

But it was. As she got closer, she recognized his hands, his long, delicate fingers. Tears ran down her face as she sat by his bed and held the hand of what was left of her brother. She sat there with him for the next three days until he died.

She could not be sure if he was even aware that she had been there, but at least he did not die alone in a charity ward.

For those three days she felt so helpless, had such a sense of deep despair. To think that Theo, of all people, who could have brought such joy and beauty to the world, should have ended up like this. That he would have been so tortured, been driven to murder all because of that one drop of blood. Poor Theo. Every bone in her body ached with regret that she had not done more to help him.

Two days later she stood shivering in a cemetery on the outskirts of Vienna, looking down at the small headstone:

THEODORE KARL LE GUARDE
MUSICIAN
1916–1959

It was all over. She had done everything she had to do. Now she could go home to Dena.

As she walked back through the cemetery, a sudden wind kicked up, and she thought she heard a small limb or twig snap off a tree. She turned to look, but she did not see anything. She had not slept for days and was now burning with a raging fever, but as she continued on, she began to feel an odd sense of relief, almost as if something heavy had been lifted. At that moment she looked up and noticed how blue and clear the sky had become.

She had been so occupied with Theo that today was the first time she actually realized: She was home! Suddenly it seemed that the entire city had come into sharp focus. Colors looked brighter to her, and sounds seemed strange and amplified.

She walked over to her family's old apartment house in the Lothringerstrasse, looked up, and remembered the good times, the music, the laughter. She walked over to the Alsarstrasse, past the general hospital where her father and grandfather had practiced medicine, and along the Elisabethstrasse Promenade beside the Danube, past the Central Café, the Café Mozart, and everywhere she went, she heard music. Vienna was now occupied by French, English, American, and Russian soldiers, but she did not notice them. She saw only what she remembered. Her beautiful city seemed almost exactly as she had left it. She felt ten years old again and happy.

It was late afternoon when she walked back to her hotel. Fifteen minutes later she stepped into a tub full of warm water. Despite the fever, she felt so relaxed and yet so alive. She reached up and opened the small window and heard the sounds of the city below. She could hear a soprano rehearsing in the Staatsoper House across the street. She smiled and leaned back and waited until all the water had gone down the drain.

For the first time in years she wasn't afraid. It had come to her this morning at Theo's grave that she was the last of the Le Guardes. The only one left. The one last drop of blood in her was the only link that could connect Dena with the Le Guardes. She closed her eyes and squeezed the razor blade in her hand. She knew what she had to do.

It was so simple. Why hadn't she thought of it before?

Where was it? she wondered. Where was it lurking? Did it stay in one place, or did it travel thoughout her body? She would just get rid of it once and for all. First the left side, the ankle, then the wrist. She must let it escape. Then the right side. There, it was done. She leaned back and waited. She felt a strange calm come over her as the blood flowed out of her, so red against the stark white tub, past her, and on down the drain. Oh, what a relief to finally get it out. Then she and Dena would be free. As she lay waiting, a faint tune began to play over and over again in her head, a sad sort of waltz. She began to softly hum the tune.

What was it? Oh, yes, now she remembered. It was an old waltz, "Vienna, City of My Dreams." A waltz from her childhood. Yes, soon she heard the music, softly at first, and then it became louder and louder until the sound of an entire orchestra filled her ears and the words sang to her from so long ago. . . .

She had only been trying to get rid of one drop of blood. She had meant to go back to the little girl who now sat in the apartment in Chicago waiting for her—and live happily ever after. She had not meant to kill herself. It just happened.

The Decision

ELMWOOD SPRINGS, MISSOURI   1978

THREE weeks after Dena had been to Washington, the phone rang. "Miss Nordstrom, it's Richard Look."

She closed her eyes and waited for his next sentence. "I have some news about your mother, and I'm afraid it's not good news."

She sat down and listened while he read her the report. Then he said he would send it to her. Three days later, when the large, ominous-looking envelope arrived, she put it down on the kitchen table. She did not want to open it. The facts inside were so shocking, so brutal, so final.

Her mother had destroyed herself over something that in a few more years might not even matter. It was unfair that a person's life could be changed so dramatically by just a simple matter of timing. If only her mother had been born in a different time, she would have been spared all that unnecessary misery. Just a few years later and Dena might have had her mother back.

She opened the envelope. Inside was another envelope, with a letter attached:

Dear Mr. Look,

Pursuant to your inquiry, we have obtained the following information:

Le Guarde, Theodore: 43 years of age, cause of death unknown. Central Cemetery, plot 578.

Le Guarde, Marguerite Louise: 39 years of age, cause of death apparent suicide by multiple razor cuts, Hotel Sacher.

The whereabouts of Marguerite Le Guarde's remains have not been located. She was most probably buried in one of several municipal gravesites. I am sorry that our investigation could not have brought you happier news.

As the inquiry was made on behalf of a family member, we have enclosed some heretofore unclaimed personal effects.

Sincerely,

Dieter Kleim, Director of Forensic Files

Vienna, Austria

The envelope inside had been closed with a red wax seal. Dena took a deep breath and broke it open. Inside was her mother's passport. Underneath her picture was written "Marguerite Louise Le Guarde—born, Vienna, Austria, 1920." A train ticket and about two hundred American dollars, a folded sheet of Hotel Sacher stationery. Dena unfolded it and read the note her mother had hurriedly scribbled across the page to herself: "Pay hospital bill. Call Dena. Tell her to wait at apartment."

Seeing her mother's handwriting after all these years—and realizing that her mother had intended to return to her—was a shock. If only she could have told her mother that nothing mattered, that she loved her and needed her. But she couldn't. All she could do was sit there and cry while the cat, upset because Dena was upset, kept rubbing up against her, over and over.

DR. DIGGERS had told Dena not to make any important decisions, that she needed to take time to think before she did anything. After she found out about her mother, she did just that. She had a lot of things to think about. She felt sad, but mostly she felt as if she was not the same person she had been just a few weeks earlier. Everything she thought she knew as fact wasn't. Everything she had believed was important wasn't.

Today she was out in Aunt Elner's backyard, walking along with her as she watered her tomato plants.

"Aunt Elner," she said, "do you like people?"

"Oh, lands yes, honey, sure I do." She cocked her head to the left. "Come to think of it, I guess you could go so far as to say that people are my pets. They just tickle me to death. There is nothing cuter to me than a pack of Brownies or Cub Scouts or a table full of oldsters." Aunt Elner looked up at the sky, which was turning slightly gray over to the west. "You watch. As soon as I water, it rains. Anyhow, yes, I like people. To tell you the truth, I feel sort of sorry for most of them. Poor little old human beings—they're jerked into this world without having any idea where they came from or what it is they are supposed to do or where they are gonna wind up after that. But bless their hearts, most of them wake up every morning and keep on trying to make some sense out of it. Why, you can't help but love them, can you? I just wonder why more of them aren't as crazy as betsey bugs."

"Do you believe in God, Aunt Elner?"

"Sure I do, honey. Why?"

"How old were you when you started believing?"

Aunt Elner paused. "I never thought about not believing. Oh, I know a lot of people struggle, wondering is there really a God. They sit and worry over it all their life. The good Lord had to make smart people, but I don't think He did them any favors, because it seems the smart ones start questioning things from the get go. But I never did. I'm one of the lucky ones. I thank God my brain is just perfect for me—not too dumb, not too bright. You know, your daddy was always asking questions. I remember one day he said, 'Aunt Elner, how do you know there is a God. How can you be sure?' "

"What did you tell him?"

"I said, 'Well, Gene, the answer is right on the end of your fin-

gertips. Think about it. Every single human being from the beginning of time has a completely different set of fingerprints. Not two
alike. Not a single one out of all the billions is ever repeated.' I said,
'Who else but God could think up all those different patterns and
keep coming up with new ones year after year?' "

Dena smiled. "What did he say?"

"He said, 'Yes, but Aunt Elner, how do you know that God's not
repeating old fingerprints and reusing them on us?' " She laughed.
"See what I mean? Yes, God is great, all right."

THE network lawyers had informed Sandy that unless Dena came
back within a week, they would cancel her contract and replace her.
Today was the day she had to make the decision, and it had not
been as hard as she thought. In the end she had no choice.

Her agent, Sandy, was in his office waiting for the call.

"Sandy, I've thought about it, and I couldn't come back even if I
wanted to. I wouldn't be any good at it anymore."

"What do you mean? You're the best in the business. You could
be back on top in a few weeks. You haven't lost all that time."

"No, but I don't have the drive I had. I know too much, Sandy.
Once you've been on the other side of this thing and know how it
feels, you can't go back." Dena drew a deep breath. "Before, I was
able to do my job and just keep moving. But not now. I'd hesitate.
I'd think too much. I couldn't ask the questions I need to ask anymore without thinking about the damage I might be doing."

"What will you do?"

"Get out of the way, I guess, and sit down for a while."

"What about your apartment?"

"I'm going to give it up."

"Where will you live?"

"Here. In Elmwood Springs."

A MONTH later, on the morning of Dena's thirty-fifth birthday,
Norma called her on the phone. "Dena, have you been outside?"

"No, why?"

"You need to go outside—and look up."

"Why?"

"Just go out. That's all I can tell you."

Dena walked into the yard. She looked up in time to see a huge gray blimp, its sign spelling out in gold lights over and over HAPPY BIRTHDAY. YOU'RE ALL THE WORLD TO ME. LOVE, GERRY.

She had to grin. She suddenly remembered the look on Gerry's face when he had sung to her at Carnegie Hall, and a warm feeling came over her. She went inside and called him.

"Gerry, I got your message. Now here's mine: You are insane."

"That's not exactly the clinical term I would use, but close enough. How are you?"

"Fine. Listen, Gerry, why don't you come down here, maybe stay the weekend. Can you do that?"

"This weekend? Is there a hotel in town?"

"You can stay here. I have four bedrooms."

There was a slight pause. Then he said, "I'll be there."

Gerry had been a good friend. They had talked on the phone often since she found out about her mother. It would be good to see him. As a matter of fact, as the few days went by, she couldn't wait to see him. Late Friday afternoon, when he was on her front porch and just about to ring the bell, the door opened and an arm grabbed him by the tie and pulled him inside, and Dena put her arms around him and kissed him. And it was as if they had been kissing for years. Dena didn't know if it was because she had been alone for so long, but he looked good to her. Better-looking than she remembered.

It wasn't until some time after he arrived that she realized that if you have a guest, you have to feed him, so she made the only dish she knew—ravioli straight out of a can, heated—and Gerry said it was delicious. After dinner they sat and talked until one thirty in the morning. When they got ready to go to bed, Gerry said, "I just want you to know I am fully prepared to sleep in the back room like a gentleman. All right?"

She was relieved in a way. They said good night.

After twenty minutes she called out, "Gerry? I think it will be all right if you come in here and sleep with me. We won't do anything. We'll just sleep together, all right?"

Gerry came down the hall carrying his pillow, wearing a pair of blue bunny pajamas with the feet in them, and when she saw him, she burst out laughing. "You fool. Where did you get those?"

"Elizabeth Diggers sent them over to my office on Thursday." He modeled for her. "Like them?"

"You are the silliest man I ever met. Get in the bed."

He took his glasses off and got into his side of the bed and lay down and felt her body next to his. And he was so relieved to finally be where he had wanted to be for so long that he relaxed completely for the first time since she had telephoned, and he fell sound asleep. The next morning at seven Dena woke and looked over at him sleeping beside her like a child in his blue pajamas, and the next thing she knew, they were making love. This was the first time in years she had gone to bed with someone when she was stone-cold sober. It was a new experience, and she liked it.

Gerry, who had been thinking and imagining such moments for a long time, was completely amazed. Making love with Dena was even better than he had imagined, and that was going some. Dena had gone back to sleep, but he was too excited to sleep. He went down the hall and showered and shaved, got dressed, and came back. He sat in a chair and stared at her, still astonished that it was really Dena and that he was really here.

She opened her eyes. "Hey . . . how long have you been up?"

He came over and sat on the bed. "For about an hour."

He leaned down and gave her a long, sweet, tender kiss, and Dena, who never liked to be kissed in the morning, liked it.

Gerry came back the next weekend, and although Dena didn't know how she felt about that, she was glad to see him. This time he stopped and brought groceries and cooked dinner for her. The thing that impressed her most was his salad. He had actually made a salad from scratch. The main course was baked chicken in a cream sauce, green beans, and new potatoes, and dessert was a cheesecake he had brought on the plane from New York. Between bites she said, "This is delicious. Where did you learn to cook like this?"

"I don't know. It's not that hard. Just follow the recipe."

"I don't know how to cook. We always ate out."

"I worry about you not eating right. You need fresh food, not all that frozen stuff you have in the refrigerator."

"I eat at Norma's two or three times a week, so I figure—"

"Dena, you need to take the time to fix yourself something healthy every day. Do you eat fresh fruit?"

She made a face.

"Well, you need to eat some fruit and vegetables every day. You need to start building yourself back up."

"The next thing I know, you'll pull down a chart of the basic food groups and give me a lecture with a pointer."

THAT afternoon Gerry started walking through the house. He was in the den knocking on the walls when Dena came in. He said, "Look at this. This is Georgia pine. And these floors are oak. This house is as solid as a rock, you know that? They don't build them like this anymore. This is a *great* house."

Dena found herself pleased. He seemed to like the house as much as she did. "I wonder how old it is."

"I'd say it was built sometime in the early '20s." He pulled at the pocket doors in the den. "I think this used to be a parlor at one time. Wouldn't you love to know who all lived here and what all went on in this house?"

"The woman I'm renting it from grew up here, and her mother used to have a radio show in the living room. There used to be a big radio tower in the backyard."

"I'll be darned."

"I'm thinking about buying it."

"Really? Well, it's a great house."

The next weekend Gerry took everybody to the Pancake House for dinner. On the way over, Norma, in the back seat, remarked, "I just want you to know this is a first for me. I have never even met a psychiatrist, much less had a pancake dinner with one."

Gerry glanced in the rearview mirror. "Is that so?"

"Yes. We have never had a psychiatrist in Elmwood Springs. Not that we don't need one, but nobody would go if we did have one."

"Why is that?"

"Because everybody knows everybody else's car. Nobody would dare park in front."

Aunt Elner was sitting in the front seat holding her purse in her lap, happy to be going. She piped up in defense of Elmwood Springs. "We had a crazy person here once. Mabel Bassett. She was as crazy as anybody. Don't you remember, Norma? She kept batting at imaginary flies." Aunt Elner turned to Gerry. "I'll bet you have met a lot of crazy people, haven't you?"

Dena had her eyes closed and was biting her lip.

Macky spoke up. "I think he's just met a couple of them."

"Oh, don't pay any attention to Macky," Norma said. "And if anybody is crazy, he drove me to it."

After Gerry had gone back to New York on Monday, Norma called Dena. "Well, it's none of my business, but he seems like a very nice person. And that's all I'm going to say. . . ."

But of course it wasn't.

AND so, at the age of thirty-five, Dena Nordstrom, who thought she could never love anything, had fallen in love with a house, a town, and a psychiatrist. It turned out that she was more surprised than anyone.

When she told Sookie the news, Sookie screamed over the phone, "You're getting married! Hurray and hallelujah. I have my matron of honor dress picked out and ready to go. It's peach. And we can get the girls little matching outfits. Oh, Dena, why don't you come do it here? At least let me give you a shower. Wait a minute. Who are you marrying?"

"Gerry O'Malley."

"That New York psychiatrist? Oh, dear."

Dena laughed. "Yes, he's the one. But the good news is that his mother is from Virginia."

"Virginia." Sookie sounded a little bit hopeful. "Well, that is a border state, but . . . What was her maiden name?"

"Hold on. Gerry, what was your mother's maiden name?"

"Longstreet, why?"

There was a gasp on the other end of the phone. "Dena, this is very important. Try not to embarrass him, but ask him if they were the cotton Longstreets or the lumber Longstreets."

"Gerry, were they the cotton or the lumber Longstreets?"

"Cotton. Why?"

"He said cotton."

Sookie screamed, "Oh, Dena! You are marrying a direct descendant of General James P. Longstreet, one of the most famous Confederate generals that ever lived. Don't tell me I don't have a personal friendship with Jesus Christ!"

In the meantime, back in New York, the network had gone on without her. They had hired another beautiful blonde. Just as Wall-Cap Productions had hired another beautiful blonde to anchor their first show, and they were off and running. The ratings shot through the ceiling. Evidently the public was ready for a tabloid "news" show. And soon other copycat shows started popping up everywhere, until the usual network news seemed as dull as Sidney Capello had predicted.

Every once in a while Dena would wonder where Capello was, and as it turned out, he wasn't anywhere at the moment.

That fall it had rained in New York City for five days straight. Capello, who had been working late on a story involving a movie star's love child, came out the door, started to cross Forty-eighth Street, fell into an open sewer, and landed in the icy-cold raging water. Before he knew what hit him, he was shooting under Manhattan at sixty miles an hour. Capello screamed, but the storm and the roar of the water was so loud he was not heard. He was swept under and did not stop until he was in the Hudson River, headed to Jersey, where his body would be found three days later.

His funeral was well attended for a man hated as much as he was. But as several, including Ira Wallace, said, "They came just to make sure the s.o.b. was really dead."

In the end, Capello's paranoia and greed saved a lot of reputations. He had been so neurotic about someone in the office sneaking into his files, where future scandals were still cooking in the oven, he had taken them home and hidden them between his old income tax files. After he was buried, a cleaning crew came in and threw out everything. Information and rumor, true and false, waiting to wreck careers, including Dena's file, would never be aired.

LIFE in Elmwood Springs went on pretty much the same. Every once in a while someone would come to town and inquire about Dena Nordstrom, ask where she lived, but the answer they always got was, "Gee, fella, I really don't know. Not sure she even lives here anymore."

Years later, when Dena and Gerry went to New York to take Elizabeth Diggers to dinner and to see a few shows, Dena was walking down Fifty-eighth Street when a woman stopped her and asked, "Hey, aren't you that girl who used to be on television?"

Dena grinned and answered, "No, I'm afraid that wasn't me."

As she continued down the street, Dena realized that she barely remembered that girl at all anymore.

And she smiled all the way back to the hotel.

Epilogue

ELMWOOD SPRINGS, MISSOURI   1987

IN THE early '80s something wonderful happened, thanks to Norma Warren's Elmwood Springs Is a Good Place to Live campaign. *USA Today* ran a story naming Elmwood Springs one of the ten best places in America to live. Yuppies and others who were trying to get away from big-city crime and back to small-town America came pouring in. New schools were built; downtown was restored; the Elmwood Springs movie theater reopened and sometimes showed a foreign film. Nordstrom's Bakery was taken over by a young couple from Boston and renamed Bread & Things, and Macky over at the hardware store had a cappuccino machine. A junior college sprang up, and Gerry became head of the psychology department and did not have to commute to Kansas City anymore. And Dena actually signed up for a cooking class and liked it.

Every day, of course, there were thousands of newspapers and news shows screaming and shouting murder, scandal, conspiracy, doom and gloom. And every day between Malibu and Manhattan millions of nice people, happy and good-natured, were quietly living their lives and not paying much real attention. As a matter of fact, many had begun to turn off their television sets or to watch old movies. But perhaps the best news locally was that in 1986 a radio tower was put up in Neighbor Dorothy's backyard and a woman whose voice sounded familiar started to broadcast from her home. It wasn't much of a show, merely lots of different things—news, guests, interviews, even recipes. But even though WDOT was only a seven-hundred-watt station, because the land was flat, on cold, still days when the skies were crystal-clear and it was really good radio weather, its signal could tear a hole straight through the Midwest, all the way up into Canada and on out to all the ships at sea. And the news was mostly good.

FANNIE FLAGG

Though new to Select Editions, Fannie Flagg is a veteran author, having begun writing and producing TV specials at age nineteen, then distinguishing herself as a writer and actress in television, film, and stage. Her previous novel *Fried Green Tomatoes at the Whistle Stop Cafe* was a best seller, and her script for its popular film version received a 1991 Academy Award nomination.

Yet Flagg, who grew up in Birmingham, Alabama, is as relaxed about her work as her southern roots would suggest. "I never know what I'm going to write until I sit and just let it come through me," she says. "The most important thing is to write with my heart." She writes with her heart from her home in Montecito, California.

ROBERT J. MRAZEK

SHENANDOAH VALLE

Harrisonburg

Cross Keys

Port Republic

Rockfish Gap

STONEWALL'S GOLD

124SW
New Market
Front Royal
Luray
Manassas
73 W
RBA
Shannessy

Shenandoah Valley, 1864. The final, fierce winter of the Civil War.

One young man has a desperate scheme for helping General Robert E. Lee and his tattered band of soldiers.

But can he pull it off in an uncivilized land where laws no longer apply and death lurks around every corner?

One

CONSTABLE Kilduff has told me to put the whole thing down in writing, and that is exactly what I'm going to do. He said if I could offer enough evidence to prove it really happened the way I said it did, then everything would come out all right in the end. He said he thought Judge Burwell would not go hard on a fifteen-year-old boy, even for the murders.

When I'm finished writing it all down, he'll take it to the judge over at the courthouse in Harrisonburg. After that Constable Kilduff said I would likely be able to start life again with a clean slate.

Don't ask me why this happened to me. My mother said it was part of God's plan. If it was, I'd say He needs a lot more practice. Anyway, it all started in those last few months before General Lee surrendered at Appomattox.

Jubal Early and his Shenandoah army were finished once and for all in the valley. A week after they got whipped by the Yankees for the last time, a long train of hospital wagons arrived here in Port Republic, Virginia, and the wounded were laid out in the fields around Fairfield Hall. A lot of those men were buried in the same fields. Most of the others had slipped across the Blue Ridge to join General Lee for a last stand around Richmond and Petersburg.

In late October the Yankees swarmed all over, burning or destroying almost everything in their path. On the day I turned fifteen, they came to our place. After piling straw around the barn, the soldiers drove our two milk cows inside, shut the doors, and set it on fire. Then they killed the chickens and stole all the cured meat. The whole matter took less than ten minutes.

We had our first hoarfrost a few days later. By late November people were saying it was the coldest winter they could ever remember. In mid-December we began having fierce storms almost every day, with snow squalls and ice rain.

It wasn't much past four o'clock on the afternoon the stranger came. The sky was already turning dark. With another bitter night coming on, I was making sure our last horse, Jupiter, was safely bedded down in the run-in shed near the back of our house.

The stranger rode slowly across the yard to the hitching post near our back porch. He never looked in my direction, although Jupiter whinnied out a friendly greeting as he dismounted and tied up his stubby, narrow-chested horse.

He wore a high-crowned beaver hat and a long military greatcoat. The insignia had been ripped off, but I knew it was an officer's coat because my father was wearing one just like it when they brought him home after he was shot at Chancellorsville.

A short-barreled carbine hung across the stranger's back. His spurs made an odd jangling sound with every step he took up to the back porch. He knocked loudly twice on the kitchen door.

When my mother answered it, he said, "They told me in the village you had room, Miz Lockhart." His voice was loud enough to carry over the wind. It was deep and grizzly.

The next thing I saw, he was heading inside.

I know my mother would never have rented him our room if we weren't so hard up. Not that it was any palace. When my grandfather built his fruit cellar into the side of the hill behind the house, he constructed a large room above it as a place to store tools. Later my father fixed it up as an office before he began teaching at the Mossy Creek Academy. My mother started renting it after the Yankees captured Winchester for the first time and prices at the store in town doubled for just about everything. The room was available now, but we didn't need any more boarders. I knew the war couldn't last much longer, and my father would be coming home again soon. I couldn't wait for things to be just like they used to be.

I finished currying Jupiter and headed inside. After hanging up my coat, I went through the back pantry into the kitchen. The stranger was sitting in my father's chair in front of the fire. I saw that the sole of one of his boots was sprung wide open, but that wasn't unusual. Dr. Cassidy had said more than half the Confederate soldiers were completely barefoot.

He was by far the hairiest man I've ever seen. The roots started growing out of his forehead just above the brows of his fearsome black eyes. Like some kind of pelt, his hair rose straight back over the crown of his head and fell way down below his shoulders.

My mother was telling him what she always said when she didn't like the looks of someone who asked to stay.

"My husband is away at the moment, but we've received word that he is on his way home. I regret that he is usually accompanied by another officer who will have need of our spare room."

At this the stranger broke into a smile that shattered the ice particles frozen into his long black beard.

"I reckon I cain understand that," he said. "Don't want to get in the way of no homecomin' party. No, sir. Now I was with the artillery myself. Back in '62 I fought right here under ol' Stonewall hisself, right across them fields yonder," he said, pointing in the direction of the battlefield.

"Well, I'm truly sorry, but—"

"I'll pay three hundred dollars the week if'n you let me stay."

Of course, he was talking Confederate. Three hundred was barely enough to buy a good pair of pants, but it was five times what she would usually have asked.

Then he said, "I don't need it for mor'n a week at most."

I was about to ask him what was so special about any old bed in Port Republic when my mother said, "If we have to ask you to leave,

I will return the unused rent. You're welcome to take meals with us."

"That's mighty kind of you, ma'arm. My name's Blewitt. Corporal Blewitt." The black eyes stopped on me. "An' how old are you, boy?" he demanded.

"Fifteen."

"Fifteen!" he repeated. "Mite small, ain't you?"

I said nothing in return. It was regrettably true.

"I'll say this," he said. "You as pretty as a girl."

My face got hot. Then my mother said, "Jamie, please go tend to Corporal Blewitt's horse while I finish preparing supper."

Putting on my coat again in the pantry, I was about to walk out when I heard him say, "They tell me you a Yankee lady."

There was a pause. "I'm originally from New York," she said so low I could barely hear. "I've lived here for sixteen years."

I went outside and led his mare back to the run-in shed. She seemed grateful when I took off the saddle. In the light of a guttering candle I saw why. The saddle was U.S. Army issue but in very bad condition. Someone had made a hasty repair to the girth buckle, and it had chafed a big raw spot on her belly. I also found a cluster of scabby wounds where the man had dug in his spurs.

Right from there I hated Corporal Blewitt. I would hate anyone who could be so heartless to an animal that carried him everywhere without complaint and asked nothing more than to be treated decently. After dressing all the raw spots, I groomed the mare's mangy coat and gave her a handful of cob corn.

It was raining hard again as I headed across the yard in the dark. The stranger was at the woodpile gathering an armful to keep his room warm. We ignored each other. When I got back to the house, my mother was slumped over the kitchen table, her face cradled in her hands, sobbing. I put my arms around her shoulders.

"Don't worry," I said. "The war will be over soon, and then Pa will be back. You'll see."

EARLY the next morning I was up to check the horses. It was another rainy day, with a harsh wind blowing up the valley between the Massanutten and the Blue Ridge. I decided to let Jupiter rest in his stall in the shed. He was twenty-eight years old and no longer enjoyed the cold. He was my best friend.

Jupiter was also one of the fastest horses in the valley in his younger days. In 1849, the year I was born, he won the match race at the Rockingham County fair for the fourth year in a row with all two hundred pounds of my father on his back. When the war came, though, Jupiter was just too old to fight. He still had plenty of go in him but tired easily. We still had a lot of great adventures together, roaming the dark forest trails on the Massanutten, traveling northeast to camp along the summit of the Blue Ridge. Whenever the Yankees were swarming, I would tether him far up Loft Mountain, where they could never find him.

Now, with all the crops destroyed, it was almost a full-time job to find enough food to keep his weight steady. But even when I wasn't successful, he never complained. He would just stare at me, his big kind eyes like twin moons in the increasingly jagged face.

Going back outside, I wrapped my muffler close and headed off on foot for the village. An hour later I was lying in the window seat of Dr. Cassidy's front parlor and reading *Robinson Crusoe* in the pale light of the rain-filled sky.

"Hell's brimstone," thundered Dr. Cassidy, who was seated across the room by the fire. Hurling down the newspaper, he snatched up his cane, limped over to the walnut sideboard, and poured himself another drink from the pitcher. "Jeff Davis, that pigheaded fool!" Limping back across the room, he dropped heavily into his chair.

"Remember the words of the great Augustus, Jamie? 'Varus! Varus! Where are our legions now?' Thanks to those idiots in Richmond they lie slaughtered on a hundred fields. And today our remaining few are as Leonidas and the Spartans. Those poor noble boys." He finished his drink with two long swallows.

" 'Among the blind the one-armed man is king,' " he muttered.

"Eyed," I corrected him.

"I'd what?" he asked, confused.

"The one-eyed man."

"You're not making sense, Jamie," he said, shaking his head sadly. Knowing he was locked in the embrace of John Barleycorn, I turned back to *Robinson Crusoe.*

Dr. Cassidy was tutoring me in the classics as a favor to my father after they had closed the school in the village when the older boys went off to fight. There were very few books on Dr. Cassidy's shelves that I hadn't finished. The authors I liked best were Shakespeare and Cervantes. My mother was keen on the tutoring for another reason. During the hours Dr. Cassidy spent studying with me, he didn't drink quite so much as he did the rest of the time.

That wasn't the way he used to be. I remember my father once saying he was the finest doctor between Lexington and Winchester. When the war started, he had become an army surgeon on the staff of his friend General Longstreet. He came back after Chickamauga with a bullet through his kneecap, his hair turned completely white. By then his boys, Harry and Peyton, were lying in soldiers' graves. After that Mrs. Cassidy seemed to just dry up and get all wrinkly before she passed on.

With the exception of Dr. Cassidy and a few others, my parents were pretty much outcasts in Port Republic. The reason was my mother. Not only was she the prettiest woman in the valley but she had the misfortune to be a Yankee from Corning, New York. My father met her at a teachers' conference at Elmira College up there.

It wasn't just the Yankee way my mother talked that got people upset. It was what she talked about. The thing that really bothered her was slavery. That caused some big rows between her and my father, although he was against slavery too and called it the curse of the South. But he also thought the Yankees were two-faced, since they had sold their slaves for good money before they decided it was evil. My father was no fire-eater, but when the war came, he, like General Lee, considered himself first and foremost a Virginian.

People put up with my mother as long as my father was around. When he was elected to be one of the officers in the 10th Virginia, you would have thought we were the most popular family in Port Republic. But as soon as he left, everything changed overnight.

THE STRANGER HAD BEEN WITH us for a few days when all the excitement began. I stopped at the Port Republic store for our mail and found half the village crowded inside, everyone shouting.

"Grave robbers, that's what I think," yelled Mr. Hannum, his voice hoarse with agitation.

"Can't be," said Jack Rainey. "They's Confederate boys buried up there. Ain't nothin' on 'em to steal."

"Well, those graves from '62 are sure messed with."

"The ground is turned over real strange," wheezed old Mrs. Miller. "Like it's been done from underneath."

Monk Shiflett said, "You think those boys are crawling out of their graves so's they kin go kill more bluebellies, Hannah?"

"I don't know about ghouls or bodies coming out of the ground," said Mr. Sherrard, who owned the bank and was the richest man around. "I did see someone on the road before dawn this morning. When I started for him, he ran toward the river."

"We've got to do something," shouted Mr. Hannum. "We could go up there tonight and wait for whoever it is who's doing it."

It got real quiet then, and in those few seconds the answer suddenly came to me that it was Corporal Blewitt who was the one disturbing the graves. I don't know how, but I just knew it.

I left the store and walked up to Fairfield Hall. The graves of the dead from the 1862 battle lay in a line near a low rock fence.

There were fourteen in all. Most of them were still marked by small crosses made with hand-hewn pine boards. If there were ever any names written on the boards, they had faded out in the years since. At least five or six graves had been tampered with.

I searched for a place where I could conceal myself if the need arose. The other side of the rock fence looked like the best possibility. After looking it all over, I walked home.

THAT night my mother went to her room a little after nine. At ten I got into my winter coat and slipped out to hide on the porch. Two hours must have passed before the door of the corporal's room creaked open. There was no time to celebrate my successful discovery as his form moved past my hiding place carrying what appeared to be a spade and pickax. Then he was gone.

There was no hope of actually following him in that black starless night, but I felt sure I knew where he was going. After crossing the river, I skirted the roads and came up by way of the foundry toward the fields beyond Fairfield Hall.

When I reached the rock wall, I ducked behind it and crawled slowly forward on my hands and knees. When I heard his voice, I dropped flat to my stomach. He sounded as if he'd gone mad.

"I'm comin' for ye, Lieutenant Shawnessy," he sang out.

For a long while I listened to the regular rhythm of the spade thudding against earth. Finally it stopped.

"So let's see who we got hidin' down here," said the corporal.

A moment later he uttered a string of violent oaths. Then, like a demon possessed, he began toiling again, the pickax striking the frozen ground like a never-ending drumbeat. I knew he was coming closer when frozen clumps of earth began raining down around me.

"How is it in the nether regions, Lieutenant Shawnessy?" he called out. "Don't try to hide from me—not old Blewitt."

The corporal's voice now seemed to be coming from below the ground, and I took the chance to peer over the wall. To my disappointment I still couldn't see anything through the blackness. About this time the flying clods of dirt stopped falling. I thought I heard the sound of cloth ripping and then a striking flint.

"Well, what do we have here?" I heard him say. There was a brief flare of light from what might have been a taper. "Give it up. Give it up. Give it here," he said as if fighting something alive.

He was breathing hard when he climbed out of the hole, and I heard him gathering up his tools. I knew he was coming closer because my nostrils were suddenly filled with the smell of the grave. He came over the fence, and then he was standing beside me, no more than a few inches away. A merciful providence kept him from tripping over me, and a moment later he was gone.

By the time I made my way home after giving Blewitt a head start, it was past four o'clock in the morning. Smoke was coming out of the corporal's chimney, so he had obviously gotten back too. My mind was racing with questions, but I was completely worn out. Dropping to my bed, I was quickly carried away in deepest slumber.

WHEN I woke up, it was snowing again. There were already a couple of inches on my windowsill. It felt good to be burrowed in my warm quilts, and I was falling back asleep when a muffled voice set in motion the event that changed our lives forever.

It was a man's voice but too low for me to hear the words. Then I heard my mother, hers loud and nervous.

"That will be enough, sir. I must ask you to leave."

I was out of bed in an instant. Going to the door, I cracked it open to hear Corporal Blewitt say, "You got to be mighty lonely with yer man away so long."

"Get out of my house," she said.

He was slowly backing her into the corner of the kitchen by the chimney. "You be nice to me'n I'll make it worth your while," he said as I stepped through the doorway.

"Keep away from her," was what I wanted to shout, but it came out as more of a screech.

He spun around, obviously surprised to find me there.

"I thought you was off larnin' yer lessons, boy," he said. Then his whole manner began to change, like he had just arrived at Mr. Sherrard's bank to see about a loan. "Miz Lockhart, I didn't mean nothin' with them words."

"Corporal Blewitt, you will pack your things and leave my home," said my mother.

"It's jess that it's been so long since I seen my—"

"Now! This instant." She cut him off.

"My pa's coming home tomorrow," I declared.

He looked long and hard at my mother and then at me. "Well, if there ain't no room for me no more, I guess I got to move on."

He walked outside into the driving snow. I went over and locked the door behind him. A moment later my mother was in my arms and holding me like she would never let go.

An hour later there was still no sign of the corporal's leaving. I convinced my mother to let me find out what he was waiting for.

The door of his room was open a crack, and I swung it in far enough to look inside. He was just lying on his bed.

"Found this down in the fruit cellar, and right good it is," he said with a laugh. He was holding a tin dipper and pointing it at a half-empty crock of hard cider that was sitting on the floor.

I said, "We need this room. I have to clean it now."

"So your pa's comin' home," he said with a low chuckle. "He an officer, ain't he?"

"Lieutenant colonel," I said proudly.

"Well, the high an' the mighty," he said, scooping up another dipper of cider and finishing it in one swallow. Then he started laughing again. "Your pa ain't never comin' home, runt. He's daid. Didn't your mama tell you that?"

"He's not dead," I yelled back at him.

"Course he is," he went on. "Why, she told me so hesself."

It was all I could do not to strike his hairy face.

"You needin' a new papa," he said. "Think I'll enlist meself."

That's when my anger caused me to blunder.

"I'll see you in prison first," I shouted. "You try anything with us, and I'll tell this whole town what you did up at Fairfield Hall."

He sat up and slid his feet onto the floor. His hand moved faster than a darting snake. In a second it had fastened itself around my throat. As in a fog I heard a voice shouting, "What do you know, you little devil?" and then the world went dark.

I don't know how long I was unconscious, but as my wits returned, I could still feel the pressure of his hand around my neck. I was lying on the cold floor of his room, and the door was wide open. My next thought was for my mother. Standing up, I lunged through the door and out into the snow-covered yard.

When I stepped inside the kitchen, I found it warm and peaceful. A pan of water bubbled silently on the stove. I looked around for something to fight the corporal with and picked up my mother's flatiron, which was lying on the edge of the stove.

I went through the parlor into the back hallway. There I spied something on the floor. It was one of her shoes. At the end of the hallway I could see that her bedroom door was not quite shut.

Moving silently forward, I craned my head and looked inside. Corporal Blewitt was kneeling over her on her bed.

I gave him no quarter. He never saw me coming, because all that hair covered his eyes like a black curtain. Gripping the flatiron tightly in my right hand, I swung it as hard as I could in a wide sweeping arc. The edge of it landed with a sickening crunch on the side of his head. He collapsed without a sound. I dropped the iron and hauled him off the bed. He fell with a great thud to the floor.

Released from his weight, my mother rolled to the other side of the bed and sat up. I saw that her hair was unpinned and the back of her dress was ripped completely to the waist.

"Is he dead?" she asked, her voice steady.

I knelt down next to him and put my ear to his chest to see if he was still breathing.

"He's dead, all right," I said, standing up again.

"Good," she replied. Gathering the bedspread around her shoulders, she took some things from her closet and went out of the room. A few moments later I heard her pouring water from the pan on the stove into a washbasin.

I couldn't stop staring at his body. As the sweet smell of his blood reached my nose, my legs began to shake so hard I had to sit down on the bed. I was a murderer. Yet I felt no guilt. I found myself trying to pray for forgiveness, but nothing came.

My mother called out to me from the kitchen. I found her sitting at the table in front of the fire. She had put on her other dress and one of my father's old flannel shirts. Her face was very pale. She reached out and took my hand in hers.

"He told me Pa was dead," I said.

"He lied, Jamie. He lied about everything."

"Well, I killed him," I said.

"You saved our lives," she replied, and took me in her arms. Then she said, "Jamie, you know how people feel about me in the village. I'm not sure they would believe what happened here. Do you understand? We will never tell anyone about this—not even your father."

"I understand," I said.

THERE was a boggy area about a quarter of a mile from our house, and that's the place where I decided to bury him, along with his hat, carbine, and a few spare clothes. Suddenly it struck me that whatever he had stolen from the lieutenant's body was probably still in his clothes. In his pockets I found a handkerchief, a knife, and a tobacco pouch. I shoved these in my coat pocket and finished what I had to do. The snow had turned to sleet, and by the time I covered him, the place had become as muddy as a sinkhole.

Back at the house, my mother had removed every trace of his blood from the bedroom floor and also cleaned his room. I had one last job to do. Putting the corporal's saddle and bridle on his poor knobby horse, I rode her north toward Swift Run Gap. When I reached the crossroad leading to Conrad's Store, I dismounted and tied the horse to a sapling. There were so many people desperate for a horse I figured someone would be sure to steal her before long.

When I got home, my mother made me take a long bath in the hottest water I could stand. Afterward I told her the whole story about following the corporal to Fairfield Hall.

Together we went through his possessions. The only thing that seemed unusual was the tobacco pouch, and that was because neither of us had ever seen him smoke. I dumped out the tobacco onto the kitchen table and carefully sifted through it, but it was just what it appeared to be. It was only when my mother turned the pouch inside out that she found the map. Actually it was nothing more than a small piece of white bunting or sackcloth someone had carefully sewn into the bottom of the pouch.

There were a series of crude markings and diagrams covering its surface. In the state we were in, neither one of us could make the slightest sense of it, and we finally gave up. That night we slept in the same bed for the first time since I was a boy.

Two

A FEW days later two men from Richmond came looking for Corporal Blewitt. At least that's where they said they were from. I was at Dr. Cassidy's when they came to the house. According to my mother, the older one said Blewitt had deserted from his artillery unit. I had no doubts about that and a lot more besides. Yet it seemed strange that the army would send two men all the way from Richmond just to track down one deserter.

My mother told them he had ridden off three days earlier. Where had he gone? they demanded to know. She said she had no idea. The two of them then spent an hour nosing around his room and the run-in shed before they finally left.

That was the same day I showed the map to Dr. Cassidy. Although I hated to lie to him about how I got it, that was the promise I had made to my mother. Things might have turned out a lot differently if I had told him the truth right from the beginning. We'll never know now. What I did say was that the map was inside a tobacco pouch I had found while exploring the battlefield. I unfolded the cloth bunting and laid it on his desk.

"Let's have a look at it," he said. Leaning down, he began to examine all the markings through a magnifying glass. He spent a good ten minutes eyeing it before rendering his verdict.

"Assuming this is authentic, which I am not prepared to do, it would appear that to the one who can decipher the code, this is the key to locating something of significant value."

"Why would you say that?" I asked.

"He wouldn't have gone to the trouble of making a coded map unless it was important enough to warrant one. Also, the instructions are recorded in a way that preserves the secret from anyone who is not in possession of certain critical information."

He explored the map again intently. "Whatever was hidden is

probably located somewhere near Sudley Springs, not far from Manassas."

"How can you tell?"

"Look here," he said, pointing to the upper left-hand corner. "These are obviously the four points of the compass. Then there is the date, July twenty-second, 1861. That was the day after the battle of First Manassas. Now, I believe these lines represent the Warrenton Pike and just north of it the stream at Bull Run. The marks to the west obviously suggest a dense wooded area, and the cross inside the square is a church. Sudley Church, if memory serves. The rest is some sort of cipher. These things here."

There were numbers and words scrawled in ink around the borders of the cloth. Things like "200SE" and then "73W" and then "the Mouth of the Devil." Below that was a black half circle that looked something like the entrance to a train tunnel. At the bottom of the cloth was written "RBA" and then "Shawnessy." I recognized the name as the one used by Blewitt at the grave.

"What could the letters mean?" I asked.

"Rockbridge Artillery, if I'm not mistaken."

I remembered Blewitt had claimed to be in the artillery.

"They were a unit of the original valley brigade. Ike Trumbo served in that battery until he was invalided out."

"Mr. Trumbo who used to work for my father at the academy?"

"The same, although I believe he is now operating some sort of roadhouse near Harrisonburg. You know, Jamie, if I'm right about Sudley Springs, then you may as well forget about searching for what was hidden there. That whole area is forty miles behind the Yankee lines."

By the following morning my curiosity about the secret of the map was whetted sharper than ever. I pestered my mother until she agreed that I could ride over to Harrisonburg to see Ike Trumbo. She packed me a lunch of biscuits spread with corn syrup, along with a bag of sour pears for Jupiter. The *Almanac* was predicting another December gale, and she made me take a second shirt and spare socks in case I got drenched. I also took along a large piece of gum cloth with a hole cut for my head that I could wear over my winter coat if it got real bad.

Jupiter was in high spirits at the chance for an outing. Although I also started the trip in high spirits, what I saw along the road west out of Port Republic changed my mood very quickly.

It wasn't the same valley I had grown up in. The first thing I noticed were the fences. They had all disappeared—ripped down, I supposed, by both armies for cooking fires or to stay warm. The road looked strange and bare without them.

Crops had been destroyed, and many of the places I passed along the road seemed abandoned, gray, and cold-looking, although at one farm a man was plowing a rocky field behind a harnessed mule. It seemed pretty crazy to be doing that in December, but the war had made people funny in different ways. I wondered whether things could ever be put back the way they used to be.

ON THE northern end of Harrisonburg I found Ike Trumbo's tavern. It was a low, flat-roofed log building set in a copse of white birch trees. Several horses were tied to the rail outside. I gave an old man sitting on the porch a dollar to keep his eyes on Jupiter.

Inside, it was warm and smoky. There was a big blaze burning in the open fireplace, but it was some kind of trash wood, and big cinders kept popping out and landing on the packed-earth floor.

Several men were standing in front of a rough-cut wooden slab that ran waist-high along one length of the room. From behind it Ike Trumbo was serving drinks. One other man sat hunched over his own bottle at a small table near the fireplace. I made my way over to the end of the wooden counter, and Mr. Trumbo came over.

"Is that you, Jamie?" he asked with a look of concern on his good square-jawed face.

I nodded yes.

He was wearing a hat with long flaps on it to cover the cavity on the side of his skull, but you could still see most of it.

"What are you doing over this way?" he asked. "Your pa all right?"

I said yes, as far as we knew. Then I said, "Dr. Cassidy thought you might be able to help me with a map I found. It could have something to do with the Rockbridge Artillery."

"Sure," he said.

"It's kind of a secret."

"All right, Jamie."

With that, I spread the cloth bunting out. He looked at it for a few minutes, turning it to read the words along the edges. The other men paid no attention.

The first thing he whispered was, "I think this might have been drawn by Lieutenant Shawnessy, but I wouldn't know why." His face darkened. "He was killed at Port Republic, you know."

I nodded. "Can you tell me what any of it might mean?"

" 'The Mouth of the Devil,' " he slowly read aloud, and then shook his head.

The front door creaked open on its leather hinges, and everyone turned around. My first thought when I saw him was Jack and the Beanstalk. Pretty much everyone looked big to me, but this man had to bend down to come through the door, and once he was inside, his slouch hat almost grazed the ceiling beams. He walked to the bar, and Ike went over to pour him a drink.

The men standing next to him resumed talking about the war.

"What about old Jube?" said one.

"He's long gone. Hightailed it way the hell south."

"They say Pat Cleburne may be coming up this way from Tennessee to give that little Sheridan the boot."

"Cleburne's dead," said Ike Trumbo.

"Says who?"

Ike pointed to the man who was sitting at the table by the fire. "This officer says Cleburne was killed with a whole passel of our generals down at Franklin, Tennessee. That right, Major?"

The officer was clean-shaven, with a dark, bronze-colored face. His black hair was thick and straight and looked like it had been chopped off by a dull knife. I had never seen anyone so dark-skinned wearing a Confederate uniform with a star on the collar.

"Unfortunately true, yes," he said with an accent I'd never heard before. His hooded black eyes seemed very tired.

When I looked back at the others, I saw that the huge man was staring hard at the bunting, which was still spread out in front of me. I carefully folded it up and put it in my coat pocket. Then Ike Trumbo came back, his body blocking out the huge man's face.

"We were talking, I think," Ike said with a smile.

The next voice I heard was very deep. "Come here, boy."

Ike turned around to face the huge man. "He isn't doing anything, mister," said Ike to put him off.

"You want another hole in your head, you'll leave it well enough alone," the huge man answered, continuing to stare at me. "Come on, boy. You got what belongs to me. Bring it here."

Ike reached toward the shelf behind him, and the huge man slid open his coat, revealing a big Colt pistol stuck in his belt.

"Step away from there," he said, and Ike did.

The huge man walked over to me. He was reaching down toward the pocket of my coat when the voice with the strange accent said, "Leave the boy alone."

The huge man stopped and looked around. Out of the corner of my eye I saw the Confederate officer rising to his feet at the table. My heart sank when I saw that his right sleeve was pinned to the side of his uniform. Upon seeing that, the huge man smiled.

"I didn't know the army had no nigger officers," he said.

"Je suis de la Bayou La Frenière, mon grand cochon."

"What?"

"My parents, sir, were from the Attakapas—Acadians, if you will. That race of which Longfellow sang in 'Evangeline.' "

"All the same to me. Keep out of this or I'll kill you."

"I don't believe it's possible for you to do that, my ignorant friend," said the officer, his piercing black eyes now afire. "If you leave now, I will allow you to live. Otherwise you shall pay a small price for those poor manners—your life."

"That's brass comin' from a one-armed nigger," the huge man said, and with amazing speed drew the pistol from his belt.

Almost in a blur, the officer's left hand flashed behind his head to the collar of his cloak and then arced forward again, grasping the tip of what looked like a small sword. I swear I heard it sing through the air before it buried itself in the huge man's chest.

"Louisiana toothpick!" Ike Trumbo cried out.

The huge man stared down at his chest with a puzzled grin on his face. Then he started to sway and, slowly tipping over backward, crashed to the earthen floor like a felled tree.

IKE Trumbo carefully approached the one-armed man. "You ever fight with the Louisiana Tigers?" he asked, extending his left hand.

"Yes, I did," said the officer as he shook it firmly. "Major Alain de Monfort, formerly of Roberdeau Wheat's battalion."

I offered him my left hand too. "My name is Jamie Lockhart," I said as he took it. "Thank you."

He looked down at me closely and smiled. Then, moving over to the dying man, he began to drag the weapon out of his massive body like King Arthur removing the sword from the stone.

"I hope it was worth your life, my large friend," he said.

The huge man neither complained nor uttered a sound. I only knew he was still alive because tears flowed freely down his cheeks. Finally his lips began to move.

I leaned close. "Stonewall Jackson's gold," he murmured.

"What'd he say?" demanded one of the men.

"He said he's cold," said Major de Monfort, who was the only other person beside me close enough to hear him. Then the huge man's eyes went lifeless; he shivered and lay still.

At the same moment the door flew open again, and the old man who had been watching the horses limped into the room.

"Riders comin' hard, Ike," he called out.

We all stepped out onto the porch. Now I could hear the pounding hoofbeats of many horses coming up the Dayton road.

Major de Monfort whispered to me, "I would not be surprised if they were the friends of the gentleman who is lying inside on the floor. I gather you have something of value to them."

I didn't say anything.

"You are welcome to ride with me," he said as he mounted the large bay mare tethered on the porch rail.

Jupiter was tugging at his looped reins as if he also knew it was time to go. I untied him and climbed into the saddle. As I looked back down the Dayton road, I could now see six riders.

"They will probably stop here to learn what they can," he said. "Do you know another route to the Valley Pike going north toward Winchester? One they might not know?"

"Follow me," I cried. With the slightest nudge in the flanks Jupiter sprang forward, and we were off. We rode east for about a mile and then turned north on the Keezletown road. Farther on we cut back across several open pastures until we reached the old forest trail that skirted the western base of the Massanutten. By late afternoon we were out of the forest and resting the horses in a small meadow along the ridgeline. From there it was possible to look back almost a mile in the direction we had come.

Spreading out my gum cloth, I lay on my back in the grass. The whole sky was now one massive cloud of gunmetal blue.

"Have you ever seen a sky this color before?" I asked.

The major shook his head. "There is a tempest brewing up there, and we will see it before long. The wind is coming up too."

I closed my eyes and a moment later was asleep. I came awake to someone jostling my shoulder. The major said, "Wake up, Jamie. They are coming."

I sat up and looked back down the ridge. Sure enough, no more than half a mile away, six riders were coming toward us.

"How could they—" I began, but the major didn't wait.

"One of them is a tracker," he said, mounting his horse and grabbing the reins in his left hand. "We have to fly."

It was a race for our lives. That was the long and short of it. Of course, Jupiter loved to race. He was snorting in anticipation. But at his age how far could he run before he was played out?

As we rode along at a steady lope, I couldn't stop thinking about what had happened at the tavern. Over and over I kept seeing the huge man falling and then, before he died, hearing him whisper, "Stonewall Jackson's gold."

Maybe it sounds crazy now, but right then I decided I would try to find the gold and take it to General Lee. I thought of how many winter coats and how many pairs of shoes it would buy for my father and the rest of his men in that scarecrow army. And there was one other thing. I knew I couldn't go home again without Corporal Blewitt's friends following me there to take back the map. Then I would be putting my mother in danger too.

"Did you hear what that man at Trumbo's really said before he died?" I asked the major as we rode.

"He said 'Stonewall Jackson's gold.' "

"That's right. Do you have any idea what he meant?"

"No, but I assume you're about to tell me," he answered.

"There is gold buried somewhere around Sudley Springs," I began. Then I guess I lied, saying I had found the map on a battlefield and taken it first to Dr. Cassidy and then to Ike Trumbo. I concluded by asking him whether he would go with me to find the gold and then take it through the Yankee lines to General Lee.

"Well now, tell me this, Jamie," he said. "How did your friends back there find out about it?"

For a moment I considered telling him everything. Then I thought about my pledge to my mother. "I don't know," I said.

He gave me a brief, hard glance. "I will think about the matter."

The darkening sky had turned to night when the heavens finally released the incredible rainstorm that followed. Major de Monfort spurred his horse faster, and Jupiter sped up to meet the challenge. We did not slow down for several miles. Suddenly I felt Jupiter give out a great shudder, and he began to quickly drop back.

"Keep that horse moving," demanded the major as he reined in his own animal. We were just approaching New Market.

"He can't keep going like this," I cried. "He's twenty-eight."

His face softened. "We will rest the horses for a few minutes."

I took the chance to ask, "Will you go with me, sir? To Sudley Springs?"

He paused before he said, "Jamie, I regret that I cannot. There is something I am required to do in Winchester."

"But the Yankees hold Winchester," I protested.

"That is so," he said, adding nothing further about it. "You are welcome to ride with me, but otherwise I must take leave of you."

"I'm going anyway," I said.

He looked down for a moment. Then he said, "The New Market mountain pass is treacherous at night, and I do not like the thought of a boy your age on the road alone with those men after you. But if you're determined to proceed with this idea, my suggestion would be for you to go through the gap as far as you can. Stay off the main road after daylight."

I nodded my understanding. He edged his horse close to Jupiter and grasped my hand. "If you find yourself in trouble, I want you to remember that on the other side of Massies Glen you will come to a settlement called Calvary. Ask for the house of a man named Gamage and tell him that Montague sent you there for help."

Who is Montague? I wondered, but there was no time to ask.

"One last thing, Jamie. If those men do catch up and find that map on you, they will kill you. Do not doubt that for a moment. Try to commit the map to memory and then destroy it. The knowledge will give you something to bargain with."

He slapped Jupiter on the rump, and we were off without him.

"I can promise you a good head start," he called after me. Turning around in the saddle, I saw him slide what looked like a Sharps rifle out of his blanket roll. Then he disappeared into the wall of rain on the far side of the road.

IN NEW Market I reached the junction that led east toward the high mountain pass. To get out of the rain, I pulled up under the extended roof of a seed-supply warehouse. Still in the saddle, I lit the stub of a candle, removed the bunting from my coat, and once again studied the map. After a minute I laid it down. Closing my eyes, I tried to bring it all back in my mind. And there it was, as clear as could be. I held the bunting to the flame.

It was then I heard the first report of gunfire. It was quickly followed by the crack of more rifles.

Suddenly the information on the map disappeared from my brain. As hard as I tried, I couldn't bring it back. I snuffed the flame before the cloth actually took fire. There would be time to memorize the map later, I decided, shoving the refolded square beneath Jupiter's saddle blanket. Then we trotted out into the pouring rain and up toward the black mountain.

It was about two miles from the town of New Market to the base of the mountain, and I knew we had reached it when I felt the ground sheer upward as Jupiter started to climb the steep grade.

The air was definitely getting colder, and soon the rain turned to sleet, slashing at my face and finding its way through the neckhole of the gum cloth. It hurt to breathe, and my whole body ached from soreness and the cold.

The anger of the wind rose steadily as we climbed higher into the black night. Maybe it was the combination of riding thirty miles and the exhaustion of the chase, but in spite of everything, I fell asleep as Jupiter kept gamely working his way toward the summit.

I awoke to find we were no longer moving. Jupiter's head was drooped low to the ground, motionless, as if his great body were paralyzed. Dismounting, I tried to lift his head, but it hung there like dead weight. His eyes were half open and unseeing. I examined his legs and found he was bleeding badly from one of his fetlocks. When I put my ear to his breast, I became sick with fear. I could hear the congestion in his lungs as he labored to breathe. Even worse was the sound of his heart, which was beating fast and fluttery.

As hard as it is to admit it now, my whole body began to shake from fear. It wasn't the fear of what would happen if those men caught up to me. It was my terror of what I would have to do if Jupiter broke down here in this godforsaken place on the mountain.

There was really only one thing to be done, and that was to get Jupiter off the mountain as soon as possible and find a place for us to lay up and rest. I took up the reins and gently led him on foot until we finally reached the summit. Although the wind and sleet continued unabated, the going became easier as we began our descent. Climbing back into the saddle, I leaned forward and buried my face in his mane, keeping it there as he headed down toward the Luray valley. Soon I was asleep once more.

I awoke to feel the prodding of Jupiter's nose at my right knee. We were stopped on the road again, but this time I sensed the danger was over. Everything around me was covered in mist. Dawn would be breaking soon.

The landscape around us was densely forested. It seemed like a good place to hide. Dismounting, I led Jupiter away from the road and along a fast-running brook to cover our tracks. Farther on we cut through the thick undergrowth to go deeper into the forest. Eventually we came to a small glade near another stream. Removing Jupiter's bridle and saddle, I first let him drink and then fed him all the sour pears in my satchel bag while I ate the last of my mother's biscuits. After treating his cut leg with one of Dr. Cassidy's ointments, I left him to forage and rest.

In a soft mossy spot between fallen trees I rolled myself up in the gum cloth. Fog was coming down through the trees around me like a woman's veil. It was perfect. No one could find anything in this muck. I thought of my mother at home and hoped she wasn't too worried about me. A few seconds later I was dead to the world.

Three

LIFE doesn't always work out the way you plan. The next thing I felt was a hard kick to my ribs.

"Get up, boy," said a raspy voice.

I stuck my head out of my lair to find that thick fog still covered the scene. The same voice said, "Where'd you hide it?"

Another kick brought me to my feet. How could they have found us? I wondered. Men moved toward me out of the fog like ghostly images. One of them was already going through my satchel bag. He was a stocky man with big powerful arms.

"This cold is cutting right through me," said the next one, who was old enough to be my grandfather. He had a mane of white hair and a greasy beard. "You mind if I build us a fire, Cole?"

The man he addressed was still hidden by the fog, but I heard him say, "Might as well. We could be here awhile."

The one searching my satchel bag had thrown it on the ground. "Ain't'eer," he said. He then picked up my saddle and began to examine its seams. It was only then I felt a surge of fear as I remembered Major de Monfort's warning to destroy the map, lest they find it and then have no further use of me.

I risked a glance toward Jupiter's wet saddle blanket lying just a few feet away. The folded square of bunting lay beside it, resembling a handkerchief more than a map, and was partially hidden by a sock that had been hurled down during the search.

The one called Cole came swimming into focus through the fog. He was around six feet tall and about the same age my father was when the war started. His was a manly, unblemished face with a full head of shiny brown hair and wide-set black eyes.

"You must have thought you were well hidden, I'd venture," he said in a friendly way. He pointed to the old man, who had already managed to somehow start a fire with wet sticks. "Nothing to be ashamed of. You were tracked by Claude Moomaw. During the Indian wars Claude scouted for Jim Bridger. He could have found you if you'd gone to Hades and back."

All in all, Claude Moomaw didn't look like he could track his way out of the kitchen. A great lard belly splayed out from under his fringed buckskin coat as he leaned over to stoke his fire.

Two more came up then. They both had red hair and looked like brothers. The older one was called Thurman and was around twenty-five.

He said to Cole, "Laddy and me waited like you told us, Captain. Ain't no troops on the road east toward Luray."

The old man's fire was now burning well. The stocky man with the big muscles came over and stood next to it.

"It's got to be on him," he said. "Ain't in none of his things."

The captain stared at me and smiled.

"I'm Cole McQuade," he said. "I already know your name."

I returned his gaze for a few seconds and then looked down.

"How did you kill Blewitt?" he asked as if discussing a fallen head of livestock. Again I said nothing.

"Your mother is a very brave woman, Jamie. She refused to tell us anything. However, we found Shawnessy's tobacco pouch at your friend the doctor's. Obviously, you were carrying the map when you left Port Republic. Since it may be hidden in your clothes, I must ask you to take them off."

"If you've hurt my mother—" From behind me someone grabbed my ear and began twisting it. It was the stocky man again.

"Stop it, Dex," ordered the captain.

When he let go of me, I took off my coat and handed it to him.

"I just hope the kid was smart enough to keep the paper dry," Dex said, and the words sent a thrill through me. That meant none of them had ever seen the real map and that my mother and Dr. Cassidy hadn't described it to them either.

"You won't find it," I said. "I burned it last night."

"You did that, and I'm gonna cut your heart out," said Dex.

I was down to my long underwear now. The men searched through my things like they were hunting for lice. By the time I was bare and they realized the map was not in my clothes, they boiled over in anger.

"It's got to be somewheres," yelled Thurman.

"For sure I kin git it out of 'im," said Dex.

"Put your clothes back on," Captain McQuade said to me. And then to the others, "I'll have a talk with him later."

That was when the last man of the band of six came in from tending to their horses, and I was shocked to see who it was. His name was Royal Bevinger, and he was one of my father's friends before the war. The last I knew, he was serving with one of the valley regiments. Right now there were lavender circles under his eyes, and from the way he was coughing, it was obvious he was sick.

"You all right?" asked the captain, and he nodded yes.

Mr. Bevinger came over and stood by the others, but he wouldn't look me in the eye. Thurman and Laddy dragged several thick tree limbs around the fire, and they all sat down. I sat down there too and held my hands out toward the flames.

Right then we heard a gunshot from way back up on the mountain, quickly followed by a second. The captain was on his feet in an instant and heading for the horses. "Thurman, you come with me," he called out. A minute later they rode off through the woods.

My first thought was that Major de Monfort had not gone to Winchester after all and was now on their trail. I leaned over to Laddy and whispered, "Do you know what happened to the man I was riding with yesterday?"

"What do you think?" he said out loud. "We got around behind him and shot him daid." I looked at the others, but no one said anything different. If he had told the truth, then I was on my own.

Dex came around from the other side of the fire and sat down next to me. "Tell us what you did with the map," he said.

"I told you already. I burned it last night."

"You burned it," he repeated, putting his arm around my back with a kindly hug. "Well, let's see about that."

Grabbing my left elbow in his powerful fist, he leaned me forward, propelling my arm out over the fire.

"Where is the map?" he repeated.

"I burned it, like I told you," I said, trying to keep my voice steady as he forced my hand lower over the flames.

I didn't believe he would actually hurt me until the first sickening bolt of pain raced up my fingers. At the same time Laddy got up and said, "I gotta go. Anybody still got newspaper?"

The rest of them didn't pay him any mind. He was walking past Jupiter's saddle blanket when I saw him stop and bend down to pick up the white bunting from the ground. If he saw what was written on the cloth, I knew my life was probably over.

"Agghhh," I groaned helplessly as the other men's eyes bored into mine. The pain was terrible. I kept trying to pull my arm free, but it was like being trapped in a vise.

Then Royal Bevinger said, "Don't do this, Dex."

"Shut your mouth, farmer," he said. Turning back to me, he repeated, "Now, where is the map?" I stared into his eyes in the hope I'd find pity there, but they were like brown pools of glass.

"Burned . . . it."

At the other end of the clearing Laddy was wiping his rear end with the bunting. I knew I was saved, but at that moment I no longer cared. Not being able to hold back any longer, I screamed with all the power in my lungs. *"Aaaaagggghhh!"*

As if in answer Jupiter began lunging high into the air at the place where he was tethered with the other horses. Mr. Bevinger's eyes were screwed tightly shut. I refused to look at my hand for fear of what I would see if I did.

I screamed long and loud again. And then again.

"Put a lid on it, boy," Claude grumbled loudly. "I seen Comanche squaws roasted a lot worse'n you with nary a peep."

I was out of my mind in pain when I yelled, "I know where it is! I know where the gold is!"

Dex seemed to take no notice.

"Sudley Springs!" I screamed. "It's at Sudley Springs."

Then I heard Captain McQuade yell, "Let him go, Dex."

The next thing I knew, I was falling backward off the log. Dex was lying on the ground next to me, and Captain McQuade was standing over both of us with the barrel of a revolver gripped in his right hand. Then I fainted dead away.

I CAME back into the world to find that Claude had slathered my fingers up with a greasy mess that smelled like herbs and rancid butter. He covered it with layers of moist leaves and a spare sock.

"I seen a lot worse, Cap," he said. "He'll jes lose most of the skin on three of 'em, is all."

Captain McQuade was down on one knee beside me. "We're staying here for the rest of the day," he said. "I want you to try to rest and then have something to eat. We'll talk after that."

He made me take a drink from a small stone jug and then covered me with a woolen blanket. Cradling my burned hand in the good one, I turned over on my side and fell into a fitful sleep.

When I woke again, it was afternoon, and I got up to see if Jupiter had been fed. The others were sleeping, except for Dex, who was standing guard, and the captain, who was sitting by the fire smoking a corncob pipe.

"You feeling better?" the captain said.

"I'd like to see about my horse."

He shook his head, then smiled, saying, "You're a game one."

On the way to the horses we passed close enough to Dex for me to see there was a knot the size of a goose egg on the side of his head. Jupiter appeared content as he stood with the other horses picking at what appeared to be dried timothy.

"I hope you know I wouldn't have let Dex burn you like that if I had been there," said the captain as I looked over my horse.

I didn't say anything.

"I also want you to know that your mother is safe," he went on. "So is your friend the doctor. Do you believe me?"

"What choice do I have?"

"You'll have to take my word for it," he said.

"What about Major de Monfort?" I asked.

"Who is that?"

"The one-armed officer I was riding with."

"The man who killed Big Joe Braddock. A rather wily character, as you already know. He eluded us in the storm."

I wanted to believe everything he was telling me, but there was no way to prove it. I decided to wait until I could learn more.

"Who fired those shots earlier?"

"I have no idea. Probably a hunter. We never saw a trace of any-one and came right back." The captain's eyes had a mournful droop to them that made him seem sincere. "Tell me the truth, Jamie. You memorized the map, didn't you?"

I paused for a moment before I nodded. He seemed relieved.

"Because you're the only one alive with that information," he said, "I'm going to tell you the story of how that map came to be.

It all began on the night following our first great victory at Manassas. I was a young lieutenant in the Thirty-third Virginia Infantry then, serving under General Jackson."

He stopped as if waiting for me to congratulate him. When I didn't, he went on again. "Well, that night we were celebrating what we thought was the end of the war, when Donegal Shawnessy rode up on his horse. He said if this was going to be the last fight, then he was damn well going to meet some Yankees face to face.

"We were both full of Dutch courage by then, and I agreed to go. He already had Blewitt with him, and as we were leaving my camp, Big Joe Braddock begged to come. You following this?"

I had knelt down to examine Jupiter's feet. I nodded.

"It was well after sunset when we headed up the Warrenton Turnpike after what was left of the Yankee army. By then everything was in turmoil. We were a mile or two beyond Centreville when we overtook a Pittsburgh wagon that was stopped alongside the road. We would have passed it by, but the next thing I knew, we were taking fire from the wagon, which sobered me up fast. Then we returned fire. It was over in less than a minute. There were three of them, and two were killed outright. We found the gold when we searched the wagon. It was sitting there in three big crates." He stopped to refill his pipe with tobacco.

"Why were they carrying gold in a battle?" I demanded.

"They were Federal quartermasters. The gold came from two Virginia banks the Yankees had overrun. Those quartermasters were trying to get back north when the panic started."

I could see it all in my imagination. The stranded wagon, the frightened desk soldiers trying to protect their stolen gold.

"What happened to the third quartermaster?" I said.

He paused for a bit. "He was already badly wounded."

"You murdered him, didn't you?"

"We didn't murder anyone. It was war. They were the enemy."

"You already said you thought the war was over."

He was quiet again. "That's true," he said finally, the mournful eyes looking straight into mine. "I'm not proud of it."

He must have seen the scorn in my eyes because then he said, "Wasn't it Montaigne who wrote, 'Men did not invent devils. They merely looked within themselves.' "

I guess he might have had a point. "So what did you do next?"

"A mile back up the road we ran into a detachment of our own cavalry—Jeb Stuart's boys. In the dark they took us for Yanks, and then all hell broke loose. Donegal took off in the wagon while Braddock, Blewitt, and I led them a merry chase in the other direction."

"And that's why you don't know where the gold is now."

"After outrunning the cavalry, we doubled back to find Donegal, but both he and the wagon had disappeared. There was no way to find him in the dark, and we finally headed back to camp. Well, who did we find when we got there but Donegal. He had already hidden the gold. When we got together in my tent, he told us he had made up a map so we could find it again."

"Why didn't Shawnessy show you the map right then?"

"What he did was hold up his tobacco pouch and say, 'Boys, it's right in here, and it will stay right in this darlin' sack until we go back for those pretty boxes.' As soon as he said it, I realized that was the best idea. I trusted him and didn't really know the other two. Besides, we all thought we would be coming back in a few weeks to claim it.

"Well, it didn't turn out the way we thought," he went on. "The war didn't end, and Donegal was killed in battle at Port Republic. He was in the ground before we could even pay our respects."

Maybe it was because my hand was starting to hurt very badly, but I said then, "I know how important that must have been for you. I watched Corporal Blewitt paying his respects the night he dug up Lieutenant Shawnessy's body."

He shook his head. "I figured it must have been something like that. Is that when you killed him?"

"I killed him when I found him trying to rape my mother."

"I'm sorry, Jamie. I never should have sent him to Port Republic. Drink and defeat turned him bad."

Now I knew the captain's version of the story. Some of it had to be true. But which parts? And what was he leaving out?

"Where did these other men come from?" I asked.

"You're looking at a few of the remnants of my last command. Royal Bevinger was my color sergeant. The others happened to be with Big Joe Braddock the night he got drunk a month ago and boasted he was going to be rich as soon as the war was over. We had to cut them in or they threatened to reveal the secret."

He fixed me with his sad eyes again. "Jamie, I wouldn't ask you to make me a copy of that map any more than I would have asked Donegal. But I do want your word you'll not try to escape and that you will help us find the gold when we get to Sudley Springs. For that I promise you will receive an equal share."

I knew that if anything happened to Captain McQuade, the only split I would receive from Dex and Claude would be a split skull. But my chances of staying alive were bound to the knowledge of what was written on that bunting.

"I give you my word I will not try to escape," I said.

As I lay back down near the campfire, I made the first of many attempts to bring the map back in my mind. It was no longer whole. Somehow it had become a jumble of unconnected fragments. I briefly considered going after the piece of bunting that Laddy had used in performing his ablutions but then rejected the idea.

THEY spent the rest of that day talking endlessly about the safest way to reach Sudley Springs without running into Federal cavalry. In their eyes I could see the greedy anticipation of pleasure that lay ahead of them once they got their hands on the gold. Captain McQuade never talked about his own plans.

Late in the afternoon the captain sent Thurman and Laddy to spy out the road toward Luray. They came back an hour later to say it was clear.

"Let's move out," the captain said. Because of my hand, Laddy saddled Jupiter for me. When it was done, I took a moment to listen once more to the horse's heart and lungs. He seemed to have recovered from his ordeal on the mountain. When I was about to mount him, he craned his head around to look at me. There was an intensity in his eyes, a look of total trust, the feeling that we were in this together and would see it through, come what may.

It was gathering dusk as we moved out. In spite of my pledge to Captain McQuade, the thought of escaping was never far out of my mind, and Dex seemed to sense it. He stayed beside me.

We walked the horses most of the way, stopping to water them twice as the night wore on. I was sagging in my saddle when the shadow of Claude Moomaw loomed up on the road ahead of us. "Good place to stop," he said. "Another half hour till daylight."

We left the farm road there, passing the burned-out shell of a barn. Claude led us into the field behind it and then into a dense copse of sycamore trees that ran along a small brook.

"No fire," said McQuade as we dismounted.

With my good hand I used a curry brush to give Jupiter a deep rubdown. The familiar tangy smell of his coat made me think of home, and I knew my mother must be frantic with worry.

Dex was still watching me when I rolled out my gum cloth and found a place near the captain to lie down.

Sometime later I awoke with a pleasant sense of warmth combined with a weight that felt like a heavy quilt. Peeping out from under the cloth, I was amazed to discover several inches of snow covering me and more coming down every second.

Grumpily the other men awoke and began pestering McQuade to build a fire. It was obvious Royal Bevinger was getting even sicker as he wiped fever sweat away from his pasty forehead.

"We can't chance it till we get past Luray and all that Yankee cavalry," said the captain. He got foul looks from the others.

"All right," he said. "We'll ride today and then find someplace warm to hole up on the other side of Blue Ridge Gap."

Thirty minutes later we were on our way. Claude took the lead again, far out in front. Captain McQuade brought up the rear.

Their luck ran out right away. A cavalry patrol spotted us before we had even covered a mile. My first inkling of what was happening came when I saw Claude whipping his horse back up the road and waving his right arm in a circle. We turned our horses around and spurred them in the opposite direction as he sped past us.

Claude leaped his horse across a low hedge and led us toward a distant smear of trees. I began to hear gunshots and swung around in the saddle to look back. At first I couldn't see anything through the heavy snow, but then McQuade's big chestnut came soaring over the hedge line as he raced to catch up with us.

That's when it happened. Even as I write these words, I cannot tell of it without a shudder of horror. One moment we were riding like the wind, Jupiter's powerful legs thundering on the ground. And then I felt him suddenly stagger, his head plunging in distress. Pulling hard on the reins with my good hand, I brought him up short. But before I could dismount, McQuade was by my side, grabbing the reins out of my hand and pulling them over Jupiter's head. As he savagely kicked his horse in the flanks, I screamed, "No! You'll kill Jupiter!" His grim face never looked back.

Gunfire erupted behind us again, and I glanced back to see a mass of blue riders, at least twenty or more, spread out in a rough line across the field. As more shots exploded, I prayed that one of the balls would strike McQuade. But it was not to be.

We raced on, first one mile and then another until we actually began to gain ground, leaving the Yankees behind.

And then it ended.

With one great convulsive shudder Jupiter's great heart finally gave out. We were still in full stride when his front legs suddenly collapsed. Arms outflung, I flew over his neck and turned a somersault in the air, landing on my backside.

On my feet in an instant, I ran back to him. He was lying on his side, his powerful legs flailing away. I wrapped my arms around his neck to calm him. His massive chest was heaving mightily in a frantic effort to take in air.

Then I was lifted bodily from the ground and cast over the saddle of McQuade's horse. As I looked back, Jupiter was still trying to lift his head from the snow, his grieving eyes making a last mute appeal for my help. That was when the shot rang out from the captain's repeating rifle, and Jupiter was gone forever.

Four

I HAD never truly hated before, but now I knew the full meaning of the word. I hated Captain McQuade for killing Jupiter. I hated Dex for burning me, and I hated the others for standing around doing nothing while he did it. Just like that winter world around me, there was now ice around my heart.

With his uncanny sense of ground, Claude Moomaw led us through the white landscape in a wide slant until we had circled completely around the befuddled cavalry patrol. The only thing I remember from that ride was McQuade trying to apologize.

I accused him of purposely running my horse to death. "You no longer have my word about not trying to escape," I said defiantly, but he didn't seem to take notice.

Two hours later we came out on the main trunk road a few miles beyond Luray. Captain McQuade lowered me to the ground and then told Laddy I would be riding behind him. By then I was beyond caring what became of me. Sunk in despair, I also felt complete contempt for myself, knowing that had I not gone after the gold, Jupiter would still be alive.

Claude dismounted and placed his ear to the roadbed. He said, "These parts will be crawling with Yankees anytime now, Cole. We've got to go to ground."

The murderer nodded. "Let's find a deserted house."

"That suits me," said Laddy, behind whom I was now sitting.

The snow turned back to rain as we left the main road, heading north for a few more miles until we came to a small road bedded with fine gravel and lined on both sides with old elm trees. It ran for almost a mile, ending at two high brick pillars.

I could now see it was the entrance to a large estate. A brass plate was embedded in one of the pillars, and engraved in capital letters was the name Dandridge.

"I'll do the talking if anyone is there," said McQuade.

The entrance lane ran for another half mile, tracking slowly up toward a three-story house made of gray brick with a white porch running all the way around it. As we walked the horses into the yard, I could see smoke curling from one of the eight chimneys that rose high above the slate roof.

Then a tall man and a white dog came out onto the front porch. The man had an air of authority about him, just like my father, although he was much older, with carefully parted long silver hair and a distinguished face. He did not appear to be armed. The dog looked like a cross between a wolf and a deer.

The captain spoke first. "My name is McQuade," he said in his politest manner. "We need fodder for our horses and food if you have any to sell. I'd also be greatly obliged if we could make temporary quarters for tonight in one of your farm buildings."

The courtly man smiled. Then his gaze shifted away from McQuade, and he calmly surveyed the rest of the group. The results of the inspection were revealed in his eyes.

"There is nothing for you here," he said icily. "Please ride on."

The dog bared his fangs and let out a low snarl.

"A man ain't braced got little to parley with," said Claude.

"I regret to do this, but I have no other choice but to requisition what we need," said McQuade.

"By whose authority?" demanded the man on the porch.

"Too damn cold for this," said Claude, pulling his dragoon pistol out from under his coat. "Here's arrthority."

A second later the barrel of a rifle came plunging through one of the large downstairs windows.

"Don't fire," yelled McQuade, but he was already too late.

Claude's pistol exploded first. The courtly man's face erupted in blood, and he pitched over the railing into a large bush.

When I heard the next explosion, Laddy flew out of the saddle just in front of me and landed headfirst on the ground.

Then, almost too fast to see, I saw the dog launch itself from the porch. In two bounds it was at Dex's side and with another leap had sunk its jaws into his right thigh. Screaming in pain, Dex pounded the dog's head with his revolver, but it still hung there until Dex placed the barrel in its ear and pulled the trigger.

As Laddy's horse reared up, I fell off his haunches, scrambling when I hit the ground to avoid his thrashing hooves.

Then the men were off their mounts and rushing toward the house. All except Royal and Claude. While Royal rounded up the horses, Claude dragged the old man out of the bushes. As soon as he had him clear, he began rifling his pockets.

I crawled over to Laddy. He stared up at the rain that still fell from the leaden sky while a gaping wound poured his life's blood out onto the muddy ground.

Claude had pulled off the old man's boots and was trying them on when I began to hear shouting from the house. Stepping up onto the porch, I went through the wide-open front door.

The shouting was coming from one of the side halls. They were in the library. In the middle of the room stood an enormous evergreen tree adorned with dozens of glass and ceramic ornaments. Its tangy fresh-cut smell was a sudden reminder that Christmas was coming.

The windows of the wood-paneled room faced onto the front porch, and several of the panes were shattered. A rifle lay on the floor by the nearest window. Next to it was another body. He was a little Negro man with tightly curled white hair. A thick stream of his blood was spreading out across the polished floor.

Captain McQuade had Thurman backed up against the wall, and his hands were at the younger man's throat. "The man's arms were raised," he shouted. "He had given up, damn your eyes."

"He shot Laddy," screamed Thurman. "He shot my brother!"

The only other person in the room was a slim woman in a green silk dress. She had long auburn hair, but I couldn't see her face, because it was covered by both of her hands. Then her hands dropped to her sides as if they were too heavy to hold up any longer.

When McQuade finally swung from Thurman to face her, she said, "Please take me to my father."

As she passed me, I could see she wasn't much older than me, but her green eyes were fixed and lifeless.

Royal Bevinger had dragged her father in from out of the rain and laid him out on his back in the front hall. The girl walked toward the corpse in halting steps. There was nothing distinguished about him now. All his pockets had been yanked out, and he was barefoot. His face was a horrible bloody mask.

She slumped to her knees beside him. Captain McQuade seemed transfixed as he stared down at them both.

Thurman came into the hall crying, "Where's Laddy?" Mr. Bevinger pointed toward the door, and he went out. He was back a minute later, bringing the streaming body inside. He laid him down on the other side of the hall from Mr. Dandridge and burst into tears, sobbing, "What's Ma gonna say?"

Still kneeling next to her father, the girl formed her hands into claws like eagle's talons as Thurman carried on. Then they slowly relaxed again. She pulled a white silk handkerchief from her sleeve and gently covered her father's ruined face with it before standing up. Turning about, she looked at each of us long and hard.

Her big eyes were no longer lifeless. They flashed like green fire. And then, as if none of her father's killers were watching her, she slowly walked up the curving staircase and disappeared down the hall. I heard the sound of a door shutting, and then it was still.

NO YANKEE patrols came near us during the remainder of that day, which continued stormy. Inside, the house was bitter cold. As the afternoon turned dark, I could see my breath in the light from the candle in the parlor, where I sat waiting while the killers decided what to do next.

None of them were excited at the thought of digging three graves. They did remove the bodies to the carriage shed in a small farm cart and then made a careful search of the house. There was no one else to be found, although I did notice a table in the parlor with several framed daguerreotypes on it. They showed Miss Dandridge with her mother and what I guessed were two brothers. What had become of them, I had no idea.

The search produced meager results in the way of food. There was no livestock in the outbuildings and no cured meat of any kind in the house. Then Dex came out from the pantry with a small keg under his arm.

"Lest I'm mistaken," he said, "this is Irish."

Apparently, it was a powerful whiskey, because they began tapping it hard as soon as the stopper was out of the bunghole. McQuade was the worst, taking it down in great gulps. By nightfall he was already sloppy drunk. With the exception of Royal Bevinger, the others weren't far behind. Royal just sat shivering in his chair with a blanket wrapped around his shoulders.

After a while they no longer even bothered to fetch wood for the fire. Thurman started it first. After complaining about how cold it was, he went over and picked up a mahogany gaming table and smashed it to pieces against the wall. Then he fed it to the fire. Whenever the blaze died down after that, someone would just break up another piece of furniture.

By evening they had consumed much of their keg of "Irish." Thurman was staring at one of the paintings on the wall.

"I bet they had thesselves some fancy balls heah," he said. "We ought to have that sweet belle up theah dance with us."

"That's a fine idea," sang out Dex. He lurched over to the captain, who lay insensible on the floor.

"What you say, Cap? Kin we have us a ball?" He kicked him hard in the ribs, but McQuade only mumbled.

"Cap says fine idea too," said Dex. "You go on up'n give an invite to the lady."

I could hear Thurman bounding up the stairs, and then he was knocking on her door. The knocking got louder until finally he lost patience and just battered it open. A minute later he was back with the girl, dragging her by her thick auburn hair.

Claude sat down at a little black piano. He had no idea how to play it, and the musical sounds were harsh and unpleasant.

"May ah have this dance?" asked Thurman with a deep mocking bow. He took hold of her, and she began twisting madly back and forth. "Someone give a hand," he called out, trying to hold her in place. Dex moved to pin her arms behind her back, and she began to make little whimpering noises.

When I heard the sound of her dress tearing, I didn't stop to think about what to do next. Being small has its advantages sometimes. I was able to get close up next to Thurman before I stamped my bootheel down on the side of his shin.

Right away he stopped what he was doing long enough to cuff me in the head with the back of his hand. It sent me flying across the room, but I was up again in a moment and on my way back to him when Dex dropped her arms and came forward to meet me.

Now free, the girl raked her fingernails across Thurman's face, and three tiny rivulets of blood spurted up in their path. As she stepped back, I could see the white straps of her shift where the dress had been ripped away. Then Dex was on top of me.

The deafening explosion stopped everyone in their tracks. I looked up to see Royal Bevinger holding a smoking pistol. He was still in his chair and covered by the blanket. As I look back on it now, he may not have had the strength to stand up.

"No more," he said quietly.

"You better stay outta this, farmer," said Dex, his face beet red.

"It wouldn't take much for me to kill you, Dex," said Mr. Bevinger. "I've killed a lot better than you in this war."

Dex did not have his gun. Neither did Thurman. I knew that Claude always carried his dragoon pistol in a shoulder holster inside his buckskin coat. That was where his hand was going.

"Watch out," I called to Mr. Bevinger. The sick man trained his pistol on Claude and motioned for him to give it over.

"This ain't forgivable, Royal," said the old man.

"We will see," he said as Claude tossed the pistol to him.

Mr. Bevinger turned to me with a wan smile. "Jamie, you and Miss Dandridge lock yourselves in the cellar. I'll hold the fort here until the captain comes around. Then we will come to get you. Go now."

The girl took a pewter candleholder from the mantel, and I followed her down the hall. Upon seeing the strength of the cellar door, I concluded that Mr. Bevinger may have already known that the girl and I would need a safe sanctuary. It was almost two inches thick, and the frame was equally stout.

I went down first. She followed with the lit candle and locked the door behind us. As I descended into the darkness, I could still hear the angry voices of the men. I hoped that Mr. Bevinger would have sufficient strength to hold them off.

We slowly made our way forward into the cavernous cellar. The girl led me to a trestle table and two ladder-back chairs. Sitting down, she placed the candleholder between us and said, "My name is Katharine Dandridge. I'm called Kate by my family."

"My name is Jamie Lockhart," I said.

"Why are you with them?" she asked next.

"They took me," I said, and she nodded as if I didn't have to explain any further.

By and by she told me she was eighteen years old and one of three children. Her two older brothers were serving in the army, and as far as she knew, they were both still alive. I was glad for that because she said her mother had died the previous spring. But for her brothers, she would have been alone in the world.

"How old are you?" she asked at one point.

"Fifteen," I said, and braced myself for words about my size.

Instead, she said, "You are brave and true, Jamie Lockhart. I thank you for saving my life."

From that moment on I would have done anything for her.

"I'm sorry about your father," I said, "and your slave."

"You mean Franklin. He wasn't our slave. My father owned no slaves. Franklin was a freeman. If I have to search for them the rest of my life, I will see those men dead for what they have done. What happened to your hand?" she asked then.

Before I could say a word in reply, we heard a shout, followed by heavy footfalls pounding down the hall. Someone threw the full weight of his body against the cellar door.

Kate raised the candle from the table and took my good hand in hers. She led us deeper into the cellar. "Can you swim?" she asked, which at that moment sounded like a stupid question.

"Yes," I said, trusting her to have some purpose in mind.

"Follow me," she said, and lifting her skirts above her knees, she climbed onto an old farm table that stood against a brick wall at the farthest end of the cellar. Behind us I heard the cellar door splinter with a loud crack and knew they were coming.

Now that we were both standing on the table, I could see there was a narrow space between the top rim of this brick wall and the ceiling beam above us.

"Climb over," Kate whispered. With that, she blew the candle out, and everything went dark. I felt her scrambling over the edge, and I followed a second later. Holding my bandaged hand to my chest, I tumbled headfirst into a lake of black water.

We were in an underground cistern that had been constructed beneath the house. Kate seemed to know exactly where she was going and gently pulled me along. I'm sure the water was cold, but under the circumstances I don't even remember it. When we reached the far end of the cistern, Kate slid open its locking bolt. A fierce blast of wind blew past into the cellar.

"What's that?" I heard Dex cry out behind us.

"Arr comin' from outside," yelled Claude. "They's clear."

Kate went through the opening first and helped me out a moment later. Then she took up the wet fullness of her skirts in both hands, and we began running for our lives. I knew how good a tracker Claude was, but we had a head start, and they wouldn't be able to get to their horses right away. We had a chance.

The air temperature was far colder than the water we had come through, and looking back on it, I think the two of us soon might have frozen to death if we hadn't been running so hard.

We passed a gravel drive and then an open pasture before she led me into an old stand of piney woods. There was no stopping to rest until Kate cleared the last of the piney branches. By then we had covered a mile or more.

Through the driving rain I now saw another house, although by no means as grand as the Dandridge mansion.

"Our overseer lived here," said Kate, out of breath.

Inside, the air was musty and damp. The front room was low-ceilinged with water-stained walls. "It's been empty for more than two years," she said sadly. She found matches and carefully lit the wick of an oil lamp. "Come on. We need dry clothes." She headed upstairs.

"If we hide here, they will surely find us," I said, partly to keep my teeth from chattering. "The fat one is an old Indian tracker."

"We are not staying here," she replied calmly. "As soon as I'm ready, I'm going back."

The idea was so crazy I wasn't sure I had heard her correctly. Before I could speak, however, she was gone again. I followed her to another room that was apparently used for storage. A half-dozen turtle-backed trunks sat covered with dust on the floor.

"Those are my brothers' cases," she said, pointing to several against the far wall. I went to the first one and pried it open with my good hand. Although her brothers had long since outgrown these clothes, many of them fit me perfectly.

Swiftly she went through one of the other trunks, removed a selection of things, and disappeared down the hall. Five minutes later she was back, having changed into black corduroy riding britches, a heavy shirt, and calf-length boots. Her hair was hidden under a wide-brimmed plantation hat.

Stuffing additional clothing into a canvas sack, she picked up the oil lamp and headed back downstairs.

"Let's have a look at your hand," she said when we were in the kitchen. Tenderly she pulled off the sock, which still covered Claude's dressing. It had begun to smell bad, and I wasn't sure what we would find. I guess the fingers looked a lot worse than they felt, but she never flinched when she saw them.

"Can you move them?" Kate asked, and I did.

"They're just very stiff."

"They will be that for as long as you live, I'm afraid," she said. After searching through kitchen drawers, she coated my fingers with balm, wrapped the hand again with a piece of clean cheesecloth, and slid it into a large blue mitten she had brought from upstairs.

"I must go now, Jamie," she said. "I know exactly where to hide so I can shoot those men when they go for their horses."

I guess she was the most fearless girl who ever lived.

"I'll go with you," I said, and then began to shiver.

"I can't let you do that, Jamie. Besides, you're the only witness to what they did in case I—"

"You can't stop me from going with you," I said.

She smiled at me and took my good hand in hers. It was warm.

"Have you ever fired a pistol, Jamie?" Kate asked me evenly.

"I have," I replied. "And I'm a good shot."

She led us into what must have been the overseer's office and went straight to a large cabinet that was built into the wall. Sliding open the pocket door, she removed a small six-shot revolver and handed it to me.

"Could you handle something like this?" she asked. I nodded.

"Being able to aim and pull the trigger is quite different from killing a man," she went on as she took out more weapons.

The image of Corporal Blewitt's body came into my mind. "I know what we have to do," I said.

We set out a little later, the wind lashing rain into our faces. Kate was weighted down with a brace of pistols and a double-barreled shotgun, which she carried inside a blanket roll. I carried another shotgun along with the pistol and a sack of spare ammunition.

She may not have had Claude's tracking skills, but she knew every inch of her father's vast estate. Another hour brought us to no more than thirty yards from the outbuilding where they had taken their horses, and around double that distance from the house.

Our hiding place was in the middle of a square of boxwoods that lined one side of the gravel drive. Not only was it a perfect ambush site but we were almost completely protected from the wind and rain by the thick shrubbery around us.

It was around three in the morning by then, and no lights came from the house. For now at least we were completely safe. She spread out the blanket roll, and we lay down side by side.

"This may not be of comfort to you right now," she said softly, "but in any fight surprise is more than half the battle. At least that's what Jeb Stuart once told me."

I may not have looked persuaded, because then she said, "You should also know I'm a crack marksman." In spite of the odds against us, I believed her. She was completely exhausted, though, and soon fell fast asleep. It was up to me to stand watch for the rest of the night, and I did.

Five

WHEN the first hint of dawn finally arrived, I happened to be staring at the house as it slowly came into view. A few minutes passed before I realized there was something wrong.

There was no smoke coming from any of the chimneys.

I woke up Kate and told her.

"Why does that matter?" she asked groggily.

"Those men are like spiders when it comes to the cold. If they were in there, they would have a fire going."

"Where else could they be?" Slipping from her hiding place, Kate crept to the nearest window of the outbuilding where their horses had been liveried, while I covered her with one of the shotguns. She stood up to glance inside for a moment, then shouted back to me, "The horses are gone."

"They must have cleared out while we were at the overseer's house. They've no doubt ridden ahead to Sudley Springs," I replied.

Kate motioned for me to follow her to the carriage shed. There she covered both her father's body and that of their Negro servant with white muslin sheets. Laddy was lying all by himself near the hitching post. She knelt beside the corpse of her father, her hands clasped together in a long prayer. Then she stood up and turned to me, saying, "It's time to go."

"To Sudley Springs?" I asked, and she nodded.

"First we'll need to find horses," she said. "Follow me."

I GUESS I WOULD HAVE followed her anywhere by then. Already I knew I could trust her with my life, just as I was ready to give up my own for hers if it came to that.

As we walked, I told Kate everything that had happened to me, starting with the night Corporal Blewitt came to Port Republic and how I had followed him to the graveyard. When I reached the part about how I had killed him, she actually stopped in her tracks and turned to me wide-eyed. After looking into my eyes for a long moment, she nodded once, and I knew she believed me.

A little more than two hours of fast walking brought us to a steep hill, at the bottom of which was a quaint old village.

Kate began to walk faster. "Helen Kerfoot lives here," she said.

She headed straight for a large white clapboard house that dominated the other buildings in the settlement. She mounted the stairs of the front porch two at a time, opened the unlocked door, and called out, "Helen!"

Thirty seconds later the hall was filled with a small army of women and children, all talking at once.

"Who are you?" demanded one.

"Is that you, Katharine?" asked another.

"Helen!" Kate called out again over the tumult.

A massive figure suddenly appeared at the head of the stairs. Her hair was silver, and she had a face like George Washington.

"Katharine Dandridge," she called out in a booming voice, "you look as if you've come straight from the trenches."

Then she saw the look of distress on Kate's face, and right away her manner changed. "Why, child, what is the matter?" she cried, almost charging down the stairs toward us.

"I need to talk to you alone, Helen," said Kate.

"Make room, make room," boomed Mrs. Kerfoot as she led us through the crush in the corridor. When we reached the winter kitchen, Mrs. Kerfoot closed the door behind her.

"Helen, this is my friend Jamie Lockhart," said Kate. "He needs something to eat." Mrs. Kerfoot shifted her worried glance to me for a moment and then back to Kate.

"We can fill that cavity," she said with a terse smile. Four crusty fruit pies were cooling on a pine harvest table near the stove. As she picked up a bread knife and began to cut me a piece, she said, "Now tell me what has happened, Katharine."

"Father and Franklin have both been murdered," she said. The big woman's head jerked back as if she had been slapped.

"Oh, no!" said Helen Kerfoot with a deep groan.

"Do you still have those horses hidden at Peak's?" Kate asked.

"Yes, they are still there," Mrs. Kerfoot replied.

"Could I have the loan of two of them?"

"Of course, Katharine, but surely that can wait until—"

"I need them right now, Helen," replied Kate. "As for the burial arrangements, I would ask you to see to them."

"Where are you going?"

"After the murderers," said Kate.

I expected Mrs. Kerfoot to have a fit about the idea, but it didn't seem to come as a surprise.

"I know how willful and headstrong you can be when you set your mind on something, Katharine," Mrs. Kerfoot said, "but for God's sake, leave the apprehension of these brigands to people who—"

"I will not take unnecessary risks, Helen," she said.

At that moment the far door of the kitchen burst open, and I was surrounded again in bedlam. They were army wives, all invited by Mrs. Kerfoot to stay with her for the duration. They came from as far as Martinsburg and were desperately eager to ask us what was happening at the front.

The conversation between Kate and Mrs. Kerfoot ended. Kate came over to me then and whispered, "She is sending her hired man for the horses. He should be back here in an hour."

"Who is Mrs. Kerfoot?" I asked.

"She is my great-aunt and was my mother's best friend. Helen has outlasted three husbands and raised nine children."

After I finished eating, one of the women took me to a room where someone had brought a pitcher of hot water and a precious bar of soap. Using my good hand, I tried my best to wash myself.

Kate was in earnest conversation with Mrs. Kerfoot again in the front parlor when I returned. Kate was saying, "Someone needs to get word to his mother that he is all right."

"I will take care of it," said Helen Kerfoot.

Kate asked me to compose a short letter. It struck me that telling my mother any of the story at that point would only increase her anxiety. Instead, this is what I wrote:

Dear Mother,
Please do not worry about me. I am fine and have made a very good friend. I hope you are all right and that you have heard from Father by now. I will be home soon. Love, Jamie.

As I finished writing, I heard the clatter of horses' hooves. Mrs. Kerfoot took the note and sealed it. When we got outside, there were two horses tethered to the stone hitching post.

"They're the best two I have left," said Mrs. Kerfoot. "The gray is Arabian, and the roan is out of Moon Dancer. They will take you a long way."

"Thank you, Helen," said Kate.

"Promise me, child, you will come back to us."

"I promise," Kate said with such a confident smile that Mrs. Kerfoot might have even believed it was true.

The hired man finished strapping our bedrolls and two bulging food sacks onto the saddles. Then Kate was up on the gray. I mounted the roan. He felt young and powerful and ready to run.

"God bless you, Katharine," said Helen Kerfoot.

"Good-bye, Helen," said Kate, spurring her stallion forward. I followed, looking back just once. Mrs. Kerfoot was holding a hand to her face. The other was clutching the hitching post. The hired man was running toward her as if he thought she was about to fall down.

FOR the first part of the journey we didn't see another human being. Kate had decided to avoid the well-traveled road that led up to Thornton Gap in the Blue Ridge Mountains. Instead, she was aiming to cross the mountains at a place called the Pinnacle, which was a four-thousand-foot promontory to the south of Thornton Gap. She had once explored it with her brothers on a camping trip. Kate said that beyond that peak there was a narrow trail we could traverse down to the Virginia plain, where the road through Sperryville would eventually take us to Sudley Springs.

To get there, we followed a succession of cramped country lanes that finally brought us to the first sharp incline of a forest path that led up toward the windswept blue-black mountain.

Kate led me straight to the place where she and her brothers had camped before the war. It was sheltered from the wind by massive boulders, and there was a declivity in the rocks where we could lay out our sleeping blankets in full protection from the elements while still enjoying a view of the countryside.

For supper we ate the roasted ham on thick slices of baked bread that had been packed for us by the women before we left. Later the wind came up, spraying the sparks from our fire wildly into the air. That was when I asked Kate why Helen Kerfoot had called her willful. She stared long and hard into the flames.

"I was a great disappointment to my mother," she said finally. "She always wanted me to be a proper young lady. All I ever wanted was to be like my brothers. Running free."

"A tomboy?" I said.

She nodded. "And then when I did realize I enjoyed female things," she went on, "I truly disappointed her by falling in love with a boy who wasn't suitable. It was his unfortunate destiny to believe heart and soul in the preservation of the Union."

"You loved a Yankee?" I said, shocked.

"No, he was a Virginian," she said. "He was killed in the second year of the war."

"Oh," I said. "Well, at least your mother must have been sorry for having doubted him."

"No, Jamie. You see, he was a captain in the Union Army when he died."

That ended our conversation for a while. When I looked up from the fire again, I saw she was crying.

"It's no good," she said finally, her voice trailing off. "As terrible as war is, I never imagined it would be like this."

I was numbed at the enormity of everything she had lost.

"What about you, Jamie? Have you ever fallen in love?"

I felt the blood rushing into my face and turned away.

"A man of secrets, I see," she said with a gentle smile. "Well, let's turn in before I start pouring out the rest of my family scandals."

That night alone with Kate at the Pinnacle was the soundest sleep I have enjoyed from the time Corporal Blewitt came to this very day. Maybe I should put rocks in my bed from now on.

I AWOKE shortly before dawn. Miraculously, the sky to the east was clear, although when I looked to the north, I could see another mass of low dark clouds surging toward us.

Kate and I enjoyed a breakfast of tea and fire-toasted corn bread. Then she saddled the horses, and we were off again.

The trip down the mountain was uneventful. It was near midday when we reached the foothills of the Blue Ridge. By then the sky had gotten very dark again, and a harsh wind presaged more rain.

"We should be in Sperryville soon," said Kate, shivering.

We were still in dense forest when off in the distance I saw a white church spire rising above the tops of the trees. As we rode closer, the little church itself came into view. It stood all alone in a glade that had recently been hacked out of the forest.

I remember wondering if it was Sunday, because a group of horsemen were sitting their mounts in a rough circle around the two oak trees that marked the entrance to the churchyard.

Then to my horror I realized what was happening. They were all watching a man who was hanging by the neck from one of the trees. It must have just occurred because as we drew nearer, I saw that the hanged man was not yet dead. Even though his hands were tied behind his back, his legs had been left free, and he was now kicking out wildly as if there was still a chance to run away.

By the time we came abreast of the group, he had finally finished his grotesque dance and now hung limp. He wore the blue uniform of a Federal soldier, and I guessed he was around twenty years old.

The leader of the Confederates was bareheaded, with long corn-colored hair and a freckled boyish face. The only thing old about him were his eyes. They were stone-cold gray.

"What did this man do?" asked Kate.

"I suggest you leave that be and ride along, ma'am," said the leader politely. He had sergeant's stripes sewn on his sleeves.

"But he must have been a prisoner of war," she came back. "And he was just a boy."

Then one of the others said, "Don't you waste no tears on the likes of him. His people murdered three of our men in Front Royal this week past. No trial. Just strung them up like sides of beef in the town square. We're just payin' back in kind."

That's when Kate cried out, "What is wrong with you men? Has the Confederate army lost all sense of honor?"

None of them but the sergeant would look her in the eye. "Don't preachify to us about honor," he snarled. "Talk to your Yankee friends about that. They started this kind of war."

"That makes you no better than them," she shouted back.

"So be it," he said.

For at least a minute Kate didn't take her eyes off his face. She didn't look away, even when one of the Confederates began trying to drag off the Yankee's boots.

"That'll do," the sergeant said harshly to the soldier.

The horsemen quickly formed up to move out. The Confederates had already claimed the sleek Yankee mount as a prize of war. As the men began to clatter away down the road, Kate called out after them, "I'll see you in hell, Sergeant."

He stopped his horse for a moment and looked back at her.

"I truly hope that ain't your destination, miss," he said with a final boyish grin. Then he turned his horse and rode away.

BEFORE riding on, we cut the dead Yankee down and hastily tried to arrange his body in a dignified way. Of course, there was nothing dignified about the way he had died or about what the Yankees would do next after they found him lying by the road in front of the church. It would mean even harsher retaliation against our people. Where would it all end? I wondered.

As we rode into the outskirts of Sperryville, the gale that had threatened all day finally unleashed its fury upon us. The rain pelted our faces and slowed the horses to a walk.

Much of the town lay in ruins. It had been the site of many skirmishes and repeated occupations by one side or the other since the start of the war, because it lay right at the entrance to the Blue Ridge in that part of Virginia.

We needed a place to stop until the rain abated, but Kate began to worry about what would happen if the hanged Yankee's body was discovered while we were still in town. There would be a lot of questions for strangers like us.

I reminded her of the man that Major de Monfort had told me about, living in the settlement named Calvary beyond Massies Glen. She agreed it made sense for us to head there right away, even if only for the duration of the storm.

A little more than an hour later we passed through Massies Glen. Unlike Sperryville, it appeared to be untouched by the fighting. Somehow the war had left its brightly painted cottages in peace. Most of them were gaily lit for Christmas. It was like a stab to my heart as I thought of my mother alone at home, not knowing where either my father or I was this night.

One of the houses sat right at the edge of the street. Through the windows I could see a family decorating their Christmas tree in the front parlor. It seemed so warm and inviting. A man my father's age was attaching sprigs of holly to the mantelpiece.

Then I looked over at Kate, who was gazing in the same window with desolate eyes. Seeing me, she immediately turned away. We silently rode on through the pitiless rain.

A mile past Massies Glen I began to look ahead for signs of Calvary. Kate was the first one to see light in the distance. As we came closer, I realized it was a man standing in the middle of the road waving a railroad lantern.

"Bridge is gone," he shouted. "You have to go back."

"We need to get to Calvary," I shouted to him.

"Only way to get there now is to cross the stream about a hundred yards up that way," he said, pointing to a track that headed north. "It's more'n likely too deep to cross."

We thanked him and began to turn our horses north.

"Who you got to see?" he called out.

"Man named Gamage," I yelled back.

"Gamage, you say? I don't mean to tell you nothin'," he shouted, obviously wanting to tell us something.

"Yes?" said Kate.

"Man's crazy as a coot."

The words gave us pause.

"Do you know where he lives?" I finally asked.

"Highland Manor. Yankees burned most of it in '63. You can't see it from the pike. When you're nigh on thirty rods past the bridge, look for the break in the trees on your right."

"Thank you," called Kate. She nudged the Arabian forward.

We followed the track to the ford he had described and stopped our horses to survey the crossing. The stream was rumbling wildly past in a great crescendo of noise.

We had no choice but to go forward. By now the Yankees were sure to have found the body of their hanged comrade and were probably sending patrols in every direction to arrest anyone who might have information about the murder.

Kate's warm hand clasped my own, and we spurred our horses into the maelstrom. At first the stream stayed shallow, and I thought we would make an uneventful crossing. Ten yards out it became deeper, with my horse plunging down to his chest in the turbulent mass. I was still holding Kate's hand when an uprooted tree violently struck the side of her horse and she was knocked off his back. Our hands tore loose from each other. She was gone in an instant.

I screamed her name as the roan finally found purchase on the gravel bed and began to pull us free of the water. Turning in the saddle, I saw proof that there is truly a benevolent God.

Miraculously, she had managed to seize hold of the tail of my horse, and as the roan frantically sought the safety of the far bank, he pulled her clear of the violent water.

Of Kate's Arabian there was no sign. Most of our food, along with both shotguns and spare ammunition, were lost.

I reached down to help Kate mount behind me on the roan. Her arms snaked around my chest in a tight embrace. Soaked and bedraggled, the two of us rode on toward Calvary.

Less than ten minutes later we saw the clearing in the trees the man on the road had told us to look out for. We turned off the road and followed a muddy lane until the outline of a massive structure emerged through the wall of rain.

As we drew closer, a bolt of lightning enabled me to see that the house ran at least four stories high. The left wing of it had been badly damaged by fire. We dismounted and walked stiffly toward the front entrance.

The door was ironbound and looked stout enough to withstand a battering ram. A minute of loud knocking yielded no response. In desperation I used the butt of my revolver to pound on the door, making a din that would have woken the dead.

Suddenly Kate grabbed my arm and pointed to the glass-paneled transom over the door. I could now see a wavering light, which grew stronger as someone approached. We finally heard a key moving in the lock, and the door slowly swung open.

The figure of a man peered out at us. He was holding an oil lamp in front of him, and the force of the wind made the flame gutter wildly inside its glass chimney.

" *'Speak, thou apparition,'* " he demanded in an odd jolly-sounding voice. There was a vacant cast to his face, and for a moment I thought he might be blind. Then, birdlike, the restless eyes darted in my direction and looked me up and down.

He was a wiry man, even shorter than me. A fringe of curly hair surrounded his bald skull, and he had a sharp beak of a nose.

"Mr. Gamage?" I said.

" *'Unbidden guests are often welcomest when they are gone,'* " he declared with an idiot's grin. I knew right away it was from Shakespeare but couldn't remember which play.

When I saw the door begin to shut on us, I said loudly, "Montague sent us."

Slowly it swung open again. "Who perchance is Montague?"

"A man with one arm," I said.

"And so he is. And so he comes anon," said the man. With that, he beckoned us in and closed the door behind us.

Six

IT WAS obvious the high-ceilinged front room was no longer in use. Aside from a brass chandelier with more arms on it than a sea serpent, all the furnishings had been removed. The dust on the floor was thick enough for us to make tracks in as we followed him through dark, empty corridors to the back of the great house.

We entered an immense kitchen, which was blessedly warm thanks to a black iron cookstove that took up most of one wall. In the glow of lamplight I could see a plantation table in the center of the room, with ten chairs around it.

"Sit here next to the stove," he said with another vacuous smile. "Are you hungry?" he asked.

"Yes," said Kate.

"Fine. We'll pluck a crow for you," he said, tittering with laughter. "But first I shall see to your horse."

The kitchen door was barred with a length of oak timber. He removed the plank from its braces and opened it. Outside, the storm raged unabated.

" *'Blow. Blow, thou winter wind! Thou art not so unkind as man's ingratitude.'* " He slammed the door shut and was gone.

"Without question he is a strange little man," said Kate. "But I believe he is pretending to be unbalanced."

"Why would he do that?" I asked.

"For one thing it probably keeps strangers away," she said.

That made sense, although it didn't explain the mystery of who he was and what Major de Monfort had to do with him.

When the little man returned, he went straight to a cold pantry and returned with a loaf of bread and a whole baked chicken.

"Thank you, Mr. Gamage," I said.

" ' 'Tis an ill cook that cannot lick his own fingers,' " he said.

After our meal he led us to adjoining rooms on the second floor. They appeared to have been in recent use and were clean, with heavy goose-down comforters on each bed. The shutters on the windows were bolted shut from the outside, and the windows covered by drapes, which kept out any drafts from the raging wind.

There was even an abundance of candles, and I soon had my room cheerily lit. A call from Kate brought me to a third chamber, in the middle of which there stood an enamel bathtub.

"The simplest and best of luxuries," she announced.

"I don't need a bath," I said, although I knew I did. It was the thought of bathing around Kate that made me uncomfortable.

"Why, Jamie Lockhart, you're actually blushing," she said, putting her arm around me and grinning affectionately. "I'll go first, then bring more hot water for you."

The way she looked right then has stayed in my mind ever since. It wasn't any one thing over another—the green eyes like brilliant stars or the pure ivory skin or the way her lips were parted as she glanced at me. But in that moment I knew I loved Katharine Dandridge.

After our ablutions we prepared for bed in our separate rooms and discussed the strange little man.

"Although our host definitely appears harmless," said Kate, "it is better to be safe than sorry." She tucked one of her two pistols under her pillows. I then did the same with mine. We locked the outer doors of our rooms but left the connecting door open.

Snuffing out the candles, I waited for my eyes to become accustomed to the darkness. Still wide-awake after ten minutes, I found myself reeling with emotions I had never known before.

"Good night," I said.

"Good night, Jamie," she called out softly from the other room.

I tried to think of something else to say that would allow me to make my feelings plain and hear her voice once more.

"I guess we've both read a lot of Shakespeare," I said lamely.

"Some," was the sleepy reply.

I summoned my courage and said with all the feeling I could, *" 'See! how she leans her cheek upon her hand: O! that I were a glove upon that hand, that I might touch that cheek.' "*

There was complete silence. Just when I thought she must have already fallen asleep, I heard her sweet, pure voice again.

" 'Here comes a strange beast which in all tongues is called a fool.' "

"As You Like It," I said morosely.

"Go to sleep," she ordered with mock severity, and I did.

SHORTLY after sunrise I went to the window and pulled back the drapes. I could see blue sky through the bolted shutters. The storm had blown itself out during the night.

Something caught my eye off in the trees that ringed the grounds. As I watched, a man's form burst into view from the edge of the tree line. He ran without stopping until he disappeared in the direction of the burned wing of the house.

"Kate," I called out urgently as a second heavily bundled figure emerged from the trees and raced across the same ground.

A moment later she was by my side. Even as I pointed to the spot where I had seen the first men come out, a third figure stepped from the tree line. When he was halfway across the clearing, Kate rapped sharply on the window, and he stopped in his tracks. He could not see us, because of the bolted shutters, but we could clearly see him. He was a Negro, coal black. For a second he stood frozen.

"Runaways," murmured Kate, as he too ran off to the left.

"He looked so scared."

"You would be too," she said. "If they're caught, they are publicly flogged as an example to others. Or worse."

The third man was the last we saw. Afterward I got dressed and went downstairs. Mr. Gamage came in from outside as I was brewing a pot of tea for Kate.

"You have runaway slaves hiding in the burned wing of this house," I said without inflection.

He cocked his head and said, " 'Not all these, laid in bed majestical, can sleep so soundly as the wretched slave.' "

I was tired of his Shakespeare games and said with ill humor, "Can you get word to Major de Monfort that we are here?"

"Who, pray tell, is that?" He seemed genuinely puzzled.

"The one-armed man," I said in exasperation.

"Yes, I see, said the blind man. I see."

Going straight to one of the kitchen cupboards, he reached down for something on one of the lower shelves. When he stood up and turned around, he was holding a small pepperbox revolver. His bird's eyes were no longer restless. They bored into mine.

"Please be assured I still wish to provide you with every comfort," he said amiably. "Your pistol, for example. It looks exceedingly heavy and cumbersome. Let me relieve you of its burden."

With that, he stepped across the room and pulled it from my belt. Then he marched me upstairs. A quick but thorough search uncovered both of Kate's pistols.

"I do not yet know what to do with you two," he said then. "I have no wish to harm you. In the meantime you will be forced to stay in here." As he left, he locked each door from the corridor.

We were locked inside our rooms for the next two days. Mr. Gamage brought us our meals and once each day a pitcher of water for washing. The only time he allowed us outside was to visit the privy, and that was one at a time. During those periods he covered us with his revolver until we were back.

Apart from the fact that I was regaining limited use of my hand, there was only one thing to be said for it, and that was being alone with Kate. She, however, spent most of her time brooding at the possibility we would never catch up to her father's killers.

Around midnight on the second night of our captivity I awoke to the sound of voices off in a corner of my room. At first they were muffled. Then one of them was raised in anger. I slipped out of bed and went over to the source of the sounds, an iron mesh grate in the floor. Although I have never seen anything like it before or since, my guess is that it was designed to carry heat aloft from the rooms below.

One of the voices belonged to Mr. Gamage. The other sounded like the major's voice, but it was flat and tired, drained of spirit.

I still could not understand any of their words, and a short time later they removed to a place beyond my hearing. I crawled back into bed and pondered the mystery. If it truly was Major de Monfort, why had he not come to us?

On the third morning we both arose a little after dawn and were dismayed to discover in looking through the shutters that it was snowing again. When an hour passed with no sign of life, we slowly became alarmed. Mr. Gamage had always come early in the morning to check on us. As the morning wore on, the air became appreciably colder. Soon it was possible to see our breath.

Finally we decided to act. The brass hinge plates on the solid oak doors were our first target, but the plates were mortised too deeply to remove the pins. Our next effort was centered on the windows. The shutter panels were held in place by two flat iron bars that fit into brackets on the outside wall. The only way for us to escape was to batter a hole in the shutters themselves.

Standing on a chair, Kate removed the solid-mahogany curtain rod over the window frame. Suddenly she said she thought she heard the sound of a horse out in the storm. Not knowing who was coming, we stopped what we were doing. I wielded the heavy curtain rod and positioned myself behind the door.

The slam of the kitchen door was our first notice that someone was inside. Next we heard the steps of someone coming slowly up the stairs. I could hear the sound of labored breathing as his boots creaked down the hall. Then a key moved in the lock. I braced myself as the door swung slowly open.

From my position behind it, there was no way for me to see who it was. Kate's startled eyes fixed on the person at the door.

"I am Alain . . . de Monfort," I heard him say. By the time I stepped around the door, however, his eyes had already rolled up in his head and he was pitching forward into our arms.

HE LOOKED very different from our last meeting on the Valley Pike near New Market. Then he had seemed unconquerable, like one of King Arthur's knights of old.

Now his slim bronze-colored body was gaunt, almost shrunken. The exposed skin of his face and hand appeared to be actually frozen. It was while stripping off his gray, patched military cloak that Kate found the bullet hole in his side.

"He has lost a great deal of blood," she said as we dragged him to my bed. "See if you can find any spirits, Jamie. And if there isn't a fire started, make one in the stove and put on some water."

As I raced down to the kitchen, I looked for any sign of Mr. Gamage but found none. In a few minutes I had a good fire going, after which I put two copper pans full of water on to boil.

Searching the kitchen shelves, I uncorked a jug that definitely had "potency" and ran it back upstairs. The major was still unconscious, but Kate was able to force a few spoonfuls of the liquor between his lips. After emitting a low groan, he slowly opened his eyes.

"Must leave here. Not safe," he murmured.

Kate said, "You are in no condition to ride, Major."

"Have to. Can expect guests anytime now."

"In case you didn't notice, there is a blizzard out there," she said calmly. "Still . . . Jamie, find out if the roan is still in the barn. Also see if there is any kind of farm wagon."

I went out to the shed where Mr. Gamage had taken the roan on the night we arrived. He was standing placidly in a stall, munching hay. Sure enough, there was also an ancient buckboard in there, and although it had obviously seen many years of hard use, the wheels and axles looked solid. I went and retrieved Major de Monfort's horse from the yard, and I put him in another stall.

By the time I returned to the room, Kate had finished cleaning and bandaging the major's wound, and he was talking freely.

"My brain may still be frozen, Miss Dandridge, but you have melted my heart," he said with a small dash of his old spirit.

"You will have to do better than that, Major," she responded. "I am not one of your simpering New Orleans belles."

"They are but a fast-receding memory," he declared. Turning to me, he said, "Tell me what has happened since we parted."

It took some time to tell it all. When I was finished, the major said, "You are both so brave as to be foolhardy. Are you still committed to going on?" We both nodded yes, and he shook his head in seeming wonder.

I said then, "Who shot you?"

He looked at me and said, "I can only tell you it was fairly earned."

"Who is Mr. Gamage, and what is he doing here?" I asked next.

"There will be time for questions later," interrupted Kate. "We must make preparations to leave."

"To Sudley Springs?" I asked.

The major said, "Yes. Sudley Springs. I will accompany you."

"Now we have a real chance against those men," I said.

It was with renewed hope and excitement that we began loading the wagon. When I went searching for food in the pantry behind the kitchen, I was astonished to find baskets of onions, potatoes, and apples, along with smoked venison and other meats.

Kate had heated several bricks in the oven before bringing out all the goose-down comforters from the bedrooms. Placing the bricks inside the quilts, she made a warm bed for the major in the back of the wagon. In the space that was left, I loaded the food and what remained of the horse fodder in the barn. While gathering together the harness trappings for the two horses, I found an old canvas top for the wagon. It would provide some protection from the storm.

When we finally got the major into the wagon, Kate wrapped him snugly inside the small mountain of comforters.

"Very cozy indeed," he said with a queasy but gallant smile.

Given we had many gales in December, but none of them prepared us for the blizzard that has since become widely known as Lincoln's last Christmas present. Those of us who encountered its full fury will remember the experience for the rest of our lives.

When at last we set out for Sudley Springs, the snow was already four inches deep on the road. Kate rode head down, the brim of her planter's hat partly shielding her face. It was very hard going for the horses too, and they slipped continually on the icy track.

Every thirty minutes or so I would climb into the back of the wagon to knock loose the snow that kept piling up on the canvas top. The major slept through most of the journey, although once, he looked up as I was leaning over him, and I took the opportunity to say, "You were in Mr. Gamage's house the other night. Why didn't you come for us?"

"Do not pursue this," he said, turning away from me.

As night fell, the road ahead of us became a solid gray mass. Feeling a sharp nudge from Kate, I turned to face her. Her words were nearly lost in the fury of the tempest.

"I must have missed the Amissville road," she shouted.

I saw despair in her eyes, but it was at that same moment I also saw our salvation over her shoulder.

"Look there," I called out excitedly, pointing off toward a pasture on our left. On the far side of the open field I could see what looked like an implement shed connected to an open lean-to.

Kate turned the horses, and we crossed the pasture, pulling up under the lean-to as darkness finally settled around us.

KATE and I helped the major inside the shack. It was filled with sprung barrels, crocks, and an assortment of mostly broken farm tools. One corner of the roof was missing, and snow had piled up a foot high in that corner.

The most important discovery was a gigantic cast-iron butcher kettle that stood on three legs. The major immediately saw its possibilities as a stove and had me drag it under the open section of the roof. At his direction I used the head of a broken pickax to punch three small holes in its rusted bottom. Starting with a few handfuls of wood shavings, I soon built a steady fire using the barrel staves. Then I flattened some metal barrel hoops and joined them together in a crisscross fashion. When I laid the meshed iron strips across the rim of the butcher pot, it made a perfect cooking surface.

Going back outside, Kate and I unharnessed the horses and put them in the one sheltered corner of the lean-to. We then unpacked the wagon, bringing in the comforters and all of the food.

Major de Monfort had already plugged the larger cracks in the walls using old rags, and it was becoming almost cheery inside, with the intense little fire turning the sides of the kettle a dull red. After warming her hands for a few minutes, Kate made a supper of hot corn porridge in a deep skillet we had brought with us.

The blizzard kept its strength through much of the next day. We could go nowhere until the snow receded. We just tended the fire and tried to keep occupied.

The major busied himself with his weapons, sharpening the blade of his "toothpick" and cleaning his Sharps rifle. As he regained his strength, he became more spirited. After our evening meal he spent an hour entertaining us with vivid stories of life in Louisiana's Bayou La Frenière. The years seemed to melt away from him, and I could see how handsome he must have been in his younger days.

After that the major and Kate began to converse in French, a language which, of course, I did not understand. To my keen disappointment neither one of them made any attempt to enlighten me. They were still talking in French when I burrowed under my comforters and went to sleep.

The next morning when I moved to get up, the major's eyes opened immediately. Kate stirred awake near me, and her beautiful green eyes came alive as she took us both in.

"Joyeux Noël, mes amis," she said with a radiant smile.

"Et à vous aussi, Katharine," said the major. "Happy Christmas, Jamie."

That was how I discovered what day it was, and a wave of sadness came over me. It was the first one away from home.

"What would my heroes like for Christmas dinner?" she said.

"Crawfish en croûte and a roast of beef, *très saignant,*" said the major with only a hint of a smile.

"Je regrette, Alain," she said. "And you, my young knight?"

"Fatback and beans," I said, and she laughed.

"I think I can do a little better than that."

She did far better than that. In the deep skillet she placed a slab of bacon, which right away began to crackle in the heat of the fire. Then she sliced four onions into the oil. Next came little red potatoes and a huge turnip, followed by chunks of venison and rabbit.

While the savory stew bubbled in the skillet, Major de Monfort suggested I attempt to reconstruct Lieutenant Shawnessy's map from memory. Kate handed me a charcoal pencil along with a notebook. I turned to a blank page.

After staring at it for several minutes, I finally shook my head. "It's no use," I said. "I can't make it come back whole."

"Just put down the things you can recollect," said the major.

I followed his advice and began to fill in the page. At first I could only remember the intersecting lines and the little box with the cross in it that Dr. Cassidy had said was the Sudley Springs church. As I worked, other details began to come back, and I penciled them in. The last thing I could remember was the black half circle along with the words "Mouth of the Devil."

My frustration must have showed plainly because that was when Kate said, "Don't worry about it now, Jamie. Put the notebook aside. It is time for our Christmas feast."

And what a feast it was. The major told us that where he came from, it was called ragout. To me it just looked like a great meaty stew ladled over steaming cornmeal cakes. I had my fill, after which the major had us toast the holiday with some of the liquor we had used to rouse the major back at the house.

I felt truly content and was beginning to nod off again when Major de Monfort said, "Jamie, I want to attempt a little experiment. Lie down and make yourself as comfortable as you can."

I lay back under my quilt and turned to face him.

"Good. Now I want you to close your eyes," he said. "Try to slow your mind down. Try not to think of anything at all."

I followed his instructions. "I'm falling asleep," I mumbled.

"All right, Jamie. Now I want you to think back to the day when you first showed the map to Dr. Cassidy. Go back to that very moment. Are you there?"

"Yes, I am," I replied honestly. For a second I thought I could actually smell the whiskey on the doctor's breath as we stared down at the map together.

"Do you see it, Jamie? Can you see it now?" he asked quietly.

Amazingly, I did. It was all there in front of me, every detail.

Hurriedly I opened my eyes and began to transfer the image onto paper. At first I just tried to make sure I got the letters and numbers right. After that I worked on getting the proportions as close as possible to what I saw in my mind. Finally I closed my eyes again, bringing the map alive in my brain one last time. Opening them, I looked at the paper. The images were as close to identical as I could make them. I handed the map to the major.

"Congratulations," he said. Kate came over and hugged me.

"I believe the starting point for this quest is the Sudley Springs church," the major said as he and Kate examined the map.

"Why is that?" I asked.

Kate answered the question for him. "It is the only fixed landmark, Jamie. Everything else—the streams, the roads—have no point of reference."

"Agreed," said Major de Monfort as he turned the map. "Then there are these other markings—200SE, 136S, 124SW, and 73W. Since they are scrawled on each corner of the map, it is impossible to know their proper order. Obviously they include points on a compass. The numbers—"

"Must be distances," said Kate.

"Paces?" I suggested.

"Maybe, Jamie," said the major, "if Shawnessy walked the horses and wagon very slowly, counting the paces in his head. We'll know better once we have seen the ground."

"What about the Mouth of the Devil?" I asked.

"That is clearly the hiding place for the gold," said Kate.

"And where is the devil to be found?" he asked.

"The netherworld," said Kate. "In *The Divine Comedy,* Dante portrayed hell in the underground."

"A well," I exclaimed. "He dropped the gold down a well."

"You may be proven right, Jamie, but I don't think so," said the major. "The devil resides in a place of eternal fire. And look at this," he said, pointing at the large black half circle. "If he hid the gold in a well, then why not a full circle?"

That was the end of our speculations. The major went out to check the horses. I was staring into the fire when I heard Kate say, "Merry Christmas, Jamie."

I looked up to see her holding out a lace-trimmed handkerchief. It was tied into a pouch with a green hair ribbon.

"I don't— I forgot—" I began, but she gently put her fingers to my lips.

"This is of small import for saving my life," she said. "May it keep you safe from harm."

I opened the handkerchief. Inside was a small gold cross affixed to a thin gold chain.

"My father gave it to me on my fourteenth birthday," she said.

"I can't—" I started to say, but she was already placing it around my neck and connecting the tiny clasp. "Merry Christmas," she said again, and then kissed me warmly on the cheek.

The door of the shed flew open, and Major de Monfort stepped back inside. If he noticed anything unusual in my manner, he was too much of a gentleman to comment on it.

When we awoke on the day after Christmas, it was to another of the Lord's manifest wonders. The sun was shining brightly, and the snow on the trees was disappearing in front of our eyes. As we waited for the moment we could leave, the major outlined his plans for Sudley Springs. The first thing to be done, he said, was to search for the gold. At this, Kate appeared to be taken aback. The major explained his reasoning this way.

If we went after McQuade and his gang first and there was a pitched gun battle, there would be no time to search for the gold later, regardless of the outcome of our confrontation. The Yankees would be down on us so quickly we would have to escape before having any chance to find it.

I said I agreed with his thinking, but I could see that Kate was becoming agitated. I knew she cared not one whit about the gold.

The major turned to her and said, "Once we have the gold, you have my pledge that I will go after your father's killers."

She stared at him keenly for a few seconds and finally nodded.

That was the last day we were marooned. Early the next morning we left for Sudley Springs. The major seemed almost fully recovered from the wound in his side and now rode up front in the wagon next to Kate, his Colt revolver under the blanket on his lap.

It was necessary to retrace our path to pick up the Amissville road. We passed through Ben Venue and then Amissville. Everywhere we looked, people were coming out of their forced hibernation like hungry bears, furiously shoveling snow. They were even walking along the roads again, quickly turning them into seas of mud.

Each step of our horses took us farther into Yankee-controlled territory, but the major seemed oblivious to the danger. Then again, the sight of a one-armed man, a woman, and a boy might not have seemed all that threatening to Grant's army.

Since the major thought McQuade might have sent one of his gang to watch for us at Thoroughfare Gap, we crossed the southern flank of the Bull Run Mountains at New Baltimore. It was from those foothills that I saw the end of the war in the form of a huge military camp that lay spread out like a city toward Gainesville. There must have been a thousand tents, each one large enough to house a dozen Union reserve soldiers.

In that moment I realized my father and the rest of Lee's little army were doomed. If Mr. Lincoln could afford to keep ten thousand men in shiny new uniforms sitting so far away from the field of battle, then there was truly no hope for the southern cause.

A mile or so beyond Gainesville something curious happened. We were passing a succession of seedy establishments that obviously served the military trade, when the major asked Kate to halt the wagon. Set back a little ways from the highway there was a decrepit flat-roofed log shanty. A Negro man dressed in rags was seated on a log bench under its overhanging roof.

The major slipped his Colt revolver inside the belt of his breeches. Swinging out from his seat, he dropped to the ground, sinking in the slush and mud up to his ankles.

"We need tallow for the lanterns," he said. When he disappeared through the door, the Negro man got up and followed him.

Ten minutes passed by, and still he did not reappear.

"I don't like this," said Kate, placing the Sharps rifle in her lap.

Less than a minute later the major strode out alone, carrying a small clay pot in his left hand. He handed it up to me. Sure enough, it contained a large greasy chunk of tallow.

"What took you so long?" Kate asked.

"The storekeeper had to send his boy for it," he said.

Late that same afternoon we came to the last leg of our journey, arriving at the far edge of the great battlefield at Manassas. I felt a thrill, knowing we might be following the same path my father once trod, since he had fought there. The major said it was only a mile from there to Sudley Springs.

He had Kate halt the wagon in a heavy copse of trees. She and I unharnessed the horses and spread out enough fodder to last them the night. While we set up camp and waited for full darkness, the major produced a brass-plated compass, which he experimented with in a long circuit around our campsite.

An hour later we set out on foot for the Sudley Springs church.

Seven

IT WAS a clear windy night, with huge billowy clouds racing across the dark starry sky in a silent armada. The major took the lead, with me in the rear. Each of us carried a lantern. We stayed off roads as much as possible, moving through tree stands wherever we found them along our route. In this way, we came to Sudley Springs church without incident.

Although three different roads intersected near the building, Kate and the major had both agreed the starting point for our search should be the front entrance to the building where it met the road. That was where we now stood.

Major de Monfort checked the compass heading of the road in front of the church, which turned out to be southwest. There was only one southwest heading from among the four clues on the map. It read 124SW. Accordingly, we began walking away from the church in that direction. When I was on my one hundred and twenty-third pace, the major whispered, "Here," and Kate nodded.

My lantern revealed we were standing at the intersection of another road. There were now only three compass headings left to choose from—200SE, 136S, and 73W.

The major checked the compass heading of the new road.

"Due west," he said softly. It appeared to be a logger's path, wide enough for a wagon. Right then I was convinced the mystery was solved and had already begun thinking about how we would bring the gold away.

As we paced along the road, we came up against a solid wall of trees. At that point I had only counted forty-two steps. Something was obviously wrong. It should have been seventy-three.

We made our way silently back to the church and stopped again at the front entrance. Since the first road was the only one to run in a southwesterly direction, the next possibility was to examine whether Shawnessy might have started from one of the other two.

One of them ran from north to south. It was the next one we explored. Unfortunately, when we reached the ascribed distance of one hundred and thirty-six paces, there was no break between the trees that was large enough for a wagon to pass by.

Over the next few hours we tried each of the other headings in turn. The first two had proved to be almost immediate failures, but the third one, 200SE, actually came out near a road with another southerly heading. This caused renewed hope, but when we finally arrived at the conclusion of our passage, all we found was another stand of dense woods.

By then it was past three o'clock in the morning. Cold and foot-
sore, the major and Kate decided to abandon the search for that
night and return to our campsite near the Manassas battlefield.

All of us were too tired to discuss what had gone wrong in our
search. As usual, the major volunteered to stand guard on the first
watch. It started to drizzle as I wearily climbed into the back of the
wagon. An instant later I was dead asleep.

IT RAINED steadily all the next day. Mostly we stayed in the
wagon, watching the water drip off the edges of the canvas top and
splash into the small lake that grew around us. Meanwhile, we
talked about the reasons for our failure the night before.

After hours of discussing each possible mistake, Kate said,
"Jamie, are you sure you remembered everything from the map?"

I closed my eyes then and concentrated on bringing it back in my
mind. "Yes. I'm positive it's complete," I said.

"Then that means the lieutenant deliberately left something out
that we need to know, Alain," said Kate.

"Maybe to give himself some additional security," he agreed.

"I believe it has to be the number of paces," I said. "What if he
just cut the number in half before writing it down?"

"Perhaps you're right," said the major, pausing again to examine
the map. "Well, I'm still convinced the road in front of the church
is the one he must have started out from. Tonight we will begin
from there and simply double each of the numbers on the map."

Several hours later we were back at the church, ready to test the
new theory. What we found after walking off the specified distance
was another road with a westerly bearing in exactly the right place.
One hundred and forty-six paces after that we found a wide lane
heading due south. Again doubling the paces, we arrived at what
we hoped would be the last piece of the puzzle.

I could not help myself from running ahead as we neared the req-
uisite number of steps. Unmasking my lantern, I almost shouted
with joy as I beheld another road in precisely the right place. The
major discovered it ran southeast, just as it should have.

The last four hundred paces brought us to a small country crossroads. If we were correct, the Mouth of the Devil had to be somewhere close. We could see the shadowy outlines of deserted structures on all four corners of the intersecting roads.

As we drew closer, it became obvious there had been fierce fighting here. The first building was burned to the ground, and the one directly across the road had taken a direct hit from cannon fire. We started our search in the other two, which were still intact. They were both small one-room log cabins. A quick search uncovered nothing that brought to mind the Mouth of the Devil.

The building that had absorbed the direct hit was the last place left to explore. If there was nothing to be found in or around it, then our search would again have ended in failure.

This building was much larger than the others and had been constructed of red brick. Three of the walls were still left standing, although part of the roof had collapsed and every window was blown out. While Kate waited by the door with the Sharps rifle, the major and I stepped through one of the window frames.

There was rubble everywhere, and it was difficult to move about. Aside from shattered bricks, plaster, and broken glass, most of what littered the floor appeared to be farm tools.

The major lifted his lantern high above his head and asked, "What do you think this is?"

The object before us was so strange and monstrous in aspect that I momentarily drew back in awe. Cloaked in shadow, it first appeared to be the leather hide of some enormous beast.

The major stepped closer to it. "It is a bellows, Jamie. If I am not mistaken, this place was a foundry."

"Then this must have been the forge," I said, holding my lantern in front of me as I stepped over the fallen debris. In the center of the room were two massive walls of brick. I turned the corner of the interior wall. "And here is the Mouth of the Devil," I said quietly.

The major came around the corner and stopped short. "By all that is holy, Jamie, I believe you have found it," he whispered.

The opening in the forge was almost a perfect half circle. It had to be where Lieutenant Shawnessy had hidden the gold, but there was only one way to find out for sure. Major de Monfort helped me climb through the opening into the fire pit. I knelt there in pitch-darkness until he extended his lantern inside. Over the years rain and snow had flowed down the chimney and packed the ashes into a hard coating beneath my feet.

"I'll need something to dig with," I said.

Major de Monfort went off for a minute, coming back with the head of a spade. I took it, grasped it tightly, and began striking at the hard coal-and-ash mixture, which was now almost like cement.

A few inches below the surface I found the first crate. In fact, I smashed down so hard on it that I went right through the rotted wooden lid and literally struck gold.

Each of the three crates was almost four feet long, a foot and a half wide, and eighteen inches high. They were made of thick pine boards strapped with iron bands. When we tried to move them, I realized how strong Shawnessy must have been. The three of us together were unable to lift even one of the crates.

That was when Major de Monfort said he was going back for the wagon. He asked Kate and me to move the bars one by one to a place along the side of the building where we could repack them directly into the wagon upon his return.

As soon as he left, we began the arduous task of moving the gold bars to the place where Major de Monfort hoped to back up the wagon. There were ninety-two gold bars in all, spread almost equally among the three boxes. Each bar was pale yellow and much heavier than any object I had ever lifted of that size. There were also three large cloth bags labeled U.S. ARMY, and each one of them was filled with Federal greenbacks.

When Major de Monfort returned, we worked together to quickly load the wagon and were soon on our way. Unfortunately, the sagging wagon now creaked and groaned with each step the horses took. Every harsh noise was exaggerated in my mind to a clamorous roar. I soon convinced myself that not only McQuade and his gang but the whole Yankee army would be onto us before we came to the next turn. Our luck held, however, and as light began to come up in the east, we rolled back into our campsite.

For the last time we unharnessed the horses and hobbled them in the small clearing. I immediately volunteered to stand guard but was secretly grateful when Major de Monfort said he wasn't tired and would take the first watch. My last waking thought was the notion that I would actually meet General Robert E. Lee.

IT WAS late morning when we awoke to nothing short of a revelation. As I write these words, I feel yet again the thrill of discovering that incredible secret. Before falling asleep just a few hours earlier, I remembered seeing Major de Monfort on the far side of the clearing, standing alone like my guardian angel.

Now there were two men with him. One of them was Mr. Gamage. He and the major were standing together and quietly conversing. The second man was a Negro, as destitute in aspect as I have ever seen. He was dressed in clothing scraps, and his footgear consisted of two furry animal pelts tied around his feet with drapery cords.

He too looked familiar, and it took only a moment to remember him as well. He was the man at the store near Gainesville where Major de Monfort had bought the tallow.

When the major looked up and saw me gazing at him in wonder, he began walking toward me. Mr. Gamage came with him.

"I believe you already know my colleague," he said with a warm smile.

I nodded coldly. Kate sat up next to me.

"You both deserve to know why this gold is not going to General Lee," the major said. "And why it is going to Washington."

His statement left me speechless. "Why?" was all I mustered.

"It is going to the Freedmen's Bureau, Jamie," he said. "The money will help resettle thousands of former slaves."

"Who are you?" said Kate.

"I have played many roles in the last four years, Katharine."

"You are not Major Alain de Monfort," she said.

"There is no Major de Monfort," he replied.

"And your life growing up in Louisiana?" she asked.

"That part of the story is true. I was born and raised in the Bayou La Frenière," he said. "But I was born a slave."

"You're a Negro?" I said in astonishment.

"My mother was from Jamaica. My father owned Château La Frenière along with ten thousand acres of Louisiana cotton land."

"And you were raised as a slave?" asked Kate.

"My mother was his slave, as was I. However, I was fortunate to be educated with my half brothers. When the chevalier freed me on his deathbed three years before the war began, I came north. In Boston I met a man named Frederick Douglass. Not long afterward I was inspired to begin stealing slaves and helping to bring them north to freedom."

"How did you lose your arm?" I demanded, still not able to reconcile my feelings for the man he now said he was with the Confederate hero I had believed him to be.

"Jamie, it was an honorable wound," he said. "I was bringing a group of men north from Mississippi and was shot by a bounty man. That part of me is buried in Benton, Missouri."

"And the house with the runaways?" asked Kate.

"A stop on the Underground Railroad, Katharine. Mr. Gamage is one of our most stalwart conductors."

Right then I had never heard of the Underground Railroad, but Kate just nodded in understanding.

"You have not met my other colleague," he said as he brought over the Negro man. "Underneath this hideous costume is Father James Donaldson, late of the mathematics department at Georgetown College."

He must have seen the doubt in my eyes because his next words were, "Georgetown is a Jesuit college, Jamie. The Jesuits do not allow the pigment of a man's skin to intrude on his ability to do the Lord's work."

"And the learning of calculus often requires divine intervention," said the Negro man with a grin. He held out his hand to me. Behind the heavy beard his eyes were clear and intelligent.

During the rest of that last afternoon the three of them worked to disguise what they would be carrying from any casual search. While James Donaldson went off carrying a hatchet, the major and Mr. Gamage emptied the wagon and removed its canvas top. Next they spread the gold bars out on the wooden planks of the bed. Then they placed the money sacks under the seat. Finally, they covered it all again with the canvas top.

By then James Donaldson had returned with a huge bundle of kindling tied to the back of a mule. Mr. Gamage began to carefully place the kindling in layers on top of the canvas, while the major spread a blanket on the ground and began to examine the loads in each of their weapons. He did not ask for my help, and I did not offer any. I was thus greatly angered when Kate sat down next to him.

"What is your name?" she asked.

"François Guillaume Mouton La Frenière," he said with a laugh. "I was called William."

"William," she repeated softly. I had to walk away then.

By the time they were finished with their preparations, the light was failing. The wagon now looked like nothing more than a conveyance of firewood to the fuel-starved citizens of Washington.

It turned out Mr. Gamage had brought three mules with him, and two of them were now harnessed to the wagon. After they saddled the horses, the major told us his plans.

He, Kate, and I were to ride ahead of the wagon on horseback. Mr. Gamage would drive the mule team, and James Donaldson would bring up the rear on the third mule. We would accompany the major's colleagues to the spur of the Orange and Alexandria Railroad, then return to plan a trap for McQuade and his men.

Since we would now be moving away from Sudley Springs, the major said it was very unlikely we would run into any of McQuade's gang. Nevertheless, he urged Gamage and Donaldson to be on their guard for anything. Donaldson was looking a little uneasy, and the major put his arm reassuringly around his shoulder.

"I guess you would much rather be imparting a theorem in Georgetown right now," he said.

"I will have the rest of my life to be a professor," said James Donaldson with a brave grin. "How often does one have a chance to be a philanthropist?"

THERE was still a hint of daylight in the western sky when we started off. The major rode his horse at a slow, steady pace. Mr. Gamage followed at the same speed, keeping the wagon in position about fifty feet behind us. James Donaldson remained another fifty feet or so behind him.

At the first road we came to, the major led us east on a new track. About a mile later we turned south onto a larger lane that he said would take us to the railroad spur. We never got there.

The major was the first one to notice the wagon had stopped behind us. We turned our horses and looked back. Mr. Gamage was waving at us with his right arm to come to him.

The major drew his revolver from his belt and started riding his horse slowly back down the road. We followed a few feet behind.

As we drew close enough to see him more clearly, it appeared to me that Mr. Gamage was silently laughing at us. I did not know then that it was because his throat had been cut from ear to ear. Nor did I realize that the arm that was waving at us was not his.

Everything that happened next took place faster than I am able to write it down. With a sudden motion the major raised his pistol and fired at Mr. Gamage. Then two more explosions rang out, and the major hurtled backward out of the saddle.

The man who was propping up Mr. Gamage on the seat of the wagon shoved his body to the side and stood up. It was Claude Moomaw, his buckskin tunic now drenched red.

Although he had lost his Colt revolver in the fall, the major was on his feet an instant later and running toward the wagon. Off to the right two figures emerged from the darkness of the tree line, firing as they came. The major staggered as he was hit, going down for the second time. He rolled in the dirt and somehow came up on his feet. Considering he had at least two bullets in him, I don't know how he moved so fast.

Kate was now off her horse and scrabbling on her hands and knees in the dirt. From way down the road another wraithlike figure closed on the wagon. It became James Donaldson. He was shouting something to the major in the moment before he fell, shot from behind. Thurman came up after him, his rifle pointed forward as the major reached the team of mules.

The major was reaching behind his neck just as Thurman leveled his rifle at him from a distance of less than five feet. Then another shot rang out, and Thurman dropped to his knees. I turned to see Kate, who was now standing straight as a ramrod. The major's revolver was extended from her outstretched hand.

Now the major was vaulting into the wagon, the Louisiana toothpick in his hand. Claude raised his pistol and fired. The major thrust his sword into Claude as the old tracker fired again from point-blank range.

The men who had come out of the tree line from off to the right swung around at the sound of Kate's shot. One of them was Dex. He brought his rifle to his shoulder and took aim at her.

I kicked my horse to move between them, but before the animal could react, I heard another explosion and the rifle sailed out of Dex's arms. A moment later his body lurched after it before falling hard into the dirt. Behind him stood Captain McQuade, his gun still pointing at where Dex had been standing.

"Enough," he said in the sudden quiet. "That's enough."

The whole thing had taken less than thirty seconds, and it ended the lives of five men, not including Mr. Gamage, who was already dead. Royal Bevinger had no doubt already lost his life for saving ours earlier.

The major was still alive, lying on his back in the road. By the time I reached his side, Kate already had his head cradled in her right arm and was gently stroking his hair.

"When it is all over," he said in his lilting accent, "please write to Frederick Douglass. . . . Just tell him . . . I am gone."

His eyes focused on Katharine's. He raised his hand, and I watched it hover for a moment at her cheek before falling away.

"Adieu," he said. His eyes were still on hers when all the life ebbed out of them.

As Kate passed her hand over his face, I found myself crying. It's hard now to remember the reasons why. After all, he had lied to me and then tried to steal the gold.

But none of that mattered just then. I somehow knew I had lost something far more important than the gold.

Eight

WE LEFT them all lying where they were. In the wake of the gunfire it was certain that the Yankees would soon be along to investigate. I brought matters to a head.

It may sound stupid, but I went over to the major's horse and removed the Sharps rifle from his saddle holster. Then I turned to face Captain McQuade and pointed it at his heart.

"I'm taking this gold through the Confederate lines to General Lee," I said. "If you try to interfere with me, I will shoot you down."

Maybe it was because he was finally sickened by all the violence he had wreaked, but Captain McQuade seemed completely listless. He had already dropped his gun to the ground and just stood there by the road, wearily shaking his head.

"That may be the best idea after all, Jamie," he said.

I picked up his pistol and shoved it into my belt. Kate continued to kneel by the major while I dragged Claude Moomaw's corpse out of the wagon. Blood was everywhere, and I mopped it up as best I could before spreading two blankets across the seat.

There was no resistance when I gently grasped Kate by the shoulders and helped her to climb back in the buckboard. Captain McQuade had already mounted one of the horses.

"If you don't mind, I think I'll ride along for a while," he said.

He had not attempted to pick up any of the weapons, and I just shrugged at him before snapping the harness reins.

Kate never spoke through the long journey that followed, and the only time I exchanged words with Captain McQuade was when I asked him how they had found us. He told me that Thurman had been watching one of the lanes we had taken back to our campsite after we'd retrieved the gold. They had then planned their ambush.

In the next fourteen hours we crossed the Manassas Gap Railroad line and forded Broad Run near Bristoe before riding on through Catlett's Station. My plan was to find a place on the outskirts of Fredericksburg to lay up long enough to rest the mules before a final push down to the Confederate lines at Richmond.

We were only a few miles from the outskirts of Fredericksburg when a growing clatter behind us revealed itself to be a mounted Yankee patrol. One of the lead riders fired his pistol into the air.

"Give those mules the whip, Jamie," shouted Captain McQuade. "They mean to search you for sure."

Without hesitation I snapped the reins onto the rumps of the exhausted mules, and they began to speed up. A moment later I realized there was no way to outrun our pursuers.

"Throw me the Sharps," the captain yelled as he cantered his horse in close beside us. I reached down with my right hand and tossed the rifle into his outstretched hand.

In one fluid motion he swung around in the saddle, aimed, and fired. Although one of the cavalrymen fell away from his mount, it had no impact on the others. There were a score of them at least, and now they returned his fire.

I was about to stop the mules when from up ahead of us there was a thin crackle of musket fire followed by four curls of smoke. The flashes came from a distant line of old fortifications ahead of us. I looked back to see the pursuing riders pull up short.

I turned off the road into the field on our left and headed the mules in the direction of the friendly fire. The fortifications seemed long abandoned, but finally we saw four lonely figures lying along the highest trench line.

"Heah," one of them called out. "Ovuh heah."

As we got out of the wagon, Captain McQuade tried to take

Kate's arm, but she brushed his hand away as if it were diseased. We finally reached their position along the trench line and crouched down under the log parapet they were lying behind.

The man closest to me looked like Robinson Crusoe come to life, with long, stringy hair and a scraggly beard. He stuck out a dirt-encrusted hand and said, "Sergeant Buck Wampler. Them Yanks down ta killing us for firewood?"

"We've got something they would want if they knew we had it," I said, giving his hand a shake. He must not have been a curious man, for he asked me nothing further about it.

I had often read the letters from my father in which he referred to his men as scarecrows. These soldiers were that living image. The face of the man crouching next to Sergeant Wampler was the color of a new pumpkin, and it took me a moment to realize he was yellow with jaundice.

"Back in a damn trench," he exclaimed. "The whole reason we left Petersburg, and look at us now. Right back where we started from."

"You've come from Petersburg?" I said, and he nodded.

The third soldier in the line looked away, maybe ashamed of having left his comrades. "I done my share of killin'," he said.

"No more diggin' fer me," declared the last man, who wore rimless spectacles.

"They made us into mole men," said Sergeant Wampler. "Hell's fire, we wasn't sojers no more. All they had us do was dig—forts, covered trenches, zigzag trenches, you name it."

"It give me the plague," said the yellow-skinned man.

"The ague, Jesse," said Sergeant Wampler. "The ague."

"Same difference, Buck," he replied.

A bullet whizzed loudly through the air and struck the earthen bank behind me with a loud thunk. It was still hot to the touch when I dug it out. It was almost an inch long.

"They still usin' those old muzzle-loadin' Enfields," said the jaundiced soldier. "Fifty-eight caliber. Take yer leg right off."

As we watched, a few of the Yankees started into the field in front of us. Then the men stopped as if their orders had been changed, and they went back to the road. The Yankees were just milling around there, as if still waiting to be told what to do.

"Them boys is green as a Yankee dollar," said the spectacled soldier. He pulled out a piece of wood and began whittling at it.

"You look like you was an officer," said Sergeant Wampler to Captain McQuade.

"Was is correct," he replied. "In the Thirty-third Virginia."

"Stonewall's boys," said the yellow man. "I seen him onct. Biggest feet I ever saw in boot leather."

I could now hear an officer's voice in full pitch, shouting orders at the Yankees in the road. More than a dozen of them moved into the field in a skirmish line and began to slowly trudge in our direction. At the same time I saw another group of soldiers begin moving into the trees on the other side of the road.

"They gonna try to outflank us," said Sergeant Wampler.

"Won't be hard," said the yellow man.

As the skirmish line moved forward, I heard the sound of a hornpipe playing "When Johnny Comes Marching Home."

"Won't be long now," Sergeant Wampler said. "You better git out of it if yer goin'. They's a dozen trails through those woods where you kin lose 'em sure. After that it's clear all the way to Richmond."

"Why don't you get out with us?" I said, taking Kate's hand.

"We ain't never run from a fight," he replied, standing up. "And I ain't gonna make this one from behind no trench." One of the Yankee skirmishers fired at him, and the bullet slammed into the redoubt behind us with a loud slap.

"I would be proud to lead you, Sergeant," Captain McQuade said. Kate looked up as he walked slowly to his horse.

"Well, boys, we got us an officer again who leads from up front," said the yellow soldier.

The spectacled man stood up and grabbed his musket. "Here," he said, tossing the piece of wood he had been whittling over to me. The figure was of a perfectly sculpted screech owl. As I pen these words, it is lying on the table in front of me.

I ran to catch up to Captain McQuade. As he swung up into the saddle, I heard a low, unguarded sigh escape his lips. He raised his eyes toward the line of Yankee skirmishers and then glanced down at me. I held his pistol up to him, but he shook his head, saying, "You keep it, Jamie. Might come in handy."

I didn't know what to say to him then, and he seemed to understand that. "I'm sorry about the way it all turned out," he said, touching his fingers to his hat. He spurred his horse forward.

I was helping Kate climb back into the wagon when Captain McQuade led the others toward the Yankees. Somehow the four Confederates no longer looked like tramps as they crossed the field, bent low to the ground.

McQuade looked back just once before turning to face the Federal fire. That was when the other four gave out with the rebel yell. It was the last time I ever heard it.

The Yankee skirmishers discharged a ragged volley with no apparent effect. As they worked to reload, Captain McQuade expertly lifted his horse over a gully and began galloping toward them. He was carrying the Sharps rifle straight up on his knee.

Behind him the four Confederates were now running flat out with their bayonets pointed forward, still screaming at the top of their lungs. When they were no more than ten yards away, the fifteen Yankees actually turned and began to run.

I slapped the reins, and the mules began to move. Kate and I were at the tree line when I looked back for the last time. After their successful charge the four Confederates had slipped off to the right. McQuade was all by himself now, his horse walking slowly but steadily toward the Yankees, the rifle balanced on his knee. Maybe some of them thought he was too brave to shoot. I don't know. But then there was another ragged volley.

I never saw the result. At the same moment I felt a stunning blow in my right arm. It whirled me around into Kate and almost propelled me out of the wagon. I knew right away I was shot.

Kate kept me from falling under the wagon. Grabbing the reins, she cried, "Oh, God, Jamie, say you're all right."

Glancing down, I saw that the bullet had torn away a large piece of my coat and gone straight through my upraised shoulder. It was already bleeding a lot, but as yet there was no pain at all.

"I'm all right," I said, and her eyes relaxed again. By then we were already into the sanctuary of the piney woods, which were a regular rabbit warren of trails. Kate kept moving at a good clip until she felt sure we could not be followed.

Finally she stopped the wagon and tended to my shoulder. It was still bleeding freely as she tightly bound the wound with a strip of lining torn from the inside of her coat.

That night we slept in a grove of trees near Spotsylvania Court House. The next morning we pushed on again toward Richmond.

WELL, that's pretty much the whole story, except for what happened to the gold. On the afternoon of the third day of our journey we arrived at the outer line of Confederate fortifications north of Richmond.

It had started snowing again, and by the time we got there, the landscape was completely white once more. I was feeling very poorly by then. My wound was worse than I had first thought.

We had just cleared the last interior line of fortifications when there was a loud cracking noise and the right rear wheel broke free from the wagon. As we ground to an immediate halt, the bed of the buckboard tipped so far over to the side that I was worried the gold bars would spill out onto the roadway. I climbed down and saw that the rear axle was smashed beyond repair. I despaired at the thought of how we could possibly locate another wagon.

Taking the risk of leaving the buckboard unattended in the road, I asked a boy who was passing by if he knew where we might find the commander of the Richmond Home Guard. He led us to what looked from the outside like a beaver's den. It was built directly into the side of a high earthen mound that formed part of the interior defense line. At the base of the mound there was a rope-hinged door fashioned from pine boards. Our escort rapped on it.

"What is it now?" came an angry voice from within.

"Two people asking to see you, Colonel Twombly. Their wagon just broke down coming through the lines."

"Let Lieutenant Cooksey handle it!" came back the voice.

I brushed past the boy and threw open the door. Inside the hovel the air was warm from a log fire.

"What is the meaning of this?" the colonel demanded. Although bald as an egg, his face had strong manly features.

"We are carrying a vitally important shipment for General Lee," I said.

He looked us up and down and then frowned. "A few bales of hay, I suppose, and available to the army for a fair price," he said with sarcasm in his voice.

If my arm wasn't on fire with pain, I know I would not have said what I did next. "There are ninety-two gold bars outside in the wagon, and I am delivering them to my father, who is commanding the Tenth Virginia under General Lee."

From his smug grin I knew right away he didn't believe me. It was only when Kate removed the shawl covering her head and stepped forward that his manner suddenly changed.

"He's telling you the truth," she said with the old Dandridge spirit I had come to know so well.

I gave him only the barest elements of the story. When I was finished, we walked outside so he could look for himself at what was under the snow-covered canvas. He immediately ordered several men to guard the buckboard while we went back inside.

"I am Colonel Hubert Twombly," he declared with a suddenly expansive smile. He stuck his hand out to show there were no hard feelings. When I did not respond, he glanced at my arm and said, "Why, you're hurt. That should be tended to right away. I will have you escorted to—"

"That can wait," I said, cutting him short. "Right now, Colonel, I would like your assistance in transferring the gold to another wagon so we can carry it on to my father and General Lee."

"Of course, of course," he said. "Well, you have definitely found the right man," he said. Going to his plank table, he sat down on a cracker box and began scribbling on a piece of paper. He carefully sealed the edges with hot tallow. Then he stood up.

He swung the door open and called out, "Lieutenant Cooksey!" A boy no older than me appeared at the door.

"Take our fastest horse and personally deliver this to Colonel Wilson," he said. "No one else is to read it, is that clear?"

"Yes, sir," he said, rushing off.

Colonel Twombly then sent for a doctor and shut the door. "Please come sit by the fire," he said cheerfully.

An hour later an officer knocked on the door and said he had come for the shipment. He and his men were from the commissary general's office, serving under General Mayberry.

I said I had never heard of General Mayberry and wanted the gold taken directly to General Lee. He responded that I was ignorant of army regulations and should desist from trying to hector the men chosen to carry out this important responsibility.

For the third or fourth time since we had arrived, Kate demanded to know where the doctor was. Colonel Twombly shrugged his shoulders and counseled her to be patient.

I could see that Kate was fed up with the whole business. She was also worried at the condition of my arm, which had swollen alarmingly. She urged me to go with her to the home of her aunt, who lived on Franklin Street, to get immediate medical attention for me. Colonel Twombly strongly endorsed her suggestion and offered to have us taken there. I refused. Enraged, I said, "The gold is going to General Lee, and if anyone tries to stop me, you can answer to him."

Kate said, "Let them have it, Jamie. They will take it anyway."

Before I could respond, Lieutenant Cooksey came around the table to restrain me and roughly grabbed my wounded arm. The pain was so terrible I fell to my knees, almost fainting on the spot. A moment later Kate had me in her arms and was asking Colonel Twombly for use of a carriage, which he readily obliged.

On the way to her aunt's house I began vomiting. As hard as I tried to stop, my stomach and brain would not cooperate. When they were carrying me up the front steps, I do remember thinking her aunt must be rich, because the house was a mansion. By then it was as if my body lacked even the force to hold the flesh to my bones. I lost consciousness before we were inside the door.

IT WAS dark outside when I awoke to find Kate sitting beside me on the edge of my bed. She was bathing my face with a cool moist towel, and it felt wonderful. Yet in the light of the oil lamp her luminous green eyes looked stricken.

"Jamie, I want you to know something in case we must part for a time," she said.

I looked up at her beautiful alabaster face and nodded.

"You are the most courageous young man I have ever known," Kate said. Then she leaned down and kissed me full on the lips.

At least I think she did. In the weeks since, I have relived that moment over and over. Recently it struck me that I was in such a fevered state at the time, it may have been a wondrous dream.

The next time I woke up, Dr. Cassidy was by my bed. He had come all the way from Port Republic to bring me home.

While examining my wound, he discovered that a large fragment of my coat had been driven into my arm by the Yankee bullet. After dosing me with laudanum, he successfully removed the foreign matter, allowing the wound to drain for a time before bandaging it. By then, however, my temperature was 103 degrees and the fever had rendered me unconscious again.

According to Dr. Cassidy, the trip back to Port Republic was by far the worst he has ever experienced. If so, I'm grateful to remember almost nothing about it. I was strapped on a litter and taken in a carriage to the railroad station, where we waited all day for a train. There was no longer any regularly scheduled service, and we were lucky that one eventually came.

By that time Dr. Cassidy found that my temperature was 105 degrees. He told me afterward that he wasn't sure just then whether I would make it home.

A wagon was waiting to bring us the last twenty miles home. This next part may sound unbelievable, but Dr. Cassidy swears it's true. When we arrived home and my mother rushed out of the house to greet me, she took one look at my unconscious form and said, "But where is Jamie? Where is my son?"

I AWOKE in my own bed at Port Republic two days later. Although I was still running a fever, the high temperature had broken, and Dr. Cassidy assured my mother the crisis had passed.

As he was leaving, he looked down at me and, with a kindly smile, said, "After surviving all you've come through, Jamie, it's clear you were born to be hanged." I fully returned his smile, knowing I owed him my life. That was when my mother brought me a hand mirror.

I did not recognize myself. The face that looked back at me had sad and weary eyes, with age lines etched in both corners. They stared at me with an intensity that was wholly unfamiliar. It took me a moment to realize I looked like a man.

During these last weeks I have had to compile this account for Judge Burwell in Harrisonburg. It's because my mother got so worried about me after I disappeared that she told Dr. Cassidy about my having gone to see Ike Trumbo with the map. He brought in Constable Kilduff, who came out with his tracking dogs and found Corporal Blewitt's grave. If Dr. Cassidy hadn't stood up for her right then, they would have sworn out murder charges against both of us. If Judge Burwell has any doubts about whether any of this really happened, I will ask him to contact Kate, who can at least confirm everything that occurred after we arrived at her father's home.

Since regaining my strength, I've written a letter each day to her, but have yet to receive a response. Dr. Cassidy told me that no one has gotten a letter from Richmond in weeks. I can only pray she is safe and that I will see her once more.

As far as what finally happened to the gold, I don't really know. To my knowledge at least fourteen men, including those Federal quartermasters, died trying to possess the gold. At this point I have to assume it ended up in the quartermaster general's office in Richmond. Since it was Union quartermasters who took the gold in the first place, maybe it is somehow fitting that their brethren in the Confederate army got it back in the end.

Right now my mother is trying to keep busy in the kitchen, waiting for news of my father. In this she is not alone. Perhaps tomorrow we will hear word that he is safe and coming home.

Editor's Postscript

THE preceding narrative was discovered in the archives of the Rockingham County courthouse in Harrisonburg, Virginia, part of a docket filed in 1865 by Judge Francis Channing Burwell.

According to the National Archives in Washington, D.C., Lieutenant Colonel Thomas Lyon Lockhart, the father of James Christopher "Jamie" Lockhart, was killed helping to stem the Confederate retreat after the disaster at Sayler's Creek on April 6, 1865. In that engagement more than eight thousand Confederate soldiers were captured. Three days later, on Sunday, April 9, 1865, General Lee surrendered his remaining forces. Colonel Lockhart's body was never recovered.

Readers might be interested to know that Jane Spenser Lockhart, the colonel's widow, eventually remarried. According to an issue of the *Rockingham County Register,* Mrs. Lockhart became the wife of Dr. Patrick Francis Cassidy of Port Republic, presumably the same person who appears in the narrative.

After looking through letters from that period compiled by the Port Republic Historical Society, it is evident that Dr. Cassidy was able to rebuild his medical practice. One letter refers to the hundredth baby he had delivered since the end of the war.

A fleeting reference to Dr. Cassidy's "son" in one of the aforementioned letters led my researcher to Washington College (now Washington and Lee) in Lexington, Virginia. According to the college's admission records, James Christopher Lockhart enrolled as a freshman at that institution in the fall of 1865. Mr. Lockhart was then just sixteen years old.

It was during his first year in Lexington that Mr. Lockhart and Katharine Dandridge apparently fulfilled their commitment to the dying "William" La Frenière. From among the papers of Frederick Douglass that are still catalogued at the noted abolitionist's last home in Washington, D.C., I found an important piece of information while examining his daybook.

On May 8, 1866, he wrote, "Today I finally received word about two of our operatives, Father James Donaldson of Georgetown and the legendary slave-stealer William, who disappeared without trace in the final days of the war. It is an astounding story that these two young people tell, and one I am inclined to believe, if only for their earnest desire to keep a promise to a dying man. More in my journal." The name Dandridge appears next to that entry. Unfortunately, there is no surviving record of Mr. Douglass's daily journals from 1866 through 1871. They were destroyed in the fire that consumed the rear quarter of his house.

Much of what is conclusively known about the life of Katharine Dandridge following the events in the previous narrative can be found in the papers of Helen Drummond Kerfoot, which are now the property of the Virginia Historical Society.

During the fever epidemic that swept away hundreds of citizens of Richmond in the last weeks of the war, Miss Dandridge worked as a volunteer nurse at the makeshift hospital set up by the Baptist Theological Seminary on Duke Street. According to a letter from Mrs. Vaughn Starling to Helen Kerfoot, dated March 2, 1865, she contracted the fever in late January and was in recuperation at her aunt's home on Franklin Street until June 5, 1865.

Upon regaining her health, Kate apparently returned to her ancestral home near Luray, Virginia, living there for almost two years until the Dandridge family estate was sold at public auction on April 9, 1867.

Based on numerous references in the Kerfoot correspondence, we know that Miss Dandridge and her surviving brother, Robert, left Richmond later that year on a ship bound for San Francisco, California. It was to be the first stop on a yearlong trip in which the pair decided to circumnavigate the globe. In a letter written at about the time of their departure Mrs. Kerfoot cites the determination of Miss Dandridge to find a "new passage" in her life.

On June 16, 1869, James Christopher "Jamie" Lockhart graduated with honors from Washington College. Chosen by the college president, Robert E. Lee, to deliver the valedictory address, Mr. Lockhart gave a speech that was "very affecting and well-spoken," according to a chronicler in the college journal. In a photograph of Mr. Lockhart standing next to President Lee, it is interesting to note that based on the known height of Robert E. Lee, Mr. Lockhart had by then grown to stand at least six feet tall. A follow-up article reported that Mr. Lockhart was planning to join the faculty of Washington College as its youngest instructor.

During that same summer of 1869 Miss Dandridge and her brother Robert arrived in London, where they were welcomed to the Devonshire estate of Sir Hugh Mercer, a blood relative of Miss Dandridge's mother and a barrister of some note.

The fall social season in London provided the occasion for Miss Dandridge's formal presentation at Buckingham Palace, and it was memorable enough to merit several paragraphs in Lord Blakenthorpe's *Life and Times of the Court of Queen Victoria*. He wrote that "her stunning green eyes, auburn hair and slim voluptuous figure made an immediate impression on the Queen. However it was the young Virginia woman's bold and frank opinions that truly captivated Her Royal Highness."

If there was any correspondence between Miss Dandridge and Mr. Lockhart during this time, there was no reference to it in the letters she wrote to Mrs. Kerfoot. However, in May of 1870 an event occurred in London that seems to confirm that they had indeed remained in contact.

The May 7 issue of the *Tatler* chronicles an incident that involved two particularly ardent suitors of Katharine Dandridge's who dueled with pistols on the plain of Hampstead Heath. One of the young

men was killed instantly by a ball to the brain. The other suc-
cumbed from a stomach wound three days later.

One newspaper ran an editorial referring to Miss Dandridge as a
"beguiling temptress" and condemned her actions in "precipitating
the murder of two of England's preeminent men." There does not
appear to have been any defense of her by a member of the royal
family. Shunned by British society, she reportedly left the country
with her brother Robert on a packet boat to France in June 1870.

Interestingly, James Lockhart abruptly resigned from his post at
Washington College on June 10, 1870, just one week before the end
of the spring term. There is no official explanation for his resignation to be found in the college files. It is interesting to speculate that
the reason for his sudden departure might have had something to
do with the flight of Katharine Dandridge from England. Unfortunately, there is no evidence to prove it.

In fact, it is here that the trail runs cold for both of them,
although not for lack of trying to follow it. There is no record of
either of them ever returning to Virginia. A review of the 1880 and
1890 census records shows no individuals with their names and ages
living in the state.

As is the case with so many other uncelebrated Americans, they
simply vanished into the vast world stage. Perhaps new information
in the form of letters or journals will someday emerge to shed light
on the subsequent lives of these two remarkable young people. Persons who come into possession of such information are invited to
contact me.

ROBERT J. MRAZEK

Bob Mrazek, a longtime Civil War buff, had a rare chance to help preserve a piece of history while serving as a Congressman from New York's Long Island. Learning of a land developer's attempts to turn the historic Manassas, Virginia, battlefield into a giant shopping center, Mrazek helped save it by co-authoring the 1988 law that designated the battle-field as a national park.

In 1992, after a decade-long stint in Congress, Mrazek decided he'd rather author books than laws, and he retired. He didn't have to look far for a setting for *Stonewall's Gold*, his first novel. He and his wife owned a vacation home in the Shenandoah Valley and spent many a weekend exploring the area's historic byways.

River's
End

Nora Roberts

For Olivia MacBride the forest is a sanctuary—a refuge where she can lock herself away from the terrible secrets of the past.

Now a man who is haunted by the same past is determined to uncover the truth.

Along the way he may even open Olivia's heart.

Prologue

THE monster was back. The smell of him was blood. The sound of him was terror.

She had no choice but to run and this time to run toward him.

The lush wonder of forest that had once been her haven, that had always been her sanctuary, spun into a nightmare. The towering majesty of the trees was no longer a grand testament to nature's vigor but a living cage that could trap her, conceal him. The luminous carpet of moss was a bubbling bog that sucked at her boots. She ripped through ferns, rending their sodden fans to slimy tatters, skidded over a rotted log, and destroyed the burgeoning life it nursed. Green shadows slipped in front of her, beside her, behind her, seemed to whisper her name.

Livvy, my love. Let me tell you a story.

Breath sobbed out of her lungs, set to grieving by fear and loss. The blood that stained her fingertips had gone ice-cold. Rain fell, a steady drumming against the windswept canopy.

She forgot if she was hunter or hunted. She would find him, or he would find her. And somehow it would be finished. She would not end as a coward. And if there was any light in the world, she would find the man she loved. Alive.

She curled the blood she knew was his into her palm and held it like hope. She closed her hand over the only weapon she had, and knew she would kill to live.

And through the deep green light haunted by darker shadows she saw the monster as she remembered him in her nightmares.

Covered with blood, and watching her.

One
Beverly Hills, 1979

OLIVIA was four when the monster came. It shambled into dreams that were not dreams. On a night in high summer, when the moon was bright and full as a child's heart and the breeze was softly perfumed with roses and jasmine, it stalked into the house to hunt, to slaughter.

Nothing was the same after the monster came. The lovely house with its many generous rooms and acres of glossy floors would forever carry the smear of his ghost.

Olivia's mother had told her there weren't any monsters. They were only pretend and her bad dreams only dreams. But the night she saw the monster, heard it, smelled it, her mother couldn't tell her it wasn't real. And there was no one left to sit on the bed and tell her pretty stories until she slipped back into sleep.

Her daddy told the best stories, wonderfully silly ones with pink giraffes and two-headed cows. But he'd gotten sick, and the sickness had made him do bad things. Her mother had told her he'd had to go away until he wasn't sick anymore. That's why he could only come to see her sometimes and Mama or Aunt Jamie or Uncle David had to stay right in the room the whole time.

Once, she'd been allowed to go to Daddy's new house on the beach. Aunt Jamie and Uncle David had taken her, and she'd been fascinated and delighted to watch through the wide glass wall as the waves lifted and fell. Then Daddy wanted to take her out on the beach to build sandcastles, just the two of them. But her aunt had said no. It wasn't allowed. They'd argued in those low, hissing voices adults never think children can hear. But Olivia had and, hearing, had sat by that big window to stare harder and harder at the water. And as the voices got louder, she made herself *not* hear. She would *not* hear Daddy call Aunt Jamie bad names or Uncle David say in a rough voice, "Watch your step, Sam. Just watch your step."

But it had started before that. Weeks before the beach house.

It had all happened after the night Daddy had come into her room and awakened her. He'd paced her room, whispering to himself. It was a hard sound, but when she'd stirred in the big bed with its white lace canopy, she hadn't been afraid. Because it was Daddy. Even when the moonlight spilled onto his face and his face looked mean, love and excitement had bounced in her heart.

He'd wound up her music box, the one with the Blue Fairy from *Pinocchio* that played "When You Wish Upon a Star."

She sat up and smiled sleepily. "Hi, Daddy. Tell me a story."

"I'll tell you a story." He'd turned his head and stared at his daughter—the small bundle of tousled blond hair and big brown eyes. But he'd only seen his own fury. "I'll tell you a story, Livvy, my love. About a beautiful whore who learns how to lie and cheat."

"Where did the horse live, Daddy?"

"What horse?"

"The beautiful one."

His lips peeled back in a snarl. "You don't listen! You don't listen any more than she does. I said *whore,* damn it!"

Olivia's stomach jumped at his shout. "What's a whore?"

"Your mother!" He swept his arm over the dresser, sending the music box and a dozen little treasures crashing to the floor.

In bed, Olivia curled up and began to cry.

He was shouting at her, saying he was sorry. "Stop crying right now!" He'd buy her a new music box.

Then Mama came rushing in, her nightgown glowing white in the moonlight. "Sam, for heaven's sake, what are you doing? There, Livvy. There, baby. Don't cry. Daddy's sorry."

The vicious resentment all but smothered him as he looked at the two golden heads close together. "I told her I was sorry."

But when he started forward, intending to apologize yet again, his wife's head snapped up. In the dark her eyes gleamed with a fierceness that bordered on hate. "Stay away from her."

"Don't you tell me to stay away from my own daughter. I'm sick and tired of orders from you, Julie."

"You're stoned again. I won't have you near her."

To escape, Olivia crawled out of bed and into her closet to bury herself in her mountain of stuffed toys. All she could hear were the terrible shouts, more crashing, the sound of her mother crying out in pain.

That's when Daddy had gone away.

Memories of that night could sneak into her dreams. When they did and she woke, Olivia would creep out of bed and into her mother's room. Just to make sure she was there.

Sometimes they were in a hotel instead. Her mother's work meant she had to travel. After her father got sick, Olivia always, always went with her. People said her mother was a star, and it made Olivia giggle. She knew stars were the little lights up in heaven, and her mother was right here.

Her mother made movies. Daddy made movies, too, and she knew the story about how they'd met pretending to be other people. They'd fallen in love, gotten married, and had a baby girl. When Olivia missed her father, she could look in the big leather book at all the pictures of the wedding, when her mother had been a princess in a long white dress that sparkled and her father had been the prince in his black suit.

The night the monster came, Olivia heard the shouting in her sleep. It made her whimper and twist. She woke with a scream in her head and wanted her mother. She climbed out of bed, her little feet silent on the carpet, and wandered down the hallway. But the room with its big blue bed and pretty white flowers was empty. Her mother's scent was there—a comfort. All the magic bottles and pots stood on the vanity. Olivia amused herself for a little while by playing with them. She sang to herself in the tall mirror, then, feeling sleepy again, shuffled out to find her mother.

As she approached the stairs, she saw that the lights were on downstairs. The front door was open. She thought there might be company. Quiet as a mouse, she crept down the stairs. And heard the soaring music of her mother's favorite—*Sleeping Beauty.*

The living room spilled from the central hall, flowing out with high arched ceilings, oceans of glass that opened the room to the gardens. There was a big fireplace of deep blue lapis and floors of sheer white marble. Flowers speared from crystal vases.

But tonight the vases were shattered on the tiles, their elegant flowers trampled. The glossy ivory walls were splattered with red, the polished tables overturned. There was a terrible smell.

The music crescendoed, a climactic sweep of sobbing strings. Whimpering for her mother, Olivia stepped into the living room. And she saw. Behind the big sofa her mother lay on her side, one hand flung out. Her warm blond hair was wet with blood. Her white robe was red with it and ripped to ribbons.

Olivia couldn't scream. Her eyes bulged in her head; her heart bumped painfully against her ribs. But she couldn't scream.

The monster that crouched over her mother—the monster with hands red to the wrists, with red over his clothes—looked up. His eyes were wild, shiny as the glass that sparkled on the floor.

"Livvy," her father said. "God, Livvy."

And as he stumbled to his feet, she saw the silver-and-red gleam of bloody scissors in his hand.

Still she didn't scream. But now she ran. The monster was real, the monster was coming, and she had to hide. Olivia heard a long, wailing call, like the howl of a dying animal in the woods.

She went straight to her closet, burrowed among the stuffed toys. She stared blindly at the door, sucked quietly on her thumb, and barely heard the monster as he howled and searched for her, sobbed and screamed, crashed through the house calling her name.

Olivia, a doll among dolls, curled up tight and waited for her mother to come and wake her from a bad dream.

THAT'S WHERE FRANK BRADY found her. She didn't move, didn't make a sound. Her hair was a pale, delicate blond, shiny as rain to her shoulders; her face was a colorless oval; her amber eyes were huge under brows as dark as mink pelt.

Her mother's eyes, he thought with grim pity. Eyes he'd looked into dozens of times on the movie screen. Eyes he'd found lifeless less than an hour before.

The eyes of the child looked through him. Recognizing shock, he crouched down, resting his hands on his knees rather than reaching for her. "I'm Frank." He spoke quietly. "I'm a policeman. Do you know what a policeman does, honey?"

He thought he caught a flicker in her eyes. "We help people. I'm here to take care of you. Are these all your dolls?" He smiled at her and picked up a squashy Kermit the Frog. "I know this guy. He's on *Sesame Street.* Do you watch that on TV? My boss is just like Oscar the Grouch. But don't tell him I said so."

When she didn't respond, he pulled out every *Sesame Street* character he could remember, making comments, letting Kermit hop on his knee. She watched him, eyes wide and blank.

"You want to come out? You and Kermit?" He held out a hand.

Hers lifted like a puppet's on a string. Then, when the contact was made, she tumbled into his arms, shivering now with her face buried against his shoulder.

He'd been a cop for ten years and still his heart ripped. "There now, baby. You're okay. You'll be all right."

"The monster's here." She whispered it.

Cradling her, Frank got to his feet. "He's gone now."

"I had to hide. He was looking for me. He had Mama's scissors. I want Mama."

God. Dear God, was all he could think.

At the sound of feet coming down the hall, Olivia let out a low keening sound and tightened her grip around Frank's neck. He murmured to her, patting her back as he moved toward the door.

"Frank, there's— You found her." Detective Tracy Harmon studied the little girl wrapped around his partner. "The neighbor said there's a sister—Jamie Melbourne. Husband's David Melbourne, a music agent. They live only about a mile from here."

"Better notify them. Honey, you want to go see Aunt Jamie?"

"Is my mama there?"

"No. But I think she'd want you to go."

"I'm sleepy."

"You go on to sleep, baby. Just close your eyes."

"She see anything?" Tracy murmured.

"Yeah." Frank stroked her hair as her eyelids drooped. "Yeah. I think she saw too damn much."

HE CAME back. The monster came back. She could see him creeping through the house with her father's face and her mother's scissors. Blood slid down the snapping blades like thin ribbons. In her father's voice he whispered her name over and over.

Livvy, Livvy love. Come out and I'll tell you a story.

"No, Daddy! No, no, no!"

"Livvy. Oh, honey, it's all right. I'm here. Aunt Jamie's here."

"Don't let him come. Don't let him find me." Wailing, Livvy burrowed into Jamie's arms.

"I won't, I won't. I promise." Devastated, Jamie rocked her niece in the delicate half-light of the bedside lamp. "I'll keep you safe." She rested her cheek on the top of Olivia's head. Silent tears slid down her cheeks. Julie. Oh, Julie. She wanted to scream out her sister's name. But there was the child to consider.

Julie was dead. That beautiful, bright woman with the giving heart and boundless talent, dead at the age of thirty-two. Killed, the two grim-faced detectives had told her, by the man who had professed to love her to the point of madness.

Well, Sam Tanner was mad, Jamie thought. Mad with jealousy, with drugs, with desperation. Now he'd destroyed the object of his obsession. But he would never touch the child.

Gently Jamie laid Olivia, limp with sleep, back in bed, smoothed the blankets over her. She walked to the window, stared out at nothing. The sudden flash of headlights had her heart pumping fast.

David, she realized, and, leaving the light on low, hurried downstairs. The door opened, and her husband walked in.

He stood there for a long moment, a tall man with broad shoulders, his brown hair mussed, his quiet gray eyes full of fatigue and horror. Strength was what she'd always found in him. Strength and stability. Now he looked sick and shaken.

"Jamie. Oh, sweet heaven." His voice broke, and somehow that made it worse. "I need a drink." She followed him into the front salon. His hands shook visibly as he took a decanter of whiskey from the breakfront, poured it into a short glass, and drank it down like medicine. "What that bastard did to her."

"Oh, David," she sobbed. The control she'd managed to cling to since the police had come to the door shattered.

"I'm sorry, I'm sorry." He rushed to her and gathered her against him. "Jamie, I'm so sorry." She wept in harsh, racking gasps until he wondered that her bones didn't shatter from the power of it. "I'll take you upstairs. You need to lie down."

"No, no. I'll be all right." She scrubbed her hands over her face. "I need you to tell me everything, David. I have to know."

He hesitated. She looked so tired, so pale and so fragile. "Let's get some coffee first," he said.

The maid wouldn't be in for another two hours, so Jamie brewed the coffee herself while David sat at the counter and stared out the window. They didn't speak.

She set two cups of coffee down, sat. "Tell me."

"There isn't much more than Detective Brady already told us," David began. "There wasn't forced entry. She let him in. She was dressed for bed, but it looked as though she'd been working on clippings. You know how she liked to send your folks clippings." He rubbed both hands over his face. "They must have argued. There were signs of a fight. He used the scissors on her." Horror bloomed in his eyes. "Jamie, he must have lost his mind."

His gaze came to hers, held. When he reached for her hand, she curled her fingers around his tightly. "Did he— Was it quick?"

"I don't— I've never seen— He went wild." David closed his

eyes a moment. She would hear in any case. There would be leaks; there would be the media, full of truth and lies. "Jamie . . . he stabbed her repeatedly and slashed her throat."

The color drained from her face. "She must have fought him."

"I don't know. They have to do an autopsy. They think Olivia saw some of it, saw something, then hid from him." He drank the coffee in the faint hope it would settle his stomach. "Sam's claiming he found Julie that way. That he came in and found her already dead."

THE press stalked, a pack of rabid wolves scenting blood. At least that was how Jamie thought of them as she barricaded her family behind closed doors. To be fair, many reporters broadcast the story with as much delicacy as the circumstances allowed.

But Jamie wasn't feeling particularly fair. Not when Olivia sat like a doll in the guest room or wandered downstairs as thin and pale as a ghost. Wasn't it enough that the child had lost her mother in the most horrible of ways? Wasn't it enough that she herself had lost her sister, her twin, her closest friend? But she had lived in the glittery world of Hollywood with its seductive shadows for eight years now. And she knew it was never enough.

Julie MacBride had been a public figure, a country girl turned glamorous movie princess who'd married the reigning prince and lived with him in their polished castle in Beverly Hills. Those who paid their money at the box office considered her theirs. Julie MacBride of the quick and brilliant smile and smoky voice.

But they didn't know her. Oh, they thought they did, what with exposés and glossy articles. Julie had certainly been open and honest in them. That was her way, and she'd never taken her success for granted. It had thrilled and delighted her. But they'd never really understood her sense of fun, her love of the forest and mountains where she'd grown up, her loyalty to her family, her devotion to her daughter. And her tragic and undying love for the man who'd killed her.

That was what Jamie found hardest to accept. Julie had let him in. In the end, she'd gone with her heart and had opened the door to the man she loved, even knowing he'd stopped being that man.

Would she herself have done the same? They'd shared a great deal, more than sisters, more than friends. Part of it came from being twins, their shared childhood in the deep woods of Washington State. The hours, the days they'd spent exploring together. Sharing their dreams as naturally as they had once shared the womb.

Now it was as if something in Jamie had died as well. But she could be strong. Would have to be. Olivia depended on her; David would need her. She knew he'd loved Julie, too, had thought of her as his own sister. She stopped pacing to glance up the stairs. Her parents were here now, with Olivia in her room. They would need her, too.

The doorbell rang. Jamie drew a breath in, let it out slowly. The reporters were ordered not to come onto the property. But over that long, terrible day one slipped through now and then. She marched toward the door, intending to rip off the reporter's skin. Through the etched-glass panels beside the wood she recognized the detectives who had come in the dark the night before to tell her Julie was dead.

"Mrs. Melbourne, I'm sorry to disturb you."

Jamie focused. "Detective Brady, isn't it?"

"Yes. May we come in?"

"Of course." She stepped back.

Frank Brady studied her as she led him and his partner, Tracy Harmon, into the salon. He knew now that she and Julie MacBride had been twins, with Jamie the elder by seven minutes. Yet there wasn't much resemblance. Julie MacBride had owned a blazing beauty despite delicate features and that golden coloring. The sister had quieter looks, sleek brown hair, eyes more chocolate than gold.

"Can I get you anything? Coffee?"

It was Tracy who answered, judging she needed to do something normal before getting down to business. "I wouldn't mind some coffee, Mrs. Melbourne. If it's not too much trouble."

"No. I'll see to it. Please sit down."

"She's holding up," Tracy commented when he was alone with his partner.

"She's got a way to go." Frank flicked open the curtains a slit to study the mob of press at the edge of the property. "It's not every day America's princess gets cut to ribbons inside her own castle."

"By the prince," Tracy added. "We'll get maybe one more shot at him before he pulls it together and calls for a lawyer."

"Then we'd better make it a bull's-eye." Frank let the curtain close as Jamie came back into the room with a tray. He sat when she did. He didn't smile. "We appreciate this, Mrs. Melbourne. We know this is a bad time for you."

"You want to talk to me about Julie."

"Yes, ma'am. Were you aware that your sister placed a nine-one-one call due to a domestic disturbance three months ago?"

"Yes. Sam came home in an abusive state of mind. Physically abusive. He'd been emotionally abusive the last year and a half."

"Is it your opinion Mr. Tanner has a problem with drugs?"

"You know very well Sam has a habit. If you haven't figured that out, you're in the wrong business."

"Sorry, Mrs. Melbourne," Tracy said. "Just trying to touch all the bases. We have to figure you'd know your sister's husband. Maybe she talked to you about their personal problems."

"She did, of course. Julie and I were very close." Jamie struggled to keep it all steady—voice, hands, eyes. "I think it started a couple of years ago. Social cocaine. Julie hated it. They argued about it. They began to argue over many things. His last two movies didn't do well, critically or financially. Julie was worried because Sam became edgy, argumentative. But as much as she tried to smooth things over, her own career was soaring."

"He was jealous of her," Frank prompted.

"Yes. They began to go out more—parties, clubs. He felt he needed to be seen. Julie supported him in that, but she was a homebody. I know it's difficult to equate with the image." Her voice cracked, but she cleared it. "She was working with Lucas Manning on *Smoke and Shadows*. It was a demanding role. Julie couldn't work fourteen hours, come home, then polish herself up for a night on the town. She wanted time with Olivia. So Sam started going out alone."

"There were some rumors about your sister and Manning."

Jamie shifted her gaze to Tracy, nodded. "Yes. There usually are when two very attractive people fire up the screen. But the rumors were groundless. Julie considered Lucas a friend."

"How did Sam take it?" Frank asked her.

She sighed. "If it had been three or four years ago, he'd have laughed it off, teased her about it. Instead he hounded her. He accused her of encouraging other men, then of being with other men."

"Some women would turn to a friend, to another man under that kind of pressure." Frank watched Jamie's mouth tighten.

"Julie took her marriage seriously. She loved her husband. Enough, as it turned out, to stick by him until he killed her. If you want to turn this around and make her seem cheap—"

"Mrs. Melbourne"—Frank lifted a hand—"if we want to close this case, we need to ask. We need all the pieces."

"The pieces are simple. Her career was moving up, and his was shaky. The shakier his got, the more he did drugs. She called the police that night last spring because he attacked her in their daughter's room and she was afraid for Livvy."

"She filed for divorce."

"That was a difficult decision for her. She wanted Sam to get help, and she used the separation as a hammer. Most of all, she wanted to protect her daughter. Sam had become unstable."

"Would she have opened the door to him last night if he was under the influence of drugs?"

"She must have. Despite everything, Julie loved Sam and believed if he could beat the drugs, they'd get back together."

"In your opinion is Sam Tanner capable of killing your sister?"

"The Sam Tanner Julie married would have thrown himself in front of a train to protect her. But the one you have in custody is capable of anything." Jamie's eyes were hot with hate.

"Mrs. Melbourne," Frank began. "It would be very helpful if we could speak with Olivia."

"She's four years old."

"I realize that. I don't want to upset the child, but the fact is, she's a witness. We need to know what she saw, what she heard."

"How can you ask me to make her talk about it?"

"It's in her head. Whatever she saw or heard is already there. She knows me from last night. I'll be careful with her."

"Dear Lord." Jamie tried to think clearly. "I have to be there. I have to stay with her, and you'll stop if I say she's had enough."

"That's fine. She'll be more comfortable with you there. You have my word—I'll make it as easy as I can."

Jamie led them out and up the stairs. At the door to the bedroom, she opened it a crack, saw that her parents were sitting on the floor with Olivia, putting a child's puzzle together.

"Mom, could you come here a minute?"

The woman who stepped out was small, with sun-bleached brown hair and blue eyes. Frank gauged her at early fifties and imagined she passed for younger when her face wasn't drawn with grief.

"This is my mother, Valerie MacBride," Jamie said. "Mom, these are the detectives who . . . They need to talk to Livvy."

"No." Val pulled the door closed behind her. "That's impossible. She's just a baby. I won't have it."

"Mrs. MacBride—" Even as Frank spoke, she turned on him.

"Why didn't you protect her? Why didn't you keep that murdering bastard away?" She covered her face with her hands and wept.

"Please wait here," Jamie murmured, and put her arms around her mother. "Come lie down, Mom. Come on, now."

When Jamie came back, her face was pale and showed signs of weeping. "Let's get this over with." She opened the door.

The man who looked up had folded his long legs Indian style. His hair was a beautiful mix of gold and silver. The eyes of deep amber that he'd passed to his younger daughter and to her daughter were fanned with lines and widely set under dark brows.

"Dad"—Jamie forced her lips into a smile—"this is Detective Brady and Detective Harmon. My father, Rob MacBride."

Rob rose. "What's this about, Jamie?"

"They need to talk to Livvy." She gripped his hand before he could protest. "They need to," she repeated. "Please, Dad. Mom's upset. She's lying down in your room. I'm going to stay here. I'll be with Livvy the whole time. Go talk to Mom. Please."

He bent, rested his brow against hers. "I'll talk to your mother."

"Are you going, Grandpop? We haven't finished the puzzle."

He glanced back, fighting tears. "I'll be back, Livvy love."

Livvy stared up at Frank. She knew who he was—the policeman with long arms and green eyes. His face looked tired and sad.

"Hi, Livvy." Frank crouched down. "Do you remember me?"

She nodded. Her thumb found its way into her mouth, and she spoke around it. "You chased the monster away. Can you find my mama? She had to go to heaven and must be lost. Can you find her?"

Frank sat on the floor. "I wish I could."

Tears welled up in her eyes and cut at Frank's heart like tiny blades. "Is it because she's a star? Stars have to be in heaven."

"Sometimes, when we're lucky, special stars get to stay with us for a while. When they have to go back, it makes us sad. It's all right to be sad. Did you know the stars are there even in the daytime?"

"You can't see them."

"No, but they're there, and they can see us. Your mother's always going to be there, looking out for you."

Olivia picked up the Kermit she'd brought with her from home. "He eats bugs."

"Does he like them plain or with chocolate syrup?"

Her eyes brightened at that. "I like *everything* with chocolate syrup. Do you have a little girl?"

"No, but I have a little boy, and he used to eat bugs."

Now she laughed. "He did not."

"Oh, yes. I was afraid he'd turn green and start hopping." Frank picked up a puzzle piece, fit it into place. "I like puzzles. That's why I became a policeman. We work on puzzles all the time."

"This is Cinderella at the ball. She has a bea-u-tiful dress."

"Sometimes I work on puzzles in my head, but I need help with the pieces to make the picture in there. Do you think you can help me, Livvy, by telling me about the night I met you?"

"You came to my closet. I thought you were the monster, but you weren't."

"That's right. Can you tell me what happened before I came?"

"I hid there for a long time. He didn't know where I was."

"It's a good hiding place. Did you play with Kermit that day?"

"I played with lots of things. Mama didn't have to work, and we went swimming in the pool. I can hold my breath under the water forever because I'm like a fish."

He peeked at her neck. "Yep. There are the gills."

Her eyes went huge. "Mama says she can see them, too!"

"Did you have friends over that day to play?"

"Not that day. Sometimes I do. Sometimes Billy or Tiffy come, but that day Mama and me played, and we had some cookies. And Mama read her script and talked on the phone: 'Lou, I love it!' " Livvy recited in such a smooth and adult tone, Frank blinked at her. " 'I *am* Carly. Make the deal.' "

"Ah . . ." Frank struggled between surprise and admiration. "That's really good. You have a good memory. Do you know what time you went to bed?"

"I'm 'posed to go to bed at eight o'clock. Mama told me the story about the lady with long hair who lived in the tower."

"Later you woke up. Were you thirsty?"

"No. I had a bad dream."

"My Noah has bad dreams, too."

"Is Noah your little boy? How old is he?"

"He's ten now. Sometimes he has bad dreams about space aliens. When he tells me about them, he feels better. You want to tell me about your bad dream?"

"People are yelling. I don't like when Mama and Daddy fight."

"In your dream you heard your mother and father yelling?"

"People yell, but I can't hear what they say. I want them to stop. Somebody screams, and I wake up. I want my mama to come."

"Did you go to find her?"

"She wasn't in bed. I wanted to get in bed with her. Then I—" She broke off, gave a great deal of attention to her puzzle.

"It's all right, Livvy. You can tell me what happened next."

"I'm not supposed to touch the magic bottles on Mama's little table with the mirror. I just played with them for a minute."

She sent Frank such an earnest look, he had to smile. "That's all right, then. What did you do next?"

"I went downstairs. The lights were on, and the door was open." Tears began to stream down her cheeks. "It smells bad, and things are red and wet. The flowers are on the floor, and there's glass. I see Mama, lying there, and the red and wet is all over her. The monster's with her. He has her scissors in his hand." She held up her own, a glazed look in her eye. " 'Livvy. God, Livvy,' " she said in a horrible mimic of her father's voice. "I ran away, and he kept calling. He was looking for me and crying. I hid in the closet."

"You're a very smart girl." She gave Frank a watery smile, and he drew her attention back to her puzzle, made a comment about talking pumpkins that had her giggling. He didn't want her parting thought of him to be of fear and blood and madness.

Still, when he turned at the door to glance back, Olivia's eyes were on him, quietly pleading and holding that terrifyingly adult expression only the very young can manage.

As he started downstairs, he wanted Sam Tanner's blood.

Two

OLIVIA didn't want to take a nap. She wasn't sleepy. But she tried, because Aunt Jamie had asked her to, and lay in the bed that wasn't hers. She always slept in this room when she came to visit. But it wasn't home.

She'd told Grandma she wanted to go home, that they could have a tea party in the garden until Mama came. But Grandma's eyes had gotten wet, and she'd hugged Olivia so hard, it almost hurt. So Olivia hadn't said anything more about going home.

When she heard the murmur of voices down the hall in the room where her grandparents were staying, Olivia climbed out of bed and tiptoed from her room. Aunt Jamie had said that Grandma and Grandpop were taking naps, too. But if they were awake, maybe they could go out and play. They liked to be outside best of all.

Grandpop said trees reached up and brushed the sky in Washington. Olivia had been there to visit when she was a tiny baby and again when she was two, so she couldn't remember very well. She thought she could climb all the way up one of those trees and call her mother. Mama would hear if she could just get closer to heaven.

When Olivia opened the door, she saw her grandmother crying, her aunt sitting beside her holding her hand.

Grandpop was speaking. "It doesn't matter why he did it. He's crazy, crazy with jealousy and drugs. What matters is he killed her. He'll pay for it. Every day of his miserable life. It'll never be enough."

"We should've made her come home," Grandma said. "When she told us she and Sam were having trouble, we should have told her to bring Livvy and come home for a while."

"We can't go back, Mom," Jamie said wearily. "If we could, I know I'd see a hundred different things I could do to stop it. But we can't. We have to face the now. The press— We have to take as much control as we can. There'll be speculation about Julie's marriage, about other men, particularly Lucas Manning."

"Julie was not a cheat." Grandma's voice rose, snapped.

"I know, Mom. But that's the kind of game that's played."

"She's dead," Grandpop said flatly. "Julie's dead. How much worse can it get?"

Slowly Olivia backed up from the door. She knew what dead meant. Flowers got dead when they were all brown and stiff, and you had to throw them away. Tiffy's old dog had died, and they'd dug a hole in the yard and put him inside.

Dead meant you couldn't come back.

The breath got hot and thick in her chest. Flashes of blood and broken glass, of monsters and snapping scissors, raced through her head. She started to run. And she started to scream. "Mama's not dead. Mama's not dead in a hole in the yard."

She kept running, away from the shouts of her name, down the steps, down the hall. Tears flooded her cheeks. She had to get outside to find a sky-brushing tree and call Mama home.

At the front door she fought with the knob and raced out. There were crowds of people, and she didn't know where to go. Everyone was shouting at once, hurting her ears. She pressed her hands to them, crying, calling for her mother.

A dozen cameras greedily captured the shot. Reporters surged forward, caught in the frenzy. Voices boomed out questions, commands.

"Look this way, Olivia! Over here."

"Did your father try to hurt you?"

She froze like a fawn in the crosshairs, eyes dazed and wild. Then she was being scooped up from behind.

"I want Mama. I want Mama." She could only whisper it while Aunt Jamie held her tight.

"She's just a child." Unable to stop herself, Jamie lifted her voice to a shout. "Damn every one of you. She's only a child!"

DESPITE the hours in prison and the fact that his system was jumping for a hit, Sam Tanner's looks had suffered little. His hair was dark, thick, and untidy. His eyes, a brilliant Viking blue, were shadowed. His love affair with cocaine had only added a romantic hollowed-out look to his face.

They'd taken away his bloody clothes and given him a washed-out gray shirt and baggy slacks. He was on suicide watch but had only begun to notice the lack of privacy. The full scope of his situation was still buried under the fog of shock and drug withdrawal.

The interrogation room had a single table, three chairs. Frank sat across from Sam. Tracy leaned against the wall.

"I don't remember any more than I told you before," Sam said. He'd been so sure when they'd finished talking to him the first time, they'd let him go. Let him go so he could find out what they'd done with Julie, with Olivia. Oh, Julie. Every time he thought of her, he saw blood, oceans of blood.

Frank only nodded, his eyes patient. "Why don't you tell me what you told me before? From the beginning."

"I *keep* telling you. I went home—"

"You weren't living there anymore, were you, Mr. Tanner?" This from Tracy, and just a little aggressive.

"It's still my home. The separation was just temporary."

"Right," Tracy said. "That's why your wife filed papers, got sole custody of the kid, why you had limited visitation and bought that palace on the beach."

"It was just a formality." Sam was desperate for one quick hit to clear his head. "I bought the Malibu house as an investment."

When Tracy snorted, Frank lifted a hand. They'd been partners for six years and had their rhythm down as intimately as lovers. "Give the guy a chance to tell it, Tracy. You'll throw him off."

"Okay, okay. I went home," Sam said. "I wanted to straighten things out with Julie."

"Were you high, Mr. Tanner?" Frank asked gently. "It'd be better if you were up front about that. We're not going to push you on recreational use. We just need to know your state of mind."

He'd denied it before, denied it right along. It was the kind of thing that could ruin you with the public. People in the business, well, they understood. A little coke between friends? Not a big deal, as he was forever telling Julie.

"Mr. Tanner?"

"What?" The eyes that had women all over the world sighing blinked. They were bloodshot, bruised, and blank.

Frank leaned forward. "Before you answer, I'm going to tell you that we searched your car and found your stash. Now, we're not going to give you grief about possession. If you're up front."

"I don't know what you're talking about. Anybody could have put that there. You could've planted it, for all I know."

Tracy moved fast. He had Sam by the collar and half out of the chair. "You're saying we planted evidence?"

"Easy now." Frank lifted both hands. "Mr. Tanner's just upset. You didn't mean to say we'd planted drugs in your car, did you?"

"No, I—"

Frank leaned forward. "Because that's a very serious accusation. It won't look good for you, especially since we have a number of people who'll testify you like a little nose candy now and then."

Sam worried his wedding ring, turning it around and around on his finger. "Look, I'm not an addict or anything. I just took a couple of hits to clear my head before I went home. I needed to make Julie understand we should get back together, get rid of the lawyers and fix things. I missed her and Livvy. I just wanted our life back."

"I don't blame you for that," Frank said. "Beautiful wife and daughter. A man would be crazy to give it all up. You wanted to straighten out your troubles, so you went over and talked to her."

"That's right. I— No. I went over and I found her. Oh, Julie." Sam covered his face. "There was blood everywhere, broken glass. She was lying there in the blood and glass. I tried to pick her up. The scissors were in her back. I pulled them out."

Hadn't he? He thought he'd pulled them out but couldn't quite remember. They'd been in his hand, hot and slick with blood.

"I saw Livvy standing there. She started running away."

"You went after her," Frank said quietly.

"I think . . . I must have. I think I went a little crazy. Trying to find her, trying to find who'd done that to Julie. I don't remember. I called the police." He looked at Frank.

"How long?" Tracy stuck his face close to Sam's. "How long did you go through the house looking for that little girl, with scissors in your hand, before you broke down and called the cops?"

"I don't know. I'm not sure. A few minutes, maybe ten."

"Lying bastard!"

"Tracy—"

"He's lying, Frank. If he'd found that kid, she'd be in the morgue next to her mother."

"No. No." Horror spiked in Sam's voice. "I'd never hurt Livvy."

"That's not what your wife thought, is it, Tanner?" Tracy jabbed a finger into Sam's chest. "She put it in writing that she was afraid for you to be alone with the kid. I'll tell you just how it went down. You thought about her in that big house, locking you out, keeping you away from her and your kid. Maybe you figured she's got another man. And you got yourself all coked up and drove over there to show her who was boss."

"No. I was just going to talk to her."

"But she didn't want to talk to you, did she, Tanner? She told you to get out, didn't she? Told you to go to hell. Maybe you knocked her around a little first, like you did the other time."

"I never meant to hurt her. We were arguing."

"So you picked up the scissors."

"No." Sam tried to clear the images in his head. "We were in Livvy's room. Julie wouldn't have scissors in Livvy's room."

"You were downstairs, and you saw them on the table, sitting there, shiny, sharp. You grabbed them, and you cut her to pieces. If you couldn't have her, no one was going to have her."

"No, no, no. I couldn't have done that. I couldn't have." But he remembered the feel of the scissors in his hands. "I loved her."

"You didn't mean to do it, did you, Sam?" Frank picked up the ball, his voice gentle. "I know how it is. Sometimes you love a woman so much it makes you crazy. When they don't listen, you have to find a way to make them. That's all it was, wasn't it? You were trying to make her listen, and she wouldn't. You lost your temper. The drugs—they played a part in that. You argued, and the scissors were just there. Then it happened, before you could stop it."

"I don't know." Tears were starting to swim in Sam's eyes. "I had the scissors, but it was after. I pulled them out of her."

"Livvy said she saw you. Your four-year-old daughter's a witness. The murder weapon has your prints all over it. Your bloody footprints are all over the house. The bloody fingerprints on the door-jamb of your little girl's bedroom—they're yours. There was no one else there, Sam. No burglar, like you tried to tell us yesterday. There was no sign of a break-in. There were three people in the house that night: Julie, Livvy, and you."

"There had to be someone else."

"No, Sam. No one else."

"My God." Shaking, he laid his head on the table and sobbed like a child. Then he confessed.

FRANK read the signed statement, got up, walked around the tiny coffee room, and settled for the nasty dregs in the pot. With the cup half full of what even the desperate would call sludge, he sat at the table and read the confession again.

When his partner came in, Frank spoke without looking up. "This thing's got holes, Tracy."

"I know it." Tracy sat. "But the guy's whacked, Frank. He was flying that night. He's never going to remember it step by step."

"Yeah, but it doesn't sit right in the gut. Not all the way. See here where he says he broke the kid's music box. There was no music box. He's getting the two nights confused."

"He's a cokehead," Tracy said impatiently. "His story about coming in after a break-in doesn't wash. She let him in. Her sister confirmed it was something she'd do. We got the M.E.'s report—no defensive wounds. We know how it went down. Makes me sick."

"I've been working bodies for seven years," Frank murmured. "It's one of the worst I've seen. I'd like a cleaner statement, that's all. Some high-dollar lawyer's going to dance through those holes before this is done." With a shake of his head he rose. "I'm going home, see if I remember what my wife and kid look like."

"Lawyer or no lawyer, Sam Tanner's going down for this."

"Yeah, he will. And that little girl's going to have to live with that, Tracy. That's what makes me sick."

Frank thought about it on the drive home, with Olivia's face lodged in his mind—the rounded cheeks of childhood, the wounded, too adult eyes. Then he pulled into the driveway beside his house, and it was all so blessedly normal. Noah had left his bike on its side in the yard, and his wife's impatiens were wilting because she'd forgotten to water them again. Her ancient VW Bug was already parked, emblazoned with bumper stickers. Celia Brady collected causes the way some women collected recipes. He climbed out of his car.

The front door burst open. His son raced out, a compact bullet with shaggy brown hair, bruised knees, and holey sneakers. "Hey, Dad! We just got back from protesting whale hunting. Mom's got these records with whales singing. Sounds like alien invaders."

Frank winced, knowing he'd be listening to whale songs for the next several days. "I don't suppose we've got dinner?"

"No health food! We picked up the Colonel on the way home."

Frank laid a hand on his son's shoulder. "You're telling me we have fried chicken in the house? Don't toy with me, Noah."

Noah laughed, his green eyes dancing. "A whole bucket. Mom said we'd go for it because you'd need some comfort food."

"Yeah." Frank sat down on the front stoop and loosened his tie. "I guess I do."

Noah sat beside him. "The TV's had bulletins all the time about that movie star. We saw you and Tracy going into that big house, and they showed pictures of the bigger one where she got killed. And just now, before you got home, this little girl, the daughter, came running out of the house. Dad, they got right in her face, and she was crying and screaming and holding her hands over her ears."

"Poor kid." Frank put his face into his hands.

"What are they going to do with her if her mother's dead and her father's going to jail and all?"

Frank blew out a breath. Noah always wanted to know the whats and the whys. "I don't know for sure. She has family who love her. They'll do the best they can."

Noah frowned. "She looked really scared. Why did he do it?"

"Some will say he loved her too much. Others will say that it was drugs or jealousy or rage. I'm not sure Sam Tanner himself understands why." Frank gave Noah's shoulders a quick squeeze. "Let's go listen to whales sing, and eat chicken."

"And mashed potatoes."

"Son, you might just see a grown man cry."

Noah laughed again and trooped inside with his father.

LESS than an hour after Sam Tanner wrote his tearful statement admitting the brutal murder of his wife, he exercised his civil rights. He phoned his lawyer, who claimed his client's confession had been given under duress, ordered him to remain silent, and called out the troops.

Charles Brighton Smith would head the defense team. He was a sixty-one-year-old fox with a mind like a laser who loved nothing better than a high-profile court battle with a media circus playing in the center ring. Before he flew into L.A., he'd leaked his flight number and arrival time and was prepared for the onslaught of press when he stepped off the plane. His face showed wisdom and concern as he made his sweeping opening statement.

"Sam Tanner is an innocent man, a victim of tragedy. He's lost the woman he loved in the most brutal of fashions, and now that horror has been compounded by the police in their rush to close the case. We hope to correct this injustice swiftly so that Sam can deal with his grief and go home to his daughter."

After seeing the news flash of Smith's arrival, Val MacBride shut off the television with a snap. It was all a game to them, she thought. To the press, the lawyers, the police. Just another show to bump ratings. They were using her poor murdered child.

Yet it couldn't be stopped. Julie had chosen to live in the public eye and had died in it. Now that public perception would be twisted to make a martyr out of the man who'd killed her. And Olivia was just one more tool. That, Val told herself, she could stop. She went quietly from the room to find Jamie.

The house was built on the straight, clean lines of a T. In the left notch Jamie had her office. When she'd come to Los Angeles eight years before to act as her sister's personal assistant, she'd lived and worked out of the spare room in Julie's dollhouse bungalow in the hills. They'd lived in that house together for two years, until Julie had met and married Sam. And less than six months afterward Jamie had been engaged to David. A man who managed rock-and-roll bands, of all things, Val had thought at the time. But he'd turned out to be as steady as her own Rob.

She knocked lightly on Jamie's office door before opening it. Jamie sent her a harried smile and continued to talk on her phone. Val sat in the chair across from the spacious desk and waited.

"I'm sorry, Mom." Jamie hung up the phone, pushed both hands through her hair. "There's so much to do."

"I haven't been much help."

"Oh, yes, you have. I don't know how we'd manage without you and Dad. I can't handle this and give Livvy the attention she needs now. David's shouldered a lot of the load, but he has his own work. People are leaving flowers at Julie's house. I needed to make arrangements for them to be taken to hospitals. We already have a mountain of condolences from people she knew or worked with."

"Jamie," Val said, "we have to talk. There's going to be a trial. Sam's fancy lawyer's already on TV. Some people are hot to say he couldn't have done it. He's a victim, a figure of tragedy."

"You shouldn't listen."

"No, and I don't intend to anymore." Val's voice went fierce. "I don't intend to take any chances that Livvy will be exposed to any of it. I want to take her home, Jamie. I want to take her back to Washington as soon as possible."

"Take her home?" For a moment Jamie's mind went completely blank. "But this is her home."

"I know you love her. We all do." Val took her daughter's hand. "Listen to me, Jamie. That little girl can't stay here, closed up in this house like a prisoner. She can't live like that. None of us can."

"Oh, Mom." Torn to bits, Jamie rose. "I want to raise her."

"How can you do that here, honey? With all the memories, all the publicity, all the risks. She needs to be protected from that, not locked in a house, however lovely, in the center of it all. Are you and David willing to give up your home, your work, to take her away, to devote your time to her? Your father and I can give her a safe place." She took a deep breath. "I won't have that man getting near her ever again. It's what Julie would want for her."

What about me? Jamie wanted to scream it. What about what I need, what I want? She was the one who soothed Livvy's nightmares, who comforted and rocked and sat with her in the long dark hours. "Have you talked to Dad about this?"

"We discussed it this morning. He agrees with me. Jamie, you and David could come, spend as much time as you like. She'll always be yours, too, but not here. Not here."

JAMIE had left the house for a few hours. She needed to clear her head. The minute she arrived back home, David rushed into the foyer. His arms came around her, clutched her tight. "Jamie, where were you? I was frantic."

"I'm sorry. I wanted to be alone, to think about things." She drew back, touched his cheek, and kissed him. "I don't know what I'd do without you, David."

"You'll never have to find out." He studied her for a minute. "Jamie, your father and I talked. I know they want to take Livvy north, away from this."

She pressed her lips together. "You agree with them."

"I'm sorry, honey, but yes, I do. It's going to be ugly here for heaven knows how long. I think you should go, too." He slid his hands down her arms, linked fingers with her.

"You know I can't. I'll be needed at the trial. I have to see it through, David, for myself as much as for Julie." Jamie gave his arm an absent squeeze. "Let me talk to Livvy."

She climbed the steps slowly. It hurt, she thought. Every step was painful. It was amazing, really, just how much pain the human heart could take. She opened the door to the pretty room she'd decorated specifically for her niece's visits. Livvy sat on the floor playing with an elaborate plastic castle and dozens of little people.

"Well, what's all this?"

"Uncle David bought me a castle." Sheer delight bubbled in Olivia's voice. "There's a king and a queen and a princess and a dragon and everything."

"It's beautiful. Is this the queen?"

"Uh-huh. Her name's Magnificent."

Jamie settled onto the floor. "Livvy, do you remember Grandma's house up in the woods? All the big trees, the streams, the flowers?"

"I went there when I was a baby, but I don't remember."

"Would you like to go live there, in Grandma's house? I bet you could have the same room your mother had when she was a little girl. Everywhere you look there are trees, and when the wind blows, they sigh and shiver and moan. You'll see the places where your mother and I played when we were girls. Grandma and Grandpop will take very good care of you."

"Is it far far away?"

"Not so very far. I'll come visit you." She drew Olivia onto her lap. "We'll walk in the woods and wade in the streams until Grandma calls us home for cookies and hot chocolate."

Olivia turned her face into Jamie's shoulder. "Will the monster find me there?"

"No." Jamie's arms tightened. "You'll be safe there. I promise."

But not all promises can be kept.

Three
Olympic Rain Forest, 1987

I N THE spring of Olivia's twelfth year she was a tall, gangly girl with a wild mane of hair the color of bottled honey. Eyes nearly the same shade were long-lidded under dark, slashing brows. The forest, with its green shadows and damp smells, was her world. She was most often alone there but never lonely. Her grandfather taught her how to track, how to stalk a deer and elk with a camera, how to sit quietly, as minutes became hours, to watch the majestic journey of a buck or the grace of a doe and fawn.

She spent quiet days fishing with her grandmother, and there had learned patience. She'd taken on a share of the chores at River's End, the lodge and campground the MacBrides had run in Olympic for two generations, and there had learned responsibility. She was allowed to roam the woods, to wade in the streams, to climb the hills. But never to go beyond their borders alone.

Her memories of the house in Beverly Hills were vague flickers of high ceilings and shining colors. During the first months in the house in the forest, she'd asked when her mother would come, where her father was. But whenever she asked questions, her grandmother's mouth would clamp tight and her eyes would go dark.

From that Olivia learned to wait. Then she learned to forget.

With her chores at the campground over for the day, Olivia wandered down the path toward home. The afternoon was hers. She moved into the clearing where the MacBride house had stood for generations. The mica in the old stone glinted in the quiet sunlight. The windows sparkled. It was three levels, with decks jutting out everywhere. Flowers and ferns and wild rhododendrons sprawled out in her grandfather's hodgepodge garden.

Olivia skipped up the stone walkway, pulled open the front door. She had only to step inside to realize the house was empty. She sniffed, pleased to catch the scent of fresh cookies. When she reached the kitchen, she dug into the big glass jar that held them and read the note on the refrigerator.

Livvy,

I had to run into town. Aunt Jamie and Uncle David are coming tonight. Stay at home, so you can help me with the groceries when I get back. You can tidy up your room—if you can find it. Stop eating all the cookies.

Love,
Grandma

"Sheesh." With true regret Olivia put the top back on the jar.

Now she was stuck in the house. What was she supposed to do all day? Feeling put upon, she clumped up the back stairs. Her room wasn't that bad. It just had her stuff, that was all. Why put it away when she'd only want to get it out again?

Heaving a long-suffering sigh, Olivia snatched down the old, neglected board games and jigsaw puzzles jammed on her shelves. Her grandmother had been asking her to sort through them for weeks. She'd take them up to the attic, she decided. Carefully she went up the stairs with the teetering stack and opened the door. When the light flashed on, she glanced around, looking for the best place to store her castoffs. Old lamps stood in a corner. Baby furniture was neatly stacked against one wall, along with storage boxes and chests. A wooden shelf held a family of dolls and stuffed animals.

Olivia carried her boxes to the toy shelf and stacked them on the floor beside it. She poked into some of the drawers, pondered baby clothes carefully wrapped in tissue. Technically, she wasn't supposed to come to the attic without permission.

The rain started to patter on the roof. She glanced toward the little window that faced the clearing and saw the chest. It was of cherry wood, with polished-brass fittings. It was always kept deep under the overhang and always locked.

Today, the chest wasn't shoved back, and neither was it locked. Grandma must have put something away, Olivia thought. She knelt in front of it. What was the harm in opening it and taking a peek inside? It was probably just full of musty old clothes.

But her fingers tingled as she lifted the lid. The scent struck her first. Something both foreign and familiar.

There were videos in plain black dustcovers, three thick photo albums, boxes of varying sizes. She opened one box. There, resting in foam, were half a dozen decorative bottles.

"The magic bottles," she whispered. The scent—Mama's perfume. Setting the box aside, Olivia leaned into the chest, breathed long and deep. And smelled her mother.

She reached for the first photo album. It was full of pictures of her mother when she'd been a young girl, pictures with Jamie and her parents. There was one of her mother holding a baby. "That's me," Olivia whispered. "Mama and me."

She set the album aside and reached for the next. Not family photos this time, but newspaper clippings, magazine articles. Her mother on the cover of *People* and *Newsweek* and *Glamour*. Olivia studied these first, looking deep. She'd been so beautiful, so perfect. Then her heart leaped as she paged through a series of photos of her mother with a dark-haired handsome man. There were pictures of them in a big room with glittering lights, on a sofa, with her mother snuggled into his lap, their faces close.

Sam Tanner. It said his name was Sam Tanner. As Olivia read it, her stomach cramped. It was Daddy. How could she have forgotten? Holding hands with Mama. Holding scissors bright with blood.

No, no. That couldn't be. It was a dream, a nightmare.

She began to rock, pressing her hands to her mouth as the images began to creep in—broken glass sparkling on the floor in the lights. Dying flowers. The warm breeze through the open door.

It wasn't real. She wouldn't let it be real.

Olivia pushed the book aside and lifted out the last. There'd be other pictures, she told herself. But it was newspapers again, with big headlines that seemed to scream at her:

JULIE MACBRIDE MURDERED
SAM TANNER ARRESTED
FAIRY TALE ENDS IN TRAGEDY

There were pictures of her father, looking dazed and unkempt. And of her, she saw with a jolt. Of her years before, with her eyes wild and blank and her hands pressed to her ears.

She shook her head in denial, ripping quickly through the pages now. There, another face that awakened memories. A policeman. He'd carried her out of the house where the blood was.

Because her mother was dead. She knew that. Of course she knew that. But we don't talk about it, she reminded herself. We never talk about it, because it makes Grandma cry.

She was already searching the words and pictures:

DRUGS. JEALOUSY. OBSESSION.
TANNER RETRACTS CONFESSION. PROCLAIMS HIS INNOCENCE.
FOUR-YEAR-OLD DAUGHTER VIDEOTAPED AS CHIEF WITNESS.

She remembered it all now. They'd sat in Aunt Jamie's living room, and a woman with red hair had asked her questions about the night the monster had come. Grandma had promised it would be the last time she'd have to talk about it.

Olivia turned more pages. And read another flurry of headlines:

GUILTY! JURY CONVICTS TANNER
TANNER SENTENCED TO LIFE

"You killed my mother, you bastard." She said it with all the hate a young girl could muster. "I hope you're dead, too. I hope you died screaming."

With steady hands Olivia closed the book, carefully replaced it along with the others in the chest. She shut the lid, turned off the light, and walked down to the back porch.

She didn't understand how she had buried everything that had happened. But she knew she wouldn't do so again. She would remember always. And she'd find out all she could about the night her mother died. She couldn't ask her family—they thought she was still a child. But they were wrong. She'd never be a child again.

She heard the sound of the Jeep rumbling up the lane through the rain. Olivia closed her eyes and concentrated. She tucked the hate, the grief, and the anger into a corner of her heart. Then she stood up, a smile ready for her grandmother.

BECAUSE the first night Jamie and David came to visit was always treated as a special occasion, the family ate in the dining room, with its long oak table set with white candles in silver holders and Great-grandma Capelli's china. With Val supervising, Olivia had made spaghetti and meatballs, Jamie's favorite meal.

Food was abundant, as was conversation. The dinner spun out for two hours while the candles burned down and the sun began to slide behind the trees.

"Livvy, that was just wonderful." Jamie patted her stomach.

Rob twinkled, giving Olivia's hair a tug. "She's got your hand with the sauce, Val."

"My mother's, more like. I swear it was better than mine."

"Blood runs true," Rob commented, and winked at his granddaughter. "That Italian side was bound to pop out sooner or later. The MacBride side was never known for its skill in the kitchen."

"What are they known for, Dad?" asked Jamie.

He laughed, wiggled his brows. "We're lovers, darling."

Val snorted, slapped his arm, then rose. Jamie started to get up. "No," Val said. "You don't catch KP on your first night. Livvy's relieved, too. Rob and I will clean this up."

"Hear that, Livvy?" David leaned over to murmur in her ear. "You cook, you don't scrub pots. Pretty good deal."

"I'm going to start cooking regularly." Olivia grinned at him. "It's a lot more fun than doing dishes. Do you want to take a hike tomorrow, Uncle David? We can use my new backpack."

"You spoil her, David," Val stated as she stacked dishes. "She wasn't going to get that pack until her birthday this fall."

"Spoil her?" David poked a finger into Olivia's ribs and made her giggle. "Nah. Plenty of time yet before she spoils. Do you mind if I switch on the TV? A client's doing a concert on cable."

"You go right on," Val told him. "Put your feet up."

"Want to come talk to me while I unpack?" Jamie asked Olivia.

"Could we take a walk?" Olivia had been waiting for the right moment. "Before it gets dark?"

"Sure." Jamie stood, stretched. "Let me get a jacket."

Even in summer the nights were cool. The air smelled of rain and wet roses. Jamie took a deep breath and smiled at her father's garden. "It's always good to be home. When I was a girl your age, I thought this was the whole world."

"But it's not."

"No. But it's one of the best parts. I hear you're a big help at the lodge. Grandpop says he couldn't do without you."

"I like working there." Olivia angled away from the house toward the trees. "Lots of people come. Some of them don't know *anything*. They don't even know the difference between a Douglas fir and a hemlock, or they wear expensive designer boots and get blisters. A lot of them come from Los Angeles."

"Ouch. Direct hit." Amused, Jamie rubbed her heart. "But L.A. can be exciting, too. Beautiful homes, wonderful palm trees, shops, restaurants, galleries."

"Is that why my mother went there? So she could shop and go to restaurants and have a beautiful home?"

Jamie stopped short. "I— She— Julie wanted to be an actress. It was natural for her to go there."

"She wouldn't have died if she'd stayed home."

"Oh, Livvy." Jamie reached out, but Olivia stepped back.

"You have to promise not to say anything to anyone. Not to

Grandma or Grandpop or Uncle David. You *have* to promise."

"All right, baby."

"I'm not a baby." But this time Olivia let herself be held. "Nobody talks about her, and all her pictures got put away. I can't remember unless I try really hard. Then it gets all mixed up."

"We didn't want you to hurt. You were so little when she died."

"When he killed her." Olivia drew back, her eyes glinting in the dim light. "When my father killed her. You have to say it out loud."

"When Sam Tanner killed her." The pain reared up, hideously fresh. Jamie sat beside a nurse log. "Not talking about it doesn't mean we didn't love her, Livvy. Maybe it means we loved her too much."

"Do you think about her?"

"Yes. Yes, I do. We were very close. I miss her every day."

Olivia sat beside her. "Do you think about him?"

Jamie shut her eyes. "I try not to. He's in prison."

"He used to tell me stories. He used to carry me on his back. I'd forgotten, but I remember now. Then he got sick and went away. That's what Mama told me, but it really was drugs."

"Where are you hearing these things?"

"Are they true? Aunt Jamie, I want to know what's true."

"Yes, they're true. I'm sorry they happened to you, to Julie."

"Is what happened why I can never visit you? Why Grandma teaches me instead of my going to school with other kids? Why my name's MacBride instead of Tanner?"

Jamie sighed. "We decided it was best for you not to be exposed to the publicity, the speculations. We wanted to get you away from all that, to give you a chance to have a safe, happy childhood."

"Grandma locked it all away."

"It was so hard on her, Livvy. She lost her daughter. Protecting you was so important. You can't blame her for it."

"I don't want to. But it's not fair to ask me to forget everything. I can't talk to her or Grandpop." Her eyes stung horribly as she forced back tears. "I need to remember my mother. How will I know who I am?"

"You're right. You're right." Jamie draped an arm around Olivia's shoulders and hugged her. "You can talk to me. I won't tell anyone else. And we'll both remember."

Content with that, Olivia laid her head on Jamie's shoulder. "Aunt Jamie, do you have tapes of the movies my mother was in?"

"Yes."

"One day I want to see them." She rose, her eyes solemn as she looked at Jamie. "We'd better go back in. But first I'd like to ask you for a favor. I need you to get me an address. It's for the policeman who took me to your house that night. I want to write to him."

"Livvy, why? There's nothing he can tell you I can't."

"Even if I can only write and tell him I remember he was nice to me, I'd feel better. And . . . he was there that night, Aunt Jamie. I want to talk to him. I'll tell him my grandparents don't know I'm writing. I won't tell lies. I only remember his name was Frank."

Jamie felt her heart sink a little. "His name is Frank Brady."

FRANK Brady turned the envelope over in his hands. Olivia MacBride. Little Livvy Tanner, he mused, a young ghost out of the past.

Eight years. He'd never really put that case aside. He'd tried. He'd done his job, justice had followed as best it could, and the little girl had been whisked away by family who loved her.

Closed, finished, over. Despite the stories that cropped up from time to time, it was done. Julie MacBride would be forever thirty-two and beautiful, and the man who'd killed her wouldn't see the outside of a cage for another decade or more.

Why would the kid write to him after all this time? Frank wondered. He frowned at the envelope while phones shrilled and cops moved in and out of the bull pen. Then he tore it open and read:

Dear Detective Brady,

I hope you remember me. My mother was Julie MacBride, and when she was killed, you took me to my aunt's house. You made me feel safe, and you helped me then. I hope you can help me now.

I asked Aunt Jamie to give me your address. I didn't tell my grandparents, because it makes them sad. We never talk about my mother or what my father did.

I have questions that nobody can answer but you. Will you talk to me? I thought maybe if you wanted to take a vacation, you could come here. Our lodge has a swimming pool and is really nice. You can go fishing or hiking or boating.

Please come. I have no one else to talk to.

Yours truly,
Olivia

Frank carried both the letter and the memory of the girl with him all day. He decided he'd write her a gentle response. He could tell her how Noah was starting college in the fall and how he'd been named Most Valuable Player in his basketball tournament. What good would it do to go to Washington State? It would only upset everyone involved. He was a cop, not a social worker, he reminded himself as he turned down the street toward home.

He pulled into the drive behind a bright blue Honda Civic, both bumpers crowded with stickers. Flowers danced around the house. Lord knows where Noah had gotten the green thumb, Frank thought as he climbed out of the car. Once the boy was away at college, Celia would kill the blooms within a month.

He stepped in the front door to the sound of Fleetwood Mac. His heart sank. Celia liked to cook to Fleetwood Mac. She stood happily in the kitchen stirring something on the stove. There was a fresh loaf of some kind of tree-bark bread on the counter.

But she looked so pretty, he thought, with her bright red hair pulled back in a smooth ponytail. She carried a look of innocence, but there was nothing Celia Brady wanted to accomplish that she didn't manage to do. Unexpectedly he came up behind her and hugged her tight. "I love you, Celia."

She turned in his arms and gave him a quick kiss. "You're still eating black beans and squash. It's good for you."

He figured he'd live through it—he had minipizzas buried in the freezer. "I still love you. Where's Noah?"

"Out shooting hoops with Mike. He's got a date later."

"Again?" Frank didn't bother to sigh but took the light beer she held out to him. "Celia, do you remember the MacBride case?"

"Julie MacBride?" Celia's eyebrows lifted. "Of course. You still get sad if one of her movies comes on TV. What about it?"

"The little girl."

"Yes, she broke your heart." Celia rubbed his arm. "Softy."

"Her grandparents got custody, took her up to Washington State. They own a place up there—lodge, campground on the Olympic Peninsula. Attached to the national forest."

"The Olympic National Forest?" Celia's eyes went bright. "Oh, that's beautiful country. I hiked up that way the summer I graduated from high school."

He reached in his pocket for the letter. "Just read this and tell me what you think."

After reading the first few lines, Celia murmured, "She's so sad. And so brave. You know, Frank, a family vacation before Noah heads off to college would be good for all of us. And we haven't been camping since he was three and you took an oath never to spend another night sleeping on the ground."

Half the weight the letter had put on his shoulders slid off. "I really do love you, Celia."

OLIVIA did her best to behave normally, to tuck the news and excitement away so her grandparents wouldn't notice. Inside she was breathless and jittery. The Bradys would be there soon.

She'd been relieved when her grandfather had been called to the campground right after lunch to handle some little snag. It hadn't been hard to make excuses to stay behind instead of going with him, though she'd felt guilty about being less than honest.

The guilt had her working twice as hard as she might have. Olivia weeded the nasturtiums outside the lodge dining room as she kept one eye on the turn toward reception.

She saw a big old Buick bumping up the drive but noted that the man driving it was young. He wore a cap and sunglasses. His hair was wavy and sun-streaked brown. The woman in the passenger seat was pretty. His mother, Olivia guessed, though she didn't look very old. Then she spotted another figure in the back seat.

Olivia got to her feet as the car coasted around the turn and parked. When Frank stepped out of the car, she knew him right away. Her knees trembled, but she forced a smile, came forward. "I'm Olivia." Her voice sounded very far away to her own ears. "Thank you for coming, Detective." She held out her hand.

How many times, Frank wondered, would this one little girl break his heart? She stood so poised, her eyes so solemn, her smile so polite. And her voice shook.

"It's nice to see you again, Olivia." He took her hand in his, held it. "Livvy. Don't they call you Livvy anymore?"

"Yes." Her smile warmed a little. "Did you have a nice trip?"

"Very nice. We decided to drive, so we needed my son's car. It's the only one big enough to be comfortable for that long. This is my wife—Celia."

"Hello, Livvy. What a beautiful place. I camped in your campgrounds once." Celia smiled. "Noah, this is Livvy MacBride."

He glanced over, nodded. "Hey," was all he said. Behind the dark glasses, he took in every feature of her face.

"Noah's a man of few words these days," Celia said soberly, but her eyes laughed. "I remember taking pictures of this lodge years ago. It looks as if it grew here, like the trees."

It was grand and old and dignified—three stories, with the main section under a steeply pitched roof. Windows offered guests stunning views. The wood had weathered to a soft brown and seemed as much a part of the forest as the giant trees that towered over it. The grounds looked appealingly wild and untouched.

"My great-grandfather built this. He named it, too. There's no river that ends here or anything. It's a metaphor."

"For finding rest and shelter at the end of a journey," Celia suggested, and made Olivia smile.

"Exactly. It was an inn first. Now it's a resort. But we want that same restful atmosphere and are dedicated to preserving the area."

"You're talking her language." Frank winked. "Celia's a staunch conservationist."

"So is anyone with brains," Olivia said automatically.

"We're going to get along just fine." Celia grinned. "Why don't these big, strong men deal with the luggage?"

Olivia glanced back at Frank as Celia led her off. Impatience all but shimmered around her, but she did as she was asked and opened one half of the great double doors.

Celia turned a half circle in the main lobby, admiring the floors and walls of pine and fir, the great stone fireplace. Chairs and sofas in soft earth tones were arranged in cozy groups, where several guests were enjoying coffee or wine. There were Native American rugs, and copper pails that held generous bouquets of flowers.

"Oh, but this is lovely," Celia said with a sigh.

The front desk was manned by two clerks in crisp white shirts and hunter-green vests. Daily activities were handwritten on an old slate board. While Celia checked in, Frank came in with Noah, loaded down with luggage and backpacks.

Olivia offered to show the Bradys to their rooms. She led the way down a hallway off the lobby, turned right. At the door to their rooms she stood back.

Celia let out a gasp of pleasure. "It's great! Just great! Oh, Frank, look at that view. It's like being in the middle of the forest." She moved to the patio doors and flung them open. "Why do we live in the city?"

"It has something to do with employment," Frank said dryly.

"The master bedroom is in here, and the second bedroom there," Olivia said. "You'll want to unpack, get settled in."

Noah headed off. "I'll go dump my stuff."

"Is there anything I can get you or any questions . . . There are some short, easy trails if you want to do any exploring."

"Frank, why don't you play scout?" Celia smiled, unable to resist the plea in Olivia's eyes. "Noah and I will laze by the pool for a bit. Livvy can show you around, and you can stretch your legs."

"Good idea. Do you mind, Livvy?"

"No. No, I don't mind. We can go right out this way." She gestured to the patio doors.

Frank kissed Celia. "See you in a bit."

"Take your time." She walked to the door after them, watched the tall young girl lead the man toward the trees.

"Mom? Why didn't you tell me?"

She turned. "Tell you what, Noah?"

"That's Julie MacBride's kid, isn't it?" Noah stood in the doorway of his room, his eyes alert and just a bit annoyed.

"Yes. Why?"

"We didn't come up here to play in the woods and go fishing. Dad hates fishing, and his idea of a vacation is lying in the hammock in the backyard."

She nearly laughed. It was exactly true. "What's your point?"

"He came up to see the kid. Does that mean something new's come up in the Julie MacBride murder?"

Celia lifted her shoulders. "Olivia has some questions. I don't think her grandparents have told her much, and I don't think they know she wrote your father. So let's give the two of them a little room."

"Sure." Noah gazed toward the forest. "I was just wondering."

THE trees closed them in, like giant bars in an ancient prison. Frank had expected a kind of openness and charm and instead found himself walking through a strange world where the light glowed eerily green and nature came in odd, primitive shapes. Dampness clung to the air. He'd have been more comfortable in a dark alley in East L.A. "Ever get lost in here?" he asked Olivia.

"No, but people do sometimes. You can get lost in the city, too, can't you?"

"Yeah. Yeah, you can."

She looked away now, slowing her pace. "It was nice of you to come. I wasn't sure you'd even remember me."

"I remember you, Livvy." He touched her arm lightly. "I've thought about you, wondered how you were."

"My grandparents are great. I love living here. People come for vacation, but I get to live here all the time." She said it all very fast before she turned a corner. "You have a nice family."

"Thanks. I think I'll probably keep them."

"I have a nice family, too. But . . . That's a nurse log." She pointed. "When a tree or branches fall, the forest makes use of them. Nothing's wasted. That's a Douglas fir, and you can see the sprouts of western hemlock growing out of it, and the spread of moss, the ferns and mushrooms. When something dies here, it gives other things a chance to live." She looked up at him, her eyes shimmering behind a sheen of tears. "Why did my mother die?"

"I can't answer that, Livvy. I can never really answer the why, and it's the hardest part of my job."

"It was a waste, wasn't it? Of something good and beautiful."

"Yes. Yes, she was good and beautiful."

Olivia didn't speak until she was certain she'd fought back the tears. "But my father wasn't. He couldn't have been good and beautiful. But she fell in love with him, and she married him."

"Your father had problems."

"Drugs," she said flatly. "I read about it in newspapers my grandmother put away in our attic. He took drugs, and he killed her." Her voice was fierce. "He says he didn't do it. But he did. I saw him. He would have killed me, too, if I hadn't gotten away."

"I don't know." How did he answer this child, with her quiet voice and old eyes? "It's possible."

"You talked to him after. Is he crazy?"

Frank let out a sigh. "Livvy, I think he was weak, and the drugs played into that weakness. They made him believe things that weren't true and do things that weren't right. Your mother separated from him to protect you."

"If he wasn't living there, why was he in the house that night?"

"The evidence indicated she let him in."

"Because she still loved him." Olivia shook her head. "Will they keep him in jail forever?"

"He was given a sentence of twenty years to life, the first fifteen without possibility of parole."

"Does that mean he can just get out in seven more years?"

"No, not necessarily. He'll go before a panel, like a test."

"But the people on the panel don't know. They weren't there. It won't matter to them."

"Yes, it will matter. I can go." And he would, Frank decided, and speak for the child. "I'm allowed to go and address the panel because I was there."

"Thank you." The tears wanted to come back, so she held out a hand to shake his. "Thank you for talking to me. I'm really glad you came. I hope you and your family have a good time. If you want, I can sign you up for one of the guided hikes here."

Frank smiled. "We'd like that but only if we can hire you as guide."

She studied him soberly. "Skyline Trail's only thirty-one miles." When his mouth fell open, she smiled. "Just kidding. I know a nice day hike. A couple of miles. You'll see beaver and osprey."

"Sold. How about tomorrow?"

"I'll check with my grandfather, but it should be all right. I'll come by about eleven thirty."

OLIVIA arrived at the lodge exactly on time. She had her compass, her knife, bottled water, and a first-aid kit stowed in her pack. She walked around to the patio entrance of the Bradys' unit and saw Noah sitting in a chair, wearing headphones. His legs were long, clad in jeans and stretched out to cross at the ankles in high-top Nikes. He wore sunglasses. His hair was damp from the shower or the pool. It was casually slicked back and drying in the sun.

She thought he looked like a rock star. Shyness wanted to swallow her, but she straightened her shoulders. "Hi," she said.

His head moved a little. "Yeah, hi." He reached down to turn off the cassette that was singing in his ears. "I'll get the troops."

When he stood up, she had to tip back her head to keep her eyes on his face. "Did you try the pool?"

"Yeah." He grinned and had the woman's heart, still sleeping in the child's breast, stirring. "Water's cold." He opened the door. "Hey, the trailblazer's here." There was a muffled response. He turned to

Olivia. "You might as well sit down. Mom's never ready on time."

She lowered herself to the stone patio and fell into silence.

Noah studied her profile. She interested him because of her connection to his father, to Julie MacBride, and, he admitted, because of her connection to murder. Murder fascinated him.

He would have asked her about it if he hadn't been certain both his parents would have skinned him for it. If he hadn't remembered the small child with her hands over her ears and tears flooding her cheeks. "So . . . what do you do around here?"

Her gaze danced in his direction. "Stuff." She felt the heat climb into her cheeks at the foolishness of the answer.

"Oh, yeah, stuff. We never do that in California."

"Well, I do chores. I hike and fish. I'm learning about the history of the area, the flora and fauna, that sort of thing."

"Where do you go to school?"

"My grandmother teaches me at home."

"At home? Some deal."

"She's pretty strict," Olivia mumbled, then leaped to her feet in relief when Frank and Celia stepped out. "Good morning. If you're ready, we'll get going. You can stop me anytime you want to take pictures or rest or ask questions," she began as she started the walk.

She identified trees for them but got the feeling only Celia was interested. However, when Olivia cut over to the river and the world opened up a bit, all three of her charges got into the spirit.

"This is the Quinault River," Olivia told them. "It runs to the coast. The Olympic Range rings the interior."

"It's beautiful. It takes your breath away." Celia had her camera up. "Look at the way the mountains stand against the sky."

Olivia scrambled around in her head for what she knew about the mountains. "Ah, Mount Olympus is actually less than eight thousand feet at its peak, but it rises from the rain forest at almost sea level, so it looks bigger. It has, I think, six glaciers."

She led them along the river, pointing out the stringlike petals of wild goldthread, the delicate white of marsh marigold. They passed other hikers on the trail, singles and groups.

When Olivia managed to catch a red-legged frog, Celia took pictures, laughing in delight when it let out its long feeble croak. After Olivia released it, she picked a shady area off the trail where they could sit and watch the water. The air was warm, the sky clear, in one of those perfect summer days the peninsula could offer.

"I'm going to walk down a little more," Olivia said. "I'll see if I can spot some beavers. If I do, I'll come back and get you."

"Poor thing," Celia murmured when Olivia walked down the trail. "I don't even think she knows how lonely she is."

"Her grandparents are good people, Celia."

"I'm sure they are. But where are the other kids? The ones her age she should be playing with on a beautiful day like this."

"She doesn't even go to school," Noah put in. "She told me her grandmother teaches her at home."

"They've put her in a bubble. A spectacular one," Celia added as she sat down, "but it's still closed."

Noah looked around. "I think I'll walk down, too. Never seen a beaver."

"He has a kind heart," Celia commented, smiling after him.

"Yeah, and a curious mind. I hope he doesn't try to pump her."

"Give him some credit, Frank."

"If I didn't, I'd be going to look for beavers, too." With that, he stretched out and laid his head in his wife's lap.

NOAH found Olivia sitting on the bank of the river, very quiet and still. It made a picture in his mind very much like, yet so different from, the one he had of her as a small child.

Her head turned at his approach. She kept her gaze steady on his face, those rich eyes of hers solemn, as he sat down.

"They don't mind people too much," she told him in a low voice. "But you have more luck if you don't make a lot of noise."

"I guess you spend a lot of time just hanging around."

"There's always something to see or do." He made her feel odd in a way she couldn't decide was pleasant or not. A kind of drumming just under her heart. "I guess it's nothing like Los Angeles."

"Nothing at all. It's okay, though. Mostly I like my nature in the city park, with a basketball hoop."

"I bet you've never even been fishing."

"Why should I?" He sent her a quick flash of a grin. "I can walk right into McDonald's and buy a fish sandwich."

"Isn't the city crowded and full of noise and traffic?"

"Sure. That's why I love it. Something's always happening."

"Something's always happening here, too. Look."

A pair of beavers swam cheerfully upriver, their slick heads skimming the surface. Then, like a dream, a heron rose up over the opposite bank with a majestic flap of wings.

"Bet you never saw that in the city."

"Guess not." He decided the beavers were really pretty cute.

"You know about my mother."

Noah looked over sharply. There'd been a dozen questions he'd wanted to ask, but now he found he couldn't. "Yeah. It's rough."

"Have you ever seen any of her movies?"

"Sure. Lots of them."

"Was she wonderful in them?"

"Haven't you ever seen one?" When Olivia shook her head, he shifted, not sure how to answer. "She was really good. I mostly like action flicks, you know, but man, she was beautiful."

"I don't mean how she looked. Was she a good actress?"

"Sure. Really good. She made you believe."

Olivia nodded. "She left here because she wanted to act. I just wanted to know if she was good. 'She made you believe.' " Olivia murmured it, then tucked that single statement into her heart. "Your father—he came here because I asked him to. He's a great man. You should know that. You have parents who care about things, about people. You should never forget that." She got to her feet. "I'll go get them so they can see the beavers."

Noah sat where he was. He hadn't asked her the questions in his head, but she'd answered one of them. How did it feel to be the daughter of someone famous who'd died in a violent way?

It felt lousy. Just lousy.

Four
Washington State University, 1993

NOAH checked the address of the trim two-story house. He parked his rental car at the curb, combed back his hair with his fingers. He'd thought about getting a trim before coming here, but hey, he was on vacation. More or less.

Two weeks away from the newspaper, where his struggle to make a name for himself as a crime reporter wasn't as satisfying as he'd thought it would be. Politics, print space, editors, and advertising got in the way of stories he wanted to tell. That was why he was here. To write the one story he'd never been able to forget, and to tell it his way—Julie MacBride's murder.

This off-campus house and others like it accommodated those who didn't look for the pace and companionship, the bursts of energy in college life. Personally, he'd loved his years on campus at U.C.L.A., where he'd gotten his degree in journalism.

And if after three years he'd learned he wasn't a reporter at heart, he was still a good one. He'd done his research. He knew Olivia MacBride was majoring in natural resource science, that her grades were a straight 4.0. He knew she belonged to no clubs or sororities. But there were things he couldn't research—what she wanted, what she hoped for, what she felt about her parents.

To know all that, he needed to know her. To write the book that fermented in his heart and mind, he had to get inside her head.

The images of her that burned brightest in his mind were of the child's tearstained face and the young girl's solemn eyes. As he walked into the house, he wondered what he would see now.

He climbed the steps, noted the small plaque that identified apartment 2-B. No name. The MacBrides still guarded their privacy. "Here goes," he muttered, and pressed the buzzer.

He had a couple of plans of approach in mind, believing it best to be flexible until he gauged his ground. Then she opened the door, and every plan, every practical thought ran out of his mind.

She wasn't beautiful, not if you measured her by her mother's staggering image. It was almost impossible to do otherwise when you saw the eyes—rich golden brown under slashing dark brows. She was tall and slim but with an efficient toughness to her build he found surprisingly sexy. Her long hair had darkened but was shades lighter than her eyes. She wore jeans, a W.S.U. sweatshirt, no shoes, and a vaguely annoyed expression. He found himself staring foolishly, unable to do anything but grin at her.

She cocked one of those killer eyebrows, and a surprising kick of lust joined his sheer pleasure at seeing her. "If you're looking for Linda, she's across the hall. Two-A."

"I'm not looking for Linda. I'm looking for you. And you just put a huge hole in my ego by not remembering me."

"Why should I remember . . ." She focused those fascinating eyes on him as she hadn't when she'd thought he was just another nuisance man who flocked around her neighbor across the hall. As she did, her eyes warmed. "You're Noah Brady, Frank's son." Her gaze shifted over his shoulder. "Is he—"

"No. It's just me. Got a minute?"

"Yes. Yes, of course. Come in." Flustered, she stepped back. She'd been deep into the writing of a paper on the root symbiosis of fungus. Now she went flying back over time, into memories. And into the crush she'd had on him when she'd been twelve.

"I can make some coffee, or I probably have something cold."

"Either's fine." Noah took the first-time visitor's scan of the comfortable room, the organized desk with its humming computer, the soft cream walls, the deep blue sofa. "Nice place."

"Yes, I like it." Olivia stood looking at him as if she didn't know quite where to begin. "I'll just be a minute."

"No rush." He followed her into the kitchen.

"Coke or coffee?" she asked when she'd pulled open the fridge.

"Coke's fine. Thanks." He took the can.

"What are you doing in Washington?"

"I'm on vacation." He smiled at her, and the drumming that had been under her heart six years before started up as if it had never stopped. "I work for the L.A. *Times.*"

"You're a reporter."

"I always wanted to write." He felt her wariness slide between them and decided there was no hurry about telling her what he'd come for. "The friend I was going to flake out at the beach with couldn't get away after all. So I decided to head north."

"You're not up here on assignment, then."

"No." That was the truth, he told himself. "I'm on my own. I decided to look you up, since you're the only person I know in the entire state of Washington. How do you like college?"

"Oh, very much." Olivia led Noah back into the living room. "I miss home, but classes keep me busy." She sat on the couch.

He sat beside her and companionably stretched out his legs. "What are you working on?" He nodded toward the computer.

"Fungus." She laughed. He was wonderful to look at—the untidy sun-streaked brown hair, the deep green eyes, the easy sensuality of his smile. "I'm a natural resource science major."

He started to tell her he knew, stopped himself. "It fits."

"Like a glove," she agreed. "How are your parents?"

"They're great. You told me once I should appreciate them. I do." He shifted, his eyes meeting hers, holding hers. "More, I guess, since I moved out, got my own place. Do you still work at the lodge?"

"Yes. Summers, over breaks. I— Did you ever learn to fish?"

"No." He grinned. "It's still fish sandwiches at McDonald's. But I can occasionally do better. How about dinner?"

"Dinner?" She had a paper to finish, a test to study for. And he had the most beautiful green eyes. "That would be nice."

"Good. I'll pick you up at seven." Noah got up, giving her hand an absentminded squeeze as she rose to lead him to the door. He grinned again before he left.

Olivia quietly closed the door, turned to lean back against it. For the first time in longer than she could remember, she had a purely frivolous thought: What was she going to wear?

HE'D BRING UP THE SUBJECT of the book during dinner. Gently, Noah told himself. He wanted her to have time to consider it, to understand what he hoped to do. It couldn't be done without her cooperation. Without her family's, he thought as he climbed the steps to her apartment again. When Olivia understood his motivations, the results he wanted to accomplish, how could she refuse? The book wouldn't just be about murder, but about people. The human factor. The motivations, the mistakes. The heart, he thought.

He pushed the buzzer of 2-B, and the door opened. He forgot the book. He very nearly forgot his name.

Olivia stood in the doorway wearing a dress of quiet blue. She'd left her hair loose, so that it fell straight as rain and gave him a glimpse of glints of gold at her ears.

"You look great."

He held her hand all the way down to the car. Then he skimmed his fingers over her hair, brushing it back as she started to climb in.

Her heart stumbled, and fell right at his feet.

NOAH had found an Italian place just casual enough not to intimidate. White candles flickered on soft salmon-colored cloths.

He was easy to talk to, the first man outside of family Olivia had ever had dinner with who seemed actually interested in her studies and her plans to use them. Then she remembered his mother. "Is your mother still involved with causes?"

"She and her Congressmen are on a first-name basis. I think the current focus is the plight of the mustang. Are you going to let me taste that?"

"What?" She'd just lifted a forkful of portobello mushroom. "Oh. Sure."

He took her wrist, guided her hand toward his mouth as his eyes watched hers over the fork. "It's terrific."

"There are a variety of edible mushrooms in the rain forest."

"Yeah. Maybe I'll make it back up there one of these days and you can show me."

"I'm— We're hoping to one day add a naturalist center to the lodge. There'd be lectures and talks on how to identify the edibles."

"Edible fungus—it never sounds as appetizing as it is."

"Actually, the mushroom isn't the fungus. It's a fruiting body of the fungus organism. Like an apple from the apple tree."

"No kidding?"

"When you see a fairy ring, it's the fruit expanding year after year and—" She caught herself. "And you can't possibly care."

"Hey, I like to know what I'm eating."

Olivia smiled, relaxing back as the waiter served their main courses. She sampled her angel-hair pasta with tomato and shrimp. "They always give you more than you could possibly eat."

"Says who?" Noah dug into his manicotti bursting with cheese.

It amazed her that he managed not only to do justice to his meal but also to put away a good portion of hers, then still had room to order dessert and cappuccino. "How can you eat like that and not weigh three hundred pounds?" she wanted to know.

"Metabolism." He scooped up a spoonful of the whipped cream and chocolate concoction on his plate. "Here, try this."

"No. I can't—" But he already had the spoon to her lips, and she opened them automatically. "Hmm, well, yes."

He had to pull back a little. The half-closed eyes, the just parted lips made him realize he wanted his mouth on hers.

"Let's take a walk." He scribbled a tip and his signature on the bill, pocketed his credit card. He told himself he needed a little air to clear the fantasies out of his head. But they were still there when he drove her home, when he walked her to her door.

She saw it, clear and dark in his eyes—desire for her, the anticipation of that first kiss. A tremble shivered up her body. "This was nice. Thanks," she said.

"What are you doing tomorrow night?"

"Tomorrow?" Her mind went as blank as glass. "There's . . ." Studying, another paper, extra lab work. "Nothing."

"Good. Seven, then."

Now, she thought. He would kiss her now. "All right."

"Night, Liv." He only touched her arm, then walked away.

WHEN HE TOOK HER TO McDonald's, she laughed until her sides burned. She fell in love with him over fish sandwiches and fries, under glaringly bright lights, riding that wonderful crest of first love.

She told him what she hoped to do, describing the naturalist center she'd designed in her mind and had shared with no one but family. He listened. What she wanted seemed to matter to him.

Because she fascinated him, he put aside his work—the sketchy outline for the book, the plans for interviews—and just enjoyed her. They talked about music, about books. When Noah discovered Olivia had never been to a basketball game, never watched one on television, he looked totally shocked. "Liv, I'm sending you copies of my tapes of the Lakers." He held her hand as they walked to his car.

"They would be a basketball team."

"They, Olivia, would be gods. Okay." He settled behind the wheel. "We've managed to introduce you to fast food. We have the only true sport heading your way. What's next?"

He took her dancing.

The club was loud, crowded, and perfect. Noah had already decided that if he was alone with her, he wouldn't be able to stop himself from moving too fast. It had taken only one evening for him to realize she was every bit as lonely as the young girl he remembered. And that she was completely untouched. She wasn't ready for the needs she stirred up inside him. He wasn't sure he was ready for them himself.

He saw her dazzled and wary look when they shoved their way through the crowd. Amused by it, he leaned close to her ear. "Mass humanity at ritual. You could do a paper."

"I'm a naturalist."

"This is nature." He found them a table, leaned forward to shout over the driving music. "Basic courtship rituals."

She glanced toward the tiny dance floor, where dozens of couples writhed together. "I don't think that qualifies as courtship."

But it was interesting enough to watch. The music was loud, but it meshed nicely with that drumming under Olivia's heart. She found herself smiling. Noah tugged her to her feet.

She tried to pull her hand free. "I don't dance."

"Everyone dances."

"No, really. I don't know how." The panic came, fast and hard, to fill her chest.

They were on the edge of the dance floor, and his hands were on her hips. His face was close. "Just move." His body did just that against hers and turned her panic into a different, deeper, far more intimate fear. "It doesn't matter how."

Her hands gripped his shoulders. Her face was flushed, and her eyes were dark and wide on his. Through all the scents—the clash of perfume, sweat, spilled beer—he smelled only her. Fresh and quiet, like a meadow.

He had to have her, if only one taste. His arms wrapped tight around her waist. He felt the quick intake of her breath and the tremble that followed it. And hesitated, drawing out the moment, the now, the ache, and the anticipation until they were both reeling from it. Then he brushed his mouth over hers, soft, smooth.

The music crashed around them, but she floated, drifted, glided. He ended the kiss, then nudged her head to the curve of his shoulder. While they swayed together in the melee, Noah wondered what the hell he was going to do now.

He kissed her again at her door. Then he closed it between them and left her staring blankly at the solid panel of wood.

She pressed a hand to her heart. It was beating fast, and wasn't that wonderful? This was what it was like to be in love.

NOAH worked through the morning. And thought about calling Olivia a dozen times. Then he shut down his laptop and changed into shorts. The punishing workout he subjected himself to in the hotel's gym helped purge some of his guilt and frustration.

He should never have gone this far down this road with Olivia, he decided as he did a third set of curls with free weights. He had no right to touch her. However horrible an experience she'd been through, she'd lived eighteen years of her life completely sheltered. He was years older. He had no right to take advantage of that.

As Noah switched to flies, the practical side of his mind reminded him that Olivia was also smart, strong, and capable. She was ambitious, and her eyes were as ancient as a goddess's. Those traits appealed to him every bit as much as the shyness she tried to hide.

He set the weights aside, mopped his face with a towel. He'd call her as soon as he'd gone up to his room and showered, ask her if they could meet for coffee. Then he'd tell her about the book. He'd explain things carefully, how he was going to contact everyone involved in the case. He'd do what he now realized he should have done as soon as she'd opened her apartment door to him.

Feeling better, looser, he bypassed the elevator and took the stairs. And jolted to a halt when he saw her standing in front of his door, digging through an oversized purse.

"Liv?"

"I was just about to write you a note." She sent him a smile and stood there looking neat and fresh in jeans and a boxy jacket. "I hope you don't mind that I came by."

"No. Sorry. I just wasn't expecting you. I was down in the gym." He dug his key card out of his pocket, slid it into the door. "Come on in."

"I had some time between classes. I was going to invite you over for dinner."

"Oh, yeah?" He tried to think. He could talk to her more privately at her apartment. She'd be more comfortable there. She was obviously nervous now, standing in his cramped hotel room.

"I just have to pick up a few things at the market," she said.

"Tell you what. Give me a chance to take a shower, and we'll both go to the market. Then I can watch you cook."

"All right."

He grabbed jeans and a shirt, then dug socks and underwear out of a drawer. "Give me ten minutes."

"Take your time." The minute the bathroom door closed, Olivia lowered herself to the edge of the bed. Her knees were shaking. How was she going to manage this and not make a fool of herself? What if she'd misread what she'd seen in his eyes the night before?

She let out a breath and got up to pace. She wandered to the desk, where Noah had set up his computer and piles of disorganized notes and files. He hadn't talked very much about his work, she thought. She'd ask him how it felt to see his words in print and know that people read them. She thought it must be a wonderful, satisfying feeling and smiled as she tidied his notes.

The name MacBride, scrawled in black ink, caught her eye, had her frowning. She lifted the sheet of paper. Within seconds her blood had gone cold and she was riffling through his work without a thought for his privacy.

NOAH rubbed a towel over his hair and worked out exactly what he would say to Olivia. Once they'd come to an agreement on professional terms, they'd work on the personal ones. He could go to River's End and spend some time with her that summer. To do the interviews, certainly. But to be with her. He'd never known a woman he was so compelled to *be* with.

Noah stepped into the bedroom and heard the world crash around his ears. Olivia was standing by his desk, his papers in her hands and a look of iced fury in those amber eyes.

"You scheming, calculating bastard," she said quietly. "You're here as a reporter. It was all for a story."

"No." He stepped to the side to block her before she could stride to the door. "Just wait. I'm not here for the paper."

She crumpled his notes in her hand and tossed them in his face. "Just how big a fool do you think I am?"

"I don't." He grabbed her arms. He expected her to struggle. Instead she went rigid.

"Listen, it's not for the paper. I want to write a book. I should have told you. I meant to tell you. Then . . . Liv, the minute I looked at you, everything got confused. Every time I looked at you, I went under."

"You used me."

"I'm sorry. I let what I felt for you get in the way of what's right."

"You'd have slept with me to get information for your book."

"No! What happened between us had nothing to do with the book. I wanted you, Liv, from the minute you opened your door, but I couldn't touch you until I'd explained everything. I was going to talk to you about it tonight."

"Were you? That's very convenient, Noah." Olivia's eyes were a burning gold. "This is my life, not yours. My business, no one else's. I won't cooperate with your damn book." She shoved him back. "Stay away from me."

"I've hurt you," he said. "I'm sorry. I didn't realize what I'd feel for you. I didn't plan what happened here, between us."

"As far as I'm concerned, nothing happened between us. I despise you. Keep away from me." She snatched up her bag, shoved by him to the door. "I once told you that your father was a great man. He is. Beside him, Noah, you're very small."

She didn't even bother to slam the door. He watched it close with a quiet click.

Five
Venice, California, 1999

NOAH Brady figured his life was just about perfect. Thanks to the critical and popular success of his first book, he had his trim little bungalow on the beach and the financial resources to live pretty much as he liked.

He loved his work—the intensity and punch of writing true crime with the bent of sliding into the mind and heart of those who chose murder as a solution. It was much more satisfying than the four years he'd worked as a newspaper reporter. And it sure paid better, he thought as he jogged the last of his daily three-mile run along the beach. With his second book just hitting the bookstores, the reviews and sales solid, he figured it didn't get much better.

He was young, healthy, successful, and blissfully unattached, since he'd recently untangled himself from an annoying relationship. Who'd have thought that Caryn, self-described party girl and wannabe actress, would have morphed into a clinging female who sulked every time he wanted an evening on his own?

He knew he'd been in trouble when more and more of her things started taking up permanent residence in his closet. He'd come dangerously close to living with her by default. No, not default. *His* fault, Noah corrected, because he'd been so preoccupied with the research and writing of his next book, he'd barely noticed.

Which, of course, is what sent her into a raging, tearful snit when she'd tossed accusations of selfishness and neglect at him while tossing her things into a tote bag the size of Kansas. She'd broken two lamps—one nearly over his head—before walking out on him.

That hadn't stopped her from leaving messages on his machine that ranged from snotty to raging. What was wrong with her? She was a stunningly beautiful woman in a town that worshipped beautiful women. She was hardly going to spend time alone.

It never occurred to Noah that Caryn might have believed herself to be in love with him. His mother would have said that was typical of him. He was able to see inside strangers, victims, witnesses with uncanny insight and interest. But when it came to personal relationships, he barely skimmed the surface. He'd wanted to once, and the results had been disastrous. For Olivia, and for him.

It had taken him months to get over those three days he'd spent with Olivia. In time he'd managed to convince himself it had been the book, the thirst to write it, that had tilted his feelings for her into something he'd nearly thought was love. When he thought of her, it was with regret, guilt, and a wondering about what might have been. So he tried not to think of it.

Noah jogged toward the tidy two-story bungalow the color of buttermilk. The sun splattered over the red tile roof. The floods of color in his flower beds were the envy of his neighbors.

He got his mail, went inside, and dumped it on the kitchen counter. He glanced at his answering machine, saw he'd already accumulated four messages. Fearing at least one would be from Caryn, he decided to make coffee before he played them back.

While the coffee brewed, he sat at the counter and worked his way through the usual bills and junk mail. There was a nice little packet of reader mail forwarded by his publisher, his monthly issue of *Prison Life,* and a plain handwritten white envelope. The return address was San Quentin.

He received mail from prisoners routinely, but not, Noah thought with a frown, at his home address. He opened the letter, and his heart gave a jerk that was both shock and fascination.

Dear Noah Brady,

My name is Sam Tanner. I think you'll know who I am. You may or may not be aware that your father has attended all of my parole hearings since I began serving my sentence. You could say Frank and I have kept in touch.

I read your book *Hunt by Night.* Your clear-sighted and somewhat dispassionate look into the mind and methods of James Trolly made his West Hollywood killing spree more chilling and real than any stories in the media.

I've come to believe that you're interested in the truth, in the real people and events that took place. I find this interesting, given my connection to your father. Almost as if it's been fated. I've come to believe in fate over the years. I would like to tell you my story. I'd like you to write it. If you're interested.

Sincerely,
Sam Tanner

"Well, well." Noah read the letter over again. "Oh, I'm interested, Sam. I've been interested in you for twenty years."

He had files stuffed full on Sam Tanner, Julie MacBride, and the Beverly Hills murder. He'd put the book aside, not his interest in the case. But he'd put it aside for six years because every time he started to work on it again, he saw the way Olivia had looked at him when she'd stood by the desk in that little hotel room with his papers gripped in her hands. This time he blocked that image out.

He'd need a list of everyone involved—family, friends, employees, associates. Court transcripts. Police reports.

The thought of that brought him up short. His father. He wasn't at all sure his father was going to be happy with the idea.

THE Brady house hadn't changed a great deal over the years. It was still the same pale rose stucco, the lawn nicely mowed and the flowers on the edge of death. Since Frank Brady had retired from the force the year before, he'd become involved with the local youth center. Most afternoons he could be found there, coaching the kids on the basketball court. Mornings he spent in the backyard reading the mystery novels he'd become addicted to since murder was no longer a part of his daily routine.

That's where Noah found him, stretched out in a lawn chair. He wore jeans and sneakers, and his thick hair had gone gray.

"Do you know how hard it is to kill geraniums?" Noah glanced at the withered pink blooms struggling along the back deck. "It almost has to be premeditated." He unwound the hose, switched it on, and gave the desperate flowers another shot at life.

Pleased to see his son, Frank set aside the latest John Sandford novel. "Didn't expect to see you until Sunday. You're still going out to dinner with us for your mother's birthday?"

"Wouldn't miss it."

"You can bring that girl you've been seeing if you want."

"That would be Caryn. I'm steering clear of her."

"Good. Your mother didn't like her. 'Shallow,' 'snooty,' I believe, were the words she used."

"It's annoying how she's always right." Noah turned off the hose and carefully wound it back on its wheel.

Frank said nothing for a moment. "You know, I was a pretty good detective. I don't think you came here to water my flowers."

"I got a letter this morning. Guy in San Quentin wants me to tell his story."

"And?" Frank raised his eyebrows.

"I'm interested in this case. Been interested for a while." Noah met his father's eyes levelly. "It's Sam Tanner, Dad."

There was a hitch in Frank's heart rate. "I see. No, I don't see," he said immediately, and pushed out of his chair. "I put Sam away, and now he writes to you? He wants to talk to the son of the man who helped send him over, who's made sure he stayed over for twenty years?"

"Why did you go to all his parole hearings?"

"Some things you don't forget. And because you don't, because you can't, you make sure the job stays done." And he'd made a promise to a young girl with haunted eyes in the forest.

"He can't hurt me, Dad."

"I imagine that's just what Julie MacBride thought that night. Stay away from him, Noah. Put this one aside."

"You haven't. I remember how it was. You'd pace the floor at night or come out here to sit in the dark. Nothing ever followed you home like this one. So I never forgot it either. I guess you could say it's followed me, too."

"If you write this book, Noah, do you realize what it might do to Tanner's other victims—the parents, the sister, her child?"

"I thought about what it might do to you. That's why I'm here. I wanted you to know what I'm going to do."

"It's a mistake."

"Maybe, but it's my life now and my job."

"You think he'd have contacted you if you weren't my son?" Fear and fury turned Frank's eyes hard. "The s.o.b. refuses to talk to anyone for years—Brokaw, Walters, Oprah. No interviews, no nothing. Now he offers you the story on a plate. Damn it, Noah, it doesn't have to do with your work. It has to do with mine."

"Maybe." Noah's tone chilled. "And maybe it has to do with both. Whether or not you respect my work, it's what I do."

"I never said I didn't respect your work."

"No, but you never said otherwise either." It was a bruise Noah just realized he'd been nursing. "I'll see you Sunday."

Frank started to speak. But Noah was already striding away.

NOAH'S foul mood drove home with him, like a separate energy, an irritable passenger in the stone-gray BMW. He hated the sudden discovery that he was hurt because his father had never done a tap dance of joy over the success of his books. Murder made entertaining fiction. But stripping down real killers for public consumption—that his father couldn't understand.

Just now Noah's mood teetered on the edge of vile. Spotting Caryn's car parked in front of his house tripped it over the rest of the way. He found her sitting on his back deck, her eyes brimming.

"Oh, Noah. I'm so sorry. I don't know what came over me. I've been so unhappy without you." She rose and went to him.

"Caryn, why don't we just say it was fun while it lasted?"

"You don't mean it."

"Yes." He had to nudge her back. "I do."

"There's someone else, isn't there? You bastard. All the time we were living together, you were cheating on me. You've already had another woman in our bed." She rushed past him, into the house.

"No, there's no one else. And it's not *our* bed. It's my bed." He was more weary than angry until he walked into the bedroom and saw she was already ripping at his sheets. "Hey! Cut it out."

She grabbed the bedside lamp and heaved it at him. He blocked it so the base didn't rap him between the eyes.

The sound of glass crashing on the floor snapped the already unsteady hold on his temper. "Okay, that's it," Noah said. "Get out. Get the hell out of my house and stay away from me."

"You never cared. You never thought about my feelings."

"You're right, absolutely." He went for her as she made a bee-line for his prized basketball trophy.

"I hate you!" she shrieked. "I wish you were dead!"

"Just pretend I am. And I'll do the same for you." He shoved her outside, shut the door, then leaned back against it.

NOAH'S first glimpse of San Quentin made him think of an old fortress now serving as a thematic resort complex. Disneyland for cons. The sand-colored building with its towers and turrets stretched out over San Francisco Bay with a faintly exotic air.

He'd opted to take the ferry from San Francisco to Marin County and now stood at the rail while it glided over water made choppy by the wind. It had taken him only hours to clear through channels for permission to visit. He'd read his file on the MacBride murder to refresh his memory. He knew the man he would meet as well as anyone from the outside was able.

At least he knew the man Tanner had been. A talented actor with an impressive string of movies under his belt by the time he'd met Julie MacBride, his co-star in *Summer Thunder*. He'd also, by all accounts, had an impressive string of females and been seriously involved with Lydia Loring, a very hot property during the '70s. He'd enjoyed his fame, his money, and his women. And he'd continued to enjoy the first two after his marriage. There'd been no other women after Julie. Or, Noah mused, he'd been very discreet.

Insiders called him difficult, then had begun to use terms like "explosive temper," "unreasonable demands" when his two films after *Summer Thunder* hadn't done well with audiences.

In 1975 he'd become the top box-office actor in the country. By 1980 he'd been an inmate in San Quentin. It was a long way to fall in a short amount of time.

Staggering wealth and fame, easy access to the most beautiful women in the world, the cheers of fans—how would it feel to have that sliding through your fingers? Noah wondered. Add arrogance, ego, mix it with cocaine, jealousy over box-office rival Lucas Manning, and you had a perfect formula for disaster.

The ferry docked. Noah drove his car to the prison and parked. At the visitors entrance he gave his ID and filled out the required forms, then was shown into a small, cheerless room with a table and two chairs. The door was thick, with a single window of reinforced glass.

And there Noah had his first look at what had become of Sam Tanner. Gone was the pampered screen idol with the million-dollar smile. This was a hard man, body and face. He sat, one hand chained, the bright orange prison jumpsuit baggy and stark. His hair was cut short and had gone ash gray. The lines dug deep in his face gave him the look of a man well beyond his age of fifty-eight.

"Glad you could make it, Mr. Brady."

Noah sat as the door closed and the lock snicked into place. "How did you get my home address, Mr. Tanner?"

"I still have some connections. How's your father?"

"My father's fine. I can't say he sends his best."

Sam's teeth bared in a fleeting grin. "A straight-up cop—Frank Brady. I see him and Jamie now and again. . . . Got any reals?"

Noah lifted a brow. He knew most of the basic prison terms. "No, sorry. I don't smoke."

"Lousy California." With his free hand Sam reached inside his jumpsuit, carefully removed the tape that affixed a cigarette and match to his chest. "Making prisons nonsmoking facilities. Where do they come up with this crap?" He lit the cigarette. "Used to be I had resources. Now I'm lucky to get a carton a month."

"It's lousy the way they treat murderers these days."

Sam's cold blue eyes only glimmered. He blew out a stream of ugly-smelling smoke. "You know, I've had a long time to think about that. I read a lot to get through the bad times. I used to stick to novels, pick a part in one and imagine playing it when I got out. I loved acting. It took me a long time to accept that that part of my life was over."

"Is it? What role are you playing here, Tanner?"

Abruptly Sam leaned forward, and for the first time life sprang into his eyes, hot and real. "This is all I've got. You think because you come in here and talk to cons, you understand what it's like? You can get up and walk out anytime. You'll never understand."

"There's not much stopping me from getting up and walking out now," Noah said evenly. "What do you want?"

"I want you to tell it, to put it all down. To say why things happened. Why two people who had everything lost it all."

"And you're going to tell me all that?"

"Yeah." Sam leaned back, drawing out the last of his smoke. "I'm going to tell you all of it. And you're going to find out the rest."

"Why? Why me, why now?"

"I liked your book. And the irony of the connection seemed almost like a sign. But there's fate, and there's timing."

"You want to consider me fate, okay. What's the timing?"

"I'm dying." Sam crushed the cigarette on the floor.

Noah skimmed his gaze coolly over Sam's face. "You look healthy enough to me."

"Brain tumor." Sam tapped a finger on his head. "Inoperable. The doctors say maybe a year, and if I'm lucky, I'll die in the world and not inside. My lawyer's working on that. It looks like the system's going to be satisfied with my twenty now that I'm dead anyway." He seemed to find that amusing and chuckled over it. "If you're interested, you'll have to work fast."

Noah tapped a finger on the table. "I'll think about it." He rose.

"Brady," Sam said as Noah moved to the door, "you didn't ask if I killed my wife."

Noah met his eyes dead on. "Why would I?" he said.

NOAH sat in prison supervisor George Diterman's office. With his thinning patch of hair and black-framed glasses, Diterman looked like a man very low on the feeding chain of a mid-level accounting firm, not the head of one of the country's most active prisons.

He greeted Noah with a brisk handshake and a surprisingly charming smile. "I enjoyed your first book," he began as he took his place behind his desk. "And I'm enjoying the second."

"Thank you."

"I assume you're here gathering information to write another?"

"I've just spoken with Sam Tanner."

"Yes, I'm aware of that. Tanner's authorized me to give you access to his records and to speak to you frankly about him. According to reports, he had a difficult time adjusting when he first came here. There were a number of altercations between him and other prisoners. Inmate Tanner spent a large portion of 1980 in the infirmary being treated for injuries."

"He got into fights?"

"Consistently. He was in solitary several times the first five years. He also had an addiction to cocaine and found sources in the prison to feed that addiction. But for the past several years he's settled in, keeps to himself. His work in the library appears to satisfy him."

"He told me he has an inoperable brain tumor. Terminal."

"Around the first of the year he complained of severe, recurring headaches, double vision. The tumor was discovered. Tests were run, and the consensus is he has less than a year."

"If I decide to pursue this, I'll need your cooperation as well as his. I'll need names, dates, events. Even opinions."

"I'll cooperate as much as I'm able. To be frank, Mr. Brady, I'd like to hear the entire story myself. I had a tremendous crush on Julie MacBride."

"Who didn't?" Noah murmured.

AFTER settling into a hotel room with a view overlooking San Francisco Bay, Noah ordered up a meal and set up his laptop. Once he'd plugged into the Internet, he did a search on Sam Tanner.

For a man who'd spent two decades behind bars without granting a single interview, there was a wealth of hits: movie summaries, his roles, and critiques. There were books on the case, including unauthorized biographies of both Sam and Julie, and articles on the trial, mostly rehashes. He found nothing particularly fresh.

When his meal arrived, Noah ate his burger and typed one-handed, bookmarking any areas he might want to explore again.

He'd seen the photographs before—the one of Sam, impossibly handsome, and a luminous Julie, both beaming beautifully into the camera. Another of Sam, shackled, being led out of the courthouse during the trial, looking ill and dazed.

Both of those men, Noah thought, were inside the cool-eyed and calculating inmate. How many others would he find? That was the irresistible pull. Who lived behind those eyes? What was it that gripped a man and drove him to butcher the woman he claimed to love, to destroy everything he swore mattered to him?

Noah began a new search on Julie MacBride, then on impulse changed it to River's End Lodge and Campground. When their home page came up, there was an arty and appealing photo of the lodge, a couple of interior photos. There was a chatty little description, which touched on the history and beauty of the national forest.

Another click took him to the recreational offerings—fishing, canoeing, hiking, a naturalist center. He paused. She'd done it, then. Built her center. Good for you, Liv.

He skimmed down. The proprietors were listed as Rob and Val MacBride. Nowhere did he find Olivia's name.

You still there, Liv? Noah wondered. Yeah, you're still there. With the forest and the rivers. Do you ever think of me?

Annoyed he'd had the thought, he pushed away from the desk and flicked on the TV, just for the noise. He let out a short laugh when Julie MacBride, young, gorgeous, and alive, filled the screen. Those striking amber eyes were glowing with love as she raced down a long sweep of stairs and into the arms of Sam Tanner.

Summer Thunder, Noah mused. Last scene. No dialogue. The music swells . . . He watched, hearing the flood of violins as the couple embraced, as Sam lifted Julie off her feet, circling, circling in celebration of love found.

Fade-out or fate? Noah thought.

THE same guard took Noah to the same room. This time he'd brought a notepad and a tape recorder. He set them on the table. Sam glanced at them, said nothing, but Noah caught a quick glint in his eyes that might have been satisfaction. Or relief.

Noah took his seat, switched on the recorder. "Let's go back, Sam—1973."

"*Fever* was released in May and was the biggest moneymaker of the summer. I got an Oscar nomination for it. I was unofficially living with Lydia and having great sex and monumental fights. Pot was out. Snow was in. There was always a party going on. And I met Julie MacBride." He paused. "Everything that had happened to me before that moment took second place."

"You were married that same year."

"Neither one of us was the cautious or patient type." His gaze drifted off. "It didn't take us long to figure out we wanted each other. For a while that was enough for both of us."

"Tell me," Noah said simply, and waited while Sam took out his contraband cigarette, lit it.

"We met in the director Hank Midler's office. She came in, wearing jeans and a dark blue sweater. Her hair was pulled back. She was the most beautiful thing I'd ever seen." His gaze shot straight into Noah's eyes. "That's not an exaggeration. I was used to having women. One look at her, and she might have been the first. I think I knew, right then, she'd be the last. You may not understand that."

"Yes, I do understand it." Noah had experienced that rush, that connection when this man's daughter had opened her apartment door and given him a faintly annoyed frown.

"Later she told me it had been exactly the same for her," Sam said. "We talked about the script, went about business as if both of us weren't reeling. Afterward I asked her to dinner. When I got home, I told Lydia it was over. I wasn't kind about it, wasn't cruel. The fact was, she'd simply ceased to exist for me. All I could think of was that at seven I'd see Julie again."

"Was Julie involved with anyone at that time?"

"She'd been seeing Michael Ford. The press played it up, but it wasn't serious. Two weeks after we met, we moved in together."

"Did it bother you that Julie's name was linked to a number of men at that time? Ford was just the latest."

"I didn't think of it then." Sam pulled the stub of the cigarette out of his mouth, crushed it out with restrained violence. "Later, when things got out of control, it was all I could think about. Who was she turning to when she was turning away from me? Lucas Manning. I knew there was something between them."

"So you killed her to keep her."

Sam's eyes went blank. "That's one theory."

Noah gave him a pleasant smile. "We'll talk about theories some other time. What was it like working with her as an actor?"

Sam lifted a hand to rub his face. "She was good. Solid. A natural. She didn't have to work as hard as I did. She just felt it."

"Did that bother you that she was better than you?"

"I didn't say she was better." His gaze whipped up.

"Julie won the New York Film Critics Award for her portrayal of Sarah in *Summer Thunder.* You were nominated but didn't win. Did that cause friction between you?"

"I was thrilled for her. She'd wanted it more than I had. We'd been married less than a year at that time. We were completely in love, completely happy, and riding the wave."

"And the next year, when she was nominated for an Oscar for best actress for *Twilight's Edge* and your movie got mixed reviews. How did that affect your relationship?"

"She was pregnant. We concentrated on that. She wanted a healthy baby a lot more than she wanted a statue."

"And you? What did you want?"

Sam smiled thinly. "I wanted everything. And for a while that's just what I had."

NOAH headed back to L.A. and set up an appointment to see Jamie Melbourne at her lavish home. He understood that Jamie's publicity firm, one of the most prestigious in the entertainment business, had branches in Los Angeles and New York and represented top names. He also understood that prior to her sister's death, Jamie had represented only Julie and had worked primarily out of her own home.

Noah drove through the gates to her elaborate estate in Holmby Hills. The main house was three stories, in wedding-cake white, with a long, flowing front porch. Rooms speared out on opposite sides, with walls of glass winking out on richly blooming gardens. Two golden retrievers bounded across the lawn to greet him.

"Hey, there." He opened the car door and was bending over, happily scratching ears, when Jamie walked over.

"They're Goodness and Mercy," she said, holding up a ratty tennis ball. As one, both dogs quivered and sat, staring up with desperately eager eyes. She sent it sailing for the dogs to chase.

"Good arm," Noah murmured.

"I keep in shape." She turned, heading away. "It's too nice an afternoon to sit inside. We'll walk."

She was fifty-two and could have passed easily for forty. Her eyes were dark, intelligent, and unflinching. Her hair was a soft brown, cut in a wedge that set off her face.

"How is your father?" she asked at length.

"Fine, thanks. He retired last year."

Jamie smiled now, briefly. "Does he miss his work?"

"I think he did until he got involved with the neighborhood youth center. He loves working with kids."

"Yes, Frank's good with children. I admire him very much. If I didn't, you wouldn't be here now."

"I appreciate your taking the time to see me, Ms. Melbourne."

She didn't sigh out loud, but he saw the rise and fall of her shoulders. "Jamie. Your father helped me through a tremendous loss, saw that my family got justice. He's an exceptional man."

Noah nodded. "I think so."

They skirted a large, fan-shaped swimming pool. He could see the deep green of tennis courts in the distance.

"I don't like your work," Jamie said abruptly. "Your father dedicated his life to putting people who take the lives of others in prison. You're dedicating yours to glorifying what they've done."

"Have you read my work?"

"No."

"If you had, you'd know I don't glorify the people I write about. Writing lays it out," Noah corrected. "The people, the acts, the motives, the whys. How and when aren't always enough. Don't you want to know why your sister died, Jamie?"

"I know why she died. She died because Sam Tanner was jealous and sick and vicious enough not to want her to live."

"But they loved each other enough to marry and make a child. Enough, even when they were supposedly having serious marital difficulties, for her to open the door to him."

"And for that last act of love, he killed her."

"You could tell me about her the way no one else can. About what she felt, about what turned her life into a nightmare."

"What about her privacy?"

"She's never had that, has she?" Noah said it gently. "I can promise to give her the truth."

"There are a lot of degrees in the truth." Jamie looked at him wearily. "Why is he talking to you after all these years?"

"He's dying." Noah said it straight and watched her face.

Something flickered across it, glinted in her eyes, then was gone. "Good. How long is it going to take him?"

"They diagnosed brain cancer in January, gave him a year."

"So he wants his brief time in the sun before he goes to hell."

"That may be what he wants," Noah said evenly. "What he'll get is a book written my way, not his."

"You'll write it with or without my cooperation."

"Yes, but I'll write a better book with it."

She believed he meant it. He had his father's clear, assessing eyes. "Maybe so. I spoke with my husband about this after you called. He surprised me. He thinks we should give you interviews. To make sure whatever ugliness Sam's formed in his mind doesn't stand on its own. So yes, maybe I'll talk to you, Noah."

Six

S AM Tanner and I drank hard, played hard, worked hard. We had vicious fights. Outrageous sex." Lydia Loring sipped her mineral water and lime from a tall, slim glass of Baccarat crystal and chuckled. Her eyes, a summery baby blue, flirted expertly with Noah and had him grinning back at her.

"Drugs?"

"Rehabilitated," she said. "My body's a temple now, a damn good one." She recrossed her very impressive legs.

"No arguing there," Noah responded, and made her purr. "But there were drugs."

"Honey, they were passed out like candy. Coke was our favorite party favor. But after Sam fell for Julie, she put a stop to that."

"How did you feel about her?"

"I hated her." Lydia said it cheerfully, without a hint of guilt. "Not only did she have what I wanted, but she came off looking like the wholesome girl next door while I was the used-up former lover. I was thrilled when their marriage hit the rocks, when Sam started showing up at clubs and parties again."

Her gaze turned inward. "He said at one party that he knew she was sleeping with Lucas Manning. He was going to put a stop to that, and she was going to pay for cheating on him." Lydia sighed. "Two days later she was dead. He made her pay."

"Did he ever hit you?"

"Sure." The humor came back into her eyes. "We hit each other. It was part of our sexual dance. We were violent people."

"But there weren't any reports of abuse or violence in his marriage until the summer Julie died. What do you think of that?"

"I think she was able to change him for a time. Or that he was able to change himself. He really wanted to be the person he was with her. But he was a weak man who wanted to be strong, a good actor who wanted to be great. Maybe he was always doomed to fail."

"One last thing. Was Julie having an affair with Lucas Manning?"

"I don't know. At the time, there were two camps on that subject: the one that believed it, and the one that didn't."

"Which camp were you in?"

"Oh, the first, of course. But later, years later, when Lucas and I had our obligatory affair—" She lifted her brows when his eyes narrowed. "Oh, didn't dig that up, I see. Yes, Lucas and I had a few memorable months together. But he never told me if he'd slept with her. But Sam believed it, so it hardly matters."

It mattered, Noah thought. Every piece mattered.

WHEN Noah arrived home that day, he parked his car, jingling his keys in his hand as he walked to his front door. The door was unlocked and not quite closed. He gently nudged it open.

Noah stood staring in shock at the destruction of his house. It looked as if a team of mad demons had danced over every surface, ripped and torn every fabric, smashed every piece of glass. He leaped inside and felt a flutter of relief when he saw his stereo equipment still in place.

Not a burglary, then, he thought, hearing the buzz of blood in his head as he waded through the mess. Papers were strewn everywhere; glass crunched under his feet. In his bedroom, the mattress had been shredded. Drawers were upended and thrown against the wall. When he found his favorite jeans sliced down to their frayed hems, the buzz turned to a roar.

"She's crazy. She's totally insane." Then anger turned to sheer horror. "No, no, no," he hissed under his breath as he raced from the bedroom into his office.

His basketball trophy was now stuck dead-center in his computer monitor. A message was taped to the base of his trophy: "I won't stop until you do."

Rage washed through him like a tidal wave. He dug for his phone, then found the receiver smashed. "Okay, Caryn, you want war, you got war." He stormed back into the living room for the briefcase he'd dropped and tore through it for his cell phone.

It was one tedious routine followed by another, telling his story first to his father, then to the police. Later he called his insurance company; then he locked himself inside his house and wondered where to begin.

Noah ordered a pizza, got a beer out of the fridge, and studied the living room. He was wondering if it wouldn't be better to just hire a crew to come in with shovels and haul the mess away, when someone knocked on his door.

"Hey, Noah, don't you ever return phone calls? I've been—Whoa, some party. Why wasn't I invited?" It was Noah's oldest friend. Mike Elmo had been part of his life since grade school.

"It was a surprise party."

"I bet. You get ripped off?"

"Just ripped. Caryn's a little irritated that I dumped her."

"Wow. She do this? Seriously twisted." Mike shook his head, his chestnut-brown eyes soft and sad. "I told you."

Noah snorted. "You told me she was your fantasy woman."

"So my fantasy woman's twisted. What're you going to do?"

"Eat some pizza and start cleaning it up."

"What kind of pizza?"

"Pepperoni and mushroom."

"Then I can give you a hand." Mike plopped his chunky butt on a torn cushion. "Hey, it's only stuff."

Noah scowled. "She broke my basketball trophy."

"Not the MVP from the championship game of '86?"

"Yeah. She broke it by shoving it into my computer monitor."

"That sick, evil broad broke your computer?" Mike was up now, stumbling through the wreckage to Noah's office.

Computers were Mike's first love. Women could come and go—and for him it was usually the latter—but a good motherboard was always there for you. He actually yelped when he saw the damage. "She mutilated it. She should be hunted down like a dog."

"I called the cops. Think you can salvage anything off the hard drive? She trashed every stinking one of my disks."

Mike shook his head sadly. "I'll see what I can do, Noah, but don't hold out any hope."

A NEW computer was a priority, and with Mike egging him on, Noah bought a system that sent his friend into raptures of envy. He outfitted his house with cargo furniture, ordering straight out of a catalogue. Within two weeks he could walk through the rooms without cursing. And he had managed to track down Lucas Manning.

Noah met Manning at his Century City suite of offices. It always slightly disillusioned Noah that actors had big, plush executive offices. They might as well be CEOs, he thought.

Manning greeted Noah with a smile and gestured to a chair. The years had turned his gold-coin hair to polished pewter.

"I appreciate your taking the time to talk to me."

"Julie was quite a woman, Mr. Brady, and even after all this time it's not easy for me to talk about what happened to her."

Noah took out his recorder. "You worked together."

"One of the happiest experiences of my life. She was a brilliant natural talent, an admirable woman, and a good friend."

"There are those who believed, and still believe, that you and Julie MacBride were more than friends."

"We could have been." Manning eased back in his chair. "If she hadn't been in love with her husband. We were attracted to each other."

"Sam Tanner believed you acted on that."

"Sam Tanner didn't value what he had." Manning's voice hardened at the edges. "He was jealous, possessive, abusive."

"Did Julie confide in you?" Noah asked.

"To an extent. I knew she was troubled. At first she made excuses for him. Then she told me in confidence that she'd filed for divorce to force him to get help."

"Why haven't you set the record straight before now? You've refused to discuss Julie in interviews since her death."

"I set the record straight in court, under oath. But the media, the masses were never satisfied. The idea of scandal, of illicit sex, has as much fascination as murder. I refused to demean her that way."

Maybe, Noah mused. Or maybe the mystery of it gave your rocketing career one more boost. "And now?"

"Now you're going to write the book. Rumors are that it'll be definitive. So I'll answer the question I've refused to answer for the last twenty years—Julie and I were never lovers. The fact is, I'd have been delighted if that had been true. The morning I heard what had happened to her remains the worst day of my life."

"How did you hear?"

"David Melbourne called me. Julie's family wanted to block as much media as possible, and he knew the minute the press got wind of it, they'd start hammering me for comments."

"Were you in love with her, Mr. Manning?"

"Completely."

Manning gave him two full hours. Noah had miles of tape, reams of notes. He believed part of Manning's interview had been calculated, rehearsed. But in it there was truth. And with truth there was progress. So he decided to celebrate by meeting Mike at a bar called Rumors for a couple of drinks.

"She's giving me the eye," Mike muttered into his pilsner.

"Which eye?"

"The *eye*, you know. The blonde in the short skirt."

Noah considered his order of nachos. "There are one hundred blondes in short skirts in here. They all have eyes."

"The one two tables over to the left. Don't look."

"Okay." Noah shrugged. "I'm going up to San Francisco again in a couple of days."

"Why?"

"Work. The book. Remember?"

"Oh yeah, yeah. I'm telling you, she's definitely eyeing me."

"Go make a move, then. Are you going to eat any of these?"

"After I talk to the blonde. I don't want nacho breath. Okay, that was five full seconds of eye contact. I'm going in."

As Mike swaggered away, Noah sipped his beer. And spotted Caryn crossing the dance floor toward his table. She'd decked herself out in a leather dress of electric blue.

"You set the cops on me." She leaned down, planting her palms on the table. "You got some nerve, Noah, getting your father to call out his gestapo friends to give me grief."

"You think you can trash my house, destroy my things, and I'll do nothing? You keep out of my way."

"Or what? Going to call Daddy again?" Caryn raised her voice. "I never touched your precious things. I wouldn't lower myself to go back in that house after the way you treated me. If I'd been there, I'd have burned it down—and I'd have made sure you were inside."

"You're sick." He was pushing his chair back when she slapped him. His eyes went dark and flat as he got to his feet.

"We got a problem here?"

Noah merely glanced at security. The man's shoulders were as wide as a canyon. Before he could speak, Caryn had launched herself against the boulder of his chest. "He wouldn't leave me alone. He grabbed me."

"That's a lie." This from Mike, who'd hopped to Noah's side. "She's a lunatic, wrecked his house last week."

"I don't know what they're talking about." Tears slid gracefully down Caryn's cheeks. "He hurt me."

"I saw what happened." A brunette with amused eyes strolled up. "This guy was having a beer, minding his own business. She came up to him, started yelling abuse. Then she slugged him."

The outrage had Caryn shrieking. She took a swipe at the brunette, missing by a mile as the bouncer nipped her around the waist. Her exit, kicking and screaming, caused quite a stir.

"Thanks," Noah said.

The brunette's smile was slow and friendly. "Anytime."

"I'm going to get you a fresh beer. Sit, relax." Mike fussed around him like a mother.

"Your friend's sweet." She offered Noah a hand. "I'm Dory."

"Noah."

"Yes, I got that from Mike already. He likes my friend." She fluttered a hand toward the table where the blonde sat. "She likes him. Why don't you join us?"

She had a voice like cream, and skin to match, intelligent interest in her eyes, and a sympathetic smile. And he was just too tired to start the dance. "I appreciate it, but I'm going to take off. Thanks again, and tell Mike I'll catch him later."

SAM'S nerves slithered under his skin like restless snakes. To keep them at bay, he recited poetry—Sandburg, Yeats, Frost. It was a trick he'd learned during his early stage work, when he'd suffered horribly, and he had refined it in prison, where so much of life was waiting, nerves, and despair.

When he'd come up for parole the first time, he'd actually believed they would let him go. That the faces and figures of the justice system would look at him and see a man who'd paid with the most precious years of his life. He'd been nervous then, but beneath the fear had been a simple and steady hope.

Then he'd seen Jamie, and he'd seen Frank Brady, and he'd

known they'd come to make certain the prison doors stayed locked.

Jamie had spoken of Julie, of her beauty and talent, her devotion to family. Of how one man had destroyed all that out of jealousy and spite. How he had endangered and threatened his own child.

She'd wept while she addressed the panel, Sam recalled. Then Frank had had his turn—the dedicated cop focused on justice. He'd described the scene of the murder, the condition of the body in the pitiless, formal detail of policespeak. Only when he'd talked of Olivia did emotion slip into his voice.

Sam had known, as Frank had looked at him, that parole would not be granted. He'd known this same scene would be repeated year after year. In his rage he'd gripped the Robert Frost lines like a weapon: *I have promises to keep, / And miles to go before I sleep.*

For the last five years he'd formed and refined those promises. Now the son of the man who'd murdered his hope was going to help him keep them. That was justice.

Over a month had passed since Noah had first come to see him. Sam had begun to worry that he wouldn't come back, that those promises that had kept him alive and sane would shatter. But he'd come back, was even now being led to this miserable little room.

The locks slid open. Noah entered, walked to the table. He took his tape recorder, a notebook, and a pencil out of the briefcase and, when the door was locked at his back, tossed a pack of Marlboros and a book of matches in front of Sam. "Didn't know your brand."

Sam smiled. "They all kill you, but nobody lives forever."

"Most of us don't know when or how it's going to end for us. How does it feel being someone who does?"

"It's a kind of power, or would be if I were in the world."

"Regrets?"

Sam opened the cigarettes. "I regret I won't have the same choices you do when this hour's up. I regret I can't decide to have a steak tonight, medium rare, and a glass of good wine to go with it and strong black coffee after. Ever had prison coffee?"

"Yeah. It's worse than cop coffee. What else do you regret?"

"I regret that when I'm finally able to make that choice again, have that steak, I'm not going to have much time to enjoy it." He slid a cigarette out of the pack, opened the book of matches, struck one to flame, and drew in that first deep gulp of Virginia tobacco. "I need money. I'm getting out when my twenty's up—my lawyer's done that dance. I'm going to live on the outside for maybe six months, and what I've got isn't going to run to that steak."

"How much?" Noah asked.

"Twenty thousand—one large one for every year I've been in."

It wasn't an unusual demand, nor did Noah consider it an unreasonable amount. "I'll have my agent draw up an agreement. Do you plan to stay in San Francisco when you're released?"

"I think I've been in San Francisco long enough."

"L.A.?"

"Nothing much for me there. I want sun, privacy, choices."

"I spoke with Jamie Melbourne."

Sam brought the cigarette to his lips. "And?"

"I'll be talking to her again," Noah said.

"Have you talked to your father?"

"I'm doing background first." Eyes sharp, Noah inclined his head. "I won't agree to getting your approval on who I interview or what I use in the book. We go with this, you'll have to sign papers waiving those rights. Your story, Sam, but my book."

"You wouldn't have a book without me."

"Sure I would. It'd just be a different book." Noah leaned back. "You want choices? There's your first one. You sign the papers, you take the twenty thousand, and I write the book my way. You don't sign, you don't get the money, and I write it my way."

There was more of his father in him than Sam had realized before. A toughness the beach-boy looks skimmed over. "I'm not going to live to see the book in print anyway. I'll sign the papers, Brady." His eyes went cold. "Just don't mess me up."

NOAH ordered a steak, medium rare, and a bottle of Côte d'Or. As he ate, he watched the lights that swept over San Francisco Bay and tried to imagine what it would be like to be eating that meal for the first time in over twenty years. Would you savor it, he wondered, or feed like a wolf after a long winter's famine?

Sam, he thought, would savor it, bite by bite, sip by sip. He had that kind of control now.

How much of the reckless, greedy-for-pleasure, out-of-control man he had been still strained for release inside him?

It was smarter to think of Sam as two men—the one he'd been, the one he was now. Pieces of both had always been there, Noah imagined. So he could sit here, try to picture how the man he knew now would deal with a steak and a glass of fine wine. And imagine the man who'd been able to command much, much more.

After Noah finished his meal, he booted up his laptop, rose to turn on the television, and stopped by the phone. What the hell, he thought, and dug out the number for River's End. He made reservations for the following week.

Sam Tanner had yet to speak of his daughter. Noah wanted to see if she would speak of him.

HE WORKED until two. There was just one more chore on his agenda before going to sleep, and though he knew it was just a little nasty to have waited until the middle of the night to deal with it, he picked up the phone and called Mike in L.A.

It took five rings, and the slur of sleep in his friend's voice gave Noah considerable satisfaction. "Hey, did I wake you up?"

"What? Noah? Where are you?"

"San Francisco. Remember?"

"Huh? No. . . . Sort of. It's two in the morning."

Noah heard another voice, slightly muffled, definitely female. "Congratulations, Mike. The blonde from the club?"

"Ah . . . Hmmmm."

"Okay, okay, not the time to go into it. I'm going to be away at least another week. Take care of my flowers while I'm gone."

"I can do that. Look, give me a number where I can— Whoa."

The low smoke of female laughter had Noah raising an eyebrow. "Later. You let my flowers die, I'll kick your butt."

The response was a sharp intake of breath, a great deal of whispering. Rolling his eyes, Noah hung up on a wild burst of laughter.

NOAH was surprised he remembered it so well, in such detail, with such clarity. He'd driven this way once before, but he'd been only eighteen. It shouldn't have been like coming home after a trip away, like waking up after a dream. He'd done his research, he'd studied photographs, but somehow he knew they couldn't prepare him for this deep, silent forest where the grand trees ruled.

He arrived at the lodge by three in the afternoon. He traveled up the same bumpy lane, first catching glimpses of stone and wood, the fairy-tale rooflines, the glint of glass that was the lodge. Then he spotted a smaller stone-and-wood structure nestled in the trees.

The wooden sign over the door read RIVER'S END NATURALIST CENTER. There was a walking path leading to it from the lodge. Wildflowers appeared to grow as they pleased around it, but his gardener's eye detected a human hand in the balance. Olivia had designed it so well, it seemed to have grown there.

Noah parked his car. He swung on his backpack, took out his suitcase, and went inside the lodge. He didn't see any dramatic changes in the lobby. The check-in was efficient and friendly, and Noah assured the clerk he could handle his baggage himself.

He'd requested a suite. There was a nap-taking sofa, a sturdy desk. The watercolor prints of local flora were better than decent, and the phone would support his modem. He dropped his suitcase at the foot of the sleigh bed. In the adjoining bath he considered the shower—he'd been in the car since six a.m.

He stripped, then diddled with the shower controls. Right decision, Brady, he thought as he let the hot water beat on his head. And after a beer in the lobby bar he'd scope out the place.

He wanted to go over to the center, find Olivia. Just look at her awhile. He'd do that in the morning, he thought.

Noah toweled off, tugged on jeans. There was a hard rap on the door. He grabbed a shirt and carried it with him to the door.

He recognized her instantly. She'd certainly changed.

Her face was thinner. Her mouth was firmer. He might have noted it wasn't smiling in welcome if he hadn't been dealing with the ridiculous and completely unexpected flash of pleasure.

Her hair had darkened to a color that reminded him of caramels. And she'd lopped it off. Lopped off all that gorgeous shiny hair. And yet it suited her better this way. The short, straight cut could have been called pixyish. But there was nothing fairylike about the woman in the doorway with her tall, athletic build.

He felt a foolish grin break out on his face. "Hi."

"Compliments of River's End Lodge." She thrust a stoneware bowl filled with fruit straight at him.

"Ah, thanks."

She was in the room in one long stride that had him backing up automatically. "You have a lot of nerve, sneaking in here this way."

Okay, he decided, it wasn't going to be a friendly reunion. "You're right, absolutely. I don't know what I was thinking of, calling ahead for reservations, registering at the desk that way."

"I told you to stay away from me."

"And I damn well did." The flash in her eyes had him narrowing his own. "Now we can sit down and discuss this like reasonable adults, or we can just stand here and snarl at each other."

"I have nothing to discuss with you. Go away and leave us alone."

"That's not going to happen." Noah sat. "I'm not going anywhere, Olivia. You might as well talk to me."

"I'm entitled to my privacy."

"Sure you are. You don't tell me anything you don't want to. We can start with what you've been doing the last half-dozen years."

Smug, smirky jerk, she thought. Olivia hated that he looked so much the same—the sun-streaked hair, the full mouth. "If you were half the man your father is, you'd respect my mother's memory."

That edgy little barb winged home. "You measured me by my father once before," Noah said. "Don't do it again."

"Money. They'll pay you big bucks for this book, won't they? Then you can bounce around the talk shows and spout off about your valuable insights on why my father butchered my mother."

"Don't you want to know why?" He spoke quietly.

"I know why, and it doesn't change anything. Go away, Noah. Go back and write about someone else's tragedy."

"Liv." He called out to her as she strode toward the door. "I won't go away. Not this time."

She didn't stop, didn't look back, but slammed the door smartly enough to have the pictures rattling on the walls.

THE food was great. Noah gave the MacBrides high marks on the lodge kitchen after two passes through the breakfast buffet. His bed had been comfortable, and if he'd been in the mood, he could have chosen from a very decent list of in-room movies.

He'd worked instead and now felt he deserved a morning to piddle. Trouble was, he mused, looking out the dining-room window at the steady, drumming rain, the weather wasn't quite as appealing as the rest of the fare.

Noah had already made use of the health club and had found it nicely modernized since his last visit. He could get a massage. Or he could do what he'd come for and start poking around. He could hunt up Olivia and argue with her again.

The bark of male laughter had him glancing over to a man dressed in a flannel shirt and work trousers, with thick silver hair. He worked the dining room, stopping by tables of those who, like Noah, were lingering over that last cup of coffee.

Rob MacBride, Noah thought, and sat back waiting for his turn. It didn't take long. "Pretty day, isn't it?"

"For ducks," Noah said. He was rewarded with that deep laugh.

"Rain's what makes us what we are here. I hope you're enjoying your stay."

"Very much. It's a great place. You've made a few changes since I was here last, but you've kept the tone." Noah held out his hand. "I'm Noah Brady, Mr. MacBride."

"Welcome back."

He saw no hint of recognition. "Thanks. I came here with my parents about twelve years ago—Frank and Celia Brady."

"We're always pleased to have—" The flicker came now and, along with it, quiet grief. "Frank Brady? Your father?"

"Yes."

"That's a name I haven't thought of in a very long time." Rob sat and skimmed his gaze over Noah's face. "Your father's well?"

"Yeah, he's good. Retired recently."

"Did you go into police work, like your dad?"

"No. I'm a writer."

"Really." Rob's face brightened. "Nothing like a good story. What sort of things do you write?"

"I write nonfiction. True crime." He could see the awareness moving over Rob's face. "I'm writing a book about what happened to your daughter. A few weeks ago Sam Tanner contacted me."

"Tanner. Why won't he let her rest? You think he'll tell you the truth?" Bitterness crackled in Rob's voice like ice.

"I can't say, but I can tell you I don't intend for this book to be Tanner's. I'm talking to everyone who was involved. That's why I'm here, Mr. MacBride—to understand and incorporate your view."

Rob rubbed his hands over his face. "Noah, do you have any idea how many times we were approached after Julie's death? To give interviews, to endorse books, movies, television features?"

"I can imagine, and I'm aware you refused them all."

"All," Rob agreed. "They offered us obscene amounts of money, promises, threats. The answer was always no. Why do you think I would say yes now, after all these years, to you?"

"Because I'm not going to offer money or make threats, and I'll give only one promise: I'll do right by your daughter."

"Maybe you will," Rob said after a moment. "I believe you'll try to. But Julie's gone, and I have to think of the family I have left. The wound still aches." He let out a long sigh. "A part of me, I admit, doesn't want what happened to be forgotten."

"I haven't forgotten. Tell me what you want remembered."

THE naturalist center was Olivia's baby. It had been her concept, her design. She'd supervised every aspect of the center, from the laying of stone to the arrangement of seats in the small theater, where visitors could watch a short documentary on the area's flora and fauna. In the year since she'd opened its doors to the public, she'd never been more content.

But that morning her mind was only half on the job as she took a group of visitors on an indoor tour of the local mammals. "The Roosevelt, or Olympic, elk is the biggest of the wapiti. In a very real way we owe the preservation of this area to this native animal, as it was to protect their breeding grounds and summer range that President Theodore Roosevelt issued the proclamation that created Mount Olympus National Monument."

She glanced up as the main door opened, and felt her nerves fray.

Noah gave her a slight nod, then began to wander around the main area. As a matter of pride, Olivia continued her lecture, moving from elk to black-tailed deer, from deer to marten, before she signaled to one of her staff to take over.

She wanted to go lock herself in her office, but she knew it would look cowardly. Instead she walked over and stood beside him as he examined an enlarged slide with apparent fascination.

"So that's a shrew."

"A wandering shrew, quite common in this region. We also have the Trowbridge, the masked, and the dusky shrew."

"I guess I'm only acquainted with city shrews."

"That's very lame humor."

"Yeah, but you've gotta start somewhere. You did a great job here, Liv. I knew you would."

"Really? I didn't realize you'd paid attention to any of my ramblings back then."

"I paid attention to everything about you, Olivia."

She shut down. "I'm not going back there. Not now, not ever."

"Fine. Let's stay here, then. Want to show me around?"

"You don't give a damn about natural science, so why waste each other's time?"

"Pardon me, but you're talking to someone who was raised on whale songs and the plight of the pelican."

Because Olivia wanted to smile, she sighed. "I'm busy."

"No, you're not. You can take a few minutes."

"I don't intend to discuss my family with you."

"Okay, let's talk about something else. What's in here?" Noah moved through a wide doorway. "Hey, this is cool." Centered in the room was a scale model of the Quinault valley. "Hawk's-eye view," he said, leaning over it. "Here's the lodge, the center." He tapped his finger on the protective dome. "There's the trail we took that day along the river. Your grandparents have a house, though, don't they? I don't see it here."

"Because it's private."

His gaze seemed to drive straight into hers. "Are you under this glass dome, Liv, tucked away where no one can get to you?"

"I'm exactly where I want to be."

"My book isn't likely to change that, but it might explain what happened that night. Sam Tanner's talking for the first time since the trial, and a dying man often chooses to clear his conscience."

"Dying?"

"The tumor." Noah watched with shocked alarm as her face went sheet white. "I'm sorry. I thought you knew."

"Are you telling me he's dying?"

"He has brain cancer. He only has months left. Come on, you need to sit down."

He took her arm, but Olivia jerked herself free. "Don't touch me." She turned quickly and strode through the next doorway.

Swearing under his breath, he went after her and caught up just as she turned into an office.

"This is an employees-only area," she said. "Take a hike."

"Sit down." He steered her around the desk and into the chair behind it. "I'm sorry." Crouching down, he took her hand without either of them really being aware of the gesture. "I wouldn't have dropped it on you that way. I thought Jamie would've told you."

"She didn't." Olivia looked down, saw her fingers linked with his. Mortally embarrassed, she shook free. "Stand up. All I need is someone coming in here and seeing you kneeling at my feet."

"I wasn't kneeling." But he straightened up, then opted to sit on the corner of the desk. "Sam wants to tell his story. If he doesn't, it dies with him. Is that really what you want?"

"It doesn't matter what I want. You'll do it anyway," she snapped. "And as for him, he wants to purge himself before it's too late and look for what? Forgiveness? Redemption?"

"Understanding maybe. I think he's trying to understand himself how it all happened. I want your part of it, Liv. You're the key. Your grandfather claims you have a photographic memory."

"My grandfather?" She leaped to her feet. "Stay away from him."

"He came up to my table after breakfast, which, from what I observed, he's in the habit of doing with guests. If you have a problem with his talking to me, you'll have to take it up with him."

"He's seventy. You've no business putting him through this."

Damn it, would she forever make him feel guilty? "We had a conversation. Then he agreed to a taped interview in my room. When we finished, he looked relieved, Liv. Sam isn't the only one with something to purge."

"He spoke with you? He never talks about it." She ran a nervous hand through her hair. "What's going on? I don't understand."

"Maybe it's just time. Why don't I tell you about my wild and exciting life and all my fascinating opinions? Once you see how charming I am, you'll have an easier time talking to me."

"You're not nearly as charming as you think you are."

"Sure I am. Let's have dinner."

Oh, they'd gone that route before. "No."

"All right, I'll just have to hire you to take me on a hike."

"Forget it."

"Oh, no. I'm a paying customer. Now, do you want to recommend a trail, or should I pick one at random?"

"You want to hike?" Oh, she'd give him a hike, Olivia thought. "Make the reservation out at the desk for seven tomorrow."

"That would be a.m.?"

"Is that a problem, city boy?"

"No. Just clarifying." Noah eased off the desk and found himself a great deal closer to her than was comfortable for either of them. And though he told himself not to do it, his gaze lowered to her mouth just long enough to make him remember. "Well, hmmm." He stepped aside. "I'll see you in the morning, then."

JUST after nine p.m. Mike entered the beach house. He'd meant to get there earlier, to give Noah's flowers a good watering before full dark, but one thing had led to another. Namely, one of his co-workers had challenged him to a marathon computer game of Mortal Kombat. But victory was its own reward, Mike thought. And to sweeten the pot, he'd called his date and asked if she'd like to meet him at Noah's for a dip in his hot tub.

He moseyed into the kitchen to see if Noah had any wine suitable for hot-tub seductions. He studied labels, chose one with a French name. He set it on the counter, then opened the refrigerator, wondering if Noah had any interesting food stocked. He was debating between a package of brie and a plate of sad-looking fried chicken when he caught a flash of movement out of the corner of his eye.

He straightened fast, felt a brilliant burst of pain. He reached up, thinking he'd bashed his head on the refrigerator. His hand came away wet; he stared dumbly at the blood. The second blow buckled his knees and sent him down into the dark.

Seven

IT WAS still raining when Noah's alarm buzzed at six. He slapped at it, opened his eyes to the gloom, and considered doing what any sensible man did on a rainy morning—sleeping through it. But a few hours' cozy oblivion didn't seem worth the smirking comments Olivia would lay on him. He rolled out of bed, stumbled through a shower, then dressed for the day.

Noah decided anyone planning on tromping around in the trees in the rain had to be crazy. He groused about it all the way down to the lobby, where he found several small groups of people suited up and helping themselves to complimentary coffee and doughnuts.

At seven, riding on a caffeine-and-sugar high, he felt nearly human. He snagged one last doughnut and headed out.

Olivia stood in the gloom with a big yellow dog, rain pattering on her bush-style hat. She acknowledged Noah with a nod, told him the Labrador's name was Shirley. "You set?"

Noah took another bite of his tractor wheel. "Yeah."

"Let's see." She stood back. "How long have those boots been out of the box, ace?"

Less than an hour, Noah thought. "Unless we're planning on climbing the Matterhorn, I'm up for it. I'm in shape."

"Health-club shape." She pressed a finger against his flat belly. "This won't be like your StairMaster. Where's your water bottle?"

Already irritated with her, he held out a hand, cupped it, and let rain pool in his palm. Olivia only shook her head. "Hold on a minute." She turned on her heel and headed back into the lodge.

"Is it me, or does she browbeat everyone?" Noah asked Shirley.

Olivia jogged back out with a plastic water bottle. "You always take your own water." She nimbly hooked it to his belt.

"Thanks for the personal service."

She nearly smiled, then attached a leash to the dog's collar. "Let's go."

Fog smoked along the ground, slid through the trees, tangled in the fronds of ferns. Rain pattered. The gloom thickened as they entered the forest. Noah felt suddenly small, eerily defenseless.

Olivia took out a flashlight, shined it straight up. "The overstory here is comprised of Sitka spruce, Douglas fir, and western red cedar. The trees and the profusion of epiphytes screen out sunlight and cause the distinctive green twilight."

"What's an epiphyte?"

"Like a parasite. Ferns, mosses, lichen. In this case they cause no real harmful effect to their hosts. You can see how they drape, form a kind of canopy in the overstory."

She switched off her light, pocketed it, and continued her spiel as they walked. He listened with half an ear. It was enough, he realized, just to look. Despite the rain and fog, there was the quiet green glow. Everything dripped and shimmered.

Olivia stopped abruptly and motioned for him to angle behind the wide column of a spruce. Then Noah heard whatever had alerted her, and felt the dog quivering between them.

Fifteen enormous elks, their racks like crowns, stepped out of the gloom.

"Where are the girls?" he muttered, and earned a quick glare.

One let out a deep bugling call that seemed to shake the trees. Then the elks slid into the shadows, their passing a rumble on the springy ground. "The females," Olivia said, "travel in herds with the younger males. More mature males, such as what we just saw, travel in smaller herds until late summer, when they become hostile with each other in order to cull out their harem."

"Harem, huh? Sounds like fun." He grinned. "So were those Roosevelt elk? The kind you were talking about yesterday?"

"Yes. We often see them on the trail this time of year."

They continued on. Olivia didn't hurry but gave Noah time to look, to ask questions. Rain sprinkled through the canopy, but the fog began to lift, thinning, tearing into swirls. The trail began to climb. The light changed subtly, until it was a luminous green pearled by weak sunlight that fell through small breaks in the canopy onto wildflowers.

"It reminds me of snorkeling off Mexico," Noah said. "The light's odd, not green like this really, but different, and the sun will cut through the surface, angle down. Everything's soft, full of shapes. Ever been snorkeling?"

"No."

"You'd like it."

"Why?"

"Well, you're stripped down to the most basic of gear, and you're taking on a world that isn't yours. You never know what you'll see next. My friend Mike and I spent two very memorable weeks snorkeling in Cozumel a couple of years back. So what do you do for play these days?"

"I take irritating city boys through the forest."

"I haven't irritated you for at least an hour. I clocked it. Wow! There it is."

"What?" Thrown off, she spun around.

"You smiled." He patted a hand to his heart. "Now I'm in love. Let's get married and raise Labradors."

She snorted out a laugh. "There, you irritated me again."

"No, I didn't. You're starting to like me again, Liv. You're not going to be able to help yourself. You ever get down to L.A.?"

"No." Olivia didn't quite meet his eyes.

"I thought you might go visit your aunt now and then."

"They come here at least twice a year."

"I got to tell you, it's tough to imagine Jamie tramping through the woods. Still, I guess since this is where she grew up, she'd slide back in easily. What about her husband?"

"Uncle David? He loves her enough to come and to let my grandmother haul him off to fish on the lake. He hates fishing. Once, we talked him into camping. I think that's how Aunt Jamie got her pearl-and-diamond necklace. It was his bribe that she never make him sleep in the woods again. No cell phones, no laptops, no room service." She slid him a sidelong glance. "You'd relate."

"Hey, I can give up my cell phone anytime I want. It's not an addiction." He was getting a little winded.

"You're starting to chug, ace. Want to stop?"

"I'm not chugging. That's Shirley."

The world opened up, with smoky peaks and green valleys, with a sky that was like burnished steel. The rain had stopped.

"What's this place?" Noah asked.

"We switched over to Three Lakes Trail."

He could see how the river cut through forest and hill, the jagged islands of rock pushing up through the stone-colored water. The wind flew into his face and was swallowed up by the trees.

"If we follow the trail another three and a half miles," Olivia said, "we'll come to the lake area. Or we can turn back."

"I can do another three and a half miles."

"All right, then."

Olivia hiked ahead as if she were strolling down Wilshire Boulevard. He tried not to hate her for it. In less than a mile his feet were screaming. She hadn't bothered to mention the last leg was straight up. Noah tried to keep his mind off his abused body by taking in the scenery, speculating on what Olivia had brought for lunch.

A hawk sailed overhead with a regal spread of wings and a single wild cry that echoed forever. There was the glinting black passing of a raven and the first thin patch of snow.

"We can stop here." Olivia shrugged off her pack. "I didn't think you'd make it, at least not without whining."

"The whining was a close call a few times, but it was worth it." He looked out over the three lakes, each one the dull silver of an old mirror. Softly reflected in them, the mountains rippled on the surface, more shadow than image.

"As your prize for not whining, we have some of my grandmother's famous beef-and-barley stew."

"I could eat an ocean of it."

She pulled a small blanket out of her pack. "Spread that out and sit down. You won't get an ocean, but you'll get enough to take your mind off how much your feet hurt."

"I brought some of my complimentary fruit." Noah smiled as he snapped the blanket. "In case your plan was to starve me."

"No. I thought about just ditching you in the forest and seeing if you ever found your way out. But I like your parents."

"You could learn to like me, too." He ruffled Shirley's head as she came over. "Your dog likes me."

"She likes drinking out of toilets. Her taste is not to be trusted." Olivia got out a widemouthed thermos, poured the stew into bowls.

"Wow, that smells fabulous."

"My grandmother's a hell of a cook."

"So can I come to dinner?"

Olivia kept her gaze focused on the thermos as she replaced the lid. "When I got home last night, she'd been crying. My grandfather had told her you were here, what you wanted, and that he'd talked to you. I don't know what they said to each other, but I know they haven't said much to each other since."

"I'm sorry for that."

"Are you?" She looked up, her eyes hot. "You're sorry that you brought back intolerable grief, caused a strain between two people who've loved each other for over fifty years?"

"Yes, I am." His eyes never wavered from hers.

"But you'll still write the book." She stirred her stew.

"Yes." Noah picked up his bowl. "I will. If I back off, Tanner's just going to tell his story to someone else. That someone might not be sorry, sorry enough to tread as carefully as possible, to make sure what he writes is true. He wouldn't have the connection, however tenuous, to your family to make it matter to him."

"Now you're a crusader?"

"No. I'm just a writer. A good one."

Had he been this sure of himself before? She didn't think so.

He studied her as he spooned up the stew. "I won't crowd and push. We'll take it at your pace."

"I don't know if I'll agree or not," Olivia said after a moment. "But I won't even consider talking to you unless you leave my grandmother out of it. She can't handle it. I promised her that you won't go over to the house asking her to talk."

"All right." Noah sighed at her suspicious frown. "What? You want me to sign it in blood?"

"Maybe. Don't expect me to trust you."

"You did once. You will again before we're finished."

"You're annoyingly sure of yourself. There's a pair of harlequin ducks on the lake. You can just spot them on the far side."

He glanced over. He'd already figured out that she shifted over into the nature mode when she wanted to change the subject.

"I'll be here through the week," he said. "If you haven't decided by the time I leave, you can call me. I'll come back."

"I'll think about it. Now be quiet." She gave Shirley a dog biscuit. "One of the best parts of being here is the quiet."

Satisfied, Noah dug into his stew. He was toying with asking if there was more when a scream had him flipping the bowl in the air. "Stay here," he ordered, leaping up. "Someone's in trouble."

Olivia scrambled to her feet as he turned to run toward the sound. "Wait!" She grabbed his sleeve. "It's a marmot." She fought back a laugh. "It isn't a damsel in distress, but a— There." She gestured.

There were two of them, with grizzled coats of gray-brown, their heavy bodies lumping along. One of them stood up on its hind legs, looking at dog and humans with a jaundiced eye.

"Terrific." Noah turned his head, eyed Olivia narrowly.

"Well, you were really brave. I felt completely protected from any terrifying marauding marmots."

"Smart aleck." He tapped his fist on her chin, then left it there. Her eyes were deep and gold with humor, her lips curved and soft. Color glowed in her cheeks, and the wind ruffled her hair.

He saw the change in her eyes, the darkening of awareness, as he'd seen it years before. He didn't calculate the move. He just made it. As his mouth closed over hers, his mind clicked in and shouted *mistake!* Her lips warmed under his. He deepened the kiss.

Olivia had meant to stop him, but the rush of feelings stunned her. The way it had been between them before. Exactly as it had been. Both of them had changed, yet the need was exactly the same. He eased away, wanting to see it.

She took defense in temper. "This isn't going to happen again."

"Liv"—his voice was quiet and serious—"it already has."

No, she told herself. Absolutely not. She spun around and began tossing everything back in her pack.

Noah couldn't pull all of his thoughts back in, but he managed to walk over, turn her around. "Listen—"

"Hands off." She knocked them away. "Do you think I don't know what this is about? If you can't convince me with your charm, add some physical stimuli. Just like before."

"Oh, no, you don't." With a wiry strength she'd underestimated, he held her still. "You know damn well I didn't hike for four hours just so I could move on you. I'd have done it in some nice, warm room before I had blisters."

"You did move on me," Olivia corrected icily. She glared at him, while Shirley whimpered and bumped her body between theirs.

"I didn't plan it. It just happened." Noah let her go. "How long are you going to make me pay for a mistake I made six years ago? How many ways do you want me to apologize for it?"

"I don't want an apology. I want to forget it."

"But you haven't. And neither have I. Do you want to know how many times I thought of you?"

"No," she said quickly, the single word a rush. "No, I don't."

ON THE walk back, Olivia became the impersonal guide again. As the lodge came in sight, the light was fading to a pearly gray with wild streaks of color in the western sky. But Noah wasn't in the mood to appreciate it. For heaven's sake, he'd only kissed her.

As he pulled open the door to the lodge, he turned to her, started to make some blisteringly polite comment on her ability as a guide, when the desk clerk hurried over.

"Mr. Brady, you had a call. Your mother said it was urgent."

Everything inside him froze. "My mother?"

"Yes. She called this morning and again at three. She asked that you call her at home as soon as you came in."

"You can call from in here." Olivia took his arm gently. The blank fear on his face set off alarms in her head as she led him into a back office. "You can dial direct. I'll just—"

She started to step back, but his hand clamped over hers. He said nothing, just held on while he dialed the number. It rang once, twice, before he heard his mother's voice.

"Mom?"

"Oh, Noah, thank goodness."

His fingers tightened on Olivia's. "What's wrong?"

"It's Mike. He's in the hospital, in intensive care. He's in a coma. They're doing everything they—" She began to weep.

Noah felt his guts slide. "What happened? A car accident?"

"No, no. Someone hurt him. Someone hit him and hit him. From behind, they say. He was in your house last night."

"At the beach house? He was at my place?"

"Yes. I didn't hear about it until early this morning."

"I'll be there as soon as I can. I'll take the first flight out."

"We'll be at the hospital. Maggie and Jim—" Celia's voice broke when she spoke of Mike's parents. "They shouldn't be alone."

"I'm on my way. I'll come straight there." Noah hung up the phone, then just stared at it. "My friend— He was attacked. He's in a coma. I have to go home."

She felt his fingers tremble. "I'll book you a flight. Go pack what you need. I'll get you to the airport."

"Just get me a seat, whatever gets me to L.A. quickest. I'll be ready in five minutes."

He was as good as his word and was back at the office before she'd completed the booking, carrying his backpack and laptop.

"You're set," Olivia said. "It's a private airstrip, friends of my grandparents. They'll take off as soon as you get there."

She headed out of the office, jogged to a Jeep in the side lot, unlocked it, and climbed in as he tossed his pack in the back.

"I appreciate it."

"It's all right. Don't worry about the rest of your things and your car. We'll deal with it." She drove fast, her hands on the wheel, her eyes straight ahead. "I'm sorry about your friend."

Noah laid his head back against the seat. "I've known him forever. Second grade. Pudgy kid, a complete dork. He's the sweetest person I know. Loyal and harmless." He pressed his hands to his face, then pounded his fist on the dash. "He's in a damn coma! And it's my fault. I sent him over there. I didn't take her seriously enough."

"Who are you talking about?"

"I was seeing this woman for a while. It wasn't serious on my end, but I just sort of drifted along. When it got complicated, I broke things off. Then it got nasty. She trashed my house."

"That's horrible. Why didn't you have her arrested?"

"Couldn't prove it. Everyone knew she'd done it, just her style, but there wasn't much to be done about it. A few days ago she tossed a few more threats in my face, made another scene. Then I go flying off and tell Mike to water my flowers while I'm gone."

Olivia could feel the pain coming off him in shaky waves. And couldn't stand it. She wanted to pull over to hold him until he found some comfort. Instead she tightened her hands on the wheel and punched the gas.

NOAH was running on nerves alone by the time he rushed off the elevator in ICU. He saw his mother and father sitting on a bench in the silent hallway. Guilt and fear balled in his throat.

"Oh, Noah." Celia got up to throw her arms around him.

"I need to see him. Can I—"

"There's no change." She rubbed Noah's back. "We've been taking turns going in. Jim and Maggie are in there now."

Swamped with grief, Noah lowered to the bench, his head in his hands. "I'm going to find a way to make Caryn pay for this."

"That's not what you need to focus on now," said Frank.

"You know she did this." Noah straightened, stared at Frank with burning eyes. "You know she did."

"She'll be questioned as soon as they locate her." He gripped Noah's shoulder. "She can't be charged without evidence. But I'm telling you, as your father and as a cop, to stay away from her. If you follow through on what you're feeling right now, you'll only make matters worse. Let her box herself in, so we can put her away."

If Mike died, Noah thought, they wouldn't be able to put her away deep enough.

NOAH stayed at the hospital, and every time he went into the tiny room, he saw Mike still and pale, his head swathed in bandages.

The next day, as morning swam toward afternoon, rage built inside him. He couldn't let Caryn get away with what she'd done. He couldn't do anything but hope and pray and stand at his friend's bedside. She'd wanted a shot at him. Hell, he'd give it to her. He strode to the elevator, with hate blooming black in his heart.

"Noah?"

"What?" He glanced at the brunette. She wore a lab coat with a stethoscope in her pocket. "Are you one of Mike Elmo's doctors?"

"No. I—"

"I know you," he interrupted. "Don't I?"

"We met at the club—you, Mike, my friend, and I. I'm Dory."

"Right." The pretty brunette who stood up for him the night Caryn had come in. "You're a doctor?"

"Emergency medicine. I'm on break and wanted to see Mike. You look like you could use some air. Let's take a walk."

"I was just heading out."

"Let's take a walk," she repeated. She'd seen murder in a man's eye before. "Mike's tests have been good." She punched the elevator button. "He's critical, but he's also young and healthy."

"He's been in a coma for a day and a half."

Dory nudged Noah into the elevator with her. "Sometimes a coma is just the body's way of focusing in on healing. And he did come around once in the ambulance on the way here. It was brief, but I think he recognized me, and that's a very positive sign."

"You? You were with him?"

She stepped into the main lobby, led him outside. "I was meeting him at your house. When I got there, the door was open. Mike was on the kitchen floor, facedown. Glass all over the place. Wine bottle. I had my bag, did what I could on the scene."

"Is he going to die?"

She turned her face up to the sun. "I don't know. Medically, he's got an even chance, maybe even better than even. Still, medicine has limits, and it's up to him now. I'm half crazy about him."

"No kidding?"

"Yeah. I know he started off that night with this thing for Steph. But they sort of ran out of steam, and I felt sorry for Mike. We started talking and had this big click happen."

"That was you the other night on the phone?"

"Yeah."

"Mike Elmo and the sexy doctor." Absurdly pleased, Noah shook his head. "That's terrific."

She laughed. "He thinks you walk on water. I didn't say that to make you sad," she hurried on when the light went out of Noah's eyes. "I said it because I think he's a great guy, and he thinks you're a great guy. So I figure he's right. And I figure that when I ran into you upstairs, you'd had enough and were going to go find that lunatic Caryn and do something that wouldn't solve anything."

"She wanted to hurt me. She didn't give a damn about Mike."

"She did hurt you. She hurt you where it matters most. Let's go back up. I only have a few minutes left, and I want to see him."

They went back inside and moved into the elevator. His mood almost light, Noah stepped off on Mike's floor. Then his heart crashed to his feet as he saw Maggie Elmo sobbing in his mother's arms.

"No!" Yanking free of Dory's restraining hand, he raced down the corridor.

"Noah, wait!" Celia shifted to block his path before he could shove through the doors into the ICU. "Maggie, tell him."

"He opened his eyes." Maggie held out both hands to Noah. "He looked at me and said 'Mom.' " She laid her head on his shoulder. "He woke up, Noah. He woke up." Noah buried his face in her hair.

Eight

S O WHEN were you going to tell me about Dr. Delicious?"

"Is she a babe or what?" Mike grinned.

"A brainy babe. Why's she hanging around with you?"

"She digs me. What can I say?" Mike still tended to tire easily, and the headaches came with tedious regularity. But they'd jumped him up to good condition and into a regular room. "I think I'm in . . . you know. With her," he said.

Noah gaped. " 'You know' is a very big thing. You were only seeing her a little while before you had your head broken ten days ago. You've been stuck in a hospital bed ever since."

"I asked her to marry me."

"What?"

"She said yes." Mike's grin turned into his puppy-dog smile.

"We're going to get married next spring, because she wants the works. You know, the church, the flowers, the white dress."

"Wow." Noah figured he'd better sit down, then realized he already was. "Wow. You really mean it, don't you?"

"I want to be with her. And when I am, I keep thinking, This is right. It feels exactly right. I don't know how to explain it."

"I guess you just did. Nice going, Mike." With a sudden laugh Noah surged to his feet. "Married. And to a doctor. Good thing. She'll be able to stitch you up every time you trip over your feet. Does she know you're a complete klutz?"

"Yeah. She loves that about me."

"I guess you won't be coming over and raiding my fridge every other night after . . ." He trailed off, remembering.

"It wasn't your fault. You didn't know Caryn was going to go postal. Jeez, I wish I could remember, but I keep coming up blank. Maybe I saw her. If I could say I saw her, they'd lock her up."

"They'd have to find her first. She skipped. None of her friends know where she is, or they're not saying. She packed clothes, got a cash advance on her credit cards, and split. I guess if the police come up with some evidence, they might take a look for her."

"So now that you know I'm going to live and that crazy broad is off somewhere, you better get back to work."

Noah wandered to the window. "I've been thinking about getting Jamie Melbourne's husband to talk to me."

"So do it."

"I'm waiting for my car." He knew he was stalling. "Someone's driving it down from the lodge tomorrow. You kicking me out?"

"What are friends for?"

OLIVIA sat in the car and studied Noah's house. It wasn't what she'd envisioned at all. It was pretty, almost feminine in the soft tones of wood. His garden wasn't some haphazard bachelor attempt to brighten up his real estate, but a careful, clever arrangement.

She'd been right to follow her impulse to take the chore of returning Noah's car herself. Even though it had caused difficulties with her grandparents, she'd done the right thing. She slipped out of the car, intending to go straight to the door, knock, give him his keys, call a cab, and get on her way to her aunt's as quickly as possible. But she couldn't resist the flowers—the charm of verbena, the chipper Gerber daisies, the bright reliable petunias.

He hadn't been quite as conscientious with the weeding as he might have been, and her gardener's heart had her crouching down to tug up the random invaders. Within a minute she was humming and losing herself in a well-loved task.

NOAH was so happy to see his car sitting in its usual spot that he overtipped the driver and bolted out of the taxicab.

"Oh, baby, welcome home," he murmured. Then he spotted Olivia. She looked so pretty, kneeling by his flowers.

He started toward her. "This is a surprise," he said, and watched her head snap up, her body freeze. "I wasn't expecting to see you weeding my gummy snaps."

"They needed it." Furiously embarrassed, she got to her feet.

"What are you doing here, Liv?"

"Returning your car. You were told to expect it."

"I'm not complaining. Come on in."

"I just need you to call me a cab."

"Come on in," he repeated, and unlocked the front door. Noah jabbed a code into a security panel. "Just had this installed."

Liv followed him inside. "I can't stay."

"Uh-huh. I'll just get us a glass of wine while you think of the reason you can't sit down for fifteen minutes after driving all the way down the coast."

"My aunt and uncle are expecting me."

"This minute?" he asked from the kitchen.

"No, but—"

"Well, then. You want chips with this? I think I have some."

"No. I'm fine. I'm glad your friend's going to be okay."

"It was touch and go the first couple of days. But yeah, he's going to be okay. In fact, he's going to be great. He got his skull fractured, fell in love, and got engaged—not necessarily in that order—in just over a two-week period. Let's drink to Mike."

"Why not?" Olivia touched the rim of her glass to his, then sipped. "Pouilly-Fuissé on a weekday evening. Very classy."

His grin flashed. "You know your wine."

"Must be the Italian from my grandmother's side."

"And can the MacBride half build a Guinness?"

"I imagine." It was just a little too comfortable being here with him. "Well, if you'd call—"

"Let's go out on the deck." He took her hand, went over, opened the sliding door. "Too early for sunset. You'll have to come back."

The breeze fluttered in off the ocean, whispered warm over her face. The water was bold and blue, chopping in against the shore.

"Some backyard."

"I thought the same thing about yours when I saw your forest." Noah trailed a finger down Olivia's arm, from elbow to wrist, in the absentminded gesture of a man used to touching. She stepped back, the deliberate gesture of a woman who wasn't.

"I really have to go. I called Uncle David from Santa Barbara, so they're expecting me by now."

"How long are you staying?"

"Just a few days."

"Have dinner with me before you go."

"I'm going to be busy."

"I like seeing you. Give me a chance, Olivia."

"You want a story. I haven't decided if I'm giving it to you."

"I want a story. But I said I liked seeing you, and I meant it. I've thought about you, Olivia, for years. Maybe I wish I hadn't, and you've made it clear you'd rather I didn't think of you at all."

"It doesn't really matter what I'd rather." She finished the wine, set it aside. "I have to go."

"Then I'll drive you."

"All right."

He took her hand again as they walked through the house, a habit she was almost getting used to. When they got in the car, he asked her, "So did you have any trouble finding your way down here?"

"I had a map. I'm good at reading maps. And this is a great ride," she added. "Handles like a dream."

"You open her up?"

She gave him a wisp of a smile. "Maybe." Then she laughed, enjoying the rush of wind as the car picked up speed. "It's a bullet. How many speeding tickets do you collect in the average year?"

He winced. "I'm a cop's son. I have great respect for the law."

"Okay, how many does your father have fixed for you during the average year?"

"Family doesn't keep track of small acts of love."

WHEN Noah swung up the drive, Olivia smiled as the Melbourne mansion came into view. "We have pictures of it, even videos, but they don't come up to the in-your-face."

"A nice fixer-upper priced for the young marrieds."

She laughed, then got out of the car as soon as he stopped. David Melbourne came out of the house, and she let out a whoop of delight, half leaping into his arms for a fierce hug.

"Welcome, traveler." He laughed, cupped her face. "Let's look at you. Pretty as ever." He'd aged well, Noah thought. He'd either discovered the fountain of youth or had an excellent cosmetic surgeon.

"Missed you."

"Goes double." He kissed her, then, hugging a protective arm around her shoulder, turned to Noah. The cooling of voice was subtle but unmistakable. "It was nice of you to deliver my girl."

"My pleasure."

"Uncle David, this is Noah Brady."

"Yes, I know."

"I just need to get my things out of the trunk," Olivia said.

"I'll get them." Noah unlocked the trunk, took out her bag.

David took the case from Noah. "Jamie got caught on the phone. She should be off by now. Why don't you run in, Livvy?"

"All right. Thanks for the lift, Brady."

"No problem, MacBride," he said. "I'll be in touch."

525

She said nothing to that, only jogged up the stairs and inside.

David set Olivia's suitcase down, glanced toward the house. "You seem to have established some kind of rapport with Livvy."

"Is that a problem for you?" Noah asked.

"I have no idea. I don't know you."

"Mr. Melbourne, I was under the impression you were supportive of the book I'm writing."

"I was. I thought enough time had passed, and I believed that a writer of your caliber could do justice to the tragedy."

"I appreciate that. What changed your mind?"

"I didn't realize how much this would upset Val." Concern clouded his eyes. "My mother-in-law. I feel partially responsible, as I did support it, and that support certainly influenced Jamie into giving you her cooperation. Val's one of the most important people in my life. I don't want her hurt."

Protection, Noah mused. The family was a puzzle made up of pieces of protection and defense. "I've already given Liv my word that I won't ask her grandmother to talk to me."

"The book itself pulls her into it," David said. "Noah, I'm going to do my best to ease my mother-in-law's feelings over it. Then if I can, I'll talk to you. You'll have to excuse me now." He picked up the suitcase. "I don't want to miss any time with Livvy."

BY THE time Olivia crawled into bed that night, she was worn to the bone by the drive, the elaborate dinner her aunt had arranged, and the nonstop conversation as they'd caught up with one another. Still, her last thought, before sleep sucked her under, was of Noah standing on the deck of his pretty house, his back to the sea.

FRANK was sitting in his kitchen enjoying a beer. On a notepad he drew circles, squiggles, *x*'s as he toyed with a play for the basketball team he coached.

When the doorbell rang, he left his beer and his doodling on the table, thinking it might be one of his players.

It was a young woman, with the tall, rangy build he could have used on the court. A little too old to fit into his twelve- to sixteen-year-old league, he thought; then images overlapped in his mind and had him grabbing her hands. "Livvy! You're all grown up."

"I didn't think you'd recognize me." And the fact that he had, with such obvious delight, warmed her. "I'd have known you anywhere. You look just the same."

"Never lie to a cop, even a retired one. Come in. Sit down."

There was a pressure in her chest, heavy, tight. "I told myself to call first. Then I didn't. I just came."

"I'm glad you did. I knew you were grown up, but every time I picture you, even when I read your letters, I see a little girl."

"I always see a hero." She let herself go into his arms, let herself be held. And her jitters eased. "I knew I'd feel better. I knew it would be all right if I could see you."

"What's wrong, Livvy? Is this about Noah's book?"

"Part of it. As much as I didn't want to, as much as I told myself I wouldn't, I trust him to do it right. It's going to be painful for me to talk to him, but I can do it."

"You can trust him. I don't understand his work, but I understand Noah."

Puzzled, Olivia shook her head. "How can you not understand his work? It's brilliant."

Now Frank was confused. "I'm surprised to hear you say that. How you could feel that, as a survivor of a murder victim."

"And the daughter of a murderer," she finished. "That's exactly why. I read his first book as soon as it came out. I don't know if I can say I liked it, but I understood what he was doing. He takes the most wicked of crimes, the most unforgivable. And he keeps them that way. When you read about a murder in the paper, you say, oh, how awful. Then you move on. He humanizes it, makes it so real that you can't. He strips down everyone who was involved to their most desperate and agonized emotions."

That, she realized, was what she feared about him the most—that he would strip her to the soul. "He makes them matter," she continued. "So that what was done matters." She smiled a little, but her eyes were horribly sad. "So that what his father did, every day, year in and year out, matters. You're his standard for everything that's right and strong."

"Livvy . . ." Words clogged in Frank's throat. "You make me ashamed that I never looked close enough."

"I'm nervous about talking to Noah. I'm going back home tomorrow, so he'll have to deal with me on my turf. I wondered if you and Mrs. Brady would like to come up sometime, have a couple of free weeks at the lodge. I know he gets out in a few weeks. I thought, somehow, if you were there, just for the first couple of days after, it would be all right. I haven't let myself really think about it, but the time's coming. Just a few weeks—" Something in Frank's face—the grim line of his mouth, the shadow in his eyes—stopped her. "What is it?"

"It's about him getting out, Liv. I was contacted this morning. Whenever there's something new about Tanner, I get a call. Due to his health, the overcrowded system, time served in prison—"

"They're letting him out sooner, aren't they? When?"

Olivia's eyes were huge, locked on his. Frank thought of the child who'd stared at him from her hiding place. This time he could do nothing to soften the blow. "Two weeks ago," he told her.

THE phone shattered Noah's concentration into a thousand irretrievable shards. He swore at it, stared at the last line he'd written, and tried to find the rhythm again. Finally he snatched it up. "What the hell do you want?"

"Just to say good-bye. Bye."

"Wait, Liv. Wait. Don't hang up. You don't return my calls for two days, and then you catch me at a bad moment. You got my messages?" All ten thousand of them, he thought.

"Yes. I haven't had time to return them until now. And I only have a minute as it is. They're already boarding."

"What? You're at the airport? You're leaving already?"

"Yes. My plans changed." Her father was out of prison. Was he already in L.A.? Is this where he would come first? Olivia schooled her voice to sound casual. "I have to get back, and I thought I'd let you know. If you still want to talk to me regarding your book, you can reach me at the lodge."

"Go back in the morning. Olivia, I want to see you."

"You know where to find me. We'll work out some sort of schedule that's convenient for the interviews."

"The book isn't everything that's going on here between us. Change your flight. I'll come pick you up."

"I don't want to be here," she said flatly. "I'm going home." To where it was safe. She broke the connection.

OLIVIA didn't relax until the plane was in the air and she could nudge her seat back, close her eyes. If and when Noah contacted her, she'd deal with it and him. Telling him her memories would only be words, words that couldn't hurt her now.

The monster was loose. The warning seemed to whisper in her ear, edged with a kind of jumping glee.

It didn't matter. She wouldn't let it matter. Whether or not they'd unlocked his cell, he'd been dead to her for a long, long time. She hoped she'd been dead to him as well. That he didn't think of her. Or if he did, that every thought caused him pain.

She turned from the window and willed herself to sleep.

SLEEP didn't come easily to some. It was full of fear and sound and bloody images.

The monster was loose. And it cavorted in dreams, shambled on thick legs into the heart, and poured out in bitter tears. The monster knew there would be no end without more death.

Livvy. The name was a silent sob. The love for her was as real as it had been from the moment she'd been born. And the fear of her was as real as it had been on the night blood had been spilled.

She would be sacrificed only if there was no choice.

"OUT? What do you mean he's out?"

"He got out two weeks ago. His lawyer filed a hardship plea, and they bumped up his release date." Frank settled down on a deck chair. His son had taken advantage of an overcast day and a quiet beach to work outside.

Noah paced from one end of the deck to the other. "He must have known the last time I went to see him. He didn't tell me. Well, where the hell did he go?"

"Actually, I thought you might have that information."

"He hasn't given me his forwarding address. Early release?" He looked at Frank. "Not parole, so he doesn't have to check in."

"The state of California considers him rehabilitated."

"Do you?"

"Which you is asking the question? My son or the writer?"

Noah's face closed up immediately. "Never mind."

"I didn't mean I wouldn't answer, Noah. I was just curious."

"You're the one who compartmentalizes what I am and what I do. For me they're in the same drawer."

"You're right. I've been giving that some thought recently." Frank sighed, laid his hands on his knees. "I thought you'd be a cop. I guess I had that idea in my head for a long time."

"I know I disappointed you."

The instinctive denial was on his tongue. Frank paused and gave his son the truth instead. "I had no right to be disappointed, Noah, but you were always interested in what I did when you were a kid. You'd ask me all these questions about a case and write it all up. I didn't see that for what it was."

"I never wanted to close cases, Dad. I wanted to study them."

"When you started writing books, started digging into things that were over and done, I took it as a reflection on what I had done, as if you were saying that it wasn't enough to do the job, gather the evidence, make the arrest, get the conviction. I let my pride get in the way of seeing what you were doing and what it meant to you. I want you to know I'm sorry I never gave you the respect you deserved for doing work you were meant to do, and doing it well."

"Well"—emotion slid through him—"it's a day for surprises."

"I've always been proud of you, Noah. You've never been anything but a joy to me as a son and as a man." Frank had to clear his throat before he embarrassed both of them. "Now I'm going to give more consideration to what you do. Fair enough?"

"Yeah, that's fair enough."

"I'll start by telling you I'll do that interview sort of thing, when you have the time for it."

"I've got time now. Just let me get a fresh tape."

IN HIS office, Noah was typing up his notes from the interview with his father when the phone rang. He jolted, and realized that he'd been working for hours. The first streaks of sunset were now staining the sky through his window as he answered the phone.

"It's Sam Tanner."

Noah snatched up a pencil. "Where are you?"

"I'm outside watching the sun go down over the water."

"Are you in San Francisco, Sam?"

"I was in San Francisco long enough. I wanted to come home."

Noah's pulse picked up. "You're in L.A.?"

"I got a room off of Sunset. It's not what it used to be."

"Give me the address."

"I'm not there now. Actually, I'm down the road from you. Watching the sun set," he said almost dreamily. "The place serves tacos and beer and salsa that makes your eyes sting."

"Tell me where you are. I'll meet you."

SAM wore new khakis and a chambray shirt. He sat at one of the little iron tables on the patio of the Mexican place and stared out over the water. Noah ordered tacos, another beer for each of them.

"What does it feel like?"

With a kind of wonder Sam watched an in-line skater skim by. "Part of me keeps expecting someone to stop me, take me back, say it had all been a mistake. Another part is waiting to be recognized, to have someone run over for my autograph."

"Do you want to be recognized?"

"I was a star. You need the attention, not just to feed the ego, but to stroke the child. If you weren't a child, how good an actor could you be?" Sam gave a small, sick smile.

The waitress clunked their food and drinks down. Once she'd walked away, Noah leaned forward. "Coming to L.A. was a risk because someone's bound to recognize you sooner or later."

"Where else would I go? It's changed. I got lost twice walking around. New faces on the street, on the billboards. People driving around in big, chunky Jeeps. And you can't smoke anywhere."

Noah had to laugh at the absolute bafflement in the statement. "I imagine the food's better than San Quentin's."

"I forgot places like this existed." Sam picked up a taco, studied it. "I'd forgotten that before I went inside, if it wasn't the best, I wasn't interested. If I wasn't going to be seen, admired, envied, what was the point?" He bit in, crunching the shell. For a few moments he ate in concentrated silence. "I was a jerk."

Noah lifted a brow. "Can I quote you?"

"That's what this is about, isn't it? I had everything—success, adulation, power, wealth. I had the most beautiful woman in the world who loved me. I didn't value what I had, so I lost it."

Noah sipped his beer. "Did you kill your wife?"

He didn't answer at first, only watched the last sliver of sun sink red into the sea. "Yes." His gaze shifted, locked on Noah's.

"Why did you kill her?"

"Because I couldn't be what she asked me to be. Now ask me if I picked up the scissors that night and stabbed them into her body."

"All right. Did you?"

"I don't know." His eyes shifted to the water again. "I just don't know. I remember it two ways, and both seem real. I stopped thinking it mattered. Then they told me I was going to die. I need to know, and you're going to figure out which of the two ways is real."

"Which one are you going to tell me?"

"Neither, not yet. I need the money. I opened an account at this bank." Sam brought out a scrap of paper. "That's my account number. They do this electronic transfer. That'd be the best way."

"All right." Noah pocketed the paper. "It'll be there tomorrow."

NOAH CALLED OLIVIA THE next morning, caught her at her desk at the center. The sound of her husky voice made him smile.

"Hello, Ms. MacBride. Miss me?"

"Not particularly."

"I don't believe it. You recognized my voice too easily."

"Why wouldn't I? You talk more than any three people I know put together."

"And you don't talk enough, but I've got your voice in my head. I had a dream about you last night, all soft, watery colors and slow motion. We made love on the bank of the river."

"That's very interesting. That riverbank is a public area."

He laughed. "I'm becoming seriously crazy about you, Liv. Did you like the flowers I sent?"

"They're very nice and completely unnecessary."

"Sure they were. They make you think of me. I want you to keep me right in the front of your mind, Liv, so we can pick things up when I get there."

"The lodge is booked well in advance this time of year."

"I'll think of something. Liv, I need to tell you I've seen Tanner, spoken with him. He's here in Los Angeles. I thought you'd feel better knowing where he is."

"Yes, I suppose I do. I have to go—"

"Liv, you can tell me how you feel. You can talk to me."

"I don't know how I feel. I only know I can't let where he is or what he's doing change my life."

"You may find out some changes don't have to hurt. Keep thinking about me, Olivia."

She hung up, let out a long breath. "Keep dreaming," she murmured, and skimmed a finger over the petals of a sunny daisy.

She hadn't been able to resist keeping them in her office. She'd recognized what he'd done, found it sweet and very clever. The flowers he ordered were all varieties he had in his own garden. The garden she hadn't been able to resist. He had to know that looking at them would make her think of him.

She'd lied when she'd told him she didn't miss him. It surprised her how much she wished they were different people in a different situation. Then they could be lovers, maybe even friends, without the shadows clinging to their relationship.

There was a knock on her door. Olivia answered it with a grunt.

"Was that a come in or go to hell?" Rob wanted to know as he gently shook the package he carried.

"It's come in to you. What's in the box?"

"Don't know. It looks like an overnight from Los Angeles to you. I'd guess it's from the same young man who sent you the flowers." He set the package on the desk. "How's my girl?"

"I'm fine. Don't worry about me, Grandpop."

"I'm allowed to worry. It's part of the job description." She'd been so tense when she'd come back from California. "It doesn't matter that he's out, Livvy. I've made my peace with that. I hope you will."

"I'm working on it." She rose to tidy some files. "Noah just called. He wanted to let me know he'd seen him, spoken to him."

"It's best you know. This young man"—Rob nodded toward the flowers—"he's bringing you an awful lot to face at one time. But he's got a straight look in his eye, makes me want to trust you with him." He headed for the door. "Aren't you going to open the package?"

"No. It'll only encourage him." She grinned.

After Rob left, Olivia used her Leatherman knife to break the sealing tape. She lifted the lid and probed through the Styrofoam chips. Glass or china, she thought. Some sort of figurine. She wondered if Noah had actually tracked down a statue of a marmot, was laughing at the idea when she freed the figurine.

The laugh died in her throat. She dropped the figurine as if it were a live snake, poised to strike.

And stared, trembling and swaying, at the benevolent and beautiful face of the Blue Fairy atop the music box.

"I NEVER wanted to be alone." Sam held the coffee Noah had given him and squinted against the sun. "Being alone was like a punishment to me. A failure. Julie was good at it, often preferred it. She didn't need the spotlight the way I did."

"Did or do?" Noah asked, and watched Sam smile.

"When we separated, the prospect of living alone was terrifying."
He glanced back at Noah's house, then out to the ocean. "You like
it here, being alone?"

"My kind of work requires big chunks of solitude."

Sam only nodded and fell silent.

Noah had debated the wisdom of conducting interviews at his
own place. In the end, it had seemed most practical. They'd have
privacy and, by setting up on the deck, give Sam his wish to be outside. He hadn't been able to come up with a good argument against
it, as Sam already had his address.

He waited while Sam lit a cigarette. "Tell me about the night of
August twenty-eighth. You remember it two ways."

"I didn't want to be alone," Sam said again. "I was angry at Julie.
Who the hell did she think she was, kicking me out of the house
when she was the one messing around? I did a line to prime myself
up, then got in the car and headed into L.A.

"I don't know how many clubs I hit. It came out in the trial, different people seeing me at different places that night. Saying I was
belligerent, looking for trouble. I did another line in the car before
I drove to our house. I'd been drinking, too. I had all this energy
and anger, and all I could think of was Julie. We'd settle this, damn
it. Once and for all. I remember the way the trees stood out against
the sky, like a painting. I could hear the sound of my heartbeat in
my head. Then it goes two ways."

His eyes, blue and intense, stared into Noah's. "The gate's locked.
When she comes on the intercom, I tell her to open the gate, I need
to talk to her. I'm careful to keep my tone calm. I know she won't let
me in if she knows I've been using. She tells me it's late, but I per-
sist, I persuade. She gives in. I drive to the house. And she's standing in the door, the light behind her, wearing the white silk
nightgown I'd bought her for our last anniversary. She tells me to
make it quick, she's tired, and walks into the parlor. There's a glass
of wine on the table, magazines, and the scissors. She picks up her
wine. She knows I'm high now, so she's angry. 'Why are you doing

this to yourself?' she asks. 'Why are you doing this to me, to Livvy?' "

His hand began to claw at his knee. "I tell her it's her fault because she let Manning put his hands on her, because she put her career ahead of our marriage. She says she's through with me, she wants me out of her life. I make her sick. I disgust her." Still the actor, he punched the words, used pauses and passion.

"She tells me she's never been happier since she kicked me out, and has no intention of weighing herself down with a has-been with a drug problem." Sam's eyes went glassy.

"The scissors with the long silver blades are in my hands. I want to stab them through her. She screams. Blood pours out of her back. She stumbles. There's a crash. I just keep hacking with the scissors. Then I see Livvy in the doorway, staring at me."

Sam's hand shook as he picked up his coffee. He sipped, long and deep. "I remember that night another way, too. It starts off the same—toking up, cruising, letting the drug feed the rage. But this time the gates are open when I get there, and the door of the house is wide open, too. I walk in, hear the music from the parlor.

"There's blood everywhere. There's broken glass, smashed. My head's buzzed from coke and vodka, but I'm thinking, There's been a break-in. And I see her. Oh, God, I see her on the floor." His voice broke, wavered, quavered, just as perfectly delivered as the stream of violence in his first version. "I'm kneeling beside her, saying her name, trying to pick her up. Blood—there's blood all over her. I pull the scissors out of her back. And there's Livvy, staring at me."

He lit another cigarette. "The police didn't buy that one. Neither did the jury. After a while I stopped buying it, too."

"I'm not here to buy anything, Sam."

"No. But you'll wonder, won't you?"

THE next day Noah decided to swing by and see Sam. He wanted to ask him a few more questions before heading to Washington the following day. This time he'd fly up, then rent a car. He didn't want to waste time on the road. Noah parked his car and walked down Sunset. He pushed through the entrance of the apartment unit and climbed the stairs. The paint was peeling, the treads grimy. He knocked on the door of the second-floor apartment.

"If you're looking for the old man, he split."

Noah glanced around, saw a woman strolling down the hallway. "Split where?"

"Hey, I don't keep tabs on the neighbors, honey. You a cop?"

"No. I've got business with him, that's all."

"Look a little like a cop," she decided. "Parole officer?"

"I just want to talk to him."

"Well, he ain't here. Packed up and moved out yesterday."

LONG after the center had closed for the day, Olivia worked in her office. The paperwork had a nasty habit of building up.

She caught herself staring at the phone again and muttered curses under her breath. It was humiliating, absolutely mortifying, to realize that part of the reason she was working late was the hope that Noah would call. Which he hadn't done in two days.

She glanced toward her little storage closet. She'd buried the music box under the packing, stuffed it in the closet. Why had he sent it? Was it a peace offering or a threat?

When the phone rang, Olivia jumped foolishly, then rolled her eyes in annoyance. It had to be Noah, she thought. Who else would call so late? She let it ring three full times. When she picked it up, her voice was cool and brisk. "River's End Naturalist Center."

She heard the music, just the faint drift of it, and started to laugh. Then found herself unable to speak at all. She recognized it now— Tchaikovsky's *Sleeping Beauty*. The soaring, liquid, heartbreaking notes of it took her back to a warm summer night and the metallic scent of blood.

Her hand tightened on the receiver while panic filled her head. "What do you want? I know who you are." Terror swam into her belly. She wanted to crawl under her desk. Hide. Just hide. "I'm not afraid of you. Stay away from me. Just stay away!"

She slammed the receiver down and ran.

The doorknob slipped out of her hand, making her whimper

with frustration until she could cement her grip. The center was dark, silent. She nearly cowered back, but the phone rang again. Her own screams shocked her, sent her skidding across the floor. She had to get out.

And as she reached for the front door, the knob turned sharply. The door opened wide, and in its center was the shadow of a man.

Olivia's vision went gray and hazy. Hands closed over her arms. She felt herself sway, then slide through them into the black.

"Hey, hey, hey, come on. Come back."

She felt little pats on her face. It took her a moment to realize she was on the floor, being rocked like a baby in Noah's lap. "Stop slapping me, you moron." She lay still, weak from embarrassment and the dregs of panic.

"Oh, yeah, that's better. Good." He covered her mouth with his, poured an ocean of relief into the kiss. "That's the first time I ever had a woman faint at my feet. Can't say I like it one bit."

"I didn't faint."

"You did a mighty fine imitation, then. I'm sorry I scared you."

"Let me up."

"Let's just sit here a minute." Noah shifted her so he could grin into her face. Then just the look of her clear amber eyes, pale skin, had something moving inside him. "I really missed you." His hand roamed through her hair. "Do you know how much time we've actually spent together?"

"No."

"Not enough," he murmured, and lowered his mouth to hers again. This time Olivia's lips were soft and welcomed him. Her arms lifted and enfolded him. He felt himself sink, then settle, so that even the wonder of it seemed as natural as breathing. "Liv, let me close the door."

"Hmm?"

Her sleepy answer had sparks of heat simmering inside the warmth. "The door. I don't want to make love with you in an open doorway."

She made another humming sound as she slapped at the door in an attempt to close it herself. Then the phone rang, and she was clawing to get free.

"It's just the phone." He clamped his arms over hers.

"It's him. Let me go! It's him."

He didn't ask whom she meant. She only used that tone when she spoke of her father. "How do you know?"

Olivia's eyes wheeled white with panic. "He called before."

"What did he say to you?"

"Nothing." Overwhelmed, she curled up. "Nothing."

"It's okay. Stay right here." Noah nudged her aside and strode into the office. Even as he reached for the receiver, the ringing stopped.

"It was him." She'd managed to get up, walk to the door, but she was shaking. "He didn't say anything. He just played the music. The music my mother had on the stereo the night he killed her."

Nine

NOAH had booked a room but had been warned it was only available for one night. There were a couple of campsites still available, though. He was going to have to snag one if he meant to stay.

His original plan had been to rent a snazzy suite in some hotel within reasonable driving distance, where he could work in comfort and seduce Olivia in style. After what he'd learned, he wasn't willing to stay that far away. The only way to keep an eye on her was to stay put and to be more stubborn than she was.

There'd been a test of that the night before. She'd told him about the phone call, the music box, and her fear had been alive in the room with them. But after she'd gotten it out, she'd toughened up again. She'd gotten all fired up when he'd said he was taking her home—she knew the way, he'd get lost on the way back, she didn't need a bodyguard. And wouldn't be *taken* anywhere by anyone.

Noah stepped out on his tiny first-floor patio and scanned the deep green of the summer forest.

He'd never actually dragged a woman to his car before. He wondered if he should be ashamed of having enjoyed it so much. He'd gotten Olivia home safely, had managed to block her last punch long enough to punctuate his victory with a very satisfying kiss.

He rubbed his bruised ribs absently. Hoping she'd cooled off, he went to find her.

OLIVIA hadn't cooled off. In fact, she was nursing her temper as a devoted mother would a fretful baby. She'd take spit-in-his-eye temper over the sick, shaky panic she felt every time her office phone rang. So she nurtured it, all but wallowed in it.

When Noah walked into her office, she got to her feet slowly, her eyes cold, steady. Like a gunfighter, she shot from the hip. "Get your sorry hide out of my office and off MacBride property. If you're not checked out and gone inside of ten minutes, I'm calling the cops and having you charged with assault."

"You'll never make it stick," he said with a cheer he knew would infuriate her. "I'm the one with the bruises." He shut the door at his back. "Now, I've got a deal for you."

"A deal for me?" She bared her teeth in a snarl.

"I want to do some hiking and camping in the backcountry with you."

Her laugh came fast. "The hell you do."

"Three days. You and me. We get away for a while. You do what you do best. And so do I. You agreed to interviews, so we'll talk. You love this place, and I want you to show it to me."

"For the book."

"No. For me. I want to be alone with you."

Olivia could feel her resolve, and her temper, melting. "I've rethought that situation, and I'm not interested."

"Yes, you are. You're just mad at me because I outmuscled you last night." Noah glanced down at her hand and saw the faint trail of bruises above her wrist. "I guess I'm not the only one with bruises." He lifted her wrist, kissed it. "Sorry."

"Cut it out." She slapped his hand away. "All right, I'm mad because you saw me at my worst and my weakest. I'm mad because you wouldn't leave me alone, and I'm mad because I like being with you even when you irritate me."

"You can count on staying mad for a while, then. Let's go play in the forest, Livvy."

"Twenty-four hours, you'll be crying for your laptop."

"Bet?"

"Hundred bucks."

"Deal." He gave her hand a squeeze.

FOLLOWING Olivia's instructions, Noah bought all the gear they'd need. By the time he was done, he figured he packed thirty-five pounds, and imagined after five miles it would weigh like a hundred. With some regret he locked his cell phone and laptop in the rental car. "I'll be back, boys," he murmured.

"I'm going to win that hundred bucks before we leave."

"That wasn't whining. It was a fond farewell."

He turned and studied her. Olivia wore jeans, roomy and faded; a River's End T-shirt; and sturdy boots with impressive nicks and scars. She carried her backpack as though it were weightless.

She jerked her thumb. "Let's get started," she said.

Noah found the forest more appealing, if no less primitive, without the rain. He remembered and recognized much of it now—the varied bark on the giant trees, the vast, nubby carpets of moss. They crossed a narrow stream, then began to climb the long, switch-backing trail that would take them into the backcountry.

"Look." Olivia stopped abruptly and crouched, tapping a finger beside faint imprints on the trail.

"Are those—"

"Bear tracks," she said, and rose. "Pretty fresh, too."

"How do you know that? They always say that in the movies—the tracks are fresh," he said in a grunting voice. "He passed through here no more than an hour ago wearing a black hat, eating a banana, and whistling 'Sweet Rosie from Pike.' "

He made her laugh. "All the bears I know whistle show tunes."

"You made a joke, Liv." He kissed her. "Congratulations."

She scowled at him. "No kissing on the trail."

"I didn't read that in my camper's guide." He started after her.

Olivia had chosen this trail because other hikers rarely chose to negotiate it—long switchbacks led to steep terrain. They moved through the lush forest, climbing up and down ridges, along a bluff that afforded views of the river. Wildlife was plentiful here.

They crossed over a wide stream, where the water ran clear and fast. Dotting the banks were wild foxglove and columbine. The scenery took a dramatic turn from the deep green of the river basin to the stunning old-growth forest where light speared down in shafts and pools. The ancient trees grew straight as soldiers, tall as giants, their tops whispering in the wind that couldn't reach the forest floor.

Saying nothing, Noah dragged off his pack.

"I take that to mean you want a break."

"I just want to be here for a while. It's a great spot."

"Then you don't want a sandwich?"

His brows went up. "Who says?"

Olivia lifted off her pack and unzipped the compartment that held sandwiches and vegetable sticks.

"How often do you get out here?" Noah asked as he started to eat.

"I take groups out four or five times a year."

"I didn't mean a working deal. How often do you get out here like this, to sit and do nothing?"

"Not in a while." She breathed deep, leaning back on her elbows and closing her eyes. "Not in too long a while."

She looked relaxed, he noted. As if at last her thoughts were quiet. He had only to shift to lay his hand over hers.

Her heart sighed as she opened her eyes to study him. "You're starting to worry me a little, Noah. Tell me, what are you after?"

"I think I've been pretty up front about that. Right from the beginning of all of this I've had feelings for you."

"How healthy is it that this connection you believe in has its roots in murder? Don't you ever ask yourself that?"

"No. But I guess you do."

"I didn't six years ago. But yes, I do now. It's an intimate part of my life and who I am. Monster and victim—they're both inside of me. You need to think about that before this goes . . . anywhere."

"Liv." His hands caught her face firmly, his mouth crushed down on hers. "You need to think about that. Because this is already going everywhere, and for me at least it's going there pretty fast."

She stood up. "Sex is easy. It's just a basic human function."

He kept his deep green eyes on hers as he rose. "I'm going to enjoy, really enjoy proving you wrong."

She decided it was wiser not to discuss it.

The sunlight grew stronger as they climbed, the light richer. At the next wet crossing the river was fast and rocky, with a thundering waterfall tumbling down the face of the cliff.

"There. Over there." Olivia gestured, then dug for her binoculars. "He's fishing."

"Who?" Noah narrowed his eyes. He saw a dark shape hunched on an island of rock in the churning river. "Is that— It's a bear!"

He snatched the binoculars Olivia offered and stared through them, studying the bear as the bear studied the water. In a lightning move one huge black paw swept the stream and came out locked around a wriggling fish that flashed silver in the sun.

"Got one on the first try! Man, did you see that?"

She hadn't seen. She'd been watching the surprise and excitement on his face, the utter fascination in it.

Noah shook his head as the bear devoured his snack. "Great fishing skills, lousy table manners." He lowered the binoculars and caught Olivia staring at him. "Something wrong?"

"No." Maybe everything, she thought, is either very wrong or very right. "We'd better go make camp before we lose the light. We follow the river now. About another hour."

When they reached the site, Noah liked it. They were tucked among the giant trees, with the river spilling over tumbled rocks.

"I'm going upstream to catch dinner." As Olivia spoke, she took a retractable rod out of her pack. "If I get lucky, we eat like bears tonight. Can you set up the tent while I'm fishing?"

"Sure. You go hunt up food. I'll make the nest. I have no problem with role reversal whatsoever."

THE tent didn't come with instructions, which Noah thought was a definite flaw in the system. Setting up camp took him triple the amount of time and energy it would have taken Olivia. But he decided he'd keep that little bit of information to himself.

She'd been gone more than an hour by the time he was reasonably sure the tent would stay upright. With nothing left on his chore list, he settled down to write in longhand.

It was Olivia he concentrated on. Would she have been more open, more sociably inclined if her mother had lived? Would she have been less driven to stand on her own if she'd grown up the pampered child of a Hollywood star? Would all that energy and intelligence have been channeled into the entertainment field, or would she still have gone back to her mother's roots and chosen isolation?

She would have come back, Noah decided. Perhaps her life wouldn't have been centered here, but she would have been pulled back to this time and again. As her mother had been. She would have needed this place, the smells and the sounds of it. She needed it now, not only for her work and peace of mind. It was here she could find her mother.

He wrote down his thoughts, his impressions. When his mind drifted, he stretched out on the bank and slipped into dreams.

OLIVIA had caught three fine trout. She'd also found a nice bramble of huckleberries. Her hat was full of them as she wandered back to camp. She saw Noah sleeping by the stream and smiled. She'd pushed him hard, and he'd held together. A glance around camp showed her he'd done well enough there, too. She settled down beside him to watch the water.

He sensed her, and she became part of his dream. He shifted toward her, reached out to touch. She pulled away, but the half-formed protest slipped back down her throat as his eyes opened, green and intense. Her breath caught at what she saw in them.

"Look, I don't—"

He shook his head to stop the words, and his eyes never left hers as he drew her closer, as his mouth covered hers. She trembled. His hands moved from her face, through her hair, over her shoulders as the kiss roughened. Panic scrambled inside her to race with desire that had sprung up fast and feral. She pushed at his shoulders to hold him off. "I can't give you what you want. I don't have it in me."

How could she not see what he saw? Not feel what he felt? His lips brushed hers, teasing, testing. "Let me touch you." He closed his fingers lightly over her breast. "Here in the sunlight."

He said her name, only her name, and she was lost. To him, to herself. As something inside her went silky, her mind went blissfully blank. With a kind of lazy deliberation that sent her head reeling, Noah's hands began a long, savoring journey. Pleasure shimmered over her skin, warmed it, sensitized it. She was willow-slim and water-soft. The lovely line of her throat drew his lips.

Muscles quivering, he held himself over her. "Olivia." Her name was raw in his throat and full of need. "Look at me." His eyes were as green and deep as the shadows behind them. "Look at me. Because it matters. It's you. It's always been you."

Then his mouth took hers in a fierce kiss.

OLIVIA couldn't move. Not only because Noah pinned her to the ground with the good, solid weight of a satisfied man, but because her own body was weak from the sensory onslaught.

She'd lost control, not only of her body but also of her will. She needed to get it back and lock it away again. But when she started to shift, to push him aside, he simply tucked her up, rolled over, and trapped her in a sprawl over him.

She wanted to lay her head over his heart, close her eyes, and stay just as they were forever. It scared her to death. "It'll be dark soon. I have to get the cook camp set up, a fire started."

He stroked a hand over her hair. "There's time."

She pushed off. "Look, pal, unless you want to go cold and hungry, we need wood."

He tugged her back. "I'll get it in a minute. You want to pull away, Liv. I won't let you. Not again." He tried to disguise his hurt. "You want to pretend that this was just a nice, hot bout in the woods, no connection to what we started years ago. But you can't."

"Let me up, Noah."

"And you're telling yourself it won't happen that way again," Noah said angrily. "That you won't feel what you felt with me again. But you're wrong."

"Don't tell me what I think, what I feel."

"I'm telling you what I see. Right there, in your eyes." He lifted her aside and rose, then went to gather firewood.

As Olivia began setting up the cook camp and cleaned the fish for dinner, she wondered why she'd ever believed she could handle him or herself around him. He was angry with her for something she couldn't, and wouldn't, change.

But later, when the meal was finished and the forest dark and full of sound, it was she was who turned to him, she who needed arms around her to chase away the dreams that haunted her and the fear that stalked with them. And he was there, to hold her in the night, to move with her in a sweet and easy rhythm.

So when she slept, she curled against him, her head in the curve of his shoulder. Noah lay awake, watching the play of moonlight over the tent, listening to the call of a coyote. He wondered how it was possible that he'd never stopped loving her.

GROGGY, achy, Noah woke to birdsong. He sat up, tugged his jeans on. Through the sharp scent of pine and earth he caught the wonderfully civilized aroma of coffee. Olivia had built a campfire and had the coffeepot heating. One long sip had his eyes clearing. "Where are we going today, Liv?"

She frowned. "I assumed you'd want to start on the interview."

"We'll get to it. Which trail do you like from here?"

She shrugged. "There's a nice day trip up into the mountains. Wonderful views, some good alpine meadows."

"Sounds like a plan."

Olivia fixed powdered eggs, and they polished off the pot of coffee. Carrying light packs, they left the camp and started the climb. A rough track led to rougher ridges. With the forest marching toward the sky to the left and the river winding below, they maneuvered the dizzying switchbacks, moving up into cool, crisp air where eagles soared.

Olivia stood by, silently amused, when Noah drew to a halt and stared as the trail curved and the sky was swept by mountains.

"If you planted a house here," he said, "you'd never get anything done. How could you stop looking?"

Why couldn't he be shallow and simple? "It's public land."

"Work with me here, Liv. We put it up there, with big living-room windows looking out this way so we catch the sunset at night. We need a big stone fireplace in there. I think we should keep it open, really high ceilings, no closed spaces. Four bedrooms."

"Four?"

"Sure. You want the kids to have their own rooms, don't you? Five bedrooms," he corrected, enjoying the way her eyes widened. "One for a guest room. Then I need office space, good-sized room, lots of shelves and windows. Where do you want your office?"

"I have an office."

"You need a home office, too. You're a professional woman. I think it should be next to mine, but we'll have to have rules about respecting each other's space. We'll put them on the third floor." His fingers linked with hers. "Just think of it for a minute. We're the only two people in the world, and we've landed here. We could spend our whole life right here, with our brains dazzled."

Blue, white, green, and silver. The world was made up of those strong colors and the blurred smudges of more. Peaks, valleys, and the rush of water. The feel of his hand warm in hers, as if it was meant to be. Nothing else. No fear, no pain, no memories, no tomorrows.

Because Olivia discovered she could yearn for that, she drew away. "You wouldn't be so happy with it in the dead of winter, when you'd freeze your tail off and couldn't get a pizza delivery."

He looked at her, quiet, patient, and made her ashamed.

WHEN THEY REACHED THEIR destination, Noah filled himself on the view. It was an ocean of flowers, rivers of color flowing through green and washing up toward a slope of forested peak that shot into the blue like the turret of a castle. At the highest points curving pools of snow shimmered through the rock and trees. Butterflies danced, white, yellow, blue, flirting with the blooms.

"Amazing. Incredible. This is where we put the house."

This time she laughed.

"What are those? Lupines?" Noah asked.

"You have a good eye. Broadleaf lupines—the common western blue butterfly prefers them. Those are mountain daisies."

"And yarrow." He studied the flat white blossoms.

"You know your flowers. You don't need me up here."

"Yes"—he took her hand—"I do." He turned and caught her unprepared with a soft and stirring kiss.

She started to turn away, but he eased her back around. "Don't." She closed her eyes before his mouth could capture hers again.

"All right." Instead he lifted her hand to his lips and watched confusion join the clouds in her eyes.

"What are you looking for, Noah?"

"I've already found it. You just have to catch up." He was afraid there was only one way for that to begin. "Let's sit down, Liv. This is a good spot. It's a good time." He shrugged off his pack, sat on a rock, and opened it to find his tape recorder.

Seeing it in his hand, she felt her breath go thick and hot in her lungs. "I don't know how to do this."

"Sit down," he said gently. "And tell me about your parents."

"I don't remember much about my father."

Noah said nothing.

"He was very handsome," Olivia said at length. "The two of them looked beautiful together. I remember how they'd dress up for parties and how I thought everyone's parents were beautiful and went out to parties, had their pictures in magazines and on TV.

"They loved each other. I know that." She spoke slowly. "They loved me. I can't be wrong about that. I remember how they shimmered with what they felt for each other. Until it started to change."

"How did it change?"

"Anger, mistrust, jealousy. I wouldn't have had words for it then. They fought. Late at night at first. I'd hear not the words so much, but the voices, the tone of them. It made me feel sick." She smiled a little. "But it wasn't always like that. I remember when he'd pick me up. 'Livvy, my love,' he'd call me, and dance with me around the living room. And when he'd hold me, I'd feel so safe. When he'd come in to tell me a story—he told such wonderful stories—I'd feel so happy. I was his princess, he'd say. And whenever he had to go away to a shoot, I'd miss him so much, my heart would hurt. When he came back, he'd leave a white rose on my pillow."

Olivia pressed a hand to her mouth, as if to hold in the words and the pain. "That night when he came into my room and broke the music box and shouted at me, it was as if someone had stolen my father, taken him away. It was never, never the same after that night. That summer I waited for him to come back, for everything to be the way it was. But he never did. Never. The monster came." Her breath caught. "I can't." She barely managed to get the words out. Her eyes were huge with pain and shock. "I can't."

"It's all right." He wrapped his arms around her. He could feel her heart race, feel the sharp, whiplash shudders that racked her.

"I can still see it—him kneeling beside her, the blood, and broken glass. The scissors in his hand. He said my name. I'd heard her scream. I'd heard it. Her scream, breaking glass. That's what woke me up. But I went into her room and played with her bottles. I was playing in her room when he was killing her."

There was nothing he could say. There was no comfort in words. He held her, stroking her hair.

"I never saw either of them again. We never talked of them in our house. My grandmother locked them in a chest in the attic, and I spoke of her secretly to Aunt Jamie and felt like a thief for stealing the pieces of my mother she could give me. I hated him for that— for making me have to steal my mother back in secret whispers."

Noah pressed his lips to her hair, rocking her as she wept. He drew her into his lap, cradling her there until she went lax and silent.

Olivia's head ached, and her eyes burned. But the agonizing pressure in her chest was gone. Tired and embarrassed, she pulled back from him.

He brushed a tear from her cheek. "You look worn out."

"I never cry. The last time I cried was because of you."

"I'm sorry."

"I was so hurt when I found out why you'd really come. After you left, I cried for the first time since I was a child. You had no idea what I'd let myself feel about you in those two days."

"Yes, I did," he murmured. "Just as much as what I'd felt for you. Olivia, the first time I saw you, you were a baby. Something about that sad image of you reached right out from the television screen and grabbed me. It's never let go. I didn't see you again until you were twelve, gangly and brave and all haunted eyes. But I never forgot you. You were in and out of my head. Then you were eighteen. You opened the door of your apartment, tall and slender and lovely. A little distracted, a little impatient. Then you smiled at me and cut me off at the knees. I've *never* been the same.

"I know I hurt you. I didn't understand you or myself well enough then. Even when I came here and saw you again, I didn't understand it. I just knew seeing you thrilled me."

"You're mixing things up, Noah."

"No, I'm not." He touched her face. "Liv, there's one thing I'm absolutely clear on. I'm so completely in love with you."

Joy and terror clogged her throat. "I don't want you to be."

"I know. It scares you. But you are what I'm looking for. Next step is to figure out what you want. Meanwhile, just tell me one thing. Is what you're feeling for me just a few sparks?"

It was warmth she felt, a steady stream of it, and a longing so deep, so aching, it beat like a heart.

He saw the answer in her eyes. "I love you, Olivia."

THE man was so carelessly cheerful, Olivia thought, it was all but impossible not to respond in kind. It didn't matter that the next morning had dawned with a thin, drizzling rain that would undoubtedly have them soaked within an hour of the hike back.

He woke up, listened to the drumming, and said it was a sign that they should stay in the tent and make crazy love.

She couldn't come up with a logical argument against the plan.

Then he nuzzled her neck, told her to stay put, that he'd see to the coffee. She snuggled into the warm cocoon of the tent and wallowed in the afterglow of lovemaking. She hadn't let herself be pampered since childhood, believed that if she didn't take care of herself, she'd be handing control of her life to someone else. As her mother had done. Love was a weakness or a weapon, and she'd convinced herself that she'd never permit herself to feel it for anyone beyond family. Didn't she have both potentials inside her? The one to surrender and the one to use it violently?

Noah nudged his way back into the tent, two steaming cups in his hand. His sun-streaked hair was damp with rain, his feet bare. The wave of love swamped her, closed over heart and head.

"I think I saw a shrew." He passed her the coffee and settled down with his own. "Don't know if it was a wandering or a dusky, but I'm pretty sure it was a shrew."

"The wandering's found more often in the lowlands," she heard herself say. "At this altitude it was probably a dusky."

"Whichever, it was rooting around for breakfast."

"They eat constantly. Very like some city boys I know."

"I haven't even mentioned breakfast. I thought about it, but I haven't mentioned it. So how about a date when we get back?"

"Excuse me?"

"A date. Dinner, a movie, making out in my rental car."

"I thought you'd be heading back to L.A. soon."

"I can work anywhere. You're here." Noah smoothed her tousled hair with his fingers. "Is that a problem for you?"

"Yes, but not as much as I thought it would be. Not as much as it should be." Olivia took a breath, braced herself. "I care about you. It's not easy for me. I'm no good at this."

He pressed his lips to her forehead and said, "Practice."

SAM TANNER LOOKED OUT THE window of the rented cabin. He'd never understood what had drawn Julie to this place, with its rains and chill, its thick forests. He looked at the minirecorder he'd bought. He intended to speak with Noah again, but wasn't sure how much more time he had. The headaches were raging down on him with terrifying regularity. He suspected the doctors had over-estimated his time, and the tapes were his backup.

A headache began to build in the center of his skull. He shook pills out of bottles—some prescription, some he'd risked buying on the street. He had to beat the pain. He couldn't think. And he had so much to do yet. So much to do.

Olivia, he thought grimly. There was a debt to pay.

He set the bottles back on the table, beside the long, gleaming knife and the Smith & Wesson .38.

WHEN they reached the lowland forest, Noah started dreaming of a hot shower, a quiet room, his computer, and a phone. "You've lost the bet," he reminded her. "I never whined for my laptop."

"Yes, you did. You just did it in your head."

"That doesn't count. Pay up. No, forget I said that. We'll call it even if you find me a place I can shower and change. I'm in line for a room at the lodge if you get any cancellations, but meanwhile I'm relegated to a campsite and public showers. I'm very shy."

Olivia giggled. "We can swing by the house," she said. "My grandmother should be out with one of the children's groups for a while yet. Then she generally goes marketing. You've got an hour, Brady. I don't want her upset."

"That's not a problem. But she's going to have to meet me eventually, Liv." He grabbed her hand. "At the wedding anyway."

"Ha-ha." She tugged her hand free.

Noah saw the flickers of color first, through the trees. Dabs and dapples of red and blue and yellow. When he stepped into the clearing, he stopped. The house looked like a fairy tale with its varied rooflines and sturdy old wood and stone, flowers flowing at its base. There were two rockers on the porch.

"It's perfect," he said.

"It's been the MacBrides' home for generations."

"No wonder it's your place. It's exactly right." He settled his lips softly, dreamily on hers. As her arms came up and around him, she heard an engine laboring up the lane. She jerked away. "Someone's coming. My grandmother."

The truck was already rounding the turn. Too late to ask him to go, Olivia realized. Too late even if the glint in his eye told her he wouldn't have quietly slipped into the trees. She turned away, braced herself as the truck pulled up. "I'll handle this."

"No." He took her hand in a firm grip. "We'll handle it."

Val sat where she was as they walked to the truck.

"Grandma." Olivia stopped at the driver's side.

"So, you're back."

"Yes, just now. I thought you'd be with the children's group."

"Janine took it." Rage had her whipping the words out. "Did you think to sneak in and out before I got home?"

Stunned, Olivia blinked, stood numbly as Noah shifted in front of her. "I asked Olivia if I could shower and change, since the lodge is booked. I'm Noah Brady, Mrs. MacBride."

"I know who you are. This is Livvy's home," she said shortly. "If she's told you that you can use it to clean up, that's her right. But I have nothing to say to you. I have groceries to put away."

She drove to the back of the house. Noah started after the truck.

"Where are you going?" Olivia asked.

"To help your grandmother carry in the groceries."

"Oh, for heaven's sake, can't you see how I hurt her?"

"Yeah, I can. And I can damn well see how she's hurt you. I'm not backing off. You're both going to have to deal with that."

He strode to the back of the house and, before Val could protest, plucked a bag out of her hand. "I'll take this in." He carted it onto the porch and let himself into the kitchen.

"I'm sorry." Olivia rushed to Val. "I'll make him go."

"You've already made your choice." Val's back was stiff.

"I wasn't thinking clearly. I'm sorry. I'll make him go."

"No, you won't." Noah came back out, took the remaining two bags. "Any more than I'll make you do anything."

"Noah, would you just *go?*"

"And leave you here feeling guilty and unhappy?" He gave Olivia a long look before turning back to Val. "I'm sorry that we disagree about the book. I'm sorry that my being here upsets you. But the fact is, I'm going to write the book, and I'm going to be a part of Olivia's life. I hope we can come to terms about both, because she loves you. She loves you enough that if it comes down to a choice between your peace of mind and her own happiness, she'll choose you."

"That's not fair," Olivia began.

Val lifted a hand. She wanted to dislike his face, to find it cold and ruthless. She wanted to see self-interest. Instead she saw the glint of anger that hadn't faded since she'd snapped at Olivia. "That book will not be discussed in this house."

Noah nodded. "Understood."

"There's perishables in those bags," Val said as she turned away. "I have to get them put away."

"Give them to me," Olivia began, then hissed in frustration when he simply walked past her and into the house behind Val. Left with no choice, Olivia dragged off her pack, hurrying in after them.

Unloading bags, Val glanced toward the door as Olivia came in. She saw nerves, ripe and jittery, in her granddaughter's eyes. It made her feel ashamed. "You might as well take that pack off," she said to Noah. "I imagine you're sick of carrying it by now."

"If I admit that, Liv will smirk at me. She wants me to think she thinks I'm a shallow urbanite who can't tell east from west."

"You can't," Olivia murmured, and had Noah grinning at her.

"Are you?" Val asked. She'd seen the bond in the look that passed between them. "A shallow urbanite?"

"No, ma'am, I'm not. I've fallen in love, not just with Liv, but with Washington. I've already picked a spot where we could build our house, but Liv says it's a national park."

"He's just babbling," Olivia managed. "There isn't—"

"But I'm flexible." Noah leaned against the counter. "This is where she's happy. This is home for her. As soon as I saw this place, I thought she'd like to get married right here in the yard, between the flowers and the forest. That would suit her, wouldn't it?"

"Oh, stop it!" Olivia burst out. "There isn't—"

"I wasn't talking to you," Noah said mildly, then offered Val an easy smile. "She's crazy about me, but she's having a little trouble, you know, settling into it."

Val couldn't help but begin to warm to the young man who obviously adored her little girl. "You're a clever one, aren't you?" She sighed a little. "You might as well go get the rest of your things. You can stay in the guest room."

"Thanks." He kissed Olivia warmly. "I won't be long."

"I—" The screen door slapped smartly behind him, and Olivia threw up her hands. "You didn't have to do that. He'll be fine at the campground."

"Are you in love with him?" Val asked.

"I— It's just . . ." She trailed off helplessly.

"Are you in love with him, Livvy?"

She could only nod as tears swam into her eyes.

"And if I said I don't want you to have anything to do with him, that you owe me the loyalty to respect my feelings?"

Olivia went rigid. "I'll go . . . I'll go tell him he has to leave."

"Oh. Oh, Livvy." Val covered her face as she burst into tears. "He was right. You'd turn away from him, from your own heart if you thought it was what I needed. I wanted him to be the selfish one, but I'm the one who's been selfish."

"No. Never."

"I've hoarded you, Livvy." With an unsteady hand Val brushed at Olivia's hair. "As much for your sake as mine in the beginning, but . . . as time passed . . . just for me. I lost my Julie, and I promised myself nothing would ever happen to you."

"You took care of me."

"Yes, I took care of you. I loved you, and Livvy, I needed you. I needed you so desperately. So I never let you go."

"Don't cry, Gran." It ripped Olivia to shreds to see the tears.

"I'm ashamed that I pulled back from you when you chose to cooperate with this book. I could see it was something you needed, but I pulled back and made you suffer for it."

"I have to know why it happened."

"And I've never let you. I've never let any of us." Val drew Olivia closer. "I still don't know if I can face it all. But I do know I want you to be happy. Not just safe. Being safe isn't enough to live on." Val rubbed the tears away. "It's best if your young man stays here, where I can keep an eye on him and see if he's good enough for you. If I decide he's not, I'll see that your grandfather whips him into shape. I'd better go up and check that the guest room's in order."

"I'll do it. I'll just take my pack up." Olivia hefted it. "Gran, I love you so much."

"Yes, I know you do. Go on. I need to make myself presentable. We'll talk more, Livvy," she murmured after Olivia started upstairs. "It's long past time we talked."

Olivia's step was light as she crossed the upstairs hall and flung open the door of her room. There, on the pillow of her bed, bathed in a quiet stream of sunlight, lay a single white rose.

Ten

S HE couldn't breathe. Her head rang—wild, frantic bells that pealed down her spine. There was a terrible urge to crawl away.

The monster was here. In the house. He'd come into the house. And her grandmother was down in the kitchen alone. Olivia's hand shook, but she reached for the knife at her belt and unsheathed it. She wasn't a helpless child now. She'd protect what she loved.

She slipped out into the hall and moved quietly from room to room, as carefully as she would when tracking a deer. She searched each one for a sign, a change in the air. Her knees trembled as she crossed to the attic door.

Would he hide there? Would he know somehow that everything

precious of her mother was neatly stored up those narrow stairs? She imagined herself going up, seeing him there with the chest flung open, her mother's scent struggling to life in the musty air.

Olivia would raise her knife and drive it into him, as he'd once driven the scissor blades into her mother. But her hand lay limply on the knob. She wanted desperately to weep and couldn't.

At the sound of a car rounding the lane, she slid the bolt home under the knob and ran to a window. She saw Noah climb out.

A few minutes later, when Olivia heard his step on the stairs, she slid the knife back into its sheath and moved into the hall. "Let me give you a hand with that." She reached out to take Noah's laptop case and left him with his bag. "The guest room's in here."

"Thanks." He followed her, dropped his bag on the bed. "This is a lot more appealing than a pup tent. And guess who's here?"

"Here?"

His eyes narrowed on her face at the thready ring to her voice. "What's the matter, Liv?"

She shook her head. "Who's here?"

"My parents. At the lodge," Noah said. "They'd booked a room a while back." He took her hand. It was clammy and cold. "I want you to tell me what's wrong."

Her cheeks were pale. "My father. He's been in the house, Noah. There's a white rose on my bed."

A coldness came into his eyes. "Stay here."

"I've already looked through the house. Except for the attic. I couldn't go into the attic—"

"Damn right." The idea of it made Noah's stomach churn. "You stay in here or go downstairs with your grandmother."

"No, you don't understand. I couldn't go up, because I wanted him to be there. I wanted to go up and kill him. Kill my father. God help me, I wanted it. I wanted it. What does that make me?"

"Human." He snapped it out, the word as effective as a slap. "He's not here, but you'll feel better if we make sure. Lock this door, Olivia, and wait for me."

Despising herself, she did just that. Hid, as she had hidden before. When he came back, she looked at him with empty eyes.

"There's no one there. We need to tell your grandparents."

"It'll frighten my grandmother."

He took her face into his hands. "She has to know. See if you can track down your grandfather at the lodge. I'll call my parents."

HE'D taken such a risk. Such a foolish and satisfying risk. How easily he could have been caught. He sat in his room, lifted a glass of bourbon to his lips with a hand that still shook slightly. But not with fear. With excitement. With life.

For twenty years he'd followed the rules. Done what was expected. Played the game. He could never have anticipated what it was like to be free of that. It was terrifying. It was liberating.

She would know what the rose meant. She wouldn't have forgotten the symbolism of it. *Daddy's home.*

What timing. He'd barely left the house by the back door—wasn't it wonderful that such people left their doors unlocked?—when he saw them step out of the trees. Little Livvy and the son of the cop, that was irony enough for any script. The cycle, the circle, the whims of fortune that would have the daughter of the woman he loved connect with the son of the cop who'd investigated her murder.

Julie, his beautiful Julie. The thought of her caused such pain.

How could he have known after all these years that he would look at Livvy, as she turned to another man, and see Julie? Julie pressing that long, slim body against someone else? How could he have known he'd remember in a kind of nightmare frenzy what it was to destroy what you loved? And need so desperately to do it again? He picked up the knife and turned it under the lamplight.

"YOU'LL need to take basic precautions." Frank sat in the MacBride living room. Back on the job, he thought.

"For how long?" Olivia asked.

"As long as it takes. You're going to want to avoid going out alone. And start locking the doors."

Olivia nodded. "There isn't anything we can do, is there?"

"So far, Livvy, he hasn't done anything we can push him on."

"Stalking," Noah snapped out.

"First you have to prove it. A phone call with no specific threat, a gift, and a flower put into an unlocked house. He could argue that he just wanted to make contact with the daughter he hasn't seen in twenty years. There's no law against it."

"He's a murderer." Rob laid a hand on Olivia's shoulder.

"Who's served his time. And the fact is"—Frank scanned the faces in the room—"the contact may be all he wants."

"Then why didn't he speak to me over the phone?"

Frank focused on Olivia. She was a little pale but holding up well. "I can't get into his head. I never could. But what we can do is ask the local police to do some checking. Do what they can to find out if Tanner's in the area."

Olivia nodded. "And if he is?"

"They'll talk to him." And so will I, Frank thought. "If he contacts you, we may be able to push on the stalking." He hesitated, then got to his feet. "Remember one thing, Livvy. He's on your ground. Out of his element. And he's alone. You're not."

It bolstered her, as it was meant to. She rose as well. "I'm glad you're here." She smiled at Celia. "Both of you."

"We all are." Val stood. "We'd like you to stay for dinner."

"Then why don't I give you a hand?" Celia draped her arm over Val's shoulders, and they started out.

"I haven't even offered you a drink." Rob struggled to slip into the role of host. "What can I get you?"

"Wouldn't mind stretching my legs a bit first," Frank said. "Noah, why don't we take a walk?"

"Sure." He turned to Olivia, kissed her. "Be right back."

Frank waited until they were outside. "I take it there's more between you and Livvy than the book."

"I'm in love with her. I'm going to marry her."

"Next time, son, remember my age. Tell me to sit down first."

Noah was braced for a fight. "You have a problem with that?"

"No. Anything but." Calmly Frank studied his son's face.

"There's something else, Noah. They found Caryn in New York, hooked up with a photographer she met at a party."

"Hope she stays there. A whole continent between us ought to be enough." Then he thought of Mike. "Did they pull her in?"

"She was questioned. Denied it. She has an alibi for the night Mike was hurt—the party. A couple of dozen people saw her at this deal up in the hills. We have the time of the attack narrowed to thirty minutes. During that half hour Caryn was snuggled up to the photographer in front of twenty witnesses."

"That doesn't . . ." Noah trailed off, felt his insides lurch. "Tanner? He knew where I lived. He was out by then, and he knew where to find me. The bastard. What was the point?"

"Could be he wanted to see where you were heading with your work. And you'd have names, addresses in your files."

"Revenge? Does it come down to that? Getting back at the people who testified against him?"

"I don't know. He's dying, Noah. What does he have to lose?"

HE HAD nothing to lose. So he sat sipping his drink and watching night fall. The pain was nicely tucked under the cushion of drugs, and the drugs were dancing with the alcohol. Just like old times.

It made him want to laugh. It made him want to weep.

Time was running out, he thought. Funny how it had crawled for twenty years, only to sprint like a runner at the starting block now that he was free. Free to do what? To die of cancer?

He lifted the gun. No, he didn't think he'd let the cancer kill him. All he needed was the guts. Experimentally he turned the gun, slipped the barrel like a kiss between his lips.

He could do it. But not yet. First there was Livvy.

THROUGH the meal Noah gazed at his mother with admiration. She drew Olivia out, asking her opinion about everything, from the plight of the northern pocket gopher—where did she get this stuff?—to the mating habits of osprey.

Val passed herbed potatoes to Frank. "Have some more."

He helped himself. "This is a fantastic meal, Val."

"Frank tolerates my cooking," Celia put in.

"Cooking?" Frank winked. "When did you start cooking?"

"Listen to that," Celia said as she gave him a playful punch. "All the years I've slaved over a hot stove for my men."

"All the tofu that gave their lives . . ." Noah murmured. "But you sure are pretty, Mom. Isn't she pretty?" He kissed her hand.

"You think that gets around me?"

He scooped up potatoes. "Yeah."

And that's what did it for Val. She nearly sighed. How could she hold back against a boy who so clearly loved his mother? She lifted a basket, offered it. "Have another roll, Noah."

"Thanks." This time when he smiled at her, she smiled back.

THE next day Olivia was leading a hike. As she guided her group through the trees, she'd done a head count of fifteen, Celia among them. The fact that she was there had been enough to help Olivia convince Noah to take some quiet time to work.

She explained the cycle of survival, succession, tolerance of the rain forest. Olivia let her audience crane their necks, murmur in awe, snap their pictures while she talked of the overstory. She pointed out the deep-grooved bark of the Douglas fir, the faint purple cast of the western hemlock cones.

As she lectured, she scanned faces to see who was listening. A tall man caught her eye. He wore a hat, a long-sleeved shirt, and jeans so new they could have stood on their own. She couldn't see his eyes through his sunglasses but sensed they were on her face.

Oliva smiled at him, an automatic response to his attentiveness.

She had an avid amateur photographer in the group who was crouched by a nurse log, lens to fungi. She used his interest as a segue, identifying the oyster mushroom he was trying to capture on film. The man in the sunglasses moved closer and stood silent. As if waiting. She could see sweat on his face.

"The cool dampness—" Why was he sweating? she wondered. "The cool dampness in the Olympic rain forest," she began again, "provides the perfect environment for exuberant growth. It supports the greatest weight of living matter in the world."

The call of an eagle had everyone looking up. Though thick canopy barred the sky, Olivia shifted to an explanation of birds.

The man in the sunglasses bumped against her, gripped her hand. She jolted and saw he'd tripped in a tangle of vine maple.

"I'm sorry," he whispered. "I didn't mean to hurt you."

"You didn't. Are you all right? You look a little shaky."

"I'm . . . You're so . . ." His fingers trembled on her arm.

"You're very good at your job. I'm glad I came today."

"Thank you. We want you to enjoy yourself. Do I know you?"

"No." His hand dropped away. "No, you don't know me."

"Miss! Oh, Miss MacBride, can you tell us what these are?"

"Yes, of course. Excuse me a minute." Olivia skirted over to a trio of women who huddled around a large sheet of dark red lichen. "It's commonly called dog lichen. You can see, if you use your imagination, the illusion of dog's teeth in the rows."

She caught herself rubbing her hand where the man's fingers had brushed. She knew him, she told herself. There was something . . . She turned around to look at him again. He was gone.

Heart pumping, Olivia counted heads. Fifteen. She'd signed on for fifteen, and she had fifteen. But he'd been there, first at the edges of the group, then close in. She walked over to Celia. "Did you happen to notice a tall man, short gray hair, sunglasses? Good build. Mid-sixties, I guess."

"I haven't paid much attention to the people. Lose someone?"

"No. I . . . No," she said. "He must have been on his own and just joined in for a bit. It's nothing."

WHEN she got back to the center, Olivia was pleased to see several members of her group head to the book area.

"Why don't I buy you lunch?" Celia asked.

"Thanks, but I really have to work." She caught the look, sighed. "You don't have to worry. I'm going to be chained to my desk. Then I have two lectures scheduled and another guided hike."

"What time's the first lecture?"

"Three o'clock."

Celia kissed her cheek. "See you at three."

Olivia walked through the center to her office. She stepped inside. Then two paces from her desk she froze. And stared at the single white rose lying across the blotter.

His face had changed. Twenty years in prison had changed it. Breathing shallowly she rubbed the hand he'd touched.

"Daddy. Oh, God."

HE'D been so close. He'd touched her, and she hadn't known who he was. She'd looked into his face and hadn't known him. His daughter, and she'd given him the absent smile of a stranger.

He sat on a bench, washed down pills with bottled water. Wiped the clammy sweat from his face with a handkerchief.

She *would* know him, he promised himself. Before the day passed, she would look at him and know him. Then it would be finished.

NOAH shut down his laptop and walked downstairs through the empty house. Olivia would be finished with her guided hike by now. And he could use a break from the book. He checked the doors as he left, making sure they were secured.

He detoured toward the garden. At the sound of a car, he remembered he hadn't thought to hook his knife onto his belt. The wavering sun glinted off chrome and glass, then cleared, so that he recognized Jamie Melbourne at the wheel.

By the time he'd walked to the car, she'd shoved the door open and jumped out. "Are they all right? Is everyone all right?"

"Everyone's fine."

She leaned weakly against the fender. "All the way up here I imagined all sorts of things. My mother said he'd been here. Inside the house. She didn't want me to come, but I had to be here."

"No one's seen him, at least not that I've heard. Liv's at the center, and your parents are at the lodge with mine."

"Good. Okay." She heaved out a long breath. "I'm not a hysterical person. But I came very, very close to losing it last night. David was in Chicago, and I couldn't reach him for hours. Nothing ever sounded so good as his voice. He's on his way. Canceled the rest of his meetings. We all need to be together until . . ." Her eyes went dark. "Until what, Noah?"

"Until it's over," was all he said.

"Well, I'd better get my bag inside."

"I'll get it for you."

"No. It's just a carry-on. And, to be honest, I could use a few minutes on my own to pull it together."

"I just locked up." He pulled the key out of his pocket. "I'm going to see Liv."

Jamie took the key. "I think you're good for her." She studied his face. "You're a sturdy one under it all, aren't you, Noah Brady?"

"She'll never have to worry if I'll be there, never have to wonder if I love her."

The fatigue seemed to lift from her eyes. "I know just how important that is. It's funny, Julie wanted that—no more than that—and I found it. I'm glad her daughter has, too." She opened the trunk and pulled out a tote.

Noah waited until she was in the house, until she'd locked the door. With his senses alert he then followed the trail to the center.

AS QUIETLY as possible, Olivia had asked every member of the staff if they'd noticed anyone going into her office. When each time the answer was no, she walked outside and started toward the lodge.

"Hey!" Noah came across the parking lot toward her. She gave him a smile, but there was strain at the edges.

"There's another white rose. It was on my desk in my office."

"Go in the lodge." Noah's voice was cool. "I'll look around."

"No, wait. I questioned the staff. No one noticed anyone going into my office. But a couple of them did notice a tall man with short gray hair wearing dark glasses and stiff new jeans when I was setting up the group out here. I noticed him, too, during the hike. He slipped into the group. He spoke to me. I didn't recognize him. He looked years older than he should, but part of me knew. And when I saw the rose, his face was right there—my father."

"What did he say to you, Liv?"

"It wasn't anything important, just that I was good at my job, that he was glad he'd come. Noah, he didn't look like a monster. He looked ill and tired. How could he have done what he did? How could he be doing this now and just look tired?"

"I doubt he knows the answer to that himself, Liv."

Noah caught a movement, a bit of color, shifted his gaze. And watched Sam Tanner step out of the forest.

Olivia saw him, too, just when he stopped short on the far edge of the parking lot. They stared at each other in the windy silence, as they had once stared at each other across a bloody floor.

Then he turned and walked quickly toward the trees.

"Go find my father," Noah said, unsnapping her knife sheath from her belt. "Tell him what happened here, then stay inside. Call your aunt at the house. Tell her to stay put, too."

"What? Aunt Jamie?"

"She got here just as I was leaving. Do it now."

Olivia watched in horror as Noah strapped her knife to his belt. "Don't go after him. You don't know what he's capable of."

"He doesn't know what I'm capable of either. Love isn't enough. You have to trust me. Let's deal with this."

NOAH had to rely on his senses. His hearing strained to catch the rustling of brush. To the left? The right? Straight ahead. As he moved deeper, the false green twilight fell. He could hear the low rumble of thunder. A storm was brewing.

"There's no point in running, Tanner," he called out as he closed his hand on Olivia's knife. "You'll never get her." Rain began to hiss through the canopy. "She's your own daughter. What good will it do you? What point is there in hurting her now?"

"None." Sam stepped out from the bulk of a fir. The gun in his trembling hand gleamed dull silver. "There was never a point. Never a reason. I thought you knew."

OLIVIA HIT THE DOORS OF THE lobby and burst inside. She looked frantically right and left. Guests were milling around or parked on sofas and chairs. She didn't know where to find Frank.

She spun on her heel, raced to the front desk, and grabbed the clerk. "Listen carefully. I need you to find Frank Brady. He's a guest here. Tell him that Sam Tanner went into the forest. The east side, Lowland Trail. Have you got that?"

"East side, Lowland Trail."

"Tell him Noah went after him. Get one of the staff to call my house. My aunt's there. It's vital she stays inside and waits to hear from me. No one's to go into the forest. Make an announcement."

"But why—"

"Just do it," she snapped. "Do it now."

She sprinted into the rear office. She needed some kind of weapon. A defense. Frantic, she yanked open desk drawers. She saw the scissors—the long silver blades—snatched at them, and slid the blades under her belt. Was it justice? she wondered. Or was it fate?

The rain began to fall as Olivia raced into the trees.

NOAH'S mind was clear as glass, detached from the physical jeopardy of the gun and focused on the man. "No point, Sam? All of it, all those years you spent away come down to you and me standing in the rain?"

"You're just a bonus. I didn't expect to talk to you again. I've got some tapes for you. For the book."

"Do you think I'll let you walk out of here, give her one more moment's pain? You'll never touch her."

"I did. I was so close. She grew up so pretty. She has a stronger face than Julie's. Not as beautiful, but stronger. She didn't know me. Why would she? I've been dead to her for twenty years."

"Is that why you arranged all this—to come alive for her? Start me on the book to dig up old memories. Put you back in her head, so when you got out, you could start on her."

"I wanted her to remember me. I'm her father. I wanted her to remember me. I've got a right. A right to that at least."

"You lost your rights to her." Noah edged closer. "She was a baby, innocent, and taking that innocence wasn't enough? You sent the music box to remind her that you weren't done. And the phone calls, the white roses."

"Roses. I used to put a white rose on her pillow. Music box?" Sam's eyes narrowed abruptly. "What music box?"

"The Blue Fairy—the one you broke the night you knocked your wife around in Olivia's room."

"I don't remember. I was coked to my eyeballs." Then his eyes cleared. "The Blue Fairy—I knocked it off her dresser. I remember. She cried, and I told her I'd buy her another one."

"You're sick and tired. Put the gun down. I'll take you back."

"For what? More doctors, more drugs? I'm already dead, Brady. I've been dead for years. I just wanted to see her again."

"Put the gun down."

Sam glanced down at the gun in his hand. Then he began to laugh. "You think this is for you? It's for me. I didn't have the guts to use it. And you know what, Brady? You know what I figured out when I stuck the barrel in my mouth, when I had my finger on the trigger and couldn't pull it?" His voice became confident and clear. "I didn't kill Julie. I've been gutless all my life."

"Let's go talk about it." As Noah stepped forward, reaching out for the gun, there was a crash in the brush, a blur of movement. He felt pain rip along his shoulder, heard a scream that wasn't his own. He saw David Melbourne's face as the force of the attack rammed him against Sam, tumbling them both to the ground.

Noah rolled aside, agony spearing through his wounded shoulder as he caught the wrist of David's knife hand. The blade stabbed into the rain-slimed moss, a breath away from his face. Rearing up, Noah bucked him aside, then rolled for the gun that lay on the ground. As he snatched it up, David fled into the trees.

"I never thought of him." Oozing blood, Sam crawled over. His eyes were glassy from the pain rolling inside his head. "A dozen other men she would have looked at. That was my delusion. But I never thought of him." As he spoke, he fumbled to tie his handkerchief around the gash in Noah's shoulder. "He should've just waited for me to die instead of trying to kill me."

Noah winced against the pain. "Not you. It's Olivia he wants."

"No." Fear coated over the agony in Sam's eyes. "No, not Livvy. We have to find him. Stop him."

There wasn't time to debate. Noah hesitated only a moment. "Take this." He unsnapped Olivia's sheath. "They're looking for you by now. If my father comes across you with a gun—"

"Frank's here?"

"That's right. Melbourne won't get far. You head toward the house. I'll do what I can to pick up his trail."

Noah checked the gun and raced into the green.

OLIVIA wanted to rush headlong into the trees, shout for Noah. It took every ounce of control to move slowly, to look for prints.

There'd been dozens of people in that edge of the forest, leaving crisscrossing prints. He'd come in at a sprint, she remembered, and judged the length between strides. Noah had long legs. So did her father. She headed due south into the gloom.

A thin fog skimmed over the ground. She moved quickly, trying to outpace the fear. Every shadow was a terror, every shape a threat. She hurried deeper into the forest.

When she heard the scream, fear plunged into her heart. She forgot caution and ran as though her life depended on it. Her feet slid wildly over the moldering ground. She went down hard.

Rain soaked her hair, dripped into her eyes. She blinked it away and saw blood. It was soaking the ground. Shaking, she touched her fingertips to the stain and brought them back, red and wet.

"Not again. No, not again." She rocked herself as the fear hammered at her like a storm of ice. "Noah!" Shoving to her feet, she shouted it once, listened to the grieving echo of it.

With her only thought to find him, she began to run.

THE gun was familiar in Noah's hand now. He never doubted he could use it. Life and death, the cold-blooded will to survive.

Twenty years the man had hidden what he was, what he'd done. He'd let another grow old in a cage, had played the devoted husband to his victim's sister, the indulgent uncle to her daughter.

Murder, bloody murder, had been locked inside him while he prospered, while he posed. And when the key had started to turn in the door to Sam Tanner's cage, it had set murder free again.

The break-ins, the attack on Mike—an attempt to stop the book, Noah thought as he moved through the teeming woods. To beat back the guilt, the fear of exposure. And once again he'd turned the focus on Sam to point accusations at an innocent man.

But this time it was Olivia he hunted. Fear that she'd seen him that night, would remember some small detail that had been tucked in a corner of her mind all this time, a detail that might jibe with the story Sam wanted to tell. But Olivia couldn't remember if she was too afraid. Or if she was dead.

Then he heard her scream his name.

THE monster was back. The smell of him was blood. The sound of him was terror.

She had no choice but to run and this time to run toward him.

The lush wonder of forest that had once been her haven, that had always been her sanctuary, spun into a nightmare. The towering majesty of the trees was no longer a grand testament to nature's vigor, but a living cage that could trap her, conceal him. The luminous carpet of moss was a bubbling bog that sucked at her boots. She ripped through ferns, rending their sodden fans to slimy tatters, skidded over a rotted log, and destroyed the burgeoning life it nursed. Green shadows slipped in front of her, beside her, behind her, seemed to whisper her name.

Livvy, my love. Let me tell you a story.

Breath sobbed out of her lungs, set to grieving by fear and loss. The blood that stained her fingertips had gone ice-cold. Rain fell, a steady drumming against the windswept canopy.

She forgot if she was hunter or hunted. She would find him, or he would find her. And somehow it would be finished. She would not end as a coward. And if there was any light in the world, she would find the man she loved. Alive.

She curled the blood she knew was his into her palm and held it like hope. She closed her hand over the only weapon she had, and knew she would kill to live.

And through the deep green light haunted by darker shadows she saw the monster as she remembered him in her nightmares.

Covered with blood, and watching her.

Fury that was as much hate as fear spurted through her in a kind of power. "Where's Noah? What have you done to him?"

He was on his knees, his hand pressed to his side, where blood spilled out of him. The pain was so huge, it reached to the bone.

"Livvy." He whispered it, both prayer and plea. "Run."

"I've been running from you all my life. Where's Noah? I swear I'll kill you if you've taken someone else I love."

"Not me. Not then, not now." His vision wavered. "He's still close. For heaven's sake, run."

They heard it at the same moment, the thrashing through the brush. She spun around, her heart leaping with hope.

At her feet Sam's heart tripped with terror. "Stay away from her." Sheer will pushed him to stand.

"You should have died in prison." David's face was wet with rain and blood. The knife in his hand ran with both.

"Uncle David." The shock of seeing him, his eyes wild, his clothes spattered, had Olivia stepping forward.

With a strength born of desperation Sam jerked her back. "He killed her. Listen to me. He killed her. Don't go near him."

"Step away from him, Livvy. Come here to me."

"I want you to run," Sam said urgently. "Run the way you did that night, and find a place to hide. Find Noah."

"You know better than to listen to him." David smiled. "You saw what he did to her that night. He was never good enough for her. I've always been there for you, haven't I, Livvy?"

"She never wanted you." Sam's voice slurred and slowed as he fought to stay conscious. "She never loved anyone but me."

"Shut up!" David's face flushed. "It should have been me. She would have come to me if you hadn't gotten in the way."

"Oh, my God." Olivia stared at David. "You. It was you."

"She should have listened to me! I *loved* her. I always loved her. She was so beautiful, so perfect. I would have treated her like an angel. He dragged her down, only thought of himself."

"You're right. I treated her badly." Sam slumped against Olivia, murmured, "Run." But she continued to hold on to him.

"I would have given her everything." Tears slipped out of David's eyes now. "I settled for second best and gave Jamie everything I would have given Julie. Why should I have settled when she was finally going to divorce you?"

"You went to the house that night," Sam said.

"Do you know how much courage it took for me to go to her? She let me in and smiled at me. She was doing her clippings. I poured my soul out to her. I told her I wanted her, always had, that I was leaving Jamie and we could be together. She looked at me as if I were insane. Pushed me away, told me to leave and we'd forget I'd ever spoken of it. Forget." He spat the word out.

"She loved my father," Olivia murmured.

"She was *wrong!* I only tried to convince her she was wrong. If she hadn't struggled against me, I wouldn't have ripped her robe. Then she turned on me, shouted at me to get out of her house. She said she would tell Jamie everything. The scissors were in my hand. Then they were in her. I think she screamed. I only remember the blood." His eyes focused on Olivia. "It was an accident, really. A terrible mistake. But I couldn't take it back, could I?"

She had to be calm. She would stand, protect. And pray for help to come. "You held me while I cried for her."

"I cried, too! If she'd only listened, it would never have happened. Why should I have paid for that? He's the one who hurt her. I had to protect myself, my life."

"How did you get out of the house and back home?" Olivia asked. "Aunt Jamie would have seen the blood."

"I went outside to the pool and washed the blood away. There were always spare clothes in the changing house. It wasn't until after the police brought you to Jamie and me that I wondered if you'd heard or seen me. Twenty years I've wondered. I've waited."

"No, I didn't see you. I never knew."

"It would have stayed that way. Until the book. How could I know for sure that you hadn't heard my voice, that you hadn't looked out the window, seen my car? It ruined my life."

"You let my father go to prison."

"I was in prison, too." Tears leaked out of his eyes. "I was paying, too. I knew you'd be just like her. I knew when it came down to a choice, you'd choose him. But that's over now. I have to protect myself. I have to end it."

He lunged toward her, leading with the knife.

NOAH kept running until it felt as if his heart were bursting out of his chest. The bone-numbing terror that he would be too late drove him harder. She was somewhere in the vast, twisting maze of the forest.

He stopped, leaned against a hemlock, and stood very still. Was that the murmur of voices or just the rain?

This time, when she screamed, he was close.

SAM shoved Olivia clear and, with the little strength he had left, drove his body into David's. When the knife sliced through him again, he felt nothing but despair as he staggered and fell. Olivia tried to catch him.

It happened quickly, her father slipping out of her hands, the sound of running feet slapping against the saturated ground. And the quick prick of a knife at her throat.

"Let her go." Noah held the gun in the classic police grip.

"Drop the gun. I'll kill her. You know I will."

"And lose your shield? I don't think so." Noah saw the shock in Olivia's eyes, the thin trickle of red sliding down her throat.

"Put the gun down!" David jerked Olivia's head up with the flat of the blade. "Do you hear me? She's dead if you don't do it!"

Olivia saw Noah's hands start to lower. "He'll kill me anyway," she said. "He'll kill me no matter what you do. Then he'll kill you. Don't let him take someone else I love. Don't let him win."

Her hand closed over the cold metal eyes of the scissors, drew them out, then plunged them viciously into David's thigh.

He screamed, his knife hand dropping. She yanked the scissors clear, then held them out as he leaped near her.

She heard the bullet ring out, one sharp snap. Saw the bright blossom of blood bloom high on his chest as he fell toward her. The killing point of the scissors slid silently into his belly.

The weight of him bore Olivia to the ground. Noah pulled her up and against him. "You're all right. You're okay." His arms quivered as his hands ran shakily over her. "He cut you. Oh, Liv."

She was crushed against him, burrowed into him. Her head went light. "I thought he might have killed you. I saw the blood and I thought . . . No!" She jerked back. "Daddy." She pulled away and stumbled to the ground beside her father. "Oh, no, no, no. Please. I'm so sorry. I'm sorry, Daddy." She had nothing but her hands to press against his wound.

"Don't cry, Livvy." He reached up to touch her face. "This is the best way for me. My time's running out anyway. I needed to see you again. It was the last thing I had to do." He smiled a little.

She pressed her face to his neck. "Don't talk. We have to stop the bleeding. They'll find us soon." Her hands fumbled with scraps of cloth Noah gave her. "We'll get you to the hospital."

"You know better." His eyes were clouding over, but they shifted to Noah. "She's a smart one, isn't she, Brady?"

"That's right." Noah pressed another scrap of his shirt to the wound on Sam's side. "So listen to her."

"I'd rather die a hero." Sam's short laugh ended in a racking cough. "There's enough of the old me to rather enjoy that." The pain was floating away. "Livvy"—he gripped her hand—"when I was looking for you that night, I wasn't going to hurt you."

"I know. Don't leave me now that I've just gotten you back."

"I'm sorry, Livvy. In the end, I kept you safe. Maybe that makes up for all the years I didn't." His vision wavered and dimmed. "Take care of my little girl, Brady. Kiss me good-bye, Livvy love."

With tears flooding her throat, she pressed her lips to his cheek. And felt his hand go lax in hers. Noah sat with her while she cradled her father's body and wept in the rain.

OLIVIA slept, and when she woke, logy with grief and shock, it was midday. Opening her eyes, she saw Noah sitting beside her.

"You didn't sleep."

He was already holding her hand. "I did for a bit."

He looked so wonderful, she thought, with his exhausted eyes and stubble of beard. "You saved my life."

He leaned down to kiss her. "Don't make me do it again."

"That's a deal. How's your shoulder?"

"Well, I could say it's nothing, but why lie?"

She sat up, tugged up the sleeve of his T-shirt, and pressed her lips to the bandage.

"Thanks. Why don't you try to get some more sleep?"

"No. I really need to get out. Walk in the forest with me, Noah."

When Olivia was dressed, she held out a hand for his. "My family? Your parents?"

"Your grandparents were up with Jamie until almost dawn. They're still asleep. My parents are in the spare room."

They went downstairs and left through the kitchen door.

"Your father," Olivia began. "When they found us, I don't think he knew whether he was proud of you or horrified."

"I think he was both. He taught me how to handle guns, to respect them. I know he hoped I'd never have to use one."

"I don't know how to feel, Noah. All these years I thought my father was a murderer, the worst kind of murderer. I lost him when I was four, and now I have him back. I have him back in a way that changes everything. And I can never tell him."

"He knew."

She tightened her hand on his as they moved into the trees. "This time I didn't run and hide. I can live with all the rest."

"Liv, you gave him exactly what he wanted at the end of his life. You looked at him, and you knew him."

Olivia nodded. "All my life I loved my uncle. I admired him, trusted him. He wasn't what I thought he was, any more than my father was what I thought he was." She let out a sigh. "I was afraid I wouldn't be able to come in here again. But I can. It's so beautiful. So alive. No monsters here. I love this place."

It had sheltered her, given her life. Now she had a choice—to stay with the old or start the new. She let go of Noah's hand. "But there's this other spot, along the coast—heavily wooded, excellent old forest with a view of the Pacific raging up against the cliffs." She stopped, met his eyes soberly. "That's where we should build the house."

He stared at her in quiet joy. "Okay. Stone or wood?"

"Both." Her lips twitched; her eyes glowed.

"When?"

"As soon as you ask me to marry you." She laughed as he hauled her into his arms.

"I've waited a long time for you." He brushed his lips over hers. "Don't make me wait anymore. Marry me."

"Yes." She framed his face with her hands. "Between the forest and the flowers. And soon." She smiled at him, drawing him close to touch her lips to his cheek. "I love you, Noah. I want to start a life with you. Now. We've both waited long enough."

NORA ROBERTS

Long regarded as the reigning queen of romance, the amazingly prolific Nora Roberts has published over 126 books and was recently honored with the Romance Writers of America's Lifetime Achievement Award.

Roberts's own courtship could have come straight from one of her novels. When the author decided years ago to remodel her house in rural Maryland, she fell in love with Bruce, her carpenter. They have been happily married ever since and still live in the house that brought them together. But Bruce has gotten out of the carpentry business and now owns a bookstore. And like a true romance hero, he loyally makes sure that his wife's best-selling novels are always prominently displayed.

The volumes in this series are issued
every two to three months. The typical volume
contains four outstanding books in condensed
form. None of the selections in any volume has
appeared in *Reader's Digest* itself. Any reader
may receive this service by writing
The Reader's Digest Association, Inc.,
Pleasantville, N.Y. 10570
or by calling 800-234-9000.

Visit our Web site at
http://www.readersdigest.com

ACKNOWLEDGMENTS

Pages 166–167: Bill Farnsworth.
Pages 236: Grateful acknowledgment is made to Warner Bros. Publications U.S., Inc.,
for permission to reprint excerpts from "You're All the World to Me" by Burton Lane
and Alan Jay Lerner, copyright © 1949 by Metro-Goldwyn-Mayer, Inc., and copyright
renewed 1977 by EMI Miller Catalog, Inc. All rights reserved. Reprinted by permission of
Warner Bros. Publications U.S., Inc., Miami, FL 33014.
Pages 330–331: Dan Gonzalez.
Pages 424–425: Rene Milot/Renard Represents.

The original editions of the books in this volume are published and copyrighted as follows:
The Hammer of Eden, published at $25.95 by Crown Publishers, Inc.
© 1998 by Ken Follett
Welcome to the World, Baby Girl!, published at $25.95 by Random House, Inc.
© 1998 by Willina Lake Productions, Inc.
Stonewall's Gold: A Novel, published at $22.95 by St. Martin's Press
© 1999 by Robert J. Mrazek
River's End, published at $23.95 by G. P. Putnam's Sons
© 1999 by Nora Roberts